Threatened River was first published
in Australia by Acacia Rose Media.

PO Box 136
Thredbo NSW 2625
Australia

———

Threatened River
Rose, Acacia
ISBN: 9780957805415

———

Also by Acacia Rose:
Midnight Pearl
Journey With The Flame

Typeset in Hong Kong by Jeremy Smart.

Printed and bound in Australia by
McPhersons Printing Group.

Papers used are from well-managed
forests and other responsible sources.

———

EDITOR

Meredith Goulding

———

ART DIRECTION

Aerostorie Studio
aerostorie.com/studio

———

PHOTOGRAPHY

Mike Edmondson
mikeedmondson.com.au

———

COVER ARTWORK

Notion Press
notionpress.com

PROLOGUE

The black stallion whinnied in the late evening light; soft rays penetrated clusters of eucalypts, and struck against the metal bars of the trap yard. The evening was still apart from the sound of a lone yellow-tailed black cockatoo screeching in the silence that was dusk in the Snowy Mountains. Thunder hesitated and pawed at the ground. The steam rose from the fresh pile of dung adjacent to the trap yard, the clear signal to any of the young colts that, this was his territory. The mares shuffled together nervously, feeling suddenly insecure that they could not reach him, the father of their foals, the strong and muscular head of the herd who was also their possessive protector. Thunder screamed, this time rearing onto his hind legs and shaking his neck from side to side. His left eye absorbed the terrible reality that his mares and foals were trapped. With his right eye he watched carefully for any signs of a contender coming up from the Cascades Valley to claim his territory. One of the mares skittishly cantered around the yard her foal attempting to cling to her flank as he ran behind her.

The sound of the mechanical beast, the gears crunching the wheels turning on the rocky track and the clunk of the trailer broke into the tense atmosphere startling the troubled herd. Thunder by now knew the sound and the smell that came with it. This was one contest he could not win, not at the moment, not now. Carefully, he retreated into the bush, stepping over fallen bark, his dark coat disappearing amongst shadows that gathered around the gnarled and whitened gums. This was his territory and he knew every tree, every rocky outcrop, where the streams flowed and trees formed bands thick enough to hide several horses at a time. Only his eye stood out brightly against the black of his forehead and the white of the tree. But the man did not see Thunder, he only saw his catch, four mares and three foals, lured by the square salt block in the corner of the trap yard.

Thunder breathed heavily, tormented by the man backing the truck towards the yards. The man opened the back of the trailer crashing it carelessly onto the ground. The horses huddled at the back of the yards. He pulled up makeshift sides to block any escape from the yards before opening its spring-loaded gate. Then he walked quickly around the back of the yards waving his arms and forcing the terrified mares towards the new trap. The mares, scared by his smell, stumbled and pushed one another up the ramp except for the lead mare. The man climbed into the yards and ran towards the truck shouting and forcing three of the mares and two foals into the trap. They started to turn, their eyes wild with fear and rage. Quickly he lifted the back of the tray and slammed it shut.

Thunder screamed as he charged towards the open yard, his neck extended and his teeth bared. The man yelled, waving his arms at the stallion realising that he himself was about to be trapped by the horse. He scrambled to the metal palings and forced himself through the yards hurting his shoulder as he hit the ground. The horse headed straight for him his hooves striking the metal bars close to where the man lay winded on the ground. The brumby catcher cried out in fear and rolled away from the flint-black hooves. Thunder turned to his lead mare, nipping her flank and forcing her out of the yards and back into the wilderness away from the smell of the man and the sound of death. Slowly, the man pushed himself to his knees and crawled away from the horse dung and wet earth in the yards and pulled himself into the cabin of the truck. His face was white with fear and his heart thumped in his chest. For several minutes he sat in the truck, looking in the rear vision and side mirrors for a sign of the horse that he never thought he would see. The Black Stallion. Legendary with the local farmers. No-one had been anywhere near him with a rope let alone loaded him onto the back of a truck or a horse float. Then the man grinned to himself. He didn't have the stallion, but he had two of his foals.

MAGIC DAY

'Tom, bring your line up here. I think we will have a better chance.' The old man winked and carefully steadied the rod with his right hand ready to cast into the river.

'OK gramps.' Tom pushed himself away from the river bank and turned to walk up the lightly worn track winding along the Snowy River. 'The river seems pretty dead. Can't seem to catch anything at all.'

'You could say that again Tom.' His grandfather drew his breath in through his teeth creating a soft whistling sound. 'Mind you, I remember when we would cast into any section of the river from Dalgety to the mouth and pull in a strong haul of any number of fish; blackfish, Gippsland perch, bream, salmon — you name it — the fish were here for the taking!'

'You old guys have fished us out then.' Tom grinned as he stepped onto the bank beside his grandfather.

'Well…' his grandfather quickly cast with his fly rod touching the surface of the water a few times. 'Here we go, we're on!' He danced the lure onto the river teasing the Tailor to bite. 'He's a beauty.' Expertly, the fly fisherman played the fish until it took the lure. 'He's ours!'

'Nice.'

Red Thompson played the fish towards the bank, the sunlight glinting on its sleek back. 'A mature old fellow. Let's pop this one back Tom. We still need breeders in the system.'

'Like you were saying — there was a lot more fish back in your day.'

'Seems like it is still "my day" lad.'

'Just lucky.' Tom retorted.

'I tell you Tom, when the Snowy River ran from the mountains to the sea, when the snowmelt started in late September and continued all the way through to mid November, in the days before any dams and tunnels, that's when the fish would always bite.'

Tom cocked his head curiously as if trying to work out what it was like when the Snowy River ran from the mountains to the sea. 'I'm not sure I can see it like you did gramps.'

'You could hear it Tom. You could hear the river running from miles away. The sound was like thunder as the river ripped through the gorges. You could almost feel the rocks tumbling on the river bed.' Red paused and looked upstream as if he could invoke the river to flood the plains that stretched all the way to Orbost. 'You wouldn't stand here if the river was running. You couldn't. The logs... the size of the logs were enormous! Natural habitat for fish mind you — but you wouldn't want to be in the river or too close to the bank when some of those monsters came down in the big floods.'

'Geez gramps. Sounds terrifying.'

'Terrifying? Nah. It was more than that. It was awesome.' Red paused as if listening for the river. 'It was unbelievable Tom, witnessing the raw power of nature.' The old man blew out his breath as if he still couldn't believe the past that was the true Snowy River.

'D'ya think we will see it again gramps?' Tom asked innocently.

'Do you think...boy. Do you think.' Red corrected his grandson. 'Do I think we will see that again? Not in my lifetime that's a sure thing. Not since they built the Snowy Scheme and built a whole agricultural community on the other side of the mountains. It would be too cruel to them to wind that back.'

'But what about us? What about the fish?' Tom defended his rights.

'Aye lad. There's a thought. What about the river and what about the fish.' Red played his line on top of the water. 'You know Tom, once upon a time, you could draw a bucket of fresh water right out at sea, just off the coast here.'

'No way!'

'Aah yes. You ask any of the old timers.'

'You mean like you.' Tom grinned cheekily.

'Yes like me and my granddad before me. The stories back then were amazing. The old men would go out in their hand-crafted boats and just follow the flow of the Snowy. They could drink straight from the sea and fish straight from the sea. No matter if you were marooned overnight you could survive easily.'

'Sounds like a legend gramps.'

'A legend it was Tom, better probably than the legend of the "Man from the Snowy River". He was upstream of course. Riding his horses around.'

'I bet he would have liked to have been where we are now gramps. Catching fresh fish and all.'

'Hmmm. The mountains were his lure. Fresh air, storms, long winters, the spring melt…'

'The spring melt. So it doesn't happen anymore?'

'Yeah. It happens alright. But the water doesn't come here, not much of it anyway.'

'So we couldn't like row out to the edge of the continental shelf then gramps, and catch us a whopper and drink straight from the sea?'

'Not any more lad. Not anymore. Here we go!' Red felt the jerk on his line. 'I've got him. A beauty.' He flicked the line and played the fish. 'This one we can take home for dinner.'

Tom flushed with excitement. 'Not a bad one gramps. Just like the old days yeah?'

'The size of the fish then boy. No need to 'throw them back' or any concept of bag limits.'

'So you could live off the Snowy River if you wanted to.'

'Yes you could and yes the Aboriginal people from here did. Fish, eels, freshwater crays, possums from the rainforest…'

'How did they catch the fish if they didn't have fishing line like us?'

'You would be surprised how advanced they were young man. Building stone houses down here around the time that we arrived, plus they built fish and eel traps. Pretty organised in my opinion.'

'So where are they now?'

'Good question Tom. Good question. There isn't the annual spring migration of the Gunaikurnai people from Marlo to the mountains any more — if that's what you mean.'

'Oh.' Tom looked perplexed. 'Could we build an eel trap?'

'We could. Not much good if most of them are trapped upstream in Jindabyne Dam though.'

'Get rid of the dam?'

'Let some more water out at least. You know that the big eels used to migrate all the way to the Coral Sea to breed then swim back here to the Snowy River?'

'No I didn't. Maybe they just surfed north on the currents.'

'Tom, you like surfing?'

'Yeah.'

'Most of the beaches up north got their sand from right here in the Gippsland.'

'No.'

'The Snowy River. The silt and sediment for tens of thousands of years washing downstream as the mountains eroded, travels north. Plus the ancient deserts of course, gradually washing into the river system. It's called a 'sand river'. Flows up the east coast of Australia and builds beaches for young fellas like you.'

'No way. Just for me.' Tom laughed out aloud.

'Just for you. Mind you, the sand could run out if we don't get some water back in this river.'

'Right gramps, I'll do something to put the sand back.' Tom kicked the river bank with his foot.

'That should get things started again.' Red smiled at his grandson. 'You're looking a bit brighter Tom.'

'Yeah. This is heaps better than hanging around the city on the weekends.' Tom sounded rueful.

'Everything alright at school son?'

'Nuh. Hate the place.'

'Anything bothering you there?' Red felt concerned about the mood swings he had recently noticed in his grandson.

'The priests and stuff. Don't really like any of them.' Tom shrugged.

'I see.' Red pursed his lips. 'Did you talk to your Dad about changing schools?'

'He wouldn't hear of it gramps. They're his mates. You know how it is. They do favours for each other. That's how he got me into the school in the first place.' Tom allowed his hurt to surface.

Red remained silent. He had had his suspicions that all was not well when the boy changed to a new school. The free spirited kid he knew well was suddenly sullen and withdrawn.

'So they're not your type Tom.' Red said wisely. 'I bet none of them know anything about horses.'

Tom grinned. 'Yeah. They spend their lives on their knees with their eyes closed. They probably couldn't work out the front from the back of a horse.'

Red laughed. He watched his grandson carefully at the same time, noticing the colour return to his cheeks. 'And I bet they couldn't crack a whip properly.'

'I reckon not gramps. Maybe we could teach them how.' Tom looked up at his grandfather, his eyes smarting at the memory of the priest.

'That's my lad. Dish it straight back to them. By the way are you hungry?'

'Yep.'

'Reckon we could head off home and cook us up a nice feed of fish then Tom.'

'Reckon we could gramps.'

RUNNING WATER

Cassandra's phone buzzed in her left hand trouser pocket.

'Cassandra speaking.'

'Cassie?'

'Yup.'

'Patrick here.'

'Patrick!' Cassandra could almost feel her friend grinning down the phone.

'Hey.'

'Hey. What's doing?'

'Just got the word there will be a release from Munyang Power Station in a couple of days.'

'Cool.'

'You going to ride it?'

'Will talk to some friends Patrick, yeah.'

'Thought you might.' Patrick chuckled.

'Good to be in the know.'

'You know how it is Cass. Privileged information.'

'Yeah I know. It sucks. Boys club or what!'

'Do you need anything Cass?' Patrick sounded suddenly sober, concerned.

'Should I?'

'Not sure. Gut feelings I get about you.'

'I know. Anything to worry about Patrick?'

'Hmm. Take it easy yeah? Tell me what the Snowy River feels

like beneath your paddle again.' Patrick chirped up. He never felt completely happy about leaving Cassandra camping alone at Island Bend. At least when she lived in Dalgety, he could easily check up to see that she was safe at work. That was Patrick. Diligent, attentive, protective.

The flames suddenly shot upwards as they caught the dry tea-tree bark in the tiny teepee of kindling, shards of dead tea-tree and dried out eucalyptus twigs, some with dead leaves hanging limply in flammable bunches, ready to fuel the rapidly growing fire.

Cassandra carefully fed the fire with larger pieces of wood scavenged from the banks of the Snowy River dumped by over 60 years of releases, and before that, the giant floods that were part of the character of the river. Some of the wood looked like it was hundreds of years old — the knotted and gnarled branches stripped of bark by the force of the ancient river. In an instant, several pairs of hands added fuel to the campfire. Before long, the wood began to sing as the fire consumed the smaller then larger pieces, eventually forming bright coals. Cassandra needed help to lift the enormous cast iron camp-oven — stacked full with pasta, vegetables and rich tomato and basil sauce — onto the fire. It would be a feast for kings; kings of the very Snowy River that was about to run unfettered once again, in a short and glorious burst of freedom.

The stars sprayed upwards disappearing into the blackness of the deep night. A Powerful Owl hooted mournfully and the plop of fish broke the silence. Cassandra turned over in her sleeping bag and switched on her head torch. She shone it briefly at the Garmin GPS watch carefully placed by her pack. It was midnight. Another five hours and they would be lighting the fire once again, bringing the charred coals to life before boiling the billy for tea, cooking toast on the Kookaburra mesh toaster and frying mushrooms and tomatoes in the blackened, cast iron frying pan. The morning could not come soon enough and Cassandra struggled to keep her excitement in check. Half a dozen of her friends instantly responded to her SMS message, packed up their responsibilities, shoved their camping equipment into the back of their four wheel drives and hoisted whitewater kayaks onto roof racks. It was part of the deal to seize the moment when the river ran.

'Cassandra, watch the Island Rapid.' Josh yelled above the roar of the River. 'There's a couple of new holes that have opened up.'

'Thanks Josh.' Cassandra yelled back. 'The storm must have pushed a few boulders around.'

'You good to go Cass?'

'Yeah! You?'

'I'll see you further down. I'm going to put in along the Rafter's Track with the Pack Raft. It's a bit wild here.'

'OK Josh. Catch you below the boulder garden.'

'Catch you Cass.' Josh watched as Cassandra moved swiftly into the heart of the river, lifting her paddles high and expertly balancing her craft as it began to take on a life of its own along the course of the first rapids.

She relaxed and pushed her butt deeper into the seat and back band of her Dagger Jitsu. Reflexly she rotated her wrists and momentarily flattened her paddle before digging in on the right blade to straighten up for the first drop. The kayak responded and dropped softly down the waterfall. She felt the kayak lift out of the friendly hole and surge forwards skimming lightly with the wash over a boulder in the middle of the garden. Cassandra grinned and looked briefly to the side of the river. There was no-one scouting this section. Her friends were competent and were already downriver heading towards the Island Rapid. She made an instant decision that as soon as she was through the rapids, she would pull into the Rafter's Track and look for Josh. It was his first time in the

Pack Raft and she wanted him to enjoy the ride downriver with her as his safety net. Her concentration naturally kicked in on the next set of rapids and she carefully scoured the drop offs for large holes. Ahead, two blue kayaks rocketed into mini-chutes, the riders lost in the waves and surges, all but their helmets covered by the wash. Cassandra followed their line, confident that their scouting expedition the day before, had the river sorted. She breathed deeply then relaxed as the water covered her completely, keeping her line and relaxing her hips and legs to feel the fine movements of the water beneath her. Carefully she dipped her blades then dug deeply to keep her momentum through the next series of holes emerging after boulder and chute drop offs. She lost track of time and suddenly, shot into calmer water and pulled towards the bank of the river. Josh was waiting and watching, holding his breath then grinning at her.

'You got it Cass! Nice ride.'

'Hey Josh. That was fun. But I reckon that was the right decision to put in here.'

'Bit wild Cass?'

'The new holes weren't as friendly as usual. Had to concentrate and paddle hard to get out.'

'Right.' Josh said soberly.

'OK, let's do it Josh. You ready?'

'Ready as I will ever be.'

'Hey, you're good at this!' Cass smiled at him.

'Yeah. Change of horse. You know what I mean.' Josh needed the confidence kick.

'Come on. I'll sweep for you.'

'Let's go.' Josh pushed off the bank and into the river.

The buzz at the camp was electrifying as the paddlers recounted their individual challenges and mini victories riding the river.

Cassandra stoked the fire and looked around for the jaffle iron.

'I am but hungryyyy!' She laughed.

'Over here Cass.' A hand reached forwards with the iron and a loaf of home baked bread. Cheese, tomatoes and baked beans suddenly materialised from the back of vehicles and eskies.

'Anyone got some oil?' Cass looked up smiling as she cut a couple of thick pieces of crusty bread.

'So Cassie when are we going to get this river permanently?' Tyler shoved the last of his baked beans jaffle into his mouth.

'Well...that's the question Tyler.'

'I don't know Cass.' Josh was still mulling over the highlights of his run down the Snowy in the pack raft. 'If the river runs all the time, maybe we won't get these surges when they generate from Munyang.'

'Hmm. Food for thought I suppose.' Tyler mumbled.

'Well if you look at the size of the boulders and the high water mark of the river when she floods, I'm not sure that any of us would be running it.' Cassie's smile looked as wide.

'You got that! Reckon the waves would be massive. Would hate to get caught in a vortex. That would be the...end!' Josh imagined the ride.

'Raft or Dagger Josh?' Tyler made the friendly jab.

'Ha ha ha Tyler! Build a circular raft and let her spin her way to the pondage.'

Cassie said suddenly. 'Has anyone run the Burrungabugge recently?'

'I wish!' Tyler brightened up.

'I know that Rob and his mate got in last spring when it was spilling. Said it was the real stoke.' Josh said.

'Yeah. That's what we are after. Release all the major tributaries in the Upper Snowy.'

'Why can't you Cassie?'

'Some concoction they put out for public consumption that there isn't enough water in the "portfolio"!' Cassandra shook her head in disbelief.

'Portfolio? It's a river!'

'Well yeah it was a river. But they do these complex sums and then say that there is not enough water for the river to run. I reckon they just have to legislate to let the Upper Snowy flow. Or at least update the Snowy Water Licence and make the Catchment and Montane Rivers' health mandatory.'

'Montane?'

'Mountain.' Cassie pointed upriver.

'Why can't they just use English?' Tyler complained.

'Seems as though they need a special river advisor and translator to sort her out.' Josh concluded.

'That job could be yours Cass!' Tyler agreed.

'Could be. Needs a bit of work to restore this river though.'

'Just needs water.' Josh stood up and threw another piece of wood on the fire. 'The Snowy just needs water Cassie and I reckon you're the person who can do that for the river.'

'And for us! Don't forget the paddlers Josh.' Tyler added.

'Maybe,' Cassandra said quietly, 'what this river needs is the Ngarigo people back here. You know, the original custodians of this land. They would let the river live.'

'Yeah, they would. Where are they anyway?'

'Mostly down the coast. Once they settled there, it was probably too hard to come back. Mind you, they seemed to follow the rivers as a part of their annual migration from here to the ocean.'

'Running water. They must have a name for it.' Josh looked up at Cassie.

'Must have.' Cassandra nodded thoughtfully at her friends.

ABANDONING IRELAND

'To Seamus Keating.' Angus bellowed out the toast to the wharfies gathered in the pub, some of them still dirty after their late shift, others grateful for the chance to be off the wharf for a few hours to relax and mingle. 'To Seamus Keating and to a free wharf, a wharf clean of snoops, pimps and traitors!'

'To Seamus Keating and a free wharf!' A voice echoed from the pub floor.

Pool cues thumped on the floor and several men pounded closed fists on the bar, lounge tables and walls.

Angus and Sean continued to toast the future freedom of their people, tossing down the rough ale and planting their glasses on the bar for another round.

'That was pure gold Sean.' Angus's thick Scottish drawl slightly blurring his meaning.

Sean looked at the man who had become almost his father. Since the death of Seamus Keating, Angus Wallace had become increasingly important to him, the man who was both his friend and mentor. And now, he was right beside him at the end of the long fight that had gone on for decades, the fight that had trapped generations of men and their families to a below-subsistence existence, the fight against poverty.

Angus wiped the froth from his lightly stubbled chin. At 62 years of age he felt youthful and ready for another round. He grinned at his partner.

'Your father always enjoyed a wee drop of ale Sean.'

'That he did Angus, but he's not here anymore to enjoy it with us, is he.' Sean could not keep the anger out of his voice.

'Sean, there are ways and means to revenge his death. Remember, Seamus Keating was always a good man first, his own man. Yes, he fought for his family and his men here at the wharf. But you should know better than anyone that trouble always followed him and it was only a matter of time before the law caught up with him.

'Aye, he was a good man Angus, but he didn't deserve to die, not like that.'

'It's too soon for you Sean to see clearly that Seamus would not have done anything different under the circumstances.' The older man put a gentle hand on Sean's arm as he nodded quietly to the barman. The ales appeared almost instantly. 'At least we can toast his life and vow that his great work will never go to waste.'

Sean looked into Angus's sympathetic eyes, grateful for the chance to continue the worship of Seamus Keating, his father, the father who was always at the waterfront, fighting for the rights of workers, taking on the bosses, challenging them to share their profits and if they lacked the heart to do that, then at least improve conditions for the men and their families who relied on them. Tears sprang to his eyes at the sudden show of emotion and courage at the pub. Seamus Keating wasn't just his father, but he was a man who spoke for all of them. He had put food on more than one table in his fight to free the wharf workers of Ireland from poverty and subservience.

Angus smiled broadly, tossing back the ale and turning to the bar, one arm loosely about Sean's broad and steady shoulders. 'When you're through your grieving son, you'll have to face up to the ugly side of your father, the side that's in your blood too. None of you Keating men are mild mannered. Not you, your father or his father before him, Sean. Your father knew more than a thing or two about those recent murders here at the wharf. He loathed any pimp that put the future of his men at risk. You know that don't you?'

'Game of pool Angus?' Sean deflected the suggestion of the reality he knew all too well. In his heart he was a Keating to the core. Anger burned brightly at the slightest provocation and here in Ireland the coals of conflict were never doused.

The room was filling with smoke; the red patterned carpet darkened with spilled ale and years of tired feet tramping to and from the bar between work shifts. Here, the men had precious moments to relax and talk amongst themselves. This was the pub that brought them together as one, where they felt free from the iron first that ruled them. Hunger and anger seemed to go hand in hand and it wouldn't be the first time that Seamus Keating would be the subject of conversation for his fight to win workers' rights, only now he was gone.

Angus turned to Sean. He knew that Sean was grieving more than just the death of his father. It was grieving the wasted years of boyhood when his father was at sea, or lost to him fighting another campaign on the docks.

'Sean. There was never a better father and you never forget that.' Angus saw the tears spring to Sean's eyes. He pulled him towards the pool table. 'You break.' Angus gave him the pool cue, dropped a coin into the slot and watched the balls tumble together into the shaft.

Sean steadied himself and set the balls squarely within the neat triangle on the pool table. The green felt was almost as beautiful as the open spaces of Ireland. He never wanted to leave Ireland, but he knew that Angus was right and that he must get away from the past, the darkness and anger that followed him around especially here at the docks.

Sean leant onto the table, setting his eye on the tip of the perfect triangle of balls. He pulled the cue backwards then quickly jabbed the white ball, setting the group spinning right and left and dropping two of the coloured balls into the back pockets.

'Great start man.' Angus clapped him on the back. 'You get another shot.'

Sean, tight-lipped yet pleased that he hadn't lost his eye for the game, set up another ball, placing it close to the cushion and cornering the white ball so it was virtually impossible for Angus to drop a ball without it bouncing off the edge.

'You certainly haven't lost your touch.' Angus leant forward, wincing at the awkward angle, bouncing the ball off the cushion and neatly pegging the shot.

'You're not too bad yourself then Angus.' Sean grinned. His sombre mood suddenly lifted as if it were nothing more than the smoke haze settling under the pool table lights. Sean moved like a cat to the other side of the table, eyeing the spread of balls for his next shot. 'Your shot Angus.' Sean's eyes twinkled with the challenge.

'An old hand like me.' Angus feigned a weary sigh. 'As if any of us have a chance against you young fellas.'

'Steady on! I'm not that young,' Sean protested.

'Aye. That's true laddie. You had better not lose what you've got left. If your father had a little more sense, he wouldn't have set the mob onto the bosses and he would be still here with us today.'

'You're convinced he was murdered.' Sean stated flatly.

'Aren't you Sean?'

'I don't know. He always took risks and it didn't surprise me that the vehicle rolled.'

'Ahh, but you didn't check to see whether it had been tampered with.'

'Did you?' Sean stood up suddenly, squaring against Angus, looking him straight in the eye.

'That I did son. That I did.' Angus said carefully.

Sean felt the anger rising, a dark anger that could explode any minute.

'You have to play your hand like you play pool Sean. Never lose control. Always keep your cool and plan carefully.' Angus drew in his breath and held it, then slowly breathed out counting …two, three, four, five. He drew in his breath again.

Sean understood. He counted inwardly to ten as he thought about his next shot, pacing slowly around the table. He positioned himself carefully, setting up the shot.

'Perfect.' Angus's voice was ice-cold sober.

'So it was payback Angus?' Sean kept his control.

'That it was son. He stuck his neck way out and they lopped it off.'

Sean's eyes turned to ice.

'You can't do anythin' about it Sean. Not now. They'll be watching you like a hawk. You're better out of the country for now.'

'What do I do? Sail around the world until kingdom come?'

'There will be work for you elsewhere. Anyway it might pay off to broaden your network.'

'I'm not sure that I need a network Angus.' Sean rubbed some chalk on the end of his pool cue. 'Then you're right as usual. I'd be far better to leave now before the anger starts again.'

'You'll need it in the future, and so will the men. Come with me to Australia.'

'Maybe I can continue the fight from there. But I do know that the men still need my father with them here now Angus. They needed his courage and his protection when he was alive and they need it now. I can fight for them just like he did. I can fight for their rights and make sure that at least there will be some bread on their tables at the end of every night and every week.' Sean felt his heart bursting against his ribcage. His lungs hurt as the emotion took over.

Angus shrugged nonchalantly, trying to defuse the bomb that was ready to explode inside Sean. 'Well, let's say that you could have a well-earned holiday Sean. The fresh air would do you good. You'll like Australia. The coasts are free and there are plenty of open spaces for a man to carve new dreams on.'

Sean listened, breathing carefully to control his outburst, letting the anger settle and Angus's words soothe his brain.

'Then there's the land. I've seen none better than the Monaro where I have my handkerchief selection. You know Sean,' Angus was suddenly gripped with enthusiasm 'the place would still be all kangaroos, wombats and crows without your ancestors and mine. Some of it, especially just under the mountains, is almost as beautiful as here. Come back with me. It would do you good.'

'Maybe you're right Angus. Maybe I need a new perspective. Maybe there's some sense in a having a break from all of this.'

'You can't go wrong Sean. It's not all roses, not by any means, but it will work out.' Angus quickly built on his advantage. 'Besides working at the wharf, you know I've been asked on another assignment. I'll need you at my back Sean. You're the only person I can really trust and count on for that work. You know that don't you'

'Oh?' Sean looked up, the anger suddenly lifting.

'Hmm.' Angus nodded quietly.

'Looks like things are heating up down south. A bit of surveillance work. Nothing in the conflict zone, but enough to keep our wits about us.'

'Then it looks as though we're heading to Australia.' Sean put down the pool cue. For the first time since the death of his father, he felt a sense of peace. His eyes glinted with the prospect of a new challenge. Angus was right. There were bigger fish to fry and the change would do him good.

VICTORIA, AUSTRALIA

The journey by sea to Australia was longer than Sean had expected. Angus had lined up meetings at different ports around the world and he was meticulous in his research at each one. There was an unfolding pattern at each of the docks, — the gradual removal of workers' rights, the sale of infrastructure to private companies and at the same time, the gradual erosion of security. Without the stronghold of the unions, the ports were fast becoming open portals for the illegal trafficking of goods, people and terrorists.

It was six weeks before they berthed in Tasmania, the entry into the harbour along the Derwent River was shrouded under the black cloak of night. The gentle lap, lap of the incoming tide against the hull was strangely comforting as they slipped into port. There was no hurry here to be noticed or to do anything that would draw attention to themselves. Angus especially wanted Sean to remain undercover, hidden until he was in position to start the surveillance work. The running of illegal shipping in the Southern Ocean, the pilfering of rare fish and the trafficking of goods was on the increase. Hobart was the closest port of call for the ships roaming the furthest oceans, but it was Melbourne where the transactions took place. And it wasn't just illegal goods, it was guns that they were after.

The boat drew next to Constitution Dock. In the dead of night, only the clanking of rigging against masts and the occasional light told them that there was life this far south towards Antarctica.

Hobart was asleep as if settlement had never taken place.

Sean could sense the power of isolation here. There was still the ancient aura of settlers and convicts huddled together at the port, hoping to find purchase in this far away land. He could almost hear the mournful echo of iron leg chains rattling amongst the boats moored at the dock and the cries of famine and torture. The sounds were no different to those he left far behind in Ireland where hunger, desperation and slavery ruled over men.

'Secure the berth.' Angus said quietly. 'We'll be OK here for the time being. Maybe we can get ourselves a fresh feed in the morning and a good cup of coffee.'

'Tops.' Sean sprang into action and in moments they were berthed and ready to sleep. Sean knew it would only be a matter of days, weeks at the most, and the memories of the war in Ireland would fade and he would find his feet in this new land. Here they would spend the remainder of the night and the following morning. After a hearty breakfast, piping hot coffee and the morning paper, there would be time to explore the wharf and the town. The thrill of a new start was as good as a totally new life. Sean knew that Angus was right. It was only a matter of twenty four hours before they would head up the east coast of Tasmania towards the mainland. Bass Strait, Angus warned him, was as rough as the North Sea and as cold as the Atlantic.

The remote Victorian coast was silent. The night was as dark under a cloudy and moonless sky, the southern stars hidden as if wrapped in black velvet. Sean felt an immediate sense of calm. His nerves, usually raw from endless campaigns on the Irish wharves, where guns, knives and blunt instruments were as common as words, instantly responded to the strange and empty shoreline. Angus left him at Flinders Island to cross the final leg of Bass Strait alone.

'I'm flying out from Flinders Sean. I need to do some preparatory work in Melbourne. But I'll pick you up at Marlo. The estuary on the Snowy River is open so you won't have any problems getting in. The captain will wait for the incoming tide. I'll be there.'

For the most part, the wild expanse of coast was empty, other than a scatter of small settlements and infrastructure that stretched from Green Cape to Melbourne. Sometimes, Custom's vessels hugged the shores and ports hoping to make a catch — capturing drug-carrying tugs and yachts brave enough to wander along the wild Victorian shore. But those vessels rarely ventured into the storms. There was enough history of shipwrecks to warn even the most adventurous of sailors and drug runners to stay well clear in a storm.

Sean was both weary and excited. He knew that his grandfather once hoped to escape the poverty of Ireland for himself and his family by sailing to Australia. But his chances were thwarted by the lack of means or opportunity or both. It seemed fair that Sean now had that chance, albeit on the back of Angus's connections.

The thick coil of rope flew across the widening gap and Sean watched as the strands landed neatly on the boat.

'Stern rope next' Angus shouted.

Sean steadied himself to jump onto the wharf, carefully timing the rise and swell of the boat on each wave. He leapt outwards catching his hand on the berth pole. The sensation of rope burning his fingers as he slipped and regained his footing was both a welcome reminder of his mortality and tangible evidence of arriving at the shore.

'Here's your pack.' The burly and wind-chiselled captain of the fishing trawler hurled the haversack onto the jetty then tossed the sleeping bag straight at Sean. The man looked as though he could stop a bull, his shoulders thickset and powerful after years of hauling in nets and longlines and of heaving baskets of fish onto the wharves. He grinned. 'Don't want to get your swag wet mate!

Welcome to Australia.'

Angus released the bow rope. He heard the soft thud of the stern rope as it landed on the deck. The trawler was already unreachable to the two men at the wharf as she drifted away from the jetty. Then the engine kicked into life, steadying the drift of the boat. Diesel fumes filled the air as the trawler suddenly turned and headed back into the night.

'That's that then Sean.' Angus turned and thumped Sean on the back. 'You won't be seeing her again son. She's gone as if she were never here. No lights, no flags, no foghorns.'

Their arrival in Australia seemed so sudden after the long journey from Ireland and everything in between. The final transfer to the Tasmanian fishing trawler on the East Coast of Tasmania meant that they were at last, close to the Australian mainland. After days of waiting for calm weather they finally crossed Bass Strait and steamed over the edge of the continental shelf and straight into the mouth of the Snowy River.

As he stared into the darkness, all Sean could see was the soft rooster tail of the trawler glinting in the light of dawn as she headed back towards Tasmania. He watched the bow spray rising like ancient mists from the tiny boat; insignificant against the endless blackness of the sea. All seemed lost in the vast expanse of water. Then rising from the waves, he imagined he saw the outline of a horse. The stallion emerged from the sea like Bucephalus, his mane trailing starkly across the white of the bow spray, his eyes shining brilliantly like dawn stars. As he rose above the swell, the horse held his head high, the white star blazoned on his forehead visible, his magnificent eyes staring straight at Sean.

Sean felt his own eyes lock with the stallion's. An involuntary shudder ran down the back of his spine as he recognised in the horse something of himself: a fierceness and readiness for battle, a destiny far greater than the expanse of the widening sea that had taken him far from his original home. Both he and the horse were the same; untamed and free.

Angus stopped, witnessing the veil of silence surrounding Sean. Only the flicker and sparkle of offshore rigs broke the stark scene. He touched Sean quietly on the shoulder, pulled the keys to the truck from his pocket and walked quickly to the end of the wharf.

'Get in.' Angus did not even look over his shoulder. 'Toss your gear in the back. We're out of here. No lights until the highway, then it's about three to four hours to Port Melbourne. We'll be there in time for a breakfast at the pub and you can lie low in the hotel until the evening.'

Angus turned the key in the ignition and the engine kicked over quietly and surely. 'I'll come and get you when I'm ready Sean. I have to get the payment sorted.'

Sean said nothing.

The road wound slowly to the right and climbed over the low range towards Melbourne. It would only be a matter of time before the traffic intensified. The Victorian countryside contrasted starkly to his own land — the harsh and often mournful Monaro. Here, the rich soils yielded agricultural spoils year after year bringing consistent wealth to landowners. Generations of farmers thrived on the land all the way from East Gippsland to the Mornington Peninsula south of Melbourne.

Angus changed down a gear as he drew closer to the first set of lights outside the city. Sean stirred at the change in the low tone of the engine, his eyes rested but mouth uncomfortable with dryness and the taste of stale smoke.

'You'd better chew more gum. That will get rid of it.'

'Are you a mind reader or what?' Sean felt stiff and rough.

'Nope. You sure lost a lot over the side though.' Angus spoke pragmatically.

'You're not wrong there.' Sean winced as he pulled himself into a full sitting position. 'My ribs are still sore.' He managed to smile.

'We'll soon be in Melbourne for hot coffee and breakfast at the pub.'

'Sounds great. And a great drive too.'

'Nothing you'll ever remember.' Angus swung the wheel. 'You were fast asleep for most of it Sean.' Angus laughed. 'You'll be fine Sean. There are enough rough Irish lads here already so you don't have to hide yourself beneath fancy accents or the like.' Angus prepared him for a 'normal' adjustment. 'Just be yourself. It always works best.'

'I'll do that. Seemed to work OK wherever else I've been.' He smiled widely.

Angus nodded quietly. He flicked his glance to the right hand mirror looking quickly for unmarked police cars. He knew which cars cruised through this patch and where to look for them. There was no use in bringing unwanted attention to themselves by driving too fast. The main game was to deliver Sean quickly into the hotel and place him under wraps.

Sean caught his mood and stared straight ahead, not looking as if the world around him did not exist.

'Want another smoke?'

'That will do nicely Sean.' Angus responded.

Angus expertly negotiated the early morning Melbourne traffic straight into the heart of the city and the docklands. 'We're here. This is it Sean. The wharfies' pub.' Angus smiled as if he had built the hotel himself.

'Looks flash to me.'

'She's old and gracious Sean. Nothing fancy, but the men are safe here. No one asks them questions. Once inside the pub, the police keep their distance. They are polite and won't press the point if there is a bit of a scuffle from time to time. They know there will be less trouble that way so we keep our place and they keep theirs.'

'Can't imagine any copper being polite if you don't mind my saying so Angus.'

Angus grinned. 'We keep the ones happy who watch our turf and they leave us alone if you like.'

'Neat arrangement!'

'Not all of them are quite so cooperative but the ones who drink with us have their own interests to attend to. That way everyone is happy.'

Angus pulled up and yanked on the handbrake. 'Inside and upstairs. Room 115. Have a shower and shave. See you in the dining room in half an hour.'

Sean got out of the truck, pulled his pack out of the back and headed straight into the hotel and up the stairs. He looked as though he knew exactly where he was going. He memorised the position of the stairs, carpeted in the dark red of the King George pattern. The numbers ran left to right with the odd numbers on the right. The door to Room 115 was open and the key on the telephone table. Sean shut and locked the door and walked straight to the shower, turning the hot water on full. He walked back into the bedroom and across the room to the window. Carefully, he drew the curtains closed and quickly checked the room, the lights, ceiling and wall plugs and turned on the radio. The room looked clean. Angus was true to his word. He threw his clothes on the bed and stepped under the stream of steaming hot water and washed away more than just the days of travel and the memories of rough nights on ocean freighters and fishing trawlers.

The sun poured in through the dining room window and spilled onto the carpet. Angus sat at a table where he could see the door, the door to the toilets and the food counter. There was nothing that escaped him. He knew all the exits, how long it would take to walk to the car and who was sitting where. When Sean entered the room Angus nodded imperceptibly to the table with cereals, fruit and the toaster. It was 'help yourself' to as much as you wanted and Angus already had a good serve of cereal and fruit and slices of thick toast with honey. Sean glanced quickly at Angus's setting and did the same, choosing different cereal, no fruit and peanut butter.

'Could you do us a couple of 'cinos Joyce?' Angus smiled at the woman who walked up to their table. 'This is my close friend Sean, Joyce.'

'Good to meet you Sean. Cappuccino?'

'Thank you Joyce. Nice to meet you too.' Sean smiled and dipped his head.

Joyce quickly noticed the instant charm and handsomeness of Angus's friend, the finely chiselled nose and high cheekbones with grey flecks in his neatly cropped hair adding a touch of distinction to his natural Irish appeal. Joyce blushed. It was not often that Angus brought such refined-looking guests into her bar or breakfast room. This man was different, but she sensed a coldness in him that made her shiver despite herself. Angus caught her flinch and smiled warmly thanking her for the extra service.

'Sean, there's a Labor Party function on today, so there will be a mixture of people, businessmen, union leaders, politicians — that sort of thing. It's an important occasion. We survived Regan's 'axe the union campaign' so we're celebrating. You mark my words, there's also some serious business going down.' Angus looked straight into Sean's eyes. 'The government is trying another round with non-union, foreign labour running the freight lines along the coast. The Ukrainians are being hauled in to run our lines and we'll not only lose the dockyards but also the trade along the coast. We can't survive the competition and be damned if we're going to lose a hundred years of hard won wars. They're determined to destroy the unions because that way, they'll finish the Labor party if you see what I mean. It's dirty out here, real dirty. So we have to win at their game to keep ourselves employed.'

'Sounds just like the home country Angus.' Sean shook his head in disbelief.

'Yup. As we have discovered Sean.'

'Anyone important coming along I should know?'

'There will be people with links to the old country Sean. But we don't want to encourage that sort of trouble out here. There's enough going on already.'

'I understand that Angus.' Sean pronounced each word slowly and clearly.

'Good. Then we'll all get along fine. Still, it is important that you know who's who and for them to get to know you. Could be some useful relationships developed tonight. You won't have the profile you had at home, but with your skills to hand, you could find yourself quickly in demand.'

'I'd like that' Sean said quietly.

Joyce shepherded a kid to a table near the door. 'You sit down here Tom,' then walked across to Angus and Sean's table.

'Here are your coffees Angus.'

'Who's the kid Joyce? Didn't know you and Richard had any kids.'

'He arrived last week. I'm looking after him for now.'

'Oh?'

'Richard did a friend a favour and who got him out of school. He needed a place to stay.'

'What happened?'

'A priest.' Joyce looked at the floor.

Angus stiffened, the blood draining from his face and jaw tightening under now dangerously white skin. His fists clenched involuntarily pulling the tablecloth toward him and spilling some of the coffee.

'Angus…' Joyce placed a hand on his soldier.

'Leave it to me Joyce.' Angus's voice was gripped with anger. He took a few minutes to control himself then jerkily drank his coffee.

Sean tensed up, the bitterness rising in his throat. 'Bastards.'

'You can say that again Sean. Makes me sick.'

'My grandfather knew what to do with them at home.' Sean felt the rage sitting hard in his chest.

Angus looked across to the table where the kid who seemed to be nothing more than a ghost of himself was slowly eating cereal. Joyce hovered close by, as if he would suddenly vanish.

'Poor kid. Wish I could get my hands on the whoever got to him' Angus bristled with rage.

Joyce came over with more toast.

'I've lost me appetite Joyce. Thanks anyway.'

'Sean? More toast?'

'Thank you kindly Joyce.' Sean met her eyes.

Joyce drew in her breath sharply when she saw the ice in his eyes.

'Angus?'

'Leave him to me Joyce. I think Sean has seen this sort of thing before and my guess is that he also has zero tolerance.'

Joyce nodded. 'Just don't get yourselves into any trouble Angus.'

'Aye lassie.' Angus attempted to lighten the atmosphere. 'Take it from me, there are ways to work these things out.'

PAYBACK ON THE MELBOURNE DOCKS

The pub had already filled to three-quarters capacity by the time Sean was ready to make his entrance. The ale flowed freely from the taps behind the bar, keeping the conversations sparking between the assortment of union leaders, politicians and their minders. The atmosphere was charged with celebration but Angus knew that this meeting was also about survival. No one had come here tonight under any illusions, that the fight to save the unions was over. The union movement was under a double threat, sandwiched between the Liberals determined to do everything in their power to emasculate and destroy the 'new-look' Labor Party on the one hand and the corporate heavyweights on the other.

Angus was already at the bar. He ordered a schooner of light and loosely wrapped an arm around Sean's shoulder. Joyce had found Sean some 'evening' clothes, nothing too fancy, nothing too casual so he would feel at home here in Melbourne at the pub. As an "engineer", Sean would be cashed up and expected to look as good in his civvies as his working gear. The coat Joyce found him hung easily off his broad and well-defined shoulders, if not a little short at the sleeve. The length and cut of the Tweed was just right, matching the dark blue-cuffed trousers. Sean looked casual yet smart, the clothes matching a hint of grey in his hair.

'You look good. Relax and I'll introduce you to the boys.' Angus smiled at Joyce. 'Pity you can't dress me up like this Joyce.'

'You always look handsome just as you are Angus.' Joyce blushed.

'You can't have her Angus. Besides, who would pull your beers if she eloped on one of your antipodean escapades?' The publican smiled. He was a big man with a shock of blonde hair and shoulders almost the width of a door.

'This is as antipodean as you can be Richard if you ask me, and it isn't as if I am about to take you on for any reason!'

'I reckon we're fairly sophisticated in these parts don't you Joyce?' Richard winked at his wife. 'This grand old lady has hosted more parties than there are grey hairs on your lawless Scottish head.'

'Aye, she has that Richard, but lawless? Not since we Scots have our crown and throne safe and secure from you British lads. The boot's on the other foot now!' Angus was ready for a light and friendly skirmish with the publican. On the other hand, just shaking his hand was a sobering experience.

'Hey, I didn't mean you personally. I wouldn't be wantin' to meet you in battle at that! What do you think Sean? Are the Scots not a marauding and lawless bunch of thieves?'

Sean laughed but his humour was muted by the fresh memory of the fights in Ireland.

'Aye they are at that.' Sean spoke soberly and quietly. 'I would never hesitate for a moment though to put my life in the hands of any of them if they are as keen as Angus.' Sean made firm his public 'thank you' to Angus.

'C'mon then Sean. Let's leave these royals to their fine carpet and gilded views and we'll join the plebs.'

'No plebs here!' protested Joyce.

'Nothing but the finest and the best can be found in your pub Joyce.' He nudged Sean quietly into the centre of the gathering where he would blend in as 'one of the boys'.

'Angus, how are you doin'?' A smoothly dressed man in dark grey put out his hand.

'Andrew! How are you? Sean this is our Labor Party representative.

This is his night of nights you could say. Gathering of the party faithful at his home pub.'

'Glad ter meet you too Andrew.'

'What are you drinking?' A taller man broke in.

'Sean?"

'Guinness, thanks.' Sean nodded in acknowledgment.

'Angus? Don't tell me you're on schooners tonight?'

'Just the one James. I'll have a scotch if ye don't mind, and water, but just a little, of the water that is.' Angus grinned.

'My pleasure.' James walked quickly to the bar.

Angus carried on with introductions then looked soberly at Sean. 'James, is our local policeman. Helpful fellow.'

'Party member?'

James stepped back in the circle. 'Sure am. Labor Party like my father before me and his father before him. The unions and Labor runs in our blood. Isn't that right Angus?'

'You are right about that James.'

James turned smoothly towards the well dressed men gathered in the pub. 'To the Union!'

The politician stepped forward on cue, his dress contrasting with the faded hues of the working men gathered to hear him speak. He raised his glass 'To the union!'

'To the union.' The pub echoed with an urgent reminder that with pleasure came business.

'May she live long!' Angus whispered to himself.

'Long live the union and long live the Party.' A man in priest's attire joined Angus's circle.

Angus tensed very slightly but Sean, standing inches from him, felt the prickles on his neck.

'Father John' Angus feigned hearty pleasure putting his hand out. 'And Father Thomas'. Angus nodded at the second Priest. 'This is Sean. Sean Keating, a close friend of mine.'

'From the homeland?' Father John raised an eyebrow at Sean.

'Always close at hand though miles by sea,' Sean mused.

'Then we'll have a lot in common Sean.'

Sean felt a cold sweat forming down his back. His muscles reflexly tautened. With the maximum of self-control, he casually raised his glass in toast and took a swig of the Guinness, quietly shaking out his left fist so the fingers were loose and unclenched.

Richard had noticed the priests walk into the circle and quietly excused himself from behind the bar. 'Sean, come and meet some of the crew. I see that you make friends easily.'

'I make a few.' Sean was working hard to keep his voice cool and to control the sweat now gathering behind his trouser belt.

'Don't worry about Tom. The boy is safe with us.'

Sean was too angry to speak.

'Come with me. We'll spend a few quiet moments on the machines.' Richard ushered Sean expertly to the group of pokies.

Sean was momentarily mesmerised by the machines They were nothing more than false hope for souls desperate for meaning at the end of a long and joyless road.

'You only need tens on this one. Here's a dollar's worth. Play them slow, real slow.' Richard positioned himself next to Sean.

He put the first coin in and very slowly pulled the handle. The coin clattered as it dropped into the box and the array of cards rolled and arranged into a shabby line of colour.

'That's right Sean. One at a time. Just take your time.' Richard's voice soothed him as Sean placed another coin into the slot, drawing in his breath as he pulled the handle, his eyes focused on the cards stacking up in front of him.

'OK now?' Richard was careful, wary.

'I'm fine. Thanks Richard.' Sean pulled a clean handkerchief from his pocket and wiped the sweat from his forehead then carefully folded the handkerchief and placed it back in his pocket, all the time working to steady his hands shaking with unspoken rage. 'We'll go back in then?' Sean said quietly.

Richard looked directly at Sean. 'Let's join Angus. This speech will stir them up a bit, then there'll be drinks all round and plenty of pub talk before the night is through.' He tried a touch of humour but a grey pall of fear was visible on his cheekbones and eyes were drained of light.

'Sean.' Angus waited for the men to join them, then turned to listen to Andrew rallying the voters with his rousing speech. He briefly caught Richard's eye and his face told him everything he already knew.

'Comrades, we are here to celebrate the anniversary of Flanagan's Stevedoring defeat at the wharf.'

The men cheered loudly.

'It isn't just this one victory that we're here for.'

The dull sound of assent and the smell of sweat filled the room. The politician looked around the room with the eyes of a fox, watching and wondering whether his turf was safe. It was important to keep these men happy or there would be more than just seats lost at the next election. 'This is not the only time we'll have to protect our jobs.' He waited to hear the expected response, cheers and the sudden ease in tensions at the subtle emphasis on the our. 'We're here to make sure that non-union labour does not work these wharves or run our freight lines.' Now the men cheered and whooped.

Angus used the moment of wild enthusiasm as cover to give instructions to Sean. 'You won't be hanging around here son after what you are about to do. There's nothing I can do to stop you so you had better take the truck keys. The truck is in the back alley, through the dining room and the courtyard. Take the kid with you. We don't want anybody from the school snooping around the pub giving Joyce trouble. I'll tee it up with her after this. Drive north towards the city and follow the signs. There's a map in the glove box and the kid should know his way north out of Melbourne. Take the airport road and then head up the main highway until you come to Albury; then head for Corryong and Khancoban. It's about four or so hours drive from here. You can make camp for a couple of days and let the dust settle here. My property is over the mountains, on the NSW side of the divide.'

'Comrades, this is the one and only chance we have to keep our jobs. You will never be betrayed by Labor. Not while I'm on the job in any case.' The men cheered.

'You want to make bloody sure of that mate!' A swarthy-looking man yelled.

Richard noted the mood to kill and nodded to the politician to continue.

'No matter what else happens in the camp, I'm with you all the way. These new Labor types have another thing coming if they think that we're going to back away from our promises. Labor stays 60:40 union to non union and that's the bottom-line.'

Angus broke into the cheering, speaking urgently and quickly. 'Keep away from the main centres except for fuel and food. The farm is on the back road out of Berridale. They know me at the café. You'll get directions easily enough and everyone knows the truck.' Angus slipped the keys into Sean's coat pocket. 'No questions asked. Stay within the law on the main roads and you won't be stopped. Once you're there, it's safe to drive the country roads. I'll send the word out that you and the boy are minding the farm while I'm at sea. Understood?'

Sean kept looking forwards to the speaker and nodded. From the corner of his right eye he noted the two priests, about four men away from where he was now.

'Are we going to fight to the last?' the politician knew he was now on safe ground and he had the wharfies in the palm of his hand.

'To the last!' the men roared and suddenly Joyce appeared at the bar, pulling the first beer of the rush that was about to come. The men had plenty to celebrate and another war to win.

'I'll buy this round.' Sean spoke politely to the priests. 'Scotch?'

'Thank you Sean. Good speech?'

'Good enough.' Sean smiled but his mood was completely blank. He walked to the bar and Joyce immediately served him, knowing it would not help to keep an angry man waiting.

'Three scotches Joyce. Make mine straight.'

'Straight it is Sean.'

'Angus said he'd talk to you about the kid. We'll be leaving at 11 p.m. I want him packed and ready, with his gear and my gear in the truck, if that's alright with you Joyce. We're out of here after the do.'

'I see. Angus is the right person to give Tom a fresh start away from here. And if you are a friend of his Sean, then so are you.'

'We'll look after him as if he were our own Joyce. Now don't you be worryin' about a thing.' Sean handed her the money for the scotch and slipped his hand back into his pocket. As he picked up the first two glasses in one hand he dropped a couple a sachets of powder into the first glass.

'Where did you get that stuff Sean?' Joyce asked.

'Don't you mind Joyce.' Sean tried to speak gently to her but his eyes already told her to back away, carefully.

She stepped back to the bottles of spirits and poured one for Richard. 'Get the boy ready Richard. They're leaving.' Joyce's voice was barely audible against the din.

'Thanks Joyce.' Richard took the drink. 'I'll take a quick break upstairs then my turn behind the bar.' Richard swung open the bar half-door watching Sean. Sean rejoined the group of men and handed the first drink to Father John, then Father Thomas. Sean took his own glass in his left hand and placed his right arm around Father John's shoulder.

'Excuse me Father' Sean spoke to Father Thomas. 'There are just a few matters I need to discuss with Father John. Being a bit new here, I need to know where the services and all are. Then there's the question of my dying mother. It's the cancer you know. She hasn't got that long to live.'

'Of course. I'm sorry to hear about your mother Sean.'

'Thanks. Father John?'

'Sean. Where do you want to talk?'

'I don't think Joyce will mind if we use the dining room for now.' Sean was emphatic in his choice.

Father John looked at Joyce. Her head was bowed as she pulled a round of beers.

'No, I don't think she'll mind. Let's go then.'

Sean dropped his hand from the man's shoulder and ushered him towards the closed door linking the two rooms.

'There. This table looks good enough.' Sean pulled out a chair for the priest, noting the exit to the back courtyard and the internal locking system. It would be a simple matter of turning the handle. No noise, nothing broken.

Angus understood the routine. He had heard enough and seen enough. Sean would need cover. Their exit was unnoticed, but the other priest would have to be taken care of as well. Quickly, he made his way to the bar.

'Joyce, I'm going upstairs and will phone you from my mobile phone. I need you to call that priest over.'

'Are you sure Angus?' Joyce trembled slightly.

'His mind is set.' Angus was resolute.

'If you think it's the right thing Angus.'

'No-one has answers to this one Joyce, not you, not me, not Richard and definitely not our slick politician over there, or his police friends. They're all in this together if you want my opinion. So we'll keep it amongst ourselves shall we? Just you, Richard and me. No one else needs to know.'

Joyce could not speak for a moment. 'Tom is the one we should be thinking about.'

'Exactly. Tom.'

'What are you going to do about your conscience Angus?'

'My loyalty comes from the heart Joyce. My loyalty is to the truth and not to these pedophile priests or to their fake politician friends who don't give a shite about any of us here.'

'You'd kill for that truth?'

'As I said Joyce. This is a different war.'

'There must be goodness in the man at least. You of all people must know that Angus.'

'I know this much Joyce. There's a kid in your hotel who was subject to something evil. His is the life here that is worth saving and the journey of the man Sean has taken out of our company, does not count. He has had his chance at a good life and he blew it apart all by himself.'

'The phone's on the second landing.'

'Thanks Joyce.' Angus slipped away from the bar.

No one saw him leave and already Richard was back at the bar, placing a hand on Joyce's arm then around her waist.

'Why don't you take a break darling? Join them on the floor for a while.'

'OK Richard. Angus is going to ring the bar to call over Father Thomas.' Joyce nodded as if in the direction of the priest, but did not look.

'I'll handle it.'

Joyce looked gratefully at Richard, then firmly closed the dining room door and walked from behind the bar into the gathering of men.

'What can I do for you son?' Father John spoke in his most calming and soothing manner.

'Thank you Father. First, a toast to the Union.'

'A toast!'

Sean downed his drink in one gulp and waited whilst Father John drank the first draught of his.

'I see you like your drink just as the Irish do.'

'Shall I get another while you catch up Father?'

'There'll be no need.' Father John knocked back the rest of his scotch.

'Father. I have to be honest with you.' Sean wasted no time. 'There's a problem with a young man I know, who is thinking of taking an overdose. He's only about 16 years old. He says it's been going on for a while.' Sean waited for the effect of the words to sink in.

'Go on.' Father John encouraged him through tired eyes.

'I think you know him Father.'

'One of the boys at my school?'

'Yes, Father. You must know about it.'

'Me know about what? If it is drugs on the school campus there would be nothing I would not do to get them out of the school.'

Sean said nothing, but stared at the priest.

'I don't quite get your meaning Sean?' Father John went to stand up but could not move from his chair. Sean stood up a second before the thought to move had time to form in Father John's mind. Already he was behind the priest, yanking his chair out from the table and hauling him to his feet.

'Let's just go out the back shall we Father.'

'I'm not sure…'

'You're not sure about what Father?' Sean pulled the man to his feet and with one arm pulled the priests' right arm behind his back and pushed him forward.

'Are you not sure that you're willing to come along or are you not sure which boy it is?

'Steady on.' Father John was quickly losing his grip, his mouth dry and speech beginning to slur.

'I'll steady you all right.' Sean spat the words into his ear. 'I'll put you right on the straight and narrow.' Sean gave the man a shove in the back so that he winced in pain. He opened the back door out of the pub with his free hand making sure it was unlocked for his return.

'The boy...' fear was plastered on the Priest's face and in his eyes.

'There will be no more boys where you're going Father. I'll make very sure of that.' Sean pushed the priest to the back gate, opened it and forced him into the alley. The truck was jammed against the wall leaving just enough space for him to open the driver's door. He pulled Angus's car keys from his pocket and opened the passenger door.

'Now get in!'

Sean shoved the Priest into the truck and slammed the door shut. He walked around the bonnet, opened the driver's door and placed the key in the ignition, watching the alley in front and behind. No one was there. He turned the key and pulled out from the courtyard keeping the lights off until they moved into the street leading to the wharf. He couldn't believe how easy it had been. The man hardly knew what had happened to him, but Sean reckoned in the five minutes left of his life, he had just enough time to think and put two and two together. If he was really lucky, there could be a few extra seconds to ask forgiveness of his 'god'.

The drive to the wharf took minutes only. Sean already had a rough idea of the public and 'private' wharf areas from what Angus had described to him on the way over from Ireland. The private wharf was not lit up but probably secure. Sure enough, as he drove down a long and narrow road leading to the loading bays he came to a locked gate. The Priest was already slumped forward, his head lolling on his chest as he began to lose consciousness. Sean jerked the Priest's head back, putting one hand onto the collar behind his neck to keep him upright; that was for now anyway. He stopped outside the security box and kept the engine running.

'Special delivery.'

The gate opened without question and Sean accelerated towards the line of containers awaiting shipment off the wharf. This was smoother than what he was used to at home where you had to pay off half a dozen people to get the job done. Here, there was no one around to pay, no one to put him into the corner with blackmail and if he was really lucky, no extra people to take care of if they were unlucky enough to be in the wrong place at the wrong time. Sean toyed for a moment with the thoughts of where to dump the body. The Priest was carrying in his blood enough white powder to kill two men twice his size and Sean knew that there was no need for anything more than what he had done already. There would be no extraneous marks, no signs of struggle, no blood. He preferred it that way. End of story. His immediate problem was to get rid of the body and make sure there were no links back to Angus's truck. Sean drove to the end of the loading bay and swung the truck around reversing it as close as he could to the water. There was no one around. He sat and watched for any sign of life. The wharf was clean and quiet. Softly, he opened the driver's door then took out the wheel jack. He fitted it under the back tray, dropping the spare wheel onto the tarmac and holding it steady so that there would be no noise when it fell. He untied the chain holding the wheel and wound it back into position without the tyre. He moved the wheel to the right of the dropped tailgate to make room for the preparation and last rites of the priest.

The guard was out of sight and Sean imagined that if he was able to see the truck, he would be discreetly looking in the other direction. He had probably come across a range of 'specials' and this was a closed wharf. His job was to keep the wharf clean of snoops and non-union snouts, all too ready to find 'performance loopholes' that could break their advantage and, ultimately, their livelihoods.

Sean opened the door to the cab and pulled the priest's head off his chest. The priest's eyes rolled back. There was little point in looking for a pulse. The man was gone. He could easily dump him then call an ambulance. The thought had crossed Sean's mind. He did not want to murder. This was intended as payback where the law refused to acknowledge abuse and deliver justice.

The body lay face upwards, arms crossing the chest and eyes closed. The frothy saliva gathered at the lips cyanosed by lack of oxygen. Sean stepped over the body and lifted the wheel onto the chest. It was a 'generic' that could belong to any of a dozen brands of similar truck, and it was unlikely that anyone would be trawling the bottom of the harbour for a child molester.

Sean Keating worked quickly. He wrapped a length of fencing wire around one edge of the wheel then rolled the body onto the wheel. Within seconds he wound the rest of the wire around the priest's body and secured it to the wheel.

A light rain began to fall. There would be a dozen or more movements only on and off the wharf for the time being and there was no reason for anyone to come looking here for the priest. Angus could be relied upon to develop a watertight alibi so it would be difficult to trace the last movements of the Father John. If Father Thomas were to start poking around for answers, the word would be put on him about the 'activities' of Father John that would bring unwanted attention to a school competing for both students and funds. No school or for that matter, no institution, could afford the scandal.

Without hesitation Sean dropped the priest into the dark waters of the harbour. He didn't even look to see if there were any bubbles rising or if the body had disappeared. He closed the tailgate, stepped into the driver's seat, engaged the gears and released the handbrake. Sean accelerated smoothly towards the gate switching on his headlights as he did so. The guard saw him coming and had the gate open in time for Sean to drive through without stopping. If anyone noticed anything, he felt confident that no one was going to say so.

There were a few women now present in the bar, arriving at the suggested time for light snacks after the official 'men's business' was complete.

Joyce said nothing. She felt the change in the atmosphere, a quiet chill. Sean had been gone for about 15 minutes. Richard suddenly called across for Father Thomas as Sean moved back into the gathering, mixing easily with the union men watching the football on the big screen.

'It's for you Father. Something urgent I think.' Richard handed him the receiver.

'Thanks. Hello, Father Thomas here.'

'Father' Angus disguised his voice by adopting a polite and cultured voice. 'Father John said that he'll meet you at the College and could you make your own way back.'

'Right you are. Thanks for calling.'

The receiver clicked as Angus replaced the phone and slipped quickly down the stairs.

'Father, can I get you another drink?' Richard detained him at the bar.

'I'd better not have another one thank you Richard. Father John has left early. I'll stay about another half hour then catch a cab back to the college.'

'You won't have to do that. Angus, do you know anyone who's going up Caulfield way?' Richard yelled above the crowd.

Angus was already in the centre of the group.

'Anyone going to Caulfield?' Angus shouted into the crowd.

There was a rally of 'Caulfield?' until someone came up to the bar.

'Father Thomas will need a lift home if you're going that way.'

'My pleasure Father. What time did you want to go?'

'About half an hour?'

'Half an hour will be just enough time for us to finish this round. My wife will be driving of course. Join us for the rest?'

'Thanks. I'd like that.'

Richard looked carefully when Sean walked in. His hair was unruffled, jacket still hanging in the same sculptured line off his broad shoulders as when he entered the pub earlier in the evening. There was nothing to give him away, nothing about his manner that suggested the tone of his actions except for the icy emotions mirrored in his eyes.

Sean unlocked his room and tossed his clothes onto the bed, flicked on the TV and turned the volume control up sufficiently to deter unwanted visitors. He walked into the bathroom and stepped under the shower, grateful for the heat striking the back of his neck, relaxing his shoulders and allowing his hands to shake free. He washed himself carefully then wrapped a towel around his waist. He walked back into the bedroom and pulled on his brown corduroy trousers and pullover. Then he picked up the tweed coat and dark blue trousers and took them into the shower. He shook both the coat and trousers vigorously shaking off any hair into the cubicle and ran the shower again for five minutes. The hair would probably be from him, but he was taking no chances. He then folded the coat and trousers neatly placed them in the bag exactly as he found them when Joyce delivered them that afternoon. Joyce would have them dry-cleaned before returning or discarding them.

Sean's identity was now totally different. Outwardly, he was again the Irish ex-mercenary crossing the world to leave behind his past as well as inwardly unmoved by what he had just done. Usually, he had to talk himself into 'forgetting' but this time, he felt that justice had been served and he found no challenge from his conscience for his actions.

It was 10.30 p.m. Sean rested lightly on the bed, television muted to low volume; his eyes were closed but he was not asleep. All his senses were alert, watching and waiting for the signal to leave. They had to have time to close the pub. By law they could open until late, but Joyce preferred the 6 to 10 pm trade, men who drank socially and who were not the hard core alcoholics that were likely to frequent the pub at lunchtime until they had to be dragged from the bar or pokies and put into a taxi to take them home again.

The soft knock at the door told him it was time to leave.

Sean was at the door in two strides looking through the security eye before opening the door wide to let Angus in. Once Angus was inside the room, Sean quietly closed and locked the door again. He said nothing, his eyes ready for instruction, his body warm and relaxed after the shower and short sleep.

'Good. You're ready. I'll have the engine warmed by the time you come downstairs and Tom and his gear will already be in the car with me. We'll do a swap around the corner. I drive to the end of the alley. Joyce will show you through the side door and you meet me there, around the corner and out of sight of the hotel.'

'Good man. How do I thank you Angus?'

'You don't. Just look after my sheep and keep the dogs off them. There's a rifle and shells in the tractor shed. You might need it. Look after the boy too. Joyce will want to hear some news from time to time. She'll ring you when she needs to know.'

'OK then. I'm ready.' Sean put out his hand and Angus pulled him into a brief bear hug before picking Sean's pack and the truck keys up off the bed and turning back to the door. Sean opened the door just enough to check that no one was in the corridor. He swung the door inwards to let Angus out then closed it quietly and walked back to the bed. Joyce would be here soon and he would say nothing to her. She only needed to know that the boy was safe.

Already, Angus had collected Tom and his things from his room. They made their way quietly back into the pub and to the dining room where Tom had sat over his breakfast earlier that morning. Angus unlocked the door and led Tom into the alley behind the pub. The truck was where he left it. Nothing had changed. He threw Tom's bag into the back tray and opened the passenger door for him. 'This is it then son. You'll be better off now. A whole new life for you!'

'Thanks Angus.' The boy looked strained but relieved.

'Don't you worry about your parents. Joyce will talk to them. You're old enough to leave school and to work. Just phone them up from time to time or send them a postcard, but not from the farm. I won't be far behind you and Sean.'

'OK.'

'You won't miss your parents?'

'Maybe a bit.'

'You're quite sure that this is what you want?"

'I'm sure Angus. I want to get the hell out of Melbourne. I hate it here.'

'In the truck then.'

Angus moved quickly to the driver's door and got in. He allowed the engine to rev gently so there would be no stalling at the other end of the alley. The truck pulled off the kerb and Angus carefully negotiated the corner. Joyce and Sean arrived just as he pulled into the left-hand side of the street. Angus alighted and Sean jumped in closing the door, pulling out almost immediately and hardly checking the mirror to catch Angus and Joyce walking arm in arm back to the hotel as if they had just returned from an evening stroll.

'You're going to be OK with me. Right?

'Yeah. I'm alright.'

'Good. I'll need you to navigate. There's a map in the glove box.'

'Got it.'

'Let's head for the hills son.'

LEGENDS AMONGST THE ROSES AT BENALLA

Sean concentrated on following the signs and obeying the road rules. The boy was alert and flicking quickly through the pages of the printed Melways Road Directory to find the page that would lead them out of Melbourne.

'Follow this road through. Stick to it and bypass the turnoffs to the airport. We're heading straight out and along the main highway.'

'That's what Angus said.'

'He'd know. He goes up there often enough Joyce said, but mostly on the other road past Suggan Buggan and Ingebyra.'

'Suggan what?'

'It's the back road through the Snowy Mountains. You follow the river through the rough country apparently and come out behind Jindabyne.'

'Then we'll go that way.'

'No, we're already heading north and Angus said not to do it, not this time anyway. Not until we know the roads. Apparently it gets slippery after rain and there's been early snows so the road might be churned up with ice and mud by the time we get there.'

'Hmm. What about the other road?'

'The Alpine Way?'

'It's all right, but they had a fair landslide there a few years back.'

'So what's new with roads? That's why my people prefer the rail.'

'Where are your people Sean?'

'All in good time son. First things first. I just want to get us out of here and onto the farm.'

Tom studied the Melways quietly for a few moments.

'You know Sean, we could do it tonight if you want to.'

'Drive to the farm?'

'Yep. I reckon we could. There are plenty of servos on the way so we can eat and fuel up whenever we want to.'

'Aye, that might be so Tom but I think we'll pull over for a bit of a kip just the other side of the city and stop somewhere decent for breakfast. What do you think?'

'Sounds OK to me. Where do you want to stop?'

'That bit's up to you. Look for a truck bay once we're out of the built up area then we'll decide from there.'

'Cool.' Tom shut the directory and put it back in the glove box snapping the lid closed.

'You boys over here eat McDonald's yeah?'

'Yeah, but not for breakfast.'

'They're bound to have something else on offer.' Sean grinned.

'There's a camera on the next bridge.' Tom pointed upwards.

'Meaning?'

'You have to use the e-tag otherwise they fine you.'

'They fine you for crossing the bridge?'

'So we've got one?'

'See that?' Tom pointed to the tag attached to the windscreen. 'Looks as though Angus has it sorted. But the cameras along the highway means that the truck leaves an electronic trail.'

'I see. But then no-one knows you or me or the fact that we are in Angus's truck Tom. So we should be cool.'

'Yeah. That's what I hoped.'

'Your folks don't know that you were staying with Joyce and Richard?'

'Nope. They have no idea where I am or who I am with.'

'You'd better send a note from somewhere to tell them you are safe and happy so no-one comes looking for you.'

'Or for you Sean.' Tom said glumly.

The road swung onto the broad, ascending bridge with sweeping views of the city lights. Sean marvelled at the urban beauty and was suddenly happy at the turn of events. They were quickly past the best of the lights and heading up the main drag to Albury.

'We drive for about another hour Tom. Keep a look out for a truck stop then we'll have a few hours kip and breakfast after that.' Sean decided.

'Okey dokey.' Tom was excited. 'You know Sean, this sure could beat school.'

'I'm sure it could Tom.'

'Did you finish?'

'Finish what?'

'School.'

'No such luxury from where I come from. Once we were fourteen we were old enough to work. I was down the mine with my father on my fifteenth birthday then my grandfather took me on the railway. I learnt everything I know from him. There was no need for me to go any further at school Tom.'

Tom looked quietly through the window, aware that he was leaving his home and all that he had known. 'Guess you're right there Sean.'

'You'll be right son. You'll be looked after and there will be something on the farm for you to be sure.'

'Thanks.'

The boy seemed comforted by the present company taking him away from the Diocesan school, away from the uneasy comforts of Melbourne and into the adventures of his dreams.

Sean glanced across to Tom settled in his seat, his long face quiet with the dark shadow of early manhood already forming around his jawline. The eyes were troubled but still held some of their natural youthful fire. Sean knew that he had a fighting chance with him, but it could prove to be tough, not only for Tom, but also for him.

An hour along the highway, instinct warned Sean that now was the time to rest. If the police were alerted to the death of the priest, it would be better to lie low for a few hours. There was no way that they would link either Angus or himself to the disappearance of the priest, but he was not about to draw unnecessary attention to Angus's truck and to himself for now.

A truck parking bay appeared unexpectedly. It was as good a place for a kip as any they would find. Tom was already dead asleep and Sean wanted to let him sleep as long as he needed to. Quietly he pulled into the bay, killed the lights and engine, then got out and opened his pack. He pulled out the windcheater for himself and a spare pullover to sling over the boy. It could get cold and without the engine running, the temperature in the cab would soon drop close to zero. He got back into the cab and closed the door quietly, careful not to disturb the boy as he draped the pullover over his shoulders.

Sean did the same for himself, draping the windcheater across his front then settled in for a few hours sleep.

Dawn broke while the man and boy slept in the cab, their presence almost obliterated by the steady build up of condensation on the glass. Sean woke first.

Tom stirred just as Sean turned over the engine, turning up the throttle and using the accelerator to pump life into the diesel. The cab was cold and Sean looked around for something to wipe the glass free from the heavy dew on the inside of the windscreen.

'I've got a travel towel in my pack, will that do?' Tom offered.

'Thanks son. How did you sleep?'

'Cold. I slept OK though.'

'Good. We're out of here in a few minutes. Just give the engine time to warm up. Are you hungry?'

'Yep.' Tom got out of the cab and started searching his pack for the towel. He came back with two travel towels and another pullover. 'This one do?'

'Thanks. Do you want to put on the other pullover?'

Tom pulled on his jumper and started to wipe the condensation from the windscreen, squeezing the excess off onto the ground. 'That should do her.'

'Sean placed the towel on the dash to dry out as the engine heated up.'

'OK then. Find us a town to eat Tom.' Sean grinned.

'I could eat a whole cow but I'm not sure about a whole town!'

'Better you eat the town than the town eat you, son.' Sean engaged the engine into gear and drove towards the exit. The early morning traffic was light with a few cars and mostly trucks hauling freight out of Melbourne. The morning sun was weak, but it would warm up soon enough. Sean wanted to get as far from Melbourne as he could. He was a bit edgy and the prospect of a bush camp for the next couple of days appealed.

Tom fished the Melways out of the glove box.

'What about this town? Benalla.'

'Benalla?'

'Yeah. It's about there.' Tom pointed to the position of the town on the map and Sean noted that the mountains were a good drive further north.

'That looks about right. We'll need to buy a bit of food and a sleeping bag for you Tom. We can stick a mattress in the back of the tray. That way you'll be off the ground and I'll get a cheap tent; or we can swap. Angus left us a tarp to cover the tray so the dew won't touch you at night.' Sean pumped up the camping event a bit.

'Great. We've been up this way with school and there are mobs of camping shops in Albury. Should be able to get what we need there.'

'OK. Done. First, breakfast!'

Benalla was quiet and tidy.

'This looks quite civilised for us bush boys Tom. Sure you can handle the crowds?' Sean teased. Tom felt reluctant to leave the warm safety of the cab, but hunger got the better of him.

'I think I can Sean. Can't see a Maccas though.'

'Not to worry. Let's try the café over the road. Looks kosher to me.'

Sean pulled the truck into the off road parking bay next to a posh looking rose garden complete with a kids' rocket and paths winding through the garden and around to an art gallery.

'These people certainly know how to put a town together.' Sean's soft admiration was a welcome break of atmosphere.

'There's Weary Dunlop. Over there.' Tom pointed to a statue edged by the garden and road. 'Do you want to see him?'

'Yeah. Why not? Who is he anyway?'

'Fought in the Second World War. He rescued mobs of our injured men. Weary's famous in these parts, although not as much as the Anzacs.'

'The Anzacs?'

'You don't know about Anzac Day Sean?'

'Can't say that I do son.'

'The First World War. They were massacred. British used them as cannon fodder.' Tom was simply repeating what he had heard.

'Cannon fodder eh?' Sean laughed. 'Sounds like what they did to our mob.'

'Your mob? What do you mean?'

'The British. We Irish folk died in our tens of thousands during the First World War.'

'Oh.'

'And it looks as though you Aussies were massacred all over again in the Second World War.'

'This guy dragged them out so I guess so.' Tom conceded, standing slightly in awe of the sculpture.

Sean walked up to the carved soldier. The atmosphere at the outdoor shrine was strangely reverent and respectful. The soldier emanated a sense of deep surrender to his cause, the ultimate sacrifice to save the wounded from the war. Sean was no stranger to fighting for the cause, yet the image of this man touched him to the core. Weary was a humble monument to sacrifice rather than the wild warrior type he was used to. He walked around the statue, noting the inscriptions carved at Weary Dunlop's feet. For a moment, Sean paused aware that he was lost in another time, a familiar but different world. Power emanated from the soldier's image: it carried the souls of the soldiers safe in its soft visage, their pain and sacrifice etched into the eyes. This was one of the most beautiful things that Sean had even seen, the stooped Warrior standing still amongst the roses.

Then, in his mind he heard them: their cries of victory and their death, the firing of guns and screaming of men caught before they fell one by one into the dust of history. He tried to block out the sounds of fresh fire from the guns in Belfast and the dying of young men. For a moment Sean was overcome by the stench of petrol bombs that had gutted Ireland in a bitter war. It was useless. There was no end to war, no end to the hatred, no end to the deaths.

Sean caught himself just in time. He pulled himself away from the vivid memory, the flashback to Ireland, the past he had only just escaped. He touched the soldier with his hand. Suddenly the grief for his father surfaced only to be absorbed by the compassionate eyes carved in bronze, eyes that seemed to shine love and tired wisdom into Sean's soul. The sympathetic and safe shoulder of the Soldier surprised Sean, nearly reducing him to tears. He looked around him and saw the vast expanse of rose gardens scattered across the park and the river winding under the bridge. The roses were almost finished, but the symbolism was not lost on Sean: the pain and suffering of war sculpted amongst the fragrance of foreign yet familiar blooms.

'It's quite lovely Tom.' Sean noted the strange language coming automatically from his mouth.

'He's a beauty all right. They don't have a special ceremony for the guys in the Second World War. I did go to the last Dawn Service in Melbourne with my grandfather though. His father was at Gallipoli.'

'A long time ago now.'

'Yeah, but we'll never forget it.' Tom remarked evenly.

Sean noted the ready pride in the young man and the ready respect for his ancestors. Suddenly, he didn't feel as bad about his past as he always had, with its long and bitter wars. Ireland was his home and his heart would always be there.

The Benalla café, as promised, was warm and lively with the office breakfast people downing coffee and raisin toast. The waitress looked busy and smiled briefly at Sean before talking to Tom. 'You look hungry young man. Anything special?'

'Thanks. What's on the menu?' Sean broke in.

'I'll have the lot.' Tom grinned.

'The lot it is. You sir?'

'I'd better go the same.'

'Best choice on the menu. You've obviously been to Benalla before!'

'I've heard about it and we had to do something for Art on the Gallery. It was some travelling exhibition of native culture, but I'm not much into art.' Tom confessed.

'Are you 'into' anything in particular then?' Sean asked, the humor sparkling in his serious grey eyes.

'Not much. A bit of sport I suppose.'

'Horses?'

'Not where I come from. The racetrack is in Caulfield. I reckon that trade is a bit cruel though. They just put them down when they've made their money. The industry is corrupt anyway. They still drug the horses and rig the races.'

'And just how did you get all this information?' Sean had to smile.

'One of the Priests likes to bet a bit.'

'Oh? I guess that's not part of the curriculum then' Sean commented, hoping to change the subject. 'So you've never been on a horse.'

'Not yet. Our school is into swimming, football and tennis in a big way though.'

'Angus didn't mention a swimming pool in Berridale, but there's bound to be a footy field.'

'Bound to be. Not that I'll be playing though.'

'Why not?

'I'm not at school now am I.' Tom's voice quavered for a minute.

'There will be a local team for sure.'

Tom brightened quickly, realising that he had unwittingly taken the first real step to independence without having to sit any exams.

'So we'd better down these hamburgers with the lot.'

The waitress returned. Sean noted she was young but smart enough to see the young man needed a bit of attention.

'Would you like orange juice with that or chocolate milk?'

'Juice thanks.'

'Sir?'

'Just coffee.'

'Have you seen the exhibition then?'

'No.' Tom was all innocence.

'Over there. At the gallery.' The waitress nodded through the window. 'Ned Kelly. He's the original hero yeah?'

'Yeah, he is. Robbed a few stage coaches.' Tom's eyes lit up as he explained to Sean.

'Thanks for the inspiration!' Sean said with more than a touch of irony in his voice.

The waitress laughed. 'Nothing like a bit of history with breakfast.'

'Then we'd better eat up kiddo. Won't be another feed until we're past Albury.'

CAMPGROUND AT CORRYONG

Night closed in rapidly as the truck pulled into the campground. The drive through to Albury for a quick stock up with food, a spare jerry can of fuel and camping equipment was fast and efficient, just as Sean had planned. They had enough food for two big men for over a week, but they would be camping, in Sean's estimation, for less than a couple of days. This was simply the lie-low space until it was safe to move off to the farm. If the police were looking for the truck, the word would soon be out that Angus and his friend were already well out to sea. Unless the police had hard evidence — and there was none of that apart from the unlikely chance that they would drag the harbour and find the wheel attached by tie wire to the body — they had nothing to go on. Life would continue on as usual apart from one less Priest at the private school. Angus would be well out of the way and no more questions would be asked. The Priests at the school would make sure of that. They had quotas to meet and budgets to keep so a police investigation would not only be unwelcome, it would be a positive thorn in the side of the well-heeled and highly respected school.

The campground was rough and ready but someone had had enough sense to build the fireplaces and stock a bit of wood. Sean had his wits about him. First build the fire and then pitch the tent. They could put the tent up by torchlight and Sean wanted to stow the wood out of any possible rain so that they could have a fire every day that they were there.

'This is it then Tom. You up to a fire man?'

'Sure am. Let's get started.'

'You do the kindling. I'll lay the paper and fire starters.' Tom needed little encouragement, the air beginning to chill him and the prospect of a warm sleeping bag decidedly enticing after the events of the last two days. He skirted around the edges of the camp, looking for bits of bark and twigs that would lay the foundation of their fire. Sean had already piled sufficient fuel for the night next to the fireplace and was crumpling The Age newspaper into flammable portions ready to take the kindling. He then quickly stowed another two days worth of cut fuel under the truck in case it rained. They would only use what they needed, and then replace it, as had the camper before them.

Tom busily arranged the bark and twigs.

'Make sure there is plenty of air and light under the kindling and put the match to the fire starter son. Then you have to watch it and blow at the bottom of the flame to keep it going.' Sean threw him the matches.

'Will do.'

'Potatoes in foil?'

'You bet!' Tom could easily imagine being famished enough to eat ten.

The fire burnt bravely with enough smoke to wake the district as Sean wrapped the potatoes in strips of foil. He put them near the fire and pulled out the billy from the truck along with a folded map carefully placed in a waterproof plastic cover.

'Water run clean in these parts Tom?' Sean spread the map on the ground.

'This runs off the ranges so yes.' Tom pointed at the source of the creek. 'Let's boil it just in case there are foxes or brumbies upstream. In any case that's what the stockmen used to do when they brought their cattle up here.'

'Oh? You do this bit then. Boil the billy.'

'Yep. And when it boils, we ad half a handful of tea, swing the billy and let it settle.' Tom looked over to his new friend. 'You know mate, "Billy Tea"! That's what we do out here in the bush.'

Sean chuckled and went back to the makeshift kitchen on the tailgate. There was bread ready for the mesh toasting-iron and a jar of peanut butter. From what Joyce had told him, Australian kids liked peanut butter. That would do the trick for now. He had picked up a couple of rabbit traps and fishing line in Albury. Tonight he would lay the traps and in the morning, they would try their hand at fishing. There would be no guns in this camp and he didn't want the boy to get the wrong idea about being dependent on shop bought meat. Survival first and luxury later.

Tom was content to sit on the fallen log next to the fire. The first stars pricked the dark night and it seemed an impossible distance over the top of the mountains and to freedom. The glow from the moon looked like a floating band of silver in the night sky above the blackness of the range and Tom knew that tonight would be clear with a good chance of a heavy morning frost. The last calls of currawongs searching for the end-of-season cones from the she-oaks echoed off the back of the mountain. Their calls were caught in the tops of the trees around the campground, like the haunting wails of wandering spirits, longing for their past and mournful for their future. A sharp cry meant that, more than likely, there were feral cats and foxes on the loose far from the guns of farmers, desperate to complete their autumn feed before the cruel months of winter robbed them of critical body mass and warmth. The night movements of the wombat rustling amongst fallen leaves, scratching for forest food, was far more comforting than the howls of wild dogs. These once tame, domestic pets were now like wandering wolves, roaming in packs, sometimes raiding farms for ewes or lambs and at other times, hunting small native animals from their long-protected wilderness homes. The possums were in abundance evidenced by their droppings near the fire as they raked over hasty campers' departures, eating scraps of bread and meat. Once, these lofty locals had enjoyed a pure diet of forest fruits and leaves. The possums, Tom thought, could provide more than enough food and clothing for a small Aboriginal tribe and he wondered if he and Sean could survive out here too, if they had to.

Sean came over to the fire with the toasting mesh, big enough to hold two pieces of bread at a time. He had relented against his better judgement and included a kilo of sausages in the shopping trolley, but was now glad that he had done so.

'Throw these on the plate kiddo, and when they're ready, jam them between the bread. There's butter if you want it and tomato sauce on the tailgate. Potatoes last. We have to wait for the coals to form before they'll cook through. Are you feeling all right?'

'Yeah, thanks. This is great. At least we have a fire tonight.' Tom grinned.

'And a good one at that.' Sean slapped him on the back.

'You keep watch over the dinner and I'll put up the tent. Flip a coin for the best berth?'

'Heads I win, tails you lose.' Tom was quick.

'Take your pick.'

'I'll go the tray tonight. I'd like to see the stars.' Tom's voice brimmed with adventure.

'Fair choice.' Sean left him at the fire and went in search of the tent. They had bought a couple of full-length close-cell foam mats, one for the tray and the other for the tent. The Irish miner's son wanted to build trust and the kid would need space to feel safe.

Sean was careful with the tent. There was no point in pitching a tent to have it collapse or simply blow off the face of the earth in the middle of the night. He adjusted the fly and hammered the tent pegs firmly into the ground with a rock. Then he secured the zipper so no curious spider or snake seeking the steady warmth of a sleeping and unsuspecting mammal could make an unannounced entry. He knew it would be warm enough with the cell mats below them and the "five below zero" sleeping bags hugging their bodies in separate cocoons of warmth and security. There was nothing as primal as a sleeping bag, a tent, and a roaring fire. Here, they had all that and one another's company to keep them safe. With the billy boiled and hand-held fishing lines tempting trout, there was little more a man could ask for. The vision of fresh fish leaping to the lure stayed with Sean, since he had abandoned his Irish fishing haunts for Australia.

The campground was a haven. The quieter, softer stands of trees drooped to the creek and dripped wet bark from every trunk. From their crowns, choruses of birds proclaimed the bush as theirs, not least the kookaburras calling the loudest 'King of the bush is he!' From the mountains, the surging streams carried spring snowmelt and memories and tales of the ancient tribes.

Sean knew from his traipsing across the Irish bogs and mountains that nature would do its work on the boy. He would say little or nothing and allow the early morning rays of muted light to deliver him hope as if they were personal letters from heaven. Even now at dusk, the soft shadows and stark bush sounds would empty Tom's heart and soul of pain and give him time to think. It was time for them both to experience their new beginnings, alone, and yet in one another's company; in the companionship of the bush.

The fire burned down to hot coals, smoke signalling the contentment of their camp. Pieces of half-burnt bread and sausage fat dropped between the spaces in the mesh and onto the fire, crackling into charcoal and disappearing beneath the coals. There was nothing as beautiful as the night sounds, the clear and star-struck sky, the freedom and friendship found only in the company of kindred souls, both men fugitives from their own private and ugly wars.

Sean poked at the coals with his firestick already shortened by flames that burst at the end from time to time. He thrust the smoking stick into the soil to extinguish the fire then poked beneath the coals for the potatoes. The potatoes felt soft to the end of the stick. Carefully, Sean rolled one towards him to test if it was ready.

'Got a knife son?'

'Only my pocketknife.' Tom dug into his jeans pocket and untied the spring cord that kept his trouser belt and knife securely attached.

'That will do. What a beauty!' Sean turned over the knife, checking the weight and balance. 'This must have set you back a bit.'

'Birthday present. From gramps.' Tom shone with pride.

'Let's see if it does the job with these potatoes.' Sean flicked open the blade, gently broke the foil seal and pressed the steel into the soft core of the potato. 'This one's done.' Sean wiped the blade carefully on his trousers making sure that it was completely clean and snapped it back into the sheath. 'Thanks.' He handed the pocketknife back to Tom. 'Let's see about the rest. Give us a hand will you. Just roll them out nice and slow or you'll find they'll disappear back under the coals without you knowing it.' Sean smiled, pleased that the rest of their meal was worth waiting for.

'Geez it's hot!' Tom pulled his hand back.

'Use a longer stick. The coals are a lot hotter after an hour or two' Sean laughed.

Tom prised out another potato, the black foil crust breaking slightly.

'Easy does it!' Sean protested. 'We want them whole you know.'

'How many in there?'

'About half a dozen I reckon.'

'That's five of them. I don't think I'll find number six.'

'Five of the best. Leave the other one 'till we've knocked off this lot then we'll have another poke. Otherwise, you can eat it cold for breakfast if you want to.'

'Yuck.' Tom was not keen.

'Just testing. Stick the pot on kiddo. Nestle it on the cool part of the coals and we'll have another cuppa before bed.'

'You sure make a good brew Sean.'

'Grandfather taught me.' Sean smiled wryly. 'Seems as though grandfathers have it tonight. Do you see your grandpa often.' It was more of a statement.

'Not enough.'

'Where is his place?'

'He's got a property near here, Corryong.'

'Oh?'

'Yep. Cattle and horses. Not much else. Says the country is too rough where he is for sheep. It's not that far from here.'

'From this camp?'

'Well, we came through Corryong on the way, sort of near the farm.'

'Son you should have said so! We could have stopped there. You'd probably be better off with your granddad than wandering into the bush with a man you don't even know!'

'Best not. He'd tell my old man then they'd drag me back to Melbourne.'

'That bad?'

'Yeah.'

'What's your father do?'

'Me Dad?'

'Yes. Your Dad, does he work?'

'Yeah. 'Spose he does.' Tom sounded a bit vague.

'Look if you don't want to talk about him…'

'It's not that, it's more like…' Tom seemed hesitant

'What's up kiddo?' Sean prompted him gently.

'Well, he's a State politician and good friends with…'

'Your father's a politician?'

'Yeah. Not that that counts for much.' Tom sounded bitter.

'And what does that mean?' Sean smiled kindly.

Tom returned Sean's smile with a mournful stare. 'He's friends with the wrong sort of people if you know what I mean. I don't like it when he brings men home and I don't like them anywhere near me.'

Sean felt himself go instantly cold with intense rage. The burden of silence suddenly broke the warmth of their campfire. With immense effort Sean forced the words out of his throat. 'Try one of the potatoes son. Cut them open on the rock. I'll get the butter.'

Sean stood up slowly, aware that his legs were shaking with anger. His knees felt like crumbled pieces of coarse granite as he moved, stonily and sombrely to the truck. The butter and salt sat casually on the open tailgate, next to the remnants of Tom's sausage-sandwich enterprise.

Sean caught a broken image of himself as the firelight flickered in the rear window. Now the fire of anger had coursed through him surely and steadily. Slowly, Sean picked up the butter and salt, drawing the night air deeply into his lungs. He turned to see the boy poking at the fire, waiting for his return with the butter and the salt. On the rock, the potatoes sat neatly carved and steaming, opened by the pocketknife Tom's grandfather gave him.

'Got it?' Tom could hardly wait to try the potatoes.

'Yup. Got it.' Sean measured his steps and voice. 'Put it on the rock son.' Sean handed him the butter and salt and avoiding the boy's eye turned quietly to the fire. The flames flicked from time to time, blue lights bursting from the coals like the ethereal Clouds of Magellan.

'Do you want one?' Tom was absorbed in keeping his hands from being burnt as he passed a potato, still half wrapped in foil, to Sean.

'That's great. Who taught you to cook?'

Tom grinned. 'Guess I must have learned it from gramps. Taught me most of the useful things that I know.'

Sean relaxed. The burning fierceness suddenly left his heart and his throat cleared. He took the coal-consecrated food reverently from Tom, his eyes brimming with unspent tears, grateful that the night hid him from the boy, hid emotions deeper than he cared to show.

They sat together on wooden logs beside the fire, savouring the hot potatoes straight from the fire, burning their lips and mouths.

'Man, that was good. Another one?' Tom was on his feet and Sean remained quiet, enjoying the kid's spontaneous enthusiasm. Tom came back with the rest of the potatoes cupped in his hands and sat them on the tree stump between them. Then it was time to speak and for listening again.

'And anyway, my dad's friends with the priests at the school' Tom muttered his mouth full of potato.

Sean absorbed the information quietly poking the fire with the toe of his boot.

'Can't go home then can I? They'd really do me in.'

'What about your grandfather? He must know son.' Sean worked to keep the inflection of his speech low and neutral, hiding his quiet, cold fury.

'Nope. The old man would have a heart attack if anyone else knew so it's a sort his secret if you know what I mean.'

'Tom, don't you have a mother?' Sean controlled the familiar stirring of rage in his chest.

'Not any more. She divorced the old man about ten years ago. She didn't like his boyfriends. She's in Queensland now. Doesn't want anything to do with him or us. Guess she just couldn't handle it.'

'So you were shunted off to boarding school.'

'Yeah. Dad thought it was best 'cause he's never home anyway. I just go home on weekends and sometimes to gramp's place.'

'Weren't you lonely?'

'Yeah. You get used to it Sean, don't you.' Tom's approach was mildly imploring.

'You never get used to some things son. Never.' Sean picked up the last of the potatoes. 'Go you halves?'

'Nuh. I'm full. All yours.'

'That billy has boiled again. Do you want more tea?'

'Yeah. Add more of that condensed milk stuff?'

'Does the job. Can't do that much without a fridge. Not that you'd need it out here. It's getting cold. We'd better think about bunking down kid. After the tea. We'll throw the rest of the gear in the cab.'

'What about the fire?'

'I'll damp it down. Gotta find a tree then give the ivories a scrub. Clean my teeth! Let's finish off that brew first.' Sean felt the anger settling. Tom was free of the school and there was one priest less to ruin the lives of other boys. He could smile a little now. It seemed easier out here. The silence absorbed him, calming him with alternating waves of solitude and space. Even though the kid was here he felt totally alone and, for the first time, aware that the cleansing had begun, the washing of his soul free from other people's hatred and wars.

Sean gathered the foil from the potatoes and screwed them into a single ball. Then he took the mug of steaming and sweet tea from

Tom, sipping it gently and enjoying the curved rim of enamel and the hotness of metal against his hands and tongue. The tea slipped easily down his throat, warming his gullet and softening his mood.

Tom sat next to him, enjoying the quietness of Sean, aware that this man was going to protect him and not destroy him as the Priest and his friends had begun to do. Tom felt safe, a little nervous still and unsure of the future, but happy that tonight he would sleep alone in his sleeping bag. There would be nothing other than the calls of owls and howling of wild dogs to breach the silence and nothing to threaten his security. Sean had already proven to him that he was a good man, good enough to take him as far as humanly possible from Melbourne and to promise not to return him anywhere close to his family, not at any cost.

MURRAY RIVER BAPTISM

The morning chorus of bird life began the dawn bush-awakening. The first strands of light filtered through the tops of the trees and glistened on the wet bark and leaves scattered around the campground. The ground was wet after heavy falls of rain overnight. By five a.m. the rain had eased and, almost like the curtain call on a natural drama, the clouds lifted high over the camp and formed towers about the peaks. There would be snow later on for certain.

Sean stirred in his sleeping bag, bone weary from the long journey. His legs ached from being curled into himself against the cold and his face felt like a piece of ice cracking; even so he was dry, completely dry. That was the main thing. It didn't matter how sub zero the temperature was, as long as the tent and fly did its job and the buildup of condensation did not form into large droplets and spoil what should be an illusion of an impenetrable cocoon.

It was time to get up and he was glad that the wood stacked underneath the cab was probably still dry. The arch of the tent allowed him sufficient space to sit up and stretch his arms in front, then rub his sore back, unused to the hard ground despite the padded cell mat. He pulled on his trousers and positioned himself far enough forwards in the tent to put on his boots. Without dislodging any drops of condensation, he lurched into the tent vestibule and forced himself out into the cold morning air.

'Shiiit…sure is cold out here.' Sean looked around. There was no movement from Tom. The boy was probably still asleep and Sean noticed that the tarp was pulled up and secured over the tray. With a bit of luck, Tom would be dry and cosy. Sean's instinct was to check on the boy, however he looked around the camp instead. It wasn't going to be a helluva lot of fun here today; holed up in a small tent with nothing much to do except tramp about the wet bush or drop a line into the river gushing with icy water. Fresh trout would be a treat, but it could wait. There was breakfast to think about, and, a wash.

'Christ! A man needs a fire on a day like this!'

'Did you say something Sean?'

'Was I speaking aloud son?' Sean smiled.

'Yep, and I'm not asleep. Cold night!'

'That it was. Are you getting up or am I going to drive off with you in the back?'

'Shit I'm sore. Must have rolled off the mat.' Tom grimaced.

'Can't be that bad if you're not complaining about anythin' else.'

'Yep. I'm jake.'

'Jake?'

'I'm OK.'

The running water distracted Sean. 'I'm having a wash. What about you?'

'Where?'

'In the river.'

'In the river, you must be mad!'

'Not mad, just itching for a wash. Are you game or not?'

'Yeah. I'm game.'

'OK then. First one in gets the big breakfast.'

'You're on Sean.' Tom tussled with the cords of the tarpaulin, pulling the top end down over his body until he was free to the knees. The light was comforting but without any warmth. 'Jeez it's cold.'

Sean was already at the river, peeling off his clothes, boots first, and piling them neatly on a rock where they would remain dry. Almost immediately, the colour of his skin changed to a light blue and he rubbed his arms vigorously before braving the first couple of steps into the river. There was no point in waiting for the slow chill effect to set in so he plunged forwards, submerging himself into the fresh snow waters.

The water closed around him like a vice and for a moment he thought he would lose consciousness as his feet lifted off the bottom. Then he realised that the water was no deeper than his waist and pushed off the riverbed with as much strength as he could muster. For a second, he was almost fully out of the water until he crashed back into the river losing his balance as he fell. The coldness forced him upright, gasping for air as he clawed out of the river. His towel was dry and warm as he rubbed his limbs until they felt red raw. Then he dropped the towel and picked up his clothes one by one from the pile, dressing quickly and for warmth.

'Mate, that's not the way to go!' Tom protested.

Sean looked over his shoulder, unaware that the boy had watched the performance of dousing and dressing. 'Feels wonderful now. Gets the blood going that's for sure. Are you in for it?'

'Don't know.' Tom felt like chickening out.

'Have it your way. I get the big breakfast.'

'You beat me in anyway.'

'You win the booby prize!'

'Yeah?'

'Hot shower at the campground after a morning's fishing.'

'Cool. I'm in.' Tom found his own rock and began to undress, taking less care than Sean to keep his clothes in a pile.

'Stack them neatly or they'll slip off the rock and you'll be wearing a pair of wet trousers and socks.'

'Jesus it's cold!'

'Wait until you get in.' Sean guffawed.

He turned away and suddenly walked back to the truck. There would be time to start a small fire and get the billy boiling and do a small pot of porridge.

Tom returned to the truck within minutes. He was in and out of the water in almost less time than it took Sean to lay the fire and strike the first match.

'How was that?'

'Maaate.' Tom towelled his head furiously.

'Steady. You'll kill the fire!' Sean teased him.

'Do we have to do that every morning?' Tom could not contain his teeth chattering together behind blueish lips.

'Yep.'

The glint in Sean's eyes told the boy that he was having him on big time.

'Yeah right. The initiation ceremony.'

'Something like that. Feel like toast or porridge?'

'Porridge?'

'Thick and hot with a good dose of brown sugar and a bit of that milk we had last night.'

'Yeah. I'll be in that.'

'We'll leave the camp here today Tom. I'm not sure about the road up over the mountain and I want to check out a few more things before we go onto the Monaro.'

'Such as?'

'Such as make sure the cops aren't looking for one truck with a bloke of my description.'

'What about me?' Tom sounded wounded.

'It's mostly about you let me tell you, but they don't know where you are, do they? They don't know you were at Joyce's place and they don't know that you left there either. For all they know you are dead and gone, dropped over some cliff by bandits.'

'Bushrangers you mean. My grandfather reckons there were a few in these parts!' Tom was beginning to enjoy the adventure.

'Your grandfather probably was one for all you know.'

'He did mention something about his father duffing other people's cattle.'

'Did he now? Then he sounds like a right ruffian. Just the sort of company you want to keep.' Sean remarked with a grin.

'Said he knew all about Jack Riley too.'

'Jack Riley? Sounds like one of my clan.'

'Yeah. He's buried in Corryong. Good rider though.'

'Jack Riley.' Sean stirred the porridge with a stick he had just de-barked.

'You know. Banjo Paterson's poem, 'The Man from Snowy River'.'

'Thought you didn't like art.'

'That's history and bush poetry. It isn't art, it's…'

'It's..?'

'It's legendary.'

'What's this 'ary' business? Where I come from it's legendry. There are no 'airy fairies' in my family.' Sean scoffed lightly.

'Are you a Riley?'

'I didn't say I was and I didn't say that I wasn't.' Sean spoke tonelessly. 'Since we've both just been baptised, I reckon it's about time for a new name. What about Keating? Sound good enough to you now?'

'Yeah I reckon. How are you going to prove that one?' Tom challenged him.

'I reckon son that I'll have to find myself some new papers as well. Just keep this fire going for a minute Tom and stir that porridge. Nothing worse than burnt porridge stickin' to the sides of the pot.'

Sean returned from the truck with his wallet, passport, the

brown sugar and condensed milk, enamel mugs and enamel plates that doubled as bowls and some spoons.

'Here. Dish it up into these when it's ready then put the billy on to boil.'

'What are you doing?' Tom noticed Sean pulling papers out of his wallet.

'Let's say, what they don't know they can't prove can they.' Sean gathered his old identity into a bundle and threw it into the fire then quickly poked it under the burning sticks.

'How will you get away with that? You have to have a driver's licence don't you?'

'That's right. If I play my cards right, no one will be asking any questions. I'll just grow me a beard like Angus and be his double for the time being until he gets back up this way. He has contacts who'll be able to provide me with a completely new set of papers.'

'Sean!'

'Don't worry. Hey, what are you going to do?' Sean felt emboldened by the swim and the immediate ceremony of burning and burying his long past in the fire. The flames licked on his passport and he kicked more fuel on top so that there would be no trace of him left after this morning.

'I'll chuck away my past too Sean.' Tom bolted to the truck and dug around for his wallet. 'Here you go. Let's get rid of this.' Tom pulled out the cash and stuffed it into his trouser pocket then hurled the contents of his wallet into the fire.'

'Nothing like a fresh start Tom.'

'You can say that again!' Tom kicked the coals, suddenly feeling brighter as if a weight had been lifted from his shoulders. 'This morning feels pretty fresh.' He grinned at Sean.

'Yep. Sure is. Good wash and a good breakfast. Clouds are lifting. Couldn't be better. So what are you going to do now?'

'Call myself Tom Keating.'

'What!' Sean nearly choked on the hot tea.

'Tom Keating. You've just adopted me as your nephew haven't you.'

'By god kid. You're not short on smart answers.'

'Got my father to thank for that haven't I.' Tom quipped.

By nine in the morning, Sean and Tom had packed up their camp.

Tom relaxed in the cab, trying his hand at rolling Sean a smoke.

'I'm trying to give it away son. Do you smoke?'

'I'm old enough.'

'Hey. I didn't say you weren't!'

'They do everythin' at the school I went to. Drugs, alcohol, the lot.'

'So you're smokin' or drinkin' or usin' or the lot?'

'Dunno. Want nothin' to do with any of the creeps at that school and whatever they were into.'

'That's the spirit son.' Sean drove on in silence.

'Here it is. The best fishing spot for miles.'

'No joke!'

'Apparently Fisheries have just stocked the Khancoban Pondage and they're pulling four pounders out of the lake.'

'Shiit. Then we're up for fishing?'

'You got it. Hire a tinny for the day. Looks magic yeah?'

'Smooth as glass.'

Sean expertly wheeled off the highway and into the caravan resort. The row of kayaks and tin outboards were upturned, washed clean by the overnight rain. There were a few people camped ready for the drive up to the high country and an assortment of jeeps parked next to the hire caravans and cabins. The pondage was as still as a sleeping baby, the mist rising softly off the water. Tree-lined cliffs abutted the far side of the dam, reflected fortress-like in the dark waters. The curved dam wall threw back images of granite and gravel, contrasting with the immaculate beauty of the lake.

Sean pulled on the brake and switched off the engine.

'Come on son. Let's see how much these boats are to hire.' He walked quickly up the ramp cluttered with rods, lifejackets and fishing paraphernalia and stepped into the tiny shop.

'Mornin'. Anyone home?' Sean's spirits were up, buoyed by the beginning of a new life.

'Hellooo. Be there in just a sec.' A woman's voice chorused from the back of the shop. 'Just shutting off the emails.' A slim and strong looking woman walked into the shop. Her hair gleamed with gold and red lights. Sean noticed her broad smile highlighted by a smattering of freckles and a cute nose. 'Hello. What can I do for you?'

'You wouldn't have a boat for hire and a hot shower would you?'

'We have both. Which would you like first?'

'I'd like the shower first please. It sure was cold in the river.' Tom smilingly volunteered.

'You went for a swim? In the Murray?'

'His idea.' Sean joked.

'Was not!' Tom took the bait.

'Now now! No fighting in my shop.' The woman joked. 'Gabby.' She stuck out her hand.

'Sean. And this is Tom, my nephew.'

'Glad to meet you both.'

'How much to hire one of your boats for half a day?' Sean was determined to postpone the shower.

'The tinny or the kayak?'

'The tinny.' Sean looked seriously interested in the brochures on the counter.

'Thought you'd be the type to try white water.' Gabby tried. 'There's some amazing trips on the Mitta Mitta, and on the Upper

Murray for that matter.'

This time, Sean took the bait. 'Hey little lady. One dip is enough for one day.'

'Did someone say 'little lady'. That she ain't.' A man, his glasses still in 'read paper' mode on the end of his nose, t-shirt loose over his trousers, walked into the shop.

'Guys, this is Ian, my husband.'

'Sean. Sean and Tom. Keating.'

'Good to meet you both.'

'You don't sound related though, not with that broad accent of yours.' Gabby was on a roll.

'I'm the lad's uncle from across the seas. We're heading north to where it isn't quite so frosty.'

Gabby broke into chortling laughter. 'A bit rough though. Did you canoe across from Canada?'

'From Ireland as it happens.' Sean rolled his rrrs.

'From Ireland? Welcome home.' Ian commented dryly.

'So I've heard. There are plenty about these parts.'

'None too many. Good workers, any one of them. We've hired a couple for the winter — general maintenance, barbeque duty, clean out the loos.' Gabby decided to spar with Sean.

'Did you say barbeque?' Tom cut in.

'Kangaroo steaks done in an earth oven. Interested?'

'You bet. I'm starving.'

'You'll be hungrier by the time we get back from fishing.' Sean cut in.

Gabby smiled and decided to let them off for a while. 'Ian will you put one of the tinnies onto the back of the Jackaroo. They're going fishing today. Bit too cold in the bush.'

'Gabby, may I do you the honour of providin' the lady of the camp with some fresh trout for her table?' Sean bowed.

Gabby laughed and quickly seized the opportunity. 'Then you'll be needing some better rods and lures.' She quickly led Sean to the fishing section of the shop and in no time had them fitted with gear. 'A few rainbows will do nicely thanks Sean.'

'Jackaroo's ready. Boys?' Ian offered.

'Yep. We're out of here. See you for lunch.'

'Three o'clock and she'll be fired up and ready to go.'

The three men left the shop and squeezed into the truck, the tinny precariously balanced, with oars jutting off the tailgate of the truck.

'Have to use a four-wheel drive down this track. Gets really muddy and if you stop to sneeze you go down.'

'Beautiful spot you've got here Ian. Been here long?'

'Long enough to know that I like it better than any of the resorts, or Cooma for that matter.'

'You from Cooma?'

'Yeah. My old man has worked in town for years. I'm a bit of a loner. Like the bush if you know what I mean.'

'I do know what you mean.' Sean was emphatic.

'What about you nephew?' Ian quietly asked Tom.

'Oh, I'm just starting a new career you could say.'

'You look a bit young to be having a career if you don't mind my saying so Tom.' Ian's voice was compassionate and gentle.

'Well, I've just…' Tom was unseated by the sudden softness of this man.

'He's having a break from the tradition you might say, Ian.' Sean's voice was equally soft, quickly reassuring Tom.

'Then you'll like the fishing here. Does a man the world of good.' Ian smiled looking more out the window and into the rear view mirror than at either Sean or Tom.

Tom breathed with relief. The boy stuff was over and he was in the company of men, real men.

Ian pulled up on a grassy flat and reversed the trailer towards the water. Within minutes the tinny was floating above a bed of reeds.

'Take your time Sean. Gabby's a bit of a stirrer and she won't mind what time you come in. Enjoy yourselves.' Ian reassured him as he gave the tinny a quick push into the pondage.

'Thanks Ian.' Sean was genuinely grateful.

'Come on Tom. Give us a heave ho and we'll get this baby into the water. Got the rods?'

'You two hop in and I'll push you out. See you around 2.30 ish if you like. I'll drive the truck back down and pick you up.'

'That sounds great. We'll be starving by then.' Sean allowed himself to be practical.

'Tom?'

'Yeah. 2.30 is good. Trout as well as kangaroo steaks for lunch!' Tom stepped carefully into the boat then sat dead centre on the tin seat.

Sean stepped into the boat deftly and placed a hand on the rudder bar.

'Easy does it until you're clear of the reeds.' Ian gave the boat a firm push away from the shore and the shallow water. 'See you both later.' Ian waved them off and walked back to the truck. He got back in and looked briefly in the mirror before carefully turning the truck and trailer. The ground was boggy and there was no point in having to dig out the vehicle by himself, not on a day like today.

'Gabby!' Ian yelled into the shop. 'I'll be down on the open ground laying the fire.'

'OK. Drag a couple of logs across can you? Could do with some more seating.'

'Yep. Anything else you need?'

'Nope. That's about it. What do you make of the boy? Bit young to be ferrying around the countryside don't you think?' Gabby sounded concerned.

'Gabby. I think that the kid's been through it. From what I can make out he's on the run.'

'How did you work that out?'

'Sean. He said nothing much except that they were 'breaking with tradition'. But the kid looks a bit traumatised to me. Could be anything, school woes, parent woes. Who knows!'

'It's hard when you are Tom's age. Adolescence can be a rocky road.'

'Sean looks like he could be a bit moody.' Gabby said soberly,

Ian laughed and slapped her gently on the back. 'Gabby, I couldn't ever imagine any man wanting to hurt you and if he tried, before I could get to him you'd turn him into mince meat.'

'Seriously. He's been through it. The look in his eyes. Don't ask!'

'Perhaps you had better not ask either of them then. Some things are best left well alone. Anyway, we've got that barbeque to get ready and two hungry Keating men to feed.'

'Kids recover from stuff. Looks like Tom's just getting started.'

'He's got a long way to go then.'

'I'd say so. Sean looks as though he's got a handle on the situation though.' Ian closed the conversation.

By early afternoon, the sun was peaking, the warmth of midday breaking up the effect of the slight wind ruffling the surface of the pondage. Tom had already landed three impressively sized trout, one rainbow and two browns. Sean's luck was not in and he knew it was because his mind was just not on the game. He needed the precious time to think and out on the water there was little interference other than the reflections on the lake and the soft rustle of gum leaves as they rowed close to the western shore where the waters dropped deeply against the cliffs. For a long while he was happy to dangle the line and observe the scenery and, on the far side, track the line of the rapidly descending white pipes that appeared to feed water through a power station and into the pondage. Upstream from the river flats that were covered in reeds and waterfowl, the river was quite beautiful, edged by willows and rich green farming country. Further away, the soft blue hues of the mountains near Corryong spoke of a thousand memories as if the bushrangers and horsemen still rode the steep and wooded slopes. It was some of the wildest country in the district. This was better here than in Ireland, the landscape surrounding him infused with a virgin beauty that he had not seen for a long time. The sudden light chop on the surface of the pond told him that the weather was changing. The wind started to gust and felt like it was carrying the cold of the Southern Ocean and Antarctica, a sensation he thought he had left behind in Bass Strait. It was time to move. Quickly, he increased the revs on the tinny, turning the boat for the shore where Ian would collect them. He pulled his coat collar up high and set a course 90 degrees to the chop. Tom sat in front of him, quickly hauling in the lines and setting himself in the balanced position on the middle seat of the boat. It would be only moments and they would be back in the truck and heading off for the kangaroo steaks on Gabby's barbeque, now supplemented by fresh fish from Tom's catch. A really hot shower would follow and a very welcome bed in one of her heated cabins.

ACROSS THE GREAT DIVIDE

The evening at Khancoban sitting around the earth oven with Gabby and Ian was both grounding and rewarding. Sean absorbed the warmth of the fire and the upbeat company noticing at the same time, a visible wave of relaxation crossing Tom's face. The mild temperatures of the late afternoon and early evening lapped the edges of the camp and added to the general sense of ease. The next day however, broke with a sudden drop in temperature, the chill winds blowing off the snow and driving the cold air into the valley. It felt like the coldest of alpine mornings as the air plummeted in sheets from the snowy crags and plunged into subzero pools at the base of the Geehi walls.

The drive was slow going. There were patches of black ice on the corners, unlikely to receive sun until the middle of the day. The largest of the gumtrees, the mountain ash, stood like sentinels holding centuries of soil in their roots, soil that would otherwise wash into the swirl of snow melt as it rushed down the valleys. There was plenty of evidence of the unstable slopes with rocks of all sizes strewn across the road in places where recent slips had evaded the efforts of the graders. It was a daily job to check the road and from time to time, to clean the boulders strewn over the thin strip of road.

They could not rush the drive so Sean pumped up the heater and switched on the radio to make them as comfortable as he could.

Tom was all eyes, watching the corners and looking off the edge of the road until he realised that Sean knew very well how to drive for these conditions. The truck ground steadily forwards, the tyres gripping well and only slipping after a sudden gear change or an unexpected sheet of ice. There was no traffic coming the other way. Either it was too early, or the weather warnings had discouraged wayward travellers from exploring further.

'Turn up the radio if you like Tom. News should come on soon.' Sean wanted to hear the best and the worst, if there was worst!

They were still tuned to the Melbourne station with the lead news: rising interest rates on the back of the housing sector boom and a warning to borrowers to beware.

Then can the news 'police are searching for Caulfield Priest Father John McDonald who was last seen at the Wharf Hotel on Friday night. After attending a function at the Hotel he was called to a drug overdose in Burke Street. If anyone has seen the Priest or has information that will help police investigations, please call your local police station or Crime Stoppers.'

Sean hardly flinched.

'That was Father John!' Tom was shocked more than alarmed.

'Father...' Sean feigned curiosity.

'He was the one. He was the one...' Tom started putting it together. 'You were there Sean. He was at the hotel...'

'Now he's missing. Strange that. Who did you say he was?' Sean concentrated on the wheel.

'That was the Priest who did me over.'

'No joke?'

'No joke! He was the bastard...' Tom instantly transformed.

'He deserved what was coming to him then.' Sean made the mammoth effort to keep any emotion out of his voice.

'You're not wrong there Sean. Bastard!'

Sean realised that Tom had made the connection. He kept his silence and focussed on driving.

'Shit this drive is long. When do we get there?'

'We're going to stop at the top and look at the view. Find the music station Tom.' Sean suggested quietly.

The final ascent to Dead Horse Gap was mostly smooth with the occasional patches of ice. Then, a totally new page in the book of mountain landscapes opened before them; the magnificent v-shaped river valley, its sides dressed in gums and a rocky river bed along the course of the valley that led towards plains over thirty kilometres into the distance. Intermittent sunlight reflected off the blanket of white snow, the rays piercing the lower cloud cover drifting eastwards. The wind picked up as they reached the gap. This was a different world. The road had been ploughed earlier in the day, with fresh snowfalls pushed to each side and the wet tar gleaming black in the sun. Sean pulled over deftly into the roadside parking spot. Fresh and steaming horse dung was arranged in heaps as if someone had come along with a shovel.

'That's how they do it Sean. Gramps reckons horses have more sense than men sometimes.'

'Never seen that before. Horses must be close then.'

'Look, off to the right. There's a mob heading along the track.' Tom pointed towards a snow bound track leading from Dead Horse Gap to the southeast. The horses struggled from time to time with deep and soft drifts collecting against the embankment or a clump of gums. The wind picked up flurries of white, tossing the light top powder into the air, white flags that fluttered and evaporated as they formed. The lead mare, a sturdy chestnut with good girth sometimes broke through the snow cover almost to her belly. The herd followed her lead, their heads bent low and tails pressed close to the body as they turned away from the wind. Where the old matron struggled to climb out of the drift traps the other horses trod more carefully, testing underfoot before lunging across the larger patches of ice and snow. The line of the valley as it disappeared into the wilderness was broad and gentle with good tree cover on both sides, the boughs weighted with wet and heavy snow.

'Must be cold for them out here. Coats look good though.'

'That's their winter coat. They won't stay for long up here. They'll have to move off the mountain to where there's more feed.' Tom, it seemed, was filled with plenty of knowledge and information about the wild horses.

'Your grandfather?'

'It's a hot topic in these parts. The wild horses.'

'How's that son?'

'The conservationists want the horses completely out of the park. Takes years apparently to repair the ground once the horses have been there. Causes untold soil erosion and churns the boggy parts up something terrible.'

'Looks all right here, except for all that shit.' Sean commented. 'Want to camp here tonight Tom?'

'With the horses Sean? Not if the Parks plan another aerial shoot. Caused mayhem. Some of the mares were pregnant!'

'Not good!' Sean remarked.

'No It wasn't. Not with most people at least. You can't just shoot the problem Sean. That's like maiming women and children at war and leaving them to die. Well, it's the same in my book anyway.'

'You do feel strongly about it then Tom. What do your folks think?'

'Gramps has been a horseman all his life. He would never shoot any horse except if it could not be saved from a serious illness or injury. You just don't do it. His father served in the Light Horse. "Your horse is your life" was his motto.'

'Conflict of loyalties!' Sean remarked. 'Whose side are you on then?' he could sense the unsolvable.

'I love horses and I love the mountains. The horses have to live somewhere you know.' Tom sounded mildly indignant. 'Anyway gramps taught me to ride on the farm. He always wanted me to go in "The Man From the Snowy River Bush Festival", camp draftin' and that sort of thing to meet the local kids, but I just enjoyed ridin' for meself and on the farm and stuff.'

'Where does this mob come from?'

'They could have come from Corryong way or from Cowombat Flat, you know, where the Murray River starts. Some of the mobs go back to the mid-1800s. The wild horse bloodlines are probably thoroughbred in their own right. Some of them are from Omeo. The best horses are from Corryong though.'

'Where your legendary Man from Snowy River belongs Tom?' Sean teased.

'Well, you would never find a better horseman than Jack Riley, but some of the old timers are fairly good themselves. Charlie Carter ran with the last re-enactment apparently. Looked as though his bones would break if he sneezed, so he wouldn't want to fall off. He did it anyway though.' Tom laughed.

'Your grandfather ride?' Sean was impressed.

'Not the re-enactment. He still rides and breeds them. When he was younger though, he drove the horses through to Omeo. Tells me his sisters used to ride from Corryong to Geehi just for fun.'

'Hardy women!' Sean whistled.

'They used to spend up to three months at a time in the bush.'

'Living where?'

'Gramps and grandma slept in the covered horse buggy and the kids in tents.'

'Thought that was reserved for the wild, wild, west!' Sean laughed.

'Don't laugh. They loved it! Grandma used to cook in a camp oven, custard puddings, damper, meat, porridge and after that, scrub up all the kids in a metal tub.'

'We have something in common then.' Sean could see the irony.

'Does he still camp out?'

'Yeah. Likes the solitude he says.'

'So if he's not running horses off the mountain and duffing other people's cattle, what does he do!' Sean grinned widely.

'He's into bush poetry and stuff.' Tom said seriously.

'So there are strands of the artist in the family.'

'S'pose.' Tom admitted.

They stood silently watching the mob make their way through the trees. Then from behind the mist hanging like a shroud amongst the stunted gums, quite close to them, Sean spotted a large, strongly built grey horse, probably a stallion. He stood alone, ears pricked well forwards and nostrils flared as if he had not long caught their scent.

'See him?'

'What?'

'The stallion over there.' Sean pointed slowly.

'Can't see him.' Tom peered into the heavy cloud-like mist.

'Behind the first clump of trees. He has a colt with him. Look Tom. Bet he's sniffed us out already. Surprising in this wind though."

Tom looked again but there was no stallion, not that he could see. From the copse of grey-barked trees, a smoke-grey colt emerged alone. The colt trembled with fear as he stepped through the snow grass, his legs awkward yet strong, his head proud and mane contrasting with his coat. The young horse froze in his tracks as he saw the truck. Tom was already out of the open door of the cab, his hand held towards the horse.

'Come on fella. Come on.' Tom clicked his tongue urging the colt closer.

The horse stopped and pawed the snow raising a cloud of wind-drift around his legs. Then he raised himself up high and turned his neck towards the herd filing slowly down the track. He looked back to Tom; his dark eyes were captured in the boy's. Then he turned on his hind legs, front legs twisting through the air before they hit the ground.

The stallion suddenly galloped through the trees towards the track. His mane, white like his tail and hocks, flew from his neck sharply contrasting with the charcoal-grey coat. The horse steadied himself before crossing the chilly river. Then he stopped and tested the air for a long moment, turning to call the colt. The colt shook his head then reared onto his hind legs again, revealing his soft underbelly to Tom. As his feet connected with the ground, he turned and lunged after the stallion, crossing the Upper Thredbo River at its narrowest section. Close on the tail of the older horse, he kicked out his hind legs and powered through the snowdrift on the far bank to join the herd.

'One day that horse will be yours.' Sean found himself watching the display in awe, noting that the stallion was in one moment visible, then, as if only a mirage, was absorbed into the canopy of trees, The colt was close to its flank, but soon flurries of windblown snow obscured both of the horses. A curtain of snow fell, shutting out the view on either side of the Alpine Way.

THREDBO CAFÉ CULTURE

'Christ it's cold. Let's get out of here.' Sean pulled the collar of his jacket high against his neck.

Sean and Tom got back into the truck brushing off their coats. Sean immediately kicked over the ignition and a welcome blast of air from the already well-heated engine blew onto their faces.

'Need gloves in this part of the world,' Sean remarked. 'Maybe we'll find some in the village.'

'Jeez look at that wind. Don't reckon I'd be out on the snow today. Not for quids.' Tom was happy for the safety of the cab.

'You're not wrong there son. Let's go find us a feed.'

'Yep.'

'Been here before Tom?'

'Never. Never ventured outside of Victoria before in my life, never been on this side of the border.' Tom replied.

'Always a first time for everythin' then.' Sean pulled away from Dead Horse Gap onto the Alpine Way winding towards Thredbo village.

'That must be where the horses are headed. Up creek from where we are. That must be the main river through this valley.' Tom pointed to the creek rampaging towards Thredbo.

'Guess it must be.' Sean concentrated on taking the line of the curves efficiently and cleanly. There was still no traffic on the road. Sean noted the rock bolting and a series of plastic drains and pipes.

'Seems as though they have their act together better on this side.

No rock falls to speak of here.'

'That's because of the road collapse here a few years ago.' Tom said simply.

'Road collapse?'.

'Yeah. Bit of the road just above the village slid down the hill.'

'Oh. The rain wouldn't help anyways. Look at the pitch of that slope and even now it's gushin' like a spring.'

'Heard it rained cats and dogs day before yesterday. Maybe that's why there's so much water around.'

'Looks like more snow on the way today. Those clouds are something else.' Sean nodded towards the bank of clouds hanging off the mountain obscuring the ridgeline.

As they drove towards the village, it was clear that this was not going to be a picnic. The wind came in strong with erratic gusts ripping at the tree tops and hurling the crows along the valley as if they were no more than feathered toys. Suddenly they came to a steep embankment, completely built over with rockwork and held securely by long rows of wire mesh.

'Now that's something my grandfather would like to see.' Sean whistled. 'Always liked a good bit of stonework. Here we go then, this must be the entrance into the village.' Sean took the left turn down a steep road that seemed a one-laner at best. 'Steep and slippery I bet. Going to chog her down to four-wheel. This surface looks a bit dicey.' Sean slowed right down and took the corners slowly. 'Cute village though.'

'Looks precarious to me.'

'Shit, this road goes all over the joint. Where do you park?' Sean was not impressed. Already cars were jammed next to walls and into sparsely allotted car parks.

'Try the other side of that oval.' Tom pointed to a green area with a patchy covering of wet snow and a double row of cars on the far side.

'Let's give that a go then.' He followed the curve around and went for the far end of the car park. 'This is more like it.' Already the car park was nearly full.

'This will do.' Sean pulled in and nestled the truck between a couple of expensive looking four wheel drives.

'There's a bit of money in those!' Sean cast his eye over the line up of vehicles.

'Half of them are probably on credit or leaseback.'

'Could be right there Tom. Where's the food mate?'

'Dunno. But there's some steps over there. Looks as though we won't be heading up to the top of the mountain but. Chair lift's not running.' Tom sounded mildly disappointed.

'Must be the wind. Sure is blowing a gale out here.' Sean slammed the cab door behind him. 'C'mon. Let's get out of the wind. Steps it is.' Sean headed off sure that Tom would follow, but the boy strode out ahead taking the steps three at a time. Sean almost had to run to keep pace as they pounded up the next set. Tom stood at the top of the second flight.

'This is it.'

The Café was full with a sizeable crowd of skiers dressed in a colourful bonanza of winter clothes. The buzz was upbeat and friendly and one of the floor staff spotted the new customers.

'Would you like a table sir?'

'Thanks.'

He waited until they sat down before pulling out the menus tucked under his arm. The waiter didn't look much older than Tom and probably wasn't. Most of the staff looked as if they were in their late teens or early twenties.

The heat in the Café was oppressive after the sharp chill of winds blowing off the mountain. Sean stood up and hung his coat on the back of the chair.

'OK Tom?'

'Yeah Sean.'

The waiter returned to their table with a young man at his heels. 'You don't mind if he shares your table?'

'No. I don't.' Sean was less wary than taken aback.

'Hi. I'm Jaydon. 'Jeez, but it's cold up there! Had to shut the main chair so they gave me time off for breakfast before we start shovelin' snow.'

The guy didn't look much older than Tom. His hair was cropped and bleached and he wore a neat row of rings down the side of his left earlobe. He was dressed in company all-weathers with knee length and well insulated rubber boots. He glanced at the numb stare plastered on Sean's face.

'So I'm going for a second breakfast. Altitude 1380 will do me for now!'

'Oh.'

'Too icy to board.'

'You board?' Tom asked.

'Yeah. You?'

'Nope. Did a fair bit of skiing though. Hotham. That was in my youth.' Tom grinned.

'Were you good then? I mean in your youth?' Jaydon grinned back.

'Yeah it was good.'

Sean said nothing noting that Tom and the kid had already found common ground. The coffee was strong, hot and black. The liquid burnt the back of his throat as he took the first few gulps.

'Ah. That's better. Should warm up the belly. How's yours?'

'Good yeah.'

'So you like working here?' Sean raised an eyebrow.

'Yeah. Usually I'm on the top chair.' Jaydon openly offered the information with pride.

'Must be cold then.' Sean said.

'Too cold for me. It is today anyway. Blowing a gale on top. About 80 ks they reckon.' Jaydon filled them in.

'They close it down whenever it gets like this?' Tom asked.

'Have to. People could die of hypothermia out there if you let them, but it's mostly 'cos it's too dangerous. She swings about a bit in the wind.'

'We were going up the top for coffee.' Tom remembered.

'You wouldn't be today. Sometimes they get them off half way through the day. Chair closes down and you have to get all the staff off the mountain.'

'Jeez. How high is it then.' Tom was impressed

'Oh…' Jaydon didn't seem to know. 'It's not always like this though. When it's pumping it's mad up there. It's unreal. Some of the runs are out of this world.'

'Sounds good. This where the road collapse was?' Tom opened.

'Yep. Over there.' Jaydon pointed through the wall.

'We saw the rockworks as we came in.' Sean added.

'Heaps good yeah? Took them a few years. Some of me mates got jobs during the summer cartin' concrete and stuff up the hill. Said it was hardest work they ever did. Kills ya legs.'

'Can imagine.' Sean smiled widely.

'Wouldn't catch me doing that.' Jaydon added. 'Any case, I'm not into carting shit up hills in summer. Rather go surfing.'

'Is that what you do?' Sean suppressed a laugh.

'Yep. Down south. Sometimes get work with the lifeguards at Merimbula. One of them Jeff works up here on the mountain in the winter and on the beaches in the summer. Gets me work when I want it. If I want it.' Jaydon stuffed the first bite of his 'Big Brekkie' into his mouth almost in the same second that the waiter put the plate in front of him.

'Cool.' Tom cheered up with the prospect of beaches.

'Ask Jeff if you want work. Knows heaps of people down there. You'll catch him on Friday Flat. Does the ski school. Kids' stuff.'

'Where's Friday Flat?'

'Other end of Thredbo. Kids and beginners' slopes and stuff.'

'Stuart Diver still here?'

'Stuey?' Jaydon asked. 'Yeah.'

'Stuart?' Sean inquired.

'Only person who survived the slide.' Tom filled Sean in. 'He's a legend man.'

'Only one survivor?' Sean measured each word.

'He was stuck under the rubble for days. Took a lot to get him out. In the end they used the heat sensors. Man, was that epic.' Jaydon started on his coffee.

'You wouldn't believe it was possible. Coming out of that I mean.' Tom held is fork in mid air.

'Stuey is unreal. Must have had the snow gods on his side though.'

Sean had to suppress a laugh. 'You believe in snow gods Jaydon?'

'Don't you Sean?' Jaydon sounded injured.

'Believe in fate.' Sean sounded noncommittal. 'But the hills do look steep here. To build on that is.' Sean said thoughtfully. 'Do you know why they built there Jaydon, since you are local and all that?'

'How am I supposed to know? Nowhere else to build I suppose.'

The waiter returned with a plateful of food in either hand.

'Here you are boys. That will get you started!'

'Jeez that looks good mate!' Jaydon glued his eyes onto Tom's pile of bacon, eggs, baked beans and toast.

'Sure looks like a good feed.' Sean smiled at Jaydon. 'So you think they had nowhere else to build Jaydon?' Sean picked up the conversation again. 'Here, grab some of my beans.' Sean shovelled half of his breakfast onto Jaydon's plate.

'Thanks mate!' Jayden's face lit up. 'Stuey got his life back. That's the main thing.' Jaydon dug into the extra breakfast courtesy of Sean, determined not to spill the beans. 'Anyway, it's history now. People always want to live on the sunny side, especially if it has a view!' Jaydon seemed satisfied that that was as good an explanation as any.

'Where do you live Jaydon?' Sean was easy and friendly in his questioning.

'Staff accommodation. Bit cramped. Charge you an arm and a leg to stack you like sardines. It leaves travelling up the Alpine Way for dead but. Wouldn't catch me on that road after dark. Too many lunatics.' Jaydon was all innocence.

'Could have fooled me Jaydon.' Sean laughed. 'No-one on the road when we came in.'

'Yeah but youse don't have to go home every night after work. Heaps better to live on the mountain if you could afford it all year round. Not enough work though in summer. That's why I head for the beach.'

'Where are your folks?'

'I was shackin' up with me girlfriend in Jindy for a bit. Needed to go away for a bit. Just got back.'

'Right. Why did ya go away?' Tom asked.

'Me girlfriend. Killed in a car accident last year. Went off the side of the road. Fell asleep or something.'

'No way Jaydon.' Tom put his head down.

'Sorry to hear it son. That's tough.' Sean placed a rough hand on Jaydon's shoulder.

'It's cool. You lost anyone Tom?' Jaydon looked up, his mouth crammed full again.

'Not really.' Tom wasn't sure how to answer.'

'Everyone has something or another to deal with son.' Sean

looked at Jaydon.

You have to get over it and get on with your life if you know what I mean.' Jaydon wiped his mouth with the back of his hand. 'Gotta go. They want me to shovel snow off the boardwalks for the rest of the morning. Then I get the rest of the day off. Cool yeah? There's a party in the pub tonight.' Jaydon's voice dropped a couple of levels. 'There's some big stuff going down. Youse comin'?'

'Thanks for the invite.' Sean cut in.

'See ya then.' Jaydon pushed his chair away from the table spilling crumbs from his red work jacket onto the floor. 'See ya Tom. Check out Jeff if you want a job.'

Sean paid for their breakfast and headed towards the concourse. The double sliding glass doors kept the wind off the steps and he could see people crossing the square, beanies and gloves keeping them warm against the biting wind. The shops looked colourful and well patronised as people searched for something to do other than attempt the wild weather on the slopes. A basket of gloves for sale caught his eye and he quickly rummaged around until he found two large pairs that fitted his own hand. The second pair would do Tom until they had time to shop for clothes.

'Is that cash sir?' A middle-aged woman smiled from the shop.

'How much?'

'Last season's stock. Fifteen dollars a pair. They're good quality for the price.'

'Thanks. I'll take both pairs.' Sean fished out a fifty from his pocket noticing the newsagent through the shop window.

'Daily paper?'

'Melbourne, Sydney papers.' The proprietor responded.

'Thanks.' Sean made a quick dash across the courtyard into the newsagent. The shop was full with people looking for small gift items so it was easy to pick up a couple of papers.

'Weekend Australian and The Age?'

Sean pulled out a five-dollar note.

'Here's your change.' The salesperson noted that he was not part of the usual ski crew. A pleasant looking man though. 'Have a good day.'

'Thanks.' Sean's eyes lit up, his natural charm surfacing for the first time since he had set foot on the shore of this old, yet for him, very new continent. He felt uncannily happy as if there were good omens here for him.

'What d'ya get?' Tom opened the driver's door from the inside of the truck.

'Gloves. Try them on.' Sean switched on the ignition. He pulled the second pair over his hands and checked the rear view mirror before reversing out of the parking bay. 'They fit?'

'Yep. Thanks.' Tom rubbed his face with the gloves.

'Check the map will you Tom. Want to see how far we have to go.'

'Where are we going?'

'Berridale son. Angus said to ask there at the village and we'll get directions to the farm.'

Tom pulled open the glove box and opened the map. 'Here we are.' He pointed to Thredbo. 'Jindabyne is there and Berridale about 30 klicks further on.'

'But first, some fresh supplies!'

'This is shit Sean.' Tom struggled with the trolley.

'Never been shopping?'

'Not like this.' Tom persevered, narrowly missing an end of the aisle display of chocolate biscuits. Their trolley was over half full when Sean suddenly got cold feet. There he was, on the other side of the cash registers: the local cop.

Sean felt his hands instantly begin to sweat. He hadn't had time to read the papers and he wasn't taking any chances. There would be no description of him. unless one of the people at the hotel had decided to link him to the disappearance of the priest, and that was unlikely — the hotel's political patrons probably had more secrets to hide than they cared to think about. But Sean wasn't taking chances. He put his head down and found his money. At least they had a couple of bags of potatoes, tomatoes, corn, a full-sized pumpkin and some fruit as well as the toiletries they were after, a few packet cakes and cereal. He could buy milk locally. Right now he didn't care what they had and what they didn't have. He just needed to get out of the shop and into the truck and keep moving until they found the hideaway.

'Listen son, can you pay for this lot. I'm just going to check out that real estate board for future reference. Meet you at the truck in ten?'

'OK.'

'This should be enough.' Sean handed him another fifty.

'This one's on me Sean.' Tom pushed away the money. I cashed up in Melbourne when I left the boarding school. Kept it hidden with me gear.'

'Good thinking.'

'Bit of work and we'll be tops.' Tom drove the trolley past Sean and towards the check out.

'See you outside. No more than ten minutes, OK?' Sean walked to the shortest aisle, picked a pack of gum off the rack, paid and headed right. The police officer was not looking and Sean was not going to risk a glance to check. He quickly stopped at the real estate board not bothering to read the text, hoping it just looked that way. Then he skirted around the side of the shops and went straight back to the truck. He would wait quietly until Tom arrived. Sean quickly opened a few of the ties and dropped the tailgate. Tom would get the message.

Tom came towards the truck, fighting the sideways pull of the trolley. Sean immediately turned the key in the ignition and waited until Tom had heaved the shopping into the tray, pulled up the tailgate and secured the tarp. Tom ran the trolley off the parking lot, caught the opened door and jumped in beside Sean as he reversed the truck.

'You're in a hurry. Something to do with the cops over there?'

'They make me nervous son.'

'You running?'

'Let's say that I don't have papers anymore.' Sean only referred to what Tom already knew.

'Mr Sean Keating. Let's find that farm!'

'Dalgety or bust!'

DALGETY

'Could we stop here for half a sec Sean?' Tom suddenly saw the viewing points over Lake Jindabyne.

'Make it quick. You need a leak?'

'Nope. Got something else in mind.'

Tom got out of the truck at the far end of the Jindabyne Dam Wall. He walked to the edge of the tarmac and onto the embankment. He unclipped a silver chain from his neck. For a moment it nestled in his hand, the inscription 'Tom, from Dad' teasing him with a thousand memories. Suddenly, Tom swung his hand back, his mind steeled with cold determination. He flung the chain as far into the air as he could. The sunlight glinted briefly against the silver. Then the chain caught the water and disappeared into the lake. Tom walked back to the truck and got in.

Sean quickly turned back onto the road and accelerated up the hill. 'What was that all about?'

'Nothing left to link me with the past. End of an era you could say.'

'Who gave it to you Tom?'

'Me Dad.' Tom paused for a moment. 'Why would I want him hanging around me neck? Anyway I'm not a kid anymore Sean.' Tom stated it flatly. 'You mean more to me than me old man.' Tom's eyes shone with a force Sean had not seen in the boy before.

'Well Tom, you've got more courage than many from the old country — walking away from your past if you know what I mean, from the abuse.'

'Thanks.' Tom said simply. 'But you're walking away from your past too aren't you Sean?' Tom grinned quickly.

'You are quick Tom. You know where I came from, they dropped anyone like that priest of yours from Melbourne straight into the bogs'

'Serious? What do you mean by the bogs?'

'Out of sight and out of mind and leave just like that.' Tom felt the old rage catching in his chest.

'So you can buy me a new chain and get it engraved 'Tom Keating.' Tom drove his point home.

'That I can.'

'So from now on it's you, me and Angus.'

'Right you are young Tom.'

'This road is cool Sean' Tom said changing the subject. 'Not like that stretch up from Khancoban.'

'Scared of heights?'

'Nup. Just like to see where I'm going.' Tom had another look at the map. 'Hey Sean, did you think about unmarked cars?'

'What cars?'

'The D's. They don't advertise you know. It's the long weekend. The place will be crawling with cops.'

'Shiiit. Didn't cross me mind to be honest.' Sean eased off the accelerator. 'You didn't think to tell me in Victoria.'

'I didn't know you then. You get to spot them pretty quick. In Victoria they like dark blue. My old man mixes with them a bit.' Tom commented lightly.

'That's great. Do you want to call him up for a list?'

'They won't stop you in this pile of junk. If I know anything about the coppers, they want to go for a spin so they'll chase the fast numbers. Mate, you'd better believe it! You're safe in this.'

Tom opened a packet of gum. 'Used to give them heaps, the ones who'd drop around home. You know, stuff a gob of blue tack up the exhaust pipe. That sort of thing.'

'You did that?'

'Yeah. That's nothin'. Can show you are few tricks if you like.'

'Tom!'

'Geez man, you really are jumpy. Why don't you just drag a flag behind you 'My name is Sean. A couple of days ago I did in a priest.'

'Shit.' Sean banged his fist on the dash.

'Look out. Do yer want me to drive or something?'

'Tom. What do you know?' Sean was beginning to panic.

'Put two and two together. It was you. Wasn't it? The missing priest.'

'Christ.' Sean dragged the back of his hand across his forehead.

'Well?'

'The less you know, the better it is.'

'But I do know, don't I.'

'Yeah. It seems so.' Sean raised his eyebrows.

'Thanks.'

'What?"

'I said thanks!'

'Jesus Tom. Can't work you out.'

'My dad never could.'

'S'pose you might have a point there.'

'Yeah. He never would have got me out of that joint neither. So here I am on the run with a crim. Cool.'

Sean laughed in spite of his anger. 'Cool for you maybe but I'm the one who'll end up in the clink for life.'

'Could be worse Sean.'

'Yeah thanks. Paroled after fifteen years for finding a solution to the major social problem in the priesthood over the past century!'

'That, and the rest.' Tom said soberly.

'What do you know?' Sean realised Tom had more experience than his years.

'Nothing you'd ever dream about. I'll get me own back. One day.'

'Yeah be careful though. You'll end up dead if you try to be the hero.'

'You're the hero aren't you? I'm just the company.'

'Well, that suddenly puts you in a fine position! Sean was exasperated. 'Accessory after the fact or whatever!'

'The perpetrator and accessory to the crime is the school and the Church in my opinion — and their mates. I always thought rape was a punishable offence. Criminal act. You just mopped up afterwards.' Tom stated simply.

'You've got a point Tom.'

'Well isn't it? They raped me and who knows who else so they should be in gaol yeah?'

'If only. Church seems to be above the law here and everywhere else it seems.'

'One set of rules for them and another set for everyone else. Just use the church and do whatever you want: rape, murder, terrorise and generally stuff people right up.'

'Doesn't get me off the hook son.'

'You know what I reckon Sean? I reckon those drags have peas for balls. Otherwise they'd land themselves a proper woman.'

Sean laughed. 'Where's this town?'

'We're here. Berridale Federation Settlement.' Tom squinted as he read out the sign. 'Leftie Sean.'

'Not a lot here. Looks all right though.' Sean negotiated the grid and drove up the rough dirt driveway.

'In here.' Tom saw the ice-cream sign. 'Bullshit! This is great.'

'Hello.' A tall man in his early 70's walked from behind the counter. 'Passing through?'

'Nope. We're finally here. Berridale!'

Eddy laughed. 'You wish.'

Sean walked into the café.

'Sean, this is it' Tom announced.

'Gidday.' Eddy stretched out his hand. 'Welcome to town. You stopping for lunch?'

'Thanks. Hadn't thought that far ahead.'

'Cup of tea?' A woman's head popped out from the kitchen.

'This is my wife Belle.'

'Hi. Tom.' Tom put out his hand.

'Hi Tom. And…'

'Sean. Sean Keating.'

'You boys new in these parts?' Eddy suppressed a grin.

'You know. Looking to settle in the district. Heard there was a lot of work about town.' Tom kept the story going.

'I need a labourer.' Eddy suggested. Building another cottage. 'We're expecting a sudden influx for the snow season;' he suddenly guffawed.

'He's having a lend of you Sean.' Belle said. 'This isn't Berridale. We're just a small heritage village. Eddy built it himself. He's a bit of an artisan and collector.'

'So I see. The workmanship is superb.' Sean looked around him noting the clean timberwork. He felt the edge of the doorpost. 'Use an adze?'

'All original period tools. You build?'

'Stonemason.' Sean lightened up noticeably.

'Show you around then.'

'We'll be back for a coffee Belle.'

'OK. You joining them Tom?'

'Might just warm up by the fire if that's OK with you.'

'Course. Sit down.' Belle pulled a polished stump close to the fire. 'Eddy always sits here. Sometimes for hours at a time. Just thinking and reading.'

'Sure is cosy. Thanks.'

'My grandfather built this cottage and I've made a few changes to take it back to the original.'

'This is sweet.' Sean looked closely at the joining of timbers.

'My wife added all the bits and pieces for the shop. The rest is workmanship. You in a guild?'

'Me?' Sean looked sharply at Eddy.

'Thought you might, being a mason.'

'Stonemason. Not a member of the order though. Freemasons around these parts?'

'Good history of them. Let's go to the workshop. Got an old forge there.' Eddy went through the back door. 'Mind your head Sean. They must have been mighty little folk a century ago.'

Sean laughed. 'You don't quite fit yourself Eddy. You Irish or Scottish?'

'Scottish. You are from Ireland Sean.'

'With a name like mine? And proud of it.

'So where are your people from?'

'Giants Grave Downland, County Tipperary.'

'Glon Mel?' Eddy asked.

'Yes. You know the area?'

'No. Some of the settlers in the area are from the same County though.'

'Well there you go.' Sean said 'It is small world.'

'Have ye come to find your Irish roots in Australia Sean?'

'I'm interested in my clan of course, but this is more of a working holiday you might say.' Sean flattened the spike of interest before Eddy found out more than was healthy for him to know.

'There's always a surprise around the corner now, isn't there.

Think you've escaped to the ends of the earth and you find someone from your very own home town down at the local pub.'

'It seems to work that way.' Sean conceded and was careful to sound totally unfazed. 'My grandfather would have loved this place though.'

'He's a builder?'

'Worked mostly on the railways, but he could turn his hand to anything. Always appreciated fine workmanship though. Who trained you?'

'Picked up skills from my grandfather. Most of it though comes naturally.' The pride was noticeable in Eddy's voice. 'He was a smithy. The original smithy's shop is in Dalgety. Not much of it left now.'

'Is that where you picked up the anvil?'

'She's a beauty all right. Still make horse shoes here, though I prefer the building side now.'

'My father was a farrier but I never learnt the trade. More interested in building and what my grandfather had to offer.'

'I prefer the building side too Sean.' Eddy confided.

'Might look you up when I come to build something for myself. Good stone around these parts?'

'The granites are the best. Now they use the old quarry pit as the Jindabyne rubbish tip. Complete and utter waste. Council could have made a fortune from that one.'

'Are there any more quarries in the area?'

'We'll find you the stuff. I've got a cottage on the go up the hill. Next time you're around I'll take you up there.'

'Thanks. I might need it.'

'No doubt you might Sean. Where are you staying?'

'Angus Wallace's property. Looking after the farm for a while. I'd prefer to keep a low profile for the first couple of months while we settle in, if you know what I mean.'

'I know the property. You can turn off at Boundary road or go into the village and go straight down Myack St and follow the signs out to Dalgety. He's up on the Bobundara Creek. I'll draw you a map inside if you like.'

'Thanks. That would be handy.'

'Coffee?'

'Yeah. Could do. The boy must be inside.'

'Your son?'

'Nephew as it happens. Came out to meet him and spend some time with the lad. He's had a bit of trouble at home.'

'Then Angus's farm might be just the thing for you both.'

'You're back then Eddy. You two up for coffee?'

'Sounds good. Thanks.'

'We'll be joinin' you.' Eddy was always ready for a cup. 'Come on over to the table and I'll put that map together for you.'

'If this is Berridale, what's the rest of the town like?' Tom asked.

Eddy roared with laughter. 'Well half of it isn't as well built as this shack. You couldn't find any of those union boys spendin' the time it takes to do it properly' he said dryly. 'Bit of sandstone though. Quality stuff. You might take a look one-day. Let's do you the map. Have you got a spare sheet of paper out the back Belle?' Eddy pulled a half pencil out of his top pocket and drew in the air before roughly sketching the highway up the left side of the paper. Then he marked in a big cross and wrote 'Berridale' next to the cross. 'We're about here.' Eddy marked a smaller cross on the highway.

'You mean we aren't in Berridale?' Sean shook his head laughing.

'Not yet. If you are heading to Dalgety you could have gone the back way through Jindabyne, along the Barry Way. Why did you come to Berridale?'

'Angus suggested it. Said people there knew him.'

'It makes sense I guess, that people know there is someone on the farm. OK. Here it is. These are the escape routes, for want of a better term.' Eddy looked up and smiled broadly. 'This is Boundary Road and this is Myack. They both link up with the main drag to Dalgety. Don't take the left fork. Just continue right on. You'll come to Dalgety. Pretty little town on the Snowy River. First is Iona Gardens, the empty servo, then the pub. Yeah?'

'Sounds simple enough.' Sean followed.

'Stop at the pub if you like. The owner shares a boundary with Angus. You can't miss the turn off in any case. Left is the wrong way and right takes you over the Snowy River on the old bridge. Take the right. It's the back way to Jindabyne. Angus's place is about there.' Eddy circled a point on the road that approximated the dirt road entry.

'His place is opposite the Church. If you hit the graveyard you've gone too far. Bit too soon for you to stop there by the look of you.' Eddy cocked his head at Tom. 'Angus's is the neat as-a-pin shack. Got the picture?'

'Pretty clear. You're ace, Eddy. Thanks for that.'

'Don't mention it. You'll be OK for access. Not much rain in the past few weeks. There's plenty of drinking water, but don't hang about the gullies after heavy rain. She rages something fierce down the creek. Drains into the Snowy. Angus's lost a few stock after the rainstorms. There!' Eddy looked up from the table, pleased with his work, handing Sean the map.

'Cool. Can I see?' Tom asked eagerly.

'Sure. Keep it 'til you learn it son.' Eddy offered. 'Can't really get lost in these parts. All roads lead either to the coast, the escarpment or the mountains. If you drop off the edge of the escarpment, you've forgotten to stop at Numbula or Jimenbuen and then you're into Victoria.' Eddy grinned.

'He's got electricity out there?'

'Got everything. He mostly uses the generator though. Diesel. Wood stove with a gas bottle as well. Light, gas lamps, candles that sort of thing. Bush dunny. Don't need much else unless of course you're looking for Windsor Castle.'

Sean broke into a smile. 'Well, we folk were never one for the royal classes now were we.'

'You'll like it here.' Eddy agreed. 'Not too many toffs in these parts anymore. Them that were, gambled and drank away the family fortune, so three or four generations later the kids are left with a patch of useless dirt and bugger all else after they've carved up the estate. Some of them sold it off in bits to pay their gambling debts. Mind you, the stock around here is pretty rare. Good quality wool. You'd never beat it, even though the blokes around Yass and Goulburn reckon theirs is better. Their stock would never last the distance here. These Monaro rams are indestructible, probably immortal some of them and they would, in my estimation, far outclass your English inbreds, if you go as far to call those blokes breeders.'

Sean roared with laughter. 'We have an enemy in common. Yeah, the British breed junk with knock knees and teeth too long for their gobs. Anyway, that mad cow thing should sort them out for a while.' Sean was suddenly very happy to be a long way from the British Isles. 'Pity you couldn't add a bit of swine fever to the water supply!' he added.

Eddy chuckled. 'Used to be a few piggeries around here. You'll see the sheds rusting on some of the farms. There's one up on the hill behind Berridale. Just nettles, sheep shit and kangaroo gullies now.'

'Your family been here for a while Eddy?'

'You could say that. There are a good number of us original families here. Some of them are as tough as old wethers. Quite a few of the old birds are already hitting the 90's. Pendergasts were probably the first family around here in the early 1820s. My lot started out a bit later with over 30,000 acres to work. We still have extracts from my Grandfather's diary. How they earned money and that sort of thing. Ended up making gravestones and coffins to keep the family going.'

'So he branched out into stonemasonry?'

'Aye. He was good all right. Built up the Gegedzerick graveyard. Mostly pioneering families. His are signature headstones.' Eddy looked around at his own handiwork. 'Then he handed the skills down and now I'm doin' the crafting.' Eddy sounded prouder of his grandfather than he was of himself.

Belle walked in with a foolscap folder wrapped in thick plastic.

'Here it is.' She opened the book. 'These are his accounts, or some of them.'

Eddy fingered the neat writing and short columns of monthly takings.

'Christ. You'd work hard for the pound!'

'They worked hard — all of them — can you imagine what it was like then, but there's not much left of the original estate now. Although there are a few of the old homesteads still around. Now there's a thought for one day Sean.' Eddy brightened to the thought. 'Take you on a local history journey of buildings as they used to be built.' Eddy looked seriously over his glasses.

'Might do that. Might do that. We'd better be movin' for now thanks all the same.' Sean stood up. 'There wouldn't be a fuel stop nearby would there Eddy?'

'Berridale. You drivin' Angus's diesel?'

'Yep.'

'He treats it a bit rough but keeps it serviced. You might want to check that there's enough antifreeze in the radiator. The Berridale pump has winter fuel. Some of the trucks used to get holed up all morning until the fuel tank thawed out before they changed the diesel.'

'Great.'

'Nothin' like that in Ireland?'

'Always cold where I'm from.' Sean suddenly checked himself. He felt he was giving away information about himself he didn't want folks to have. 'And thank you Belle for the lovely cuppa. Tom?'

'Yeah, thanks Mrs...'

'Just call me Belle, Tom.' Belle smiled at her husband.

'Thanks Eddy.' Tom put out a paw with jam and butter still smeared on his fingers.

'Thanks is fine without the handshake.' Eddy's shoulders shook in time with his deep and raucous laugh.

'Yeah.' Tom noticed the cream on his fingers.

'Here Tom.' Belle produced a blue napkin. 'Have a couple of extras.' She handed him a bunch. 'Now you two get going before it's too late to light the fire.'

Sean and Tom left the Federation Settlement, their spirits considerably raised since the morning report on the radio news about the Priest and their close encounter with the Jindabyne police.

'We're nearly there son.' Sean was visibly relieved.

'Reckon. Just look out for that sign yeah?'

'Yeah. Need fuel first though. We'll take the Myack turnoff. Got it marked?'

'Yep.'

They turned onto the highway and within ten minutes, pulled into the greater bush metropolis of Berridale.

'Is this it!' Tom counted the shops as they drew off the highway and into the first entrance. The road immediately became a broad car park with a row of shops set back well away from the highway. 'One, two, three, how many shops do you reckon Sean?'

'More than the last village we stopped at.' Sean said dryly.

'Yeah. Them scones were pretty good.'

'Those scones Tom; those scones were great.'

'Yeah. Those. What's this? The local alfresco joint? Hey don't run over them Sean.' Tom put his hands forward on the windscreen expecting a sudden collision, as the green plastic table and chairs with a group of women sipping coffees loomed larger than life.

Sean neatly turned to the right and angle parked opposite the café.

'What an en-trance!' Tom unbuckled his seat belt.

'Is this a town?' Sean stepped out of the cab. 'Let's see what this lot are about.'

Tom walked into the café. 'Video Sean? Anything interest you here?'

'Don't know if he has one, do we. Angus I mean.'

'Yeah, that's a point. We're not in the city any more are we!' Tom laughed.

'Can I get you something?' A woman in her 30's with attractive brown hair got up from one of the tables in the café.

'Thanks. Just looking. See you have a good selection of videos here.'

'We try and keep them moving' the woman said.

'Sandy, another hot chocolate for outside' a man yelled in through the hanging strips of plastic, there more for effect than flies it seemed. There was a fair breeze blowing, however the women seemed happy sitting outside, rugged up in fleeces, vests and scarves. A couple of them were smoking which, Sean thought, accounted for the outdoor dining choice.

'Thanks Dan. Tell them I won't be a moment. Just doing these chips.' The woman in the back of the shop counter grappled with a basket of steaming chips and upturned them onto the classic butcher's wrap before liberally sprinkling salt and vinegar over the lot. 'Sauce?' she yelled through the square cut into the wall between the kitchen and servery.

'Thanks heaps Sandy.' A couple of children peeked their heads just above the counter far enough to nick a few of the chips off the pile before they were wrapped and out of reach.

Sandy smiled. 'That the lot then?' She walked back into the café and slapped the boys' booty on the counter. Mind when you cross the highway. There are some crazy drivers at this time of year.'

'Mmm.' The kids were already charging out of the shop, the parcel of hot chips securely tucked under one of the armpits. They headed across the highway looking just long enough to beat the truck and aimed for the skatepark.

'At least you can see what they are up to from here.' Sean noted.

'They're all right' Sandra said. 'Kids don't have a lot to do around here.'

Already there was a mob of about five youths dancing across the concrete on their skateboards and another group huddled together on the grass.

'That's it then? The skatepark?'

'That's about all they have' Dan picked up the conversation as he walked into the shop with a tray of empty mugs. 'They could use a gym. The pool's closed most of the time. Council can't afford it. Insurance. It's not heated in any case.'

'Real battle then.' Sean nodded his head. 'Listen, can you tell me where the petrol station is?' Sean decided it was time to get a move on.

'About five metres away.' Dan grinned and pointed with his left hand further into the settlement of shops.

'Right. Then I won't miss it.' Sean was never one to be on the end of someone else's humour.

'Not like you nearly missed us.' A woman walked into the shop her blonde hair highlighting her broad and cheerful face.

'Taa Anna' Sandra took the pile of plates from her. 'Leave the chairs out if you like. Jo is coming later.'

'You new here? Can't remember seeing you before' Anna studied Sean closely.

'Sorry about the fright. When Tom said 'alfresco' I realised that we'd finally arrived in Berridale.'

Anna laughed. 'Well just don't forget where the brakes are. I thought you'd end up as the latest installation in the art gallery!'

'I didn't and I won't any other time.'

'Driving like that it's a wonder you see anything at all. You're driving Angus's truck.'

'You know it?' Sean was not sure whether to feel alarmed or acknowledged.

'Angus's truck? Yeah. I dinged his tailgate unless you haven't noticed the dent.'

'Right. Then you must live close by?' Sean probed for the zone of privacy.

'Close enough. Gotta go.'

'Nice to meet you.' Sean's eyes twinkled.

'You too. See you Sandra.'

'Anything else then?' The shopkeeper asked politely.

'Huh? Oh. No. I mean yes, a couple of packs of salt and vinegar chips.' Sean fumbled for the change.

'This enough?' Tom handed coins across the counter.

'You staying at Angus's?' She asked.

'Seems as though everyone knows your business in Berridale before you know about it yourself.' Sean shook his head in disbelief.

'See you next time then. Do you know the way to the farm?'

'Yes. Thanks. The guy in the Federation Settlement drew me a map.'

'Eddy?'

'Yeah.' Tom helped Sean out again.

'That way.' Dan pointed down Myack Street.

'Have to get some fuel first remember Sean.'

'That way.' Dan pointed in the general direction of the bowser.

'You know son, I don't think that we're going to be able to keep much of a low profile out here.' Sean commented as they pulled away from the diesel pump. The events of the past twenty four hours seemed to him to be a mini roller coaster of practically every feeling known to a sane or insane man.

'She's cool man. They'll forget about us in about five minutes I reckon. Out of sight, out of mind.'

'Hope you're right. Got everything we need?'

'Must have by now. Let's find the farm!'

The road was as Eddy described, easy to follow and Sean made sure that he continued straight on, ignoring the left fork on the outskirts of Berridale. The road then curved left and followed a ridge-line before dropping off the ridge and over a bridge. Within a minute they were upon a small settlement with the Post Office Café on the left as they drove in. Sean was past it before either of them had noticed. The road seemed to be going nowhere fast so he pulled up at an intersection.

'Buckley's Crossing Hotel' Tom read out the sign.

'This must be Dalgety then.' Sean let out his breath.

'There's the Snowy River! Not much of a river. Looks as though a dog couldn't even paddle in it.'

'Probably that's their piddle.' Sean pulled up. 'This is Dalgety? Smaller even than Berridale.'

'Got a pub. That counts!' Tom rubbed his hands together.

'Which way?' Sean gazed past the collection of houses on the top of the road heading left from the pub into the rural distance and the tennis courts over the road.

'I'm lost! Too many choices.' Tom decided. 'Better ask the bloke in the hotel.'

'Bloke?'

'You know. The barman.' Tom shook his head in disbelief.

'Getting late in the day Tom. You ask.'

'Yeah OK.' Tom shrugged and walked up the steps to the broad wooden verandah. The hotel was a single story solid brick building with a snug foyer, anteroom and a bar big enough to fit in about fifteen people at a squeeze. There was no one inside other than the owner drying a rack of glasses.

'Know where you are son?'

'I don't. That's why I'm asking you.' Tom replied.

'You're underage aren't you. So that means you're lost. Mostly people are lost or regulars.'

'I'm lost.'

'Then who are you looking for?'

'Angus's place.' Tom pulled the map from his pocket.

'And that would be his ute I take it.'

'Yep. Sure is.'

'Well he lives about here.' The barman pointed to the map. 'Down from the Boloco Church. You come at it from the bottom end of the valley. Cross the bridge here then take the right fork. Follow the road to the second letterbox and take the road in a few kilometres. Stay to the left on top of the ridge. If you drop off to the right, you'll end up in the Snowy River, or what's left of it. Angus's place is off to the left. Past the shearing shed, then you'll come to his place. Nice spot.'

'Thanks. How long do you reckon?'

'You'll do it in under fifteen.'

'I'll tell Angus that you're looking for him. What did you say your name is?'

'Tom. Tom Keating. Nice to meet you.'

'And you Tom. Keep an eye out for 'roos on the road. Dusk and dawn. Catch you 'round.' The barman nodded quietly.

'Got it Sean,' Tom yelled from the verandah. He leapt off the steps in one stride. 'That way.'

'OK. Then we're nearly home son.' Sean got back into the jeep and, for the first time since the camp, felt happy. He whistled quietly to himself as they left the pub and negotiated the ancient looking yet solid bridge over the river.

'There Sean. That's the turnoff. Then we follow this road down and we're home!' Tom was triumphant.

'Got it. This is it. We've got plenty of time to relax now. We'll just take the last few kilometres nice and easy. Light's fading.' Sean's smile was as big as a Cheshire cat's.

They came to a shearing shed and a few hundred metres further on they had arrived at the farm proper. Sean switched off the engine, his eyes firmly planted on the essentially wooden structure that reminded him of the 'artisan' work of the Federation Settlement. The outer boards were plainly cut and grooved together and the tin roof neatly capped and waterproofed the very basic and homely hut. Sean let out a slow whistle.

'Well. This looks like home Tom. A little more, shall we say, salubrious than our tent affair.'

'Looks cosy and dry. She's got a cool chimney. Must be a wood fire!'

The rough slab construction and the broad stone chimney butting into the sky like a sentinel of domesticity could not have been more welcoming.

'Out you get then Tom. Can you light the fire?

'Yep. Got some matches in me pocket. Hut looks pretty basic.'

Sean laughed. 'Wouldn't surprise me knowing Angus.'

Sean let Tom find his way into Angus's bush home, before he opened the truck door and loosened the ties on the tarp to get their gear out of the back.

In the dimmed light slanting through half-frosted windows, Angus's slab bush hut was, on first appearances, a cosy nest of perfection, the doors crafted it seemed, from old packing cases, the roof rafters exposed and running over the verandah and long cedar interior wall planks snugly fitted together. The rough and unpolished hardwood kitchen floor had a minimum of furniture, a round table and four chairs. There was nothing else in the front room of the hut, which served as both kitchen and dining room. The only furniture was an old and deep ceramic sink, chipped on one corner, and the almost overpowering yet welcome presence of the Canberra Wood Fuel Stove snugly contained in what had been the open granite fireplace. The firebox was already neatly stacked, and the woodbox adjacent to the stove was filled to capacity with carefully split timber, sized to fit the stove and ready to burn. Another lantern hung by an old butcher's hook from a rafter nail and somehow the collection of kitchen utensils, delicately perched on a leaning wood ledge, defied the law of gravity.

That Angus clearly had plenty of basic kitchen common-sense, without too many frills or indulgences, was evident in his interior design and decoration. The pantry, leading off to the right of the kitchen, was well stocked with bottled fruits, dried fruits and nuts, stainless steel containers filled with an assortment of grains, flours and oats, and plenty of cans of milk, beans and vegetables. Sheaves of lavender and rosemary hung next to the stove and a loose arrangement of ginger, pumpkin and potatoes on a layered wooden rack in a cooler section of the naturally dark pantry meant that there would be a hearty meal tonight. An old 1950s wireless on its own shelf near the sink completed the picture of domestic peace. The doorway through the kitchen led into a long and narrow hallway, again featuring rough, yet worn, unpolished hardwood boards and with more planks of cedar on the walls. There was a high ceiling where the exposed rafters ran across the hut. The effect was like being inside a wood-crafted womb, complete with warm and soft hues. There was nothing much else in the hut, no pictures, wall hangings or paraphernalia. The neatness of his home stamped Angus as a man of taste and simplicity. He was a man who liked home comforts without fuss, an uncomplicated retreat from the world.

'Neat pad.' Tom busied himself at the fireplace crumpling an old newspaper into a burnable shape to place under the already laid wood. The firebox had beside it a small tomahawk, to make a few splinters for kindling.

'Since you've got that in hand, I'll check out and see where our digs are.' Sean quickly walked down the hallway, noting which was Angus's room. There were four rooms, all with single beds and freestanding wardrobes. The bathroom was at the far end of the cottage. A cast iron tub consumed most of the space, with a wash stand and chest of drawers to complete its service. The toilet, Sean noted, was outside.

'Find a cot?' Tom had the fire going, his lungs working like bellows to force the flame over the newspaper.

'Plenty of those. You can find your own room. 'Bathroom's that way.' Sean pointed down the hallway. 'Actually, you can take the last room on the left, the one with the view.' He grinned and threw Tom his bag. 'Hot water is hooked to the gas bottle. This man has his priorities worked out.'

'Thanks. What's for dinner?'

'Feel like a stir fry?'

'Can you cook?' Tom wasn't sure whether that was an advantage for a man.

'Nothing gourmet. I reckon I can put us together a feed though. Noodles, can of chopped pineapple, mushrooms that sort of thing, bit of chilli sauce.'

The night closed in quickly around the cottage and Sean checked the windows, looking to see where the stationary lights were that marked neighbouring properties and would give him a reference point for moving lights. If anyone decided to come snooping, he wanted to know about it first. There would be no encouraging unwanted visitors and if he had his way, he would also discourage friendly 'drop ins'. It was going to be as dark as Hades tonight except for the stars drawn in celestial curtains across the night sky. That was both uplifting and reassuring to him. They would wash, eat, and hit the cot. Early.

NEW LIFE BY THE SNOWY RIVER

The morning broke in silence over the vast expanse of the frost-covered Monaro. This was a timeless land long-forgotten by wandering tribes. Only the kangaroos remained generation after generation, keeping a gentle foothold on the remaining native grasslands that had escaped European impacts. The land belonged to the past. There was nothing that even the famers could do to ease the yawning emptiness, the open and treeless plains, the vast star-ridden night sky and the bitterly cold winds that sheeted incessantly off the mountains.

Inside, the cottage was a haven. The wood fire burnt bravely throughout the entire night and into the early morning. Now the wood coals had little heat left. Sean stirred in his bed, noting the condensation frosted on the windows in his bedroom. The familiar sound of a plover nesting nearby was a pleasant reminder of his once civilised existence, albeit marred by violence and unwanted encounters with the law. The farm was a hidden haven and Sean felt in his bones that they would be safe. There would be time to heal and time to plan a future for them both.

The morning lifted as it always did over the broad back of the Monaro tablelands, the first light spreading to expose its breadth, a vast and cold footstool to the great expanse of the Dividing Range.

Sean dragged himself off the bed and pulled on his jeans and thick pullover. His boots and socks were next to the door as was his habit: easy to find and neatly placed. The cottage was totally quiet.

Tom was still asleep and the runaway Irishman was content to let him be. Sleep was nature's medicine and Sean understood that it would take the boy a while to get a handle on his new situation. It was more than just a change of scene. As Tom said himself, this was a totally new life. The past was well and truly behind him. Sean was pleased, yet unsurprised, to find he was whistling — a cheerful and spontaneous response to feeling good and for the first time for decades, free from worry.

It was not every day that he had awoken without needing to check the windows and door, wary of booby traps planted during the night by men with plans on his life; or the end of it. Sean was on the hit list of more than a few governments around the world, not just because of suspicions about his own activities, but also because of the company he kept and their links to the IRA.

He made for the verandah door and the outhouse that appeared to have a specially positioned building site all of its own. The air was clear and sharp with the sun breaking in a symphony of gold and red above the assortment of morning clouds. The view was unexpectedly stunning and for the first time in years, Sean felt at home. The childhood memories of space, freedom and innocence sprang into his awareness. He felt his heart almost physically lift out of the cave of sadness that had confined him for so long and his mind release from the very real concern to cover his tracks every living second of his life since the first skirmishes on the picket line.

The toilet was blissfully simple, and with a view to live and die for. The farm and its buildings were far better than Sean had anticipated. The open air and sense of freedom was way better than the tight and steamy constraints of the trawler with the sweaty presence of a dozen other men, and of course far better than being perpetually on his guard or on the run in Ireland.

Sean emerged from the shed zipping his fly as he stepped into the morning light. He breathed long and deeply, stretching his arms as wide as they would go and above his head. He opened his lungs to taste the chilled sweetness of clean oxygen. There were no smoke stacks out here, no dirty tack-tack of engines belching out poorly burnt diesel, no stench of stagnant waterways clogged with the dead cargo of industrial waste, sewage and algae, no dying cities or the depressed citizens that lived in them.

This was the land for saints. He could see further than the horizon it seemed and there was nothing except an uninterrupted expanse of calmness and silence. Sean's natural impulse was to look around and explore on foot; he wanted to get a sense of the place. He knew that on more than one occasion his intuition had done the work to save him from premature death. His sixth and seventh sense told him to watch how the birds flew, where the winds blew in from and the direction of the smoke as it trailed from the chimney into the valley. All these were the signs that back-dropped the normal roll of day and night. These were the pointers that would tell him whether they were being observed at any time or whether there were unwanted and unwelcome visitors lurking in the shadows or on their doorstep.

Angus was a tidy man and already the two visitors brought change to the quiet routine of the farm. Sean was aware that the local people, although relaxed and nonchalant, were keenly observant of any newcomers in the area. They would of course be noticed. Sean had found the locals friendly enough, yet in his experience there was no village in the universe that did not have either its secrets or its snoops. He would have to suss out both and figure out who could be trusted and who could not.

Sean went back into the cottage, and cleared the bags off the kitchen table then stowed the rest of the food. The pantry was as well stocked as any he had seen and Sean made a note to keep it filled. There would come a time when they might not be able to travel in to the towns for stores and would have to more-or-less close the doors to the outside world. There could easily be times when they would have to remove all traces of their existence and disappear out of the place, and fast, without leaving any careless, tell tale signs.

Though the classic wood fuel stove graced the kitchen, Angus, a man of practical sense and experience, had built alongside the wood stove, a separate two-ring gas burner on a plank of wood. The standby 'fast food' option was handy for a quick brew or meal. For now, Sean was in no hurry and the cold morning begged for a warm kitchen fire and eggs broken straight onto the stove plate. The scent of a sausage sizzle wafting down the hall would encourage Tom out of bed and straight into a world that was far better than anything he had ever experienced before.

Sean busied himself with the fire. He blew softly at the base of the smoke curling up from the tiny splinters of kindling. He left the firebox door wide open until he was sure the flames were hot enough to keep the wood ignited. Then he gently closed the firebox door and opened the flue to charge the fire.

'Tom!' Sean bellowed down the hallway. 'Am I eating yours as well as mine?'

'What?' Tom's muffled voice was music to Sean's ears.

'Breakfast. Do you want it?'

'Great! I'm famished.' Tom was already out of bed, pulling on his trousers and sweater and halfway down the hall by the time Sean had sussed out the salt and pepper part of the pantry.

'Where to start!' Tom followed Sean's lead, abandoning the knife and fork and wrapping both hands around a toast sandwich of sausages. 'Shit, this is good!' Tom complimented the chef between mouthfuls.

'More?'

'You fattening me up for something Sean?'

'Nope.'

'Got anything planned today?'

'Yep. We'll take it easy. Check out the view. Angus's got a few thousand acres here so there's plenty of space for a walk. He said there's a brumby with his old mare and a donkey in the top paddock.'

'Cool. D'ya reckon there are any saddles around?'

'You could have a poke in the shed, see what you can find.'

Tom was tempted by the adventure of finding the brumby and decided that after breakfast he would look around the farmhouse and sheds for a bridle. The farmhouse was set amongst the trees on a hill and around it, uninhabited space. A shrubby ridge stretched from behind the house towards the road they had driven along to find the farm. Tom wanted to explore, but not yet. Everything that he knew was gone and he felt like sticking around Sean for the time being until he got a better feeling of where they were and what was around them.

'Wash up?'

'Stick the pot on the stove. No point wasting gas when we've got the fuel stove going.'

'See ya point. Where's the outhouse did you say? Outside?'

Sean flicked a thumb over his shoulder. 'Good view.'

Sean chuckled and switched on the radio. The farmhouse was a haven, but clearly connected with the real world. He tuned into the early morning news bulletin.

'In scenes reminiscent of the bitter waterfront dispute, police have broken a picket line at the Hastings Street BHP-Billiton plant in Victoria resulting in violent clashes.'

'Sheesh.' Sean whistled out through his teeth and turned up the dial.

'Mounted police broke through picket lines using a Federal Court injunction to break striking workers. Once the cordon was broken, a convoy of over twenty trucks moved in with the first supplies of steel in three weeks, destined for the General Motors Holden car manufacturing plant.

'Well there you go! You can change your country but you'll find the same pile of horseshit politicians wherever you go!' Sean flicked off the radio.

'You say something Sean?'

'Reckon we might just lie low for a few days son. What do you think?'

'Sounds good to me. Brought me book.' Tom offered.

'Sounds perfect. I brought me knitting.' Sean grinned.

By Friday, Sean and Tom had walked the length and breadth of Angus's property. The shale hill was topped with a workable quarry, lightly dug and with plenty of materials for a good-sized building. The hill dropped away to the south, with rough-barked, dark trees married it seemed, to less common, smooth-barked white trees. The ground was slippery with loose shale and eventually dipped towards a long gully, now drenched in sun and green with new shoots of grass after the recent rains. The only horses on the property had already found the fresh feed and were too preoccupied with eating to notice the men's arrival. The horses shared a long and open valley running north to south along the line of the creek. To the far south, Sean noted a couple of buildings on the horizon. He pulled Angus's binoculars from around his neck and studied the view. He could see a church with an elegant shale roof and a small outhouse that must be the toilet. Adjacent, to the church was a cluster of pines, planted to break the fierce, southerly winter winds. To the right, another group of trees bordered the otherwise open graveyard — groups of graves randomly clumped in a section of native grassland. Sean swung the glasses forwards following the creek line back towards the farmhouse, noting its private and relatively safe location.

The horses finally caught the scent of the men on the morning air. The mare saw them first as they descended the deepening gully below the base of a small shale cliff. She looked at them steadily, her eyes resolute and unmoving. Her faded white and strawberry-flecked coat was still long and shaggy from the winter and her grey-white mane was bedraggled and studded with grass seeds and burrs. A donkey hung closely to her rump and a young brumby stood apart from them, watching the men.

Sean handed the binoculars to Tom. 'Look son. There he is. He's a beauty!'

Tom took the glasses and sighted them to the horses, adjusting the lenses to his eyes. 'Wow. He's in condition all right.'

The horses looked back at Tom, uncertain about the visitors in their paddock, yet curious at the new scents. The morning light shone on his steel grey coat, and his hide rippled with nervousness at the sudden appearance of the men. He had the telltale signs of white hairs above the eyes and sported an elongated white star from the forehead to his nose. The black mane was softened with white streaks, and his tail raised high in the anticipation of flight. His hooves were neat and compact, black against white socks that rose all the way to the hock. The young colt had all the markings of a beauty, hidden far away from the world in the semi-wilderness that was Angus's farm. There was plenty of space here, yet the colt could never be as free here as he was in the mountains. The setting was nevertheless magnificent with Guise's Range striking roughly to the west, an umbilical cord to the mountain wilderness from where the colt came.

'Look at his hooves Sean.' Tom handed him back the glasses.

'Gramps said the wild horses are far better than even the best breeders can produce. Only the tough survive on the mountain. Darwin's law.'

Sean took the glasses and studied the feet of the young brumby and the hooves of the mare. He noted the colt's compact, intact hooves compared to the mare's ragged and slightly split hooves. At least here the ground was well drained, with an assortment of loose basaltic rocks on the surface that would naturally trim their hooves.

'Got it Tom.'

'I wouldn't mind breaking a wild one in, like me gramps taught me.'

'Oh.'

'Horses he bred himself.'

'Right. So you know horses?'

'Yeah. Used to ride a lot on the farm, checking the boundary fences, moving stock around, that sort of thing.'

'Well that's good then?'

'Yeah. I am an alright rider.'

'Do you want your own horse?'

'D'ya think we could catch a couple Sean?'

'Can't see why not. Might have to wait until Angus comes back. They'll know where the horses are around here and how to get their hands on a couple. You sound like you could be up for it'

'Yeah. Sure am Sean. I'd love a colt. I don't really want to geld him though.'

'Maybe you won't have to. Just depends on how you handle him I guess.'

'Give a horse enough space to run and he'll be OK. Christ I hate fenced paddocks! Half the horses in this country don't even have ten cents worth of mud to spin on and even then it's shared with a dozen or more.'

'You feel trapped son?' Sean asked mildly.

'This is awesome.' Tom breathed out looking up the valley to the church then across to the race. 'One day we'll take some horses up there Sean, across that range and into the mountains. Might take this little fella if Angus'll let me.'

The next morning broke with fresh and gusty winds tearing at the wings of a Great Harrier as it hovered close to the ground searching for rabbits, native mice or dead lambs. The sun made a strong entry, warming the chilly air blowing off the fresh snowfalls on the range.

For the last few days, Sean had ventured far enough along the Creek to note a scatter of farmhouses fed by dirt roads. There were no power lines. The only signs of life were the thin streams of wood smoke signalling the easy and rough lives of the high country dwellers. There was little coming and going during the day and the night-lights of the local people were an unexpected comfort to him. It was obvious that few cars came this way. Sundays may be a different story, but Sean didn't mind traffic at a distance. He was not ready for total isolation. He had never experienced 'life in the bush' as Angus called it and did not want to spoil it by feeling he was hiding like a thief and murderer. He did not want to carry the scent of a man running from himself; he did not want to run. Sean felt free for the first time in his life. He was determined also that Tom would live as a free man, not as a runaway, or an escapee from the law or his previous life. This is where they would begin their new lives. They would be a part of the rural community and enjoy weekly visits to the isolated town of Dalgety on the Monaro, its tiny Post Office Shop and Cafe, the fuel bowser and pub. From Angus's noticeboard he learned of the Dalgety and District Community Association and the occasional gathering in the community hall and barbeque on the banks of the Snowy River.

He was always a careful man. He never said much and would be on guard so that his behaviour was as normal and predictable as every other man in the locality. He was not from here, however he would try to behave as if he was Monaro born and bred. He would quietly observe habitual patterns of the town, the comings and goings of people, the style and lilt of language and the social norms that distinguished one community from the next. It was clear to him that the four towns, Thredbo, Jindabyne, Berridale and Dalgety were very different from one another, separate identities joined it seemed, by the common thread of the Snowy River and its tributaries such as the Boloco Creek. Angus obviously had more reasons than just the stunning scenery to choose the isolated head of the Boloco Creek for his farm. Here, on this land, there would be enough water to sustain the men long enough even if they had to survive on water from the creek or what had been captured in the rainwater tanks that were part of every farm. Angus had prepared himself and the farm to survive for months at a time with no need whatsoever to rely on the towns or cities.

Sean completed their morning routine of breakfast, stacking the dishes for Tom. The heavy iron kettle boiled on the stove ready to fill the single deep ceramic sink.

'Maybe go to town a little later on Tom. What do you think?'

'Town?'

'Yeah. Thought we could do lunch at the pub, you know, Dalgety.'

'Has it got a pool table?' Tom was suddenly interested.

'Might do. We'll have to check it out. Go meet some of the locals. However we say naught, son.'

'Say naught?'

'That's right. Tell people nothing: nothing that they already know and nothing that they don't know!' Sean had already softened the Irish in his accent.

'Sounds good to me. Talk about the weather I suppose.'

'We can check out the work scene if you like. See what interests the locals. Get the drift?'

'Do I ever. Reckon I could get some work with Eddy?'

'Maybe son. Let's just go with the flow. See what turns up.'

'Mmm. I suppose I will have to register with Centrelink.'

'Centre who?'

'Centrelink. You know, the dole office.'

'You want to?'

'No. But…'

'Then let's just let that one hang for now. We'll go for some odd jobs son. Keep a low profile and get a few pennies for a feed. Don't need much else do we?'

'No.' Tom couldn't think of anything.

Sean slung his pack into the back of the truck and kicked over the ignition. This was the first time in several days the two men had ventured beyond the farm. Sean found in himself an unexpected regression to his boyhood days, as if being with Tom was the trigger for childhood freedoms. They were innocent and free together, untroubled by time and duties other than the day to day rhythm of keeping house, of lighting the fire and cooking meals, of sleeping to the sound of the wind and waking to the raucous cry of the white cockatoos. So it was with some trepidation that Sean drove the truck to the gate and the narrow strip of the Snowy River Way that defined 'civilisation'. The red and rocky feeder road to the gate was access for the cluster of properties adjacent to Angus's farm; the road surface was firm, blending in almost invisibly with the soft light brown of the native grasses.

Tom wound down his window and hung his elbow out the window. The air was fresh and as they drove along the ridge, he let out a low and appreciative whistle.

'Can you beat that Sean!'

'Not bad son. That must be Dalgety on the far side of the ditch. Didn't know we were so close!'

'You wouldn't know it out here.'

The road suddenly dipped and they came to the loosely locked double white gates, one of the gates bent, probably by an eager bull bar on a wayward ute.

'I'll get the gates.' Tom leaped out of the door before Sean had time to pull up. He shoved them back as far as he could against the pile of dirt and the gate dropped on its hinge. Sean drove through and waited for him at the edge of the road.

'We're onto it Sean.'

'Looks like it. Ten minutes and we'll be crossing the Snowy River.'

The road was now smooth, an unmarked black scar snaking across the grasslands, a perfect complement to the minimalist development on the Monaro. The gracious pastoral vistas dropped on all sides towards the line of the river. As they approached the Snowy River, the simple span bridge — clearly from a bygone era — was the main access route to the village. The broad, timber planks danced under the truck wheels as they crossed the bridge. A low lying weir ran parallel to the bridge, spilling barely sufficient water to fill a garden pond into the river downstream.

'That's it then Tom. The mighty Snowy River!'

'Could have fooled me. Bridge is good though.'

'You're not wrong there. Nice piece of workmanship. Looks as though it's lasted a good while. Although, you can't ever beat a stone bridge in my opinion.'

'Do you build bridges Sean?'

'Had to. Some rail lines cross gorges and rivers and they need good solid bridges to carry them.'

'Seen the Sydney Harbour Bridge?' Tom took a jab at his new friend.

'Well of course I know it. The stone was quarried near here wasn't it? From Moruya on the South Coast if I recall, then sailed up to Sydney. That's how I know. Freight and wharf tales down the ages. I heard that the stone mason didn't get a stone wrong or out of place. The stones were so perfectly worked that not a single stone needed trimming. He was a Scotsman from Aberdeen; the stone mason.' Sean was on solid ground.

'Oh.' Tom was momentarily lost for words.

Sean drove across the bridge and immediately they were in the centre of the town.

'Well, not too many choices in parking. Outside the pub here or outside the pub there.' Sean headed for the nearest edge of the verandah. 'No point locking our stuff up. Got your brass?'

'I've got enough.'

'And just how are you going to prove age without proof of identity?'

'They don't know me.'

'What did you say your name was?'

'Tom. Tom Keating.'

'Give you a sip of mine.' Sean teased.

'Yeah! No thanks.'

'I knew you were off the milk.'

Sean slammed the door and headed for the steps up the verandah.

The building was a low-lying brick construction, over a century old and somewhat sad. The tin roof sheeting was rusting but it shaded two wide verandahs. To Sean's experienced eye, there were a range of add-ons to the original structure of the hotel. Buckley's Crossing Hotel was nevertheless a pleasant sight and no doubt the hub of the local farming community.

Sean and Tom walked through the open main door. A small lounge to the right had a few tables tucked together under some old photos from another century. On the far wall of the lounge was a well built fireplace, stocked and burning brightly even though it was still early in the day. The pub walls were littered with treasures, probably from outlying farms: rams horns, horseshoes, stirrups and whatever else could be crammed onto every nail hammered into the wooden walls. Sean assessed the layout of the pub and walked to the bar.

'Gidday son. Hello.' The barman acknowledged Tom first then Sean.

'Gidday. This is Sean.' Tom introduced his partner.

'Hello. Sean nodded seriously and sat at the bar.'

'Can I get you anything?'

'One milk and one beer.' Sean tried not to smile.

The barman broke into laughter. 'I'm Barry. Baz. Will that be two beers?'

'Make mine a schooner.' Tom said deciding that he would break with his own tradition of sticking strictly to apple juice.

'Got your ID?'

'Lost it in a fire.'

Barry smiled resolutely. 'Yeah. Last year's wildfire. No proof of age. No sale.'

'He can use mine.' Sean offered politely.

'Where's yours?' Barry's intrigue was aroused.

'Same fire.' Sean laughed.

'OK then. You want a beer and you're underage.' Baz decided. 'So that'll be one beer?'

'I think you get the gist. He'll drink air and I'll drink the beer. The smell of it isn't against the law I take it.'

Baz said nothing and wisely held his counsel; he poured the beer.

'Thanks.' Sean paid. 'Counter lunches today?'

'Fine dining's open. I'll bring it out here if you'd like. Joan's out the back.'

'Tom? Chips?'

'The lot.' Tom smiled brightly sitting up as straight as a rod.

'Two of 'the lot' and he's paying.' Sean placed his order.

Baz laughed. 'And you also expect him to only smell the steaks and chips along with the beers?'

'Drinkin' outside isn't against the law is it?' Tom tried.

'I'll be busy watching the dart game and if your friend here drops some into your mouth, then that's his business and not mine.' Baz turned to face the servery hole to the rear of the bar. 'Take this through to the kitchen would you Nance. Thanks.'

'Darts?' One of the three men sitting at a table with two women offered Sean a dart.

'Tom says he's a champ.' Sean moved to a free table and sat down.

'Hi Tom. That's Ray and I'm Jenny.' She put her hand out to shake his. 'Game?'

'Yeah thanks.' Tom took the dart and positioned himself at a good distance from the dartboard. He tested his aim holding the dart close to his eye. Then with a short, yet true jerk of his arm, flung the dart in a tight trajectory towards the bull's eye.

'Clooose.'

'Jenny?'

'Yeah. Thanks.' Jenny picked up a dart, smoothing the feather as she walked to shooting distance from the board. She stood feet slightly apart and, with complete concentration in a single smooth and well aimed shot, threw the dart. It fitted closely behind Tom's dart the point quivering as it embedded itself in the board.

'Looks as though we've got a true competition on our hands at last.'

'Another fight. It's on!' Jenny sounded more cynical than pleased.

Sean cocked an eyebrow in her direction looking at the same

time at Ray.

'She's been at the forefront of another particular fight for years now.' Ray explained

'Oh?'

'Jenny's one of the drivers for freeing up the flows.' Ray pointed his finger towards the river. 'The Snowy River of course. Just out the door there. She's up against the Federal Minister for Natural Resources or whoever signed off on about forty nine agreements or something equally as ridiculous — to seal the fate of our Snowy River. Did it at Parliament House the other week. They're just about ready to corporatise.' Ray elaborated.

'Mate, we just don't trust them.' Baz said from behind the bar. 'Meet the folks from the "Snowy River Alliance".'

'It's a bit...what did you say your name was?' Ray put out his hand.

'Sean. You've already met the champ. Watch your back Jenny.'

'Yeah. Play you for your pint Sean.' Tom chided.

'You could always drink from the river son. By the sound of it there might be more in it soon.'

'Well, we're not sure about that are we Ray. They promised to return 28% of natural flows to the river. Then at the last meeting, we heard that it could be scaled back to 12% of flows. Can't trust them. They're always fiddling the figures and when they say 28% they mean 21% and when they say 21%, that's only in a wet year and then only if there is enough water out west in the Murray Darling.'

'Complicated! Who's them then?' Sean asked.

'The Feds. Water rights are protected under Section 100 of the Constitution. "The Commonwealth shall not, by any law or regulation of trade of commerce, abridge the right of a State or of the residents therein to the reasonable use of the waters of rivers for conservation or irrigation." Jenny read it from a piece of paper on the table. 'Theoretically, the whole bloody scheme is illegal! Can you imagine, taking out a billion dollars of water over the life of the scheme and virtually giving it away out west! Then they tell us that we have to buy back water for the Snowy River? It's a bit rich isn't it!'

'Is this a war cabinet?' Sean was pleased with the discovery. The people gathered in the pub were not who he had expected. They were farmers no doubt, but he didn't expect the passion or the anger bubbling beneath the surface.

Jenny smiled and dropped her head modestly, however her grin said it all. Her smile was as wide as the Snowy in flood, stretching from side to side of her face. The evidence of a tough life was chiselled in lines from the high point in her cheeks to the corners of her mouth. Her slightly greying and fine hair hung softly over her shoulders and the brown eyes sparkled with a mixture of humour and grim determination. The woman was barely five feet tall with a wiry and slight build. Her clothes were relaxed and casual; jeans, loose jumper and boots somehow completing the story of a seasoned and wise campaigner.

'Jenny is our frontline warrior at the moment. There's a group of us though. Snowy River Alliance and yes, this is sort of where we make our battle plans.'

Sean looked around the small group and noticed the quick and intelligent eyes, the hardy faces and the sense of honesty about them.

'There was a meeting of around 50 of us the other week. People came all the way from Victoria, from Orbost and Marlo where the Snowy flows into the sea,' Ray explained. 'You can see how big the river used to be from space and where once the Snowy would surge out into the ocean and cascade over the continental shelf at a place called Snowy Falls. The fishermen know it well and water there is still fresh even though it is by then part of the sea.'

'That's what me gramps said too!' Tom was suitably impressed.

'Yep. She used to really flow. So the Snowy River Alliance put up one of the fishermen as their very own candidate, an Independent who was voted in about three years ago. He holds the balance of power in the Victorian State Government and the plan was basically to have the leverage to sort out some of the outstanding issues for the Snowy. Otherwise, the process was more or less stalled.'

'Sean, you want a shot?' Tom interrupted.

'Can't steal your spoils son. Play, win and then eat.' Sean grinned.

'Your shot Jenny.' Tom held a dart out.

'Thanks. Yeah.' Jenny paused to take aim and this time, shot with much greater force bedding the dart deeply in the first outer ring.

'Look out for a lady on the war path!' Ray noted.

'Your lunches will be ready in about ten.' Barry announced from behind the bar.

'Thanks.' Sean looked back to Ray. 'Joining us for lunch?'

'Jenny?' Ray asked.

'Why not? Not going anywhere today. We'll just shift these tables together.' Ray got up, lifting a couple of chairs over to one of the tables.

Jenny grabbed another dart. 'Come on Tom. Finish this round?'

They played off the game with Tom edging higher in points.

'You're good.' Jenny commented.

'I'm Ookaaay.' Tom agreed reluctantly.

'No. I mean it!' Jenny encouraged him further.

''Nother match?'

'Yeah. Maybe after lunch. You live around here?'

Tom looked instinctively at Sean.

'We're minding Angus's farm for a bit.' Sean said smoothly, aware that there was no point hiding the fact that they were there and not to be fazed in his response would mean less suspicion aroused around the district.

'Angus Wallace?'

'That's him.'

'Tom has taken a liking to his brumby.' Sean smiled widely at his partner.

'Oh. You ride?' Jenny softened to the lad.

'Yeah. My grandfather was good with horses. I wouldn't mind a couple of brumbies to break in.'

'Could be organised.' Ray said. 'Probably do a wild horse run in the spring if you're still around then.'

'Yeah, could be.' Tom looked interested.

Ray took a swig of his beer. 'Here's to the Snowy!'

'The Snowy!' Barry chorused across the bar.

'Yep. When she starts to flow we'll party!' Ray added. 'Mind you, irrigation is worth millions Sean and the NSW irrigators are up in arms already, having to cut back their water access. Some of the rice farmers pull in a million dollars for each crop. It's far more than they would ever make from sheep.'

'Can see your point.'

'Then there's the cotton growers — cotton means arsenic. The soil blows all the way to the mountains and so do the moths and bingo, you have a big problem.'

'True?'

'Yep. The Bogong moths carry the arsenic in their systems all the way from the black soil country and then the pygmy possums feed on the moths. Apparently the snowmelt concentrates the poison up to 1,000 times. It's just as well that there aren't any of the Ngarigo people up there anymore otherwise they'd be poisoned too. Top of the food chain thing.'

'Ngarigo?'

'The Aboriginal people. They don't really come to the high country anymore. Most of them live down the coast where it's a bit warmer. At least there aren't any moths in Bega!' Ray was sympathetic to the first inhabitants of the land; the majority living a life of landless dispossession, of cultural loss and familial separation. Once, the Ngarigo were the caretakers of the Dreamtime, and passed on their stories from generation to generation, no doubt also the water stories, where the water came from, the importance of springs, wetlands and waterways including the great Snowy, Murray and Murrumbidgee Rivers and their tributaries.

'Now, as well as destroying the wetlands and drylands, practically every rivulet in the mountains has an aqueduct on it so nothing flows freely for that long. Even the high country streams can be polluted by foxes or campers, so the whole system is basically stuffed and that's what you get.' Ray pointed out the window to the water hardly flowing under the bridge.

'This land is a bit dry.' Sean noted.

'That's the problem. Once it wasn't. According to the original people and the real locals, the Monaro used to be really lush. The tricky bit is that no-one seems to remember the stories anymore. It's a long time since Ngarigo people lived on this land.'

'Maybe if they returned, the land would speak to them.' Sean offered.

'You surprise me Sean! That's quite an insight for a newcomer.'

'Perhaps so. But it makes sense doesn't it? Return the original people to the mountains and the Monaro and bingo — they start to remember.

'Possibly so Sean. Possibly so.' Ray mused for a moment. 'Especially so now that the Songlines are open.'

Lunch was unexpectedly refreshing and friendly and Tom managed to surreptitiously sip at least half of Sean's beer. He didn't lose a single point of awareness, resolutely determined to appear completely sober and unaffected by the amber fluid softening his gullet. Sean was equally alert, watching everyone and everything around him, albeit unnoticed. He instinctively measured the mood and waited for the right moment to gently exit.

There was no point forming deep relationships, not yet at least. He wanted to be able to move in and out easily from any gathering without leaving a trace of himself or Tom in people's minds or on their emotions. He knew his Irish charm usually pulled women like moths to a brilliant flame and he did not want that. Sean was not immune to the fairer sex, but chose for the time being to put his sexual ambitions on ice.

'That really was wonderful.' Sean picked the serviette off his lap and wiped his mouth.

Jenny noted the gentlemanly habit and manners of the Irishman and grinned at Ray. 'We'd better be going too. Got to prepare for the next battle and be ready for whatever may come.'

'Gotta feed the kids and the dogs more like it.' Ray laughed.

'Good luck.' Sean stood up shaking Ray's hand and bowing ever so slightly to Jenny. 'Good luck with the River and I look forward to hearing the result.' Sean became emotionless, readying himself to effect a seamless exit. Tom got up and walked straight to the door, anxious not to lose sight of Sean. From the doorway he suddenly realised that he hadn't said goodbye and turned back to Jenny.

'See ya Jenny. Bye Ray.' Tom said easily.

'See you Tom. Give you another game sometime.' Jenny smiled.

'Bye son.' Ray nodded.

'And keep off the milk!' Barry tossed him a parting shot from behind the bar.

'Ya gotta raise your age son.' Sean said as they left the pub.

Sean and Tom braced against the afternoon gusts blowing fresh air from the mountains. The cold weather front was moving very slowly with dark clouds gathering and forming before dumping heavy loads onto the tops. The wind on the Monaro was characteristically cold, but the sun thankfully took the cold bite out of the afternoons. Sean was not one for hanging about and backed the truck away from the verandah wall, turning it quickly towards the bridge and back to the farm.

'Well, we didn't make it to Centrelink Sean.'

'Next time, matey. Next time.'

SERENITY ON THE MONARO

Sunday dawned, a silent and gentle affair of the rising sun set against the rolling and majestic landscape of the Monaro. The mist barely lifted from the deepest valleys and the frost continued to sit in cold hollows over the vast plains. Only the elevated and eastwards aspects of the farm were free from frost and mist, the earth now warming under the soft glow of the morning sun.

Angus shook himself into wakefulness. The trip back to the farm from his fishing boat moored at Eden had been uneventful and he was keen to make sure that Sean and the boy had settled in without any dramas. He had got in late two nights ago and the bed was safe and cosy, pulling him further into sleep. Now, he desperately wanted to get up and once again, feel the earth of the Monaro beneath his feet. He pushed himself off the bed, put on his moleskin trousers and boots and pulled on his lumberjack's coat. The early morning was brisk and his breath formed streams of condensation as he walked to the kitchen. Tom and Sean were still sleeping, yet at the sound of the crackling fire and kettle whistling to the boil, Sean would be first up followed by Tom, curiously linked (it seemed), to Sean's every movement like a cat following its master in a somnolent dream. Angus had noted the link between the men, Sean the master of them both, yet Tom very much the mover of Sean's emotions.

He put some full cream milk in a saucer for the stray cat that at times wandered close to the house, and turned to the fire. Angus was more than happy. He realised within himself that living close to the land and the sea fed his dreams and more so, his soul. This morning, he felt his spirits rise and his heart bursting with a new zest for life, a new pleasure in being on the farm, feeling the first breath of morning and on his back, and the warmth of the rising sun.

The day after an epic storm at sea that nearly took his boat Aurora — and his life too — Angus walked the perimeter of his property, checking the fences, looking for the monster holes, made by the wombats, that could easily break a horse's leg. He rubbed the leaves of the manna gum between thumb and forefinger, relishing the sharp and acrid scent of the eucalyptus and marvelling at the patterns of bark spilling onto the forest floor. Most of the property was grassland — rocky underfoot with broken streams of basalt and shale — with only remnants of gum trees remaining in the gullies and along the ridges.

Today was to be celebrated. Life too good to waste. After breakfast they would go to the Boloco Church and celebrate with friends. Although Angus was never a religious man, in his own way, he wanted to give thanks with his friends and neighbours for a safe return to the enriched life he led on the farm. There was no better way that to do so than here. The church was a testament to his ancestors as they too struggled to find a foothold on the harsh yet beautiful landscape that became their farms, towns and lives.

Back in the hut, he opened the door of the old fuel stove. There was still some warmth in the coals and it would not be long before new flames would burst from the remains of last night's cheery and welcome fire. He went outside with the kettle filling it from the rainwater tank's overflow and returned to the stove. The kitchen was warming up quickly. Gratefully, Angus placed the kettle on the stovetop then set about preparing for the three of them a solid breakfast of bacon, eggs, toast and porridge.

Sean stirred and turned over aware that the dawn light had already touched the iron roof of the shack. His first thoughts turned to Tom, wondering what to feed the boy today. Then he remembered that Angus was home, the scent of freshly cooking bacon wafting through the shack. Sean smiled, realising that Angus had beat him to the task of preparing their morning meal, a Sunday celebration of the good life on the land. He dressed quickly and warmly, with the casual discipline of his former life, his life before he left Ireland, before he left for the farm.

'Mornin' Sean.' Angus caught the footfalls in the hallway as Sean approached.

'Mornin'. Smells good!'

'Fire's warm.' Angus smiled as he looked up from the pan.

Sean nodded. 'Thanks Angus. Always appreciate a good fire! Thank you Angus for your fire and your farm.' Sean said sincerely. 'We've felt safe here. So far.'

Angus remained silent for a few minutes, stirring the pot of porridge and turning the toast from time to time. 'Going to the Boloco Church this morning Sean. You coming?'

'Church?' Sean almost burst out laughing.

'No. I'm serious. Something tells me I need to go. Want to say my thanks if you know what I mean.'

'I know for sure Angus, but church?'

'Boloco's not really a church. Not in the sense that you'd normally think of. It's where we all meet on the weekend. Up on the hill. At the top of the valley.' Angus vaguely waved towards the valley.

'I know. We've seen it through the glasses. Tom says he likes old buildings. I'm not sure if I do though. Not that much!' Sean jested.

'Come. The service is short. We just gather for a gabble and then go home. Some of them go down town to the pub for lunch and a few go on to the Iona for a coffee.'

'The Iona?'

'Yeah. The shop at Dalgety where you collect my mail. In any case, I'd like to go and you're welcome to come if you want.'

'Sure. Might as well. Beautiful mornin' and it might be a good chance to meet some more of the locals.'

'You mean someone spiritual.' Angus grinned.

Sean looked taken aback then burst into laughter. 'Angus, I didn't know that you were a believer.'

'I'm not man. I can tell you this though. It's more than once that the Aurora has survived a heavy sea. There was something or someone else outside of me that steered me safely to shore.'

'I don't doubt you Angus. Though in my humble prayer book of life and death, both are pretty straightforward.'

'Well whatever or whoever is out there, they were happy to get me back home one more time to the farm.'

'Your farm Angus.'

'Not now, not anymore. It's ours Sean, if you're fine about that. When I'm not here, Tom also needs a place to put his head and this is as good as we've got, our own home and our own family unless you've found something better.'

'Nothin' better Angus. This place is…well it's…'

'It's a haven on this earth; yes, I know. There's something strange and magical about these hills, not just because of the isolation and the beauty of this valley. It's not just the hidden creek or the Snowy River. No, Sean, it's more than that. It's almost as if the primordial has touched this place and that essence still survives today.'

'I've felt it Angus. There is something otherworldly about the farm, but I can't quite put my finger on it. I would swear that this land is more ancient than Ireland herself.'

'Now that's saying somethin' Sean.' Angus broadened his Scottish vowels.

'So ye think that your Protestant god is better than our Catholic one then, protectin' us from the British all these years?'

'Sean. We have the same god of that I'm sure, and I was never into the Orange March. I was never into war for that matter, and as far as I'm concerned, God owns this earth out here and so therefore it's as much yours as it is mine.'

'I'm not sure how to thank you man.'

'Then don't. Just enjoy it. That would be sufficient thanks for me, and for my Protestant god I'm sure of it.' Angus grinned and flicked the toast onto an enamel plate.

Sean reached across and picked the kettle off the fire and poured a good measure into the teapot, warmed and already waiting with a handful of the best tea from Angus's pantry.

'Call the kid. He'll be hungrier if he misses out on this feed.' Angus continued to play with the bacon then turned to set the table. His manner was as easy and civilised as a man could possibly manage in a post as far from the city as this.

The journey up the Boloco Creek was more relaxing than any meditation Sean could imagine. Angus led the way, sure-footed on his own land, careful to avoid the steep and shaly slopes and mindful of the pull of the horses for Tom, who was still visibly overwhelmed by their presence. Tom, quick to sense the horses were alert to him, looked at Sean, then at Angus. As they approached the gully, the horses stopped, catching their scent and turned towards Tom. Angus nodded towards the horses.

'Go to him son. Give him some bread.' Angus pulled a couple of buns from the pocket of his jacket and handed them to Tom.

Sean and Angus stood for a moment as Tom walked away from them towards the horses, crossing the wide erosion gully; it was big enough to drive a horse and dray along. As he reached the other side of the divide, Tom looked up to see the colt waiting, his nostrils quivering and his ears pricked forwards.

Tom clicked his tongue, urging him close. 'C'mon boy. C'mon.' Tom reached out his hand and in the other, held the bread rolls.

The horse hesitated, noticing Sean and Angus standing still in the paddock then looked again at Tom. The colt walked to Tom's open hand, nuzzling him softly.

'That's a fella. Here. Try one of these.' Tom opened his other hand with the bread and the colt flicked one with his teeth to the ground and for a moment pawed the bread, snorting and testing its texture with his lips. Then he picked it up and threw it upwards. He lifted his head, ears pulled back and eyes stretched and wary. Then he picked the bread off the ground where it fell.

Tom patted the colt's neck moving his arm under and to the other side. The colt stood still, his legs rigid at the first sense of the closer touch by the young man. His ears moved forward and then back to his neck as he relaxed. He flicked his ears from side to side, more curious than afraid. Tom gave him the other roll, and let go of the horse's neck. The horse turned his rear to the men, paused, and picked up the bread, wheeling around to check that the young man was still there. The colt threw his head into the air, his eyes fixed to Tom and without warning, broke into a sudden canter up the hill and back to the familiar comfort of the old mare and the donkey that kept them company.

'Let's go Tom.' Angus called out across the gully.

'Yeah.' Tom watched the horses move off the ridge and towards the long-drop of Boloco Creek. He crossed back to the paddock and walked quickly to catch Angus and Sean, waiting for him and ready to move on up the valley to the Boloco Church.

'There you are son. You've made yourself a friend.' Angus opened.

'He's a beauty all right.' Tom smiled and without breaking his step walked in pace with Angus and Sean placing himself in the centre as they made their way to the church.

'I hear you can ride pretty well.' Angus grinned at Tom.

'Yeah. I love horses. I hear you do too.' Tom noted.

'Well, being on the land and all, horses are a part of the deal.' Angus said dryly.

'Can you break him in?' fresh enthusiasm broke into Tom's voice.

'My son is best.' Angus replied. 'When he comes down here, he'll teach you as much as he knows in the time that he has.'

'Cool' the kid returned.

'Angus thinks that you might find work in these parts Tom. To ride horses and to strain fences could be useful to you then.'

'I'd like that Angus. Thanks.'

'Don't mention it. Might talk to a few people this morning then.' Angus looked across Tom to Sean. 'Could you bear a chat?' Angus enquired of Sean.

Sean laughed. 'Could probably do so. So long as it's over a pint and not over a prayer Angus.'

'You don't pray do you Sean?' Tom asked.

'Angus does.' Sean jested.

'Well, mostly at sea so the fish will come to me and not the other way around.' Angus was far away in his thoughts.

'What are you going to do now Angus? I mean, are you still going to sea?' Tom asked innocently.

'Well let's see what the good Lord has in store for us today shall we?' Angus furrowed his brow.

'You don't really believe in that stuff Angus.' Tom insisted.

'I'm not dragging you up here just to look at the architecture Tom.' Angus huffed.

'Nor the graveyards of your ancestors.' Sean added.

'More like yours, Keating!' Angus noted.

'Didn't Sean tell you he's changed his name?' Tom said. 'Keating.

We're both Keatings.' Tom informed him filled with clan pride.

Angus laughed. 'That's a good one!'

'Let's just call it judicious.' Sean cut in.

'Does anyone else know you as Keating?'

'Word gets around Angus. You of all people should know that.' Sean said softly.

'Guess you're right about that and not a bad thing too with the rural wire the way it is. Not much, escapes people in these parts and you'll probably still need a fairly low profile. My cousin from another shore!'

They topped the hill and climbed over the fence. The thin strip of tarmac was empty of traffic; the cars and utes were already collected around the church ground. The bell tolled persistently, its hollow sound echoing solemnly along the valley to the west and down the Boloco Creek from where they had come.

'Just in time then.' Angus said.

'Long service?' Sean was slightly nervous.

'Not if you have a clear conscience.' Angus laughed then suddenly became more serious as the Minister welcomed them at the door.

'Angus. Good to see you. Your friends?'

'Sean and Tom.' Sean placed a hand in hers.

The Minister said nothing more and the men walked in and took their seats.

The service started in the tradition of the Protestant church, the congregation content on the wooden pews, comfortable with familiar words and hymns crafted and consolidated over time to suit their beliefs.

The Minister stood at the pulpit to deliver her sermon, her eyes slightly moist and a soft smile gracing the corners of her mouth. 'Our thanks for the safe return of Angus from the sea and for his bountiful catch of fish.'

That was Angus's way. He always brought home part of the catch to Dalgety to share with his friends and neighbours.

'Thanks be to god.' The congregation replied in unison.

Tom didn't know where to begin but he wanted to tell Sean that he needed to get out of the church. Now! He had felt claustrophobic immediately they entered through the tiny doorway into the church foyer. The body of the church was however, strangely peaceful and simple in décor. He could imagine it could be peaceful here except for the clasping feeling over this throat, the scream that was half-formed and rising further as they moved into the service. It was the sudden wrenching of unexpected tears from his eyes that became too much for him to bear.

Sean felt the boy stiffen. 'Come on son. Let's get some fresh air.' Sean pulled his elbow and moved him out of the pew and down the aisle. A few of the parishioners noticed them leaving and said nothing. These were new people in the district, guests in their church and it was never polite to ask anything more than people join them in the routine prayer and worship once a month in their humble gathering.

Angus remained stationary in his place. He knew that Tom had felt a sudden reaction to the presence of the Minister and was grateful that she was only a dim reminder of his pain, not a more direct reminder of the perpetrators who had stolen his faith and his youth. Angus wanted desperately to leave with Sean and Tom, but something held him still against his will and again, he felt the hand of god.

'Shit' he muttered under his breath. The conflict was massive. Here he was thanking 'god' for his life and at the same time, cursing under his breath the same 'god' that was indirectly the cause of the boy's psychological trauma. The Minister noted the departure of

Angus's friends and knew that there was something more than pain in the young man. He had the haunted look of many a young man who had lost his way, who had lost his innocence.

'God be with you.' She announced.

'And with you.' The congregation replied.

The congregation were quietly cautious of the new men yet openly grateful for the presence of Angus. Many of them came to shake his hand, to give him a hug before leaving for their farms and homes, adjusting their coats against the morning wind and stepping into their utes and cars. It was only the young Tom and his friend Sean who stood back, waiting while Angus thanked his friends for their prayers, stepping seamlessly into the role of minister of the faith as if it were he who were ordained and charged with their spiritual care.

The Minister watched as Angus placed a careful arm around the boy's shoulder and turned to point at the horizon, perhaps the bottom of the valley. Sean turned and met her eyes. He nodded briefly, then the three men left, walking over the road towards Angus's land.

'That's that then Sean.' Angus said. 'Church is good from time to time.'

'They certainly noticed your presence Angus.' Sean said quietly.

'As I said, the bush telegraph is mighty fast in these parts. Besides, we're all close here. We drink together, go to the same auctions, the same races, the same church.' Angus pressed the top wire of the fence closer to the ground so the men could step over easily. 'Tom. I'm not sure that you like church.'

'You mean god.' Tom retorted, smarting with anger.

'Son. It's going to take time.' Angus broached the subject as openly as he could.

Tom was too choked to talk.

'There's no hurry.' Sean repeated the assurances offered by Angus.

'Thanks,' Tom muttered. He was genuinely relieved.

'You don't have to believe in god if you don't want to either.'

'I don't' Tom answered flatly and straightly. He looked up for the first time and faced Angus. 'Thanks Angus. Thanks a million. I mean it.' He said sincerely.

'That's all right son.' Angus answered gently, placing a hand on his shoulder. 'Anytime. You have that colt to break and no doubt he'll keep you busy enough.' Angus looked at him with eyes that said he meant what he said. 'As I said, just take your time. We'll make a good rider out of you first then think about the rest. Understood?'

'Thanks man.' Tom was genuinely touched and grateful for the chance to forget about the church and the past.

The three musketeers wandered back down the Boloco Creek towards the farmhouse. Eventually, Tom walked towards the horses, leaving Sean and Angus to watch from a distance. The boy had no food for the colt this time; his open hand was all that he needed to draw the horse to him. He whistled softly and the brumby turned towards him, ears pressed forwards and alert. Tom whistled again and the colt sprang forwards, cantering towards him, and slid to a stop just a metre away. The colt gathered himself onto his hind legs and pawed the air in front of Tom's face. Tom stood still, his left hand motionless at his side and right hand, extended gently forwards. Then the colt stood quietly and observed him. Tom stepped forwards, soothing the colt's mane, talking softly and calmly to him. He looked straight into the horse's eye and placed his nose against the colt's.

'There's a good boy. I haven't got anything for you this time mister. Bring you some hay next time I come.'

The colt threw his head up eyes staring at Sean and Angus

then dropped his forehead to let Tom explore his forelock and ears, twitching in delight to his touch. Tom sensed his friends approaching on the other side of the gully and quickly patted the horse on his neck and slid his hand along its back to the top of the rump. He walked to the front of the horse and smiled, then walked back to join Sean and Angus. The colt, unsure of Tom's sudden departure stood alone; vulnerable yet fiercely proud. The mare whickered from behind him and the colt suddenly cantered towards her, safe in the company of his adopted mother and the donkey that followed them around wherever they went.

'That's it then son. The horse is yours.' Angus announced.

'Gee thanks Angus.' Tom was close to tears again.

'Don't think of it. He's a beauty all right. Can't see that the donkey would look any better, even with Jesus Christ on his back, so there's no point in ridin' him.'

Tom laughed in relief. 'He's a bit of an odd ball. What are you doing with a donkey anyway?'

'Good company for the horse. Until the colt arrived of course. What are you going to call him?'

Tom looked at Angus in surprised. 'Haven't had time to think about it Angus.'

'Take your time then. He's not going anywhere. Not yet.'

'Great.' Tom was visibly over the worst of the trauma he had felt at the church.

Angus grinned. 'Well, we'd better get a hike on. Got a few things to do around the house this morning then later, I want to take you both to the pub for lunch.'

Sean smiled broadly. 'My shout.'

'No, mine. Really.' Angus insisted. 'The feast of St Clementine.'

Sean laughed long and loudly. 'Christ man. You are full of surprises!'

'None that you can't have seen before Sean.' Angus replied. 'Besides, there's another person I want Tom to meet. A young friend of mine.'

'Oh.' Tom looked innocently at Angus.

'Her name's Cassie. She's a darlin'.'

Tom blushed. 'She can probably teach you to ride that horse of yours better than anyone else I know.'

'What about your son?' Tom asked.

'He doesn't really have time.' Angus dismissed the thought. 'He works overseas in the ski resorts during our summer and spends the winters on ours. There's no time for the farm between ski seasons so the horse is yours. He'll be happy for someone to take an interest in him.'

By lunchtime, Angus had Sean and Tom crammed into the truck and were on way to the pub at Dalgety. Sunday lunch was his favourite when the pub served up a hot roast meal and the locals gathered for a game of pool.

'Angus. Good to see you man.' The republican extended a hand across the bar.

'How are you Barry?' Angus returned the greeting. 'Sean, and Tom.'

'Hello again lads.' Barry nodded to Tom and extended a hand to Sean.

Tom put his hand across the bar. 'Hi.'

Barry took the shake. 'Well, what will you have boys?'

'Three schooners thanks Baz.' Tom cut in quickly.

'Three it is.' Baz was already pulling the first beer.

'Where's Cassie?' Angus asked.

'Up at the Iona. Andrea needs her.'

'Oh?' Angus took the beers and paid.

'Doing a special lunch. Pumpkin soup or something.' Barry

smiled at Tom. 'Why don't you go up there?'

'We were planning the special roast for lunch.'

'Can always do it another time. The weather's good today and it's very pleasant sitting out on her verandah.'

'Yeah, OK, but we'll finish this drink. Tell me your news Baz.'

'Yours first.' Barry smiled.

'He nearly carked it.' Tom broke in. 'Big seas apparently.'

'We heard.'

'We sure got a thumping.' Angus shook his head wearily.

'Sorry about the damage to the Aurora.' Barry quietly observed Angus.

Sean sat watching the exchange, respecting Angus's right not to talk. He sipped on the beer and looked at Tom. 'Taste all right Tom?'

'Beer's good thanks.' Tom responded.

Angus took a few sips, gulping down the bitter liquid, unable to talk, nevertheless grateful for the company.

The door suddenly opened and a young woman walked in.

'Cassie.' Barry turned around, spotting her in the mirror.

'Just popped down for some more rolls Baz. Hello.'

The young woman with a stunning head of dark hair with a natural bronze tint, turned at the sound of her name. Her petite body was graceful and feminine, softly exaggerated by the cut of her jeans. Suddenly she became quiet, her face sad then in a moment radiant with her beautiful smile. Cassie placed a soothing hand on Angus's shoulder. 'Welcome home sailor.'

Angus was too choked to talk.

Cassie turned to Angus's friends. 'Hello. I'm Cassie.' She put her hand out to Sean.

'Hello Cassie. I'm Sean and this is Tom.' Sean nodded across the table.

Barry stood behind the bar, watching the subtle chemistry,

understanding that Angus had it figured, that these two youngsters would quickly become friends.

'They're coming up for lunch Cassie. You'd better tell Andrea to put on another pot of soup by the look of the appetites sitting here.' Barry suggested.

'Yeah, sure. See you up there then.' Cassie walked out of the bar and headed towards the pub kitchen.

'Good kid Cassie. Couldn't do without her here.'

Angus came back to himself. 'Yeah. She sure is. Reckon pumpkin soup could build a man.' Angus patted his stomach. 'You eat veggies Tom?' Angus teased.

'Mostly spuds. I like the way Sean does them, in the fire. Pumpkin soup sounds good though.'

'With freshly baked bread rolls!' Barry added, a wicked glint in his eyes.

'We'd better be off then.' Angus finished off his beer. 'Sean?'

'Yeah. I'm ready.' Sean chuckled.

Tom drained the rest of his beer. 'Steady on mate. I'll help you up.' Angus joked.

Sean grabbed him under the other arm and together, they pretended to drag the boy out of the pub.

'Just don't come here between 8 and 9 on a Friday night. That's when the cops do their regular run.' Barry called after them.

'Thanks Baz.' Angus yelled over his shoulder. 'Come on then. Race ya up the hill.'

Tom sprinted ahead of Sean and Angus.

'God. Anyone would think he was keen!' Angus said as they caught Tom at the cafe.

Cassie was already at the door. 'Come in Tom. We'll find you a table outside in the sun.'

'Thanks.' Tom beamed spontaneously.

Set amongst the bookshelves stacked with groceries and jam,

the fuel stove burnt brightly.

'This is just like home Angus.' Sean said.

'Andrea's a whiz all right.'

The café and verandah were jammed with tables. Outside, a well stocked nursery and garden with its promises of life and colour drew the visitors in.

'Hi Angus.' Andrea said cheerily as she walked out from the kitchen, one of her kids in tow.

'Hello Andrea.' Angus gave her a peck on the cheek. 'Hello to you too young man.' Angus picked up the child and swung him up and over his head. 'You're getting too big. Your mum will have to put you to work soon.'

'This is Sean and Tom.' Cassie introduced them.

'Hello guys. Where are you sitting?'

'Outside.' Tom had already found a spot in the sun.

'Sure is lovely. Angus, do you want a coffee to start?'

'That would be excellent. Tom will have chocolate milk...' Angus couldn't resist the teasing.

'Three cappuccinos thanks Andrea.' Tom spoke for them all.

'OK three it is. Cassie, can you set them up. Andrea went back into the kitchen to get their drinks.

'This is really cool.' Tom looked around at the gentle garden edging both sides of the corner block.

'Where all the best folk meet.' Angus grinned at Cassie. 'Sean?'

'Pumpkin soup. With the lot. Thanks Cassie.'

'Three pumpkins with the lot.' Tom cut in falling easily into Sean's trap.

'Yeah. Right.' Cassie placed a friendly hand on Tom's shoulder. Her dark eyes laughed silently. Her infectious smile captured in the frame of her face shone directly at Tom. 'I'll bring you some bread rolls to get you started.' Cassie started to move back into the cafe.

'Shit you two.' Tom shook his head.

'Nothin' like a bit of entertainment son.' Sean winked at Angus conscious that Cassie would see the exchange.

Cassie blushed, her hair sparkling like silk unfurled in the winter sun. She quickly shook off any sense of embarrassment and turned inside with their orders.

'Angus, I heard about the trip. You OK?' Andrea inquired softly as she came out with the coffees.

'Doin' all right thanks Andrea. With a little help from my friends.' He smiled at Sean.

'Thanks be to good friends.' Andrea sounded serious. 'Need anything up on the farm Angus? I'm expecting a delivery of vegetables this afternoon if you want any.'

'That would be good Andrea. What do you have?'

'Potatoes, sweet potato, pumpkin, carrots, you name it.'

'A big box of mixed veggies would do very nicely thank you. Any bags of spuds?'

'In fact, yes.'

'We'll take a bag. Might light up a bonfire and invite you and Cassie up.'

Andrea laughed. 'There's a dance on at the Nimmitabel woolshed next Saturday night. 'You coming?' she asked lightly.

'Why not. Sean?'

'We're coming.' Sean spoke for them both.

'Cassie coming?' Angus asked.

'You'll have to ask her yourself. Here she is. Cassie?'

'What?'

'Tom's askin' if you want to come to the ball on Saturday night.' Angus said as soberly as he could.

Cassie laughed. 'I thought you'd be asking me Angus. See you there around eight?'

'Eight o'clock it is. Sean?' Tom sounded unsure.

'We'll be there. Eight o'clock on the dot.' Sean was deadly

serious.

As the women went back inside, Tom gave Sean a quick kick under the table.

Sean threw his hands up into the air. 'Hey, it wasn't me. Honest.'

'Nor me.' Angus said.

'Must be this Sunday lunch thing.'

The men broke into laughter and Tom, despite his reservations, could not help but join in. The mood was broken only for a split second as the soup arrived at the table. Then the revelry continued with Sean and Tom jostling for Angus's attention as he related tales of the sea since last they met at Port Melbourne.

UNDER THE
SOUTHERN STARS

Saturday night arrived with Sean taking the toss to sort out who would cook them tea.

'Heads I win Sean.' Tom suggested.

'Tails I lose?' Sean knew Tom well enough by now. 'Either way, I get to cook yeah?'

'Yeah.'

'What about me? I can still cook up a mean meal.' Angus offered.

'What about we eat out?' Sean saw an exit plan.

'You mean at the dance?'

'Could do. Better than that rehashed mash of yours Tom.'

'Thanks. You guys can. It'll be meat all the way won't it?'

'Cornish pasties, sausage rolls, veggie pasties. Whatever.'

'Yeah OK. Let's do it.' Tom needed little persuasion.

'Do you want to ring Cassie to make sure she's coming along? You don't want to be disappointed do you Tom?' It was Angus's turn to tease.

'Hey. Who said I was taking Cassie?' Tom sprang on the defensive.

Sean grinned. 'Thought she was taking you. She likes you Tom in case you didn't notice.'

'We only just met! Give it a rest.'

'Angus and I will dance between ourselves and that'll leave you free without any apron strings to hold you back.'

For a minute, Tom thought he was looking at a couple of old

queers, then he burst out laughing. 'Can't imagine you doin' an Irish jig Angus.'

Angus waltzed on a sixpence on the kitchen floor. Come on then Sean. Show us your stuff.

'Not me. Can't dance to save me life.'

'Ohhh. You're not pikin' are ya Sean.' Tom taunted him.

'Not yet. Just waitin' to see me partner's form before committing meself to something I might regret.'

'Regret? No time for regrets Sean.'

'Right you are Angus. Then we'd better put on our dancin' shoes. Git ya boots on son.' Sean emphasised the Australian country drawl.

'Jeesus! We're outa here!' Tom whooped and dashed down the hallway to the bedroom.

'Hope Tom and Cassie hit it off.' Sean wiped his brow.

'They will. Whaddya call it. "A match made under the southern skies".'

'Hope you're right Angus.'

'Doesn't matter if they don't. They're both young and should be out just to have a bit of fun. You're not going to get all maternal on me are you Sean.'

'You're the mothering type Angus, not me. The kid doesn't need me smooching all over him.'

'Whatever.' Angus grinned.

'Whaddya mean?' Sean looked perplexed.

'He hardly leaves your side in case you hadn't noticed.' Angus smirked. 'Protective instinct?'

'Hey. I'm no mother type. Just a rough and ready mercenary from the other side of the seas.'

Angus chuckled. 'We'd better find you something else to do also Sean, before you go nuts in this place. I've got a few friends in the district who are in the building game. Fancy a bit of work?'

'Yeah. That could be good.'

'Stone masonry? Could you handle it?'

'Eddy mentioned something about that.'

'Eddy?'

'At the Federation Settlement. Told us where we would find your farm. We thought his joint was Berridale.'

Angus guffawed until his sides hurt. 'You sure are green man. Berridale is hardly a flutter on the map, let alone Eddy's.'

'In any case. He has a keen hand at the forge and adze.'

'That he does. Did he offer you any work?'

'Yes, sort of. Said he would help us build a shack if we needed to.'

'Could be handy. This job's in Jindy though. New estate going in. Some dude with a bit of cash wants a fancy place finished off with some neat and clean stonework. You know the score.'

'OK then. Done.'

'He might be there tonight. I'll introduce you if you like.'

'Thanks. I'd like that.'

Tom came in, boots gleaming brown from a fresh coat of polish and his dark jacket handsomely offset against the cream moleskin trousers.

'Impressive! What about us?' Angus made a joke of his own gear.

'Can't have ya outdoing me Angus. Not at your age.'

'Couldn't anyway son. You look great. Well, let's git a hike on then.'

'Sean?'

'I'm ready. Got some cash.'

'Good oh. Who drives home?'

'You have the first couple of beers and I'll have the rest.' Tom said.

'You haven't got your licence have you?'

'Didn't say I couldn't drive.'

'That's true. Well, one of us will have to stay sober and you've already put your hand up so Sean and I can have a good time yeah?'

'Yeah.' Tom was sweet.

Sean flicked an eyebrow at Angus then headed for the door.

'Do you think the kid is ready for you know, women!'

'Ready, as he'll ever be. Might surprise us Angus.'

The dance hall was well lit, and at the far end the band was in full force pumping out some classically bush music. The beat was up and the mob on the floor didn't seem to care if they were in time or not. Tom looked around as they walked in to see if they could see Cassie. It was still early and he was surprised to see that she was already on the floor, her hair loose and catching the dimmed lights as she danced it seemed with someone she already knew. The young man smiled at her and held her, Tom thought, too close and for too long.

The music stopped and the band announced a short breather.

'The barbeque is ready out the back and lads, please use the gents as the wee police are ready and waiting outside.'

Someone got the joke and laughed and the crowd dispersed.

Tom walked straight for Cassie.

'Hi Cassie. You up for a meal?'

'Hey Tom.' Cassie was slightly out of breath; her cheeks flushed rose red from exertion of dancing.

'Good. Let's go then.' Tom totally ignored her partner. He put his arm through hers and drew her in the opposite direction and towards the exit door before she had time to think or change his mind. Cassie struggled to catch her breath, allowing herself to be guided outside by Tom.

'I've gone veg. Do they have anything like that here?'

'Veg?'

'Yeah, you know. No meat. What are you eating?'

'Same.'

'Who's the bloke?'

'Adam?'

'That his name? Can't dance for nuts.'

Cassie looked at him. 'Can you?'

'Not like that sissy stuff. You want a beer?'

'Thanks Tom. Where's Angus and Sean?' Cassie smiled the colour in her cheeks deepening more with pleasure than from her dancing.

'Over there.' Tom pointed to the steak sandwich queue. Suddenly he was silent, as if he had run out of words and the instant inspiration to rescue Cassie from the jerk had taken out his punch.

'You still working?'

'Sort of. You?'

'Yes. I love it.'

'Oh. Weekends?'

'Paddleboard in summer, snowboard in winter.'

'Yeah. Cool.' Tom was not sure how he felt.

'Two veggie pasties thanks.' Cassie called out as they reached the food counter.

'No sauce. You want sauce?' she remembered Tom liked sauce on his pie.

'Yeah. Thanks. I'll pay.'

'No. I don't mind.'

'No really.' Tom handed over a ten-dollar note and waited for the change. 'Anywhere to sit down here Cassie?' He looked carefully at her face.

'Fire's the best spot.' Cassie smiled and headed them towards the bonfire.

Tom found a space in the circle and pulled a couple of crates from behind the woolshed for them to sit on.

'Thanks.' Cassie sat down and stared into the fire. Her face was composed into a portrait of inner thought, her hair dropping softly across her shoulders, the curls blazoning in soft whorls in the firelight.

'The pasty's pretty good.' Tom said through a mouthful.

'Not too bad. Have you always been veggo?'

'Not really. Just went off meat all of a sudden. Last few days really. Before I caught up with you again.'

'Oh?' Cassie smiled.

'Nothin' premeditated. Not like I'm trying to get healthy or anything.'

Cassie looked past Tom and saw her brother walking towards them.

'Hey Cass, I've got some stuff if you want.'

Cassie went a deep pink and looked into the fire. 'No thanks Will. Will this is Tom. Tom, Will.'

'Tom. You from around here?' Will suddenly switched his attention from his sister.

'Sort of.' Tom said warily.

'You could persuade Cassie for me.'

'She said no thanks.' Sean was suddenly by Cassie's side.

'What's it to you?'

'What's it to you? If she said no, she meant no!' Sean had Will by the top of his fleece.

'Get off me.' Will yelled.

Sean flew in faster than he had time to think and landed a solid blow in Will's solar plexus. Will went down gasping for breath.

Sean suddenly, felt a strong hand pulling him off by the back of his jacket.

'Cool it Sean. Not here, not now.' Angus had a firm grasp.

'Shit.' Will brushed himself off.

'Hello Cassie darling. Doing OK?' Angus walked over.

'Will. Is he OK?' Cassie pointed to Will lying on the ground, still fighting for air.

'Sean doesn't seem to approve of his behaviour tonight?' Angus tried to smother his laughter. 'Cassie. We should leave you two in peace.'

'Thanks Angus.'

Angus walked over to Will and picked him up off the ground. 'You all right son?' he asked kindly.

Will did not look all right at all. This time, it was more than just hurt pride. He was still too angry to speak but Angus caught him a full eyeball. 'You know that your sister has never taken that stuff Will. I reckon you shouldn't either.'

'How would you know what I should or shouldn't do?' Will tried out his mood on Angus.

Angus remained perfectly steady and calm, his voice ice cold sober. 'Will. Just look at it this way. You leave Cassie alone and I'll leave you alone. Got it?'

Will broke into a sweat. Angus's eyes said it all.

'Got it?'

'Yeah. She's sweet.' Will said quickly.

'Just don't forget that now will you son.' Angus let him go and walked away. 'Come on Sean, let's us have that dance.'

Cassie was reluctant to return to the shed. She was still shaken by the revelation that her brother Will was doing drugs and probably dealing.

Tom was standing where Sean and Angus left him. 'You warm enough Cassie?' Tom took off his jacket and put it over her shoulders.

'Thanks Tom.'

Tom said nothing, unsure of how to respond to her, the fire racing through his belly.

'You know Tom. I'd like to hang out with you.'

Tom's cheeks glowed warmly in the reflection of the maturing fire. 'Music's stopped.'

'You staying?'

'Not sure. I'm driving tonight. Have to check where Sean and Angus are.'

'See you next time then?'

'Yeah. Sure. You always work at the Iona?'

'Mostly. Buckleys Pub as well and sometimes Berridale Pub when they need me. Come down sometime. Footy match between the Pigs and the Crows next week. You play?'

'Not for a while.'

Cassie grinned and stood up. 'Have to go. See you.'

'See you Cassie.' Tom stayed beside the bonfire and watched her as she walked back to the shed. He noted the flow of her long hair against her back and the easy swing of her shoulders as she climbed the steps.

'You still here son? Thought you'd be showing us both how to dance.' Angus clapped Tom on the back.

'Yeah. Just talking. You know.'

'I know. You want to stay or go?'

'Don't mind. You and Sean?'

'Not a bad time to go before the road gets busy. Bit of traffic on a one lane bridge if you know what I mean.'

'Sure thing. I'm ready.'

'Sober?'

'Sober as. Where's Sean?'

'Just talking to some mates of mine. Job stuff.'

'Work?'

'You want some?'

'Could do. Not sure what though.'

'Pitch in with Sean if you like. You can be his offsider.'

'What's he doing?'

'Laying stones. Can you mix mortar?'

'Soon learn I suppose.'

'Let's go then. Here he comes.'

Angus walked Tom back to the truck and Sean joined them a few minutes later.

'I'm driving Sean. You two can nookie in the back.'

'Steady on. He's the one who can dance. Not me.' Sean protested draping his legs between the two front seats of the cab.

'Just stick to the road son, and the rules.' Angus tightened his belt and settled in for a quiet ride home.

COOMA

'Shit Sean.' Tom began the morning's conversation.

'What? Bad dreams son?'

'No, money.'

'What.'

'I said I'm running out of cash.'

'Then it's probably time to get you working.' Angus chipped in over his toast and cheese.

'Thought you said you had somethin' lined up for me anyway?'

'I did and I do; if you still want it, that is.'

'Course.'

'You get what you ask for in this life son.' Sean jeered softly.

'Done you heaps good then. Ending up in the backwaters with us.' Angus sided with Tom.

'Hey. I'm in this too!' Sean feigned shock defence and put both hands on the table in front of him. 'Willing hands ready to work.'

'Good. I asked Barry for you Tom. Hope you don't mind.' Angus began.

'Asked him what?'

'If he needed a hand around the place. You know. Bit of maintenance, keep the pub grounds tidy. That sort of thing. Maybe do the parking on Friday and Saturday nights!'

Tom laughed. 'Buckleys!'

'It gets a bit wild there at the end of the week and he could use a hand.'

'Right. What did he say?' Tom was suddenly all ears.

Sean managed to keep a judicious silence and the smile creeping along the corners of his mouth from widening into a revelation that Tom could not ignore.

Angus smiled. 'Well, he said that Cassie could use some help in the kitchen when the dining room is open. Some of the work is too heavy for her it seems.

'Sure.'

'OK then. I'll call him. Can you start this week?'

'Yeah. OK.'

'Then you won't need to go to Centrelink Tom.'

'Shit no. That would be good. Wouldn't mind visitin' Cooma though.'

'Cooma?' Angus inquired.

'Heard that the flicks are OK.'

'Anything special on?' Sean asked.

'Rabbit Proof Fence.' Tom chomped into his toast.

'Rabbits?' Sean seemed amused.

'It's about the Koori kids. You know. Stolen generations and stuff.' Tom was heading for the second breakfast.

'Steady on. What about the rest of us?' Angus flicked Tom's hand away from the hottest piece on offer.

'I'll make some more.' Sean got up.

'Toss you for it.' Angus suggested pulling a coin from his pocket. He flicked the coin and slapped it onto the back of his left hand. 'Go on. Call.' He prompted the kid.

'Hmm. Heads.' Tom took a punt.

'Heads it is. You wash up!' Angus roared laughing and swiped the toast.

'Hey. That was mine!'

'No way. That call was for the washing up.' Angus chuckled. 'You'd better get in practice anyway if you're going to impress

Cassie.'

Tom blushed and got up from the table. 'Thanks Sean.' He took another couple of pieces of toast from the top of the fuel stove and sat back down. 'Toss you for it?'

'Go on. Eat up son.' Angus's eyes twinkled as he observed the strengthening spirit of the young man.

'So are we going to Cooma?'

'Can't see why not.'

'Flicks?' Sean offered.

'Yeah. Could do, or just walk around.'

'Show you the shops then. You boys must be starved for civilisation.' Angus laughed.

'No. Not really.' Sean answered.

'Nor me.' Tom reiterated the sentiment.

Angus threw his hands in the air. 'Suits me. Can't always kick around the farm for the rest of our lives.'

'We'll come.' Tom jumped in before the opportunity was lost.

'OK. We're out of here then. Take you the back way. Bring a coat. Looks windy out there.'

Angus foraged around for a spare jacket for Sean. The cupboard was well stocked with woollen knits including a couple of balaclavas and beanies. Fishing aside, the wind was ferocious on the Monaro and anyone who had spent more than a few years toughing out the cold knew to build up a supply of woollies; that and stack the woodshed full before winter. He dragged out a bedraggled Drizabone and gave it a rigorous shake. The crumpled cloth relented and gradually, the coat took on the shape and dimensions of a solid all-weather coverall. Of all the coats he had, these were still the best all-rounders in Angus's experience. The biting Monaro winds and driving rains always seemed to penetrate the synthetic fleece jackets. During the lambing season, a farmer simply had to have the best outdoor clothes. The long, cape-like Drizabones were simply the best of the winter coats on the market.

'Here Sean. Stick this on your Irish frame.' Angus handed him the coat, now looking almost respectable despite its wear. 'Tom. You got something warm to wear?'

'Yeah. Can we buy some hay?'

'Hay?'

'For the colt; or carrots.'

'Might as well, but not from the Cooma main street.'

'Oh?'

'Got someone who cuts it off his farm. He'll deliver it straight to the hayshed. Now are you going to drive or not?'

'What about the coppers?'

'We'll go the back way. Arable Road. Magnificent scenery and nothing to worry about apart from a few stray mobs of Aberdeen Angus.'

'Just as well for the bullbar.' Sean said.

'You'll love it Sean. Take you right home. Land out here is magnificent. Come on then. Into the truck.' Angus tossed Tom him the keys.

Tom felt more exhilarated than he remembered. He hardly noticed the drive out of the farm and the long winding stretch of smooth tar to the Dalgety pub. As they crossed the Snowy River, he tooted the horn almost losing sight of the direction from Angus to take a left at the pub.

'Steady on mate. We want to cross the river, not swim it.'

'Sorry Angus. Mind must have been somewhere else.'

'Cassie is probably at the Iona Café. Toot your thing.' Angus said.

Tom blushed despite himself and as they drove past the café, Sean suddenly leant forward and leaned hard on the horn then settled back into the back seat. He turned his head to look out the back window to see where Cassie was.

Cassie was clearing the tables on the verandah, looking up just long enough to catch the disappearing back end of the truck as they pulled up the hill and out of sight.

'Was that Cassie waving?' Sean asked innocently.

'Didn't see if it was.' Tom answered.

'I was asking Angus.' Sean spoke with a musical lilt to his voice.

Angus smothered a laugh, as he looked sideways at Tom. The kid was blushing more deeply, hands gripping the wheel intensely. 'You drive well Tom. Just don't rip the wheel off.' Angus broke into laughter to ease the tension.

'Can't you two guys leave us alone.' Tom smiled despite himself.

'We're heading towards Cooma, not heaven.' Angus remained lightly on Tom's case.

'Cooma or bust.' Sean added dryly.

'Yeah, or bust. How d'ya get there?'

'Keep on trucking son. Up ahead a few klicks there's a turnoff. The Arable Road. Beautiful stretch of dirt with no blues to worry about.'

'How do I get me licence?' Tom sounded keener than he was worried.

'We'll sort that for you son.' Sean eased himself into a more comfortable position, his boots resting on the dash.

'Cool.' Tom released his grip and skilfully negotiated a bridge. He chocked back the gears then accelerated out of the gully and started the climb on the other side. For a few seconds he tested the mirrors, adjusting the rear view and opening the side window to pull the mirror closer to the car. 'Shit you're ugly Sean.' Tom remarked.

'Thanks. Glad it's me and not you. Can't see Cassie falling for a grey haired Irish bastard like me.' Sean grimaced, running a hand through his hair. 'Could do with a shave I suppose.'

'Could do with a total makeover you mean.' Tom worked on his advantage.

'Steady on! Women like men a bit rough around the edges you know. Smooth bastards don't usually make the grade.'

Angus burst into a rumbling belly laugh. 'Wouldn't dream of calling ye smooth Sean. Far from it. Haven't heard too much about your saintly friend here Tom I take it. Would make a man lose his sleep.'

'Yeah? He looks OK to me.' Tom was unsure whether to defend Sean or take the advantage.

'Well, while we're talking character references, Angus, Customs might have a few notes on you stowed away in the hold of one of their steam-around-the-coast cruisers.'

'Me?' Angus sat up straight like a well-trained schoolboy.

'You two got some stories you want to tell me?' Tom felt distinctly pure.

There was a muted silence in the cab. Angus looked straight-ahead, eyes wide open and brows raised high onto his forehead. Sean similarly, stared forwards without a flicker of recognition on his face.

'Well?' Tom lost the edge of his confidence.

'Search me.' Angus shrugged his shoulders.

'Can't see me getting' up to too much mischief.' Sean said cheekily.

'Hey, is this the turnoff?' Tom slowed down.

'Take a right Tom.' Angus instantly became the mature man showing the younger one the ropes of life. 'Another few klicks and the road does a dog leg; take the left then the right almost straight away.'

'Smoke Angus?' Sean already busied himself rolling cigarettes.

'You smoke Tom?' Angus took the cigarette.

'Nuh. Can't stand the stuff.'

'Good.' Angus lit the smoke and drew deeply, winding down the window.

'Sorry Tom. I'll be breathing down your neck.' Sean lit his smoke and blew a long plume directly at the windscreen.

'Thanks Sean. Probably need someone like you on my case.'

'Better than the boys in blue.' Sean said

'I haven't done anything wrong!' Tom protested.

'Under age, no licence.' Sean began.

'Yeah, well.'

'Just keep a low profile. No point in attracting attention.' Angus continued the dry, no-nonsense line. 'I want to introduce Sean to some friends. You can muck around on your own for a while. Check out the local scene. You know the score.'

'Yeah OK. What are you two going to get up to?'

'Sort out some sort of ID for you mostly.'

'Wow! No joke?' Tom looked at Angus.

'No joke. It won't be if you don't stay on the road.' he smirked.

The Arable Road unfolded like a scene from a master's hand, the soft fawns of the native grasses perfectly balanced against the dust-coloured road and contrasting with the unexpected collection of orangey granite boulders. Tom, more committed to negotiating the dirt road than observing the magnificent scenery, kept both hands firmly on the wheel.

'There's nothing out here son.' Angus was mindful of the sense of deep relaxation imbuing the cab of the ute. 'This is where you go when you believe in god even if you don't know where to find him.'

'Sure can believe it out here.' Sean nodded in acquiescence.

'Can't see a living thing except for those cockies and the cows.'

'Seems like they are named after you Angus. Aberdeen-Angus stud no less.'

'Ha ha. Scottish breed of course. Finest beef in the world started by one of the local lairds.'

'Just like you are Angus. A local laird!' Sean laughed loudly.

'Well, a local landholder but nothin' as fancy as that!' Angus allowed the words to drawl over his tongue. 'What do you think of this road anyway. There is nothin' else out here except for cows, crows and rocks. You can relax son. There'll be no one on your tail lookin' for you.'

'What about when we get to Cooma?'

'When we get to the end of this road, you can let go of the wheel. I'll drive.' Angus offered.

Soon they were heading past some of the best of the region's farming estates. The road was smooth and untroubled with the landscape stretching in all directions like the vision of a great artist. The sky was lightly streaked with loose white clouds as if a flotilla of jets had trailed streams of white from south to north. The wind was light, almost indiscernible but sufficient to bring a crisp freshness to the air. They passed the main homestead of the Aberdeen Angus stud and within minutes, were at the T-junction on the highway.

'Here. Pull over. I'll take the wheel son.' Angus offered gently.

Angus turned right towards Cooma. The town rested like a heritage postcard within the broad relief of the valley. The church tower rose prominently above the cluster of houses and central business district and occasional spirals of smoke told the story of a winter's morning in the country. The highway suddenly broadened into the main street, lined on either side by high gutters and the newish retail sector before the older houses welcomed travellers to the majestic centre of the historic regional centre.

'There's the pub.' Angus pointed at the Royal Hotel.

'Not that we'll be needin' much of that.' Sean patted his stomach, now fuller after the quiet domesticity of farm life.

'Tell you what. We'll stop off at Sharp's Café for lunch then Tom, you can explore around a bit while we sort out some work for Sean.'

'Sounds like the go. Tom?'

'Yeah. Fine by me. Hey Angus, what does a man do in Cooma?'

Angus laughed out loudly. 'You can either hang in Centennial Park, or cruise the aisles of Woollies, or if you like there's the library.'

'Not much then.' Tom grinned.

'Bit short of the Melbourne mark Tom?' Sean said whimsically.

'Do you want to go back there man? Can fix you for work if you want.' Angus was quick to respond to Sean's inflection.

'No way. Wouldn't trade the farm for quids. Besides, this stone masonry deal sounds good.'

'It is. Believe me.'

'Centennial Park it is then.' Tom decided.

'More to do by half on the farm.' Sean summarised the life of Cooma.

'When it happens here it is good. Everyone has to shop somewhere and the Shire's here as well.'

'Local Government?'

'Weeds, seeds and parks,' Angus scratched his chin, 'Gutters, garbage and foot paths. Then if we don't keep down the pests, weeds included, the land goes to rack and ruin. Councils are anyway mostly about raking in the rates.'

'You never are liberated even in this world then Angus,' Sean remarked dryly.

'Keep your head down and invest at the bottom end of the market. No one sees you; no one wants anything from you. That's my motto.' Angus negotiated the angle parking outside the tourist information centre.

'There you go Tom. After lunch, you can check out what's on offer in there and that's Centennial Park.' Angus pointed directly in front of the ute.

The park was maintained to present a sense of civic order, A brightly coloured conglomeration of plastic formed the kids play centre and an older concrete half moon structure housed the public facilities. The leafy, mature trees reflecting the arrival of the immigrants, the European workers who built the giant and impressive Snowy Scheme, were exotic yet welcome imprints on an otherwise ancient landscape. Tom quickly gauged the extent of this limited urban territory and settled for a quick lunch with the men before heading into the unknown. Already, he had noted the small groups of young people, mostly his age and perhaps younger, sitting under the trees and the strange older men roaming the perimeter of the park. He was never shy in his own environment and his natural curiosity awakened him to the opportunity of new friendship and information on the local scene.

Lunch was a happy event with the casual crowds frequenting their favourite tables and attended by their customary waiters. Angus was welcomed and seated in the courtyard in the sunshine amongst the 'office' crowd, along with a couple of mothers taking a break from shopping and kids care.

Angus adjusted his feet under the table, his boots comfortably coarse and rough against the worker's socks. His foot accidentally kicked the metal leg of the table causing the coffee to spill into the saucer. Tom was completely absorbed in a ploughman's luncheon of extraordinary snow peas, avocado, cracked pepper and sea salt. His mouth grasped at the firm crust, wood-fired at a bakery that had served more than a generation of working men and women. Sean sat quietly, sipping his coffee and toying with the assembly of pastries familiar to his Irish taste. The flow of warm liquids and open nourishment salved body and soul and he was grateful for the company of the boy in particular, who had prompted him to journey from the confines of the farm to Cooma.

Tom finished his lunch and drink, and pushed his chair back away from the table.

'See you then Tom. Catch you around 2 pm?'

'Two o'clock? Sweet.' Tom stood up. 'My shout?'

'Next time. This one's on me.' Angus smiled.

'Thanks Angus. See you both at two then.'

He walked back into the café from the courtyard then carefully picked his way to the door and into muted sunshine. The street was fully parked with a steady, yet casual stream of cars traversing the roundabouts to exit Cooma for the big smoke of Canberra and Sydney. He waited his chance then skipped across the road and made for the park.

The drug dealer was waiting for his friends near the childrens' playground when he saw Tom heading across the park. For a moment, he was seized with the fever of opportunism. In the next second, his mood turned to ice cold as he decided on a more effective method to lure and catch his quarry. His heart pounded with excitement as a plan formed in his mind, a plan that would certainly deliver him victory. As much as he did not know a lot about the nature of people, he knew this much, that he had a rare talent for making people do what he wanted them to do. It was nothing premeditated, it was simply a skill that came with the role he played as one of the major dealers across the territory, privileged in his access and power and beyond reproach apart from the coppers if they had the opportunity and brains to catch him. He knew he could play the police against someone else any time he chose to do so and take the heat off himself. This was not an opportunity to be missed.

Tom reached the centre of the park and looked up at the graceful trunks of the trees, marvelling at their height.

'Hey mate!' The dealer called coarsely from the middle of the kids' playground.

Tom turned to answer and saw the young man standing with arms loosely by his side and a broad grin on his face.

'Gidday.' Tom responded cautiously. 'You're Cassie's friend Will yeah?'

'What's happenin'?'

'Nothin' much. What's it to do with you anyway?'

'Not much. Just thought you might like to score. A deal between friends.'

'I didn't know that you were a friend of mine.' Tom answered evenly.

'No reason why we can't be.'

Tom hesitated for a moment. 'I suppose not.'

Will smiled and shrugged his left shoulder. 'Smoke?'

'No thanks.'

'Don't do drugs?'

'You know how it is.'

'Not really. How do you relax and enjoy yourself?'

'Chill out. Listen to music I s'pose.'

'Cool.'

The wind suddenly picked up and Tom pulled his jacket closer to his body. 'Christ. It's as cold as hell in this place.'

'Cooma? Not as cold as Nimmitabel though.'

'Yeah. I was there the other night at the Bush dance remember?' Tom relaxed his guard.

'Wind comes off the snow and across the plains. Enough to freeze you in your tracks. Mind you, I'd prefer to be out here than in the city.' The dealer said carefully.

'What about the coast? You could always live there.'

'This is my preferred patch if you know what I mean.'

'Not really.'

'Where you from?'

'South.' Tom was noncommittal.'

'Oh?'

'Not from the coast if that's what you mean.'

'You don't know the south coast here?'

'Not really. Where do you hang?'

'Go up and down a bit, you know friends along the way, Jase and his mates. Trade stuff that sort of thing.'

'Got to earn a living somehow I suppose.'

'You got a source?'

'Might have.'

Tom felt like leaving. The conversation trending in the wrong direction and he did not want to have anything else to do with Will.

'Do us a favour?'

'If you like.'

'Tell Cassie I'm sorry about what happened the other night if you know what I mean.'

'Why don't you tell her yourself Will, she's your sister not mine.' Tom felt angry about his unwanted intrusion at the bush dance and again now in the park.

'Look after her for me.' Will grinned then stuck out his right hand to shake Tom's hand. As he did so he quickly slipped a box with his other hand into the pocket of Tom's jacket. He thumped Tom on the back to obscure the 'exchange' then turned to walk towards the corner café. As he sauntered out of the park, the dealer gave a nod to his mate sitting quietly at the bus zone. The fellow got up and walked in Tom's direction, neither acknowledging Tom or apparently noticing him.

'He's the one. He's the dealer. Got the crap on him.' The snoop continued walking towards the pub and turned at the corner towards the supermarket where he would be unnoticed amongst the shoppers and their trolleys. A man skulking in the car park walked into the park and towards Tom.

'Hey. Mate.' He called to Tom, signaling for him to come over and talk.

Tom turned to observe the slightly stooped man dressed in nondescript blue denims and a black parka. Before he could think or move away as his natural instinct told him to do, the man was onto him, pulling his right arm behind his back and forcing him against the trunk of one of the tall kapok trees, its branches spreading upwards in open surrender to the sky.

'Little birdie told me you have something for us.'

'What are you talking about? Get off me!' Tom was fuming and ready to strike.

'Settle down. Don't want to find yourself charged with assaulting a police officer do you?'

'What?'

'Come on. Give it over.'

'Get off! Give what over?'

'Where is it?' The man patted down Tom's jacket then pulled the box out the pocket.

'Well, well. What have we here?'

'That's not mine!' Tom protested.

'It's in your pocket isn't it.' The man glared at him. 'If it isn't yours, whose is it then?'

'I don't know. How should I know whose it is?'

'Come on. Don't try the innocent crap on me. Ice?'

'Look, I don't know whose it is!'

'Listen mate. This stuff is worth a fortune. I could do you on the spot for trafficking with this quantity.'

'I want to call my friends.'

'You can do that from the station. What's yer name?'

'What's it to you?' Tom was livid with fear and fury.'

'If you don't have a name, we'll have to drag it out of you won't we!' The plain clothes started to march him towards the car park. 'Just as quick to walk from here but we don't want you trying a runner mate. Get in.' He pushed Tom into the back seat of the car next to an equally innocuous looking middle-aged man.

Tom could not believe what was happening. In less than 20 seconds the car pulled out of the car park and drove the short distance to the blue 'Police' sign protruding from the same street that bordered the park. His mind whirled in dismay then in a matter of seconds managed to pull some sense out of the madness.

'Will! He must have planted the stuff on me.'

'Good story son. Tell that one to the judge.'

'What do you mean? It isn't mine!'

'Traffickable and commercial quantity kiddo. You're inside.' The police officer opened the back door and started to haul Tom out.

'I can get out myself. Leave me alone.' Tom was close to tears.

'Inside.' The man marched Tom ahead of him, past the counter and straight into an interview room. 'Sit down.'

'I want to talk to my friends.' Tom began to feel shaky.

'OK. What's the number?'

'I don't know. They're at the café. Sharp's I think. We were just having lunch.'

'Ring Sharp's.' The man ordered his assistant. 'What did you say his name was?'

Tom's brain did a backflip. The image of Sean nervous at the wheel at the shopping centre, the burning of his papers at the campfire, the night flight from the hotel in Melbourne, the image of the Priest bending over him... 'Angus.'

'Angus who?'

'Just Angus. They'll know who he is.'

'Call Sharp's and ask for Angus. He'll have to bail him.'

'Bail?'

'We're charging you with possession mate. Commercial quantity. You'll be bailed at $500. End of story.'

Tom groaned and put his head on his hands. It was Will. He was sure of it. The sleazy attempt at 'friendship', the irksome request to say hello to Cassie, the handshake. That's when it must have happened. The prick must have dropped the box into his pocket then walked off on him. It was no use. He had been here before; used, abused and disbelieved. It would be another long walk out of another horrible mess not of his own making.

The minutes dragged by. The policeman disappeared leaving him with a paper shuffler and with nothing other than the blank walls to stare at. He finally returned with the paper work.

'Name?'

'Tom.'

'Tom who?'

'Tom Keating.'

'Address.'

'Don't have one.'

'Where do you live?' The policeman spelt it out.

'Angus's place.'

'Angus's place!' He said in disgust. 'Then we'll have to wait until "Angus" gets here won't we.'

'Shiit!'

'You can shit yourself or talk. Take your pick.'

'Get off me.' Tom started to shake.

'Leave him Jim. Wait for his mate to turn up.' A mature, plain-clothes detective walked into the interview room. 'Video on?'

'Just about to turn it on.'

'Make sure it's on tape. I don't want to miss this one. Do you want a cup of coffee son?' The older man sounded more compassionate and kinder than the younger officer.

'Thanks.'

'White?'

'Yeah. Two sugars.'

'Bring him coffee and biscuits. Now, where did you say you got this stuff.'

'I don't know what you're talking about.'

'I think you do.'

'What stuff. What is it anyway?'

'This won't do. It will help if you cooperate! Now what did you say your name was?'

'My name is Tom.'

'OK Tom. Where did you get the tabs?'

'I don't know about any tabs and I don't know how they got there.'

'Where's your ID?'

'I don't have any.'

'What are you talking about? Licence?'

'I lost my ID in the river.'

'You lost your ID in the river. Do you expect us to believe that!'

'You can't prove that I didn't!' Tom managed to rally his defence.

'No, we can't.'

'Date of birth?'

'Here he is. In here.'

'A uniformed policeman walked into the interview room with Angus. Sean was nowhere to be seen.'

'What's up Tom? What are you doing in here.'

'I don't know.' Tom shook his head.

Angus looked around the room, at the plain-clothes detectives, his eyes studying them with concern. 'Would someone mind telling me what's going on?'

'You a friend of his?'

'Clearly I am. Now what's going on?' Angus commanded, aware of his and Tom's rights to protection under the law.

'Found this on the kid.'

'This meaning what?' Angus glared at the policeman.

'Traffickable quantity of tabs. Probably Ice.' The senior detective said calmly.

'This is bullshit. Tom doesn't keep any of this shit, nor does he take it.'

'Then what's he doing with it?'

'Tom?' Angus turned to the young man clearly distressed with the situation.

Tom just shook his head.

'Then I'll take him home thank you very much.' Angus walked over to Tom.

'You'll have to sign a bail form first. He's charged with possession and he will have to appear in Court. We'll get the details from you if you don't mind.'

'OK. Then take my details if you want, but make it fast. I'm going home and he's coming with me. Now!' Angus was on slow boil.

Within ten minutes, the paper work was completed and Angus signed the bail form.

'Let's go son.' He stood up and looked Tom straight in the eye. The boy was clearly suffering and confused. Angus walked up to him however refrained from putting a hand on his shoulder despite his urge to do so. He looked at him frankly. 'There's work to do at home Tom.'

'Yeah. Let's get out of here.' Tom pulled himself together.

THE SANCTUARY OF FRIENDS

The three men sat in silence as they left Cooma. But as the descending sun caught the tops of native grasses, they rippled in glorious and golden unison. The majesty and immutable beauty of nature's evening script was always a perfect lullaby for Angus and he hoped it would also calm the boy.

'Can you believe that Sean!' Angus exclaimed.

'Never seen anythin' like it before. Not even in Ireland. Must have been ordered just for us here in this old truck of yours Angus.'

'Tom?'

'Awesome.' Tom was virtually speechless.

Angus prolonged the mood allowing them time and space to enjoy the beauty around them.

'There's nothing to worry about son. You might have to face court but god knows you're as innocent as hell.'

'As if I can prove it.' But Tom sounded less disconsolate after the soothing traverse over the evening landforms.

'We'll prove it readily enough Tom. There's only one way to deal with stuff like this and that's to face it directly. At the end of the day, I believe in justice and justice is more powerful than any pile of crap that some cop or lawyer dumps on you.'

'Is that what happens out here?' Sean was surprised.

'Conviction's as good as. Who cares about who is the guilty party? Tom is innocent though so eventually he'll be off the sacrificial hook and they'll have to look for the guy who is really guilty.'

'You mean Will?'

'Little idiot. Glad Cassie is going to stay well away from her brother for the time being. I'll have a word to her and square her up. Don't you worry about it Tom. You don't have to say anything to anyone. We'll sort it out and you'll wonder how come you suddenly have so many friends in the district. Most of us hate the bastards that run that shit up here from the coast. Wrecked more than one family, that crap!'

'Drugs?'

'Ecstasy. Ice. Doesn't get any worse in my opinion. Stuffs up the kids' heads and before they know it their life is a total trainwreck.'

'How do you know about it?'

'What do you think we do down the coast Tom? Running boats along that piece of coast isn't a picnic by any stretch of the imagination.'

'You a coast guard?'

'De facto for want of a better description.'

'Is that what you were doing the other night?' Tom's curiosity was aroused.

'Put it this way son. There's more than just fishing boats shoring up at the Bermagui and Eden Wharfs. Why do you think that little prick travels up and down the coast to Cooma. He's running the stuff off the wharf. Just haven't nabbed him yet.'

'Then why didn't you tell the cops?'

'Not here, not now. My suspicion is that some of them are bent and your long term interests and safety are more important than me gaffing off to them to get you off the hook. Let them think we know nothing and that there's no one on their scent. Safer that way.'

'You can't mean...' Tom was perplexed.

'Tom. This is one savage and corrupted world. There are good and bad apples in every box. You just want to make sure that you step well clear of the rotten apples and if that means actin' even more innocent than you are, then so be it. In my opinion, you're far better off running the course. Maybe they'll land you in the clink for a couple of days, we'll definitely get you out again. You gotta play their game for a while to get yourself free of them.'

'Bastards!' Tom exploded.

'Take it easy son. You're here to live and not to fight for causes and campaigns. Besides, there's Sean to think about.'

Sean shuffled in the back seat his legs stretched to the dash. 'Why, thank you Angus.' Sean was genuinely touched.

'You'll be working around town Sean and there's no need to link you up with any cop shop even for Tom's sake.'

'That's what I thought.' Tom recalled his decision to ask for Angus.

'Clever move son.' Angus closed the conversation.

THE BRUMBY COLT: BRINDABELLA

The morning chorus of yellow-tailed black cockatoos breaking unexpectedly over the range jolted Tom to wakefulness. Their strident calls were welcome echoes of the dawn awakenings he experienced on his grandfather's farm at Corryong. Instinct warned him to move quietly without waking either Sean or Angus. He wanted to climb over the short hill that abutted the farmhouse and head back along the Boloco Creek Valley where he knew that the colt would be standing with the old mare and the donkey. He knew they would be there, shaking off the dew drops and heading for the sweet pastures on the rough and shaly hill that would remain untouched by the heavy overnight frost.

Tom swung his legs off the cot and found his trousers. Angus had left him a pile of moleskin trousers, hardly worn and now too small for his body beset by middle age, and sinewy from the years of solid farm work. Angus's legs were now as strong as tree trunks. His tough frame had been repeatedly tested against the southern Antarctic swells as he traversed the southern seas: conquering Bass Strait before passing the Snowy Falls that fell into the abyss off the edge of the continental shelf.

Sean pulled on a dark blue pair of trousers, too good to wear for farm work; they were soft and comfortable like velvet against his skin. He put on his socks, and picked his boots off the floor. As quietly as he could he padded along the creaking boards towards the kitchen then opened the door into the early morning sun. Once he closed the door to Angus's hut, he pulled on his boots and headed up the hill into the trees.

Angus, no stranger to early mornings, looked out of the window and into the morning light. The light was dim and unremarkable for the winter. He too caught the familiar sound of the cockatoos, heralding, in his long experience, good luck. Despite himself, Angus was surprised, yet glad that Tom had emerged from the trauma of the Cooma park and police station. Now he was a part of the present and exhilarating landscape that had for so long welcomed and energised him between his lonely sojourns on the sea.

Tom took his time once he reached the top of the hill that stretched in front of the farmhouse towards the Snowy River Way. The cockatoos were still slightly ahead of him, their cries merging into a haggling and hilarious conversation. He picked his way carefully over the shales until finally he crossed the eroded gully and clambered up over the lightly-grassed slope towards the three motionless horses, their backs turned to the rising sun.

Below him was the steep river terrace that bissected the ancient landscape; successive seasons of snowmelt that had filled the stream to overflowing and cutting through the rock-ridden clayey soil. The colt caught his scent pricking his ears forwards in recognition of his friend. He took the first step towards his friend, just as an eagle spread its wings wide and with a sharp shriek began its upwards path, circling towards the top of the range.

'Here. Boy. Here!' Tom held out his hand. He had left the house too quickly to consider bringing an apple or carrot and now regretted his haste.

To the young colt there was nothing sweeter than this new friendship with the boy Tom. He walked surely head slightly drooped to the ground until he came close to the terrace as it broadened into the gully.

'You sure are a beauty!' Tom opened his hand for the colt to nuzzle his palm. He ran his left hand along the colt's neck now twitching with nervousness. The colt jerked his head up and looked straight at Tom. Their eyes met and Tom suddenly smiled, noting the courage and cheeky nature of the colt. 'You can't fool me. Would never get a bridle near you let alone a saddle. Bet your father was a beauty too, just like you.'

Tom continued to rub the horse, throwing the dark mane to one side of the tender neck. The colt pulled a step backwards then pawed the ground, throwing his head to his right hoof. He rubbed his left nostril against his leg and Tom waited until he pulled himself upright again, this time keeping his hands by his sides and watching, looking the horse in the eye. He wanted to send the message to the colt that he would not touch him unless he came to him.

The colt took a step further back then turned to the old mare, grazing patiently and unconcernedly on the hill. He then turned back to Tom and nuzzled his chest roughly, almost bringing his long white-streaked nose up under Tom's chin.

For a second, Tom thought the colt would bolt. He took a step backwards and raised his hand to stop the horse moving either forwards or backwards. The colt stood still, his legs shaking in readiness for flight. Then as if he had somehow overcome the mix of fear and inquisitiveness, he rose to his true height, shaking his head and mane free from where Tom had smoothed it against his neck.

'OK fella. I won't groom you. You're too smart to let me start.' Tom chuckled. 'I don't know how I'll break you in if you're not keen on even that much!'

Tom placed his right hand on the neck of the colt then ran his hand down the shoulder to the colt's hoof. He picked up the foot and turned his body to face the horse's rear as he would if he wanted to check his shoes. The hoof was firm and hard to the touch. There was no brittleness or cracks despite the rocky terrain and tendency of the horse to canter away from the slightest foreign sound. Carefully, he placed the colt's hoof back on the ground and walked silently towards his flank, running his hand along its back as he did so. He stopped short of the hind leg, resting his hand on the rump then walked backwards towards the horse's head, keeping contact with the colt as he did so. Gradually, Tom eased himself in front of the horse's head and made eye contact, clicking his tongue and smiling into the colt's eyes. 'Brindabella. Brindabella.'

Tom tickled the bottom lip of the colt then up to the jawline and down the horse's neck. He repeated the stroke a few more times, all the while keeping eye contact. He allowed himself to relax deeply and draw in his breath. The colt remained stationary, transfixed as he let the young man through his guard. There was almost no movement between them, hardly the flicker of an eyelid or swish of the horse's trailing tail as they bonded under the spell of the timeless landscape.

'Tom.' Cassie's lilting voice broke the moment.

Tom turned around slowly, soothing the colt with his left hand. He could feel the horse stiffen under his hand. 'Shh. It's all right boy.' He carefully quietened the colt. 'Take it easy boy.'

'Hello Tom.' Cassie called from the other side of the gully. Then she noticed them together, their bond striking and tangible in the morning. 'Sorry!' Cassie suddenly realised she had interrupted the bonding of the horse and man.

Tom patted the colt more firmly and took a measured step backwards.

Brindabella half reared, then reared again, this time fully, exposing his powerful underbelly. Tom quickly stepped away. The colt whinnied as he pounded the earth with his hooves. For a second he tilted his head towards the young woman, then turned and raced up the gully, breaking his pact with Tom and at the same time shaking off the impulse to gallop back to the mare.

Tom watched the colt gallop along the base of the gully, then mount the side of the river terrace, his dark flanks challenged on the steep rise his forelegs straining for purchase on the stony, slippery soils. With all his strength he topped the terrace then stood on the high side, alone and solitary in his newfound stature. Brindabella reared again, a stark and powerful image against the morning sky.

'Hello Cassie.' Tom said simply.

'Tom.' Cassie struggled to catch her breath.

Tom broke into a spontaneous smile. 'Brindabella.'

'What?

'His name is Brindabella.'

'It suits him. I didn't know you too were such close friends.'

'Getting there.' Tom turned to watch the mare slowly making her way down the river terrace and towards the Snowy River. The mare seemed to understood that the young horse had broken the subtle umbilical cord that held them so close, a bond now reforged with the young man standing below her. The donkey, noting, lifted his head and followed at her tail, obedient to her age and discretion.

'She must have been an amazing horse in her day.' Tom said brightly.

'What about Brindabella? Related do you think.'

'Hardly think so. Angus said he came from the mountains. Near Dead Horse Gap. There are a couple of mobs of them up there. One headed by a black stallion and the other by a grey.'

'What about him?'

'By the looks of his colouring, his father is the black and mother like the old mare here, a grey.'

'How did they capture him?

'Apparently it's not that difficult. That's if you know what you're doing.'

'Do you think you can break him in?'

'Never done it before Cassie. I can give it a go though. Not sure whether I want to yet.' Tom stated simply.

'What do you mean?'

'He mightn't want to be broken.' Tom shrugged his shoulders. 'I'd rather he came to me. He did this morning.'

Cassie raised her brows. 'Can see that. No halter and no carrots.'

Tom remained noncommittal. 'It's not like that really. I don't really need to ride him I suppose.'

'Would he let you d'ya think?'

'Probably. Can't see why not, but there's no hurry.'

Brindabella, as if aware of the conversation between his friend and the young woman lifted his head from his light grazing on the top of the river terrace. He whickered at Tom and threw his head in the air and cantered around the terrace.

'Thata boy, thata boy.' Tom said into the ether. There was little chance that the colt would hear the words, yet it was clear that over the distance, they already understood one another, bridle or no bridle, saddle or no saddle.

'He's simply amazing Tom. I've never seen a horse like him?'

'Gift! Just meant to be I suppose.' Tom smiled then turned to Cassie. 'Angus said he's mine. Gave him to me last Sunday.'

'Yeah!'

'Looks as though I'm going to be around for the time being.' Tom grinned.

'That's good. I mean…'

'Yeah. It is good Cassie. Glad that you're around!'

'I am too Tom. Angus said that you might be doing some work at the hotel.' Her cheeks deepened to the rose colour she wore last time they met.

'Gotta work somewhere. The hotel's a good start. Wouldn't

mind building me own house when I have a bit of cash behind me. That's down the track though.'

'Angus told me about the other day.' Cassie placed a gentle hand on his arm.

'Not to worry. They can't put me away for something I didn't do.'

'I'm really glad Tom.'

'I'll be OK Cassie.'

'Don't do anything that puts you in more trouble.' Cassie sounded distressed.

Tom looked at the young woman standing in front of him, her long curly hair brilliant in the morning light. For a second, he was seduced by her natural beauty and tempted to pull her towards him. Cassie felt his response and instinctively removed her hand from his arm, aware that her sense of modesty was more powerful than the attraction she felt for him. The sound of thundering hooves on the river terrace broke the silence and Tom turned to witness his friend, tail flying in the wind, descend the far side of the terrace and overtake the mare with the timid donkey at her heels. He continued to gallop, aware that Tom was closely watching the perfect explosion of his gait as he raced past, finally disappearing from view and following the creek on its course to the hidden gorge of the Snowy.

'Go Brindabella, go.' Tom whispered.

Cassie remained silently by his side, the magnetic pull between Tom and herself eased by the announcement by Brindabella that he was the undisputed star of the day.

'Cheeky little fellow.' Tom spoke after the colt had overtaken the mare.

'You'll have a job to train him.'

'You know anything about horses?'

'Broken a couple on Dad's farm.'

'You have?'

'It's a part of life and around here, plenty of people throw their hand into horse breaking.'

'This little guy doesn't want to be broken.'

'We can lunge him in a round yard. Shouldn't hurt him.'

'Round yard?'

'It's the easiest way. Don't really want to get on him until he's used to you and a rope. You work it up gradually.'

'See how it goes. It's really up to him though. Let's go back for breakfast.' Tom changed the subject. 'You're here early?'

'Brought some groceries over that Angus wanted.'

'Something wrong Cassie?' Tom picked up her sadness.

'Few problems at home. My mother is on my case a bit.'

'Tom?'

'No. She's going through some sort of mid-life crisis.'

Tom laughed. 'That's supposed to be normal.'

'My mother is far from normal! Cassie lamented.

'You could leave home.'

'I wish!'

'Why don't you come and stay with us?'

'Three bachelors?'

'Sorry. Just a suggestion.' Tom sounded meek.

It was Cassie's turn to laugh. 'Not that I have anything against you blokes.' She started to walk away from the gully and back towards the shale hill hiding the farmhouse.

'Wait.' Tom trumpeted after her. 'You could stay at the hotel.'

'Could do.' Cassie nodded. 'This hill's steep yeah?'

'A bit. Easier to ride up.' Tom grinned. 'Wonder whether Brindy would mind it. You'd better teach me how to break him in then.'

'Yeah. OK. Can show you a few tricks.' Cassie brightened.

'Does your mum ride?'

'I don't care what she can or can't do. I just don't want to be around her any more. I feel suffocated.'

'Must be bad.'

'I'm the last of four. Mum's going through some attachment thing. She has to find herself again or something like that. Basically she's finding it hard to let me go.'

'Must be hard bringing up a mob of kids then losing all of them.'

'Yeah, but...' Cassie sounded more than a little exasperated.

'Don't know how I'd feel.' Tom continued to be conciliatory.

'Where's your mum?

'Don't know exactly. Somewhere in Queensland.'

'Oh? Your dad?'

'Don't care and don't want to know. Good as dead as far as I'm concerned.'

'Tom!' It was Cassie's turn to be astonished.

'He's a bastard. Doesn't care about me, just about his prestige.'

'Jeez. You sure sound sore!'

'You would be too.'

'Sorry. Looks as though you and I have shared parent woes.' Cassandra smiled her eyes lighting up.

'How far down the creek can the colt go?'

'Almost to the river. Angus has it fenced off. They can't get out and they have plenty of free space inside the boundary.'

'That's what you need Cassie. A bit of room to move.' Tom smiled at her, catching her mid-stride and gently putting his arm around her shoulder.

'Tom Keating. You certainly know when and how to move.'

'Just friends yeah?'

'Yeah.' Cassie turned to face him then broke free, running up the final 25 metres of the hill. She stopped at the top, out of breath and leant against a tree, enjoying the magnificence of the morning.

Tom soon caught up with her and flopped on the ground near the tree. Cassie sat down next to him. 'Maybe you're right Tom. Perhaps I should ask at the pub. It would be better than home for now at least.'

'You're old enough to leave home then?'

'Always have been. Should have been out of there by the time I was breaking my first horse.'

'When was that?'

'Learnt to ride when I was four. Broke in Lancelot when I was 14.'

'Lancelot?'

'Gorgeous. He was a pure bred. Died a couple of years ago.'

'No! I'm sorry.'

'It was an accident. The float rolled with him in it when we were taking him down the coast for a show.'

'Cassie!'

'It happens Tom. I've never liked floats anyway. I'd rather take a few days and ride him to the shows myself. Horses and floats don't belong together. If you can't go there on horseback, don't go. That's what I reckon.'

'Have you got another one?'

'Not yet. Thought I'd wait until I had my own place.'

'You could put one here.'

'Yeah, suppose. There's a brumby run later this spring. Thought I'd team up with some of the locals and bring one in. Another colt maybe. Some of the mares could be good breeders. Wait and see I guess.'

'That sounds tops.' Tom was enthusiastic.

'You going up for breakfast?'

'Coming?' Tom sprang to his feet and put a hand out for Cassie.

'Thanks.' She stood up and brushed the shale dust off her trousers.

Angus was had already set another place at the table, realising that Cassie would catch Tom at the horse paddock and come back with him. There was nothing as good as young friends and as much as Tom and the colt would be unbreakable in their friendship there was Angus reckoned, a place in his life for the young woman. Angus was a quick judge of human nature and sentiment in as much as he could read the quality of a character before someone had even opened his or her mouth to speak. Besides, the moment he had met her he realised Cassie had all the attributes that were essential for the civil defence team that was a part of his brief for surveillance across the Monaro and Snowy Mountains.

Tom was innately a strong and principled young man, but in need of love and companionship. He was not the sort of person, in Angus's opinion, to tolerate frivolity or fools and Cassie was neither frivolous nor foolish. They would become good friends and in Angus's reckoning, just the right medicine for one another as they leaped from adolescence into early adulthood.

Angus was acutely aware of Cassie's predicament, trapped by an increasingly lonely mother isolated in the world of her maternal fears and regrets. The young woman needed an instant breather from the pressure of stifling attachment laced with implied threats of illness from her mother, untimely blackmail that would scar her emotionally and saddle her with unreasonable guilt and worry.

Cassie was naturally bright and cheerful, however Angus noted the gradual loss of her sparkle as her mother became increasingly ensconced in her own trap of self-pity and faked illness. Her mother finally caved in to her fears; her emotions were blackened by jealousy of her daughter's youth and beauty. Then by degrees, she succumbed to envy, becoming increasingly devious to convince Cassie into believing that her mother was ill. Cassie felt trapped. Compassionate by nature and automatically sympathetic towards her mother, she was nevertheless aware that it was unfair, totally unfair, that her mother would willingly rob her of the best years of her youth.

'Cassie is a legend.' Angus stuffed a pile of bacon into his mouth. 'No one, but no one I know is out there as early as Cassie. Came up when we were hardly awake with a pile of fresh veggies and this morning's eggs.'

'Nice to know that you have an admirer Angus.' Tom was quick to beat him at his own game.

Sean burst into laughter. 'Looks as though you have scored yourself a couple Tom. The colt and Cassie.' Sean preferred the blunt and let's not muck around approach.

'He's called Brindabella.' Cassie wised them up.

'Brindabella!' Angus looked wide-eyed at Tom.

'Yeah I know, the yacht. The name suits him.'

Angus raised an eyebrow. 'Sure you know what you're taking on with a name like that Tom.' Angus stuck his fork into another piece of bacon.

'What do you mean?'

'Well, inheritin' the name of a racing yacht could prove to be a challenge.'

'He's got form.' Tom defended the choice.

'Brindabella?' Sean got his full mouth around the name.

'Sydney to Hobart Sean.' Cassie explained.

'Oh.' Sean wasn't sure that the line of conversation would be fruitful for Angus.

'Nothin' on earth like it Sean. Even the America Cup fades by comparison.'

'You ever raced Angus?'

The room filled with the sound of Angus's laughter. 'Would I really have time for the flotsam and jetsam of the shipping world Sean? My hands are already too full with the challenge of foreign labour to contend with this year and the Patrick's Stevedore debacle before that. So it's unlikely that I would fiddle faddle down the coast in a matchbox made of straw.'

'I thought Brindabella was a boat!

'Tom. If you can keep that colt under rein and not lose your poise then you're a better rider than I am a sailor. Mark my words.'

'Do you think he's too much for me?'

'I didn't say that.' Angus clamped his mouth shut over the healthy mix of eggs, toast and bacon.

'Can you ride Cassie?' Sean turned to the young lady sitting in the all-bloke camp.

'Yep.'

'Cassie's helpin' me to break in Brindy.'

'Right.' Angus nodded as if it were new to him. He looked sideways at Sean and smiled. Sean looked studiously at his plate, moving the meat off the toast then the toast over the top of the scrambled eggs, before putting a corner of toast onto the end of his fork.

'You all right Sean? Never known you to be short on appetite.' Tom noticed that Sean played a bit more than usual with his food.

Before he had time to open it too far, Sean shoved the toast into his mouth. 'Mmm.'

'Mmm what Sean.' Tom burst out laughing despite himself, realising that he had suddenly broken the link of dependency that held him to Sean, like a ship to a predictably safe berth.

'Yeah.' Sean paused for breath between bites. 'When do you and Cassie start on the colt?'

Tom, wide eyed, looked across the table at Cassie. 'Cassie?'

'Next week. Working until Monday.'

'You will be too son. Working at the pub.' Angus commented dryly.

'Yeah!' Tom threw his hands into the air. 'Too good to be true. What about you Sean?'

'Sean? Got something in store for him son. Don't you worry. We didn't totally waste our time in Cooma.' Angus grinned at his mate.

'Great. I'm out of here for the day. Cassie? You coming?'

'Where?' Cassie looked around as if the world just didn't extend beyond Angus's kitchen.

'Go for a spin to the mountains?'

Cassie shrugged.

'Go on. You'll be safe with him.' Angus nodded. 'Take the ute if you like.'

'Thanks Angus. What about you and Sean. You'll be stuck here today, just with one another.'

'Friend's coming over later. Talkin' shop.' Angus cut in.

'Work?'

'Might be. For Sean. Building job on next week.'

'Cool. See ya then Sean. Catch you Angus.' Tom pushed himself off the table.

'Leave the dishes son.' Angus said.

'I was gunna. Sean likes to wash up he said.' Tom grinned at his old mate and ally.

'Do not. Anyway, your idea of doing the washing is to chuck it in the creek or the fire I might add. Go on. Get out of here!' Sean slapped him on the back. 'Look out for him Cassie. He's been in more trouble than a pack of wild dogs since I've known him.'

'Don't know whether I want to Sean. I'm not sure whether I can help him with the drug charge either.' Cassie sounded forlorn.

'Yeah Sean.' Tom pushed his chair into the table. 'Day at a time Sean. Day at a time.' Tom noted beyond the wisdom of his youth.

'So where to Cassie?' Tom noted her easy skill at the wheel as she took the ute through its paces up the road to the Boloco ridge.

'Dead Horse Gap.'

'Really?'

'Been there?'

'Yeah. On our way over the range from Victoria.'

'Oh.' Cassie looked quickly at Tom then turned her attention back to the road, her hands in driving gloves firmly placed on the wheel.

'It was soooo cold!'

'Will probably be OK today. Not much cloud around, but there will be a fair covering of snow.'

'Why there?'

'Horses. You saw them, didn't you?'

'Yeah we did.' Tom said quickly recalling the moment they climbed the Alpine Way and pulled in briefly to witness the stunning emergence of the wild horses from amongst the mountain gums.

'Then you'll know what I mean Tom. They're beautiful yeah?'

'Have you seen the stallion?'

'There are a few up that way.'

Tom wasn't sure how to continue. He still trembled internally at the thought of the charcoal-grey colt with the deep and black eyes, the memory already imprinted in his mind.

'There is a white stallion there. Sean saw him in the trees.'

'Oh? Most of them look fairly stocky to me as if they have draught horse in them.'

Could have. Someone used to mix the wild horses with draught horses years back or so I heard.'

'Then you know more about the horses than I thought!'

'Not a lot, but there are plenty of stories floating around Corryong way.'

Cassie concentrated for a few minutes on her driving skills, testing the steering of the ute and lightly touching the brakes on the first downhill section. 'You drive Tom?'

'Did the other day To Cooma.'

'Got your licence?'

'Not yet.'

'P plates?'

'Nope. Have to get my ID first.'

'You don't have any?'

'Lost it all in a fire on the way up here.'

'That's different! Bit late in the year for bushfires I would have thought.'

'Well, it was more like a 'cleansing of the past' campfire.'

'Sounds weird. You dump your stuff in the fire?'

'Yeah. Why not? Seemed a good idea at the time. Still does. You know, make a clean break, new start. That sort of thing.'

'Running from something?'

'Wouldn't really say that Cassie, but I definitely don't want to go back to where I came from.'

'Corryong?'

'That's my grandfather's scene. I'm from further south. Melbourne.'

'You don't sound as if you're from the city. You seem OK out here.'

'This place is heaps better than home. Nothing like it.'

'So how are you going to get your ID?'

'Sean said he had it figured.'

'He scares me a bit. He's not from around here is he.'

'Ireland. Just arrived. New immigrant. Must have been a friend of Angus's way back. Both of us have Angus to thank for being here. Angus organised for Sean to get me out of Melbourne. Trouble at the boarding school. You know the score.'

'No. I don't Tom.'

'Priests...?'

Cassie's concentration slipped just sufficiently for her to catch her breath. 'You don't mean... Tom...'

'Yeah.'

'I'm sorry. That's bad.'

'Was. Doesn't affect me as much now, Cassie as it did before I met Angus and Sean. Sean's been lookin' after me. Got me over the worst.'

The ute topped the Boloco crest and Cassie changed to overdrive letting the force of gravity do most of the work. The morning was brilliant, the sun subtly lighting the tops of the grasses dancing in the breeze.

'Still can't bear the sight of a Church.'

Cassie flicked a glance in the rear view mirror. The pines of the Boloco Church were dressed with white cockatoos clamouring for the highest position as they stripped any surviving cones and new shoots off the trees.

'Look, over there.' Tom pointed through the windscreen. 'Can you see them?' Tom spotted the flock of yellow tailed black cockatoos careering ahead of them then forming a single flight formation as they made steady progress towards the range.

'Amazing birds yeah?'

'This place is unreal. No one out here at all except the stones and birds.'

'Stone the bloody crows eh?'

'Granddad said they're ravens, not crows.' Cassie defended.

'Easier to call them crows!'

'Wait 'until we're closer to the mountains. Ngarigo people reckon they're totems. Black crows and eagles.'

'Totems?'

'Yep. Spirit world stuff. Like the American Indians. I don't know much about it really, although I would like to learn more about their dreamtime and their stories.'

'You got a totem?'

'I like the crows. They always find me when I'm in the mountains.

Not that there aren't many of them there already. A couple of times I've been lost in thick fog. Have you seen yet how quickly it comes over the mountains from Victoria,? Then you don't know which way is up, down, north or south. The crows have come in and flown the path for me. I just follow. Always get me off the mountain.'

'Jeez. Wouldn't like to depend on it!' Tom was unconvinced.

'I don't. Mostly have a map, compass. That sort of thing.'

'You go out often?'

'When I can. We'll be in Jindabyne soon. Want anything?'

'Nuh. Hate the shops.'

'What happened in Cooma?'

'Your brother Will planted stuff on me. He said to say hello and to say sorry for what happened at the dance.'

'If you see him, tell him to get stuffed from me!'

'You don't use?'

'No way. Never! I don't want anything to do with Will until he is clean. He's been there so many times before Tom and he just doesn't seem to care. There is nothing I can do to help him. He has to work this one out for himself.' Cassie suddenly withdrew into herself and accelerated up the long pinch of road. She stopped at the top letting the engine idle to look at the view. 'There it is Tom. Neat view.'

'Tops.'

'Always come this way if you are in a hurry to avoid being seen. Never much traffic out here.'

'Thanks for that.'

'Do you think you'll go to gaol Tom?'

'Don't know. I'll leave it to Angus. Says he has a handle on the situation. Might have to spend a bit of time in there until he works something out.'

'You didn't do anything Tom!'

'No but I had the stuff on me, didn't I.'

The road was mercifully quiet and free of traffic.

Tom laughed, relaxing in the company of the young woman. She smiled easily and was good to talk to: understanding but not intrusive. Tom felt more at peace and the tensions of the Cooma visit began to lift the further they drove along the Alpine Way. The mountains had a reasonable snow cover and the leaves of the silvertops glistened in the sun. The air was clear and Tom wound down the window to let a gust through the window and into the ute. The bush was clean. There were only a few farms at the bottom end of the valley and increasingly less development the further they went into the valley. Cassie tooted and drove straight through the entrance gate, pointing to the annual pass sticker on the windscreen, their passport to the National Park. The woman in the booth smiled and waved and, moments later, they could see the snowfields at Thredbo.

'Looks lovely at this time of year.' Cassie said quietly.

'Lovely.' Tom had little need to talk at the present.

'We'll bypass Thredbo for now. Let's just head up to the gap. Hope your boots are waterproofed Tom.'

'Are we going for a swim?'

Cassie laughed. 'Snow can be a bit wet sometimes.'

'You planning on a hike then?'

'We could walk in a couple of klicks. Best idea if you want to see the horses. They don't always hang around near the road, although they do tend to shit there.'

'We noticed, on the way through. Thought one of the locals shovelled the stuff into piles for some reason.' Tom laughed.

'Brumbies have more sense than most people credit them with.'

Cassie continued to drive steadily passing the turn off to the village then braking sharply to avoid a crow diving across the road in front of her. She dropped back the gears then drove more slowly past the stonework holding the embankment and past the village.

The snow had receded in the slightly warm weather and with the lowest precipitation rate in decades the early snowfalls were insufficient to provide good bush cover.

The horses would have plenty to eat provided they did not attempt to go higher for feed. The river was washing coldly over boulders and the swamp was patchy with snow; grass poked through in sizeable clumps. As they neared the gap, Cassie pulled into the information bay and turned the ute around so they were facing downhill towards Thredbo.

'Never know when you can't start the engine. Nothing worse. I always park where I can do a hill start.'

'Smart thinking Cassie.'

'Too many cold starts.' She grinned. 'Come on. Let's follow the creek along. There's a good track in.' Cassie was already half way out of the car, pulling her coat on and locking the door behind her. In seconds she was walking along the track, now covered in snow and with a couple of sets of ski tracks marking the way.

Tom realised Cassie wasn't someone who mucked around and rapidly caught up with her, pulling his jacket close to the body and the parka hood over his head. Cassie was already 100 metres down the track and seemed to have a mission in mind. Tom put his head down and simply followed, negotiating the deeper drifts near the stunted snow gums and heading for the firm, icier patches of snow that could hold his weight.

The skiers had apparently reckoned on the same approach, taking the firm path rather than breaking through into soft drifts where it was both impossible to ski and to walk. The path wound slowly along the general course of the creek and from time to time, cut higher along the side of the hill and away from the river.

'Look. There they are.' Cassie stopped and pointed, breathless with the exertion of the pace she had set over the snow. 'In the trees Tom.

There are a couple of mobs.' She waited until he caught up with her. 'You can see one group heading along the creek and another closer but moving towards the trees.'

'Gotcha.' Tom followed the line of her arm until he spotted the first group of horses. 'Wow, must be cold up here.'

'Good coats.' Cassie smiled. 'Don't need rugs with their winter coats on. These horses are born in the mountains. They're much hardier than any of the stock horses as a rule.'

'Seems a bit of a shame to take them out of here.'

Cassie shrugged her shoulders. 'Some of them could be broken in and trained up. Others are probably best left alone. Not to worry. They'll be catching more in the spring. Wouldn't mind a couple. Maybe keep them at Angus's.'

'He OK about that?'

'Yeah, sure. Keeps the feed down on the property. Bit of company for the other horses. Provided you have good fences, they don't do too much harm.'

'Cool.' Tom watched the mob in the trees move higher and away from the creek line. His long-range vision was sharp and he searched quickly, before they disappeared, to see if he could see either the old white stallion or the colt.

The horses filed in a close line, behind one another, their tails close to the body and heads lowered towards the snow.

Suddenly, he heard a whinny, almost like a shriek and the mob turned, at first slowly, then grouped together, to watch a colt moving through deep snow drifts, working hard against the powder, his powerful shoulder muscles pulling his body in strong leaps over the deep snow.

Tom caught the image of an older horse, almost invisible against the white of the snow, at his rear, moving from left to right as if to keep him on track as a sheep dog would track and chase a stray ewe back into the flock.

The colt had no choice except to move forwards, his full energy and strength taken up with ploughing through and over the deep drifts until he came closer to the track forged by the other horses, clearly a marked route to and from the creek.

The grey-white horse stayed with him, his powerful hindquarters almost bent to sitting position on the snow, his forelegs dancing over the drifts, hardly connecting with and so not penetrating the soft powder in the same way that the colt broke through. Then Tom noticed that this was not any ordinary horse. Maybe the light was playing tricks, but the horse hardly seemed to touch the ground, as if he were weightless, like a mirage on the snow.

The stallion was clearly unaffected by the deepening drifts. He seemed to float like an apparition above the white blanket, a visible yet invisible part of the scene. He moved the herd forwards, guiding the mares and foals out of danger.

'That's him Cassie. Look.' Tom pointed towards the horse.

'Is that your colt?'

'Yeah. Can't you see him? The stallion?'

'There's only one horse. The grey colt and the herd on the hill. He's doing it tough down there. Must have got off track for some reason.'

'You can't see the stallion with him?'

'My eyes aren't that bad Tom. There's nothing else out there.'

'Must be the same horse that Sean saw. I couldn't see him before either. He's there all right. As clear as day.'

'Phantom horse?'

'Don't know. Never heard of one before. Have you?'

'Yeah. I have. Met a woman at the Diggings Campground about six months ago. Said she saw him up here, at Dead Horse Gap. She says that she has the gift. She sees and hears things if you know what I mean.'

'Really? Sort of like a psychic?'

'She said he's ageless. Almost as if he was placed over the land to protect the herd.' Cassie became more sober, pulling her coat closer to her body. 'Bit spooky. No wonder they've survived out here so long.'

'There he goes.' Tom almost shouted. 'The colt. He's almost made it out of the drifts. They're waiting for him.'

'He's amazing. He looks a bit like Brindabella. Maybe he's Brindy's brother. Could be by the same stallion.'

'Yeah. He's the one I want. He's amazing all right. Look at the power in his legs.'

'Maybe that's what this is all about. Showing off the colt to you.'

'You think that the stallion would do that?'

'Why not. Best of the herd. Have to cut him out from the others so you can get a good look at him.'

The colt suddenly broke through to the track, his hooves on firmer snow. He spun in a circle, frisking with delight, then he broke into an instant gallop his tail flying straight behind him as he raced past the herd, throwing his head high and from time to time, kicking his legs free as if to shake off an imaginary rider as he ran into the cover of the trees.

'Wow!'

'Reckon you could handle him?' Cassie asked curiously.

'Don't know. Never seen a horse like him before.'

'Real son of a phantom stallion.'

'Not possible Cassie.' Tom said steadily.

'Anything's possible out here Tom. Should tell you about it one day. That stallion certainly has a claim on the herd. Can't see any others in there with them. Few broken down mares. Must have been here for more than 20 years. A mob of colts and he's the best among them.'

'Got a name for him?'

'Holy Smoke? Thunder?'

'Shit. I'm cold.'

'Turn back if you like?'

'Anything more out here?'

'We could track one of the mobs for a bit if you like.'

'He is the best yeah?'

'Yeah. I reckon. Doesn't look like any scungy brumby to me. Some of them are a bit too solid. He's in a class of his own.'

'Wouldn't mind going up the hill.'

'Yeah could do. Eagles Nest?'

'Let's do it.'

The ride up the main chair was thrilling, the mountain falling away beneath as they quickly rode above the groomed slopes, the valley unfolding like a painting in motion, the thin silver stream of the Thredbo River marking the fault line towards Jindabyne. The slopes were lightly covered with the multicoloured wonder of snowboarders and skiers enjoying the fresh powder covering the groomed piste.

Below them, a couple of skiers managed a stretcher between them, a young woman lying face upwards as they gently traversed the steepest section of the run.

'You see that Cassie?'

'Ski patrol. More accidents these days. Some riders are out of control.'

'Really?'

'Well it is mostly us — the boarders. You know, you get an edge and just fang down the mountain. Anyway, sometimes the skiers are just sitting ducks. Beginners shouldn't be on this trail and when they stop in the middle of the run…' Cassie's voice trailed off. 'Can work the other way as well. Skiers who don't have the experience lose control, especially on the ice. Then it's all over.'

'Many accidents?'

'Even one accident is too many in my book! People mostly have a great time. The resort is still open, so something must be working!' Cassie said dryly.

'What about the landslide.'

'That was a complete tragedy. Should never have happened. Mostly ski school staff.'

'No way!'

'Now they just have to get on with it. Put it behind them if you know what I mean.'

'Must be hard. Did you know anyone?'

'Yeah.'

'Sorry.'

'Cassie looked sad. She raised an eyebrow and said nothing.

'Geez. I'm sorry Cassie. Shouldn't have said anything.'

'It's OK. I don't have a problem talking about it Tom.'

'You think that they still haven't found out the reasons?'

'Some of them.'

Tom was lost for words. The top of the mountain loomed closely. He was unsure of how to alight. The majority of people had either skis or boards on their feet and he noticed how the chair in front slowed and the people pushed the bar up and over their heads then simply stood up on their skis and skied off to the side.

'Walk straight ahead please.' A voice called out.

'Hiya.' Cassie called out.

'Cassie. How you doin'? Where's your board?'

'Not boarding today. This is Tom.' Cassie moved deftly off the chair and walked straight forwards. Tom simply followed, eager to be out of the way of the next chair swinging into place.

'Catch you later yeah?'

'Yeah. Going up for a drink.'

'Have one for me.' The young man smiled. He looked happy

and healthy and Tom wondered what all the fuss was about in life if you could do this, just offload people into the stunning scene around them.

'Not bad Cassie. Not bad.'

'Good spot. Snow's usually good at the top. Looks a bit thin on down the bottom at times. There is less snow around since they built the Snowy Scheme, or so they say.'

'For real?'

'Seems to be the case. Jindabyne Lake has stuffed up the rain and snow patterns.'

'Plenty of it up here.'

'I like it out back best. Take you out there one day.'

'Thanks.' Tom stared past the side of the building in their face. 'Do you board out here with anyone?'

'Yeah I have. When I was going out with my boyfriend.'

'How long did ya go out with him?' Tom smarted at the thought.

'For a while.' Cassandra said in a non-committal tone.

'Did ya love him Cass?' Tom said boldly.

'Look at that Tom. Pretty good runs yeah?'

Cassie pointed to a tow with people riding up and down the slope and to a small group of skiers who were tackling the highest point. 'We're pretty high up here. Closes down in high winds. Can't see your hand in front of your face sometimes.'

Tom grinned. 'My shout?'

'Hot choccies?'

'In here?'

'See you up the top. Just have to go to the little room.' Cassie called over her shoulder as she marched towards the toilets.

Tom saw the steps and climbed to the restaurant. For a moment, when he entered the room filled with skiers sipping their coffees and chocolates, he felt like running and at the same time, dizzy from the unexpected sensation of height dropping away sharply as if on the edge of a cliff. The firebox burned brightly at the far end of the room. Tom saw the space and headed for the warmth, where he could see both the full complement of people and the spectacular and unhindered view. The valley opened up revealing its pristine beauty with groomed slopes cascading to the valley floor between the stands of trees. A flock of crows flew overhead then shot at a giddying speed along the descent line of the slope and towards the Thredbo River. The sun burned radiantly through the wall-to-wall glass. To the front, the chairlift continued to roll smoothly, depositing passengers and returning with empty chairs to take the quick drop to the valley floor.

'Would you like a seat?'

'Thanks. For two.'

'Take this one.' A man stood up from the corner table and pulled on his gloves. He was old, in his late seventies it seemed, but fit and strong and tanned from days perhaps, on the slopes.

'Thanks.' The waitress pulled a chair out for Tom.

Cassie spotted Tom in the far corner near the window. She walked over to the table, her face fresh with the chill of the snowy air, the lights in her auburn hair blazing as she neared the fire, her eyes more intent of finding Tom's than checking out who was who and with whom in the cafe.

'Hey Tom. Good view?'

'Heaps good.'

'You ordered?'

'Thought I'd wait for you.'

The waitress, smiling even though dead tired on her feet, walked over with the menu.

'Light lunch?'

'Just a hot chocolate thanks. Tom?'

'Same. Do you have soya milk?'

'Yeah, we do. Hot chocolate on soy?'

'Thanks.'

'Anything else?'

'No thanks. Tom?'

'Sweet.'

The waitress took the menus and Cassie placed her hand on Tom's hand. 'You don't like crowds.'

'No, I don't. You noticed?'

'You looked like a rabbit caught in the spotlights when I walked in. Are you OK Tom?' Cassie smiled despite herself.

'Just been on the farm for a while. You know, you lose your skills.' Tom managed to grin.

'You'll be fine. Dalgety is quiet and there is nothing much happening except for big dining room nights. Baz will have you in the kitchen and out of the public eye.'

'Thanks. I'll get over it.'

'No hurry Tom. Really.'

'I suppose not. Wasn't prepared for being so freaked out.'

'You want to talk about it?'

'Not sure that I can. I know how I feel Cassie, but I can't quite put it into words if you understand what I mean.'

'It can be hard. I sort of know what you mean.'

'Don't feel I need to say much around you though.'

Cassie smiled gently. 'Teach you to board one of these days.'

'You good?'

'Can get down these slopes in one piece and have a bit of fun. Helps if you've been surfing.'

'Sailboarding?'

'Might help.'

'Thought I might like skiing better.'

Cassie groaned. 'Split sticks!'

Tom nodded slowly, slightly dropping his head and grinning at the same time. 'I like the art in some of those guys out there. They look smooth.'

'It's different.'

'You ski?'

'I can.' She said thoughtfully. 'Spent most of my snow time on the board though. Could give the sticks another go I suppose.'

Tom shrugged.

'Next time we come up. Hire out the gear and see if you like it.'

'Cool.'

'Hey Tom. You going to live at the farm forever?' Cassie suddenly asked.

'What?'

'You could get another place, once you're working.'

'Yeah. One day.'

'Especially in spring the place is deserted. I should be able to find a cottage around here somewhere.'

'Great idea, but I have to do one thing at a time. Start work, go to court, do time…' Tom was smiling broadly.

'After gaol Tom. I'll wait for you yeah?'

'You'll what?'

'I'll wait for you and help get you started. I might want my own place too some time. You know. After a stint in the pub.'

'Do you think you'll move into the pub?'

'Yeah. I think I will. Couldn't live there forever of course. I want somewhere to keep my own horses, grow a few herbs and veggies, that sort of thing.'

'You into all that sort of stuff?'

'What stuff?' Cassie defended herself.

'Herbs?'

'Not that junk Tom. Lavender, basil, oregano. Rosemary is my favourite herb.'

'Like aromatherapy?'

'Yeah, but for food.' Cassie gave him a "you can't wind me up" sort of look.

'Heard that you can use those bush flower essences on horses.'

'True?'

'Hot chocolates?' Soy?'

'That one's mine.' Tom almost grabbed the mug smiling cheekily at the waitress until she blushed.

'Looks as though I've got some competition Tom.'

'Didn't know you cared Cass.'

'Drink your chocolate.' Cassie sipped her drink looking over the top of the mug at Tom.

As they drove back down the Alpine Way leaving the buzz and hub of the snowfields behind them, Cassie felt a change for the better.

Soon they were past the built up section of the valley and freewheeling out of the National Park and into the grazing lands broken by clumps of trees and dotted with old huts, cottages, and lodges nestling in the bush. As they reached the broad base of the valley, a powerful eagle flew in front of the car, its wings open and almost spanning the width of the car.

'Wow.'

'That's a present from the Elders for you Tom. Good omen the eagle. You're being protected by them.'

'Why me?'

'Rite of passage. Must have you on the list Tom.'

'What do you mean?' Tom shook his head turning to watch the eagle fly off into the western bank of the Crackenback Range.

'Your time Tom. It's your time.' Cassie said no more, keeping her mind and eyes on the road until they were well past Jindabyne and climbing steadily towards the mountains breaking over the granite plains of Berridale.

'Cassie. You look flushed.' Angus announced.

'It's the sun.'

'You're both home safely, that's the main thing on these country roads.'

'Decided to come the long way around Angus. Felt a bit spooked by an eagle we saw on the Alpine Way.'

'Didn't think you got spooked by much Cassie.'

'Yeah. I don't usually but the last time an eagle flew in front of me like that, Peter rolled his car remember?'

'I do Cassie except an eagle won't cause a car to roll. That was just youthful exuberance gone wrong.'

'Angus. It's not as easy to explain away as that. He was killed 'cause the omens just didn't hang his way.'

'Wait on a minute Cassie. Thought you said an eagle was a good omen.'

'It's the way the bird was flying Tom. You always get a choice in life. Follow the law or take the punishment. I got the clear message to come through Berridale. So I did.'

'Cassie. That's freaky.' Tom was insecure on this new terrain.

'You have to listen Tom It's not like you can just do your own thing anymore. You have to listen and follow the signs.'

'I don't know whether I can!' Tom was unsure whether to be scared or irritated.

'You'll understand. One day.'

'What?' Tom began to lose patience.

'Leave it Tom. Cassie has more strings to her bow than most city blokes like you do.' Angus tried to lighten the atmosphere.

'As if I haven't enough to think about.'

'Gotta go Angus. Let Barry know I'll take a room if he asks.'

'I will Cassie. I will.'

'Shit, is she from another planet?' Tom felt out of his depth.

Angus cracked a wry smile. 'Put it this way, Cassie has hung out with more interesting people than I have in my lifetime and for someone of her age, that's saying somethin'. She also has a real feel for nature, an uncanny knack, for want of a better description, to listen to and read the landlines and songlines, especially around these mountains.'

'Spooky huh? What are songlines?'

'It's a bit like being in tune.' Angus avoided the question. 'You could learn a few things from her you know. She's a real Snowy girl.'

'I wish.'

'You'll be out of gaol son, before you know it. Like I said, we've got to play their game to get them off your tail. There'll be nothing more embarrassin' for them than havin' someone on the outside comin' on board to spring an innocent kid like you from the clink.'

'Wish I felt as confident as you Angus. I haven't got anything except my word and they've got all the evidence.'

A solitary raven landed outside the kitchen door. Angus threw it some bread and watched as the bird hungrily picked it up. He looked at Tom, his eye alert and glowing blue. The crow jerked his head from right to left sussing out the young man. He cawed loudly at Angus, then flew off towards the Boloco Church in search of the rest of his flock.

Angus watched the bird fly off then walked outside where he had picked the bread off the ground. He bent over to pick up a large, glossy black feather, perfect in formation.

'This must be for you son. Keep it with you in gaol.'

Tom took the feather, fingering it and smoothing the feather along its spine. 'Didn't know ravens had such amazing feathers.' He looked up at Angus and smiled, placing the feather behind his left ear.

PRISON

Sean felt the sweat prickle on the back of his neck, despite the early morning chill still hanging in the air. The memory of the night on the Melbourne wharf was still fresh and Sean was worried that questioning in the dock might link Tom with his relatively unknown past, more precisely Melbourne. Now the boy would be slated, with the ill-timed and undeserved encounter with the law.

Without ID, without a reasonable explanation for his life on the Monaro plains, Tom's former life would easily be uncovered and with it, questions to possibly trace him back to the hotel and the death of the Priest. Sean did not want questions, and although there was nothing to indicate that Tom had any part in the events leading to the disappearance of the Priest the worry was, that Tom had a mode of transport to the Monaro, and Sean was that mode and link.

Sean momentarily toyed with the idea of lying low during the court hearing and allowing Angus to go with Tom into Cooma to face the judge. The boy was doing well, exceptionally well with new friends and there was, in both Sean and Angus's minds, abundant hope for his future. This was a setback. Nothing more. It was a glitch that would be forgotten almost as quickly as it had happened.

Sean realised that the misadventure in the park, a humiliating appearance at the court and harrowing time in gaol, was more than likely, fate's mercy to protect him from the discovery of crime and drugs. This was the all too frequent course that young men took and especially as they accidentally uncovered the hidden pains of their respective pasts. More than one good man had died under the influence of the bottle. Tom was no exception. He would be even more vulnerable to addiction as a result of the abuse in his past. The priest had put Tom at risk. The drug dealer was different. He was a grubby little so and so as were his mates.

Sean heaved himself out of the bed and into his boots and trousers. The crows' cries continued to echo from the sides of the valley as they flew steadily northwards pre-empting the mood of the day. Tom was already up and about in the kitchen, sitting at the table and picking at his toast and eggs.

Angus tended to the fire, making as little fuss as necessary. His natural talent was to fill the morning with a sense of the normal, the everyday — routines that would calm the spirit of the boy and instil in him memories of his new home that he could draw upon whilst he was in gaol.

'Mornin' Sean. Crows are ahead of us it seems.'

'The crows?'

'You must have heard them. Big flock heading along the valley.'

'Aye, I did Angus. Mournful soundin' if you ask me.'

'If you ask Cassie, they're a good omen for Tom.' Angus sounded commendably cheerful.

Sean laughed. 'Good god man. You have some interestin' angles on life.'

'Sean, put it this way. If Cassie is right, and I think she is, then Tom's life is in good hands.'

'You mean, better than ours?'

'We are just the mortal men that house and feed him for now. There are others out there looking after this one. He's special, no doubt about it.'

Tom picked up the enamel mug, blowing softly on the hot tea

sweetened with a generous helping of honey. The tea was warming and for a moment, he was lost in the familiar comfort of the presence of the two men that he trusted and had grown to feel secure with. The toast suddenly appeared again in front of him and Tom looked up briefly to catch Angus's soft and compassionate eyes. Then he returned soundlessly to his breakfast, grateful that there was nothing between them that could be said.

'Are you comin' in to Cooma then Sean?'

'I'll be comin' in. Can't have Tom face the judge by himself now can we.'

'You'll probably get your chance to put your side of the story Tom. They'll listen. However without an alibi, in the ultimate analysis, it's your word against Will's. No doubt that little piece of horseshit will have armfuls of excuses.'

'No doubt he will.' Tom cut into the conversation. 'He will get his. Later.'

'Now don't you start thinkin' that you have to mete out justice or revenge, Tom. You leave that to the crows and those who talk to them.' Angus said with a broad smile.

Angus parked the ute outside the Courthouse and together they walked the path to the hewn steps that climbed up to the graceful old building. The Court was only used once a month when the Magistrate, at his discretion, listened to cases that could not be heard or solved otherwise. Along both sides of the steps people lounged in small groups, waiting for the big doors (that always remained firmly shut apart from hearing days), to swing open and admit them and their supporters to hear the charges.

Sean was the first to note the small group of Aboriginal men sitting on one side of the steps and among them, a young man who looked clearly distressed. The two older men sitting with him were silent, their eyes embracing the scene and at the same time, fixed far away as if on a distant point. The older of the two men looked straight into Sean. He felt a sudden chill as if the man knew everything about him, then the eyes softened with a slight warning mixed with comfort that instantly eased his fears for Tom. Angus, close to his heels, felt the exchange between the two men and placed his hand on Sean's shoulder.

'You sure you want to be here man? We can meet later at Sharp's if you want. Take a round of the town. There's no need for us both to be here.'

Sean hesitated and again, the old man met his eyes, nodding slightly and then acknowledging Angus.

'OK then. I'll disappear for now.' As he turned to go, a police officer emerged from the office of the Clerk. Sean broke his step almost imperceptibly and the old Aboriginal man rose and walked down the steps between them, shielding Sean from the view of the policeman. He stopped, fumbling with something in his pocket, stooping to pick up an imaginary coin then again rising to his full and noble height as Sean crossed the road and headed into the car park behind the hotel.

Angus stopped at the top of the steps with Tom then turned around to observe the old Aboriginal man walking steadily back towards them. He turned briefly to note that Sean was nowhere to be seen.

The Aboriginal man sat down with his group and nodded calmly.

'OK son?' Angus asked.

'Yeah I'm fine. Sean?'

'We'll catch up later. It's better.'

'Who's that.' Tom nodded towards the Aboriginal man and his group.

'Locals. They'll keep an eye out for you.'

The old man pulled a feather from his jacket and held it out to

Tom. Tom looked at him not knowing how to respond. The man smiled and indicated gently for Tom to come and claim the feather.

'Go on then Tom. He wants to give it to you.' Angus softly prompted him.

Tom stepped forward and for a few seconds was pulled to the kind old face; the lines crinkled beneath white hair, the mouth was upturned and the broad nose slightly flared with humor. Without conscious thought he put his hand forwards and accepted the feather from the old man's hand.

'For you. Keep it with the other one.' The old man said.

Astonished, Tom turned back to Angus and the old man and his friends got up and together walked down the Courthouse steps and towards the supermarket where their women stood waiting for them to return.

'Who's next?' The magistrate boomed.

'Tom Keating.' The Clerk turned to the judge. 'Charged with possession.' 'Tom Keating.' The clerk turned and shouted into the mostly empty courtroom.

Tom stood up as he would at school when his name was called.

'Up here and make it quick.' The Clerk called out.

'Go on. I'm with you.' Angus supported him.

Tom walked along the opening between the seats and stood where the Clerk motioned.

'Could you tell the court your name.'

'Tom. Tom Keating.'

'Age?'

'18 Sir.' Tom hardly blinked.

'Address.'

'Dalgety sir.'

'Occupation.'

'Pub maintenance.'

'Right. Then you were apprehended at Cooma Park on 18

June this year. You were found with a commercial quantity of amphetamines on your person. Is that correct?'

'I was in Centennial Park yes, Your Honour.'

'You were found with a commercial quantity of drugs on your person. Is that or is that not correct?'

'Yes sir, but…'

'Tom Keating. You are charged with possession of a commercial quantity of amphetamines. Do you have anything to answer?'

'They're not mine sir.'

'Then what were they doing in your pocket?'

'I don't even know how they got there.' Tom attempted.

'How did you come by that quantity of drugs son if you don't do drugs? You'd better come up with something better than that.' The judge continued. 'Do you know Mr Tom Keating, how many young lives you have probably harmed by already carrying and almost certainly dealing in drugs?'

'No sir I…'

'Do you know how long you would be spending in gaol except that this is your first offence?'

'I didn't…'

'You didn't what? You didn't have any drugs on your person when you were apprehended by the police or you didn't stop to think about how many young people's lives you have already destroyed?' The judge began to redden.

'The drugs were planted on me.' Tom blurted out.

'That's very funny, however I hardly think it's a believable story. So just who do you think planted these drugs on you?'

'I don't know sir. I was just…'

'You were just what? Waiting to meet someone in the park?' Do you know how long it takes and how much police time and resources are wasted on people like you?'

'Sir…'

'Don't interrupt. Just let this be a warning young man. I don't want you back in this court, ever. Because if I see you again, it won't just be 6 months but you can think about 5 years. Is that clear?

'Yes sir.'

Tom shrugged his shoulders feeling trapped by the emptiness of the court. There was no jury sitting and the only other 'third party' was the policeman who had manhandled him into the car and later charged him with possession.

'The police report says that this is your first time. Is that so?'

'Yes sir. I mean, no I...'

'So you're unlucky. First time. Let it also be the last time you're here in my court. I don't like drugs and I don't like dealers. As far as I'm concerned the sooner both are off the streets, the better. Six months, non-parole. Next.'

'But...'

'Next!' The judge was in no mood for arguing a case that was already closed.

Tom felt the world close in around him like a black cloud. Angus was already by his side, taking his elbow and leading him back to the seat. 'That's it then son. You will have to do some time. You're not alone, remember that. I'll be here to see you as much as I can. Cassie will come in too. Mark my words.'

'What about Sean...' Tom felt close to tears.

'We'd best keep him out of this son. He's better to lie low considering the profile he's had in the past.'

'You'll be back at sea.' Tom began to panic.

'Tom. We'll get it sorted out. Fast. I promise.' Angus looked him straight in the eyes.

Tom was literally lost for words.

'You ready to come with us son?' The police officer stepped forwards.

'No cuffs.' Angus stepped in between them.

'We'll look after him from here.' The police officer bristled as Angus glared at him.

'I'll be checking up on you also from time to time.' Angus barked back at the policeman.

'This way.' The police officer pulled Tom by the arm.

'Sean…'

'Don't worry about him Tom. He'll be OK.'

Angus watched as Tom was ushered out the back of the courtroom. He felt a momentary sense of panic wondering if this was the straw that would break the boy. He was only weeks out of Melbourne and for the first time, over the past week since Tom had met Cassie, Angus had felt any sense of genuine hope that he would emerge, from the hellhole of betrayal and desperation. The boy was deeply attached to Sean and it was clear that the sudden separation would be an additional trauma for him on top of the unfair trial with no chance for his defence. Gaol was no place for someone as vulnerable and raw as Tom.

But as Tom was led out of the courtroom, a sudden feeling of strength visited him as if willed to him from another place. The rough push of the police officer hardly registered as he recalled the dark and intense eyes of the old Aboriginal man. Tom placed his hand in his pocket and the loose fringe of the crow feather greeted his fingers like a close friend, soothing and quietening his feelings. For an instant, he toyed with the idea of breaking free from the company of the law, and running back into the wide streets of Cooma where he would find Angus and Sean, steady and sure mates who would simply take him home. Then he realised that he couldn't run, not from the gaol nor from his feelings. He would have to tough it out — forge his resolve to resist like iron any temptation to weaken within himself.

Tom awoke to the feel of a cold hand on the back of his leg almost at the point in his dream when the crow pecked urgently at the window of his room in Angus's house. He sat up in bed with a start, swivelling around and with the force of the surprise pushing the man off him and onto the floor.

'Steady on! You were crying out in your sleep. Calling for someone. Sean is it?' the man sniggered, 'I thought I had better come across and see if you were OK.' He wiped the spittle off his chin.

'What do you want?' Tom almost screamed.

'Shh. No point in waking all the rest of them. You've already had me awake for half the night.' The man hissed putting a hand on Tom's mouth.

'Get off me!' Tom pushed the hand away.

'Now now! No need to get nasty. You should thank me that you're in here with me. Had a word with the gov'. You look too green to be in there with them.'

'I don't need your help. Just leave me alone.' Tom pulled the blanket over his body and up to his chin. His eyes widened with horror as he realised that the man had almost come into his bed, his hand awakening memories that he thought that he would never have to revisit; not now, not ever. He felt himself break out into a cold sweat. Experience warned him he could flick off the unwanted attentions, with the excuse of illness if nothing else. 'Look. I'm carrying.'

'Carrying? What do you mean?'

'I slept with someone I didn't know. About a month ago. So I'm carrying.'

'What have you got then?'

'Thought you knew. Isn't that why they put me in with you.' Tom quickly put a story together.

'You little shit. You don't know who you're talking to do you.

Just mind your mouth around me and don't you make any more noise or I'll find something to tell the governor to make it real hard for you here. Then you'll be carrying more than…'

'More than what? A slug like you trying to get on me in the middle of the night?'

The man stood over Tom, his face contorted into a cruel grimace. He put his fist close to Tom's face forcing him back against the mattress, ready to pummel him on his pillow. Tom turned his face sideways, more at the fetid smell of the man's breath than the threat of a punching. He pulled his knees to his chest and kicked out, his feet moving fast as he swung his body towards the man. His right foot connected with the man's chin and the left with his stomach.

Almost the second the prisoner hit the floor, the guard was outside the cell.

'What's goin' on in there? You tryin' to wake up the entire town?' The guard yelled into the cell.'

'He tried to go at me.' Tom yelled.

'Tricky! What are you up to? Did you touch the boy?'

'Nah. Just checking on him. Kid needs a bit of comfort on his first night.'

'Get back to your own bunk or you'll be on your own for another month.' The guard was ready to take nothing.

'Said he was carrying.' Tricky rubbed his jaw.

'You got something you want to give me then son?' The guard suddenly started.

'I haven't got anything! I just want him off me. That's all.'

'OK then. I'll be looking in on you Tricky. Keep your hands to yourself if you know what's good for you!' The guard thumped his fist on the cell door. 'Back to sleep young man.' The guard softened slightly.

Tom was not entirely convinced, but climbed back onto his bed.

'Don't worry. He won't do anything while I'm here and we'll get you looked after properly in the morning. Go on. Back to sleep. Not a sound out of you Tricky. I'll throw more than solitary at you if you're not careful!' The guard warned him before slamming the cell door shut behind him.

At first light, the guard returned to the cell with another man, who looked more like a doctor than a gaoler.

'This is him. I want him away from Tricky. Only place we've got free is the sick bay.

'You said Tricky had lost his wandering hands habit.'

'I don't want any trouble. Not on my shift and not in my gaol. I want the boy somewhere out of here so they can't get to him. My application for transfer is in and I'll be buggered if old Tricky is going to put a spanner in my works.'

'Whatever you say. It had better be good though. I'll need to put something convincing in my report.'

'Just say that he had a seizure in the middle of the night. Drug withdrawal. Something like that will do. I just want him out of this cell before the change of shift. After that, there's every chance I won't be able to keep Tricky off him.'

'If you have to write your own report, just stick to the same story. Seizure. Relocated to the sick bay for observation.'

'Thanks Doc. Really appreciate it. Come on then boy. We're putting you in the hospital room until we can work out what caused you to have a fit in the middle of the night.'

Tom, too confused by the rapid change in events to argue or ask, looked blankly at the guard then at the doctor.

'Bring your things. You'll need your toothbrush. I want you in the hospital wing for the next couple of days until we sort out whether you should be here or in the main hospital.'

Tom said nothing. The good omens that had accompanied the

feather talisman were clearly working more quickly than he had imagined possible. He put his trousers on, collected the standard issue toiletries then put on his socks and shoes. He stood up and walked to the cell door feeling as much relief as when Sean whisked him out of the Melbourne pub and away from the sickening priest.

The social worker walked into the sick bay, ushered in by the prison governor.

'We're not sure what brought on the fits, if you talk to him for a bit, you should be able to work out the background. I don't want him dying on me in his first week. The prison's only just reopened and I don't need the publicity Kate.'

'I'll need to see the doctor's report.'

'I'll get it brought down to you. Try to find out what he's been taking will you. If he's in detox it could help.'

Tom lay on his back staring at the ceiling and tracing the patterns of light that broke and disappeared as the door opened to let in the social worker then closed again as the Governor departed and left them alone. He felt strangely comfortable and carefree, as if the spirit of the Aboriginal man had taken him under his wing. The unfamiliar comfort immobilised him into an unusual obedience. He felt no desire to resist or move. The thought lingered at the back of his mind to reject and refute the renewed sense of safety but the effort was not worth it. Then the social worker was talking, quietly at first, noting the details of his files, then directly to him.

'Sean. They said that you were calling out to Sean, Tom. Who's Sean?'

'Sean?'

'Hmm. You don't remember?'

'I just remember that rock spider. Tricky.'

'The social worker put down the file and pulled a chair up to the bed. 'Did you say rock spider?'

'He was climbing on top of me when I woke up.' Tom shuddered.

'You could have imagined it Tom. If you were fitting — you might have been hallucinating at the same time.'

'I wasn't hallucinating.'

'Have you been injecting?' The social worker pulled up the sleeve of his left arm.

'I don't do that.'

'You sure are a confused young man. Holding back the truth is not going to help me to help you.'

'I told you, I don't need anyone's help. I just want to go home. Angus had some work lined up for me and I want to get started. Then Sean and I are going to build a house. So we have our own place to live.'

'So there is a Sean.'

'Sean's me mate. Couldn't do much without him.'

'Tom, do you realise how serious it is to be in gaol? You don't look as though you know what you've got yourself into. Once you're in here, there's a good likelihood that you'll be back.'

'I shouldn't even be here.' Tom started to become anxious again. 'Some guy just planted the gear on me.'

'You mean you're not dealing anything?' The social worker was mildly patronising, a tone not lost on Tom.

'You don't believe me either do you? That's the difference. Sean believes in me. So that's how come I must have been dreaming about him, before the crow came to the window?'

'Crow?'

'Yeah. The crow.' Tom pulled the feather from under the pillow. 'See this. An old Aboriginal guy gave me this.' Tom stroked the feather, marvelling at its total blackness.

'Really? Did he tell you his name?

'Nope. He was sitting on the steps before I went into the Court House. He gave me this.'

'He gave you a feather. Did you know that there's an Aboriginal guy visits here? He usually does a session after Andrew and Wendy.'

'No.' Tom shook his head. 'Who's Andrew and Wendy anyway?'

'They're here this morning. Run a sort of relaxation thing. You want to go?'

'Me?'

'Can't hurt' Kate smiled, her friendly face surprising and relieving Tom in his moment of anxiety.

''Spose.' Tom smiled back.

'Good. I'll come and get you at ten. Have your breakfast. Can't meditate if you're fasting. You'd probably faint, especially if you've been fitting.'

Tom felt like bursting into laughter. The feeling of relief washing over him was like nothing he had experienced in his life. He wondered what it would be like to float off the bed and touch the ceiling. Then a warden crashed into the room with a tray covered with a metal food protector.

'Breakfast. Eat it all. There's nothing here that you can feed the crows with even if you wanted to.

'Breakfast?'

'We're not putting you in gaol to starve you! You hardly look seventeen man. How are you going to fill out without food?'

'Guess you're right.' Tom buried his head in the plate of food to avoid the topic of his age. 'Mmm. Toast and eggs.'

'Orange juice in the jug. Thought you'd prefer it to water.'

'Thanks!' Tom looked at the warden with gratitude.

The warden smiled dropping his head slightly. Then he stood quietly as Tom started on his food.

'You don't look as though you belong here Tom' he said softly.

'What did you say?' Tom looked up.

'What are you doing inside?'

'Don't know.'

'What were you done for?'

'Drugs.'

'Dealing?'

'Possession.'

'Don't look like you've had many drugs to me. Most of them on the inside look as though they are wearing their livers on their faces.' The warden laughed.

Tom allowed himself to laugh a bit with the warden.

'You know, eyes hanging down' the warden pulled the bottom lids of his eyes into a Dracula formation. 'And yellow!'

'Nothin' on my arms. Look.' Tom pushed up his sleeve.

The warden grabbed his arm and pretended to closely examine him for puncture marks. 'Hmmm. Shoot up your bum do you?'

Tom recoiled pulling his arm back from the warden.

'Hey. I heard about Tricky. We'll do him, don't you worry about it. He didn't touch you did he?'

Tom was not keen on responding, more than the memory of the prisoner suddenly intruding into his mind. His eyes clouded over and his hand shook as he tried to lift the fork to his mouth.

'Put it down Tom. Do you want to talk about it?'

'No, I don't!'

'Look. You shouldn't be in here I agree, but there's more going on isn't there. Someone do something to you in the past?

Tom said nothing as he struggled to keep the tears under control.

'OK then. I'll let you off for now. It will come out in the end. Better you talk to Kate or Wendy when she comes in.'

Tom was forlorn and confused, suddenly uninterested in eating, the feeling of dejection catching up with him faster than any prospects of being moved out of Tricky's way. The warden understood breakfast was over and packed up the mobile food camp. Tom stared at the door as the warden left him alone on the hospital bed, strangely safe although lost in the world of hopelessness and grief that he had hardly recognised, let alone come to terms with.

'You had better get dressed now Tom.' Kate announced as she walked into the room.

Tom looked up as she walked in. He had hardly moved his position since the warden left with the unfinished breakfast tray.

'Come on Tom. I'm not going to dress you. I know the colours are a bit drab.' She raised a sympathetic eyebrow.

'Yeah. OK. Give me a minute will you.'

Kate walked away from the bed to give Tom some privacy, busying herself with the curtain that masked the hospital room from the more extraordinary realities taking place in the courtyard. She smiled internally, wondering if Tom was ready for the humorous shock awaiting him.

'The toilet door is behind you. Not much furniture in there though. Do you shave?'

'Yeah, I shave.'

'Just promise me it will be a light brush and no deep cuts thanks Tom.'

'I wasn't planning to cut my throat if that's what you meant!' Tom croaked.

'Just checking kiddo. You're my responsibility for the time being.'

Tom disappeared into the 'bathroom' and flushed the toilet. Satisfied that the running water could provide him temporary cover and privacy he continued, finally relieving himself without the fear of unwanted interruption. The morning seemed to be a remake of the subconscious pattern of dysfunctional fears that had haunted him from the time that the abuse had begun. He was not obsessive, but this morning, extra careful about the timing and exposure of his bathroom visit, grateful only that Kate was a woman and therefore unlikely to approach him as the Priest or Tricky had.

He quickly washed his hands then face, checking the overnight growth forming as a soft shadow on his face. The razor was a simple, throw away blade and Tom wondered how Kate had guessed the thoughts of suicide that had already crossed his mind. Carefully, he lathered the hand soap onto his face then tentatively drew the blade across his right cheek. Then he continued over his chin before shaving the other cheek and quickly taking the light cover off his neck. Then he washed his face thoroughly, splashing more than enough water to wash off the remnants of soap and hair before turning off the tap and drying his face and hands. He walked back into the room and faced Kate.

'Do you get new underclothes in this place?'

'Thought they would have kitted you out.'

'Nope.'

'Can you handle it for this morning. I'll have a word to them.'

'Thanks Kate.' Tom sounded unusually mature.

'Then you're ready.'

'What's to do this morning?'

'Quick exercise-break in the courtyard. I'll stay with you. Then we go into the group session.'

'Group session?'

'Relaxation.'

'In the middle of the day?'

'Nothing to worry about. Just a gentle introduction to 'self' Tom.'

'As if I need to relax. I just wanna get out of here.'

'Then you definitely need to relax, Tom. You've got to learn to handle the highs and lows young man. You're going nowhere for six months, not unless the Doc decides to shift you to hospital.

'Come on then. We're going for the fresh air and exercise routine in the courtyard. Ever seen a woman's upper body?'

'What?'

'Tom. There's a trannie in the lock up. She's really beautiful on the outside, but on the inside, she's probably still a bit of a bloke. In here for drugs like you, so stay well away. They've probably got you sussed already and she might try it on you. So just look, don't perve, and keep on moving yeah?'

'What in the f' is a trannie?'

'Boy you are green. You can't tell me you've never heard of transvestites?' Kate smiled at him.

'You mean sex change numbers.'

'You got it. She sure has that sorted with lots of extra on the top half thanks to surgery. Silicone job.'

Tom laughed. 'That's one way to learn the ABC's I suppose.'

'Thought I'd better warn you. Think you've had enough shocks so far.' Kate grinned.

'Yeah.'

'OK. This is what we'll do. Walk into the courtyard. Look normal. Don't stare or make eye contact with anyone. We walk a couple of rounds, then we go to the group room and you sit down and wait. Act like you do it every day of your life all right. You'll be noticed as the new kid on the block but you gotta pretend it's like you've been here every day for the last year OK.'

'Yeah OK. If you think it will help.'

Kate walked to the door and called for the warden.

'I'm taking Tom to the group session then I'll bring him straight back.'

The warden pushed a book under Kate's nose. 'Sign here.'

Kate took the pen and signed and handed the pen back to the warden.

'I don't like new inmates in hospital. If he's not fit, move him onto secure care outside until he's fit. Too many forms to fill out when things go wrong.'

'I don't want any trouble either. I'll need more to hang secure care on than just 'fits and hallucinations'. Anyone would have bad dreams in this old castle.'

'Yeah. Tell me about it. Get out then. Both of you.'

'Follow me Tom.' Kate walked into the sunlit courtyard with Tom close at her heels. The courtyard was bare and curiously inviting as clusters of prisoners loosened up after a night in the cells. A few prisoners tossed a ball around, the rest happy to look on or do their solo exercise routines. Tom walked with his head down until a soft wolf whistle broke the morning activity buzz.

'Don't react.' Kate quickly warned.

The second whistle was louder.

'Hey new boy. She likes you.'

Tom swung around as Tricky pointed to the woman sitting, topless, in the sun.

'You'd be better with her than me mate.' Tom yelled back.

'Settle Tom. You don't want your face broken up.' Kate broke her step to stand beside him.

'What did you say you little prick?'

'Don't answer him Tom. Please!' Kate caught him under the elbow moving him quickly towards the far end of the courtyard.

'If you're looking for a screw, try her and not me.' Tom emphasized his point.

'You been touchin' up the new boy Tricky?' A quiet voice softened the atmosphere now thick with anger. 'Thought you got over that one.' A thin man with white cropped hair stepped into the courtyard. 'What's yer name kiddo? Mine's Andrew.'

'This is Tom, Andrew. He's here for group.'

'Tom is it? Good name. Tricky won't be coming today so we need another person to make the numbers match. That's good isn't it Tricky!' Andrew smiled broadly then nodded at the woman still sunning herself. 'Hi Petal. Good day for a sunbake. This is Tom and he doesn't like you. Well, that's the courtyard for today.' Andrew looked quickly around the group. 'Ten minutes everyone, except Tricky and see you inside. Tricky you can keep Petal company since she might faint if she relaxes any more than she already is.' Andrew turned around and headed back under the canopy of stone.

'That's Andrew Tom. He's all right and so is Wendy. You comin' then? Or are you going to stand there gawping all morning.'

'Sorry. Uh…'

'You've never seen a lady before.' Kate chuckled.

'She's…'

'She's naked and dealing drugs Tom. Clear?'

'What now?'

'Keep your arse and your nose clean. You'll have to learn to defend yourself and tell them to back off. No favours for or from anyone. OK? You'll be on your own and that means no give and no take. Just do what the warden tells you and mind your own business. Then you'll be out of here with a clean bill and no more scars.'

'Scars?'

'I'm thinking about the inner scars you're carrying Tom. You've obviously got a few of those so use the time to heal them and not open up new wounds.'

'This is too much.'

'Let's go and see Andrew.'

'Who's he anyway?'

'Drama teacher.'

'Drama?'

'Act out your foibles, fears and fantasies mate. Get them out of your system before they destroy you.

'Psychodrama? Thought this was just a stare at your navel session.'

Kate chuckled. 'Well, let's just see what Andrew has in store. Here we are.' Kate pushed opened the door. Andrew was busy fiddling with his CD machine, his white head bent over the buttons. A thinnish woman in track pants moved chairs into a rough circle then lit a stick of incense.

'That one sounds soothing Andrew.' Wendy announced.

'Should be relaxing enough. Do you think they'd be better lying on the floor Wendy?'

'Yeah they might. Could put the cushions around.'

'We might do some breathing before and after the relaxation part.'

'Hello.' Wendy noticed Kate and Tom in the room.

'Oh this is Tom, Wendy.' Andrew's head bobbed up from his machine.

'Hi.'

'Hi.' Tom responded still slightly nervous.

'Tom joined us last night Wendy. He's in the sick bay for a while. Fits and so on. Relaxation might help.'

'Oh. I'm sorry.' Wendy said sympathetically.

'I'll be OK.'

'Tricky had a go Wendy. So he's banned from today's session. Left him with Petal for the morning.'

Kate patted Tom on the back. 'Let's sit down Tom. We'll just wait for the others.'

'Make yourself comfortable. Andrew? You ready?'

'Huh? Yeah. Let's have some meditation before the rest arrive.' Andrew turned the music volume higher then seated himself where he could see the men entering the room and easily reach the machine. 'Aah. That's better.' Andrew raised his arms as if to a presence in the room. 'Mmm. Just relaaax...' Andrew dived into his unconscious self, his eyes already turning upwards, the lids closing in response to his well-trained meditations.

Tom drifted on a wave of notes more beautiful than anything he had heard in a long time. For some reason, he felt totally safe with Andrew, as if he'd already understood him, as if he had read his story and not reacted, taking it in the morning flow of events and allowing him space just to be. He was semi-aware of the arrival of the rest of the inmates, yet too relieved to be away from Tricky to care. He stretched his legs further in front of him, breathed in deeply, then let his breath go and slipped for a few minutes, into the haze of semi-consciousness where there were no dreams to trouble him.

'Aaaauuumm.' Andrew held the note until Wendy and one of the veteran meditators in the group began the chant. 'Aaaummm.' Andrew repeated the chant, a note lower.

'Aaaaauum.' The group began to hum, individuals finding their note one by one.

'Aaummm.' Kate joined in a little higher than Andrew and closer to Wendy's range of comfort.

The chant continued with tones moving in and out of the general hum until several of the men dropped out, leaving only the veteran and Andrew to finish the chant.

'OK everyone. Eyes open.' Andrew said. 'Everyone back here with us? Tom?'

Tom remained silent, unsure yet curious.

'This is Tom everyone. He's new and in hospital for now. You'll get to meet a bit later on. Now. We're going to do the breathe in and breathe out exercise. Find a spot on the floor. There's plenty of room so don't cuddle up too close OK?'

'Shit Andrew. Thought this was me only chance!'

'You just keep yer hands to yerself Peter. You should be meditatin' anyway, not looking to score.'

'Jeez Andrew. You spoil everything.'

'Now everyone. Lie down and find a spot on the ceiling. Everyone got that?

'Yeah.'

'Wendy, do you want to look after Tom. Kate and I'll keep an eye on the rest of 'em.' Andrew suggested.

'That's it everyone. Now just think that your legs are weighted down to the floor, as though there is a bit of lead in yer boots. Got that?'

'Might as well be lead and chains.'

'That's the idea. Watch your breath. Breathe in... and out. Breathe in... and out. Nice and slowly. In...and out.' Andrew talked them into a half somnolent doze.

The room was buzzing with a comfortable quietness that Andrew knew meant the guys were sinking deeper.

'Breathing slowly...in...and out......in...and out.' Andrew talked them deeper. 'Watch your breath. Taking a deep breath. Breathing from the bottom of your diaphragm...drawing the breath deeply to the base of your stomach. Now letting go. Let all the air out. Watch the breath leave your body. As you let the breath go, watch all the negative feelings go with it. Another deep breath. Breathing in. That's it. Let the chest wall rise by itself. This time, letting out your anger as you breathe out. Letting go, letting the chest wall fall as the air flows out.' Andrew paused for breath.

He quickly glanced around the room to make sure that the inmates were positioned, as he wanted them, on their backs and completely immobile. He let out a breath of relief.

'This time when you breathe in, breathe in the light. Let it fill your lungs and then watch the light as it travels down your limbs, down your arms, into your fingers and toes. That's right. Just fill up with light with every in breath, make it slow and steady. This time you'll notice that your feet and legs start to feel floaty, as if there is cloud around your feet.'

'No!!'

Tom's sudden cry broke the atmosphere Andrew had induced through the relaxation response.

'Let me go!'

Andrew sprung to his feet and in less than a second was beside Wendy.

'He's regressing Andrew.'

'Just take him there. Let him go through it.'

'You blokes stay on the ground.' Andrew growled at the group. 'We're going to go through another deep in breath and slow out breath to help Tom out of his trance. OK. Feeling the light circling around your toes again. Watch the light encase your body, as if you are back in your mother's womb, only this time it's peaceful. Shit.' Andrew muttered under his breath.

It was OK if they were all going through it at the same time. This was different, to have someone new, flipping back to a past life or whatever, was not on the program as far as he was concerned.

'You say somethin' Andrew?'

'Nothin' you were meant to hear. Just stay where you are on the floor and we're going to go through this together. We've all been here before. Remember…' Andrew dropped his voice to the soothing motherly lullaby … 'Remember what it was like…when you were wrapped in a cloak of warm velvet…'

'Not rebirthing Andrew!'

'It was so comfortable and peaceful, and the only sound was the rhythmic beating of your mother's heart…you felt totally safe, calm and protected…now just let yourself go…for now, you are not in a man's body…you are simply a tiny living spark of light covered by a baby's body…' Andrew paused, audibly breathing in and breathing out slowly…'Just stay there in that warm cocoon of safety…there's nothing to fear…you are totally calm…'

From Wendy's arms, the sound of soft crying filtered into the room. Andrew felt the men lying on the floor soften, their defences more disabled than anything he had achieved to date through the meditations. The reflex response to comfort Tom was universal, but Wendy held him loosely, giving him just enough support to provide him with a sense of safety, without suffocating and killing his natural instinct for comfort.

As she stroked his face, the crying gradually increased and suddenly, the boy was racked with deep and uncontrollable sobbing, his body writhing as if against a hidden trap. Wendy pulled him closer towards her, cradling him like a baby. Gradually, the crying began to abate, the young man spent of the pain that he had not even realised that he carried. Silently, he dropped into a soft doze, comforted by Wendy and supported by the surprising unspoken tenderness of the inmates, obediently lying motionless on the floor on their backs as if lined up together in a row on prison cots.

'Coming back now everyone. Slowly…breathing in deeply and hold for five, letting out the breathe for the count of five…four… three…two…one and back to the room. Everyone awake.'

Andrew was already on his feet, taking the position of command and dominance over the inert inmates, some of them rubbing their eyes, others, flexing their hands and feet as they had been taught to do in the past.

'OK, on ya feet everyone.' Andrew was quick to move the dynamic satisfied that Wendy had Tom well in hand.

'Shit, that was peaceful Andrew.'

For a minute, it was a struggle for Andrew to keep the circle together. He took another couple of deep breaths…drawing them mentally into silence. Seconds before Tom came back to wakefulness, the old Aboriginal man appeared again. He stood on top of a mountain covered in cascading tors of rocks that spilled down to the deep ravine of the valley where he and Sean camped on their flight from peril to paradise.

WINTER RAGE

Cassie sipped on the last of her apple cider, relishing its cool freshness. The DJ pumped out the last three tracks, building the vibe to a crescendo. The Jindy pub was packed to the max, the floor space limited to dancers with only a small number of drinkers lined against the bar. Cassie felt a familiar hand on her shoulder and she instinctively recoiled.

'Hi Cassie?' Will said casually.

'Will. I really don't want to see you. Tom's in gaol because of you!'

'Shit Cassie. Don't take it to heart.'

'Take it to heart? You planted stuff on him and now he's in gaol. What's not to take to heart Will?'

Will was suddenly dark, his eyes glaring with emotion. 'So he's more important to you than me.'

'I didn't say that Will. I just said that you did the wrong thing, OK?'

'Right. 'Spose I shouldn't have done it.'

'Exactly Will. Listen, what' going on with you. You have to give this shit up Will.'

'I can't. You know that. There's too much in it for me.'

'Get a job Will.' Cassie got up and walked out of the pub.

'Cassie, I'm going to Dalgety. You want a lift?'

'Thanks Sue. Can't get away from here fast enough.'

'Thought so. What happened?'

'Will. I can't stand him anywhere near me for the moment. I am just glad that we are going up snow camping tomorrow.'

'Yeah. Who you going with?'

'Chris and Jo. Why don't you come?'

'You got room?'

'Think so. I'll give them a bell and let you know later tonight. Leaving at 6.30 in the morning.'

'Shiiit. No wonder you're clean Cassie.' Sue checked her own head. 'Not sure if I'll feel this good tomorrow.'

'It happens that way. You will feel great tonight then tomorrow you'll start hitting the lows.'

'At least I have got my head together enough so I don't do drugs and booze at the same time.'

'That's something I suppose.'

'You drinking?'

'Apple cider.' Cassie smiled. 'Looks the same in the bottle so no one asks. Just tell them I'm drinking sweet champas. They think it's cool.'

'Yeah. Should try it I suppose.'

'Thanks for taking me home Sue. I'm well and truly over Will. He's been nothing but trouble and worry for far too long.'

'Hmm. Can't be easy. Still, he is family.'

'That's the trouble.' Cassie winced. 'I think he takes me for granted. You know, always there to rescue him from his latest crazy stunt.'

'Who's the new dude in your life?'

'Tom. But we're not going out or anything. Will just landed him in gaol.' Cassie said ruefully.

'No joke?'

'Yep. He's doing time for commercial quantity.'

'Holy hell.'

'That's about the size of it.'

'Come on.' Sue buzzed the auto-lock on the car. 'We're out of here.'

'You want me to drive Sue.' Cassie asked coolly.

'Thanks. That would be good. I'm still floating yeah?'

'Yep. Get you there. Want to stay at my place tonight?'

'I'd better go home. Mum and Dad will freak. You can take the car though. I'll just tell them that I was too tired and you drove.'

'Good plan Sue.'

'Don't mention it Cass.' Sue struggled to keep her thoughts in her head. 'Stay at my place if you want to.'

'Thanks Sue.' Cassie felt brighter all of a sudden. 'This road is OK at night. Look at the stars!'

'Love the stars.' Sue said deliriously.

'Reckon each star is one of us Sue. Where's yours?'

'Alpha Centuri. Gorgeous.'

Cassie laughed. 'Bit difficult to beat that act!' She skilfully negotiated the curve over the dam wall and dropped back the gears to take the long haul past the lake and towards Berridale.

'How come we're going this way Cassie?'

'Bit less risky. Just the two of us, and no cars to speak of on the back road. Besides, they do good Chinese takeaway in Berridale. Feel like some?'

'Cool.' Sue drifted.

Cassie accelerated out of the last of the long Jindabyne curves onto the plateau climbing steadily towards the range. She let the car cruise easily over Barney's, freewheeling into Berridale. Sue was totally asleep by the time they reached the tiny commercial centre but Cassie pulled in outside the club and quickly walked in to order takeaway. Five minutes later, she was back to the car heading out on the link road to Dalgety. Life wasn't all that bad. It felt good to have Tom in her life, even though this was a rough start for him, new to the area then being set up by her brother and finding himself in gaol. But Angus had assured her that they would go in to Cooma and to the gaol together to visit Tm until she felt strong enough to go in by herself. It would take time, however there was plenty of courage in her heart, enough to overcome her natural apprehension. Tom needed her and that was all she knew.

RIDING HIGH

Will skied off the bottom of the snowboard park and back onto the Cruiser Chair at Thredbo. The village was unusually quiet, the heavy and torrential rains washing away the good snow cover and dropping tons of dust blown in from the drought stricken plains of Victoria. The snow was dirty, slushy and heavy, as if someone had poured buckets of warm waste over the slopes, liberally scattering streaks of brown and turning the previously magical white winter laden mountain to a running, weather-beaten sore. Will had had enough for the morning, sick of having no challenge and sicker still now that his own sister Cassie had given him the flick. The heavy feeling of bitter anger sat heavily on his chest. He hacked up yellow-brown sputum onto the snow, muttering to himself about the total waste of time comin' up to the mountains. Might as well get something to eat then head back to Cooma where he could brag about the brilliant runs and new daredevil tricks he had learned at the snowboard park. He careered down the last run onto the Flat, nearly wiping out a beginner, swearing and veering sharply right to reach the creek bridge across to the Café. There was not much activity on the deck. Most of the board and ski racks were empty as Will quickly ran his eye over the selection, wondering about an upgrade, then decided against the move. Instead, he dropped his board into the rack, loosening off his boots and tramping the residue of slush into the café. The room was virtually deserted apart from an older looking woman, turning the pasta over and checking numbers of pasties and pies in the food warmer.

'Can I help you? The woman inquired mildly.

'What's for lunch lady? Will said rudely.

'I beg your pardon!'

'I said what's on for a feed in this crap joint.'

'Let me Felicity.' A younger woman stepped forwards. 'You've got a choice today. What would you like?'

'I like you.'

The younger woman reddened but stood her ground.'

'Standard meal is $10 a plate, includes a soft drink.'

'You want me to pay $10 for this shit?'

'You can also leave.' She remained quiet her eyes summing up the character.

'I'll leave when I want to!' Will quickly rose to anger.

'Perhaps you had better go now!' The older woman glared straight at Tom.

'Not until I say so.' Tom yelled, pulling the half-carving knife from his trouser-leg pocket.

The young woman shot behind into the kitchen and to the restaurant phone. She dialled, trying to steady her fingers and voice.

'Roslyn. Call the cops will you. There's a young guy up here who has just pulled a knife.'

'You OK?'

'Just do it please. I'd better get back out there.' She put down the phone and walked calmly back to the café.

'The police are on their way so I'd suggest you put the knife away and leave. Now!' She commanded.

The older woman was sitting on a tall stool in the kitchen, her legs shaking as she struggled to regain control.

'Can't you see she's frightened. What did you have to do that for?'

'I don't give a shit about her! Where's my lunch!' Will demanded.

'Look. Just sit down and I'll bring you something. OK? Pie and chips do ya?'

'Yeah, and a coke.'

'OK. It's coming. Sit down yeah. I'll bring it to you.'

'Will reluctantly left his staging-post and sat at a table close to the counter. Diedre knew the type. She had seen them in the horse industry, lurking around the shows, no-gooders who had come from nowhere and were going nowhere. She carefully pulled the coke from the machine, filling a litre cup and pushed it to the end of the counter so that he could see it. Then she opened the food warmer and lifted out a pie and sat it on the counter. With her right hand, she reached for a warmed plate and piled a good quantity of chips on, leaving just enough room for the pie.

'Sauce?'

'Barbeque.' Will settled down slightly.

Diedre squirted the barbeque sauce over the pie then pushed the plate over the counter until it was level with the coke. Then she walked behind the counter and into the cafe, briefly smiling at the older woman who was still shaking and sitting on the stool in the kitchen. She picked up the pie and coke and put it down in front of the young man.

'You probably won't need a knife and fork, you've already got one yeah? I'll get you a serviette though.' The manageress somehow managed both humour and courtesy.

Will nonplussed by her calm and mature nature, succumbed to the immediate challenge of chips, the pie and a coke, but kept his right hand wrapped around the handle of the knife.

'Hey you. Sit there.' Will pointed with the knifed hand at the chair, his mouth already half-stuffed full of food.

'Is this for real? You've got more than you can handle on your plate already haven't you.'

'I said sit. Don't want you pulling the kitchen hardware on me.'

'Hardly!'

'What's your name?'

'Not telling. Yours?

'Diedre.' She paused sitting gingerly on the chair opposite him, keeping her eye on the hand and knife. 'You worried about something?'

'What do you mean? I'm OK.'

'You don't look your best. You do drugs.'

'Deal. How much do you want?'

'Depends how much it is?'

'Serious?'

'Depends how good the gear is.'

'How do I know you're really it? You might be just setting me up. Shit, my head!'

'I can get you a Panadol.'

'Must have been last night.'

'Drinking?'

'Rage party.'

'Yeah? Jindy?'

'There was some good stuff going down this time. A bit rough though. '

'I'm sorry.'

'You're sorry! What about me?'

'What happened?' Diedre's tone soothed him.

'Me sister won't talk to me anymore. Some blow in she met at the woolshed dance.'

'Hmm. He must have had an influence on her.'

'Shithead. He's in gaol now though.'

'For real!'

'Did him. Planted the stuff. Cops got him.'

Diedre caught her breath the mind spinning quickly for a quick escape from the imminent explosion from the young man in front of her. 'Hell. Better turn the pasta. Want some more chips.'

'Cool.'

Tom was too self-absorbed to notice her quick exit from all hell about to break loose.

'Hey. Pass your plate will you.' Diedre successfully diverted his attention.'

'Where's the lady?'

'I sent her downstairs. She doesn't need to be here.' Diedre protected her chef, again calmly walking to the side of the counter and discreetly signally for her to disappear and lock the door behind.

'You going back up?'

'Nuh. Snow's shit. Might go to the bar for a drink.'

'Yeah. When you've had your lunch, I'll let you out the back way.

'Cool.'

'Go now before the cops arrive.'

'Yeah. Suppose I should.'

'Here. Give me your plate. I'll put the rest of the chips into a takeaway for you.' Diedre deftly lifted the lunch pack from under the counter and put out her other hand to take the plate. 'I'll just put some tape on that.' She walked towards the kitchen to check that the chef had left. She had, the kitchen was empty apart from dishes stacked ready for the afternoon shift to complete dish picking after the lunch rush.

Will followed Diedre through the café kitchen down the back steps to the riverside exit. There was the usual types of people walking along the broad footpath, some hampered by their ski boots and skis, others waiting for the resort bus that trafficked them to and from the beginner's slopes to the terminal in the village. There was nothing unusual in the flow of skiers, boarders and contractors busily carting out rubbish, linen and cleaning equipment around the various lodges. The car park was virtually deserted and Will quickly cast his eye around to see if any boards or boots had been inadvertently left out. Satisfied with lunch, yet still smarting from being shunned by his sister, he was still stewing inside. The chick at the hotel was good though, to get him out before the cops arrived. He quickly looked over his shoulder to make sure she was gone before he walked to his car and quickly got in. It was quiet, and carefully he drove out the north exit, pulling around the circle and narrowly missing a huddle of kids grappling with skis and boots as they raced to catch the next bus.

'Shithead kids!' Will looked at the rearview mirror and gave them the sign. One of the kids, face wide with shock, returned the compliment as Will accelerated angrily past the row of angle-parked cars and across the river. The short and steep climb to the Alpine Way brought him little relief as he hungered for more speed. Then, without checking for traffic coming down the mountain, Will heaved the wheel to the left, rapidly moving through the gears into overdrive and fast tracking towards the Bullock's Flat ski-tube.

He switched on the radio and flicked the dial off Triple J until he found the local Snow FM station. Maybe the snow would be better on the other side. At least, the half-pipe would be pumping and there would be a chance to take on some of the pros with his latest skills. Will whistled an out of tune reminder to himself that life was OK. He had scored a free lunch — so stuff what his sister thought about him. It was better when they were younger, they would hang out together boarding. But in the last few years Cassie didn't want to hang with him anymore and she wasn't as stoked on boarding the terrain parks as he was. That meant dragging around the backcountry on skis with her. That was nuts! Too much walking for too few thrills out there!

The road wound surely past the campgrounds and, in moments,

Will was at the National Park entry gate. He accelerated giving the booth the obligatory finger then braked sharply to take the left turn to the ski tube. The local news burst into the car.

'Police warn local residents that an armed youth who attempted a hold-up in Thredbo today is dangerous and should not be approached. The youth is described as being moderate build, fair, with a scar on his right cheek. He was last seen wearing snowboarding clothes and boots. Anyone who has seen someone of this description should contact the Jindabyne Police.'

'Snowboarding clothes and boots! Fuckwits.' Will grinned. 'Better change.' He muttered under his breath. 'The old girl must have called the cops faster than he thought.' Will's anger rose to the surface again. At least the young one with the chips and pie had got him out in time. Will couldn't figure her though. Why would she help him? 'Beats me! Women.'

Will parked so he was facing the exit, on the far side of the last row carrying cars. He liked to see behind, in front and to both sides and have a clear path if he had to move fast. He slammed the door then opened the back door and dragged out his jeans, fleece and parka. The boots would have to stay on and the board was coming with him. He pulled on his fleece beanie and boarding gloves, slung the board under his arm and headed for the Ski Tube. It would be better to keep his head down until he was on the mountain. That's when it counted. When he had a chance to show the other guys up.

'Going up today?'

'Yeah. Just for the rest of the arvo. Any concessions?'

'Same price for a return ticket. Can do you a 24 hour one if you like? You staying over?'

'Nuh. Just do a few turns in the half pipe.'

'OK. Single return. Want to purchase a half-day on the mountain?'

'Cool.' Will dug for dough.'

'Last ride down is…'

'I know. Thanks sweetheart!' Tom pasted a finger kiss on the glass.

The girl sighed. 'You're not really dressed. Weather could turn later.'

'It's cool. Know what I'm doing yeah?'

'Yeah. See you then.'

Will took the ticket and walked to the platform. It was another few minutes until the train and he didn't feel like waiting. There were a few dudes sitting together, their bags dropped on the bench behind them. Will sauntered towards them.

'You guys doing the half-pipe?'

'Might. Getting windy up there. Visibility's falling.'

'You staying on the mountain?'

'Nuh. Jindy. Just checking it out. Comp's in a few days. You ride?'

'Might. Join you guys?'

'Yeah OK. Just don't cut the track up.'

'Ridden it before. Can you do three sixties?'

'Mmm. Joey can. I'm more into aerials.'

'Flips?'

'Mostly turns. Haven't quite sorted the backflips. Working on it though.'

'You work?'

'Nuh. School. Stay in Jindy a couple of weeks for this though.'

'Do ya do stuff?'

'You mean tabs?'

'Might.'

'Want to try? Make ya riding more interestin'.'

'How much?'

'How much you got?'

'Enough for one tab.'

'Show us.'

'Show us the gear.'

Will pulled a metal box from his pocket.

'OK.'

'Twenty for one?'

'Yeah. Why not.'

Will watched closely as the kid pulled out his wallet and took out the twenty-dollar note. He kept his eye firmly on the kid as they exchanged the tab and money. The kid licked the tab then popped it into his mouth. Will watched him drop the wallet onto the top of his bag. He carefully put the twenty-dollar note into his top pocket. He watched the other kids for a while. They went back to their chatter, distracted with talk of the half-pipe and weather. The kid looked at Will and grinned.

'Good stuff yeah?'

'What's your name?'

'Max. What's yours?'

'Mine's "Minor". You're still a minor yeah?'

Max laughed. 'This should put a new spin on the game. You ride often?'

'Not if it's a slushbowl after rain.'

'Perisher's brown. Dust blew in, but the snow's still good.'

'You dropping anymore later today?'

Maybe. Got to catch up with a few people first.'

Will kept half an eye on Max and half an eye on the rest of the group. 'Don't your mates drop stuff?'

Max looked towards the rest of his friends. Will slowly reached down just as Max turned his head and plucked the wallet off his bag. He tucked it under his seat and crossed his arms.

'Some. Mostly into alcohol. Less of a downer the day after.'

'Know what you mean. You have to take caffeine in the morning to give you a boost and drink heaps of water. Then it doesn't touch you the day after.'

'Thanks for the tip.'

'Let me know if you want more.' Will said. 'I usually hang at Jindy or Cooma Park.

'We go back to Canberra after this. The bus stops for lunch at Cooma but. Next Wednesday.'

'Might see you there then. In the park. Lunchtime?'

'Yeah OK. See what gives.'

'See you later then Max.' Will reached under the seat then picked up his gear and walked towards the approaching train.

The short trip on the tube was uncomfortably long for Will. He hoped that the kid hadn't noticed that he had 'dropped' his wallet.

He had said he would ride with the guys only because he knew they would forget him the minute they stepped off the tube. The train pulled into Perisher and Will look distractedly through the window and watched the kids unload. He whistled softly under his breath and waited. There would be more mountain to lose himself in if Max suddenly put two-and-two together.

The kids were off the train and onto the platform. Will pulled the wallet out of his jeans pocket. There were three $50 notes stacked in the main section of the wallet.

'Rich kids!' Will muttered. He pulled out the notes and crammed them into his coat pocket then dropped the wallet into the cache of snowboards and bags on the floor of the train. Then he quickly stepped out onto the opposite platform and onto the Blue Cow train.

The train pulled slowly up the last stretch to Blue Cow. The wind was up and the snow blew lightly off the top of the crests. There were a few riders around, mostly school kids boarding in groups and a few veteran skiers negotiating the short downhill section from the Terminal to the chair and some people were traversing the long side of the Blue Cow Mountain.

The wind tugged at the two chairlifts and it probably wouldn't be long before they started shutting the mountain down. The steep run off Blue Cow was closed for race training and most people skied the two runs to the long chair lifting to the top of the mountain for the run to Central Valley and back to the Valley. Will traversed across to the Brumby T Bar, riding aggressively between the few skiers on the slope then caught the Pleasant Valley Quad Chair to the next level. It was a slow traverse across to the front of Back Perisher Mountain, but he wanted to board to where he could observe the half-pipe, to see if the lads were riding. The snow was slow and side boarding was never easy.

Will loosened the bindings and stepped out, walking across the face of the mountain and up the short stretch to the saddle. He locked into the bindings again, pushing off with sufficient speed to board to Mid Station, then tracking right to ride the Bull Wheel before cutting back to centre mountain. The ride down was free, the visibility dropping sharply on the final fast-board under the T-bars and cross ride to the top of the half-pipe. Will rode hard and fast. He was no slouch on the slopes and didn't give a rat's about the half-confident learners negotiating every turn as if they would fall off the mountain. The top of the pipe was empty as far as he could see, the blue jackets already descending in a pack along the pipe. The boys were performing a combo number, one after the other in quick succession, they dropped into the pipe taking two or three turns off the top. They were good. Will waited to see if they would ride up again. The snow was hard packed at the end of the day, the conditions less than inviting for solid work on their aerials. They were coming up again.

'Shit.' He pushed off the top of the pipe spinning first to the right for a one eighty then across to the left to take the three sixty. It worked. The speed on the next turn was better and he tried a one and a half, pulling it off and racing for the fourth and final turn. The boys noticed him as he dropped off the top into a free backspin, landing on the steep part of the chute then quickly manoeuvring back to the forward position.

'That was great. Going another?' Max piped up.

'Yeah. How was your ride?'

'Maate. Somethin' else! Spinning into space on the turns, diving into the ocean on the drop offs.'

'Cool.'

'Let's take another. Hey dudes. We're going again.'

'Yeah. Let's do it.'

The pack set off together, dragging their boards behind them as they climbed the slope, watching the pipe as they went to check out the talent. Max arrived first at the top of the pipe. His head felt floaty and his feet could have been a thousand miles away. It was going to be a challenge. He would need to keep his feet connected to his head on the pipe to make tight and complete turns. He wondered whether it would be a 'legs follow head' routine this time. Usually, he liked to work as an integrated unit with as little distance between his thoughts, his body and its movements as possible — where the snow felt like an extension of his feet.

As he hit the bottom, his feet felt like lead and he crouched lower than normal to take the shock off his knees and ankles at the same time pumping up the speed for the next wall. With the extra crouch speed he easily got air on the left, grabbing the board between his legs at the same time. Then he released his hands, opening and crouching for the last hit and exit on the top of the right wall.

'He's shit hot yeah?' One of Max's mates piped up. 'Reckon you can do the McTwist?'

'Savin' meself. Bigger things on next week. Been to the board park at Thredbo?' Will changed the subject.

'Nuh. Only ride Perisher. Your turn.'

Just as Will contemplated kicking off the edge, a couple of men dressed in rough bush shirts, beards half-crusted in snow and broad hats planted on their heads, raced past the half pipe, legs pumping rhythmically as they mastered deep telemark turns on their carve skis. Their swish of snow beneath them carried an authentic feel of the wilderness as they streaked past the hip boarders dressed to the nose in fashion boots and dacks.

'Bloody bushrangers! I'm down there.' Will pushed off the edge, the drop taking his breath. He swung into the first wall easily spinning off the top and taking a broader descent to limit the manoeuvres to two on this run.

He wasn't about to allow Max to show him up. Then he took the next turn and instead of spiralling back to the base, did a three sixty aerial landing on the top of the wall, a metre higher than where Max stood.

'Gotta go Max. Work to do.'

'See you in Cooma then. Like your ride.'

'Cool. See you later.' Will dropped into classic board position and rode to the front of the Terminal. If the cops were out looking for him and if the kid discovered that his wallet was missing and decided to report it, there would be more 'blue' on the mountain than he was comfortable with. Will quickly unstrapped his board and made fast tracks towards the ski tube. As he crossed the last section of the car park, he noticed a couple of cops walking between the rows of cars, checking regos and number plates.

'Holy shit!' Will turned sharp right, facing towards the Charlotte's Pass Road. The snow cover was still strong, although muddied with the dust storm. There was no way that he could run or walk up the road without being noticed and there was every chance that cops were on the lookout on the road to Jindy.

Tom spat onto the snow. He noticed the collection of skidoos parked behind the Medical Centre. The boys were unpacking for the day, some of them probably slacking off for a coffee before stowing their machines. He looked carefully over his left shoulder then walked easily towards the last of the skidoos. The keys were in the ignition of three of the machines and chances were they had refuelled a couple of times during the day already.

HELL ON ICE AND SNOW

The escape was easier than he expected. Without thinking, Will swung his leg over the saddle and kicked the machine into life. Then he steered onto the roadway, accelerating gradually, boosting the skidoo's speed for the long run up to the Gap. As he rode up the road, Will glanced quickly to the right, noting that the stations were packing down at the end of the day. The tows and chairs were winding out and soon the workers would be bringing their own skidoos back to the main shed or skiing down the groomed company road along the creekline. Then he flicked a glance in the mirror.

'Just what I fuckin' need!' Will exploded.

The duo of skidoos carving up the snow behind him meant that the missing skidoo was already noted. Will crouched low onto the seat and revved high forcing the skidoo up the steady slope. He knew he had the edge with balance riding rough. He had been on and off farm bikes from the age of ten and easily riding the off-road trails near the Lower Snowy River where the hills were rough and steep.

Within moments, the skidoo topped Perisher Gap. The strong winds roaring off the main range caught him off guard. The snow and ice blasted his face like a myriad of painful needles. Surprisingly, it was harder to balance this machine than he thought as he plummeted down the icy road on the south side of the Gap. He waited for the right moment to ride the skidoo off to the side of the road and pulled off to the left before circling left into the trees to wait out the chase.

The weather was closing in and with a bit of luck, his skidoo tracks would be quickly covered. If he had to, he would dump the skidoo behind some rocks then carry on by foot. He knew the uplands of the ski fields reasonably well, always boarding off limits and out of bounds, pushing the edge of his abilities. He quickly checked out the lay of the land and flicked off the skidoo lights. The sound of the wind shrieking in his ears was music to his ears. He knew that his pursuers would have trouble finding him.

The lights of the first skidoo beamed in long and diluted rays as it topped the rise and Will knew that it would be a few minutes before they figured out that they had lost him. He waited, listening, watching. Will knew that he had one thing on his side: his fierce determination and unshakeable focus once he set his mind on his objective. The curious and inexplicable talent he possessed always surprised him; his performance, reflexes and timing kicking in perfectly once he had set his aim. Anything was possible on a night as bad as this. His mind raced forwards a few hours to his intended arrival at Thredbo, the destination that on a night like tonight might as well have been as far off as Timbuktu.

The two men riding the company skidoos in pursuit of the joyrider found the exit over the snow embankment. They were well outside their normal terrain. The leader hesitated unable to find the tracks.

'Can't see any lights ahead. I reckon he's headed up the back of Mt Wheatley. Silly bastard. Thinks he can shake us in the trees. Probably ride to South Perisher and dump the skidoo somewhere there. Joy rider I reckon.'

'This geezer must know the terrain yeah?'

'Let's hope so for his sake.'

'You radioed back to base?'

'Nup. 'Spose it's a good time. We'd better stick together. Getting lost out in this stuff is not my idea of fun!'

'Nor mine. Shit it's cold.'

'Wind's picking up. Whiteout within the half hour I reckon.'

'Give them a call?'

'Yeah. Tell 'em to inform the cops. We'll get the bastard. Damn. I was on my way to the pub.'

It was on. Will sensed rather than saw or heard the two skidoos circle around towards Mount Wheatley. As far as he was concerned, the plan was working. The jerks would follow him for a while, then as the light faded and ever increasingly dense flurries of snow reduced visibility, they would be totally confused and unable to see the lights or tracks of his skidoo. He grappled with the steering as he negotiated the deeper snow. He would have to use his judgement and general knowledge of the pattern of drifts, gullies and cornices, of how snow banked against the windblown western side of trees sometimes leaving the leeward side more exposed with greater obstacles for the skidoo. The tors of rocks to his right appeared like omens from the white gloom. Will knew that for now at least, he was heading in the right direction.

The police station at Perisher Valley swung into action as the news of the stolen skidoo came in.

'Silly idiot. Imagine heading out in this stuff. What's his game?'

'Search me. Probably doing it for kicks.'

'Should leave him out there to learn a lesson.'

'Yeah. Then pick up the body?'

'Let's move. Two skidoos out the back. Strike to the back of The Stables and head for the Porcupine Trail. You'll need to take GPS, compass and PLBs. Hand-helds working?'

'Check that. Radio on. PLB and GPS in the can.'

'Good. Five-minute rekkies on the radio. Any problems, come straight back. Ron, you call the Fire crew. Get them to go with you on their snowplough. I'll ring Hans Oversnow. Go slow. Use the side spotlight see if you can pick this nutcase up.'

'He'll be lost in no time. Might be easier to call it off until the morning.'

'I wish. This weather would send my grandmother to an early grave.'

'Yeah.'

'Just make sure it's none of you. No risks. Understood?'

'Check that. Apprehend?'

'Usual stuff. Stolen property. Hit him with driving without a skidoo licence.'

Ron laughed. 'Well he probably won't have a licence on him.'

'Not this one, no. Too much of a risk taker. Let's move.'

The Sergeant wiped a hand across his chin. He hadn't had time to pick up the razor for the last couple of days. The runs up and down the mountain, booking drivers over the limit and getting a fix on the rage party at Jindabyne kept him awake until two in the morning for the last couple of nights. Now this!

'Police in pursuit of stolen skidoo. Suspect ditches vehicle off the edge of the mountain. Body found jammed between a rock crevice and a hard place. Sounds good for the PR.'

He grinned to himself. At least the drama broke up the usual pace of stolen equipment, drug possession and DUI. He would make this guy suffer for his lack of sleep.

The oversnow vehicles were a mountain worker's dream come true. The interior warmed within minutes of the engine starting. The ten-wheel double trackers were as stable as a tank in mud and their lights powerful enough to penetrate the darkest of dark winter nights. This time, the blizzard swirled in all directions, the light reflecting on the flakes swirling crazily in from of them.

'Terry, you take number one. I'll take the older one.'

'Right you are. What a night!'

'Seen worse. We'll have the Fire Brigade with us. They're bringing out their Haggland. We'll need everything we have. If this guy stacks into a rock, you never know what you'll find.'

'All in a day's work mate. All in a day's work.'

'Ready as you are. Fireys ready?'

'Just coming out of the shed.' Terry announced dryly.

'Race you to the gap?'

'No way.' Terry felt sober reality wash over him..

'He'll be at the Chalet before we even reach the Gap if that's where he is heading!'

'He will! He'll hole up where it's warm if I know anything about joy riders. They go for the spin then look for the nearest place of warmth, food and grog.'

'Who knows! He could be spun out on drugs. He's probably flying over Kosi by now.'

Terry laughed coarsely. 'That'd be right.' But he was nevertheless focussed on the job.

The Haggland pulled up on the road waiting for the smaller oversnow vehicles to join the convoy.

'We got radio communication with this geezer? He'll be on the resort channel yeah?'

'Everything goes through our base to police HQ. They'll pass on the messages to him if there are any.'

'Feel sorry for the kid. Probably doesn't know what he's got himself into.'

'Who said he's a kid?'

'Yeah. True. Could be anyone I suppose. It's dammed cold out there. Maybe he'll be grateful for a ride back in an oversnow vehicle at the end of this.'

'Where are the cops?'

'Right here boys. Peter and David. You get one a piece.'

'Good. You're with me then?'

'Sure am. We'll use our radio. Save yours.'

'Good work. I can concentrate on the chase.'

'In this thing?'

'They go very fast. Don't hang too far out of the window.'

'Yeah. I know. I score the spotlight position.'

'Use the left window at the rear. Wind is blowing from the sou' sou' west so most of it will hit us on the top right window.'

'Good.' Peter checked the spot and placed it on one of the seats. Then he checked his radio and patted his belt. 'Ready when you are.'

Terry flicked his headlights to give the all terrain the signal.

'Did you bring your handcuffs?'

'Doubt whether we'll need them. Whoever he is, he'll be too bloody cold to worry about resisting. That's if we find him.'

'True. Not a good night to take off into the wilderness.'

'Do we know what he's wearing?'

'Hard to say. Guys didn't really get a good look, except that he's wearing a decent jacket and has a beanie.'

'That's a start. He'll freeze out there.'

'The company boys are coming in. Reckon it's a living hell.'

Peter opened the back left window and poked the spot into the gloom. The light caught the frenzy of flakes bursting through the wall and lighting the edge of the road and tree-line. He pulled the spotlight back into the cabin, closing the window.

'Got some penetration with the light. Mostly reflected.' He remarked dryly. 'This guy is going to be one very lucky lad to be found on a night like this!'

'Shiit. Glad it's not me. We're going straight to the Chalet?'

'We are. No point plunging into Spencer's Creek on the way.' Peter snapped the light on and off.

'You got other boys out there?'

'There's a couple of skidoos heading to the back of Wheatley. They'll join us on the route to the Chalet if they don't find him. Two company guys coming in. They won't be going out again.'

'He's got the run on us.'

'Seems that way. No sign of him. Unless he's well ahead or hiding.'

Will had the edge and he knew it. The cold was now biting deeply into his reserves of energy. He didn't know how much longer he could maintain the pace with the wind whipping into his flesh. His hands began to seriously numb on the handlebars. He rocked his body from side to side to try and generate some heat. The last thing he wanted was to freeze up inside and lose his grip on the skidoo. The first snow pole unexpectedly came into view and Will was surprised how quickly he had travelled the distance. Still, time meant nothing on a wild night where there were none of the usual handles to grab — distance, definition of the mountains or the passage of the landscape around him — there was only an endless swirling of snow in front of the skidoo headlights and an ominous deepening of the cold that now penetrated to the very core of his being.

The police search and rescue captain was fidgety and tired. At least they had made it intact to the Chalet without losing any men or machines on the way. This was the last thing he needed; some idiot joyrider leading him on a merry chase into a full whiteout.

His deputy stepped forwards. 'The dude at the top of the Stillwell chair reckons he saw someone.'

'Bring him in. I want to talk to him.'

'Here he is mate. Frank.'

'You say you saw someone up there as you were coming down?'

'Yeah. There was a skidoo riding up the road towards the Pass above the resort as I was coming down. Not one of ours.'

'Are you sure about that?' Terry felt and sounded tired.

'I was last down. All the others finished their shifts about half an hour earlier. My job is to do the final sweep and make sure no one is still out there.'

'Anything else?'

'Just a fucking horse.'

'A what?'

'A bloody black stallion. Couldn't miss it! No rider though.'

'Christ. As if we need a hallucinating liftie. We're looking for a stolen skidoo and the idiot riding it, not a horse!'

'You asked.'

'Thanks. What did you say your name was?'

'Frank. Frank Josephs.'

'OK Frank. Where do you think a person on a skidoo would be going out there.'

'Stuffed if I know. Anyone with sense would head straight to the hotel and get something inside of them. You know. Food, drink, fire. The internal burner dies out there.'

'How long would you last riding out in this storm.'

'I only go out there because I have to and then it's about 10 to 15 minutes and only if I have to check some equipment. This is no joyriding weather.'

'You joyride?'

Frank blushed. 'Pop over the top after checking the top station. Don't really go too far though.'

'You familiar with the terrain?'

'Most of it. Don't you guys know this place?' Frank stood his ground.

'We do, but we might need you to pick up his tracks.'

'No chance. Wind is coming in too strong. Tracks cover over in no time.'

'If you were on the run out here, where would you head?'

'I would have stopped here.' Frank was definite.

'He didn't though, did he. You saw him go over the top.'

'Two choices only. Seaman's Hut.'

'And..?'

'Thredbo. There's nothing else out here.'

'Seaman's Hut?'

'If he thinks he's alone, yeah. Could hole out there for the night, except there might be snow campers using the hut. Sometimes they do for kicks. You know, ski up from the Chalet and spend the night at Seaman's then ski back to work the following morning.'

'It's supposed to be an emergency shelter!' The police captain was exasperated.

'Well it didn't help those young snowboarders. They never made it to Seaman's.' Frank retorted.

'Who would in the middle of a blizzard.'

'I reckon this bloke is joyriding and he may not be looking for the first comfort stop. Might pay to head up towards Seaman's Hut.' Frank made the decision for them. 'Otherwise check out the winter pole line but you could get seriously lost on a night like this and find yourselves in no-man's land on the edge of the escarpment. After that, it is anyone's guess where you end up. Steep valleys, thick forest below the treeline, rocky creeks..... Recipe for hypothermia in anyone's books.'

'Thanks Frank. Can you ride ahead in the Haggland?'

'Yeah. Sure.' Frank sounded unsure.

'Have you had something to eat?

'A cup of soup and bread roll could do me a power of good at the moment.'

'OK everyone. Five minutes max. Eat what you can. No alcohol. Then we go back up the road towards Seaman's Hut and check the area out. Straight up the road. Clear?'

Will was ready to ditch the skidoo and use his legs. The wind was enough to make you crazy, the sound howling out of the depths of who knew where, to cover him in a freezing shell of bitter despair. This was hell on ice and snow. He wondered briefly what drove him to the extremes of daredevil stuff, but he already knew the answer. The effect of drugs on him over the last few years, even in the face of the highs and the money he regularly pooled from the deals, had gradually changed his personality, making him less sure of himself, more aggressive and since his sister was no longer there to pull him back to reality; angry. He couldn't keep the anger under control and he knew that was totally the drugs. He came off a high and instantly felt depressed. But it was too late to turn back now.

'Jesus Cassie. Why didn't you stand by me?' Will screamed into the wind. 'You bastard Tom. Rot in gaol!' Will started crying, the red-hot tears burning his eyes and freezing almost straight away on his cheeks. For the first time in months he felt better, letting out his long suppressed anger, the hurt finally coming to the surface. For a moment, his concentration was broken by his emotion. Will struggled to regain control and the skidoo slipped from his grasp sliding into a rocky snow gully.

'Just what I bloody need!' he screamed in rage. He scrambled down to the skidoo and kicked the seat. The machine rested where it slid, the lights burning and the engine still going. He wrenched at the handlebars forcing himself to try to pull the skidoo away from the rocks. The weight of the machine and angle of fall was against him. He tried again. This time, carefully, placing one leg over the saddle before revving the machine. He engaged the gears hoping that the engine would do the work of lifting the machine out of the ditch. His energy was fast waning and he knew that this would be the last attempt before he would have to walk. He breathed in, opening the throttle and pulling the machine towards him. The skidoo bounced free, jerking him almost over the handlebars. He lunged backwards and caught the saddle with his groin, winding himself with the pain. He gasped in pain but he was free!

For a moment he thought he would lose control of the skidoo as he hurtled into the night. The faint glow of light visible in the storm from Seaman's Hut warned him not to stop there. Instead, he fought the sideways slide of the machine, gravity wrenching it downwards, downwards it seemed, as if he and the skidoo were destined for a bottomless abyss of ice. He pulled desperately on the throttle and the skidoo suddenly responded lurching forwards and accelerating past the hut and towards the faint shadow of the mountain.

The skidoo bucked as it slammed into the side of Mount Kosciuszko, throwing the rider and the snowboard off to the side. Will clawed at the snow to stop his fall as he cartwheeled then slid on his stomach down the steep slope. He watched in amazement as the skidoo slid a few metres towards him — its head light picking up the frozen lake — before a section of the cornice cracked and fell shutting out the light as it buried the front of the skidoo.

Instinctively Will grabbed for the binding of his snowboard as it came to a halt a metre from his body. He dragged the board under him and surfed as far downhill as the board would take him. The skidoo could stay where it was.

Will stood up for what felt like an eternity. Intuitively, he knew he was safe. He knew exactly where he was. It would be a long walk up to the Ramsheads but he was totally at one with himself and the icy mountain landscape surrounding him. He knew in an instant the way out and forwards. He allowed himself a few seconds to peer into the gloom, glancing backwards to where the machine had tossed him into the night. His mouth opened in amazement to see two sets of headlights trained on the pile of snow beneath the imploded cornice covering the skidoo that he had just ridden through the white, winter hell.

'Shit. They must think I'm in there!' Will whistled. He quickly turned to make tracks towards the Ramshead Range, but something pulled his attention back to Kosciuszko. He looked into the gloom broken by the gleaming lights. Galloping through the mist was the image of a horse, his head proud and defiant, his hooves now pawing the tumbled snow where the avalanche settled near the edge of the frozen Cootapatamba Lake. Will stopped in his tracks, uncertain, awe-struck at the vision of the horse, now looking straight at him, through him, eyes startling red, face composed and calm. It looked like the horse that came to him in his dreams, on the darkest of dark nights when the drugs had worn off and he had found himself in the depths of suicidal despair.

Will felt his heart pulled towards the horse. 'I'm here! I'm here!' Will screamed into the wind.

The horse lifted his legs to the sky, his head turned to Kosciuszko and tail streaming in the wind behind him. He struck at the blizzard, his hooves ringing like steel against the force of the wind. Then he turned, looking down the valley of the Leatherbarrel, where the storm arose. The ghost horse charged forwards, riding high on the snow and in his wake a hundred wild horses followed; some stumbling and falling in the snow, others floundering through the remains of the cornice avalanche and still others, abreast and challenging the stallion to the descent.

The horses were gone. Will picked up his board. He crossed the frozen creek and started the climb up the steep western side of the Ramsheads. He knew the route almost by heart, but he would still have to be careful. He let his instincts kick in and headed slightly left. The ground rose beneath him. The slope continued to steepen steadily. He fought the almost overwhelming desire to lie down and rest. There was no shelter out here and already, he was soaked to the skin, frozen it felt, to the core. He kept climbing, counting the steps, measuring his breath, breathing more deeply and feeling his body warm up slowly as he continued to climb. Anything but stop and give up. Five minutes, ten, it must have been at least twenty minutes at a steady pace and Will knew that he was on the first of two wind-scoured plateaus. The sudden increase in the pace of the wind plucking at his clothes told him exactly where he was. It was still blowing and gusting from the south-west. He turned his body to feel the full force of the wind on his back, then rotated ever so slightly to the right and headed across relatively level ground. There was nothing to see; nothing at all in the white gloom. Soon the plateau dipped and he knew he was on track before the next ridge on the escarpment. He breathed in, fighting back the tears. He was all alone in the winter wilderness. No-one cared. Only the horse had seen him. He carried on, step by step, counting them one by one. He crossed the next plateau and desperately peered into the white, hoping for a sign. Momentarily, the white blurred into dark grey. Will followed the line of grey upwards. The stacked rocks leading to the dark pyramid told him this had to be North Ramshead. He could hardly contain his excitement. This was it. He was out of the valley. The clouds momentarily cleared and a faint moon glinted against the black of the rocky tors. He knew where he was but he also knew he would have to move carefully along the mountain handrail, rock by rock until he came to the edge of Signature Hill. He looked for the Balancing Rock, then Lindsay's Rock where he had climbed with his mate, the elusive moon teasing him as it appeared and disappeared. In a moment the clouds rushed across the plateau obscuring any sense of where he was amongst the rocky tors and in the next, evaporated, swirling upwards as the weather began to clear. Will moved forwards until he found the Mohawk Rock. He grinned. There it was. The ice-covered solitary high boulder shining under the brightening moon. He was home and hosed. Another hundred paces. Will strapped on his board. He couldn't believe where he was. Somehow, someone or something was protecting him and sending him on the right path out of the devil's jaws into the welcome comfort of civilisation; Thredbo.

Will crested at Eagle's Nest, schussing crosswise from the top of the Basin tow. It was deathly cold and the wind howled mournfully through the transmission tower, the chairlift eerie and motionless in the dead of night. He was tempted to try his luck, then decided against an empty and locked building, a sure trap where the cops would think of looking for him anyway. He dropped in towards the Supertrail. His legs felt like water and it was unbelievably difficult to turn the board, the movement thick and stolid as he fought off his total weariness. The lights of the snowploughs caught him for a moment, but they continued on as if no-one was there. Will knew that he was just plain lucky. He felt like having more than just a feed. He felt like curling up in a warm bed for a very long time.

Exhausted, Will side slid the steep sections of the trail then let the board free run towards the village. At least he had fresh groomers to ride! Everything in him wanted to take out the last 100 metres to the Valley Terminal, except the lights and activity warned him to be careful. He skidded sideways, unstrapped his board and stepped over the fence behind the top row of the lodges. He walked between the lodges onto the snow-covered road and towards the centre of the village. Will almost stopped in his tracks. The blue lights of the local police patrol took him by surprise. He had no option other than to continue walking as if he did it every night. He put his head down, slung his board under his arm and headed straight towards the village square. The lights of the car swung to the right over the bridge from where he had just come. Will resisted every impulse to run. He knew that there was nowhere to go and he was way too tired anyway. He passed the closed shops and cafes and headed down towards the Bistro. Wearily, he stashed his board against the wall and pushed his way into the pub. The crowd was humming, the television pulsing, competing against the general throb of locals and workers, drinking, playing pool and chilling out after yet another big day on the mountain. The bizarre sight of dozens of ski instructors decked out in drag, top hats, bottomless trousers and a random variety of wild gear made him want to laugh and cry at the same time. His mood lifted and the hunger cramping at his stomach reminded him that he wanted to eat.

The Bistro food station was well and truly shut. The only option was cold, bar chips and something to drink. Will walked through the irreverent and jubilant crowd of assorted instructors and punters.

'You look as if you've just come out of hell mate. What can I get you?'

'Anything hot?'

'Not at this time. I'll do you a coffee out the back though if you like.'

'Thanks.'

'Anything else?'

'Hot food?'

'Pies are in the warmer.'

'Man. That's the best bloody news I've heard in a long time.'

'Give us a tick.'

Will turned his back to the bar looking for a familiar face in the crowd absorbed in its own craziness. The warm fuzz in his chest at the prospect of company, sanity and something hot to eat and drink reminded him that hey, this wasn't a bad life after all. The idiocy of the crew celebrating the end of the season, the crazy colours and the loud laughter jolted him out of his frozen stupor. There was nothing more that he wanted than to mill into the crowd bumping up against the pool tables where half-drunk and hilarious people tried to pot the balls.

Will grinned. At least this was a better ending than he had imagined; and he wasn't about to hitch a ride down the Alpine Way on a bloody cold night like this.

The police officer stood about a metre away, quietly watching the young man order his food and drink. He waited in amazed wonder, prolonging for as long as possible the moment when he would inevitably have to take the young freerider in. Will turned for a brief moment towards the TV screen buzzing over the heads of the local Thredbo crowd. As he looked upwards, the faintest of blue, the line of the hat, the bulging holster…

'Come on then mate. We'd better have a talk don't you think?'

Will froze, the warm fuzz turning to a cold lump in his chest. 'How did you know where I was?'

'Supertrail. The groomers picked you up in their lights.' The policeman grinned despite himself.

'Shit.' Will looked at the floor.

The policeman raised his eyebrows looking almost admiringly at his captive.

'Here's your coffee and pie mate.'

Will swivelled back to the bar.

'Oh…thanks'

'Bring them with you mate. Free ride to Jindy?'

MEN AND THE MOUNTAINS

Tom recovered from his unexpected and traumatic regression into childhood. It took half an hour for the Social Workers to organise a bed in the prison hospital, his main carer Kate heatedly arguing with the guard that he was not well enough to be in the lock up.

'Most of them are here for drugs Kate. You know that. They're all the same breed and this fella is amongst his own kind. He knows the score.'

'He does not!' Kate retorted. Tom doesn't have a clue what's going on inside his own head. If Wendy and Andrew weren't around, he'd be in deep water.'

The guard looked taken aback. He threw his hands into the air. 'OK Kate. I'll believe you. See what I can do.'

'Thanks. I'd appreciate it. I mean it.'

'You'd have them all out of here Kate if you had your own way.'

'Maybe they should be out of here. Maybe these guys need some horse whispering equivalent and not punishment to get them back on track. This is not the place for wounded souls.'

'The "Brumby Riders" program might be starting up soon.'

'Really?'

'Seems the inspiration came from America. They've got plans to set up a camp past Adaminaby.'

'Not sure that Tom is well enough for that. I'll keep it in mind though. Thanks.'

By the end of the day, the young man was moved from the main prison and safely housed in the hospital, away from the raw edge of damaged men.

The guard turned to the sound of the door buzzer.

'Hi Wendy. Glad you made it!' Kate sounded relieved as she propped Tom up on his pillows.

Wendy took one look at Tom. He looked flushed yet his eyes sparkled with deep emotion and she instantly recognised that the pathway to his subconscious self had opened. He was internally engaged with his emotions and the wellspring of inner emotional strength had burst to the surface. Tom was on the mend.

Wendy shot a look at Kate. Quietly, she stroked Tom's head. 'I don't want you in here for much longer Tom. We're doing all we can to move you out to the general hospital if we can.'

'Thanks.' Tom's response was choked.

'There's only one master of your soul and body Tom, and that is yourself. There is nothing anyone else can give, that you can't give yourself. You will find the strength to heal within yourself.'

The buzzing silence in the prison room lifted Tom away from his intense emotions. For a moment, he felt separate; suspended from his body, transported from the room. The image of the old Aboriginal man, his eyes dark, compassionate and penetrating, appeared in front of him. Tom couldn't move, trapped by the eyes immersing him in acceptance, in love without judgement.

'Hello.' Tom said aloud.

'What did you say Tom?' Wendy asked.

Tom relaxed, smiling back at the face now gleaming with pride. The old man used his mind to caress Tom's emotions, taking him higher on the plane of consciousness. This was the place where for the first time, Tom felt as though he was the observer of his own thoughts, witnessing his mind think creatively and constructively about his future.

'That was him wasn't it. Jack.' He announced.

Two days later, Tom had found himself and finally his own voice.

'Cassie. I have to see Cassie.' Tom smiled at Kate.

'Kate. I need to talk to you for a moment.' The guard pulled her aside. 'Listen, they brought young Will in last night. He's confessed to planting the drugs on Tom. Seems as though he had quite a rough ride in the storm. They can't believe he came out of it. Apparently his skidoo was buried beneath a collapsed cornice on Kosciuszko. For a while they thought he was in there with it.'

'What?'

'Will is in the lock up at the moment. He'll be charged later today. Tom's free to go. There's been a mistake in his conviction.'

Kate smiled broadly. 'Thanks. Thanks mate.' She turned to Wendy and nodded for her to come over. 'Good news Wendy. We have one free man on our hands. Tom is off the hook.'

Wendy laughed aloud, clapping her hands together and hugging Kate.

'You tell him Kate.' The prison guard suggested.

'OK. We'll tell him together.' Kate said. They walked back to Tom's room.

'Tom. Are you strong enough to go home?'

'What?'

'You're a free man Tom. They've caught Will. He's just confessed.'

Tom felt as if the chains around him were suddenly cut free. 'I can go?' He let out a cry of freedom. 'I'd better ring Sean and Angus.'

Angus was itching to return to sea. The pull of the water was more than he could resist. Despite the overwhelming sense of his powerlessness against the might of the ocean, his intimate connection with the sea pulled him towards the treacherous reaches of the Bass Strait, and he knew he would finally have to go. But in the meantime, there was the surveillance exercise and he had planned a training camp for young local men. He wanted Tom on that camp.

It was the farm however that anchored Angus to the daily routine and bound him together with his friends. Angus loved his land and he lived equally for the mountains and the endlessly changing sea. Now, he had the quiet pleasure of observing in Sean the same sense of contented wonderment and security in the majestic and powerful land they shared. It was here that Angus found peace, sanctity and safety. On the land, man could make a camp with nothing to think about or do other than to find water, to build a fire, to listen to the sound of the wind in the trees and to watch the glittering roof of night stars. He knew that Sean, torn apart by the unjust incarceration of Tom, also needed earth medicine to soothe his soul.

'Don't worry about him Sean. There's nothin' you can do at the moment. I know it's rippin' your heart out man, but you have to let this one be. Maybe it's for the better.'

Sean was close to tears. 'Yeah.'

Angus placed a reassuring hand on his friend's arm. 'Look. Why don't you take the truck out for a few days? Dump a swag in the back and go exploring. It would do you good for a few days.'

'I'm sure it would sharpen my senses spending a few days in the bush.' Sean smiled despite of himself. Besides, at some point we are going to have to catch up with our military friends Angus. We have another job to do after all.'

'You are right in that Sean. The time has come. We have work to do. In the meantime, there's a lot to see out there. It's lovely country. You'll never find another place on earth like it. Take the gun if you like. You might help the Park by potting off some of the rabbits for your dinner or finishing off some of the wild dogs.

There's a fishing rod in the shed. Trout's some of the best you'll find anywhere.'

'Well, you have me convinced now Angus.' Sean let a slow smile spread over his face.

'About pot shots at the rabbits?'

Sean laughed aloud. 'A man could do worse. There's something bothering me about Tom. I can't quite put my finger on it. Maybe my thoughts will clear up out there.'

'Don't think about him. Just do what you have to do for yourself for a while. This might be the best chance you'll get for a long time to give yourself a break man. Then there's the work ahead of you to build that house and make your niche in this territory. There are a few good masons around you can team up with and I know that you'll be one of the best. There's some building going down over the summer and it will be easy enough for you to pick up work.'

'A break will do me good Angus. Get away from my thoughts if you know what I mean.'

'Take the truck Sean. Head up to the northern end of the park and have a look around. You won't regret it.' Angus dropped the keys on the table. 'Our SAS friends want to keep you fresh and sharp so a short break before the mission will do you kindly.' Angus observed his friend closely. The last thing he wanted was for Sean to feel under pressure. The man was about to break with emotion and there was little time before the SAS training exercise. Angus just could not tell his best friend that he was about to walk into a firestorm.

'So you don't mind if I clean out the kitchen cupboard?' Sean grinned.

'Absolutely. We need to clear out last month's stores so you'd be doing us all a favour if you'd stock up the truck for your camp.' Angus grinned. 'You won't need to stop for fuel. I'll put a couple of jerry cans in the back of the ute. That will see you out for a couple of hundred kilometres at least.'

'I really appreciate it Angus. I mean it.'

'What's mine is yours Sean.' Angus said simply.

'I was thinking about building Tom and me a house.'

'You could build something solid like the Cooma gaol with your skills Sean.' Angus guffawed.

'Stone work is something I enjoy, that's for sure. My grandfather knew all the old techniques. Do you need anythin' done around here before I head out Angus?'

'Nope. I dropped the old mare, her donkey friend and Tom's colt a bit of feed this morning. They'll need building up after the winter.' Angus grinned

Sean laughed. 'OK. You win. I'm out of here.'

Sean crested the boulder-strewn hill that looked over the sparsely populated farms, then accelerated over the vast plains towards the northern end of the national park. The farms were nothing more than fragile footholds in a landscape otherwise dissected by faulting, uplifts and volcanic activity, the mountains punctuated by broad swathes of forests. In between, the farms were at best temporary niches on virgin terrain that would for decades just tolerate, yet never absorb, man. Despite its undeniable beauty, underpinning the pastoral mecca was a sense of ominous tidings, the past or future, Sean could not tell. The scars on the landscape reverberated against his awakened senses like a coarse bow on fine violin strings, the song of unfinished business.

Sean shivered as he drove on, wondering whether the privations of the early settlers had left an indelible mark on the mood of the mountains or whether its hidden Indigenous history was still resonating throughout the landscape. The road would take him deep into the northern end of the National Park, however his plan was to probe the off-track routes and camp where he could keep a wary ear to the ground. This was not the time for chance meetings with adventurers and bushwalkers. He needed time out and space. He needed the freedom to think and reboot his reflexes. He wanted to be unnoticed and unknown for now. There was a training exercise at hand and he wanted no distractions. Already, he had had to deal with an unexpected encounter with mercenaries in Cooma, people who belonged in Sierre Leone or Cuba and not in Australia. It was as unnerving to him as the drug bust was to Tom. Sean knew he was not one of them, hired killers. He was trained to protect Queen and Country, not kill for personal gain or revenge. In Australia he had maintained a discrete identity and low profile. But the Monaro was clearly a small place. It was virtually impossible to move without being noticed. The dynamic of community, the underside of gossip and networked deals, were the same as in any territory he had ever known. The only relief was that this land soothed him, almost more than his home in Ireland.

Sean eased back on the accelerator wondering if he still had the strength and presence of mind to camp in the open. He toyed with the idea of moving deeper into the mountains, once the training camp was over, far from the well patronised huts and the main routes at the northern edges of the park. He quickly flicked the map open on the dashboard, tracing his path and reckoning on his proximity to Tantangara Dam. Finally he turned onto a plain, mentally marking a spot to lay his swag.

The stars fell from the sky in a spectacular display of diamonds set against the black silk of night. Sean lay on his back, absorbed in the display of constellations. Here, in the absolute darkness, the thickening galaxy of shimmering stars drew him in, each one filled with its individual script, each one perfect against the black of the limitless night. The sound of the night owls, the occasional song of the dingo ringing in the hills and the plop of fish in the darkness of the dam, all this was sufficient sound to soothe his body and soul. Instinctively Sean put his ear to the ground. Yet instead of the hum of the earth the unexpected vibrations of history rose up and caught him in a strange spell. It was as though there was a living memory in the rocks. The sound of horror and death: the rape of women, children torn from the breasts of their mothers, men subdued like cattle, humiliated and herded together to be shot. Then he heard the audible report of a rifle, and another, ringing in his inner ear, an invisible yet open vestibule to history, as sure as the sounds of screaming and the horrific realisation etched into the faces of the old men as they tried to flee, their foreheads creased with defeat and bare chests sunken with the burden of shame. As their noble and black heads bowed in surrender, the old men, women and children dropped like crows. One by one the rifles continued to fire relentlessly reducing them to nothing more than flyblown corpses to be tidied into a gully and buried beneath the advance of another civilisation, as if one generation, one culture, one race was dispensable in the path of the next. Sean awoke, his heart racing. There was nothing here at all, no people, no horror, only deathly quiet. Sean thankfully breathed in the silence before finally dropping asleep.

Deep into the night, the unexpected sound of rapid gunfire reached Sean's unconscious mind. He woke instantly, his armpits prickling with sweat and palms moist with anticipation. The next round of fire reverberated off the mountain range, echoing across the body of water that formed Tantangara dam. Sean could hear the sounds ricocheting in the dense silence of the night. He sat up, fully awake, his senses on high alert.

The gunfire had suddenly exploded into his solitude. To Sean's well-trained ears there were at least five distinct sources of fire. He instinctively flattened himself on the ground, flicking a glance at the fire and scooping loose soil to douse the glowing coals. He did not want to become a target. The SAS were already in position, camped perhaps in the hills and mobilising on foot, their vehicles stationary and silent, as was Sean's.

The impulse to flight was as powerful as his unconscious reflex to hit the ground and douse the fire. He knew he had to move from where he was. But to run and abandon the truck would also leave him exposed. He strained to hear any signs of movement, wondering if he could recognise the make of the gun from the crack of the bullets or the thwump of the shots penetrating their target. The controlled firing and discipline of the separate groups told him that this was a professionally run and deadly serious exercise.

Carefully Sean took the rifle from under his sleeping bag and planned his strategy. The chance of exposure of the truck, particularly once mobile, was high. The chance of discovery in the hills was less, provided he made good his getaway and found sufficient cover amongst the trees.

Then the roar of Black Hawk engines suddenly broke over the crest of the dam wall. Sean instinctively rolled under the truck. A second chopper followed closely on the tail of the first, both flying on night vision, lights dimmed to avoid detection. The burst of gunfire from the first chopper backed up Sean's theory that the target was set and the air troops were closing in to take out their object. These guys were well trained, but Sean immediately sensed a mistake. The second chopper overflew the mark and had to circle to come in again. Sean carefully inched from under the truck into the open. He checked his watch, noting the time and altitude, and that the barometer was falling. By tomorrow, there was every chance of foul weather. He counted the seconds until the predicted withdrawal of the choppers. Without warning, the chopper flew back towards his truck, shattering the silence with its powerful motors. Sean gritted his teeth and rolled back under the truck gripping the rifle to his chest. It would be impossible for them to miss the vehicle. The night radar suddenly snapped on and Sean knew that there would be no point in running. His image would show up through the sophisticated lens. They could chase him through the night all the way to Kosciuszko and there was nothing he could do about it. He got out from under the truck then stood up slowly, holding up his hands just as the powerful searchlight of the chopper caught him full glare.

'Let me take him Robert.' The leader, face still covered by a navy balaclava moved in to lead the interrogation.

'Name?'

'You don't need to know!'

'Rank?'

'British SAS Commando. Irish Task Force.'

'Last posting?'

'Iraq.'

'Subsequent reconnaissance point?'

'Grid reference 51.5 degrees east, 40. 5 degrees south.'

'Anything to report?'

'Negative.'

'At ease Sean. Forward intelligence suggests activity in all main centres of southern region.'

'Negative David.'

'You are on the ball Sean. The region is covered, yet quiet. We have reason to suspect, however, undercover ops in northern section are spilling into the Brindabellas and close to the Deep Space Centre.'

'Do you have anything to add?'

'No sir.'

'Good. Keep it undercover Sean. NASA and the CIA will look after the Brindabellas.' David pulled a laminated map from his fatigue pocket. 'I need you to cover the following grids on a routine basis.' David drew a marker around the perimeter of the observation zone. 'You'll get back up later this month to probe any cells once you've penetrated their cover.' David paused for thought. 'Any further intelligence on the Croat training camps?'

'We know that they are out here. All quiet for the moment. Activity has moved to the south coast of NSW. Angus is keeping a close eye.'

'Good. Are you compromised Sean?'

'Negative sir.'

'You are compromised Sean. Where's the boy?'

'I didn't know you were watching my back for me David.' Sean barked.

'Where is he?'

'Cooma gaol. Set-up job.'

'Can you exit?'

'No. He's my responsibility now.'

'Sean, you won't be able to maintain cover if you're too close to the kid. You'll have to find an excuse to separate.'

'I won't need to. The kid has found himself a girlfriend.'

'I hope you're right Sean. We can't afford anything to put the operation in jeopardy. No ties. Understood?'

'Understood.' Sean said flatly.

Sean watched the lights of the chopper flare briefly then disappear as David and his team exited the scene. He climbed back into his sleeping bag, feeling the comfort of the rifle butt against his thigh as he settled in for the last hour of sleep before dawn robbed him of the opportunity. The drone of empty sound and space hummed in his ears, triggering a spontaneous state of detachment of his consciousness from the body, as if he were riding the low level thermals, skating quickly over the park and along the exit route to

Adaminaby.

Tom emerged from the stone walls of the Cooma gaol with cautious elation. Angus heard the news and within minutes was on the road out of Dalgety to collect him. He was as proud and as deeply moved as any father would be when his son was granted freedom. Angus opened his arms to Tom as he walked out of the prison gates.

'Tom. Glad to see you're out of here man. What a turn of events!'

'Hello Angus.' Tom accepted the embrace, turning briefly to see Kate and Wendy softly waving him on. 'Where's Sean?'

'He's out campin' for a few days son. Looked as though he needed a break as well.'

'Oh.' Tom felt the immediate pang of deep disappointment.

A man stepped across the road from the perimeter of the stone memorial.

'Hello.' Angus swivelled around instinctively, putting out his right hand to greet the man.

The dark eyes of the Aboriginal man carved from a bottomless well of compassion met his. Angus recognised the eyes, yet still was unable to detect the focal point or fathom their unreachable depths.

'This is Tom.'

'You know him?'

'They told me. That he was comin' out.'

'How did anyone else know?'

'We know.' The old man didn't elaborate.

'Tom? You know one another?'

Tom smiled recognizing the vaguely familiar face.

'I think so. Good to see you again.' Tom said simply.

'Are you comin' then? The men's camp.' The elder turned to Angus.

'Men's camp?'

'We're doin' a special initiation at the mountain.

'When does it happen?'

'We'll call you.'

'Thanks.' Angus put out his hand.

'You all right then son?' He asked.

'Feelin' better. That's for sure.'

'Keep yourself clear of Cooma for the next week. Don't want anythin' pollutin' you before the journey.'

'I'll be at home with Angus for most of it.'

'Good. That's then the right place for you, son.' The old man looked carefully at Angus before walking towards the town centre.

Early spring was always a major challenge for the herds of horses living in and around the mountains on both sides of the Great Dividing Range. Unseasonal storms, with winds gusting from the Southern Ocean would bring lashing rain, sleet and unwelcome snow. The temperatures would steadily drop under the influence of the sub-Antarctic weather systems, freezing over the pastures and forcing the horses to traverse ice and snow once again. These were the times when the oldest of the stallions, stumbled and struggled through the deepening drifts of unexpected snow. It would be only time before the maturing colts eager for leadership of the mares would challenge the stallions for control and leadership of the herd. Weary from the long winters and sudden spring storms, some of the battle weary stallions relinquished control rather than endure the bitter rivalry and deadly fights with the younger horses.

With the first signs of spring touching the high country, the snow began to melt and gradually the horses began the long journey towards the summer pastures. Many of the mares were already heavily pregnant, some ready to drop their foals just as the green shoots appeared on the Cascades grasslands. It was hard going for the brumbies, urgently in need of nourishing spring feed to build them after the long and hard winter.

The ageing black stallion knew that he didn't have much left in him. His instinct to protect and sustain the herd was still powerful, even though his solitary journey and tortuous climb along the well-trodden track to the Ramsheads had taken the last of his reserves of energy. He stumbled back to Dead Horse Gap, driven down from the mountains by the weather building behind Mt Townsend, the stormy winds changing as the cold front moved closer.

The old horse waited at the head of the Cascades Valley and whinnied, calling to the lead mare and waiting for her reply. The weather was closing in quickly, forcing the horses into a tight huddle at the edge of the tree line. The stallion wanted to lead them, as he had for so long, into the shelter and safety of the trees; however one of the younger stallions blocked him from joining the herd. The old stallion hesitated, then walked forwards towards the creek crossing. The black colt lunged forwards and with ears laid back and teeth bared, attacked the neck of the old stallion. The stallion stopped in his tracks, aware that he did not have the strength for the fight. The young colt was coming at him again, eyes wild with rage and hindquarters swivelling and striking the stallion on the ribs. The old stallion stumbled with the force of the strike, his back leg, broken at the pastern, giving way and sending him tumbling onto the snow. The colt struck again. The stallion screamed in pain as his ribs fractured under the sharp crack of the colt's hooves. He tried to push himself to his feet, his hooves sinking into the snow and the last of his precious reserves waning.

The mares pulled back, frightened by the warring stallions, the wind warning them that there was little time to move out of the exposed valley before the wild storm hit. The main herd of mares and some of the foals began to climb a granite topped hill, making their way steadily towards the shelter of trees where they could wait out the storm. The wind whipped at the top of the trees and the horses, rumps to the onslaught, huddled together for protection. One of the mares, her usually light coat streaked dark by the rain, faltered with the effort of the climb. She was close to giving birth to her foal and instinct, more powerful than her need to stay with the herd, forced her to find temporary protection behind a rock jutting through the pastures on the valley floor. There was no other choice. She knew she did not have the time or energy to climb, pain gripping at her belly as her foal was about to be born. The mare lay down behind the rock, keeping close to the ground and out of the wind. The wind groaned around the perimeter of the rock, pulling off loose lichen and shearing twigs off the trees. The wilderness home that she knew and loved was now a nightmare of a raging spring storm bringing deathly rains and renewed freezing cold.

The colt was born in the middle of the night as the wind screamed in agony forcing its way over the Snowy Mountains. The mare struggled alone, the cold biting her flesh and her instinct alone saving the colt and herself from certain death. After he was born, as much as her waning strength would allow, the mare licked the afterbirth from the coat of her foal, his tail wagging in response to the first touch of reassuring life after the warmth of the womb. The mare nuzzled his side and the colt lifted his head, instinctively looking for milk. The mare relaxed. The birth was over and the colt was alive. The colt started to suckle, taking in the first flow of her milk which was essential to prepare him for the long and hard weeks ahead.

The wind plucked at the mare's mane and she knew that they would have to move off at first light, leaving the scant shelter of the rock and to rejoin the herd. She stood up wearily and faced the first blast of cold air. The colt struggled, pushing his front hooves into the mud and snow, standing, then stumbling and falling back onto the earth. She nuzzled him again and the colt responded. On wavering legs he pushed himself onto all fours, unsteady, then finally finding his balance. The mare whickered and the colt took his first steps, wobbling as the blustery wind pushed him off balance. The colt stuck fast and took a step, then another and within seconds was at the mare's tail. She whinnied, looking for the herd. The wind whistled through the trees, the silence of the valley complete as she realised that she had lost the main group. Panicked by the separation from the rest of her herd, she broke into a canter, forging up the hill and forgetting the foal. Then she stopped, exhausted and wild-eyed, alone in the valley with her young colt.

FOOTY MATCH AT BERRIDALE

Sean found the drive back to the farm refreshing and he looked forwards to the company of Angus. The surprise news that Tom was released from goal instantly brought tears to his eyes. But it was Angus who stepped in with wide arms and the broad back to catch his unexpected emotion and Sean knew immediately that this was the strongest bond he would ever have in his life; unbreakable and real. Now, it was time for the men to rebuild themselves and to find a new release.

From the western hilltop, the sounds of a football match carried on the up-draughts like a pocket of hot air. Sean sat quietly listening to the game. The shouting and whooping of Jindabyne parents as the Pigs scored again pierced the sound of the wind wailing through the fence, its wires rusted and sagging and posts already rotten with age.

Pieces of scrap iron that once formed the roof of the piggery clattered together on the stone ground and the mob of 30 strong kangaroos ate nervously, aware of the presence of the man sitting like a stone, listening and watching. The wind picked up in strength, tugging the crowns of the scant gum trees, their growth stunted by poor soils and strong competition from grazing sheep and kangaroos. Too many mouths had already eaten all the nourishment from the soil. Then the rains came, carving deep erosion gullies along the natural drainage lines formed into the terrain.

By contrast, the neat village was tightly nestled in the base of the valley, once an ancient floodplain able to subdue the most savage of storm-fed deluges. Now the busy hub was filled with a mixture of heritage and contemporary structures designed for the essentially pub-centred town, dominated by the Snowy River Shire Council. The three main hills confined Berridale to an almost idyllic setting, often sheltered from the raging winds that excoriated the back of the mountain range and ripped roofs off the more exposed Jindabyne and Cooma houses. The relative peace of Berridale was broken only when, from time to time, the town hosted Saturday games on the footy field.

The match ended, and with it, the sounds of unanimous cheers from the Jindabyne supporters dominating the aftermath of the game and, now, the wind. Tom pulled himself off the ground for the umpteenth time. Angus reached down to give him a hand up after the final whistle had been blown.

'Well played son. I'm proud of you.'

'It was a bit of fun I suppose.'

'Good. There's someone waiting for you at the pub.'

'Oh?'

'Come on. Shower and we'll go ahead. Then you can drink with the team if you want. Pick you up around 10.30 p.m.'

'Gee. Thanks Angus.'

'Don't mention it. Got your gear?'

'Tom!' Cassie ran across from the sideline. 'I just heard you were here.'

'Cassie.' Tom caught her in his arms.

'Thank goodness you're out! They caught Will. I thought he was dead.'

'Can't keep a man down Cassie. He's over there.' Tom pointed to his opponent.

'Will's here?'

Tom nodded in the direction of the hub of Bush Pigs players. The curly top of Will emerged from the clump of mothers, players, supporters and their coaches. Instinctively he looked up, noticing Cassie, Angus and Tom. 'He's apparently out on bail. Don't know why.'

'Maybe he did a deal with the cops and told them who deals in this area.'

'Could be.' Tom was non-committal.

'He looks pretty quiet Tom.'

'Not too sure about that Cassie. He walloped me a few times on the field today.'

Cassie was transfixed by the figure of her brother now moving surely towards them. She placed her hand on Tom's arm. 'Don't say much Tom, about us I mean.'

Tom was silent as he watched Will.

'Cassie.'

'Will. Are you OK?' Cassie's voice quivered with emotion.

'I'm fine. Cass. Bit of a ride through the storm. But you know me. Always come up trumps.'

'Will I'm sorry I wasn't there for you this time. I know you needed help.'

'You know Cass. You're the best sister anyone could want. You've always looked after me and well, I guess it was just about time I learned a few lessons for meself.' Will grinned at his sister.

'Will, I…' Cassie was close to tears.

Will pulled his sister into his arms and gave her a hug. 'Don't cry Cass. I'm alive yeah?'

'Yeah. I guess you are.' Cassie laughed.

Hello Tom. Good match.' Will sounded surprisingly courteous and civil.

Angus stepped forwards. 'Hello Will. You all right son? Heard you had a bit of a scare up on the mountain.'

'Not as much of a scare as this dickhead getting himself landed in gaol. At least he won't deal drugs anytime soon.' Will grinned at Tom. 'Good luck Tom. Look after her for me will yer.' He put his hand into Tom's.

'Yeah. Thanks Will. I will.'

'OK then boys. We're out of here for a shower. See you at the pub Will?'

'Not sure.' Will reverted to the sullen, troubled boy Angus well remembered.

'Look after yourself Will and stay out of trouble.' Angus wheeled Cassie and Tom towards the ute.

Will took Angus's comment better than he thought. Usually he would go off his head and swear at any unwanted advice. But after the nightmare on the mountain, he could feel that he was different. It would be a few weeks before he had to front court again and hopefully, he could stay out of trouble and out of the clink on a suspended sentence. He sighed. It was one thing to survive the wild ride through the storm to Thredbo. It was another all together to stick to the new plan and stay clean. But he knew that the mountain had changed him deep down and that there was no going back to the past. Now, it was almost as if another person told the story of recent life; the drug deals, running supplies from the coast, the occasional encounter with foreign nationals on the deserted shorelines, the risks he took to find the right clients, the plans for break ins to some of the coastal servos. His past life read like a bad novel and as though someone else had written the script and he was just the onlooker. Somehow, Angus was in the ghost script in his memory, but he just couldn't work out how or where. Maybe he had seen him on the coast somewhere. He just couldn't put his finger on it and then his face popped up again at the bush dance and again on the footy field. What he did know for sure was that he felt so different since the night on the mountain. He swore that he would change his life, change it forever.

RITE OF PASSAGE

Sean deliberately stayed out of the football scene and away from the match. The walk to the top of the hill energised him and even though he only had a few scraggly sheep for company, he was happy and contented. The sounds of the match were amplified in the natural stadium, a bowl of land dissected by Myack Creek and surrounded by low lying hills.

He met Angus and Sean back at the farm where Tom told him bright eyed, the details of the match and about catching up with Cassie.

'You should have brought her home man.' Sean couldn't understand that she was not here.

'I will Sean. I wanted to see you.' Tom said quietly looking up into the bright eyes of his best friend.

'Me too. I am so glad you are out Tom.' Sean caught the emotion rising once again in his chest. 'Angus sent me out into the bush to forget all about Cooma and so I wouldn't stress about you too much Tom.'

'Thanks Sean. It was tougher than I thought inside. Should've been Will though.'

'Well he got a serve of the best that the mountain weather had to offer and that brought him to his knees and senses it seems.'

'Well I'm happier for Cassie than I am for Will. At least she won't have to pick up the pieces after Tom as often.'

'Let's hope not at all Tom. I think we will find that Will has certainly turned a corner. Let's get some grub and throw a line in the river.'

'Yeah. Good plan.'

Sean and Tom sat side by side on the banks of the Snowy River. Sean plopped his line into the water and dragged the lure across the surface. He watched the trail of the lure and waited for a nibble. It was quiet and relaxing thinking of nothing in particular apart from watching the soft ripples on the surface of the water and the emerald dragonflies dancing upstream, taking off like mini helicopters then landing again before darting forwards in search of prey.

'Tom, look at that fellow.' Sean pointed to the dragonfly now creating a mini vortex with its wings. 'They make it look easy.'

Tom casually cast his line and landed the lure close to the dragonfly.

'Nice cast!'

'Thanks. Me granddad taught me everything he knows about fishing.'

'Then you can bring home dinner!' Sean grinned and continued to trail his lure.

'Might.' Tom said noncommittally.

Half an hour of the lazy afternoon easily passed with no fish landed for dinner.

'Tom.' Sean called out to his fishing buddy.

'Yeah. I'm here mate.' Tom replied.

'Tom, you know how I told you that I might have some business to do in Ireland…'

'You mentioned something about it.'

'It's come up.'

'Oh.' Tom's face dropped and he looked down at his fishing rod suddenly disinterested.

'It won't be for long Tom. I just have to sort out a few things. That's all.'

'What things Sean!' Tom thrust his forehead close to Sean's face, eyeballing him and asserting his 'right' to Sean before any business overseas.

'I have to go away.'

'Says who?' Tom demanded.

'Look. I don't want to go as much as you don't want me to go.' Sean was surprised at his sudden pricking of tears.

'I just got out of the clink two weeks ago Sean. It's not as if I'm ready to see you go off anywhere.'

'I know son.' Sean softened in his tone. 'I know.'

Sean struggled with his emotion, carefully reeling in the fishing line then standing for another cast. He felt the line pull and tug through his fingers, the reel spinning freely as the lure catapulted into the water metres from the shore.

'What did you do when I was away?'

'What do you mean?'

'When you went camping in the northern end of the park.'

'Tantangara Dam? I needed the time out to clear my mind.'

'What did you do there?'

'You and Angus aren't just farmers and a lousy fisherman.' Tom started reeling in his line.

'Tom…'

'I know that Angus has more to him than meets the eye. He's a wonderful bloke and I'd be the first to say so. I'd never be here or anywhere without him, without you Sean.'

'It's nothing son. It's nothing.'

'If you're going to Ireland on business, then I'm coming.'

'You can't.' Sean snapped. 'What about Cassie. What are you going to do without your job?'

'I can work for you.'

'You can't Tom.' Sean was emphatic.

Tom stood up, throwing the rod onto the ground. He started to walk to the ute then thinking the better of his mood went back to the rod and reel. He picked up the rod, stood next to Sean and pulled some line free and easily cast into the middle of the river.

'Nice cast.' Sean said.

'If I can work at the pub, I can work for you.'

'It's hardly the same line of work.' Sean relaxed and laughed.

'You're not telling what line of work though.' Tom pressed for an answer.

'Let's change the subject.'

'You know how you murdered that priest Sean…'

'Why are you bringing that up?'

'Did he have anything to do with your 'line of work' as you call it?' Tom pushed.

Sean put his rod down very gently. He was having trouble, for the first time in a long time, controlling his anger. He could not stomach being unable to tell Tom the truth and there was also no way that he was going to lie either. The sweat broke out on the back of his neck. He was in a tight spot and he knew it. Already, his cover was considerably compromised not to mention his feelings now that he had responsibilities for Tom.

'He was human trash Tom.' Sean muttered. He walked over to the truck and pulled the tobacco from the glovebox. His hands were shaking. He sat down on the ground and slowly rolled a smoke. 'Smoke?'

'Thanks.' Tom waited until Sean had finished rolling the cigarette.

'Sit down.' Sean commanded.

Tom, surprised by the sudden change in his tone, sat next to Sean on the ground.

'The camp that is coming up,' Sean waited for acknowledgement from Tom, 'I want you to go. Angus will be there. It's a mens' workshop scene, Indigenous elders, Andrew from the prison and a couple of Angus's army friends.'

'Oh.'

'It will be a good camp son.'

Well it won't be if you're not there Sean?' The accusation was back in Tom's voice.

'As I said, I won't be here for that one.' Sean said firmly. If you get the training, if you feel comfortable about the drift of the camp, then we'll see about training you in our line of work as you put it.'

'Cool.' Tom immediately dropped pressing charges against Sean over leaving him.

'OK. That's settled.' Sean did not elaborate.

'When's the camp?'

'A couple of weeks time. Angus will take you out there. Should be good.'

'Thanks Sean. That's swell.'

'Think nothing of it son.' Sean said mentally offloading the mountain of mini worries that had built into two major anxieties, Tom's welfare and his own identity.

Angus revved along the four wheel drive track, enjoying the rage on dirt as a welcome diversion from the more measured negotiation of ocean swells. The beautiful fishing boat, the Aurora, was no more after the epic storm at sea, but he would find a way back out onto the ocean in good time. For now, even the endless rounding up of ewes for the early spring shearing was too predictable for his liking. He needed the break from his normal routines. The rough track went into terrain that he did not usually traverse, yet Angus knew it held more secrets than he could ever know.

The camp was an experiment. It was not meant to be anything more than a contemporary stab at bringing the young men home to themselves. This would be just one chance for them to find the balance of love of law by pulling them into loose social yards, where amongst them there would be leaders.

At the end of the day however, every one of them would learn to live by the law. There was no other way. The lawless scourge of young people running amok on drugs, destroying their souls in a series of social and personal disasters was more than some of the local men could stand. It wasn't just about the wasted youth. This was a fight for the souls of young men but it was also a carefully considered judgement about the future of the nation now at serious risk from the perils of war.

Angus hit the accelerator, taking the vehicle over jumps in the road, washing the tail out and fanging the wheel to the right and then left to avoid the tumbled rocks abutting the verge. Tom gripped his seat, surprised by the sudden revelation of the new qualities in the man he knew. This guy was not the totally sane and utterly reliable friend he knew. He was out of control. Angus planted the accelerator again then jammed on the brakes, taking the ute in a full three sixty before driving the accelerator to the ground and raising an impenetrable shield of dust on the road behind.

'You in a hurry Angus?' Tom attempted humour.

'You scared?'

'Shit scared.' Tom readily admitted.

'Good.'

'What?'

'I said good.' Angus yelled.

'Thanks. What's that for?'

'Scare the shit out of you Tom before we get there. That way you won't be any trouble to me, or the other camp leaders.'

'I wasn't intendin' to be.' Tom protested, his defences coming up.

Angus said nothing. He accelerated, this time slowly as Tom, clearly out of his depth, gripped the side of the door.

'Steady on Angus. I'm not interested in dying.'

'I'm not sure about that mate. You looked 'dead' to me when we found you.'

'What do you mean?'

'What do you think I mean?' Angus allowed incredulous anger to come into his voice: as if Tom could have forgotten he owed his life to Sean and him.

'I'm sorry all right. I'm sorry for what I don't know I've done yet.'

'That's good. Maybe you need a bit more sorry to you in case you get any smart ideas.'

'What the fuck are you talking about Angus?' Tom's anger began to rise.

'Don't you ever swear at me like that son. You understand?'

The tone in Angus's voice told Tom he was icily angry and that there was no room for movement in the conversation. The tone came out of nowhere on the back of a skill at the wheel that Tom had no idea Angus possessed.

'Shit.'

'Don't swear. Rule number one is that you don't swear. Not now, not ever. Got it?' Angus repeated the command, his voice just under control.

'I didn't think it was against the law.' Tom said soberly.

'It is, against the camp law Tom. That's the first rule. The other rules you will learn later. Don't any of you think about jumping the ute because you're not going to do that either unless you want me to come back for you and run these four wheels over you.'

'Christ you really mean business yeah?'

Angus deliberately ignored the blasphemy. 'Good. Now that's sorted. Relax and roll us both a smoke.'

Tom did as he was asked, carefully extracting the tobacco and papers from the glovebox and meticulously rolling the smoke as Sean had taught him.

'Light yours only. I'll light my own.' Angus said tersely.

Tom followed, wondering where his 'mate and mentor' was coming from, but did exactly as he was told anyway. Angus continued to drive in silence, drawing deeply on his cigarette then carefully butting out the residue in the ashtray, closing it tight without making any allowances for Tom if he needed to do the same. Tom knew he was caught. He couldn't stub it out on the floor of the cab or throw the butt out of the window without earning another strong reprimand from Angus. So that left the option, of drawing carefully open the ashtray to deposit the ends of the smoke.

'Stub it out properly. I don't want the dags smouldering up my nose.' Angus said without emotion.

Tom carefully butted out the cigarette then closed the ashtray, making sure that no smoke was escaping and that the tray was fully shut.

They arrived at night, the camp already lit by a fire raging, but under control, in the huge, stone-walled fire pit. A pile of logs, some sawn and others uncut, were stacked next to the fire. The tents were lined in a neat row, military style, and Tom realised that this was no ordinary 'men's camp'. It was clearly a highly planned event. He had no choice except to attend and obey. The vehicles were parked about 50 metres from the camp each car allotted a space one beside the other. Angus pulled into the bush carpark, unloading their swags and dumping them on the ground.

'Wait here Tom. You'll be told which is your tent.'

'Aren't I staying with you?'

'You'll stay in the tent where you're put.' Angus walked away without looking over his shoulder. He returned a few moments later and picked up his swag. That's your tent Tom, the one on the end. There are three other blokes in there with you. Toilet tent is down the track 20 metres and the shower tent on the other side. One shower each day. Half a bucket only. You'll be given your duty after the meal tonight. See you then.'

'Yeah. See you then Angus.' Tom walked directly to his tent aware that any transgression against time or space in the 'bush city' would be punishable. He opened the flap to throw his swag down. Four neat camp stretchers lined the dirt floor of the camp with makeshift hooks attached to the middle poles at either end of the tent.

'That's your bed Tom.'

Tom swivelled around. 'What the fuck are you doing here Will?'

'Thought you knew there was no swearing on this camp Tom.' Will said quietly.

'Who do you think you are you little prick, telling me what to do?'

'I'm leader for this tent Tom.' Will looked him squarely in the eye.

'We could have brought you all here blindfolded,' the camp leader opened. 'Take this as your first test of trust and loyalty. This is a private camp and no one else knows or will ever know, about the location. Is that clearly understood?' Peter spoke firmly to the 16 young men gathered around the fire pit. 'Do I take that to be a yes?' Peter commanded quietly.

'Yes.'

'That's one yes only?'

'Yes!' A chorus of assent broke out.

'Good. Is anyone not happy about the situation here?'

Silence pocked the air with unspoken questions.

'Then you all know why you are here? Peter commanded.

'No, I don't.' Tom was confused by the sudden change in dynamic between Will and himself.

'Good. That's one honest person. Are there any more out there?' Peter asked.

'I'm not sure.' A younger voice spoke out.

'Anyone else? This is your last chance.' Peter indicated in his tone that the patience game was over. 'Right then. All of you are damaged goods.' Peter broke the news. 'None of you — none of us — are totally clean.' He continued, 'this is a camp to show you to yourselves. This is a camp to see if you have what it takes to take responsibility for your past without blame. This is the camp that will make sure you are right here now with all your faculties awake, your senses alert and your mind in the present only. This is the place where you will gain the courage and skills to face the future — any future — without fear. Is that right?' Peter steadily addressed the gathering.

Tom felt the shock wave rock his body. The immediate dizziness, the temptation to regress back into fainting or the 'out of body' experiences in the gaol were immediately pressing upon his consciousness.

'If any of you have a problem with the fact that you are young and at risk to yourself and the community, then you had better speak to Bruce after the group meal. Bruce is a non-negotiable person you will soon discover. He has your full history, for every one of you, and if you have a problem with his assessment of your character, then you can take it up with him. You'll find that your argument will last about 10 minutes at the most. There won't be a question or an escape clause too clever for Bruce.'

'But...'

'If any of you think that you are the victims of crime, then you had better think again. This is not the victim-game camp. There are no pseudo-rescuers in the group. If anyone tries to play appeaser, peacemaker or mediator for anyone else, they will be punished. Is that understood?' The shocked silence indicated to the young men that there was no crap going down in this camp.

Peter felt the sudden paralysis in the atmosphere, setting the cue to let Andrew talk them into a broader vision of themselves. Andrew looked around the group. The young men couldn't have been more scared if they tried. He spent a long time looking into the fire, creating a powerful atmosphere of exposure with his thoughts. Finally, he broke the silence.

'This is where we dump our baggage. I'll start. Commit your past to the fire!' Andrew stood up. For a moment he focussed on an old emotional wound as he spoke. The memory was powerful, painful and in that moment, the tears of rage pricked at the corners of his eyes. He carefully, deliberately, picked up a piece of firewood and threw it into the fire and with it, mentally discarded the source of internal pain. He walked away from the edge of the fire. 'That is how you deal with pain. You pick it out before it picks you out and overwhelms you. You identify it, you look at it in the eye and you consciously let go of that pain. Let go of the humiliation, the outrage, the rage.' Andrew faced the young men seated around the fire pit. 'You face your pain and throw that pain into the fire pit. It is no longer your pain. Understood? The fire takes your pain. Let go of the pain and anger. Let it out and let it burn. Free yourselves.'

One of the young men screamed spontaneously. 'You bastard!'

Andrew deliberately allowed the young man to break into a sob, careful not to interrupt his process or provide to him the same sense of false comfort that most likely was the cause for his adolescent hate, hurt, and anger.

'You bastard.' Will screamed into the night. 'I'll get you, you bastard.' He stood up looking for something to hurl into the pit. The 'minder' at the perimeter of the circle almost as if by instinct, gave him a piece of wood. Will seized the talisman, as if gripped by another power, wanting to break and torture it, to destroy its tangible existence. The full force of his emotion rose to the surface when he realised that this thing, this symbol in his hand, represented his dependency on drugs and the guy who got him into it in the first place. The memory was real. The complete agony and humiliation and a total powerless rage caught hold of him. He wanted to drop to his knees and sob, but he couldn't do it. He couldn't allow the memory of being trapped, eat away at his soul any longer. With his anger out in the open, Will stood up and looked at the wooden talisman with complete control and contempt. He studied its shape as if it was a cannabis joint, then hurled it into the blazing fire of roughly cut bush timber.

Andrew waited for 30 seconds. He breathed in, and breathed out, taking on Will's troubles as if they were his own then breathing them out into the fire. He breathed in again, taking on the power of freedom and breathed out, mentally covering Will with the feeling of at last being freed from his past.

'Anyone else?' Andrew asked quietly. 'This is your last chance men. This is the only opportunity you will get for the rest of the camp. If you are unable to do anything about yourselves now and the pain you carry, this camp will break you. If you don't unload now, at this point and now, then the emotional damage you carry will weaken you to such an extent that you will not, I repeat not be able to withstand the next stages of your initiation.'

Andrew waited for another 15 seconds, before he closed the opportunity.

'OK. Now we eat.' Peter said in an even tone.

The camp leaders understood the value and power of nourishment after emotional exposure and catharsis. Some of the boys still looked uncertain, too shocked by the discovery in themselves and their camp mates of the depth of what lay within themselves. The contrast of Will's emotions on one hand, and the almost ecstatic aftermath of release of his tortured memories, the spilling of toxic chemistry that for so long held him a fugitive from his past and captive of the present, was almost too much for them to bear.

The arrival of roast potatoes, carefully crafted in the coals, the bounty of damper with blackcurrant jam and the serving of kangaroo meat, was the balancing power to bring them back to the immediacy of their rough and ready, yet well-structured, environment.

Will munched slowly on his potatoes. He had never remembered a time when food tasted and felt so good to his mouth and gut. The warmth of the piping hot meal suffused him with strength and the assurance that he was finally on the way out of his entrapment, thanks to Andrew: he was on the way out of hell. For some reason, his imprisonment had been delayed and it was only on arrival at the camp, that Peter indicated to him; that there would be a slight reprieve for him to get his shit together before he was committed to the lock up. If he came good at the camp, then his sentence would be indefinitely suspended. This was, as Peter insisted and impressed upon him, his chance to get even with himself before the world got even with him. It was his chance to come clean and clear with his soul, to cut the crap and at least be man enough to own his own shit. Will agreed. There was nothing wonderful about the choice of the clink. It was a crap house probably no better than the private hell in his mind created by a long habit of drug taking. The incident at the fire awoke him to the fact that it was of no use to look for the 'escape clause', that it would be better to confront his explosive rage that had been building on the bed of pain. There was nothing wrong with power and freedom, provided it remained within the context of carefully constructed boundaries. The exorcism of his ghosts that night around the fire pit was the beginning of finding his own power and the men at the camp provided the clear boundaries for him to do so without destroying himself or anyone else around him. The fire pit was the focus for recovery. That was the essential message and Will was first to get it.

In the cold morning light, Peter signalled to Jack to wake the young men. The quiet Aboriginal man with his self-contained manner, began to wake them one by one, tent by tent. The young men piled out of the tents, remembering the instruction to dress immediately for the day and wash later. No one was allowed to walk around the camp in bare feet. There was no such luxury as 'slackness' or 'accidents'. 'Medical liabilities' were considered to be a contravention of the safety of the group.

'There will be two groups of eight. The first group will go with Jack and the second group will follow my directions. By ten in the morning, the second group will traverse five kilometres of rough territory and find water for the camp. There will be no drinking of water supplies without permission. Clear?' Peter was totally calm setting the course for the morning.

'Anyone who strays from their group will be punished by confinement and deprived of his evening meal. Is that understood? Good. I take it that there are no 'nos'. These are your groups. Group one. Will, Tom, Andrew, Jase…' Peter reeled off the list of eight in the first group. 'The second group will be Adam, Shawn, Dan….'.

The two groups filed out of the camp separately, Jack indicating to the first mob to simply follow in silence along the track to 'the rock.' Peter, more attuned to the rough and ready second group, herded them together and gave them broad instructions on the landscape, drawing a rough map in the dirt.

Tom kept up with Jack, maintaining a discreet distance of about 10 metres to indicate to their "spiritual guide and leader" that he afforded him the proper respect for the occasion. Will walked quietly behind Tom, recognising the strength in his new best friend.

Tom remained slightly in awe of Jack's power, the depth of his subconscious mind that almost by instinct knew what he, Tom, was thinking and feeling. He reckoned that Jack already had him and Will fully sussed. They had passed the first stages of initiation and were on the path of tribal belonging. Tom felt the quiet compassion of the man and had the sense that Jack knew that he had been violated. He was strangely unconcerned that someone had a kind of power over him and that he had no reason or wish to challenge that power. He concentrated on his feet, carefully stepping as Jack had, along the path mindful of living creatures and of the bush signals that were the give-away for nesting sites for birds and animals.

The morning sun warmed the rock and Jack seated himself to the north, indicating to the young men in his group to form a sitting circle. The air rang with a lyrebird song and in the distance the far off sound of white cockatoos cavorting over the open plains gave spatial context to their hidden bush retreat. He could still hear the voices of his Elders, their quiet convictions and instructions tuning his spirit to the greater and bigger picture of the past, present and future of his land. He knew that seated before him young men, old in spirit although their bodies told the world otherwise.

As if still in a trance, like the Pied Piper, Jack lead the initiated men back to the camp. They arrived back in camp to the makeshift tables where a feast of damper, tea and fresh fruit waited for them. Both Tom and Will instinctively knew that this was 'the first day of the rest of their lives'. They had finally found themselves and therefore owned the past, the present and the future life ahead. They communicated quietly, both aware of the inner peace and sense of complete resolution of themselves, a spiritual awakening in the capable hands of Andrew and the Indigenous Elder Jack.

Jack called the men — elders and young initiates — to gather at the fire pit. The flames roared with freshly cut timber deepening the already glowing coals and warding off the surprising night cold that dropped over the bush camp. The men filed out of their tents and gathered quietly at the fire pit. Jack stood tall and stationary, his head lifted to the sky, his feet slightly apart as he watched and listened to the wind coming down the valley. The movement in the camp tonight, the rustling of the leaves and hurried flight of birds told him that the spirits of his ancestors, the elders guiding him in the initiation, had arrived. Jack smiled, internally acknowledging their presence. The flames flickered more brightly for a second and Jack saw Tom, clearly carved in rock, as if his face were morphed with the generations before him. Tom was first to smile at Jack catching the feeling of the man's warmth and protection. He was still glowing after the unexpected exhilaration of being part of passing all stages of his initiation and that his friend Will had now fully entered into manhood.

'Eat this bread as if it is your last. Drink this honey mead as if it is your last.' Andrew held his chalice towards the star spattered sky.

Tom nearly choked on the velvety honey mead, wondering whether he was close to laughter or disbelief. A bloody communion service in the bush! Tom allowed his emotions — a mixture of disbelief and elation — to surface and freely express themselves as he joined in the feasting on the freshly slaughtered kangaroo, the tender meat carefully prepared and cooked, almost dripping off the bone. To accompany the main meal they were treated to more bush honey mead and damper peppered with ground wattle seeds and dipped in lemon myrtle-infused macadamia oil. It was a banquet for the kings of the bush camp. Tom dipped his bread in the mead and then dropped it into the oil. The fragrance of rosemary, the sharp tang of the wattle, the mellow aromas of the rich mead made him dizzy with delight. The prospect of a permanent life camping off-road far from the endless trap that was abuse at the hands of the priest was as thrilling as it was refreshing. The drugs could go to hell as far as Tom was concerned. This was different. This was very different. The stars reflected in the wine and Tom read the future for himself. There was something important for him to complete.

'Tonight men, you are entering the next phase of your life. Drink to your health. Drink to the health of your friends and the future. Your future and the future of your country, is in your hands.'

'To your health, future and country!' Peter raised his enamel mug filled with the mellow brew of mulled honey mead and herbs.

'To health, future and country.' Tom stood to his feet.

'To our health, future and to country.' Will clinked his mug to Tom's mug, his smile as wide and bright as the heavens that opened up above them.

Jack watched from the sidelines of the firepit as the flames flickered tall and strong as Andrew sat amongst the young men. Once they finished feasting, Andrew opened with a powerful aauumm. Then Jack stood tall, raising his eyes to Terry. Terry raised his drumstick sounded the Tibetan gong. Tom felt a chill go up his spine. It was as though death had touched him on the shoulder, warning him that there was no way out, that there was no escape. He forced himself to relax, concentrating on Andrew's chant, making his mind merge into the aauumm and limbs relax under the influence of the honey mead and flickering firelight.

Tom could not control his consciousness, he felt as though he was entering another dimension filled with stars, images ... ancient stories. This was *his* dreaming. His mind filled with stories from a past far older than he knew could possibly exist, as if it stretched endlessly in both directions. He was just part of a continuum. The complete silence resounded all around him. He knew that he was totally alone, and in his aloneness, Tom sensed the presence of elders from his people and, amongst them, Jack, compassionate and caring. For the first time in his life, Tom understood the depth of the damage, the crime committed against him by the priest. He felt the deep emotion of finding Sean, the wonderful joy of meeting

Cassie and the great sadness he felt for Will, lost in his tiny world of drugs. Everything made sense. There was a purpose, a greater plan for his life and he now knew that every moment was literally his destiny. This was it. This was as close as he could ever come to realising his life path was already mapped out and that all he had to do was to stay on the path and live the proper way. He was jolted back to his body by the image of Jack's face, floating in space. He came into the awareness of the camp as if a thunderbolt had struck him down from heaven. The fire was raging higher. Andrew threw a mug of sacrificial mead into the flames. It seemed to burst into life just as Tom felt himself back inside his body.

The fire danced before his eyes and Tom saw himself seated with the men he knew he could trust. He was now a warrior, honoured amongst the elder men.

Today, they had learned about earth and water. Tonight, they tasted fire and air, and for Tom, he sampled the ether. Now they would have to sacrifice something from themselves. Only three other young men completed the journey; Will, Adam and the youngest in the group who shook like a leaf. The ceremony was complete and it was time to heal. Angus and Sean now knew which of the young men were strong, willing to follow the Law and ready to be initiated into the para commando group, their first step towards selection.

PARTNERS

Tom felt the sensational let down after the camp. He looked at his watch and sighed. It was only six in the morning, but he was already bored and looking for an outlet. He needed action as much as other people needed food and water. It was different now, since the camp. He loved helping Angus around the farm, he spent more and more time talking to Brindy, but he needed something more, something new. He just didn't know what.

'I can't stay here today.' Tom exploded one morning. He walked out of the farmhouse and onto the dirt driveway, looking across the paddocks towards the trees. Tom quickly made the decision to head into the mountains. He trotted towards the Snowy River Way.

'Hey Brindy. How are you going? I'm outa here today mate. See you tonight yeah? He kept walking up the road until there was a good hitching spot, then decided against it and continued to climb on to the long and steady pinch up to the Boloco Gap. By the time he had reached the top of the hill, Tom was hot, taking off his shirt to allow the air blowing off the mountains to cool his body. There was only a light stream of traffic and Tom did not bother hitching until he reached the top of the Range. It felt good to walk for once. He needed to stretch his legs and lungs after being confined to the farm. Out here, there was plenty of space and the sudden urge for freedom was enough to make him just keep walking. The tarmac glistened as the sun reflected back and already, he had his eye on the mountains. The snow cover was still sufficient for late skiers and boarders. He didn't feel like doing anything like that. After the camp, he could not really say that he 'respected' the mountains as much as he felt wary and needed time to 'reassess' his relationships with the world in general, especially with himself.

A small stores truck pulled up and Tom opened the passenger door.

'Jindy?'

'Yeah. Thanks.'

'Hop in. What's your name kid?'

Tom let it sit. 'Tom. Yours?'

'Roger. Doing the routine stores run today to the mountain. You look as if you've been walking out in the sun kid.'

'I'm hardly a kid anymore thanks all the same.' Tom was surprised at his unexpected good nature.

'How exactly would you define 'not a kid anymore.'

'Can fire a gun.'

'Oh really? And what were you firin' at?'

'Nothin' in particular. Rabbits.'

'Any other talents under your belt?'

'Not sure yet.'

'Could you drive this thing?'

'Yeah. Sure. Can drive all right.'

'OK. I need to make a few phone calls before I get there. Got a licence?'

'Nup.'

'Then you're still a kid.' Roger laughed. 'Hang about.' Roger pulled over then got out of the driver's door and walked over to Tom's side. 'You're driving.'

Tom enjoyed the sensation of taking control of the wheel and power of the vehicle. It was the first time in months that he had driven a car and it felt good. There was always another step upwards in a car, learning to drift around corners, doing three sixties, fanging around the long curves up to the resorts and hooning on the back roads near the farm. So far, he hadn't been caught.

'You thinking of getting a car of your own sometime Tom?' Roger said between calls.

'Maybe.' Tom was suddenly noncommittal.

'I could line you up with one.'

'Thanks. Someone is already lookin' into it for me.'

'Oh?'

'Friend of a friend if you know what I mean.' Tom's gut instinct was to shut his trap and get out of this car. This man smelt bad.

'Drop you at Gippsland Street. Is that all right with you? Take her around the back. I've got to drop off these stores.'

'Thanks Roger. See you later.' Tom slammed the door behind him and walked back over the highway to the skate-park. He felt a wave of relief wash over him. The man was bad medicine and Tom, alerted to that which was no longer good for him, made a mental note not to ever recognise him if their paths crossed down the track. He crossed the highway and in moments was standing, watching his usual bunch of friends.

The moon was high and the night clean and clear reflecting back the night sky off the lake. Tom had spent the afternoon chilling out in the shopping complex, catching up with new friends from the camp, drinking coffees and cruising the net. There was no real work advertised and the best jobs that suited his 'talent' were for "riflemen" with the Department of Defence, advertised apparently on every Centrelink site in Australia as if they were expecting an invasion at any minute.

'Thought I told you Jase. I don't do that stuff. Neither does Will!'

'Not that crap. I mean the geli.'

'What?'

'Got a mate on the mountain with his ticket and access.' Jason announced proudly.

'What do you want to do with that?' Tom asked carefully.

'Thought we'd put a hole in the dam wall. Seems like half the people around here want to do it anyway.'

'You've got to be jokin' Jase. What do you want to blow the dam wall for?'

'Kicks. Thought we'd abseil in at night. Plant the stuff. Then piss off fast.'

'Are you out of your small mind.' Tom laughed. 'The whole thing could blow up in your face then you'd be plastered all over the bottom of the Snowy River.'

'Could be too easy though. Reckon if you've got a long enough fuse, you can do anything. Roll it out and set the thing off remote.'

'Jesus Jason. Haven't you thought about doing anything useful with your life yet?'

'Could give the river a bit of a kick-start. You know, start up a white water industry. Feed the sheep and cattle downstream.'

Tom laughed. 'Yeah, and flood bloody Dalgety. See if you could ride this thing properly first. Before you start mucking around on the dam wall.'

'Come on Tom. Haven't you got any guts left? Since that camp you're different.'

'Maybe you've got too much crap in your brain Jase.' Tom was not amused by the 'mad az' plan. 'You're nuts if you are thinking of dropping the Jindy Dam wall.'

Jason laughed. 'Then you're in?'

'Get a life! When's the food turning up?' Tom asked asserting his natural rights of leadership.

'In about ten I reckon. Look. Don't tell the others. It's between you and me OK?'

'OK.' Tom looked at Jase squarely. He made a mental note to let Angus know.

The rest of the 'gang' turned up fifteen minutes later, two of them cradling large pizzas heated up in the 'midnight oven' of the flat. The water was still and Tom was amazed how beautiful the dam was, even though it was artificial as were most of the lakes in the area. Nothing could have worked in Jindy without the snow and the dam. The lake was almost as big an attraction bringing in serious real estate dollars with the stunning views along with a solid fishing and boating industry. Tom was as mesmerised as anyone by the tranquil beauty of the water, the soft plop of occasional wavelets against the contoured shoreline. He wanted badly to sail out into the middle and just sit staring into its depths. He needed to think. He finished his pizza before finding his bed for the night. There was always someone around ready to share space. It was the landlords that sometimes got the wrong end of the deal. Jase's place was a tip. He and his mates had missed out on housekeeping skills somewhere. At least Will had the commonsense to live by himself and drop the bad company once and for all.

After a couple of hours, Tom had had enough of Jason's mess and his mates. It was time to head out for some fresh air. Sitting around smoking dope and staring at walls was for dumb idiots like Jason. Even the smell of the stuff made him want to throw up. He had had enough.

'See ya mate. I'm outta here.'

'What? We only just got started!' Jason whined.

'That's the problem Jase. I only just got finished.' Tom said softly as he closed the door behind him. He walked quickly through the quiet streets and back to the shopping centre.

Tom walked to the only remaining phone booth in the town.

'Cassie?'

'Tom. How are you doing?'

'OK. Feeling a bit bored after the camp. Haven't seen you in a while Cass.'

'Uh huh.'

'The camp was something else Cass. Wish you were there.'

'Yeah. It was a mens' camp. Angus told me all about it.'

'Right.'

Cassie paused. 'How is Brindy?'

'He's going good. He responds really well to my touch. Hardly had to do a thing with him. Just comes to me every time I'm out in the paddock. Got a loose rope around his neck yesterday. I'm going to lead him soon. Long rope. Get him used to going where I want him to with it. You want to come out?'

'Yeah. Sure. Hey. Did you know the Jillamatong races are coming up?

'Nope. What's that?'

'Mountain race out of Jindy. Really cool stuff. Some of the best horses and best riders in the district.'

'Sounds OK. When's it on?'

'About a month. Reckon your horse will be ready by then?'

'Should be.'

'What you got planned otherwise?'

'Angus lined up a couple of months for me down at Tom Groggin. Said he had to go to sea and didn't want to leave me alone, not with Sean back in Ireland for now. Said I could take the brumby if I wanted to. That's if we could get him to float. There's a guy down there that's full on into the Parelli method.'

'Oh?' Cassie sounded impressed.

'Somethin' to do with natural method of horse handling. You could come and do it with me if you want.'

'I'd love to Tom.' Cassie said wistfully. 'But I've got to work.'

'Get Angus to ask them for you, you know, for time off.'

'I wish.' Cassie laughed.

'Well, let's do that race thing. Take it from there yeah? I can delay going to the Station if Angus knows you'll be around.'

'Hmm. That could work Tom.' Cassie smiled to herself.

'Might be able to swing Tom Groggin for you. I'll ask Angus.'

'Thanks! Where are you Tom?'

'Jindy. I'd rather be back on the farm I think. Jase and his friends are nuts.'

I'll come and get you if you like. See you in about an hour yeah?'

'Cool. Thanks Cass. Watch the kangaroos!'

'Yeah I will.'

Brindabella whinnied as he caught the scent of Tom in the wind. The colt stood upright, his ears pricked in anticipation of another nibble from Tom's hands. Eager to meet Tom halfway, he was already galloping across the gully as Tom descended the slate-bound hill. This time, the colt started his usual race to his new friend, when he stopped suddenly in his tracks, skidding to a halt on the dirt.

'He's got your wind Cassie.' Tom said calmly.

'Yeah. Looks as though he has bonded to you and you only Tom.' Cassie was amazed.

'You smell nice Cass.' Tom laughed softly. 'It's just that Brindy has a good nose.' Tom added diplomatically.

'Haha. Boys!'

'C'mon boy. C'mon.' Tom called.

Brindabella snorted at his right hoof, stamping it onto the dusty ground.

'C'mon boy.' Tom urged him again.

Brindabella danced on all fours in a circle, then threw his head to the ground and rose into a slight rear.

'You are a beauty.' Tom whistled.

Brindabella suddenly flew towards them, his smoky grey tail flying behind him and mane washing in the wind. Then he turned and headed back up the valley at a gallop showing his muscles and speed as if he was a well-trained show pony.

Tom and Cassie walked slowly from Brindabella's paddock back to the rough hut on the farm at Dalgety. This was more a home and haven than either of them had experienced in their entire lives. The sun warming the verandah, the light filtering through the leaves of the station gums and the sound of birds shrieking as they discovered spring delights, rang like bells of victory in their ears. Tom opened the door and turned to smile at Cassie, welcoming and reassuring her that this too was her home, that she was as much a part of his life now as were Angus and Sean.

'You up for a cuppa?' Angus said cheerily.

'Thanks Angus.' Cassie smiled.

'Cassie came over to help me break in Brindy.' Tom said

'Cassie, you are always welcome here. You know that.' Angus said smiling at his young friend. 'Besides being friends, we are sort of colleagues Tom.'

'Oh?'

'Cassie is on the same team as Sean and I. Not full time mind you.' Angus grinned broadly.

'Team?'

'Yup. She and Sean and I go a long way back, don't we Cass?' Angus opened the door for Tom to get the full picture.

'I do a bit of work with Angus and Sean, Tom.' Cassie explained clearly. 'I've been through training with them.'

'You mean ...' Tom trailed away the words.

'That's right.' Angus stepped in. 'Cassie is one of us.' He put an arm around Cassie's shoulders and clapped Tom on the back.

'You hungry Tom? Cassandra's engaging smile lifted the atmosphere.

'Tom?' Angus probed.

'Yeah. Thanks Cassie. What's on the menu?'

'As you like it.' Cassie laughed. 'What about…jeez, what do you guys like to eat?' Cassie was momentarily lost for ideas.

'Anythin' Cassie. Nothin' that's too much trouble.' Tom said meekly.

'Hmm. Toast?' Angus suggested.

'Toast? You won't break in a horse on rations Tom. Better go for something a bit more substantial. Cheese burger with the lot?' Cassie suggested.

'Yeah. No meat.' Tom added.

'Cool.'

'OK. Three cheese burgers with the lot…avocado?'

'Could work.' Tom's enthusiasm sparked again.

'You going veg Tom?' Angus wrinkled his nose.

Tom laughed. 'At least my breath won't stink like Sean's.'

'Hey. Not behind his back when the man can't defend himself!'

'Yeah. Go easy on Sean.' Cassie defended her friend.

You'll turn into a bloody rabbit Tom if you're not careful.' Angus winked at Cassie.

'Brindy only eats grass, oats and carrots and look at him!' Cassie chipped in.

'Do ya think he could win the race?'

'Jillamatong?'

'Yeah.'

'You've got a bit of work to do first Tom.' Cassie cautioned carefully turning to the stove to open the firebox. 'And the donkey.' Cassie turned to them, her face alight with humor.

'Can't forget the donkey.' Tom laughed.

'Hey, do you think that…who's that person you said could help us out Cassie?'

'Gai? Yeah. She knows heaps more than I do about horses. Give her a ring if you like. Could come down and give us a few pointers I suppose.'

Cassie served the food under the gum trees already shedding their winter coat of bark and leaves making way for the fresh shoots. The small band of friends sat down, munching on their cheese and avocado burgers and listening to the sound of the wind making light music in the tops of the trees and under the tin roof of the hut.

'I could use some company at Tom Groggin.' Tom opened.

'Oh? What are you thinking?'

'Cassie. She would be good value.'

'I'm not so sure. I'll have to ask the Station Manager.'

'OK.' Tom relaxed, happy to leave the arrangements with Angus.

'We need to race at Jillamatong first.' Tom added.

'I'm not sure that you would enjoy being out here alone Tom.' Angus said soberly.

'Cass said she would come and look after me.' Tom jested.

'I did not Tom!' Cassie protested.

'That sounds like a good plan.' Angus said evenly.

'I think so too. The camp was good yeah?' Tom suddenly changed the subject and stood up.

'Yeah the camp was good.'

'Some of those guys are planning a job on the Jindy Dam wall.'

'What!'

'Yup. Jason and his crew.'

'Are you sure?'

'Sure as Angus. Thought I'd let you and Cassie know, since you are on the same team.' Tom said quietly.

'We are. And thank you for telling me son.' Angus said quietly. He felt the blood draining from his face.

'Speed; it does your brain in. They just do stuff like that for kicks. Must send them mental.' Cassie drew on her experience of the group.

'Should put them through the camp again, only this time behind the wire.' Tom decided.

'Trouble is, most of them couldn't last the distance. Even the straight guys couldn't get close to the initiation level you reached Tom.' Angus looked at Tom squarely.

'Do you think you can stick it Tom. I mean, do you think you'll ever relapse or anythin'?' Cassie said. 'Like the emotions take over again?'

'Nope. I am a changed man. Will is too.' Tom waved around his empty plate and walked back inside. He let the door slam softly behind, muffling the low tones of Cassie's voice as she spoke urgently to Angus. Tom emerged again from the house with a flush in his cheeks and in his hands a piece of fruit and some cake.

'Looks as though our luck is in Angus.'

'Yeah. She's the best.'

Tom munched into the apple, sitting on the ground next to Angus. 'One door closes, another opens.'

'Do you mean that there aren't too many around like Cassie, Tom?'

'You bet.' Tom slapped Angus on the back and grinned.

'I reckon you two are good for each other Tom.'

'Thanks Angus. We are.'

'I mean it. In any case, you don't really need me and Sean anymore. Now that you have Cassie.' Angus grinned broadly.

Tom shrugged. He felt strangely relieved, as if he were suddenly free. He picked up a stick off the ground, pulled his pocketknife out of his jeans pocket and began to carefully craft a tip to the stick. Angus watched him quietly as the arrow began to take shape.

'You got a bow Tom?'

'Nuh. Know how to make one though. Used to shoot my own rabbits in Victoria. Pretty good shot as it happens.'

'Cool. Teach me how to make one someday?' Cassie asked.

'Maybe. After the races.' Tom grinned.

'Damn.' Gai slammed the truck door behind her. 'Forgot my long rein.'

'Hi Gai.' Cassie had come out of the hut when she heard the car approach.

'Well hi there Cassie. How's the brumby breaker?'

'He's doing this one.' Cassie smiled at Tom.

'Hello. I'm Gai.'

'Hi. I'm Tom.'

'Hello Tom. Well, we've got quite a team then. Probably a good thing since he'll have to get used to crowds if you're going to run him at Jillamatong.'

'Cool. Brindy's pretty sharp on the scents though. Picked you out a mile away.' Tom jested.

Gai laughed. 'That's a good thing then. Always better that a horse knows its master. Guess that's you Tom.' She added softly.

'Guess so.' Tom was chuffed.

'Want a drink before we go Gai?'

'Thanks Cassie. Tea?'

'Coming up. Just doing a brew. It's on the stove.'

'Great. Come and check out the gear guys. You'll need gloves for the first run Tom. If he pulls back you might get yourself a nasty rope burn.'

'Brindy's not like that.' Tom immediately responded.

'Oh?'

'He comes to me when I call. Never had a problem like that.'

'Well, we're well on the way then.' Gai said briskly, and turning away from the truck headed inside to sample Cassie's brew.

'He's a beauty all right.' Gai mused over his stance as Brindabella stood stock still, watching the three people climb out of the valley towards where he, primarily, kept guard over the mare and donkey. 'Did you say he was already on the property when you arrived Tom?'

'Yeah. You know. Angus had this thing about keeping him when his son caught him up in the National Park.'

'Jeez, wouldn't mind him myself. Look at his line. This fella ain't no inbred brumby. Looks as though he has a bit of stock horse, thoroughbred…'

'Do you reckon there's some Arab in him Gai?' Cassie piped up.

'Dunno Cassie. He wouldn't be carrying his papers I suppose?' Gai grinned.

Tom said nothing, carefully watching his breath, breathing in and out slowly as he had learnt in the gaol, keeping his emotions cool and connecting with the colt before they arrived on his turf.

'Thata boy. Hey Brindy.' Tom called softly, his whisper almost inaudible yet the intonation clearly reaching the colt. 'Hey boy. These are my friends yeah.' Tom continued to utter soft and soothing sounds to give the colt time to acclimatise to them.

'Is he always so alert Tom?' Gai asked the obvious.

'Never known him to be asleep or not watching. I reckon he knows I'm coming out to see him before I do.'

'Maybe he pulls you here Tom. Seems as though he wants a friend just as much as you do.' Gai put a friendly hand on Tom's arm.

'He's pretty good. Not sure about all of us. He seems to be handling it OK though.'

'Normally, I would just work alone Tom, however since he already knows you and Cassie, it's really only me he has to get to know and since I'm with you folk, that's probably good enough for Brindabella.'

'Do you think that they have so much sense Gai. I mean, can he distinguish who's who in a group of people?'

'Why not? We do don't we?'

'Here he comes Tom.' Cassie hadn't taken her eyes off the colt. 'Come on Brindy. Come on.' Cassie put out her hand.

'Give him some apple Cassie.' Tom pulled the fruit from his pocket. 'I'll feed the mare and you get the donkey Gai.' Tom grinned at Gai handing her a couple of carrots.

'Gee thanks Tom.' Gai stuck one of the carrots in her own mouth.

Cassie was already a couple of paces ahead, calling to Brindabella. The colt looked past her at Tom, watching to see his response. Tom noticed the exchange and nodded quietly at the colt, confirming for him that it was OK to take the piece of fruit from Cassie. Cassie stood still, waiting for him to come to her.

'Thata boy Brindy.' Cassie held out the apple on the palm of her hand.

Brindabella dropped his head almost shyly, sniffing at her hand before curling his lips around the apple. He lifted his head up suddenly, smiling with his eyes at Cassie then at Tom. He looked at Tom, putting his head down and tossing it against his leg, then stood upright to start on the apple.

'He likes you Tom.' Gai observed quietly.

'This is Gai, Brindy.' Cassie nodded to Gai to come closer to the horse.

'Hey mate. You're a fine boy yeah.' Gai instinctively put her hand on his forehead, stroking it down the side of his cheek, allowing Brindy to get her smell. Brindabella didn't move and continued to munch on the apple. Gai took advantage of his mood, running her hand quickly under his chin and down his neck and along his right foreleg. Then she stood up again, caressing the horse under his right ear and quickly moving under his chin to the other side. She repeated the procedure, carefully checking the neck and left shoulder, this time picking up the left foreleg and looking for stones in the hoof before placing his hoof on the ground again. She walked to his rump, then around him, her hand on his back until she was standing with Cassie, still at his nose. 'That's a good boy. Tom, did you bring the rope halter, I want to slip it on him whilst he is still,' Gai commanded quietly.

Tom stepped forward, putting his hand on Brindabella's forehead, clearly in charge of the horse and slipped the rope over his neck. Brindabella turned and nuzzled his shoulder, letting Tom slip the halter over his head, the noose around his nose loose and relaxed. He ran his fingers under the rope, disguising its feel until he was sure that Brindabella felt comfortable. Then he quietly clipped the rein to the ring on the halter and took a step backwards, urging Brindabella towards him. Brindabella walked straight to him and again, nuzzled him on the shoulder.

'He's a natural yeah Gai?'

'You both are. Haven't seen that for a while. Is that the first time?'

'More or less, but I reckon I could easily work him without too much fuss.'

'OK. We might just all walk together in a big circle with you and Cassie at his head. I'll follow with the donkey.' Gai joked.

'You could give the mare hers Cass.' Tom pulled an apple from his pocket.

'Thanks.' Cassie caught the apple and walked towards the mare, pushing the donkey away as she did.

'Is the mare still feeding your colt Tom?' Gai asked.

'Never thought she was!'

'I wouldn't be surprised if she came into milk when he turned up though. How old did you say he was Tom?'

'Good question. I don't reckon Brindabella is the type. This bloke is way too independent.'

'Brindabella danced on his back legs as if to demonstrate the point. Tom backed away to give him space, keeping eye contact with the colt.

'That's the boy. Keep moving, we're with you.' Tom encouraged him to find some space. When Brindabella stood still, Tom stood still, waiting for the horse to make the first move. Brindabella was content to stand, testing the rope halter against his left foreleg then lifting his head to look at Tom. Then he walked towards Tom, letting the rein go slack as if it weren't there at all. He lifted his head and looked at Gai.

'Are you sure you need me. I reckon he's telling me he's cool just the way it is.' Gai laughed.

'You could show him a few things though.'

'Might take a few days all in all. We'll put him on the long driving reins for a bit. Do you reckon he can handle it?'

'Can't see why not. How do they work?' Tom was keen to keep moving with him now that he was becoming used to the equipment and the larger group.

'OK. Cassie. Best you park yourselves a ways over there to give us all some space. You can just watch for now. Tom, I want you to stay at Brindabella's head and I'm going to walk behind him with the driving reins. We'll walk him to the top of the river flat so we can form a bigger circle. It's easier that way. Remember horses don't have good vision so give him plenty of room on the side to see properly. Keep his head up so he knows what's going on all the time.'

Gai clipped the rope on and took off the shorter rein.

'Roll that up and stick it over your shoulder for now Tom. OK my boy. We're heading uphill for a bit then onto the flat.'

Gai gave Brindabella a quick rub on the cheek then walked calmly towards his rump, stroking his spine then continued to walk without looking back until she had reached the full length of the driving rein. She turned around slowly making as little movement as possible on the rope.

'We're ready when you are Tom. Don't move him. The rope will do the work, you just keep him company for now.'

Gai clicked Brindabella forward, giving the rope a light flick. Brindabella instantly responded dropping his head for a second them taking the first easy steps.

'Stay with him Tom.' Gai urged. 'Come on Brindy. That's the boy. Walk on.' Gai flicked the rope again and Brindabella, with Tom at his head walked up onto the broader shelf of the river plain.

Gai kept them moving turning Brindabella in a wide circle always to the right. Once they had formed a full circle, she pulled firmly on the rope.

Brindabella automatically stopped, then turned to Tom as if waiting for instructions.

'Hey, she's driving you, not me.' Tom said to Brindy.

Brindabella whickered and muzzled at his hand.

'OK. OK. I did bring some.' Tom fished a couple of sugar lumps from his pocket.

'This guy has you sorted Tom. Wonder if he'll be the same when you get on his back?' Gai said. 'He's intelligent. I'll give him that.'

'Not sure about riding him yet. Bit soon don't you think? Anyway, so long as he's happy, I'm happy.' Tom responded.

'One more circle then it's your turn mate,' Gai said confidently. She flicked the rope again, this time turning the horse to the left in the opposite direction.

Brindabella, keener for fun than work, reared and skirted around Tom. Gai waited patiently with a loose rope until the horse was ready to move.

Tom stood slightly apart from the colt, giving him time, making sure he knew that this was not capture, this was entertainment and that there would again be a reward of some sort at the other end. Then they changed places, Gai walking carefully to his rump and patting him, running her hand in the reverse direction along his spine and reaching the right side of his head.

'Good boy Brindy. Good boy.' Tom handed Gai a lump of sugar and Brindabella instantly took the bait, looking at Gai and forgetting that it was she and not Tom who had caused him to take his first big step towards taking a rider.

'Don't give him too much sugar. There's only one set of teeth there for this life. You could always mash a bit of oats and molasses and give him wee tidbits that way.'

'Yeah. Sure. Good idea Gai.'

'OK. Your turn. Do the same thing. Walk to his rump. Keep your hand on his back then walk straight on until just before the length of the rope. Give him a bit of slack. When you feel he is settled and steady, flick the rope once and with luck, he'll have learnt that one and we just walk on. I'll play you for now and walk at his head.'

'OK Gai. Let's do it.' Tom followed the procedure, running his hand along Brindabella's spine and softly patting his rump then walking to the length of the rope. Then he turned, carefully lifting the reins to waist height and waiting until he felt Brindabella settle. For a moment, he could feel the tension in the colt with Gai at his head and the almost bunching of his rump muscles.

Tom reflexly flicked the rope and Brindabella shifted his weight forwards. Tom clicked his tongue and Brindabella walked on, Gai keeping a close yet respectable distance and reinforcing the original lesson for the colt.

'That was great Tom. Come forwards now.' Gai stood quietly, looking the horse in the eye, then stroking his nose. 'Thata boy. Thata boy.'

Tom reached his rump, running his hand along Brindabella's

back and reaching his right cheek. Brindabella turned and lifted his wrist as Tom went to stroke his cheek.

'What's the matter boy?' Tom stopped.

'OK. I think that's about enough for now. Let's give him a break. Tom, Cassie.' Gai called. 'We'll call it a day for now.'

Cassie was up onto her feet, putting out her hand to Tom. 'That looked unreal Gai.' Cassie said.

'Thanks. Not often you find a horse like Brindy.'

'Thanks.' Tom had to struggle not to choke on his words.

For the next three days Tom went out to the horse alone. Each time, he followed exactly the same routine, slipping on the bridle, then the saddle blanket, taking off the saddle blanket, flicking it in the wind, then mounting Brindabella bareback before finally walking him up the hill to practise the wide circles, right and left. On the third day, he sighted the church in the distance, clicking Brindabella forwards and then squeezing with his calves until Brindabella broke into an easy canter up the creek. When they were as close as they could be to the church, Tom pulled him to stand and then slid off his back. He walked around to the horse's head, talking to him, patting his neck and cheek then deliberately pulling out two, three oats and molasses treats. Then he sat on the ground, looking at the majestic view tumbling before them, the reins loosely held in his hand, Brindabella nuzzling his neck between munching on the molasses filled sweet.

Tom and Cassie talked incessantly about getting Brindabella ready for the race.

'Do ya reckon he'll take to the saddle Tom?'

'I'm not sure about that Tom. I reckon he'll handle it. I might have to ride him first with the girth loose, then gradually tighten it on the second or third circle.'

' You've sure moved fast. Didn't know it was so easy to break a horse in.'

'I'm not sure if it's not the other way around. I've learned heaps in the past week, probably more than Brindy I reckon.'

'Cool.'

'Let's have lunch out today.' Tom suggested.

'Yeah, why not?'

'Bit early. But I guess it means that we won't have as many distractions once we're out there.'

'I'd like you to drive the ute up the gully so that I can meet you at the top if it's all right. That way we can give Brindy a good feed and water.'

'Good idea. Any reason?'

'Just a hunch. Big step for a little boy.'

'Yeah, well you could just ride him half girth' Cassie suggested. 'What if he suddenly takes off and the saddle's not on properly? What do you do then? Your feet will be in the stirrups and if the saddle slides, you go with it.'

Tom laughed. 'Just like the westerns yeah. Drag me along behind him, one foot in and the other out. Brumby bolts to the boundary. Rider bounces off the ground, losing skin along the way.'

'Ouch!' Cassie protested.

'I get your meaning Tom.' Cassie smiled softly dropping her head shyly.

'OK. Lunch it is then. What's on Cassie?'

'Pub fare I'm afraid. Not the Sunday best, but it's solid.'

'That sounds tops to me.' Tom said brightly. Tom smiled at the young woman sitting beside him in the ute cab. Her hair seemed more brilliant as it caught the deflected rays of the sun through the cab window. 'Can you cook like they do at the pub?'

'S'pose if I had to. Have learnt a few things there. Sometimes they're short of a chef so waitress becomes cook. That sort of thing.

You?'

'Not me. Never have, never will.'

'Just asking'. What if we go bush Tom and it's your turn to put on the tucker?'

'That's different.'

'How so?' Cassie teased him.

'Well, blokes are blokes if you know what I mean. It doesn't matter that much how it turns out.'

'I still eat when I'm in the bush.' Cassie pressed the protest.

'Well, you know…'

'No Tom. I don't. You have to cook too.'

'Teach me sometime then Cass.' He turned the ute into the Dalgety pub where he knew for now anyway, he would not have to cook a single thing.

After lunch, they headed straight back to the farm. Tom focussed his mind on the immediate challenge of introducing Brindabella to the saddle. They dropped the bridle, saddle blanket and saddle at the bottom of the gully and continued up the valley towards the boundary near the church. The hawthorn bushes were thick with white spring blossoms and the birds already feasting on the small insects attracted to the scent. The creek appeared more deeply carved than Cassie had noted from the Church; the gully was now almost completely dried up by the long drought.

'You're good at handling the ute Tom.'

'Angus is cool. He trusts me.'

'No, I mean it.'

'Comes with spending my holidays on the farm. Part of the territory. Have to know how to handle machinery safely; drive tractors, trucks, and cars. You name it.'

'This licence at 17 or whatever is silly yeah?'

'Most of the time I agree with it, but you should see some of my friends. They're nuts Cassie. They drop stuff and alcohol together then they're out on the road. Glad I'm not spending time with them so much.'

'I know Tom. I'm glad you're safe to be with.' Cassie made her point quietly and carefully.

'I'm glad you trust me Cass.' Tom said simply.

'This looks about a good spot.'

'Thanks Cassie.' Tom switched off the engine facing the ute downhill so she could sit in the cab until the horse and rider mounted the crest of the hill. I'll be back in ten to fifteen minutes.' Tom hopped out of the ute and jogged down the hill to where he had left the saddle and bridle.

Tom whistled softy for his horse.

'Brindy, it's me, Tom.'

Brindabella's ears pricked at the sound. He whickered and dropped his head for another mouthful of dry grass, but his eyes were on the young man walking towards him.

'Hey Brindy. We're going to try something new today.'

Brindabella nuzzled Tom's hand and then his pocket.

'OK, OK.' Tom laughed. 'That was for later but a carrot now won't hurt.'

He let the horse take the carrot from one hand and slid the saddle to the ground. He kept the bridle close to Brindabella's nose and quickly slid the metal bit into his horse's mouth. Brindabella was unconcerned. Tom bent down to pick up the saddle blanket. He felt the horse's nose against his pocket but ignored the cheeky request. He placed the blanket of Brindabella's back, then the saddle.

'Good boy. There you are Brindy.' Tom followed through quickly with the saddle. For some reason, he felt more scared than the horse and couldn't figure the reason. Brindabella seemed unconcerned, happy to stand still while he negotiated both the bit and carrot now firmly between his teeth. This metal crunching between his teeth sure was welcome distraction from the belt under his gut. Tom decided to pull tighter on the girth so that it fit snugly under Brindabella. Then he tugged on the saddle, noting that it still had slippage, slippage that he could not afford if this was the first attempt at a saddle ride with the colt.

'Hey Brindy. I'm going to draw it in so I want you to hold your breath for a sec yeah?' Tom laughed despite himself. There was no point in being tense when the colt was OK about the next adventure into the necessary corsetry that would see them as able entrants into the Jillamatong Races.

'OK man. Breathe in.' Tom laughed again, patting the horse on the neck. Then he realised that Brindabella didn't have a reasonable prompt. He tugged again on the girth, this time gently kneeing the colt in the gut. Brindabella swung his head around, curious at the new signals. At the same time, as he was taken off guard, Tom pulled harder on the girth, notching it another couple of holes until the saddle felt firm and strong enough to hold his possibly moving weight.

'That's great boy. Looks OK. How does it feel?'

Brindabella pawed at the ground with his left foreleg. Tom watched, waiting to see what he would do. Then the horse shook himself from side to side, shivering as if to test the garment grasping his hide. He stretched out his neck, then suddenly let out his breath, releasing the tension of the girth.

'Hey. You haven't done this before have you?' Tom looked into the cheeky eyes.

Brindabella threw his head and snorted then lifted his tail, swishing it as far forwards as he could.

'Mate. You got me beat. I don't know where you're coming from. You're one step ahead of me. That's for sure.' Tom tested the girth again; decided against tightening it another notch then drew the reins along the horse's neck. 'I suppose I'll have to get up on this thing sometime or another. Although I'd probably prefer it just the way it was between us Brindy.'

Tom grimaced as if it were he and not the horse now saddled. He moved along the horse's back as he always did, placing pressure with his hands, this time into the curve of the saddle and tested his left foot in the stirrup. Then he took his foot out again and walked back to his head. He gave Brindabella a palm full of mushy oats, thick with the sweet molasses.

'That'll be another notch for you Brindy. Good boy.' Tom could not understand his reluctance. There was something niggling him about riding the horse with the saddle yet he couldn't put his finger on the problem. He looked deeply into the horse's eyes, looking for a slight clue, why he had reservations about the ride. There was no indication from Brindy. Nothing. Just the slightly cheeky glare back.

'Got me beat Brindy. 'Suppose we should just do it yeah?' Tom walked back to the colt's side, adjusting the reins before putting his left leg in the stirrup and quickly swinging himself over the saddle into the sitting position on the horse. Brindabella suddenly reared on his hind legs. Tom wanted to slide off the horse, and decided to stay his ground, soothing and patting his neck. Then he let the reins loose, until Brindabella, trembling as if with the sudden shock of his capture, suddenly quietened. Once he had settled, Tom slid off his back, walking to his head, patting him and feeding him another of the precious oat cookies.

'Sorry boy. You didn't like that much. It's not as though you're trapped for life.'

Brindabella looked him in the eye, almost accusingly and Tom wondered whether it was too soon, whether he had suddenly shocked the colt and broken his trust. Brindabella whickered and nuzzled his hand, searching for the comforting sweetness of the oats.

'We try again then?' Tom asserted his mastery over the horse. 'You ready. I'm going up again Brindy. Only this time stand still. No rearing yeah?' Tom quickly swung into the saddle again before he had time to lose his nerve, talking to the horse and patting his neck. Brindabella trembled for a moment, then quietened, dropping his head to his right foreleg before pulling himself into his usual proud and unfettered stance.

'Atta boy.' Tom sat still. There was plenty of time. Tom felt the waves of relief wash over him. He would wait until together they decided to move on. Tom knew that Brindabella wanted to go, however he would wait until the horse indicated to him that he felt Tom and was ready to respond to his almost invisible command.

The long minutes passed. The horse and rider stood completely still, the ages washing between them as if they had been cast long ago as one. The midday air was warm. The sound of birdsong was brilliant on the range and the glint of sun on stone reflected off the cliffs as if from another age. A wedge tail eagle spiralled on the thermals above horse and rider. Tom felt an uncanny sense of connection, as if he and the horse were one and together and that they formed part of the earth, the landscape and the sky above where the eagle continued to wheel ever upwards on silent wings. Tom didn't want the experience to finish. If this was the goal of 'breaking' in Brindy, he had achieved it. Brindy and he understood one another. Brindabella turned his head towards the head of the creek, sensing Cassie in the wind. Tom felt him flex and clicked his tongue, gently urging him with the muscles in his calves. In one long stride, the colt broke into a canter then in less than a dozen strides, galloped towards the church, Tom motionless in the saddle, legs loose in the stirrups and reins folded gently over his fingers.

Cassie couldn't tell whether Tom was on the horse at first or not. All she could see through the lens of the camera was Brindabella's astounding head, the ears forward, the perfect bunching and relaxing of his powerful shoulder muscles as the horse raced towards them.

Then, as Brindabella inclined his head, subtly as if to reveal the rider, Cassie saw Tom almost motionless, as if moulded to his horse as they galloped towards the top of the Boloco Creek.

JILLAMATONG

Tom carefully coaxed Brindabella onto the float.

'That's a good boy. Good fella.' Tom whispered, stroking the colt under his ears and running a calm hand along his neck. 'That's my fine boy.' He clucked. 'Today we do a couple of runs over the course, then tomorrow, we race.' Tom felt the excitement rising in his heart. He knew that Brindabella would enjoy the challenge. There could be no problem in Tom's mind with racing him over the course. The problem might be when the colt had to deal with the other horses, riders, floats and camping vehicles.

Tom felt like taking the risk. His reading of the colt was that he was more than just a nervous or flighty steed. This horse had wits, common sense and already Tom could ride him on a loose rein, letting the horse find his own way. Tom more than anyone was surprised at how well the colt responded to his hand and commands. Brindabella simply wanted to run.

The horse float creaked at the tow-bar as Tom eased the vehicles over the rough dirt track that made up the way to Angus's farm. He felt confident at the wheel, steady and sure as he manoeuvred out of the paddock and onto the open dirt track that edged the hill. The dip onto the bitumen was a strain on the tow-bar, however Tom knew to take it at an angle so that the ute and float would rock only slightly and Brindabella would have plenty of time and space to adjust and balance his weight. Tom had the foresight to pad the walls of the float with thick wads of hessian bags that Angus had found at a local clearing sale. The smell of old oats in the bag was as comforting to Tom as it was to the colt. Easily, he swung the wheel onto the bitumen, the float rocking then settling onto the smoother surface of the sealed road. Tom breathed out in relief.

The Jillamatong camp was already well laid out. Gai and the team had set up the essential 'bar' by the time Tom and Brindabella arrived. Tom got out of the ute and walked straight around to the back of the float. Brindabella stood quietly, his tail rhythmically swishing against the tailgate.

'Hey fella. Howya doin?' Tom called softly to him.

Brindabella lifted his head and whickered.

'That's a good boy. Won't be a second. Just have to find us a possie mate.' Tom assured him.

'Tom. You made it!' Gai called out from behind the makeshift bar, a couple of slabs of VB were ready for the early and the rest stowed in the portable fridge.

'Heya Gai. Yeah. We got here in one piece. Brindy's magic. Hardly a whisper from him all the way.'

'He travelled OK?'

'Mate. He's something else. Doesn't matter if I tug or tow him. He's as quiet as a lamb.'

'He's supposed to be a brumby.' Gai laughed. 'How do you reckon he'll go? He's hardly had time with you Tom. Let alone with us mob.'

'Dunno. Just see how he takes it today I suppose. If he likes the track, I reckon he'll be all right.'

'OK then. Where do you want to camp?'

'Not sure. Where's the best place to park?'

'You can camp next to my float.' Gai pointed to her truck and float. 'I usually dump my swag in the back of the float. Horses like to be outside at night. Freaks them being tied up all the time.'

'Thanks Gai.' Tom was deeply grateful for her assistance.

'Get you settled. I'll just finish up here at the bar.' Gai made a grandiose sweep of her arm and laughed. 'Then I'll be over to help you get started.'

'OK. That's great.' See you in a short while.' Tom smiled.

'Hey, where's Cassie. Thought she was comin'?' Gai asked.

'She said she's too frightened in case we fall.'

'Good grief. What do you expect! You'll be lucky to stay on Tom. Most of us count on a bit of good luck as well as the brilliant horsemanship in these parts.'

'I've heard all about it!' Tom grinned.

'I'll give you a few pointers on how to run later. See you in a bit.'

Tom drove to where Gai was parked, her float sparkling clean and her mount tied to the side, contented with the half bag of oats and lucerne hay by the wheel.

'OK Brindy. We're here mate.' Tom called out to the colt, patting him on the rump as he climbed back into the float. Tom felt the shiver of excitement in the colt's rump. Brindabella had already sensed the event. The excitement in the air was as palpable to him as it was to Tom.

'Steady on boy. Steady.' Tom carefully released the halter rein from the front of the float. 'We're going to back out mate. Steady as she goes.' Tom nudged Brindabella gently at the shoulder. 'Thata boy. Ease back, ease back.' Tom urged Brindabella to take the first steps onto the ramp. 'Good boy. Back down, back down.' Tom pushed a little harder against the colt's shoulder.

Brindabella gave and stepped backwards onto the ramp, his hind hoof slipping until it caught the cross rail.

'Come on boy. Another step. Back you go.' Tom looked him in the eye. Brindabella, aware of Tom's caress connected with him and catching the idea that it was safe, walked backwards off the ramp onto the ground.

'I'll run you through the course Tom.' Gai squatted on the dirt. 'This is the start line.' She drew a line in the dust. 'We race up the hill here.' Gai extended the line. 'The track starts at a fair pace. Then it takes us through the rocks and over a couple of jumps.' She suddenly looked up. 'You jumped Brindy yet?'

'Shit no. Didn't think about that.'

'Better take him through today then.'

'Yeah.' Tom said dryly.

'OK. Then it winds back down another hill. It's steep yeah. There's all sorts of shit in the way — trees, briars — it goes straight down about there.' Gai extended the line in the dirt to indicate the course. 'As you come down the hill, you reach the foreshore of the lake, that's if it's got water in it. Actually, it does today.' Gai grinned. 'Not exactly Lake Jindabyne, but there you have it. OK. This is the hard part; sometimes the water's about a foot deep otherwise it's mud and duckshit. Whatever the lake is like, you've got to drive him through it. There's still a bit of water in it Tom, and Brindy might not like the mud.' She grinned wryly at Tom. 'Come out the other side, then you've got about 400 metres to run. At that point, don't look at anything else. Just go for it. Run for the line. Kick him on. He'll take the hint. There! Did you manage him on the farm OK?'

'Yeah. The farm's a bit rough around the edges. Bit of loose shale, gullies and wombat holes. But this is more challenging by far.'

'Good. That's the way it's intended. You ready for a run through?'

'Yeah. Why not.'

'I'll come through with you. Dally will want to run. He knows the course. We'll take it at a slow canter though. Give Brindy time to learn it. Saddle up?"

'Yep.'

'Hey. We're riding stock saddles only. You got one?'

'That's all Angus had in the shed. Seems to fit Brindy like a glove.'

'You're in luck. There's no whips or curbs allowed. Animal welfare. We ride rough, and we make sure the horses don't get hurt, not if we can help it. This one is more about skill Tom and less about brute force. And you and Brindy look like a good team. Set?'

'Yeah. Give me five.'

'Have a drink before you start. Your mouth dries up if you're anything like me. Leave it hangin' open as you race.' Gai poked fun at herself.

'Easy boy. Easy.' Tom slipped a foot into the stirrup. He carefully swung his leg over the saddle, settling his full weight onto Brindabella's back.

'That's a boy.' Tom settled more deeply into the saddle, feeling the length of the stirrups and letting the reins fall loosely about the colt's neck.

'I'm ready when you are Gai.' Tom called over to her float.

'Good one. Dally needs a minute. I'll let him finish his mouthful of hay.' Gai slapped her horse on the rump. 'That's it fella. We're on.' Gai mounted her bay, the gelding revelling in her spirit. 'This guy just wants to gallop.' Gai looked towards Tom. 'I'll hold him in, but be prepared for Dally just wanting to race!'

'Can't do much then. I don't usually hold Brindy in on a tight rein. So I'll have to hold my seat.'

'Yeah you will. OK. We're out of here. Up the hill. Haa.'

Gai kicked Dally straight into a canter. He responded by breaking into a long stride and heading up the familiar track. Gai knew he would want a few long strides before settling into the 3.2 kilometre course.

She held him steadily, looking over her shoulder to see Brindabella and Tom cantering smoothly behind her. She was amazed that already they moulded together as one, Tom clearly at ease and letting the horse have his head and find his own way.

Gai thought there would be no problem with this one. The main thing would be to prime Tom for the drop down the hill where the track narrowed to 'one wide' and where it was easy to be blocked into a chute. Tom would need to use his wits a bit to make sure that nothing out of control came in behind him forcing him and Brindabella forwards faster than their set pace.

'How was it Tom?' Gai puffed as she dismounted Dally.

'That was a fast pace you set us Gai. Brindy handled it OK. I was more worried about myself.'

'You did fine. Anything too tight for you out there?' Gai waited for him to answer. 'The chute?'

'Reckon if we're positioned in front enough we won't get stuck in a crush.'

'Then you're on Tom.'

'Yeah. Never said we weren't. That's why we're out here Gai.' Tom responded in surprise.

'Looks as though I'll have some competition then.' Gai joked.

'Jeez I hope so.'

'Hi Tom. Hi Gai.'

'Cassie!' Tom dismounted smiling at her. 'Thought you'd chickened out.'

'I had to come.' Cassie smiled softly catching Tom's arm.

'Hi Cassie.' Gai waited for a break in the exchange.

'Hi. Can I help with anything?'

'Sure. Meet you over at the bar in a second. Just have to fix Dally.'

'I'll do it if you like.'

'Thanks. Can you brush him down? Make sure the sweat's off him.'

'Will do.'

'See you two a bit later. Better do my other job. Runnin' the bar in between races keeps me fully busy.'

'Thanks Gai.' Tom waved to her as she headed straight back to her other 'duties'.

'Cassie?' Tom started. 'You can share my camp tonight if you want.'

'Hadn't thought where to stay. Gai said there was always somewhere out here.'

'There's plenty of room in the float. I've got heaps of stuff to put on the floor. Just have to clean it out a bit.'

'Sweet. Heard there was a band playing tonight.'

'Should be good. You up for a drink?'

'No. Don't think so thanks Tom. Can't really get interested anymore.'

'Come on. Let's find the band. They're warming up for the shindig.'

Cassie took Tom's hand and walked across the paddock to the bush pub set up in a half tin shed under the brilliant blue mountain sky.

'What time is our race Gai? Tom found Gai at the official's tent. She was already dressed in her racing colours: long-sleeved pink shirt tucked into cream jodhpurs with dark brown chaps to protect her knees and thighs. 'Shit, you look a bit of all right Gai!' Tom said spontaneously.

'Steady on. Mitch mightn't like me getting too much attention.'

'Hello. I'm Tom. This is Cassie.' Tom extended his hand.

'Yeah. I know. Mitch. Mitch Flanagan.'

'Mitch's riding heavyweight. The Cup's on towards the end. There are about eight or nine races to run first Tom, so you'd better settle in for the long haul. Watch how the others ride for a while. Walk your horse around a bit to warm him up before the start.'

'Which races are you in Gai?' Cassie asked.

'I'm only running the Cup this time round. Saving Dally. The Ladies' Cross Country is usually fast paced, however the Cup is a mixed race. More of a challenge. Not for Dally though.' Gai added quickly.

'Anything we can do Gai?' Cassie was clearly keen to do something more than just hang about.

'Sure. You can help with the kids' novelty race if you like. Tom, you might like to team up with Mitch at the bar for a while. I'll need to spell myself before the race.'

'Yeah. Can do.' Tom nodded. Gai, like everyone else, thought he was eighteen and there was no reason for anyone to think differently. Cassie accepted that he was old enough to drink and serve behind the bar. That suited him. Less questions asked and it made life easier all around. The only cops at the race were out on holidays, supporting their friends and spouses riding the track.

'Be back by 2.30 at the very latest. Race starts 3.00 pm sharp.'

'Copy that Maa'm!' Tom saluted and grinned at his trainer.

The race clerk walked the line of horses bunched tight at the start, quickly checking race colours, bits and bridles and for crops and whips. Gai waited patiently while her colours were checked.

'You're under Gai.'

'I'm always under!' Gai half-joked. 'How much lead you giving me this time.'

'As much as you should carry.'

'Thanks. My strapper is ready. Can I go?'

'Yeah. You're right to ride Gai. Don't put yourself through too many risks. Save that brain of yours for the day job yeah?'

'Like shit!' Gai didn't pull her punches. Her tone indicated that it was a part of the familiar banter between the mountain horse racing crowd. She was well known about the place and always performed well, often pulling in the prizes. She and Dally made a superb team, Dally the 'outcast' from the Victorian racetrack, was tardy at the start, however in Gai's experience sure-footed and strong at heart with plenty of stamina. Gai pulled her stirrups short before mounting Dally. Tom saw her move, raising an eyebrow.

'Pull them short Tom. You'll have more control. The only thing you've got to hold onto is his mane and with your knees.'

'Thanks.'

'Don't pull on the bit. I only use a Tom Thumb to guide him. Don't steer your horse. Give Brindy his head. He knows what to do. You've got a good horse under you today.'

'You said it Gai!'

'Listen mate. The secret is not to worry too much about the others. Let Brindy find his own path.' Gai gave him a wide smile. 'Race you yeah?'

'You're on Gai!' Tom's spirit soared at the prospect.

Brindabella bunched under Tom, dancing on his usual square. Tom knew that the horse sensed the moment. The rest of the pack tightened against them, Gai and Dally in the middle of the set. The start 'rope' would bounce as it released and no one wanted to be in the way of its spring back. It would make for a rough and tumble lunge off the line and up the first hill.

'Ready riders? The official yelled. 'Are you set? The pistol cracked and the line broke free, recoiling away from the horses as they lunged forwards towards the first long hill.

Gai broke faster than the rest, Dally's reflexes primed by the repeat performances on the groomed Melbourne racetracks. Gai leaned forward into his neck, allowing her weight to shift to balance him. His muscles gathered and formed in a single line as he stretched towards the hill. Gai drew in deep lungfuls of fresh air. Her mount felt like silk beneath her, his gait steady and smooth with no break in his stride as he raced for the top of the hill.

Brindabella followed Dally almost by instinct. For less than a second, Tom was caught off guard then hurled himself mentally into the race, pulling up in the stirrups, his rear riding high semi-jockey style. He felt deeply for the stirrups with the balls of his feet, carefully adjusting his weight until he could grip lightly with his knees. Automatically, he took hold of Brindabella's mane to balance, allowing the reins to slip motionless in his fingers, both sides trailing delicately off the colt's neck. Brindabella put his head down with the exertion of accelerating into a gallop behind Dally. Tom lifted a little higher then dropped his entire body mass to a line along the colt's back. He put his head down, close to the horse's neck and let him go.

'That's my boy. Run Brindy. Run.' Tom whispered.

Brindabella responded to the invitation to fly after Dally. He lifted his head for a moment, opening his nostrils and striding out full length, his muscles extended to the full as he raced up the hill. Tom understood from this position that this was the horses' race and that they would simply have to stay on their mounts and stay the course. He leaned into the corner, leaving the reins loose at Brindabella's neck, yet exerting sufficient weight to urge Brindabella around. Then he dropped close to his neck, again centering his weight.

Gai was now sitting deep into the saddle, her legs as far forwards as the short stirrups would allow as Dally began the precarious descent between the rocks and down the narrow track into the chute. The horses behind were losing control, some of them already bolting. Tom remembered Gai's warning not to be in the chute if any of the horses behind were out of control.

'Haa!' Tom leaned deep into the hill urging Brindabella to the limit of his balance. Then he leant back to take his seat as Brindabella half slid through the chute, almost at Dally's tail. Dally, sensing Brindabella, sprung forwards to create a space between them, then extended towards the lake. Gai, ready for the obstacle settled to the centre of the saddle, one hand free in the air and the other holding onto her horse's mane. Tom looked up for a moment, just long enough to get a glimpse of Gai's position in the saddle. Then, as if by remote control, he too rose off the neck of his horse, balancing as he kicked Brindabella forwards and into the lake. The colt trembled almost imperceptibly beneath him and then with barely a pause, strode full length into the water, his neck extended and head held to balance as he plunged into the lake, the mud already churned into a slippery sinkhole beneath Dally. Suddenly, the horses were abreast, taking the last strides out of the lake together.

'Go Gai. Go.' Tom yelled.

Gai hardly had time to look over her shoulder at Tom and Brindabella surging forwards for the final run out to the finish line. She had a glimpse of the spirit of the colt, his eyes steady and fixed as if on a distant landscape, his tail and mane held high, catching the wind, his muscles magnificent and powerful moving like a stream of grey lightning over the bush track. Then she saw Tom, sitting upright, one hand raised in the air, his legs steady and still at Brindabella's side. The horses strode together then Dally pulled half a stride in front, Gai dropping instinctively to his neck as they raced the final 400 metres to the white line. Gai heard the crowd roar as they crossed the finish line, the blur of the commentator calling the race through the megaphone indistinguishable to her ears as she instinctively patted Dally's neck. Dally paced further with Gai sitting lightly in the saddle and easing him back to a canter, letting the reins drop. She turned back to the crowd and raised her cap and hand in victory. They came over the line, a few strides later, Brindabella and Tom the boy riding like a veteran horseman. The colt turned sharply into a circle to face the crowd. Gai nudged Dally forwards towards Tom and Brindabella to salute them. The horses quivered with sweat, the freedom shining like fire in their eyes. Then Gai turned her mount towards her strapper, cantering him forwards then slipping out of the saddle.

'Gai. You've got to weigh in. Quick.' Mitch took her arm, pulling her off the horse and running her back towards the official before any time elapsed. 'You'll be bloody off side with the stewards!'

The steward saw them coming, realising that Gai was thinking only about her mount. He kept his eyes fixed on her until she reached the circle, standing to the weigh in. Then he gave the nod and the cheer went up.

'Drinks for everyone at the bar!' Gai shouted from the victor's podium, the Man from the Snowy River Cup held high above her head. Mitch stood at her left and Tom quietly at her right, accepting his well-deserved second place.

Brindabella quivered and trembled as Cassie rubbed him down, hosing off the sweat and wrapping her arms around his neck.

'Is that your horse young man?' A neatly dressed man approached Tom and Cassie at the float.

'He is.' Tom asserted.

'How much do you want for him?'

'He's not for sale.' Tom said quietly.

'What do you call him.'

'Brindabella. Brindabella's his name.' Cassie said possessively.

'Good horse. Got anymore like him?'

'Know where to find some.' Tom said obliquely.

'I've got a buyer. He has a string of racehorses and stables all over Europe. Good blood lines. I've never seen a horse like that one though. Something in his spirit.'

'Like I said. Brindabella is not for sale. There are others out there that might be.' Tom said firmly but politely.

'Out where?'

'I'll let you know.' Tom was deliberately evasive.

'Who do you work for?' Cassie was inquisitive.

'The stables of the Aga Khan.'

'The Aga who?' Cassie asked innocently.

'Let's go see Gai.' Tom suggested quickly. 'Here.' He handed Cassie Brindabella's bridle.

'Gai. There's someone I want you to meet.' Tom opened.

'Hello.' Gai stretched out her hand. 'Gai.'

'Hello. Dariyan.' The man took her hand lightly. 'Congratulations on your outstanding win Gai. You certainly know how to ride.'

'Thanks Dariyan. It's mostly Dally though.'

'He's quite a horse. I was wondering about…'

'Tom's horse?' Gai guessed.

'Hmm.'

Gai smiled openly at Tom. 'We'll have to ask Tom about that. I wouldn't sell him if he were mine. Mind you, Tom didn't tell me he could ride so well!'

'My grandfather taught me. I have been riding since I was five on his farm at Corryong.'

'Well it certainly shows young man.' Dariyan said kindly.

'We could locate the stallion for you if you like.' Gai offered.

'You could?' The man inquired.

'The brumby herds usually stick together and Angus will know where this horse came from so it won't be hard to identify the stallion.'

'That would be excellent. Thank you.' Dariyan gave a short bow.

'Are you drinking with us?' Gai invited. 'This is Mitch. Mitch Flanagan.'

The man melted into the bush crowd settling in at the bar with a glass of soda and lime as Gai toasted their ride.

'Tom, that sure was some ride today. We're hoping to collect a few of the brumbies later in the spring. Would you like to come and work with us for a while at Tom Groggin Station?' Charlie, the station manager had finally caught up with Tom.

'Yeah. I would. I mean, thanks.'

'Don't mention it. First things first. I'll have one of my farmhands float your horse down the mountain.

'Will Brindy be OK?'

'Usually people don't take trailers down the mountain, but believe me, it's OK so long as your brakes are in good nick and you take it steady in low gear. Meet you down at the Station when you are ready.'

'That's cool. See you there. Thanks Charlie.' Tom grinned and shook his hand..

'You're welcome. Angus tells me that you're a good hand around the farm. We do need a bit of extra help at the moment. The cows are calving and I want to make sure that we keep them under a watchful eye. So you'll be up some nights watching the calving. Can't afford to have them go down. It's too much strain on both the cow and the calf. You can keep your horse in the round yard until he settles. It might take him a few days to get used to the other horses. He'll be in new territory.'

'Mmm.' Tom was thoughtful. 'What about Cassie?'

'I can't Tom. I'm expected back at work tomorrow. I managed today, but it's a bit of a push, being a weekend.'

'Sorry. Shouldn't have asked.'

'No, it's OK.'

'You're always welcome. Cassie isn't it?' Charlie inquired. 'Angus has told me lots of good things about you.'

'Thank you. Good to meet you.' Cassie felt chuffed.

'My wife Lou and I manage the station. She's great with the horses too. You'd like to meet her I'm sure.

'Tom?'

'Yeah, come Cassie. On your days off.'

'Sweet.'

'OK. Then we'd better push off. There's more to be done around the farm.'

Charlie stuck out his hand, taking Tom's hand firmly in his. He met his eyes, the quiet and sober welcome assuring Tom that the Station would be much as Angus promised; work, friends, new experiences and skills that would last him a lifetime.

'That's settled then. See you at the station tomorrow Tom.' Charlie lightly tipped his hat.

The quiet man Dariyan who had enquired about buying Brindabella suddenly joined Charlie. He smiled briefly then together, the two men walked back to their four-wheel drive, Charlie patting his dog as he got into the cab.

Tom and Cassie spent the night with Brindy at Jillamatong Station. It was easier that way, with Gai to talk to as they camped in their swags under the stormy sky. Tom wondered whether the skies would open and they would have to race for shelter in the makeshift stables where both Brindy and Dally were corralled for the night — both horses fed, watered and given an extra nosebag of oats as a treat after the race. The weather held and Tom gradually fell asleep, reluctant to let go of the beautiful scene above him; the radiant moonstruck clouds with their silvery sheen and the occasional flashes of lightning in the distance. Cassie lay beside him in her own swag, occasionally rolling towards him as if by instinct. She woke several times in the night, feeling or sensing Tom dreaming of the race, his hands reaching forwards to pat and encourage Brindabella.

The morning broke with a slight dew on the outside of the swags. Tom lifted his onto the back of the ute and rolled it out to dry in the morning sun. Then he went back to find Cassie already sitting up, her hair alight with the morning sun.

'Hey Cass. How d'ya sleep?'

'Mmm. Hey Tom. What a morning.'

'Breakfast?' Tom grinned.

'I wish. I have to be at work. Breakfast at the Cafe for me.' Cassie said sleepily.

'Here, I'll give you a hand.' Tom reached forwards, caught her hand and pulled Cassie to her feet.

'Hey! I can't walk in this thing.' Cassie laughed, jumping a few steps in her sleeping bag.

'See you then Cass. Catch up soon yeah?'

'Yeah. See you soon.' Cassie smiled and jumped — still in her sleeping bag — towards the parked cars.

For Tom, there was plenty of time for a bush breakfast with Gai — fried eggs and bacon sizzled in a cast iron frying pan over a newly stoked fire and hot coffee. There was plenty of bread, roughly toasted on a homemade wire grill with spoonfuls of plum jam sold to the race goers by the Jindabyne Country Womens' Association.

Tom grinned at Gai.

'That hit the mark then.' Gai grinned back.

'Thanks Gai. You're tops.'

'So are you Tom. And so is that horse of yours. You be careful driving down to Tom Groggin. You don't want to lose your horse on those hairpin bends. Take it very slowly and take the turns wide.'

'Thanks Gai.' Tom said soberly. 'I'd better be on my way then.'

'I'll help you load Brindy.'

'Thanks. He will probably just walk on.'

'Show me. I've never seen a brumby like a horse float before.'

Tom laughed. 'You'll see.'

Tom walked to the bush stable. Brindabella pricked up his ears and whiskered as Tom approached. 'I see you've finished your oats Brindy. Come on then. Let's show Gai what you're really made of. Walk on.'

Tom held the reins loosely and Brindabella, head slightly down, walked obediently behind him. Tom stepped aside as they neared the float. He slipped the reins off his horse's head and Brindabella walked up the ramp and stood quietly in the float.

'Well I'll be!' Gai shook her head in disbelief. 'How did you teach him that?'

'I didn't.' Tom answered simply. He walked to the front of the ute and got into the front seat.

'See you next time then.' Gai flashed a brilliant smile at the young competitor who she knew, would train to pip her at the post next year.

'See you then Gai.' Tom returned the smile. He looked in the mirror and gave Gai a final wave as he drove the ute towards the farm gate.

JOURNEY TO TOM GROGGIN

Charlie had quickly settled back into the daily work routine on Tom Groggin Station. He was filled with the energy that was always the aftermath of the Jillamatong Race meet. It wasn't just the horses and the excitement of the race that fired him up, but it was the meeting with old friends again, the bushies, the farmers, the horsemen and women and the young people — married it seemed to their horses — who lit the fire inside of him and reminded him that these mountains and its people were his home. His heart would always be here, on the rugged Victorian side of the Great Dividing Range. Here at Tom Groggin, the river flats hugged the Murray River where the tall timbers drew the eye upwards to catch the snow-capped ramparts of the Snowy Mountains. He pulled in to the station over the low lying causeway, aware that the Murray River was pumping after the rain had brought gushing flows of water and snow off the back of the mountains. This time the crossing was easy, yet, more than once, they had had to abandon the ute and cross over the surging river via the narrow footbridge. The pastures, green on virtually black soils were reflected in the plump and shining condition of the Angus herd. Charlie knew that it was time to draft out the cows and calves and push them through to the fallow paddock before the annual sales at Albury.

The summer grazing leases were a boon to the property but the time had come to relinquish them. It was an historic time in Australian agriculture, to move away from grazing the subalpine and alpine pastures and adjust to the seasonal constraints of feed. Tom Groggin Station, set within the national park, was the last property in New South Wales still with permission to graze the high country. With the imminent demise of Tom Groggin, the history of the high country cattlemen and their horses was in peril and with it their heritage. Charlie was determined to keep just a part of that tradition alive.

Charlie was not happy. He was no fool and the evidence was clear to him on both the New South Wales and Victorian sides of the Murray River, that the national park — despite the withdrawal of cattle grazing — was disgracefully, seriously becoming degraded. No matter the millions of dollars the government drew from the public each year from the National Park, they had not controlled or managed the feral animals, wild dogs and weeds along the banks of the Murray, the pigs roaming freely through the forested and subalpine areas. Now, there were deer and pigs climbing up into the true alpine area during the summer months. The season was still early, but once the Murray Valley heated up under the summer sun, the blackberries would explode into new growth, choking any chance for native grasses, flowers and shrubs to find a firm foothold along the riverbank.

Charlie drove directly to the cattle yards. The sound of distressed cows looking for separated calves broke the morning silence. The air was still cold from rain, with occasional clouds hanging over the Station in a soft shroud. Although the drought out west almost incapacitated the rural sector with its harvest of death sending shock waves through the export economy, Tom Groggin remained by comparison, immune; it was an oasis of spring growth and sure economic returns. He immediately set to work, drafting the cattle with the aid of six or seven cattle-dogs, his wife and their friends.

Slowly, over the past couple of years, Charlie had changed

the profile of the herd. The Station boasted a solidly Angus line, the cows altogether better calvers than the Herefords and with a better frame for meat. The Herefords proved to be less hardy in the alpine winter months and too prone to skin and eye cancer from the harsh summer UV rays. Gradually he consolidated the herd, trimming out the Hereford bulls and breeders, switching to a more manageable Angus herd. Eventually he built the stud, and simultaneously improved the genetics of the horses, bringing a few brumbies into the mix with their powerful muscles and sure feet.

There was nothing a man could do out here without his horse and dog, and even the collection of trail bikes and all-terrain buggies could never replace his horses. Along with the Station dogs, the horses were the ideal shepherds and 'moveable yards' for the cattle. On the long run up to the last of the summer leases at Davies Plain and Mount Hope, it was impossible without either. The dogs knew their work and Charlie hardly had to give the command before the dogs rounded up the strays wandering off the four wheel drive track and into the bush. This year, the run to the high pastures would probably be the last. The pressure was on to get the cattle off the high country once and for all.

Tom made his way carefully along the Alpine Way pulling the horse float behind the ute and using the gears, as Charlie had instructed him, as brakes on the winding corners. He drove straight through the Visitor Entry Gate waving as he did so and continued towards Thredbo. This time there would be no stopping to enjoy the view or a coffee, time though for a brief moment at Dead Horse Gap. He pulled the float into the parking bay and stepped out into the cool air. He walked quickly to the back of the float, to check that Brindy was as happy and calm as he hoped. For a moment, the tears sprang into his eyes as he looked around him. This was where he and Sean had started their new lives in New South Wales, leaving the horrors of his schooldays behind him. He looked around him searching for any of the wild horses they had seen on the way through from Victoria. He listened carefully but only heard the sound of the wind plucking at the tops of the trees, the calls of the crows and the distant hum of a car climbing towards them.

'Let's go Brindy. Tom Groggin or bust!' Tom patted his horse on the rump and got back into the cab.

The descent along the Alpine Way towards Victoria was stunning. The forest of Alpine Ash dressed with fresh and sparkling snow was magnificent. The tall trees emerged from the forest floor as straight as ship's masts, their crowns forming a loose yet complete canopy that would shield the ferns from the full glare of the hot summer suns. The loose scattering of snowdrifts on the sides of the road, the glistening of leaves wet with rain, snow and sleet under the rising sun completed the breathtaking beauty of the western face of the range.

The drop off was as steep as Tom could handle and any increase in the incline would almost certainly see him jackknife the float into the back of the ute. Brindabella held fast, his feet slithering forwards to the front of the float. He was used to tough terrain and automatically balanced and braced with his chest wall against the front of the float. Slowly and steadily, they made sure their descent to the bottom of the last of the green and fertile grazing valleys in the mountains. Tom, although anxious and careful at the wheel, was quietly jubilant after their ride at Jillamatong, and with the new beginning, the chance at last to train Brindabella with proper yards and gear, under the watchful and seasoned eye of Charlie and his crew.

The road suddenly turned towards an open grassland at an elbow in the road. In the early morning, when the dew was still hanging in droplets along the long stems of the native grasses, over a 100 kangaroos, mothers, joeys and 'old man kangaroos' gathered, most of them sunning themselves, lying casually in the open field. Tom looked wistfully at the abundant campsites abutting the river. He would like nothing better than to hang out with Brindy by a campfire, but there was work to do! He continued carefully along the strip of tarred road, negotiating the curves and changing through the gears until suddenly he came across the dirt road that was the entrance to the station. The low-lying bank of cloud that had settled over the valley during the night lifted as the morning temperatures steadily rose. Tom Groggin Station emerged as a vision of paradise set amongst the rugged and spectacular terrain of the Snowy Mountains.

'Geez Brindy. This looks good.' Tom knew he was speaking more to himself than the horse in a world of his own in the float. He changed down to second gear, easing the truck and float over the ford. The strong flow of the Murray River pulled at the wheels of the ute and Tom panicked for a moment as to whether he would lose the float. Suddenly they were across the river and pulling up the last kilometre of road towards the homestead. Even from a distance, he could hear the buzz of the cattle draft in full swing. As he pulled the float towards the group of sheds and yards near the homestead, the sharp and metallic sound of welding caught both him and Brindabella by surprise. He felt Brindy pull backwards in the float. Tom quickly cut the engine and hopped out of the ute and ran straight to the back of the float.

A chorus of farm dogs wildly yapping and barking announced their arrival.

'It's OK Brindy. We're here!' Tom couldn't contain his excitement. 'You OK boy?' Tom opened the back of the float and ran a hand along Brindabella's spine.

Brindabella shivered with excitement, his ears twitching and hoof lightly pawing at the straw on the bottom of the float.

Tom unhitched the bridle and quickly backed Brindabella out of the float and walked him around the ute and float to stretch his legs before tying him loosely to the float rail.

An old man walked out of the shed, welding mask pushed up from his face.

'Hello. I'm Tom.'

'Hello Tom, I'm Max. Charlie's father.' He grinned softly and put out his hand still in the welder's glove. 'Is that your horse?'

'Yeah. That's Brindy.'

'I heard you two did really well at Jillamatong, considering he's just a brumby.'

'Thanks.' Tom was chuffed.

'OK. Let's put him in the round yards. He'll be happier there.' Max walked up to the horse, putting out his hand and looking him in the eye.

'Hello boy. Aren't you a beauty.' The old man couldn't help himself, running admiring hands and eyes over the horse, checking his forelegs and hooves, checking the line of his back and the strength of his shoulders. 'You sure are something. Sure you don't want to sell him Tom?' Max shot the young man a glance.

'Not for sale!' Tom announced with a proud smile.

The round yards were solid, built with steel that would last 100 years. In the adjacent paddock a group of assorted horses, most of them quality bred, grazed on the light feed. The horses had already shed their winter coats; none of them were rugged during the day and mostly worked only in training.

'I'll open the gate. Bring him in.' Max walked on, pulling half a bale of lucerne hay out of the stable and tossing it into the yard for the horse.

'Come on Brindy.' Tom clucked.

Brindabella followed Tom straight into the yards, more curious than alarmed at the fresh sounds and smells at his Victorian mountain home.

Max took Tom back to the machinery shed where he was struggling to fix the trailer all but destroyed by Charlie's young bloke, Jake. The shed was packed with machinery, metal saws, welding gear, a couple of utes and tucked to one side, a separate generator shed. Within the main shed was the saddle store and outside and still under cover, an assortment of trail bikes, overland buggies, utes, floats, trucks and a couple of New Holland tractors for ploughing and pulling anything that happened to get bogged.

The picture of a strong working property, self-sufficient in everything down to billy tea, struck Tom immediately he entered. Amongst some of the almost new, hundred thousand dollar heavy tractors, was a rusted share plough lying between the machinery shed and drafting yards where the Angus and Hereford cattle were being slowly and surely sorted by Charlie and his wife.

'Hello son. Welcome.' Charlie climbed over the metal yards and walked towards Tom, his hand outstretched. 'Come on over and I will introduce you to your digs. All OK Max? Can you sort out the trailer?'

'Nearly got it sorted Charlie. Young Jake sure twisted a bit of metal running it through the river. Lucky the ute didn't go with it.'

Charlie laughed. His son was tough, bright and independent for his age.

'Come on then Tom. This is your space for the next while.' Charlie opened the door into the old Tom Groggin Hut.

'Wow. This is amazing.' Tom whistled softly.

'Sure is beautiful. We fixed her up a bit. Put in the new floor. Most of the rest of the structure is much the same as the original though. I looked at the old pictures. The verandah used to be hardwood, so we built that back on.

The hut was well built with white gum in log cabin style. Inside, exposed beams under the iron roof added to the sense of bush comfort and Tom knew that he would be happy here. A new wall separated the bathroom from the main cabin and Tom drew in his breath, as he caught a glimpse of the stunning views extending back towards Mount Hope past the Pinnibar Range. At the front of the hut the rural panorama unfolded in a majestic sweep of the Murray River as it surged full with spring flows towards Khancoban. Behind it, the steep and untamed western face of the mountains rose above the Station.

'You'll be warm enough in here. There's a stockpile of wood out the back. Sometimes we have campers come and stay for a few days while they explore the area.' Charlie explained. 'Mostly people we know. They come back each year and a few people camp on the river flats.'

'This is great Charlie. Thanks.' Tom said openly. 'This feels like home.'

'Don't mention it son. Just put your swag in here.'

'Me granddad had a place over at Corryong.' Tom said proudly.

'Oh? I might know him.' Charlie said.

'I don't think so.' Tom realised he needed to change the subject quickly. 'He isn't there anymore.'

'I'm sorry son. Hope he is OK.' Charlie placed a hand on Tom's shoulder.

'Well he had a great life but he died a few years ago and the farm was sold after that Charlie.' Tom felt a sudden surge of emotion threatening to choke him.

'Listen, come to the house for a feed. Lou likes to feed her men up.' Charlie smiled sympathetically at the young man.

'You have quite a few dogs!' Tom said brightly noticing the string of kelpies trotting after Charlie.

'Yeah. They're worth a fair bit. Some of them bring in two and a half thousand dollars each.'

'No joke!'

'We like to look after our dogs.' Charlie added dryly. 'This one's mine. Spike.' Charlie patted the tan kelpie with white socks. 'He's worth about ten times more than the rest of them put together. Could never replace him. Brings the cattle in when they head off into the scrub.

'Spose they're faster than people.' Tom offered.

'Dog is worth eight or nine men and about five women.' Charlie joked. 'Lou's a bloody good worker. She droves the cattle with us most years. You met my father Max welding the trailer?'

'Yeah. He helped me unload Brindy into the round yard.

'Good. Max knows this area better than most.' Charlie paused and looked towards the mountains. 'When he was about six or seven years old, he and his old man used to pack saddle the tin ingots out of Surveyor's Creek. It's the roughest country around. The soils were good.' Charlie grinned at his young charge. 'Dad tells me one potato out of those soils would fill half a kero drum. Doesn't talk much else about that life though. Must have been hard work back then.'

'The farm must keep you busy.' Tom said looking at the acres of green stretching around him.

'It does. I'll appreciate your help Tom. We've got the annual sales coming up in Albury and we have to drive the rest of the herd to Mount Hope.'

'That's great. I'd love to!' Tom smiled.

'Good. See you at lunch. There's hot water in the tank. Feel free. Take a shower. Whatever.' Charlie walked out the door and put his work boots back on. He whistled and two or three of the kelpies joined Spike already at his heel. Then he walked over to the main homestead allowing Tom space and time to settle in.

'That was great Lou!' Tom put down his napkin after finishing off the plate of fresh beef, potatoes and beans smothered in a generous helping of homemade gravy.

'That's alright Tom. Glad you enjoyed it.' Lou beamed at the young man seated at her table. 'Besides, you'll get an appetite around here. Plenty of work on each day.' She smiled at her husband.

'Maybe you can show Tom around the farm this afternoon Lou. Can you ride a bike Tom?'

'Yeah. I can. I rode lots on gramp's property. I had a monkey bike for a while then got onto the real thing, a Kawasaki Stockman 250. Never really took to the quad bikes though.' Tom added as an afterthought.

'Great stuff. Do you still have a bike of your own?'

'Actually I do, sort of,' Tom started 'well I mean it's Angus's bike but he has let me have it to ride around the farm. That is when I won't be riding Brindy.' Tom grinned.

'Look, why don't you head up the mountain with Lou tomorrow. She has to go and collect some saddlery she ordered. Lou could drop you off and you could ride the bike back if you want.' Charlie offered.

'Yeah. Good idea. I'd like that Charlie. It's a good bike. But it would be better if I dropped Angus's ute back to the farm. Lou can follow me.' Tom grinned.

'That's settled then. Lou?'

'Fine.' Lou smiled broadly as she cleared the table. 'We'll explore the farm this afternoon Tom if you like.'

'Yes, thanks. I would like that Lou.' Tom was almost beside himself with excitement.

Tom settled into the long ride on the motorbike up the Alpine Way. As promised, Lou had dropped him back out at the farm near Dalgety. He'd quickly found the helmet and a pair of work gloves.

His riding boots were fine for the trip, along with a small backpack with some extra food and water.

The cold air blasted his face beneath the open helmet. Once he had passed through Jindabyne and the outlying farms and lodges, he finally felt free. The invitation to the farm at Tom Groggin was a godsend and Tom knew better than to waste any time even if it meant he would not see Cassie for a while. Fate had opened up the road to Victoria and Tom seized the moment with both hands. Suddenly, he was at the National Parks Entrance Gate. He slowed the bike, stopped at the window, and reached into his pocket for the money.

'You passing through or staying in the Park.'

'Just passing through.'

'You don't have to pay.' The cashier gave him a cheery smile.

'Thanks.' Tom smiled back. He fitted his helmet and gloves again, then checked in the rear view mirror before accelerating smoothly, onto the Alpine Way. 'Fifteen minutes max', he thought to himself, 'And I'll be at Dead Horse Gap.'

The road curved to the right and Tom was aware that in less than a minute, he would rise over Dead Horse Gap and be on his way to Tom Groggin. Something tugged at him inside as he reached the information bay at the start of the Cascades track; he turned the trail bike into the valley riding past the gate and onto the rough, stony path that tracked alongside the river now tumbling with fresh snow-melt. He knew that this was definitely 'off limits' now that he was in the National Park, but something greater than his knowledge, common sense and respect for the mountains pulled him into the heart of the valley.

Tom eased the trail bike along the four wheel drive track towards the metal footbridge that crossed the river. The piles of horse dung on the footbridge puzzled him until he realised that the bridge was also a territorial marker for the horses. The opposite side was wet and boggy, so Tom rode off track until he found a narrow section of creek he could cross without unduly disturbing the soil. It wasn't so much that he didn't want to leave tracks, even though he was aware that he was literally trespassing into territory that was not cut out for trail bike riding. He crossed safely, taking the hill in low gear and ascending over the rise until the track dropped over towards another river, running strongly, the water almost at its banks.

The horses gathered at the base of the valley looked up in surprise as Tom came down the track. He killed the engine, allowing the bike to drift down the dirt towards the bridge. For a moment, the lead stallion looked warily at him, wondering whether to gather the mares and foals and head up the valley. Tom sat still on the saddle of the bike, watching and wistfully wondering whether he could catch one of the horses. He knew it was out of the question for now but he mentally traced the direction of the horses as they moved carefully up the valley. He turned to check out the terrain around him, instinctively watching for trailers. The surrounding hills looked impenetrable: the dual peaks of Purgatory and Jerusalem and the distant majesty of the Ramsheads. They looked beautiful. Before him was the sweeping Big Boggy where the horses grazed before moving more deeply into the wilderness.

Tom knew it was only a dream. The horse would have to wait. Maybe, if he hung for long enough at Tom Groggin, Charlie and Lou would help him find a friend for Brindy. Inspired, Tom gently kicked over the engine, riding high over the rocky Bob's Ridge and past the rough bush hut hidden in the brumbies' lair on the side of the Cascades Creek. It took him longer than expected, yet Tom knew that the track would eventually lead him out of the wilderness. As he rode along the broad fire trail, he probed for the sidetrack that would take him down the deep descent to the Murray, crossing to the other side of the gorge where he could again climb the rugged mountain ridge and ride to Davies Plain. As he avoided the trees that now littered the track — bent and broken by the storm — Tom realised that his experience in the mountains had smoothed the rough edges off his character and softened his personality. He was no longer the sad kid Tom, crying inside from repeated abuse. He was now Tom, the man moulded by the mountains and by the men who had taken him under their wing, Angus, Sean, and Jack — especially Jack the elder — who had the secrets of the land etched deeply into his heart. Cassie was no longer out of reach. When they had first met he was mesmerised by her eyes, her hair, her untouched beauty. Then they were together, spending time together. He could wait. If he wanted her enough — and he did — he would wait until he was sure that she felt the same way about him.

Tom was aware that the weather was closing in. Already, he could hear the sound of distant thunder tumbling about the peaks. He had long since passed the last vista of the Ramshead Range visible from the Cascades. Now, he was surrounded by tall timbers, some of them surrendering to the relentless winter winds, their trunks shattered and limbs broken like matches, some now bent and groaning against the present onslaught of the cold front sweeping onto the mountain ranges. Tom shivered. He had little protection and realised that his chances could only worsen as night closed in with this weather. It would be dark before he was anywhere close to the Tom Groggin Station half way down the Victorian side of the Alps.

The track was dangerous with large trees, sometimes up to 100 metres in length, strewn diagonally along the path, their ancient trunks rotting back into the earth, remnants of creation burying itself into the forest floor for the next generation of giants to emerge.

Then the track descended deeply over tiny cascading creeks, only to rise and climb yet another ridge. The journey seemed endless and from time to time, Tom felt rather than saw the presence of the wild horses. Suddenly, as he rounded one of the curves in the track, a black, brumby colt, clearly three years old or more, faced him, its ears twitching, nose tuned to his scent and white-socked hooves turning the soil as he anticipated Tom's approach. Tom stopped, letting the engine idle as he watched the colt.

'Hey boy. Here. Come on.' Tom talked to the colt.

The colt more curious than afraid, made to canter towards Tom, then thought the better of the adventure, wheeling around and cantering a few metres up the track. He stopped again, turning to face Tom, his eyes open and inquiring, nostrils flared and ears forwards. Tom stayed where he was, content to watch the horse and wait for it to react to him.

'That's the boy. You're a beauty.' Tom observed the powerful flanks of the horse, the well-built muscle and good frame. This horse didn't carry the inbred lines of the majority of horses in the valley. His feet though, had the telltale sign of a true mountain horse, neat and compact, unmarked and without splits. His coat was dark, almost charcoal with flecks of white on the forelock. Tom knew that he had found what he was looking for. Most of the stories were about the wild horses that were runts, underfed and undernourished on the coarse and sparse winter feed. This horse had all the signs of breeding, perhaps with a flare of Arab visible in the eyes and refined line of the nose.

'Thunder!' The name sprang from Tom's lips.

'Come on Thunder.' Tom watched the colt move. Suddenly, a second horse appeared, slightly smaller, almost midnight black; her ears less welcoming and curious than Thunder's.

'This must be your mate then.' Tom whispered.

The youthful mare, less adventurous than the young stallion, bolted off the track and into the bush. Thunder turned and stormed up the track away from Tom. Then the third horse appeared, the old white stallion, its eyes strangely wise and soft — appraising Tom. 'Holy Smoke. Here you are.' Tom said quietly. 'You are the Keeper.' Tom realised that this horse had known men and was hesitant, without curiosity or trust. He didn't, however, begrudge the stallion warning off the young mare. The horse had already seen too much: men with careless ropes catching the wild horses, some breaking their spirit, others their necks. The majority of horses were captured against their will, intuitive to the knowledge that they would be bound to a life of fences, yards and cattle.

The sudden appearance of the bush hut surprised Tom as he rounded a corner on the track. He had accustomed himself to being totally in the wilderness, not really sure of where he was or how long it would take to get to the other side, if there was another side! All he knew now, was that he was headed towards Victoria somewhere deep in the Pilot Wilderness.

The track could take him to Omeo for all he cared. At the moment, all that mattered was that there was a sign of civilisation, albeit nothing more than a roughly hewn mountain hut, the smooth planks a beautiful grey against the soft gold of the landscape. Then he noticed the second hut, also crafted from unfinished alpine timber, the vertical planks inviting him to take shelter, for now at least. The small group of wild horses grazing around the huts became alert to his presence. They moved off quietly, leaving Tom to remain fascinated by the timber constructions in the middle of an otherwise abandoned and remote part of the national park.

The mist had already settled over the valley. Tom noted the wood half-sawn, left lazily on the ground where campers had attempted to restore the supply and instead, abandoned the saw in the middle of their journeys. Perhaps there was another peak, another horizon more important than the immediate and wonderful presence of the Tin Mine Huts, complete with their open and welcoming hearths. There was a certain magic in finding a fire already stacked with dry wood.

Tom parked the trail bike carefully beside the hut. The ground was still dry but it wouldn't be long before the rain thundered down, obscuring the valley, the huts and the bike under a veil of water. Quickly, he moved inside the largest of the huts, noting the cross-saw on the far wall. There was a good supply of timber already next to the cavernous fireplace backed by sheets of tin. He hadn't even had time to think how long he would remain in the hut, yet for now, he just wanted to make sure that there would be enough wood to keep him warm and dry. With less than enough clothing and no sleeping gear, he would have to move one of the beds close to the fire to keep warm for the night. Tom frowned as he noticed a brumby skull perched on one of the bunks like the skeleton of ghosts still haunting the mountains with their sorry tales.

He went outside and selected a few pieces of dry timber, branches of larger trees that would saw into good-sized logs for the fire. He set to work, his muscles pumping until they ached and until there was enough wood for at least two days. Whatever he could not use for himself, he would stack neatly for the next travellers through the legendary country that only cattlemen and their horses intimately knew. It would not be long before dark and he needed water.

Tom remembered the smaller of the two huts. He made his way outside, walking around the perimeter of the hut until he found the doorway positioned near the fireplace. The hut was compact and simple, with more stacked firewood and a table only. Perhaps this was where campers cooked on wet and lonely nights and then retired to their tents. The fireplace here was of a better construction than the larger of the two huts. Tom lifted the billy off the hook and retreated to the creek, filling the billy away from the pile of horse dung. He knew that the water would be clean, apart from where the horses had trodden their tracks to their own drinking supplies. Tom drank deeply from the creek. The water was fresh and freezing. He refilled the billy then pulled out one of the muesli bars he had stuffed into his pockets. It would be scant rations but at least he could put something into his gut.

Tom returned to the hut that was already dark inside, the weather closing in around the mountains and blocking the final rays of sun. Two of the windows could be propped open with sticks and Tom pushed them as far as the sticks would allow, letting in the last critical light for the evening. He scrabbled around the woodpile looking for candles, matches, anything that would give him light and start the fire. Finally, he looked in the metal box containing the Hut Log, a few pamphlets and matches! Tom grabbed a pamphlet, noting the general blurb then placed it at the base of the fire. He covered the paper with bark and twigs snapped into kindling size until he had a sizeable teepee of paper, twigs and small sticks. The fire roared into a welcome blaze and rekindled for Tom, the memories and experience of the campfire with Angus and the elders. He felt safe here and the same warm feeling of coming home to himself in the company of protective friends, friends who had shown him the pathway to becoming a man from a boy.

The wind picked up, plucking at the tin in the shed, the roof shingles shaking in warning of the coming storm. The hut held fast, bolstered by the ongoing care of mountain heritage lovers. This was it. This was what he wanted. Something like this hut that he could call his own, away from the pressures of his family life where he was expected to be something he was not. He now knew that he was a simple person with few needs apart from good company and a purpose; not just as a passenger or passer-by in life. Sean, Angus and Cassie, had given him that: a home, friendship and true meaning to his life. Tom stared into the fire, poking the coals with his stick. Suddenly, quietly, and without warning, the old man came through the front door of the hut, holding the bridle in his right hand, the reins drooping loosely over his forearm. As he stepped into the hut, the door flapped against its post in the wind behind him. Tom started and turned to the sound of the door opening and shutting to the wind. The old man stood quietly observing him, his eyes moist with emotion and a love that Tom hadn't imagined possible before. Then the image vanished into the night from where he came.

Tom awoke in the middle of the night to the sound of horses screaming and the pounding of their hooves on the earth. He sat up, the sweat breaking under his armpits, his sudden movement scaring off the rats already trying to reach his backpack. Then again, the horses screamed, their high-pitched cries piercing the wind and cutting like a chill into his heart. The memory of the old man flashed before his mind, the sight of the reins carrying the message of the wilderness and within it, one man who knew how to trap and tame the horses to his will. Tom shot out of the bunk, flicking off the overpants he had loosely arranged as a cover. He walked to the door where the old man had entered, released the leather strap from the nail and peered into the wailing gloom of the night.

There he saw them, the two horses their legs flailing wildly under the clouds. For a brief moment, the clouds parted and the moon struck an eerie light over the landscape. The larger of the two horses, his mane white and coat gleaming with sweat, blood and rain, was raised to full height on his back legs. His eyes, fiery and protruding from his skull, caught Tom's eyes, the rage an unmistakable statement of his kingship over the herd, struck fire and power into Tom's heart. The big stallion reared up, and with thrashing hooves, thundered back towards the ground, his hooves striking the young stallion.

The younger horse screamed as the stallion's hooves cut him deeply on the shoulder. A stream of blood spurted from the wound and gushed down his foreleg and onto the earth, shuddering under the force of the fighting horses.

'Thunder! No! That's Thunder.' Tom screamed.

The old stallion looked through and past Tom with his wild eyes. Then he vanished into the storm like a ghostly vision, whisked into the ether by the eddies of wind shocking the valley with deathly cold.

The sound of bush birds burst through the dawn, and the scampering of the native rats looking for the remnants of food, brought Tom to wakefulness. Luckily, he anticipated the bush visitors and had hung his pack off the floor. There was a wire running across the hut, which served neatly as a safeguard from curious rodent noses. Now, he wanted nothing more than to soak up the early sun, its light filtering into a soft but vital warmth. Tom eased himself off the deeply sagging wire bed. It was at least a place to sleep without a horse skull or skeleton for a night companion. The fire still burned softly, the embers lasting through the long night and glowing welcomingly in the morning. Tom stoked the fire, adding a few pieces of wood to see him through the next hour. He picked up the billy, still half full with creek water and placed it on the fire, then stepped out onto the golden grass. There was no sign of Thunder, but the breathtaking view onto an open plain and the cry of currawongs reminded him that he was in the wilderness and he was free.

He stepped out from the safety of the bush hut, aware that the most challenging part of his ride was about to begin. Instinct had driven him onto the Cascades Trail during his trip to Tom Groggin. Now, fate bound him in his choice and he had to press on through the wilderness along the fire trails until he reached at least Victoria, where he could turn back inland and navigate back to Tom Groggin Station. He revved higher, the track for now an enjoyable escapade, the bike more than powerful enough to take the rises at a fair speed. Only loose rocks and fallen debris from the storm spoiled the track. Tom rode over the debris, righting the front wheel from time to time as it hit loose stones

The trail was well marked and clearly an open passage from the wilderness reaches from NSW into Victoria. Tom welcomed the cold bite of the morning air on his face, happy that he had at least the bike beneath him. There was little between him now and the Station. He dropped over yet another stony rise, when he heard the distinctive sound of gears crunching and the loose traction of a four-wheel drive as it began to ascend the track in front of him. Quickly he turned off the track and into the forest. The undergrowth was still navigable although the forest floor inevitably littered by decades of fallen trees and branches. Some of the trees were damaged by storms and wildfires, others simply sacrificed limbs into the forest as they pushed their crowns further towards the sunlight. Tom killed the engine, and dropped the bike onto the ground, flattening himself behind a boulder, anticipating the worst if the ranger saw his tracks. He was ready to hide for as long as it took. The ranger continued up the track, oblivious to all else other than the perfect morning, the raindrops lighting branches, trunks and leaves with a palette more splendid than any artists' with their limited repertoire of colour.

Tom waited, breathing in carefully and slowly through his nose and softly pushing the air out through his mouth. He fought to keep his heart rate down, the perspiration already smarting, his palms sweating with more than just the exertion of pressing himself flat against the forest floor. The ranger drove on, his CB crackling uselessly, the comfort of the cab buoying his enthusiasm for the bush. The ranger reached the top of the rise where Tom had ducked off to the right. He changed down a gear and the car dropped out of sight.

Tom forced himself to listen and stay attuned to any change in sound or gears that could mean his tracks were visible and he could be traced. He counted slowly to gradually calm his heart to a steady pound. He stood up, leaving the bike where it was while he looked around, gingerly checking the route back to the main trail. There was no sign of the ranger. The faint smell of diesel, the fresh tracks in the rain-softened dirt, was all that remained and Tom knew he was safe for now. Except for the arrival of this one human, clearly with a licence to bring a vehicle into the heart of this remote wilderness, there was no one out here. Sure there could be walkers, campers, wild horses and cross country mountain bikers at any time. But for now, he truly believed he was all alone. He walked back to the bike and slowly wheeled it back towards the trail. He swung a leg over the bike, kicked life into the metal horse and continued cautiously down the trail.

The track would lead him far to the south before he had any chance to turn inland over the rough terrain towards the Murray. The bush was impenetrable and the terrain far too steep. Tom had only one choice, one chance to cut the route short. He would have to take Snow Gums Trail until it ended then cut through the bush until his was on the spur that lead down to the Murray River opposite McCarthy's Trail. Angus had spent hours patiently teaching him about the mountains since the Mens' Camp, trawling over maps, showing him routes in and out of the mountains, where to camp, where he could hide unnoticed and where he could find food and fresh water.

Within minutes, Tom made his way along the fire trail. Surely it would take him all the way to the Murray River! He rode carefully, guiding the machine over the rocky track before deciding to get off the bike, engine still running to use first gear as a brake, and wheel the bike down the spur. He dug his heels into the dirt as far as he could and hung onto the handlebars. The bike slipped sideways and Tom had to use all his strength to grapple the bike back on course until finally, he was through the worst of the descent. He could now see the Victorian border, the Murray River.

The terrain was as rough as anywhere on earth, the bush straddling several climate and vegetation zones within a matter of kilometres. The mountains cascaded through the magnificent Alpine Ash country to frost-ridden high plains. Then, in deep gorges, the landscape plunged to the upper reaches of the great Murray River. He knew that he had bypassed the worst of the Pilot Wilderness and the impossible terrain with its myriad of impenetrable spurs and deeply dissected gorges leading into the Upper Murray River. Tom clung to the handlebars his wrists numbed by the incessant shattering of small rocks under the wheels and the constant need to brake. The going was tougher than he thought. His intuition kicked in and he found a line through the trees, carefully keeping his direction towards the river as he remembered it. Suddenly, he stumbled onto a green verge along the river. He found the bend in the Murray River and knew he was on target, on track to freedom. He straddled the bike and accelerated coursing through the rushing waters, the final marker between him and McCarthys Trail that would lead him onwards to Tom Groggin Station.

The track suddenly turned off out of the forest and Tom found himself at the edge of an open and grassy plain. The kangaroos, more attuned to the coming and goings of campers than most of the remotely based picnickers and adventurers, languished in the sun, grateful for the warmth of an early spring and simply content to watch their young play, thrive and grow. The new shoots of native grass were abundant, watered by the constant flow of the river washing alpine soils and the spoils of unexpected storms between the confines of its deepening banks. Further downstream, past the pondage, the Murray tumbled free-spirited, released at last from the grip of the mountains and buoyed by the diverted waters of the Snowy River.

Once, the Snowy River flowed free and rich with sediments from the uplifted ancient seabed that formed the high passes of the mountain massif. As the river passed through NSW towards the Victorian Coast, water from a myriad of minor and major lower catchments built the velocity and volume of flow, and with the additional water, minerals and microorganisms. When the Snowy reached the broad coastal plains it would dump the rich pickings from the upwaters, a bounty of silt that had built fertile farming lands over the millennia. There, the local Indigenous peoples feasted along the river, their communities thriving on the seasonal flux and flow of food. Now, the Snowy, strangled by tunnels and dams of the great engineering scheme, trickled sadly into the oblivion of sandy reaches choked with weeds and willows. It was the Murray that flowed with new life enjoying water pumped or diverted away from the Snowy River. The rich waters, diverted by weirs, aqueducts, pumps and tunnels, fled towards South Australian wastelands, thousands of kilometres from the age old destination of the Snowy River at Marlo, where the river once spilled voluminously into the sea.

He had found the way out of the mountain wilderness thanks to Angus's expert tuition. Now he was as near to paradise that anyone could be. Nature, horses, the Station folk and a few wildcard bushmen completed the picture. At the moment, he knew neither right nor wrong. For too long, Tom had hung precariously onto emotional cliffs defined by the abuse, isolated and lonely, and where he couldn't care less whether he lived or died. Now he knew love. He had been through the initiation and had experienced there the rare joy of love and respect for himself. He had found a mature, wise and strong love, especially in the friendship of Jack the Aboriginal Elder from the camp. He had found love in the strengthening friendship with Angus and in the protective mothering of Sean. He had found inspiration and he thought, possibly, love in the company of Cassie. Then last night when the old brumby runner at the Tin Mine Huts looked into his eyes, he felt pure love and a compassion that he knew would change him forever. The gnawing loneliness was gone.

'Tom!' You made it. Young Jake hurdled the fence and ran towards his new friend as he rode up the driveway to the homestead.

Tom switched off the engine, lifting the helmet from his head. 'Jake.' Tom grinned. 'Epic ride man.'

'Alpine Way? You look as though you've been climbing rocks in that thing.'

'Just about. Down the fire trails actually.'

'Sounds manic! The steed manage it OK?' Jake patted the bike's tank.

'Handled most of the rough stuff. Couldn't exactly ditch it for a brumby.'

'You saw some?'

'Yeah. Heaps. Some of them are a bit runtish. I've got my eye on a young black stallion though.'

'Cool.'

'Strange yeah. They seem to know when you're coming.'

'Come inside. Hey, have yourself a shower Tom. You look as though you could use one.' Jake grinned. 'I'll just let mum and dad know you're here.'

'Thanks Jake.' Tom said sincerely as he swung his bag over his shoulder and walked into the Tom Groggin cabin.

'Yeah. We can probably go up in a couple of days.' Charlie stuck his fork deeply into the baked pumpkin. 'Tastes good Lou.' Charlie mumbled. The farmhouse was neat with a well-kept open plan kitchen, dining and lounge room. Max sat quietly on the lounge, listening to the evening news until Lou called them to the table for dinner.

'There's more. Tom? Eat your heart out. There's plenty where that lot came from.'

'Thanks Lou.' Tom looked fresh after the hot shower and change of clothes into a clean pair of jeans and a work shirt.

'You known Angus for long?' Charlie asked between mouthfuls.

'Long enough.' Tom said soberly, wiser than his years.

'That's good. I could use you around the farm for a while. We've got our work cut out for us this season with calving coming on.' Charlie grinned. 'You seemed to handle the bike OK Tom, through that rough country. Good job.'

'Thanks. I didn't expect the last track to be quite as steep though.'

'We used to ride it a bit, before the National Parks people stopped us. In fact, there used to be a bit of cattle up in the top bush.'

'I saw someone in a 4WD driving along the track.'

'He didn't see you then?

'No.' Tom grinned.

'Good. So you can ride a horse, drive and manage a trail bike Tom.' Charlie paused as though mulling over Tom's skills. 'As a matter of fact, I've got a young filly, just broken in. She needs a gentle hand. I wouldn't mind taking her up when we look for the horses. Do you reckon you could manage both her and Brindabella: ride one and lead the other? That way we have an extra packsaddler.'

'Yeah. I would like that.' Tom looked brightly at Charlie.

'I'll saddle her up in the morning Charlie.' Lou offered. 'You'd better sort out the gear.'

'What do you take?' Tom's interest was pricked by the prospect of a trip into the mountains on horseback.

'As little as possible. We do need a packhorse on this run though for camp supplies, extra ropes, the salt blocks.'

'Salt blocks?'

'We've tried it the other way. Using ropes. Some of the horses don't like it. They panic. Had one of them go down.'

'Oh.' Tom didn't know how to answer.

'So we thought that we'd try old Charlie Carter's way. You know, drop in some bush yards. Put a block of salt in and wait.'

'Charlie Carter?'

'Yeah. Last of the mountain men, so the legend goes. Lived at the Tin Mines.'

'Really?' Tom was perplexed.

'You heard of him then.'

'Well…not really. But I did see a black horse at the huts, a real beauty.'

'Oh?'

'After the old man came into the hut, I woke up in the middle of the night and two horses were fighting, a black and a grey.'

'Awesome.' Jake cut into the conversation.

'You saw the old man?'

'I thought I did.' Tom said, suddenly unsure.

'Probably saw his ghost. Old bugger. Couldn't bear to live in town. Used to trick the horses into taking the salt, then he'd trap them. Trouble was, when he needed them most, they pissed off on him and left him out there to die. They found him face down in the door of his shack, bridle still in hand. Looks as though he was outside trying to catch one. That's how he got his stores. Usually he rode one of his 'wild horses' across to Jindabyne.

'He ran out of food!' Tom wondered about the old man appearing at the door of the hut.

'Should have learnt a bit more about bush tucker. I wouldn't be surprised if he ate a few of his horses. He'd certainly sell their skins!' Charlie said wryly. 'We won't eat any horses though.'

'Reckon we'll catch some?' Tom mused.

'Yeah. We could try the same tactic eh? Put up a few logs. That'll do for yards and see how we go. Might find your black stallion then Tom.'

'Thunder? Do ya reckon he'd come back with us?'

'Is that what you call him! Good name son.'

'Yeah.' Tom grinned from ear to ear.

CAPTURING THE WILD HORSE THUNDER

The ride out from Tom Groggin to Davies Plain was as enjoyable as any riding Tom had experienced during his short life. Only this time, Tom stuck close to Charlie and his eleven-year-old son Jake, Max bringing up the rear with Lou and the pack horses. Lou appeared jubilant, the break from the routine farm duties, the thrill of fresh mountain air — too early into the spring to be uncomfortably warm — the prospect of a bush camp enlivening her and spurring her spirit to the chase. Once they were off the plain, the track suddenly steepened and the horses fell into a steady single file walking surely and steadily between the trees.

The bush birds carolled at the approaching convoy of men, horses, dogs — and Lou. The day was brisk with floral scents, the movement of kangaroos and wombats rustling through the scrub, the far-off cry of the crows and currawongs calling them back to the high country. It was a superb scene from a heaven that few could ever hope for, let alone have as a first hand and recurring event in their daily lives.

Charlie and Lou enjoyed the liberating sense of leaving Tom Groggin for a few days at least, for one of their favourite bush haunts. There was nothing more beautiful than the mountain air, the sound of water rushing off the slopes and into rocky cascades before being bridled by the surer course of rivers.

Tom was in his element. In the few short hours that he had spent on the Tin Mines track, he felt for the first time in his life a strong sense of kinship with the land — the feeling that he had 'come home', that this was heaven and his heritage, where his spirit would finally find complete peace and rest. The temptation to whistle was almost too powerful, the sound of a golden whistler, then the mimicking lyrebird filling in the chorus of happiness that beat a powerful drum in his heart. This was the time for which he had waited for so long. He was with company he never knew he could have and along with it, a pounding sense of freedom and purpose. There was also the excitement of the prospect of catching the horse, of finding and taking Thunder as his own.

'We'll camp here for the night.' Charlie announced. 'I want to rest the horses and take it easy for the first couple of days. We'll need them to be at full strength if we want them to bring Thunder out.' Charlie dismounted, loosely hanging the reins over a low-lying branch before slipping the saddle and blanket off his horse. He put the saddle carefully against the trunk of a tree, covering the leather with his Drizabone, tucking the edges of the coat under the pommel and leaving the stirrups free. Tom followed suit, carefully placing his saddle against a tree and then Lou, quickly eyeing off the campsite, placed her saddle into the curve of her husband's saddle, making sure that there was a spare Drizabone handy to ward off the descending dew.

'Campfire Charlie?' Lou suggested.

'You and Jake could fix that Lou. I'll take Tom for a quick scout around for some saplings. We might rig up a loose yard in case the horses are spooked.'

'OK then. Potatoes and stew?'

'Sounds wonderful!' Charlie rubbed his stomach. 'Tom, you come with me.' Charlie nodded to his leading hand, already attending the horses, rubbing them down with a rough blanket, pulling the bag of oats off the pack horses and making sure that each mount had a treat until they settled into some freshly cut native grass for their evening feed.

'Charlie, what if we catch the horse?' Lou asked over dinner. 'I mean, do you think he'll come out with us?'

'Who knows Lou. We really have to just play this one by ear. If he's anything like Tom described to us, then the young spirit has plenty of life in him. He'll put up a fight no doubt. Maybe Brindabella will mean the difference to him. The horse might bond since Brindy isn't too long out of the bush himself.'

'You could be right, but something tells me this stallion will fight all the way.'

'If your sixth sense has already kicked in Lou, we're going to have to use our wits as well as the ropes.'

'I think you should put Brindabella into the yard with him. Let him settle that way. Then lead them both on foot with a loose halter rope. He'll probably walk with Brindy. I just wouldn't try leading him off another horse. I don't think it will work Charlie.'

'Women!' Charlie explained smiling at Tom. 'Trouble is, she's usually right.' Charlie was resigned to his wife's innate sense of timing and her wisdom.

'Anyways Charlie, for now we've got these potatoes to get through. Max, did you bring your guitar?' Lou asked.

'Yeah, sure as hell did Lou.' Max drawled.

'That's good then. Perhaps you could teach the boys a few of your songs.' She opened.

'What would you like?' Max turned to Tom.

'Dunno. Can't remember many songs. Mainly rap and that could prove to be a bit difficult on your acoustic.' Tom looked glumly at Max.

Max laughed. 'Then we'd better go for something more generic. Bit of a bush ballad. Made some up meself.' He said proudly.

'You and your songs.' Charlie feigned exasperation. 'He's bloody good though. OK Tom, while Max warms up the strings, we've got more work to do.' Charlie started into the bush to look for saplings to construct the makeshift and detachable set of yards, leaving Max to ponder over the evening repertoire of music that could easily rival the nightlife on the mountain.

'You know Charlie,' Tom started after a heavy, serve of damper and jam, 'I reckon that's probably the sweetest music I've ever heard.'

Charlie looked up sharply from his 'dessert' surprised by a sudden insight into Tom; the young man at first glance, he had reckoned was fairly simple. He paused for a moment, letting the significance of Tom's words ring around the campfire before he spoke.

'There's probably a bit of music in every one of us here tonight, trouble is, not many of us go to the pains to use it like Max has.'

'S'pose. Does it take long to learn Max?'

'Nup. My mum used to play the piano, you know, old time songs and that sort of thing. So I guess I was just brought up around it.' Max strummed a few absent chords on his guitar.

'Can you teach me sometime?' Tom asked.

'Can't see why not.'

'Could sit out on a log somewhere and have a go.'

'Just as long as you don't frighten the bulls off my cows, Tom.' Charlie winked at Lou.

'Let's see how your time pans out Tom. You'll have the brumby to break in. Then there is all the work around the station, and if you're lucky, Max will be free enough to teach you the ropes.' Lou suggested.

'Cool.' Tom stood up, invigorated by the prospect of learning new skills. He walked away from the fire circle towards the sapling yards where Charlie had managed to contain the workhorses along with Brindabella, close for once, to his place of birth and nurture.

The dew was already forming on the crooked lines of the yard rails, the ground wet beneath the horses' feet and the slow drop of moisture from leaves forming in small telltale pools near the base of the tree trunk.

'Charlie,' Tom began, gripping the enamel mug of piping hot tea, 'So do you think there would be enough work for me around the farm for a while?'

'Sure. We're busy at this time of year. As it happens, I was just talking to the CDEP about planting up the riverbanks. Bush regen, that sort of thing.'

'Cool. What's that?'

'You know. Catchment management. Around here, the program runs mostly for indigenous young men and women. It keeps them off the streets and out of trouble. The government pays and I gain because we look after the creeks and swamps. A few more trees brings in the birds and keeps the insects down. Lou likes the birds.' Charlie paused for thought.

'Do you mean I have to dig holes?'

Charlie laughed loudly. 'We could stick the auger on the back of the tractor Tom. Then you'd only have to pour a bucket of water in each hole and poke the tree in.'

Tom laughed.

'Yeah. I need those trees planted. Got any other skills up your sleeve?'

'I haven't got any tickets if that's what you mean.'

'You can't cook!' Lou feigned surprise.

'Well, could be useful to learn a trade, you know. Sean wants to teach me to be a mason.'

'That would be handy. A trade is good, but it isn't everything you know.' Lou said softly.

'How come?'

'Max can teach you to blacksmith. He knows a little bit about every trade that ever was since the guilds first started up. There isn't a job he can't turn his hand to on the farm. I don't think he ever got past grade six primary. Always on the road, that sort of thing. Too much hard work around for a young fella like him to be botherin' about a fancy education or getting a "ticket: so to speak.'

'Max fixed me trailer.' Jake said proudly.

'He fixed my trailer Jake.' Lou laughed.

'It's me that uses it! No one else could be bothered dragging stuff around the farm.'

'I use the trailer Jake, not me uses the trailer!'

'Jake idolises his granddad. I think it's a mutual admiration society.' Lou explained for the benefit of Tom. 'He knows how to use most of the tools already. I just don't want him near the welder quite yet.'

'Can you shoe a horse?' Tom was all ears.

'Granddad can. He has to hold the horse's hoof for me, but I know where to hammer in the nails. He's teaching me how to bend the shoes on the anvil. Especially for the brumbies, their feet are too small for standard shoes.'

'Do you need shoes on the farm Charlie?' Tom wanted to know about Brindabella.

'I wouldn't shoe your colt yet Tom. His feet are good. Just don't gallop him over stony ground. He'll be fine on the trails and there are no dramas around the farm. Best you could do for him is to leave him as he is at present and just check to make sure he doesn't get shin sore or damage his hooves. Happens mostly during and after a muster. Check him every night and every morning.'

'Right.'

'We'll do it in the morning. I'll show you how.' Charlie offered.

Charlie woke early alerted to soft neighing in the loose yards they had put together as the sun fell. Lou stoked the campfire to a full blazing fury of warmth and friendship. She placed the bush oven ready with the morning damper mix into the firepit. Charlie quickly kicked the coals around the oven and dropped a few logs under the groundsheet so they would stay dry for later. There was every reason to start the day with a good fire for the morning brew of hot coffee and 'bush cakes'.

He walked to the makeshift yards and immediately noticed the loose earth at the corner rails — signs that at least two horses had visited the corral.

'Shit. After my horses then?' Charlie checked the top rail, feeling for telltale signs of the tie wire loosened by one of the wild stallions. Brindabella danced nervously as he always did, almost on a stationary square, this time, with his butt backed into the corner of the yard and ears moving backwards and forwards, sometimes plastered against his head and then, fully forwards pricked like sensors. He was alert to the temptation of his wild friends and the life he had left behind.

'Hey boy. Hey Brindy.' Charlie called the horse. 'Steady on. These are your friends yeah?' Charlie attempted to walk closer to the black colt. 'There boy. Steady.' Charlie held out his hand.

Brindabella, excited and stirred by the smell of the horses, turned his rump towards Charlie and extended his neck over the top of the rails.

'Geez. I'd better call Tom. You're stirred mate!' Charlie retreated in case Brindabella suddenly broke through the loose yards, pulled by the wild horses.

A breathless Charlie woke Tom. 'Tom. It looks as though the wild horses have been after your colt. They've got the wind of him.'

'Brindy?'

'Check him out son.' Charlie waited until Tom sat up out of his swag and pulled on his boots. 'Take him a handful of oats if you like. He's firing!'

'Thanks Charlie.' Tom leaped up and headed straight for the feedbag of 'treats' for the horses, secured by a rope from a tree branch. He lowered the bag, pulling on the rope and stuffed a handful of oats into the pocket of his Drizabone and jerked the bag back off the ground away from the curious attentions of bush rats.

'Hey Brindy. Here boy.' Tom clucked through the palings. 'That's a fella. Come on boy.' Tom poked a hand through the rails. Immediately he sensed the restlessness in the colt and decided against climbing into the yard in case he spooked him. The last thing he wanted was to lose Brindabella in a moment of fear and panic.

Brindabella, his eyes instantly softening as he caught the scent of Tom, turned his head towards him, his ears forwards and tail held high, swishing against the railing.

'It's OK boy. They're your mates yeah?' Tom grinned at his horse. 'Here boy. Here's some oats.' Tom held out the oats on the palm of his hand.

Brindabella started towards him, then turned towards the far railing, his head and tail high, the loose earth shifting beneath his dancing legs, his rump swiping one of the railings loose. Then he skidded to a halt near the boundary of the yards, suddenly lifting his legs off the ground into a half rear. Tom, startled into action climbed through the fence, heading towards his horse as Brindabella turned and saw him. Tom looked into Brindabella's eyes, feeling suddenly frightened by the wildness in his colt. Brindabella saw him coming and raised both his legs into a full rear, pawing the air and screaming at Tom to keep his distance. His front legs thudded onto the ground centimetres from Tom. Tom dropped the oats and dived for the railings as Brindabella's hind legs struck off the top rail. Charlie raced the short distance to the yards and pulled Tom through the rails. He called for Max to bring some fencing wire to keep the horses in, most of them frenzied by the strong scent of the black colt.

'Shhiit! That was close.' Tom stated the obvious.

'Could happen at any time around brumbies.' Charlie was still breathless.

'You reckon Brindy still has too much of the brumby in him?' Tom was momentarily dismayed.

'You alright son? Nothing broken?'

'Just a bit of bruised pride Tom. Your horse's heart is still half wild.' Lou commiserated.

'You wouldn't want him totally tame though.' Jake consoled his new friend. 'A wild heart is a strong heart.'

'Now there's a bit of bush wisdom for you.' Charlie smiled and shook his head in disbelief. 'You can see where they've been.' Charlie pointed out to the two sets of hooves on the outside of the yards. 'They're after Brindy all right.'

'Cool.' Tom closely examined the hoof prints on the ground.

'Not so cool Tom, if they take Brindabella.' Lou remarked.

'You sure can see where these boys have been.' Tom stood up, wiping the earth from his hands.

'Wait until we go further in. Sometimes they make a bit of a mess around the bogs and swamps. Mostly though they have their own tracks and don't muck the territory up too much though.' Jake shared his bush knowledge.

'You OK son?' Charlie turned his attention to Tom.

'Yeah. Bit worried about Brindy though.'

'Jake will ride him if you like. He's used to the wild boys.' Charlie looked soberly at the kid, wondering if he had what it took to rein the horse in.

'No. It's all right. If he doesn't stay with me out here, I've lost him anyway.' Tom was resigned to the possibility that Brindabella was being tempted back to the wild.

'Hmm. You're probably right there son. You sure you want Thunder Tom?' Charlie smiled broadly.

'Do you think that Brindabella and Thunder will take off on us?' Tom looked disappointed.

'There's a chance son. There's a chance.' Charlie took off his hat, shaking off the drops of moisture loosened from the tree. 'Come on then boys. Breakfast time. Let's see what sort of magnificent feed Lou cooks up for us this time!'

'You don't cook Charlie?' Tom challenged him cheekily.

'Don't you start, Tom.' Charlie joked. 'I'll be the target of Lou's constant jibes if she gets wind of an opportunity. Reckons if she can last the distance out here, she should have a fair share of the hard work and we blokes should have a fair share of camp cooking!'

'Women are nuts.' Tom decided.

It was still early, but the bush kitchen was already alive, the fire burning brightly and a large pot of coffee on the brew. There was a civility to the rough bush camp as well as more life and colour than in any town or city. The sounds of birds calling and the sun breaking through the canopy created a beauty and warmth unique to the camp's abundant bush comforts. Lou was a veteran at bringing just enough to make the men comfortable without weighing down the horses and holding up their steady progress onto the mountain. She knew it was the little 'added touches' that made the difference. It was the fresh blackberry jam, the dried fruit and nuts, the rich coffee boiled to mellow perfection on the open fire and sweet loaves baked in her camp oven that buoyed the spirits of her men. Along with their own strength and spirit, her bush kitchen powered them to perform like the men before them, the generations gone, their legends and images indelibly carved into living memories. Lou was too well aware of the naked power of the mountains to neglect her kitchen — how the weather boiled in the cauldron of black and deep spaces rising to the top of the ranges to pound, pummel and soak the tops with sleeting, sheeting rains.

There was no taking chances out here. One sunny day misread could easily fool the most hardy of bushmen and women, leaving them within hours shivering under rock ledges as the mountain mists and clouds shrouded them. Despair and sometimes death followed. Always, she kept a close eye on the tops of the range, watching for telltale signs of the first clouds curling innocently over the Ramsheads or Townsend Spur, warning of the lashing to come. Now, for Lou, ironically the almost zephyr-like wind foreshadowed an impending change in the weather. There would be shelter further down the mountain, away from the now expected high winds that would tear loose branches from some of the trees and uproot others. Life on the edge was precarious and the drovers knew all too well the perils of venturing unprepared, even if it was to find a treasured horse.

So Lou came prepared with more than just the kitchen sink and special farm preserves for their bush breakfast.

'I think these yards are the ones.' Charlie announced over breakfast. 'We'll leave a couple of the palings down so they can step over them, then when they're settled near the salt block, we'll move in and close them in.'

'Do you really think they'll buy that one Charlie?' Tom was amazed at the apparent simplicity of the plan.

'Worth a try! Long gone are my days of thundering down rocky slopes after a wayward horse. You know Tom, when I look back, if I had known what I'd be doing running the brumbies I would have told myself in advance that I was completely mad. None of us would have done it. But I tell you, once the adrenaline is pumping, once you're on the chase, there's nothing and no one that will stop you. You give your horse his head and let him fly.'

'I'm the first to second that.' Lou added soberly.

'So you reckon the yards are the go then?' Tom asked again.

'We'll see how they go son.' Max cut in, saving his boss from recalling and recounting the memories of mountain dashes down deep descents that he knew he'd rather forget. More than one horse had been lost and some of them, the Station's broken mares and geldings too footsore and unsure to navigate the steepest and most treacherous of the tracks, were lost to the wilderness. No one knew whether they lay dying behind the threatening tors, their legs shattered on the devastating bluffs or limbs broken like dolls.

'Salt blocks?' Tom remembered.

'Yeah. Let's do it.' Charlie was already up and onto his feet. 'Max, can you give me a hand with the block?' He called over his shoulder.

'Tom, I need you to pack up and Jake, give the horses a rub down before we saddle up.' Lou was quick to complete the camp command.

'Yes mum!' Jake looked at her as if she had suddenly remembered him too and that he was still years younger than the rest of them.

'Don't forget Brindabella. He'll want an extra shine if he's going to bring us in his mate.'

'Shit yeah!' Jake's eyes sparkled.

'Don't swear!' Lou turned her attention to Tom. 'Listen lad. If the horse doesn't come in easily, we'll give him one run. Otherwise, it's too dangerous out here. There's no point in any of us having to break our collarbones or necks to save your brumby from himself.'

'You think he'll want to stay out here?'

'Wouldn't you?'

'Can see your point, but…'

'Let's just take it as it comes yeah?' Lou smiled and patted him on the back.

Tom breathed in deeply, grateful for the chance to capture

the colt. He felt happier now that Lou had warned him of the possibility, that at the end of the day, it was Thunder's decision whether he wanted to be captured and Brindy's decision whether he wanted to go back into the wilderness or not.

Charlie led the small party off the open plain and into the scrub to the east. Already Max had tracked the direction of the horses and they deliberately struck well away from the herd so that there would be less invasions and confusion of scents for them as they picked out the salt.

Brindabella stood alone in the yard, lightly tethered to the corner post, his stomach already filled with the rest of the lucerne hay and another handful of oats to replace the first ration he snorted into the dust as Tom tried to tempt and settle him. Charlie placed the salt block in a corner of the yard, away from the opening where he had removed the top two rails for the wild horses. They walked with the remaining horses for about two hundred metres, slowly and in single file, keeping their voices low, quietly expectant that morning would return them, if not Thunder, then at least one of the mares. The mares would be far easier to catch in the presence of the brumby colt, Brindabella, as long as Thunder stayed away. They pushed the horses well into the trees with Max to watch over them and Jake and his father silently moving to a better position to watch and wait for the brumbies.

'Dad.'

'Shh son. Not now.'

'I can slip around the back. The horses won't see me and it will be easier for me to put up the rails than it will be for you to race back to the yards.'

'OK then. Just do it quietly. Sit up a tree if you have to. Just don't let them see you and make sure you're downwind of the yards.'

'Cool.' Jake was already off, trotting around the perimeter of the clearing and towards the yards. Brindabella whickered as he sensed the boy approach, his anxiety eased at the reappearance of some company after the sudden shocking abandonment by Tom and his friends.

'Sit tight Brindy. I'm not going to leave you mate.' Jake reassured him. 'That's a fella.' Jake hopped through the rails and quickly walked up to Brindabella, patting and stroking his face, gentling him on the shoulder and chest, rubbing his foreleg and picking it up as if to check the hooves. Brindabella nuzzled him softly on the back of his neck, as Jake bent down to examine the prize horse he thought only belonged in dreams.

Half an hour later, with Jake stationed metres from the loose-rail yards in the fork of a tree, the group of horses carefully approached the yards, their feet hesitant yet inquisitive on the black soil as Brindabella began his solitary dance, his back legs drumming lightly on the earth.

Thunder, aware that Brindabella was not going to fight, came closer, pawing at the ground, still wary of his mares now in danger because of the presence of a second stallion. Brindabella neighed softly, happy to be in the company of the herd of horses to which he once belonged. Thunder stood stock-still, his front legs forwards, back legs slightly flared and with his tail held up high. Urgently he passed water and wind, clearing his system of impediments to the fight and flight response that visited him as naturally and automatically as the breeze now playing in his mane and tail. The mares caught the signal of their stallion coming to a halt and moved closer together to protect the solitary bay foal in their midst.

Thunder drew himself in, pausing and pawing the ground. He took a few faltering steps towards the yards. The enticement of the salt was more powerful than the horse's wild sense of self-preservation and the instinct to flight wherever there were men and their scent hanging in the air.

Brindabella stood quietly, not interested in the usual displays of the stallion, both warning and tempting him to show his strength and force. He dropped his head, casually rubbing his nose against his foreleg, sniffing the ground and moving as far as the loose rope allowed, towards the salt. Thunder, noticing the advance on the prize, leapt towards the yards, searching for the entry, then stepped across the rails lying in a loose 'V' towards the centre of one side.

Jake waited for a few seconds until Thunder had moved across to the far side of the yards where the salt block lay positioned at the maximum distance from the dropped rails. He dropped with a soft thud from the tree and in a few steps was at the yards, picking up the first of the rails then dashing to the other end of the row lifting, despite his size, the heavy sapling to form the top rail as Thunder swung around.

The brumby colt screamed in rage at the young boy standing between him and his mares.

Brindabella pulled back on the rope snapping it — his instinct to fight fired by the entry of Thunder into his yards. Thunder wheeled towards him, his ears laid back on his skull, his eyes wide and neck already extended to rip the exposed flesh on Brindabella's neck.

Jake was already half way across the yard, calling to Brindabella and searching with his hands for the rope. Then Jake had him, talking to him, moving under his shoulder, patting his chest, looking the colt in the eye and pushing him with his shoulder back into the corner. Brindabella relaxed, softened by the boy's touch, allowing him to walk him backwards away from Thunder, his muscles shivering and trembling, still half-ready for the fight. Jake wiped the sweat from Brindabella's chest onto the back of his trousers. Then he flicked the loose rope quickly around the top of the corner post, standing with Brindabella and settling him as

Thunder watched.

The wild horse, unsure of the defeat of Brindabella stopped and stared at Jake. He could still smell the salt and the boy was no longer between him and his mares.

'Shit Jake. That was unreal.' Tom was first back across the clearing to the yards. The mares and foal, aware that they were now separated from their lead stallion, had backed away and huddled some hundred metres from the rough bush yards.

'Take it steady Tom. He's still flighty.' Jake said evenly. 'Can you come behind Brindy and wait there. We have a stallion in the yard and they are but dangerous!'

Tom, surprised by the quiet command did as he was asked and moved cautiously to where Jake held Brindabella fast, the brumby colt now licking the salt, nervous, trapped, yet distracted by the diversion.

'Well done son. Well done.' Charlie was mildly out of breath. 'Take it easy everyone. Just walk. We want him to settle. There's your horse son.' Charlie spoke to Tom.

'He's a beauty all right.' Tom said proudly.

'You get the prize today Jake.' Max announced as he arrived with oats bag spilling with loose feed.

'Good man Max. Give some to Brindabella first.' Charlie decided.

Max climbed carefully into the yard, well away from the stallion and walked with an open palm towards Brindabella. Then he dived his hand into the feedbag, pulling out a broad fist clamped around the feed and offered it to Jake.

'You feed him Max.' Jake offered.

'Can you take some over to the stallion son.' Charlie asked Jake. 'Just walk half way and see if he takes it. He might be too spooked so make sure you've got an exit. Can't tell what these buggers will do.' Charlie was taking no chances.

'Yeah. Sure. Tom?'

'Sure thing. First things first.' Tom watched carefully at the interplay between Jake and Max and the horses. There were no sudden movements; instead they moved carefully, keeping their eyes on the horses all the time, watching their backs for vagrant hooves ready to connect with unsuspecting skulls.

'Just drop it Jake.' Charlie commanded. He didn't like the look in the stallion's eye.

'He's OK Dad.' Jake walked a step closer, holding out his hand, raising his left hand in a halt sign. The stallion, noticing the block to his attack, moved back a step his hindquarters dropping slightly in submission. 'That's the boy.' Jake calmed him. 'Come on fella. There's nothing to worry about.' Jake kept his left hand raised, then carefully dropped the oats into the middle of the yard, never taking his eyes off Thunder, then backed towards Max and Tom now standing at Brindabella's head.

Thunder looked around him. There were people gathered close to Brindabella and the mares were some distance off. He was, for now, isolated in one corner of the yard, his back against the rough rails, the oats a couple of steps into the centre of the yard. Almost to comfort himself, defenceless in capture, Thunder moved towards the oats, snorting the ground, pawing at the feed, then with quivering lips, gathering the first of the oats, and relishing the sweet scent and taste.

'He's taken it Dad!' Jake whispered hoarsely.

'That's good son. We'll let him settle for a while.' Charlie patted and stroked Brindabella along his back almost to the rump. Brindabella shuddered with anticipation, still fired to fight yet unable to move with the boy back at his head, whispering and stroking his ears. Then Tom climbed into the yard.

'Hey boy.' He talked to his colt. 'That's a boy Brindy.' Tom put a hand on his horse's neck. Jake and Charlie instinctively took a step away from the colt, allowing Tom to talk to him.

Brindabella stood quietly, calmed and comforted in the company of his friend. He was alerted to his wild past and at the same time, happy in the presence of Tom. His heart thrilled at the prospect of running with the herd, yet his loyalty was now to the young man who had befriended him and quietly tamed him to the bridle and saddle.

'Charlie. I think we ought to make a start this afternoon. The weather's coming in.' Lou offered her practical and no-nonsense advice as they sat around the campfire polishing off the remains of the damper served with lashings of blackberry jam.

'Hmm. Looks as though you are right Lou. Do you reckon we'll make it all the way down?'

'If we start early, we'll be there just on dark.'

'Not sure if I want to come in on the back of a storm though.' Charlie winced.

'Don't think we have much choice Charlie.' Max said. 'Better we get this boy down the mountain. He'll be nervy if we try to move him off in a storm.'

Already the wind was picking up in pace and Lou, not waiting for an answer from anyone apart from her common sense and experience on the land, pulled on her Drizabone. Then she adjusted her hat so that any rain would drip off the slouch onto the broad seam on the back of her coat.

'OK then. Since we're packed to go, we might as well make a move.' Charlie waited for a minute, thinking about the best approach with the stallion.

'I reckon Thunder will just follow, Dad.' Jake said quietly.

'In your dreams Jake!'

'Well, he's away from his herd. We're it for now. Just let Tom lead Brindy with a loose rope from Brindy to Thunder. They'll probably both just follow us down.'

'I guess you're right. Jake, you, Max and Lou walk your horses out in front. We'll see how it goes. Watch him. If he starts to get too edgy and stirs up Brindabella, slip him loose of the rope.' Charlie climbed out of the yard and went to the packhorse to pull off the long rope. 'This could be tricky. Best if just Tom and I are in the yards. Jake, you can climb the rails down that end of the yards. Talk to Thunder for us. I'll hand you the rope in a minute. See what we can do.'

'Why don't we walk Brindabella towards him? Give Thunder more feed. Let them get used to one another. Thunder mightn't be so scared if he sees Brindabella already roped.'

'Worth a try I suppose.' Charlie nodded to Tom.

Tom slipped the rope off the corner post, talking to his horse, patting him then clicking him forwards into the centre of the yard. He stopped for a moment, allowing Brindabella and Thunder to become used to being close. Tom stood still, the hairs automatically pricking on the back of his neck. Something was happening.

'That's him. That's him!' Tom screamed as the grey-white stallion charged towards the yards, his white mane extended like a battle flag and tail rising as he kicked out with his back legs. 'That's the phantom horse.' Tom rushed towards the mirage waving his arms across his chest warning the stallion to stop.

Thunder, suddenly noticing the flight of the phantom horse, reared and crashed his hooves into the ground, narrowly missing Tom.

Jake was already through the yards, taking the spare rope from Tom and slipping it over Thunder's neck as his hooves pounded back onto the earth. He secured the horse only to his wrist, taking his left hand into the air and halting the stallion as he readied for the second rear. The grey-white stallion was gone.

'Christ Jake. What the hell did you do that for?' Charlie was halfway over the rails.

'Stay where you are Dad.' Jake spoke with maturity well beyond his years. 'Come on Thunder. Easy.' Jake kept his hand raised high, gradually drawing in the long rope with his other hand. 'Easy boy.' Jake was at Thunder's head, stroking his nose, slipping the rope into a loose halter around the horse's head, stroking him down the front of his long neck to the chest.

'Tom. Walk in. Slowly.' Jake commanded. 'Take it real steady. Bring some more oats. Some for Brindy, some for Thunder.'

Tom did as he was told, climbing very carefully through the rails as Max handed him two handfuls of oats. He walked straight to Brindabella, holding his hand out with the oats and then to Jake.

'Come closer, nice and slow.' Jake dropped his left hand as Tom approached the colt. 'Just hold your hand out and stand still.' Jake stroked Thunder's quivering shoulder.

Tom extended his hand, keeping his eye connected with the horse. Thunder dropped his head to sniff the oats then stretched his neck, moving slightly off balance. As he took the first of the oats from Tom's hand, Jake pushed him further off balance, backing him towards the rails of the yards, then tightened off the halter, urging Tom to move in and stand with him at the stallion's head.

'Jake made that look too easy Charlie.' Max commented as they began to lead the horses off the mountain.

'I don't know where the kid gets it from Max, I swear.' Charlie said. 'Something was in him even when he was just a little fella. Sort of had some magic about him. The horses always loved him.'

'Maybe he's one of them come back for another try Charlie.' Max said softly.

'You think it's possible?'

'Anything's possible out here mate. Anything.'

THE PHANTOM HORSE

They arrived back at Tom Groggin Station unbelievably weary, yet triumphant at bringing both Thunder and Brindabella in without a fight. Jake was footsore and ready for bed but Tom, was still buzzing. He had his new horse Thunder, a friend for Brindy. Since being in the bush, he had found more strength than he had ever known or used before, more than enough to stay the distance with his horses until they were safely in the Station's yards.

'Bring them both in. First Brindy, then Thunder. Once they're in the yards, we'll let Brindy into the next set of yards. Don't want them in there together overnight where we can't keep an eye on them.' Charlie felt weary, saddle sore and desperately in need of a hot shower and shave.

'I'll take your horse.' Max offered.

'Thanks Dad.' Charlie slipped off the back of his horse, handing the reins to Max.

'Don't worry about the packsaddler. I'll fix him as well.'

Charlie opened the gate into the steel round yard to let in Jake and Tom in with their brumbies fresh from the high country. 'OK. Two of us will stay here. The rest of you can go and fix yourselves up. Max will rub down the horses. Drop your saddles inside the machinery shed for now.'

Everyone was bone weary when they walked into the homestead kitchen.

'I think you're in for a surprise.' Lou laughed gently. 'Here's the advance dinner party!'

'Nice surprise! Malcolm!' Charlie walked towards Malcolm.

'Hello Charlie. Been up the mountain?'

'Sure have. Brought home a real beauty. His name is Thunder. Belongs to young Tom here.'

'Hello Tom. Good to meet you.'

'Hello.' Tom stuck out his hand.

'Malcolm is a friend of Angus, Sean and mine.' Charlie explained.

'One of the team?' Tom twigged quickly.

'You might say that. Common interests. Horses amongst other things.'

'Okaaay.' Tom nodded. 'Yup. Horses definitely do if for me.'

'Did you see any more up there? I've got a mate who's very interested in any horse like Brindabella.'

'Yeah, the phantom horse that spooked Thunder. Tom reckons he's a real beauty. Just vanished into thin air though before anyone else clapped their eyes or put a rope on him.' Charlie joked.

'Hello Tom.' Malcolm extended his hand. 'I hear you now have two priceless horses.'

Tom grinned despite the weariness now flooding through his body. 'Yes. Thanks to Jake here. He caught Thunder.'

Malcolm smiled and patted Jake on the shoulder. 'You have a rare talent young man. I've brought down a pack of pizzas. You feel like a feed?'

'Cool.' Jake piped up.

'Looks as though you're also ready for a bath. Well, don't just stand there. Time for a feed!'

The wind roared off the back of the mountain and the thunder raged around the tops, crashing through the granite tors and frightening even the crows down to the Crackenback River. There, at least, there was some shelter in the narrow ravines. The night was black. It was the sort of darkness that blotted out memories of the day, where the light gave contrasts and shadows some shape and form to the often bleak landscape.

The dry storm raged over the Victorian mountains, crashing trees to the ground, their crowns splintering and self-destroying on impact, the roots thrusting skywards as the giants surrendered to the onslaught. The first clap of thunder cracked synchronously with the sheets of lightning scouring the sky over the high plains. Lou knew that this was a storm to be feared. At other times, when the wind crashed through the forests leaving a path of devastation that few would believe possible, they simply waited until it passed. But this was no ordinary storm. She was grateful that they had come off the mountain when they did. Now, there would be little between them and the full force of the lightning and winds tearing apart any semblance of peace on the Station.

'I'll keep watch Charlie.' Max offered over dinner. 'I don't like the sound of this storm.'

'What about the horses?' Malcolm was concerned for his own, as well as the Station horses.

'We'll keep them together in the paddock behind the round yard. If they can see one another, they'll probably be all right.'

'Malcolm, do you and Fay want to stay with us tonight?' Lou offered.

'Could be a good idea Malcolm. God knows what we'll find in the morning.' Charlie extended his wife's invitation.

'I guess you are right about that. We can take the tractor in the morning if needs be.'

'Good. That's settled.' Malcolm smiled at his wife and patted her on the hand. She was a city person unused to the hardships of the bush let alone the wild storm about to break loose over the

Station.

'What about Brindy and Thunder.' Tom asked.

'They're OK. They are bush horses after all.' Jake sounded sure.

'I'll check them every hour just in case.' Max confirmed.

'OK. Everyone else to bed! We might have a bit of damage to mop up in the morning.' Charlie assumed authority for the safe management of the Station and its staff.

By midnight, Max smelled the first signs of smoke coming from the lightning strike across the river. The sound of the wind, the smell of burning gum, the still flashing sheets and occasional lances of lightning warned him that this was serious danger. The bush was alight. He walked onto the verandah of the Station house, pulling on his gumboots and picking up the broad-faced flashlight which he peered without success into the night.

Suddenly he saw flames shooting from the trunk of one of the giant river gums, its branches choked by fire. At least on their side of the Murray, the land was cleared and sown to green pasture to the edge of the river. Not even sparks from bushfires would be much of an issue, save igniting the fence posts. Summer, still weeks away, had not browned the land and Max instantly calculated that the real danger would be to the National Park, the bushland thick and fuel — rich from years without a true fire. Since the various agencies had taken over fire management he had never been happy; the amount of forest floor detritus had built steadily year by year, to a dangerous and combustible level. With the influx of stray cats from surrounding towns into the bushland, the population of small native mammals and lyrebirds had diminished faster than anyone imagined possible. The bush litter on the forest floor that was once mulched back into the soil by the lyrebirds, continued to build each season at an alarming rate. It was too long ago that the bushmen talked of a big fire, and much longer in the distance since the local tribes periodically burnt off sections of the bush as their yearly food management program, flushing from the forests the strongest kangaroos and wombats fat with spring feed. Now the fire hazard was real. There was no use telling anyone anything different. This was going to be one almighty fire and he knew it straight away.

'Charlie, Charlie.' Max urgently knocked at the door.

Charlie rolled out of bed, pulling his sweater and trousers over his shorts and T-shirt.

'Dad.' Charlie opened the door and stepped into the hallway.

'Charlie there's a fire. Over the river. Lightning strike.'

'Just what we need!'

'How big?'

'Just started I think. The flames are fairly shooting from the top of the tree, or what's left of it. Can't see much else, but by the size of the strike it won't be long before the rest of them catch alight. Wind this strength, and who knows…' he let his sentence trail.

'Crikey!' Just what we need. We need to wake everyone up Dad. Bring over the fire-fighting unit. I'll call the Parks. We'd better see what we can do at least. No point muckin' about while they stuff around deciding who's going to come out and fight the fire.'

Max was already moving out of the house, flashlight in hand, towards the machinery shed where the fire unit was already primed, the water tank routinely checked and filled, the pumps pressured, helmets and radio readied for instant action.

They were completely snookered at the homestead. Any major fire that approached the Station from whichever direction would soon have them cornered onto a small patch of pasture or sitting in the middle of the Murray as the only available wet sanctuary. Now, with the new house on the hill, at least there was a sizeable underground water supply. They could retreat to there and hose down the built structures until the major onslaught had passed.

'You sure about that mate?' A reluctant voice replied over the phone.

'Course I'm bloody sure. Don't just ring up in the middle of the bloody night for fun. Can't you hear the storm where you are?' Charlie just managed to contain his anger. He wished he could call the Corryong crew or the Khancoban Ranger, but it was out of the question as the mob over the ranges now called the shots on fire fighting.

'OK. I'll ring the fire bloke. Give you a call in ten.'

'Make it five man. We're moving over to the river in a few minutes. We'll get this fire under control by the time you blokes think about pulling on your boots.' Charlie's temper was frayed by the knowledge that it could take hours for them to rally themselves together into some sort of fighting defence. He knew that he would be 'trespassing' taking on their fire role, but he didn't give a damn. Out here, authorities and departments meant nothing to him. It was not just the survival of the Station that concerned him, he knew that if they didn't act fast, the whole bloody mountain would go up in one of those 'once in a century blazes' that no one would ever forget. This would be the fire that would take out most of the timber as far as the wind would take it. The dry winter and the drought out west meant the winds bore a lighter moisture load. The accumulation of fuel on the floor of the forests, the lack of readiness for "the big one", and intermittent communications across the region where radio frequencies changed from service to service, spelt nothing but trouble to Charlie.

'Lou. I'll need you to keep the boys fed and watered and you'll have to manage the communications from here on in.'

'OK Charlie.' Though she was a strong and able fire fighter, this was no time to argue roles and capacities. Quickly she dressed and walked to the kitchen, stoking the fire and placing two cast iron kettles onto the top plate. She opened the pantry door, dragging out the potato box and dumping a dozen into the sink. In minutes, she had scrubbed and peeled the potatoes, halved them and along with a kilo of carrots and a pumpkin, dumped them into oiled and salted baking trays. She grabbed the Hobart mixer and put it onto the kitchen bench, carefully measuring enough flour to make dough for four day's supply of bread and damper.

Twenty minutes later, Charlie returned to the kitchen, slightly breathless and blackened by his first battle with the fire.

'It's a big one Lou. We'll have to push the stock into the clear. I'll put them in the paddock near Malcolm's house. Can you wake the boys? I want Tom and Jake to help me drive them through. You'll have to operate the two-way. Put out the hoses and fill the buckets. Ask Max to set the ladders. Keep Max with you. He's better off inside. Dad's a bit old for this caper.' Charlie walked straight to the fridge and grabbed a 2-litre bottle of water. 'See you soon. I'll check in on the radio every 15 minutes to let you know what's happening out there.'

'Take it easy Charlie.' Lou looked carefully at her husband.

'Yeah. I will Lou. I will.' He turned on his heel and was gone into the night, the horizon now lit up as the flames and sparks whisked by the wind coursed a trail of fire into the forest.

At five o'clock in the morning, Charlie, Tom and Jake returned beaten and wearied by the relentless onslaught of the fire. They had hardly penetrated the perimeter when Charlie decided to pull them back to the ford and go along the riverbank instead, quickly burning off the edges with the flame-thrower then attempting to douse the fire with water. Charlie attached the fire-truck to the river, drawing water from the Murray instead of the tanks. For two hours, he drove along the Station side of the river, spraying the water as far as it could reach until he had built a reasonable firebreak for the farm.

There was no point in going deep into the bush without backup, and with the wind moving in eddies and circles and changing direction every few moments, it would be suicide to attempt the steep slopes. Charlie hoped like hell that the Parks people would soon get a handle on the scene, and bring in the choppers. It would be easy enough to draw water out of the Khancoban Pondage and bomb the fire as it advanced up the western ridges towards the mountain tops. There was nothing worse than a fire moving up the crest of a mountain fanned by searing winds.

Tom sensed rather than heard Thunder pressing up against the steel barriers that now held him securely against escape.

'I've got to check him Lou.' Tom urged.

'Thunder? He's safe for now Tom. If the fire jumps the river, we'll move the rest of the stock up to the top house. Don't worry.'

'It's not so much that. There's something going on. I'm not sure.'

'OK. Make it quick. I need you back here Tom.'

'I will.' Tom bolted from the kitchen, racing across the back yard and through the machinery shed to the stables. Brindabella was dancing within the stable, aware that Thunder was being pulled by his herd now in danger of the fire that had crossed the Alpine Way and was moving towards the lower end of the Pilot wilderness. The fire, once it moved into the rugged terrain, could take weeks to contain. There was nothing and no one with the capacity to turn it back once it was out of control. Tom felt panicky for the horses in the mountain valleys. They were safe when the weather was calm and even in winter they had their coats to protect them.

'Hey Brindy.' Tom talked to the horse. 'Hey boy. What's the matter?' Tom quickly patted Brindabella's shoulder then moved past his stall into the round yard.

Thunder saw him coming, bolting towards him then skidding to a halt. Tom noticed where he had already bruised his shoulder on the metal rails, opening the wound he thought he saw the phantom stallion strike deeply into his flesh as they fought outside the Tin Mine Huts. The yards were too high and even a horse with Thunder's strength and determination would find it difficult to gain sufficient stride in the short distance to take the top rail.

'Steady boy. Steady.' Tom was unsure what to do. Thunder had already injured himself and Tom knew he would do so again to reach his mares. 'It's OK man. Settle.' Tom walked towards him.

Thunder, freaked by the storm, was in no mood for being calmed. He looked at Tom his eyes filled with the pain of his bruising and the need to find his mares.

'It's OK boy. I know they're calling you. You have to go!' Tom felt like crying. He hesitated for a second, thinking it could be easier for them both if he pushed Thunder into the stall next to Brindabella. In a flash Tom dashed to the far side of the round yard, headed for the gate and opened the exit for Thunder to race into the night. It would be easier for the horse to take his chances in the storm and the fire now advancing surely towards his precious herd, than be trapped by the tall iron railings against his will and instincts to save the mares.

'OK boy. You're free.' Tom screamed into the wind, the tears streaming from his eyes. Come on Thunder. Move!' Tom yelled at his horse.

Thunder, stunned by the sudden opening in the yard, looked at Tom. Tom's face was streaked with tears, hair dishevelled in the wind and coat waving like a starter's flag around his narrow frame. The horse walked almost serenely towards Tom, then just as Tom extended his hand to pat him, his sixth sense took over, the wilderness coursing through his blood, lighting his eyes with the fire that Tom knew would never leave him. The horse bolted at full stretch through the open gate, taking the fence at the end of the paddock in his stride and almost by instinct, galloped down the road to cross the Murray River ford.

'Go Thunder Go.' Tom screamed after him. He was as wild as the phantom horse returning to the mountains he knew and loved, to his mares and foals that were vulnerable and unprotected in the fire that was fanned by the unseasonal and treacherous wind.

'Tom! You let your horse go?' Charlie was incredulous. He wiped a blackened hand across his forehead, deepening the lines of weary toil and smearing more ash into his hair.

'I had to Charlie. I had to.' Tom was again on the verge of tears.

'Couldn't you just settle him. You'll have a problem finding him again.'

'I know, but you should have seen his eyes Charlie. It's as though he knew. The fire. There was nothing that could stop him and if I didn't he would probably have broken his neck trying to get out.'

'Good man.' Max patted Tom on his shoulder. 'I would have done the same any day Charlie.' Max supported the younger man's decision.

'I suppose you're right.' Charlie looked at Lou, and gratefully accepted the hot mug of tea.

'You're too tired to think about it for now Charlie. You need to sleep.'

'What time is it?' Charlie looked blankly around the kitchen.

'The fire's well out of control Charlie. There's nothing else you can do until the Parks mob get their act together. Have a good wash and a sleep. We'll wake you when there's some fresh news.' Malcolm suggested.

'Guess you're right.'

'The Station's safe. Good work men.' Malcolm praised the gathering of callused and blackened men sitting around Lou's table, drinking their coffee and wondering how on God's earth the bushfire could possibly be contained.

'They're setting up the command centre at Eagle's Nest, Charlie.' Lou informed him. 'Call came through about half an hour ago. So the weight's off your shoulders for now. Rest!'

For days, the fire burnt out of control through the steep and rugged reaches of the lower National Park where the mountains dropped in impossible slopes towards the deepest valleys at their base. Almost by instinct, the local people rallied wherever they could, some moving to Khancoban where there was plenty of water in the Pondage and enough open space to see any spot fires from a distance. Others reluctant to leave their farms and lives, holed up on their stations, continuously watering down their roofs and keeping fire-buckets full. Most of the stock were saved, the majority well away from the grazing leases that weren't open until the summer and the horses were quickly sheltered at Corryong away from both the smoke and the flames that would bring more death than any community needed so close to Christmas.

Tom and Jake waited at the farm, unsure of how to react when their haven was so abruptly threatened by the severity of the wild storm and close on its back, the unstoppable bushfire that reduced to rubble and ash the forest that was once a haven to them as well as the myriad birds, animals and plant life. It was a night that neither of them readily wanted to revisit. Tom was still sad that he had lost Thunder, yet in his heart, he knew that he had done the right thing, that there was no other course for either of them. In that moment, when the fire raged into the mountains, Thunder needed to be free and Tom needed to set free the horse that had become his, the horse that in an instant he loved more than anything or anyone in his life before. Tom looked through the binoculars high onto the mountain, watching as the eagles circled high above the Ramsheads, escaping the smoke now spiralling towards them on the tallest of up-draughts.

Monday morning broke and Malcolm arrived after hearing the news of the fires.

'Charlie!' Malcolm walked into the station dining room.

'Malcolm. Great to see you man.' Charlie stood up and accepted the strong embrace of his friend. 'Cup of tea? Lou, are you here?' Charlie called out to his wife.

'Not far away Charlie.' Lou walked down the hallway and into the dining room.

'Malcolm!' What a nice surprise. Lou hugged him quickly. 'Tea?'

'Sounds like the best plan I've heard in a long time Lou. Sorry about the fires. They're pretty extensive by all accounts.'

'They seem to be Malcolm. We've been fully focussed on saving Tom Groggin so haven't caught up what else has been burnt.'

'Great work Charlie. And the top homestead I see is intact.'

'Yep!'

'The Masters Paddock and the Pinnibar seemed to have copped it though.' Malcolm stated.

'That was the same fire as the one that started on the other side of the river. The backburn that got away, jumped the Murray and took out the Pinibar and Davies Plain and for that matter most of the mountain on the other side heading up to the high country towards Thredbo.' Charlie said quietly.

Malcolm whistled quietly. 'Not just lightning strikes?'

'Nope. Not just lightning strikes.'

'Hmm.' Malcolm thought about it for a moment. 'I've got tickets for the Spring Racing Carnival including the Melbourne Cup' He triumphantly held up the paper trophies in front of the Station team. 'Anyone interested?'

'Shit yeah.' Tom was first to speak. 'Thanks Malcolm.'

Malcolm laughed. 'Good stuff Tom. What about you and Max,

Charlie? I know that Lou will sweep the field with those looks of hers.'

'Why not!' Charlie scratched his head.

'Lou. What do you think. Do some shopping in Melbourne at the same time?"

Lou laughed. 'I could use some new shoes but I'd rather stay here this time Charlie if you don't mind. We have a few calves due to drop in the next few weeks and I'd rather be here.' Lou looked at her husband.

Charlie nodded. 'Max?'

'No. Not me. I'm too old for those capers. Besides, I've got to shoe the horses and I'm still working on a new bridle and saddle for the colt. Plus my money is on Lou needing an extra pair of hands with the calving.'

'Then that just leaves us boys then.' Malcolm concluded.

'Yeah. Cool Malcolm.' Tom was already on his feet, putting out his hand to shake Malcolm's, clearly caught up in the spirit of the moment.

'Plenty of work to do around the Station in the next few weeks Tom. Before the races.' Charlie added.

CALLED IN

Angus's satellite phone pinged in his pocket.

'Angus speaking.'

'Hello. Angus. Malcolm here.'

'Malcolm? Lovely surprise! Anything new down under?'

'There is indeed Angus. The fires are big.'

'So I heard. So I heard.' Angus clucked with his tongue.

'Listen, the Cup's on soon. Thought you and Sean would like to come along. I've got a few spare grandstand seats. It could be worth the trip.'

'Malcolm.' Angus put his hand over the mouthpiece as Sean joined him at the table.

'I take it you will have both finished your business in Antarctica in a few days.'

'Yes that is correct Malcolm.' Angus started. 'Mind you Sean is itching for some new action.'

'Then come back for the Melbourne Cup. The boys from the station are coming along, Charlie, Luke and Tom.'

'Excellent.'

'That young Tom of yours looks as though he will make the cut Angus.'

'That's what we think. Tom rose above the others. Clear choice for the team. Can't say that about all of them though.'

'Good. I think Tom misses you both. He apparently sometimes talks in his sleep.'

'I see.' Angus nodded to himself.

'Charlie said that after the fire, he could hear him calling out for Sean. You know, when Charlie's out checking on the horses — as he has the habit of doing late at night — he passes the hut on the way to the stock yards and hears Tom talking in his sleep.'

'I see. Then we'd better make sure we are back for the race.' Angus spoke soberly.

'Good. Then we'll see you at The Cup?'

'Absolutely.'

'I'll leave the tickets at the entrance for you. In your own names.' Malcolm couldn't let the opportunity pass.

'Thank you Malcolm.' Angus kept his voice flat and even.

'Don't mention it Angus. Regards to Sean.' The phone line went dead.

'We're going to The Melbourne Cup, Sean. Your lad Tom is missing you apparently. He still calls out for you in his sleep.'

'Oh?' Sean couldn't suppress the edge of anxiety rising to his throat, 'The fires must have triggered something. Fire can do that to a man. Stirs up the old memories and as they tell me, there is a connection inside between fire and the sexual side of the psyche. So you think it's triggered his memories of the abuse?'

'It could be so. Alternatively, it might be the campfire stuff. He still sees you as his anchor to sanity I would think.'

'I suppose. He seems to have done well though managing on his own and so has Cassie.'

'Cassie?' Angus sparked up at her name.

'Tom and she seemed to have thoroughly enjoyed the Jillamatong races Angus and their campout that night.' Sean winked at his friend.

Angus laughed. 'Cassie's a sweet kid all right. Anyway a boy still needs a good man in his life. Isn't that so, Sean.' Angus stood up, slapping Sean on the back as he headed for the coffee already spluttering through the filter and into the pot sitting precariously on the Polar Bird's galley stove.

THE SNOWY DAMMED

It was early morning when Cassandra had felt the slight tremor of the earth beneath her sleeping bag. Now, she was sure that there was about to be a change, in the earth below. It had to be the Snowy River. Trapped by the dam walls, the river languished in the Snowy Lakes, saturating the rock pores and lubricating the fault lines. The ground rumbled again, shaking rocks from the road cuttings and causing the billy to rattle on the gas stove. This time, the tremor lasted for several seconds and came with an audible 'bang'. Cassandra jumped despite herself. She looked quickly for telltale signs of landslips and localised 'boiling' in the river. The river flowed smoothly, a steady pulse mirroring the earth deep below the mountain massif. But she knew instinctively that the second earthquake came from the very depths of the mountains; it was a warning of more earth movements to come. The dams!

Cassandra pulled the tent flap open and pushed herself into the brisk morning air. The rush of cool air descending from the mountain, the frosty earth, and the clear crispness of birdcalls pumped new life into her limbs. The early morning sound of the Snowy River, still flushed with the last rains rushing past the campsite, filled her with a sense of exhilaration and a sense of being alive. She felt free. Cassandra knew one thing, that she was far better off here in the mountains than the many people tied to employment in large organisations. They usually became shackled to soul-destroying boredom in robotic jobs they did not want. Most organisations it seemed to Cassandra, were characterised by the toxic dynamics of internal politics. Once caught on the treadmill of paying off mortgages and striving to remain employed, people lost touch with themselves and their once innate relationship with nature. Few understood or remembered the inseparable contract of the earth with its inhabitants. For Cassandra, she knew where she belonged and could sense the eternity of the land, the timeless qualities of natural evolution and how the earth had shaped all living beings. Not the other way around. Cassandra's sense of this and the mountains was best captured by the sound of the river crashing over giant boulders and plummeting down waterfalls before humming gently as it broadened out on the valley floor near Jindabyne.

Cassandra had what most could never imagine, the capacity to listen to the earth and its abundance, the feeling of freedom and an understanding of the timeless nature of the mountains. To care for the mountains was her driving passion, her mission and her destiny. She understood things about nature that other people could not conceptualise and she knew that some of the people in the mountains probably thought she was "off her tree". However Cassandra was not ruled by the uninformed views of those who had not tasted what she had: freedom, the clean taste of pristine water iced by fresh snow melt and the scent of eucalyptus hanging in the air after rain.

Cassandra looked quietly around her. The campsite was quiet apart from the birds, and kangaroos idling grazing in the open patches of native grass. The pastures had burst into new life after the bushfires and with successive rainfalls, the plethora of dormant seeds suddenly pushed new shoots through the soil. She pulled her long light brown hair into a knot at the nape of her neck and headed towards the rounded pebbles at the bank of the river. She squatted next to the river, still icy green from a late spring melt, and dipped cupped hands into the water. The water felt silky and clean, sparkling with life and intensely cold as she splashed her face. The sun already hinted at warmth, lighting the tips of the tallest trees that clamoured for light above the forest canopy on the highest ridges.

Soon, the entire valley would be bathed in warmth, the cicadas chirping loudly and deafening the soft cries of the gang gangs, as they balanced on native grass heads almost ready to explode and distribute their bounty of seeds. After the fires, it was clear that there would be more happening in the mountains than the regular rhythm of the seasons: the glorious autumn golds of the remaining trees planted during the building of the Snowy Scheme, the scintillating clear and magical winter landscapes, the surprising burst of growth in spring and the heady scents of high summer when the fragrance of alpine heath hung on the air. The regrowth would be as exponential as it would be impenetrable, the fire scarred trees destitute of spring growth, yet rejuvenated by the emergence of coppice growth from beneath the soil.

As much as she loved the gum trees, Cassandra could see beauty in the exotic trees around her. Here, the golden shadows of leaves, turning in the autumn and falling from the poplars, the sudden bright yellow of willows struggling for the last opportunity of autumn warmth, tinged the landscape with a European hue. It was to Cassandra, a beautiful moment, the contrast of the wilderness tones juxtaposed against the measured beauty of exotic plantings. As much as she preferred the mountain's wilderness cloak of olive greens, Cassandra always felt a tingling of surprise at the seasonal splashes of colour from the introduced species: the purples, blues and pinks of the lupins that adorned the valley and the brilliant autumn cascade of poplar leaves. The eucalypts were different. Each one, adapted to the extremes, survived against the odds. Despite the sudden frost bronzing some of the shoots, and afterwards, the onslaught of insects nibbling at the new shoots, the trees somehow survived. Young leaves adorned the trunks of trees in bright colours of green. Then the more hardy and resilient shoots emerged from beneath the fragile soils, fed by the succulent lignotubers, the nutrient-rich bowls at the roots.

At higher altitudes, the icy onslaught of low pressure fronts bursting over the western side of the ranges brought blizzarding winds, then the dumping of deep snows and freezing nights forged a distinctive tree line. Despite the sometimes, good soils there was a tolerance level beyond which the eucalypts could not survive. Where the soils were any poorer in humus or without basalt spills from ancient volcanoes, there were no trees.

The Monaro was a naked widow of an ancient past: vast rivers, a myriad of mini volcanoes rich with minerals, outcrops of desolate soils, bare and devoid of life apart from the resilient native grasses. Here in the mountains, the subalpine hills were well-wooded; the trees were dressed in an abundance of green and grey leaves. Below the tree line there was a plethora of birdlife and fauna, their habitat and populations nevertheless marked by the often sudden altitude changes, the steeply ascendant mountains and high rocky ridges that drove even the hardiest of wombats to lower and more prosperous climes.

A zephyr-like wind warned of a change in the weather. Later, the wind would wrap around her tent, threatening to lift it from its tenuous position on the ground. Cassandra moved quickly, taking the largest stone with her to secure the first corner of the tent. She returned to the river's edge, collecting more weights to manage her best attempts at shelter. There was nothing certain here, there was nothing permanent. She placed the last of the quartz stone on the edges of the fly ropes then picked up a flat, heavier rock and hammered in the pegs until they were secure against the impending weather and straightened and tightened the ropes before zipping the entrance to the tent closed. For this morning, she had planned a long bike ride towards Geehi, however the inclemency of the weather, the approaching wind and possibly rain storm, forced her back to her tent. A short, fast ride along the valley floor to the dam would be sufficient for today. There was anyway, something that she needed to check. Her bike was old yet trustworthy, not equipped with the suspension of the downhill mountain bikes, but nevertheless reliable and responsive to her touch. Cassandra preferred the even balance of a strong cross-country bike that over long distances would deliver good results for her efforts both up and down the long hills of the tumbling fire trails. She knew that the loose rocks and fallen and dead timber that littered the trails was always a hazard, however an integral part of the terrain and territory. This morning, the nagging thought continued to break into her routine was that many land managers did not care about the land or its people. Especially so in the mountains.

Cassandra lit the small gas burner in the shelter of the tent. She boiled sufficient water for two cups of tea and a third to wash her breakfast things. Then she laid out the bread, coarsely cut into large slices, on her makeshift and rusting toasting rack. The burnt edges of the bread smelt incredibly appetising, probably because she was famished. She cut another four thick slices of bread for lunch and quickly made up cheese sandwiches for the bike ride. It was time to move.

Cassandra pushed hard against the pedals, the bike bouncing over the deepening potholes in the neglected, dirt road. Pieces of torn tarmac, the remnants of a former Snowy Scheme settlement, pockmarked the dirt road. All that remained of the old township of Island Bend were a few concrete slabs, some rough stone walls and a grid pattern of dirt roads, most of them eroded or laced with tyre shredding rocks. The legacy of the past was minimal except for the giant concrete walls, weirs, aqueducts and tunnels that trapped and diverted the Snowy River. Cassandra pushed harder. Soon she had left the potholed campsite road and was moving smoothly along the Island Bend to Guthega Road. The road wound along the valley floor following the contours and natural flow of the terrain towards Guthega Village. Once she had reached the ski village, Cassandra turned off to the road-bridge that ran high along the dam wall.

The sight of open water, the feeling of intense calm emanating from the dam, was paradoxically as beautiful as the free and untroubled waters of the river. Cassandra stood at the dam wall watching. The Snowy River flowed in the upwaters above the dam, but there was no water in the river below the dam wall. She looked along the depth and breadth of the dam. Then she saw what she was looking for. Yes, there! She lifted the compact binoculars to her eyes to look more closely at the telltale signs of earth movement, a distinct crack in the dam wall. Cassandra traced it to the source, where the rocks lifted out of the bottom of the dry riverbed in front of the mass of concrete that was the dam wall. She followed the signs of the crack all the way to the highest point of the dam. Cassandra waited, listening for sounds of movement and feeling, with her eyes, for signs of a fracture. She felt nervous.

She cycled carefully along the wall, keenly aware that the water level was now lower than in the early spring. The gushing snowmelt had passed and now the river was quiet. Cassandra stopped, placed her bike on the ground, pausing for a moment to observe the dam wall. There was no sign of movement. She waited to see if the birds would give her any signs. There were none. Carefully, she moved forwards, waiting until she felt sure that the dam was safe. She felt puzzled. The dam was definitely holding, however her intuition was telling her otherwise. There was something significant that was about to happen to the dam wall and there was nothing she could do to stop it from being so. Suddenly, she decided to move fast and warn her friends that the dam could go. Cassandra started running back along the dam wall towards where she had left her bike. She picked it up and ran it up the track to the road. Once out of danger, she pulled out her satellite phone and dialled.

It was months since she had had any contact with Patrick, however this was a matter of urgency. The wind had already forced most of the visitors into early retreat out of the mountains and into the shops and cafes of Jindabyne. She was alone in the village, the Guthega Hotel closed for the week after a busy weekend trade.

'Yeah. It's me. Cassandra.'

'Haven't heard from you for a long time, nature child.'

'Right oh. Knock it off' she laughed.

'What are you up to these days anyway? Heard that there was a plan to take out the Jindabyne Dam wall. That wasn't you Cassandra was it!'

'You know me better than that Patrick.'

'I know you better.' The man on the other end of the line sighed. 'What can I do you for kiddo? Coffee?'

'There is a problem out here Patrick.'

'What?'

'A major crack in the Guthega Dam wall.' Cassandra said determinedly.

'You mean that's what you hope it is.'

'Give it a rest! I wouldn't ring you unless I had to.' Cassandra grinned but felt totally stone cold sober inside. She really liked Patrick He was one of the few people on the planet who understood her sufficiently to take the mickey out of her practically every time they met.

'I know. That's why I like you Cassandra. Anything else?'

'Nothing that I know about. You could give me some of that

government money you've got your hands on. I will spend it well.' Cassandra said cheekily.

'Mercenary to the last!'

'You are mean you are!' Cassandra laughed at her colleague.

'OK. I'll have a look at it.'

'Thanks Patrick. I mean it.'

'Taa to you too. Bye babe.'

'Bye bye.' Cassandra switched off the phone.

'How about that!' Patrick turned to his boss in Canberra. 'Cassandra reckons that we have a problem. A crack in the Guthega Dam wall!'

'She would, wouldn't she!'

'You know she's rarely wrong.'

'Let's hope she is this time Patrick.'

Cassandra climbed back on her bike and headed back towards the campsite. That was that. Patrick had the picture and she knew he would share it with the right people. She knew from long experience that the world was mostly a 'boys' club' and the men simply closed ranks and simply shut out the women from key roles. She had done all she could. Now, the weather was closing in and she needed to be warm inside and not cold outside her tent. It could be quite a ride over the next short while, especially if you had a kayak. Quietly, she dialled her friends and gave them the heads up that there could be an unexpected water release into the Snowy from Guthega Dam. The whitewater troops would soon head this way and camp out at Island Bend, waiting for the big moment, if and when it happened, at least to watch if not to paddle.

ANTARCTICA

Sean winced as he pulled himself up the final metres of the ascent. He felt exhilarated far beyond his expectations that he was so close to the summit and that Angus would be on top with him in a matter of minutes. He wanted to savour the moment, to cast his eyes over the magnificent vista of the Antarctic wilderness spread below him, but for now, his full concentration was on the climb. He swung the finely chiselled ice axe into the wall and then cranked in another screw to complete the line of anchors. His heart pounded and his legs and arms ached with exertion. Quickly, he established a belay and positioned himself to protect Angus as he climbed the final pitch.

Sean was utterly amazed at the breathtaking beauty of the scene and the vastness of the Antarctic ice. From his vantage point he could clearly see the McMurdo Sound and scintillating Ross Sea, and the dominant peak Mt Erebus in the distance. Close to the climb was the tumbling crescendo of cliffs that brought them to the edge of the plateau and, across the plateau, the deep blue of the sea. Here, there was the strong sense of being at the very end of the world, lost on the edge of a wilderness of ice and snow where few humans dared to venture. Only wild animals, seals and penguins, huddled together in their tens of thousands.

There would however, be very little time to enjoy the view this time. The first whisper of wind told him that the forecast cold weather would soon turn into strong winds, then a nightmare as the temperatures dropped further below freezing. They would need to descend quickly and return to the ship.

In the distance, further than the Ross Ice Shelf, Sean picked out the Polar Bird, a dot on deep, dark blue waters, lost to the world in this polar wasteland. Now that he had reached the summit, he was acutely aware that he had stretched himself beyond his usual physiological limit. This climb had been tough, easily tougher than some of the hardest climbs in Scotland and Wales that he and Angus had trained on, and even more than some of the low altitude climbs in the Himalayas. Perhaps it was the desperate isolation of the place that scared him. But at the same time, it was also the physical and psychological boost that Sean needed right now, the sense that he was master of himself. When they had climbed together in the British Isles as a part of their SAS training, Sean always found that the Scottish mountains in winter with its mixed rock and ice climbing was the most challenging and exhilarating. Here in Antarctica, it was pure joy and Sean knew that Angus also would instantly respond to the desolate mountain landscape. They wanted to be here but they also had important tasks to complete in the deep south region that involved more than just climbing.

Angus was close on his heels, pulling himself easily like a well-muscled panther onto the ledge next to Sean. Sean signalled 'two minutes'. He wanted to begin the descent as soon as possible. Angus nodded, driving the shafts of his ice axes into the ice platform and setting up his belay with a length of cordelette attached to his harness. He pulled the hood of his down jacket over his head and thrashed his arms across his chest to ward off the cold. They would need to keep moving to stay warm and maintain their energy levels sufficiently to return to the Polar Bird.

Far below them the icy blue of the Ross Sea beckoned and warned the men. The sudden chop on the water and the formation of light blue and grey wavelets was the first indicator that the storm had come through. The promise of safety and the company on the boat was incentive enough to make good their return in one push. But for now, there was the ever-present possibility that lack of attention, carelessness or a wrong move could send them tumbling onto the shelf below.

Sean adjusted the belay, threading the climbing rope through the eye of a single ice screw. He carefully applied pressure testing the anchor. Satisfied, he grinned at Angus. Angus, who was a veteran climber, never underestimated the impact of a long, and hard climb on his body, noting over time the minute changes to his musculature and his increased vulnerability to hypothermia. Sean signalled to him again, this time to indicate that Angus would lead the rappel off the mountain first. Angus simply nodded, checking his climbing boots and crampons then deploying the double ropes with an artful skill that came from decades of experience in the British services, firstly as a cadet, then as a trainer and now, as a remote SAS officer.

He strapped the climbing axes to his climbing backpack before clipping into his descender. Both men were used to fast ascents and fast canyon-style descents, wasting neither time nor words. They did not need on this occasion to spend any more precious moments talking or discussing the climb; that would come later when they were safely off the mountain and back on the Polar Bird. Aware that the weather could at any moment close in, Angus gave Sean the thumbs up and rappelled backwards over the lip of the mountain towards the first of their belay positions below.

Sean waited until the ropes went slack then clipped into his descender ready to rappel off the top of the mountain and join Angus on the ledge they had carved for the next belay. He pulled the multifunction communications device from his top pocket and scrolled through to GPS. The reading was now steady and linked to a library of micro maps. He quickly flicked to radio transmit and blew into the mike.

'Mountain One to mountain Two, do you read. Do you read.' Sean switched to receive.

Angus heard the crackle in his communicator strapped to the shoulder strap of his pack.

'Mountain Two to mountain One, I read you.'

'Are you safe. Over.'

'Safe Mountain Two. Over.'

'Coming down Mountain Two. Over and out.'

Sean switched the communicator to 'satellite' and pressed the automatic dial. He waited until the familiar ring tone informed him that they had connection.

The wind groaned. 'Mountain One here Base. We are descending.'

'Right Sean. Hot coffee on the boil.'

'Roger that. Can smell it from here.' Sean grinned and flicked off the phone, placing it back into his jacket. He kicked off the ice platform and over the lip of the mountain, careful to avoid cutting the rope with his crampons as he rappelled towards Angus.

Five weary hours later, the men threw their ropes and packs into the shipping container that had been converted into a portable laboratory.

'Minutes to spare Sean. Angus alright?'

'I'm fine, but very cold.' Angus pushed the hood off his cropped hair.

'Straight into the pod boys. Warmer in there. Sleeping bag Angus?'

'Sounds good Roger.'

'Half an hour then we retreat to the Polar Bird.'

'Copy that. Half an hour.' Sean confirmed.

The ice pod, fixed to the floor of the great southern continent with long steel bolts was a complete haven. There was no way that any wind or blizzard would lift them off the Antarctic shelf provided they remained within the anchored pod. The wind had already picked up and the forecast gale-warning propelled the men to immediately rehydrate, eat and warm up before their final passage to the ship. The sudden protection from the weather, the warmth of the pod, the instant effect of warm fluids and glucose was the life or death detail that none of them could afford to ignore. Exposure for too long to the sub-zero winds sweeping across the ice shelf would result in hypothermia, the slowing of blood flow throughout the body and the accompanying incapacity to think clearly and act decisively. It was essential for them to take on board warm fluids, and in significant quantities, to ward off the insidious onset of 'slow death' from extreme cold. The pod was designed to maximise and trap body heat at every level.

Angus kicked off his boots, jammed his body into the sleeping bag and sat himself upright in the director's chair that was Roger's 'office.' Roger had already primed the gas stove and the familiar aroma of New Guinea roast shot into his nostrils, the caffeine immediately sparking his brain and body back to life. Barely minutes had elapsed since they had fought through the driving horizontal wind to the container door. Soon they would be eating hot soup then plunging into a short sleep before they headed out through the fierce Antarctic weather again to the Polar Bird.

The research vessel lay sluggishly off shore, obscured by the remnants of the spindrift-laden storm, with only the cold metal glinting in the diffused light. The storm blew through with predictable ferocity, ripping the guts out of any hopes to board the ship that afternoon. All night the men in the pod heard the groaning of steel as the Polar Bird struggled to hold her anchor against the force of the wind. The Captain made the call to wait out the storm and keep the men on the shore until the storm passed.

Then, at first light, it was possible to make a painful yet necessary exit from the pod. While most of the team was more attuned to the rigours of mountain life than the complexity of human relationships, invariably however, the mental and physical shock of leaving the warmth of the pod jolted them back to the value of human civilisation and company. They left as a team.

Twenty minutes after they left the comfort of the shelter, the men donned their lifejackets and boarded the inflatables. The Zodiacs bobbed across the ocean transporting the stores, scientific equipment and ice cores, along with the team of men and women, to the Polar Bird. Within moments of the inflatables being hauled on board, the engines throbbed into life and the Polar Bird set her course towards Macquarie Island and ultimately Hobart, where she would deliver her bounty of scientific findings to the waiting laboratories. The wonder of Antarctica that scientists were slowly beginning to understand was that the ice itself held the key to life on the planet; the nutrient cache of microorganisms there was capable of sustaining millions of tonnes of algae, uncountable populations of krill, fish and bird life. Deep within the ice were secrets of life and evolution that had accumulated over millennia.

The Polar Bird steamed steadily north with her precious scientific cargo and crew. Their's was an early, yet timely, exit from Antarctica's inhospitable landscape, well before the onslaught of the next storm. A departure during the summer was essential otherwise the ship could be caught as the ice floes in the Ross Sea formed into sheets and closed in around her hull. As she headed north through the great Southern Ocean, the scenery surrounding the Polar Bird remained as spectacular as it was on the ice shelf. The blue-grey of the water contrasted with the striking light coloured jade of the massive ice floes, their peaks rising ominously above the water. New to the sea was an increase in the flotsam and jetsam of ice;

dismembered pieces of the great ice shelves that once formed at the edge of the Antarctic continent were now discarded and drifting out to sea as the ocean warmed. The Polar Bird proceeded steadily on course and, throughout the night, the grey shine of the water, the shimmer of fluorescence from microorganisms as well as streaks of light from the Southern Aurora, created a world of immeasurable beauty.

The crew, feeling elated in the aftermath of a successful expedition, decorated the dining room table with an avalanche of food and drink. The ship glowed in the warmth of the festivities as it chugged doggedly towards home.

Through the mists far to the south of Australia, the Polar Bird sailed like an ethereal queen, her deck and wheelhouse strung with lights and her flags fluttering softly as the grey waters slid silently beneath her hull. The sunny shores of Australia beckoned her home and the Captain and crew luxuriated in the prospect. Even in the daytime, the captain decided to keep the fairy lights afire as if to announce her arrival home. The men dined on the last of the fresh meat and fruit. The sticky date pudding, soaked in rum, was a warm and inviting closure to the dinner. Then, the men slept as if the ocean were their cradle. The revelry and drinking had put them into their berths early and the majority were asleep by midnight.

The morning broke and Angus awoke early. He had had a troubled night and needed to nut out the information they had found on Antarctica. He walked to the coffee machine and deliberately selected 'long black' and pressed the button; the machine spluttered the dark liquid into his mug. He walked back to the lounge room and sat down, anxiety gnawing at his gut. He couldn't put his finger on the problem, but he knew that there was more information in the ice cores than they were ready for. Perhaps climate change was chasing them faster than they realised, and it would have major implications for most of the cities around the world that hugged coastlines. Australia was a case in point. His thoughts were abruptly broken by Sean, stumbling towards the coffee machine.

'Mornin' Angus.'

'Sean? I thought I was alone out here.' Angus was suddenly relieved to have Sean's company.

'I must have been dreaming. Thought I heard the earth rumbling beneath the ship.' Sean looked troubled.

'Maybe one of us was snoring.' Angus guffawed.

'Could be. Then again..'

'Well, might as well enjoy your coffee. Come and sit down.' Angus invited him.

Angus and Sean languished in the ship's lounge room, reading, drinking coffee and reviewing their trip. The primarily scientific expedition had accepted them on board to conduct their own reconnaissance of the mountains near the Ross Sea.

'Australia needs Antarctica's weather Sean,' Angus muttered, breaking into his train of thought.

'Like a hole in the head Angus. Those winds would strip the deserts and farmlands back to basically rock.'

'We've lost too much topsoil, aye. Perhaps its ending up down here in any event.'

'A bit more rain would help?'

'If the readings are right, the lows are dumping the rain over the Southern Ocean instead of the land and probably taking with them Australia's precious remaining soils.'

'What about the temperatures?'

'Too high for comfort. Shorter winters, early and warmer springs, longer summers.'

'Meaning?'

'Sea levels will rise around the world. We could lose a few islands and coastal communities.' Angus looked more concerned than grim.

'That will create some migration issues.' Sean said evenly.

'None that we can't handle. They will only be small movements of people from mostly the islands.'

'I'm not so sure about that Angus. What about the coastal populations around Australia and what about all the Pacific Islands for that matter?'

'That's a thought. That's why I am on the Monaro of course.'

'We might need to set up another camp a little further up the slope from your farm.' Sean looked squarely at Angus.

'Well, we'll do that anyway. I've been thinking the same thing — setting up the Alpine Unit — now that Tom is shaping up so well. What do you think Sean?'

'Absolutely. Water security, energy security. It's about time we looked after those assets a little better.'

They approached Macquarie Island in the dead of the following night with little movement on or below deck. Then it came, the deep rumble of the earth shaking far below the ocean it seemed, from the belly of the earth. The first shock reached the Polar Bird lifting her slightly at the stern. The wave strengthened as it passed, moving rapidly over the vast expanse of ocean. Angus awoke, sensing the stern rolling steeply forwards.

'What was that?' He leapt out of his bunk pulling his trousers off the peg then tugging a jersey over his head.

'Sean!' Angus shook Sean's shoulder roughly. 'Sean. Let's go. Something's not right.'

'You're meant to be sleeping it off Angus!' Sean muttered.

'Not this one. I'm going upstairs. This felt like an earth movement to me.'

'Out here?'

'You can feel it. The swell has picked up.'

'Here with you.' Sean was suddenly alert, his senses tuned, listening for subtle changes in ocean. Sean pushed himself to a sitting position, tugged his jacket off its hook and reached for gloves. 'Boots?'

'Rubber. If we're going onto the deck.' Angus, keen as a fox, flexed slightly onto his toes; he gave Sean the benefit of a few extra seconds, as he always had.

'Yup. You're right about the swell Angus. What do you think happened?'

'Can't say for sure. My money is on the seismograph. Coming?'

Angus climbed the ladder first, shinning lightly up the rungs. He forced himself into the cold midnight air, bracing for the first thrill of the icy wind. It was the Polar Bird dipping steeply down the giant wave that had woken him from his restful sleep. The ship was built with a heavy hull to crash through the ice, but not designed to take on giant waves that may rise out of the ocean in response to earthquakes. Angus shuddered at the thought. Anything was possible out here. Now, the feeling of the ocean moving beneath the hull of the boat meant that something was happening somewhere — perhaps the tectonic plates were moving. Water was an excellent transmitter of energy and sound. Suddenly, another wave washed under them, as though propelled from the depths of the ocean floor. Kilometres below, where the earth became liquid, and rock gave way to a molten core, the Indo-Australian tectonic plate crashed against the Pacific plate. The Polar Bird lifted for a few seconds, then slumped back just as quickly as the giant wave passed beneath her.

Angus immediately moved to the central point on the deck, aware that in these conditions a freak wave could easily tip a man overboard. It was a miracle and a half that the wave arrived front-on to the ship, the vessel shuddering to rise and fall as the wave passed. Angus pushed open the door to the wheelhouse. The Captain was already there, standing legs astride, hands lightly on the wheel and eyes scanning minutely the detail of the radar, sonar and the horizon.

'Anything on the seismograph?' Angus asked lightly in a husky voice.

'Angus! I Thought I was alone.'

Angus grinned. 'What did you get? That felt like one massive wave.'

'You're not wrong about that. Take a look at the seismograph.' The Captain paused as the roll spewed from beneath the charting pen.

'How big!' Sean inquired briskly.

'Over eight on the scale. Six kilometres below. The Captain did not sound happy.

'Christ! We must be close to the epicentre then.'

'Too close. You're right if you are thinking what I am thinking.' The Captain said quietly.

'I am. Any closer to shore and we could kiss the Polar Bird good bye.'

'Full speed ahead!' The Captain barked the order into the radio.

'Yes Captain.' The Ship's engineer was fully alert to the imminent danger.

The Captain sensed rather than heard Sean enter the wheelhouse.

'Full steam ahead might just get us out of trouble Captain. Can you judge the wave so the backwash from Macquarie Island doesn't hit us broadside?' Sean asked quietly.

'Copy that. Might not make the world of difference for a big wave though. Could tip us stern over aft.'

'I was thinkin' about keeping warm and dry and not testing the water so to speak.' Sean said wryly.

Angus looked directly at the Captain. Let's put a call through to Macquarie Island Captain. See how everyone's faring on shore.'

'Good call. Meanwhile, let's keep our wits about us. Watch and wait for the backwash wave.'

'Let's hope we're just far enough from Macquarie Island for any backwash to run out as a smooth wave. Most of the energy will dissipate as she hits land.'

The captain gripped the wheel ever so slightly. 'I just don't want the Polar Bird going into the Island unless it's essential. If they're safe, we carry on.

'Stay on course Captain.' Angus said evenly. 'We have a mission to complete. They will have medical staff on Macquarie Island and my guess is that there won't be any local tsunami on the back of this earthquake.'

'Copy that Angus.' The Captain said sombrely.

'You haven't picked up a Mayday call from anywhere?' It was Angus's call as the senior SAS office on board the Polar Bird, the ship seconded to the Navy under Angus's command for the time being.

'Not so far. Nothing.' The Captain measured his words steadily.

Angus was deeply worried. Potentially the sea and far off coastlines could be heavily impacted after the string of linked earthquakes and inevitable tsunamis. Closer to shore along the edge of the continental shelf, the steady and even swells, turned into freakish waves. Most ocean going vessels, even the biggest of the freighters and container ships, stood little or no chance. He shivered involuntarily. Intuition warned him that there would be major issues to deal with as climate change disrupted global weather patterns. Natural disasters, disruption to coastal ports, loss of valuable shipping lines and attrition of the coast posed a far greater risk to national security that a few boatloads of illegal immigrants. Provided the chaos was contained at sea and there was minimal wash up against marinas, there would be no real effect of the earthquake on Australia though the wash of the tide against the shores of Tasmania sent freak waves along both east and west coast. At Strahan, whales unexpectedly beached themselves as the earth moved below the depths of the ocean floor.

Angus waited patiently for a more detailed analysis to determine the cause and origin of the quake. He doubted nuclear testing and it seemed unlikely that the crashing of Antarctic ice into the sea would trigger alone such a quake. The most plausible and likely reason for the earth movement, was simply massive stresses building up along the fault lines between the great tectonic plates kilometres below the surface of the sea.

The Captain felt the massive wave before it reached his tiny fishing boat. Ahead of the wave, the swell started to lift the stern of the boat. Almost by instinct, he pulled the wheel starboard and pointed his vessel into the oncoming wave. He had only moments to spare before the giant wave moved under them, lifting the bow to an impossible angle. The wave seemed to go on forever. Time stood still as the fishing boat and crew remained poised in the ocean, bow to the sky now invisible as the monster wave towered over them. The deck, littered with the last of their fishing materials was awash with spray and loose items skittered to the stern and flew off into the dark sea. Suddenly the wave passed and the boat crashed with a whump back onto the ocean surface. The hull shuddered and shrieked with the impact. The Captain bent his knees deeply expecting the shock. It came. He felt as though the boat had fallen four floors and smacked onto the ocean which felt as hard as concrete. The water suddenly gave beneath the force of impact sending up spray ten, fifteen metres into the air before once again washing over the deck washing the last of the loose materials into the sea. The sudden shock of the massive sea, the force of the impact onto the ocean surface and the sheer fear of being inverted by the monster wave took its toll. The captain suddenly dry retched.

Ten minutes later the crew had assembled together with the Captain in the wheelhouse. There were injuries; a broken nose, semi-concussion and a bruised shoulder as the men were thrown around like toys by the giant wave. But no-one was missing and no-one was dead. The Captain sighed in relief. He once again set his compass and course for Tasmania. He was however unaware that in pursuit of his vessel was a powerful ship capable of outstripping them on the waters and with the authority to stop them at sea to board and search the crew and cargo. The Pakistani crew returned below deck to pick up the pieces of the galley strewn about the cabin. One of the men found the coffee pot and sat it precariously on the portable gas stove in the tiny galley. He started the burner and grinned at his companions. The cards were found and someone lit a bidi. The drama was over and they had money to make. The holds were intact and filled to capacity with their lucrative catch destined for the Tasmanian and, possibly, mainland markets. The Captain hoped this time that the catch was untraceable and not linked in any way to Australian waters. He knew if they could avoid detection, there would be enough income to maintain the boat and feed their families on the subcontinent. He pulled the sub-machine gun from its holder on the wall in the wheelhouse and set it next to his right thigh. The magazine always loaded and the cold metal familiar to his fingers. The remains of an unburnt bidi hung loosely from the left side of his mouth, the spittle causing the end to soften and almost break. He pulled the cigarette closer into his mouth, biting off and spitting out the loose ends of the tobacco.

The Captain believed that in this world, everyone was a possible thief, traitor or captor — even his own crew. He could never be careful enough. Also to carry a gun would create the necessary atmosphere of fear and apprehension in his crew. It was, he told them, as much for their security as it was for his. Only he and his second in command knew that there was a cache of high-grade, semi automatic weapons stowed deeply below the coiled ropes and nets. He expected an intercept at some point in the journey. Already Russian intelligence had increased surveillance details along the southern coast. Canberra, as far as he knew, was for now porous and he was satisfied that as long as they had sleepers in the community, they could rely on reasonable intelligence. It was a risky business running into any of the main ports, but the guns were needed ashore, and fast.

As the Polar Bird moved northwards under the thrust of her powerful engines, she made steady headway over the vast wasteland of water between Macquarie Island and Tasmania. The satellites overhead had already detected and zoomed in on foreign nationals in Australian waters. The boats, all unmarked and without identifying flags, were clearly visible on the satellite images, as were the men on board, identifiable by face scanning as originating as far north as the Arabian Sea. They were of neither African nor Arabian descent. They were not from any of the south Asia countries or islands, or from Papua, from the Pacific Islands, or Japan, Taiwan or Korea. There was nothing to suggest that they had gone off course from South America and they certainly hadn't floated in from the Arctic. The satellite images distinctly outlined the facial features and ethnic origins of the men: Northern India, Kashmir, Pakistan. Afghanistan. The image interpreters looked for signs of Mongolian descent and found none. The Customs vessel was no more than a radio call away, yet for reasons of practicality the Polar Bird had special dispensation, legal means and backup firepower to detain any crews caught in illegal fishing activity. But deeper in Angus's consciousness, nagging at his early warning system, was the real possibility that under the freezer vats filled with fish was a more sinister cargo. The chances were that theirs was a serious agenda: people smuggling, contraband, drugs, and at worst, arms. The Polar Bird could easily outpace and capture any fishing vessel, but Angus decided to follow the vessel to port to quietly observe a potentially wider network of boats and onshore contacts.

The shrill sound of the radiophone blasted into the Polar Bird's wheelhouse.

'Angus?'

'Speaking.'

'We've got them now Angus. You can proceed to Hobart without intercept.'

'David are we sure we have them.' Angus was not going to let them slip through his hands even if his boss indicated that they were on the tail of the small fishing vessel registered in Pakistan and flying a Dubai flag. Angus found he was relieved to hear the voice of his SAS superior.

'We are sure.' His boss stated flatly.

'Why Australia?' Angus cleared his throat, his fist automatically clenching around the receiver.

'We don't know for sure. Could be a stash point only. We're watching for camps along the south coast.'

'Nothing on the satellite images?'

'Nothing above ground. Not yet.' David said.

'Trucks?' Angus pushed for the detail.

'Could be. Easier to hide a cache for sure. Disembark in Hobart Angus. Mix with the yachting fraternity and enjoy yourself for a while. You're booked on a flight from Melbourne to Jakarta. Spend a couple of days getting to know the freighters and their captains. Spend a week in Kabul, Karachi then the rest of the time in Dubai.

You should enjoy the races.'

'I don't want to miss the action down south. The races sound interesting.'

'They will be. You'll be back in time, don't worry. Our friendly Sheiks, Angus, watch them carefully — who mixes with who.' The SAS commander ordered quietly.

'My face must be known to some of them surely.'

'We need to take the risk.'

'Probably not as dangerous as being out on the seas at the moment.'

'Some big waves! Yes, we heard.' David laughed softly. 'We had you covered.'

'Good. Did you find out anything else new out here?'

'One of their operatives is from Afghanistan. He's returning to Australia.' David said soberly.

'Oh?'

'The Americans may have something. We're not sure. There seems to be some evidence that he trained in Afghanistan.'

'Then we should be very careful.'

'We'll keep both eyes firmly on the target.' David said quietly.

'And use your intuition.'

'Now there's a thought.' David clicked his tongue.

'Where am I staying in Dubai?'

'The best of course Angus. For you. Always the best. A good place to make your retirement plans.'

'I'm not thinking of retirement.' Angus said tersely.

'It is getting too dangerous. You already are aware of it. You just said so yourself. Farming and fishing is a sensible retirement plan. Perhaps you can breed more horses for our Arabian brethren.'

The guffaw on the other end of the line caught Angus off guard. David had a point. He might as well have a capital venture after a life of service to Her Majesty and the colonies. Horse breeding would be rewarding, if Brindabella was anything to go by. 'Protection?' Angus suddenly realised that indeed, he was ready for retirement.

'Organised. In your hotel suite. Bathroom cabinet.'

'Thank you boss. Take care.'

'You too, Angus. Regards to Sean.' David smiled and hung up.

The Polar Bird arrived in Hobart and berthed at the new marina close to Constitution Dock. There was the usual coming and going of local yachts as well as the historic wooden boat sitting serenely at her permanent berth, her twin masts rising high above the wharf building. Far from the icy wonderland of the Antarctic, the screaming winds and freezing polar days, the colour of the yachting flags and buntings lifted Angus and Sean's spirits. At the helm, the Captain whistled to himself, happy at their arrival amidst the boat traffic that talked only of a buzzing port. It felt like a party for him, his crew and the Antarctic team after conquering one of the toughest oceans in the world. Too many had already been lost in the remote, unreachable and lonely latitudes of the Southern Ocean where only wandering albatrosses were really at home.

THE MELBOURNE CUP

'Banjo Paterson reckoned this mob were a bunch of thieves.' Malcolm announced as they sat together in the grandstand.

'Who?' Tom's ears were pricked, ready to hear the call of the race commentator. Malcolm had placed a bet for him and Tom was unwavering in his conviction that his horse would win.

'Banjo Paterson Tom. You should know his poem!' "Man from the Snowy River"?'

'Yeah, course I know it!'

'He reckoned, this mob are thieves, all of them; the owners, trainers, race goers. The whole pack of them.'

'Does that make us thieves as well?' Tom asked innocently.

'Don't know. Banjo for one thought this caper, as Max put it, is about money, not horses.' He grinned, breaking into well-tried verse, '"Come all ye bold trainers, tender my song, you mustn't train ponies for that's very wrong."'

Tom laughed. 'Have you got any race horses Malcolm?'

'Sure do. My mate that's coming over to join us is interested too.'

'That's the guy we met at Jillamatong!'

'That's him. Still looking for a brumby like yours, Tom.'

'He could have had Thunder.' Charlie teased.

'No way.' Tom broke in.

'Hey! Sean, Angus.' Tom sprung out of his seat.

'Just as well I had a couple of extra grandstand seats. Move along a couple of places lads. Let two good men in.' Malcolm grinned.

'Shift Tom.' Charlie nudged him with his elbow.

'Hello lads. Malcolm.' Sean tipped his hat.

'Mate, you look cool!' Tom looked Sean up and down.

'Don't look at me. Check out Angus.'

Tom clapped his hands whistling at Angus's fancy-cut clothes, the Akubra hat adjusted to a slight angle and Williams boots polished to the shine.

'Gidday lads. Glad to see you're in good company here.'

'When did you two get back?' Tom looked accusingly at Sean.

Sean placed a firm hand on Tom's shoulder. 'I was never far away Tom. You know that.'

'You could say it had something to do with the phone call we received. Malcolm here told us all about Jillamatong, then about Thunder and the fire. So we reckoned it was about time to come home. Isn't that right Sean?' Angus said evenly.

'That it is Angus. Couldn't keep two good men off their favourite soil for too long, not even if the old country pulled us back for a bit.'

'Nothin' that would keep a man from a fine race like this one.' Sean nodded at the last of the horses leaving the circle, their trappers guiding them to the gates. See there's a bit of competition from over the seas here Malcolm.'

Malcolm tipped his hat. 'That's why we're here I guess. Couple of my friend's best from his Irish stables. Ah, here he is.' Malcolm waved over his friend.

'Hey! That's the guy who wanted to buy Brindy!' Tom looked questioningly at Malcolm.

'Indeed Tom, Dariyan.'

Malcolm stood up. 'Dariyan these are my friends, Sean and Angus and you have already met Tom.'

'Pleased to meet you both.' The man was impeccable in his

manners, his suit cut to perfection, the tie a distinct match.

'You have your own horse racing?' Angus inquired mildly of him.

'In time we plan to bring a thoroughbred from one of the stables of the Aga Khan. We think from Ireland. Irish bred horses seem to do well on Australian turf don't you think Malcolm?'

Malcolm grinned. 'Angus and Sean have just returned from the emerald Isle as it happens Dariyan.'

'I see that there are some excellent horses running today.' Dariyan glanced briefly at the form, noting with a cross his preferred winner, then second, third and fourth.

'Then you'll have already laid your bets?' Angus let his Scottish accent do the work.

'Of course Dariyan has.' Malcolm broke in with perfect ease lightly chiding Angus. 'Indeed. It is the quality of the horses that interests Dariyan. Not just winning the races, isn't that so Dariyan?'

'We are continually working to improve our lines at the stables. Sometimes, the best blood comes from overseas. But one always looks around for stamina and good breeding in local horses.'

'Like Brindy you mean?' Tom took the bait.

'Absolutely. Your horse Tom, has that little bit extra that we always look for. — sure and steady on his feet, fire in his heart, well-muscled, good proportions, responsive to human touch....' Dariyan let the sentence hang for a moment. 'It's not just about a horse racing when he hears the starter's gun and how quick he is out of the barrier. For this race especially, the horse needs to be a stayer.'

'You could breed from Brindy if you like.' Tom continued to talk across Sean, Angus and Malcolm who were sitting between him and Dariyan, his new best friend.

'What an excellent idea.'

'Why not.' Angus was quick to support Tom's new enterprise. 'You could learn a few things from Malcolm while you are here.

There's not much he doesn't know about breeding.' Angus added.

'Brindy must have had a natural match.' Tom chipped in defensively.

'Indeed. Natural selection is a wonderful thing.' Malcolm said diplomatically.

'That too. But if you were to select a horse here today Malcolm,' Angus opened, 'What would you look for?'

'The quality of the gait, the spirit of the horse, how he or she responds to the handler, a wiling eye.' Malcolm stepped in skillfully to educate Tom. 'Watch how these horses move. The strappers are leading them into the ring now.'

'Oh.' Tom couldn't help but notice the shine on every horse, the clipped coats, polished hooves and racing colours dancing before his eyes. 'Can't see Thunder looking so dandy.'

Sean laughed. 'You got that right Tom. But don't you reckon Thunder has a little more spring to his step?'

'Spose.' Tom felt his spirits rise.

'Exactly right Sean,' Malcolm picked up Sean's lead. 'You want a horse to move naturally with an easy gait, like that bay mare with the blaze on her forehead.' Malcolm pointed towards the horse wearing gold and green colours.

'D'ya think she'll win?' Tom cut in hopefully.

'Let's see. There are more horses entering the ring now. Personally, I like a horse with spirit Tom, with intelligent eyes and independent movement. A horse that is a natural winner moves naturally without having to be pulled or pushed by its strapper. He's a starter.' Malcolm nodded at the horse just entering the ring. 'Watch how relaxed he is in the ring. No funny business or biting the bit.'

'Mmm.' I guess you have them sorted.' Tom sounded unusually complimentary.

Malcolm chuckled. 'I guess I do. A man has to make an honest

living in this world and horses are an important part of my living.'
He slapped his knee. 'We're on!' Malcolm cut the conversation. 'It
won't be long before they are ready to head out to the barriers. Tell
you what Tom, you pick the horse that you like and I'll tell you
mine. What do you think?'

'Can't see Thunder out there.' Tom hedged his bets. 'Or Brindy.
Shit! This is really it. The Melbourne Cup.' Tom couldn't believe
himself.

'Good line up Malcolm.' Angus announced loudly.

'Have you got a bet in, Tom?' Sean asked.

'I thought I'd bet on one of the Irish horses. Seemed like a good
omen to bring you back.'

'And here I am.' Sean grinned.

'Malcolm, are they friends of yours?' Angus pointed discreetly to
the polished gathering to their right.

'Yes they are. The Premier and his friends.' Malcolm smiled
secretively at Angus.

'Change of jockeys in your state I note. Do you think he'll win
his race?' Angus laughed broadly and openly, a refreshing breach of
protocol.

'At this stage of the race, I'd put my money on it.' Malcolm
responded bowing slightly towards the Premier.

'You do know them?' Angus was surprised.

'Of course. Graziers are after all Angus, the nexus of Australian
life and politics as any seasoned politician will know.'

'Here they come! The stock horses are leaving the ring.' Tom
cried.

Several banks of stock horses, their riders clasping long poles
boasting the national flag and dressed in Drizabones, cantered
steadily around the course.

'Look at the power in the shoulders Angus.' Malcolm announced.
'Give me a stock horse any day over a thoroughbred.'

Malcolm's friend nodded quietly in acquiescence, mesmerised by the powerful impression created by the Australian horses moving smoothly in front of the crowds.

'Now here come our runners for today.' Malcolm saw the first of the Melbourne Cup runners pass along the rose-lined corridor.

'There's a colourful scene for you Angus.' Sean smiled broadly.

'Almost as beautiful as your Irish greens.' Angus laughed.

'The same Irish horse is running today Sean as in the last Cup. The last time the trainer won the cup was in 1993.' Malcolm pointed to the steed.

'Good breeding, there's no question about it. The jockey is one of yours?' Sean nodded at the horse.

'Yes, it works better of course. Our lads know the track, and the race.'

'Then perhaps I should bring the horse and use one of your jockeys?' Malcolm's friend asked politely.

'You'd certainly stand a better chance.' This time Angus offered the advice.

'Some of these horses are better dressed than most people!' Sean watched as the line of jockeys dressed in race colours climbed the podium to take their bow. As each one entered the arena bursting with almost a thousand of the best that Melbourne and the overseas racing fraternity could find, a large silk jersey in matching colours was draped onto the race track.

'There's plenty to be said for Emirates oil money Malcolm.'

'Perhaps Malcolm, your friend might like to buy some of our wonderful mountain horses and train them on your farm.' Angus offered.

'Indeed. Brindabella or Thunder could run well. But my hunch is that they would be better in endurance racing.'

'Do you think we could bring some of the other brumbies in?'

'To sell?'

'Yes. They're just looking for staying power and speed. Some of the lower mountain brumbies look classy enough.'

'There's Arab in them. That's for sure.' Malcolm agreed.

'Mostly, I find the brumbies are easy to train.' Angus added from his experience.

'Can't see why it couldn't be a new industry. You know. Homegrown steeds on the banks of the Snowy River. Should be strong and supple.' Malcolm mulled over the idea.

'They used to breed horses on the Monaro for the Indian Army.' Angus smiled quickly.

'Ahh! I see Angus. You are well ahead of the rest of us.'

'My ancestors. They had a good trade going.'

'England could never have won the war without the Australian Light Horse.' Malcolm observed.

'Or the Indian Army.' Angus repeated.

'That is true. That is true. Look. They have arrived.' Malcolm pointed to the quiet gathering of obviously wealthy Sheiks arriving at the course.

'You're in the wrong trade Malcolm!' Angus laughed.

'There are definitely too few home bred horses at the Melbourne Cup!' Malcolm conceded.

'Gai's horse is good. She reckons the mountain horses are stronger than any of these thoroughbreds.' Tom defended the locals.

'Sadly Tom, they won't run next year. Insurance has all but killed off Jillamatong.' Angus said glumly.

Tom suddenly jerked forwards in his seat.

'What's wrong?' Sean suddenly sensed the panic in the young man.

'Him.' Tom pointed to the priest seating himself behind them and to the right.

'Aye lad. Father Thomas.' Sean tipped his hat towards the Priest then deliberately turned his back, placing a firm hand on Tom's shoulder and pointing towards the slightly curved barriers, the heads of the jockeys just visible over the top of the gates.

'They're off!' Tom yelled.

The horses broke from the barriers, the strongest quickly pulling out in front and moving to the fence, taking a single-stride lead over the rest of the group pumping hard to keep pace. In moments, the group broke up with the lead horses extending around the curve. The sound of thousands of cheering men and women filled the stands.

'Keep your eye on that Irish horse Tom.' Sean laughed.

'Come on. Go boy go! Tom stood up and yelled into the cheering crowd.

'Look Tom.' Sean urged him to lift his head as the horses entered the straight. 'There he is. The stallion.'

As steady as grey-white granite, the phantom stallion moved surely between the horses racing along the fence. Slowly he edged forwards until he ran neck and neck with the group of horses at the front, his nose almost over the line. As he took the line, his forelegs thrust in front of him, he raised his head, throwing his mane and tail, edged with silver white to the crowd, then vanished like a ghost back into the landscape.

Sean had seen him too. Tom knew that the phantom horse was not just in his imagination.

'Great race Sean.' Malcolm was on his feet.

'You won!' Angus slapped Malcolm on the back.

'Always knew how to back the right horse.' Malcolm said coolly. 'Media Puzzle was always going to be my pick. His trainer is Irish of course Sean. Dermott Weld.'

'What a race!' Sean's eyes shone with elation. It was the first time in years he had allowed himself to let go. 'Go the Irish!' He shook Malcolm's hand. 'The jockey was something else.' He grinned. Sean turned to Tom. 'Your horse came in second Tom!'

'Second?'

'Didn't you keep your eye on him?' Sean was still grinning from ear to ear.

'I…' Tom was still distracted by the sight of the phantom horse crossing the line his nose ahead of the winner.

'We'll collect your winnings later.' Sean slapped him on the back.

'Damien. Damien Oliver. Look Sean. They are all going crazy after him. He's beaten his stable mate Vinnie Roe.' Angus turned to his friend.

'Two Irish champions in one race.' Sean felt as though the world was behind the Irish today.

'That was one of the best battles I have ever seen Malcolm.' Charlie was still seated, in awe at the magnificence of the two Irish horses on his home turf in Melbourne. 'Can't believe you Irish can produce something like this Sean.' Charlie stood up and grinned at Sean. 'What could possibly be better than this.' He thumped Sean on the back then pulled him into a bear hug.

Sean felt the tears pricking the corners of his eyes.

'The underdog wins from time to time Sean.' Angus cast his eyes around the grandstand. People were on their feet cheering, some waving tabs in their hand and some hugging. A group of women were already making their way towards the race track to greet Media Puzzle and Damien, the elated winning jockey.

'Well lads. I am very happy for Oliver. He beat the outright favourite. This one is for his brother Jason. Too young for him to die.'

CLEAR

Tom casually flicked the beautifully knotted stockwhip at a fly sitting on top of the fence post. From a distance, the crack of leather in the still morning air, sounded like a pistol shot: decisive, short and sharp. He pulled the whip easily behind his right shoulder and this time flicked the end of the whip a few centimetres above the fence post. Cassie was constantly in his thoughts yet he wistfully conceded that Angus needed her in the mountains for the time being and not at Tom Groggin Station. Again, he lifted the whip, this time aiming for a single barb from the top strand of wire. The urgent sound of the phone in his pocket momentarily diverted his attention, although not sufficiently to distract him from his target. The wire sang and the end of the whip lifted free as Tom judged to less than a second, the point to retract the whip.

'Yo. Tom here.'

'Tom. Sean. How are you son?'

'Sean. Yeah. Great man. Where are you?'

'Around. What's happening?'

'Pretty hot out here today. Merry Christmas to you too.'

'No more fires I take it?'

'Nothing visible. A bit of haze towards the south. All looks well otherwise.'

'And you are at the Station?' Sean inquired politely.

'Yep. Breaking in another few horses. Malcolm wants more ready for sale. There are stables overseas waiting he says.'

'Then that is good news. I imagine that you are earning more than your keep then.' Sean smiled to himself.

Tom flicked the stockwhip again, allowing it to crack lightly well above his right shoulder.

'Shooting rabbits?'

'Practisin' with the whip.'

'Oh?'

'Yep. Not that there is much to use it for other than flies.' Tom stated dryly.

'Then you sound as though you could use a new challenge son.' Sean said softly.

'Yeah?' Tom innocently took the bait.

'In the mountains. We need you to set up camp. On ground surveillance. See if you can match our comms surveillance. You'll be close to Cass up there.'

'Cool. Anythin' interestin'?' Tom said hopefully.

'There might be. Nothing that I can talk about though over this line.'

'Isn't your phone encrypted mate?'

Sean grinned in spite of himself. 'Mine might be but yours certainly isn't.'

'I could use a proper satellite phone. The reception is not always that good in the mountains from what Case tells me.'

'Oh?'

'Yeah. She rings from Island Bend.'

'OK. As good as done Tom.'

'What else do I get?'

'Tent. Pack. Rations. Sleeping Bag.'

'DVDs?' Tom offered.

'Bit rich!' Sean protested.

'Not into star gazing seven nights out of seven Sean.'

'Hmm. We'll see. If you think you can get a computer out of me son, you'd better hope it can do more than just play DVDs! See if I can get you a full system.' Sean did not elaborate.

'Cool.'

'That's settled then.'

'When do I start?' Tom cracked the whip in delight.

'Tomorrow.' Sean said soberly. 'Find your way up to the village. Take the first chair up to the top. Thora will meet you at Eagle's Nest.'

'Who?'

'Thora.'

'Yeah. Name like that..'

'She's a good climber. You'll like her. On your bike then! You will have more on your plate than you think.'

'Rightio Sean. Enjoy the fishin'. Oh..' Tom added as an afterthought. 'Heard you mob ran into the earthquake down south. You think it's connected to the same one Cassie felt?'

Sean chuckled. 'Possible.' He hung up the phone.

Tom chewed on a stalk of grass as his eyes scanned the valley for signs of life. The station hands were away for the weekend. He was left in charge to make sure that the cattle did not stray through gates left open by campers, fishermen or four wheel drivers heading into the steep and rugged mountains of north east Victoria. The responsibility made Tom feel good and he knew that he was up to the mark, the man of the moment and felt he could handle anything, even another major fire. Today, there was nothing unusual to note. The sights and sounds of the summer erupting in early morning glory was almost transcendental, giddying in its beauty, seductive in its aromas of eucalyptus oil evaporating along with the rising air heated as if in a mini oven. Tom loved the valley, almost as much as he loved the mountains. But duty was the stronger pull — loyalty to Sean being the measure of him the man, and how he saw himself.

There would be little to do today, apart from a quick run around the property on his trail bike, checking gates were closed, water troughs were running, the ballcocks free from the tangle of weeds or similar impediments. The cows were well past calving and there should not be, in his estimation, anything to complicate their quiet ruminations on the plentiful and nutritious summer grasses. The flight of a flock of parrots past the Station homestead and the insolent barking of the youngest of the cattle dogs was about as much activity as he expected today.

Tom turned on his heel, leaving the sound of the river behind him and headed in for breakfast. The kitchen was quiet, clean and always left with a full fridge and freezer and he had nothing on his mind apart from a solid feed of fresh bacon, eggs and a pile of toast. That would set him right for the morning. He eased himself into his morning routine, whistling softly under his breath, switching the radio to the local news, waiting for something of interest and finding nothing in particular in the weather report. The fire danger was pretty high as usual, however that would be expected for this time of year. He was always careful, starting the bike or the all terrain vehicles away from long grass, particularly during windy weather when even a zephyr could spell disaster for an entire district.

The lights were on in the shed when Tom finally kicked over the trail bike. He had not recalled leaving the shed open and functioning, but reckoned that maybe he had forgotten to switch off and lock up after feeding the horses in the evening. The shed yards were deserted, the horses grazing quietly past the round yards, enjoying the best of the summer feed with a smaller than usual supplement of oats to encourage their spirits into top performance. Tom accelerated steadily, taking the bike towards the main drafting yards, through the gates and up to the top paddock. The view was always good, the clouds and mists over the high country enticing him as they always did. There was little sign of rain about, however the cloud and low front system warned him that out of nowhere weather systems could erupt, created it seemed, on pressure, temperature and moisture gradients.

The Kosciuszko massif formed from an ancient seabed, metamorphosed into slates, quartzes and schists was later intruded by granites, then sequential uplifts, weathering and again uplifts, created an unimaginable fortress where it seemed, creation occurred on an almost daily basis. This was the stuff of legends as far as Tom was concerned, where nature dominated man and there was no room for reckoning in between.

He allowed the throttle to ease back slightly as he neared the top end of the property. The fence line was intact, untroubled by kangaroos snapping a top wire as they leapt towards the forests leading to Mt Hope and the subalpine grazing areas. Sometimes, he had found a wire snipped by an impatient trail rider, not sure of the positioning of gates eager to head into the bush country away from the remnants of civilisation. It never worried Tom. The day was better spent straining a wire than sitting around the homestead waiting for something to happen. Today was unsurprisingly empty of little jobs, free from entanglements to other people less respectful of the rhythms of farm life.

Tom wasted little time, turning the bike towards the valley and gradually making his way down the track to the lower paddocks. The cloud over the tops had suddenly lifted, whisped into thin trails as if a feather were dragged across the main range. He listened for sounds of vehicles, but there was nothing and no jet streams at this time of day from the high fliers heading to the west. He continued on to the last gate. He was puzzled. The gate was open and he was sure that he had left it closed. An open gate was an invitation to cattle to stray into the higher paddocks. Unless a ghost was following him, Tom could not find an explanation. The farm dogs were clever, but not that clever.

He slammed the gate shut, making sure that it was secured and headed back to the shed, leaving the bike ready for the next round in the morning if he felt it was necessary. Then he checked the generator was set to switch on, in the event of a storm. The lights off, he closed and locked the door behind him.

The morning of his departure was happily quiet and free from stresses as Tom rolled over and switched on the bed lamp. The birds already alerted him to dawn, the sound of a lyrebird mimicking several species in quick succession, enough to resemble entire forest of life. The cockatoos, lazy at first, then squawking with delight, flew over the homestead and down the valley towards the next farm. The new crop of oats would take a hiding as the white horde descended, determined to make the most of the opportunity. Tom was tempted to pick up the shotgun and warn them off, then decided against it. It was not his problem. The cockatoos would return anyway. There was less feed after the fires until the native pines recovered with new cones to keep the birds happy. His pack was ready, boots treated with a few extra coats of waterproofing and jacket rolled neatly beneath the top flap of the pack. He was ready. Tom headed down the dirt farm track to the Murray River and onto the tarmac strip that climbed into the high country. This was as good as it could get. No worries, nothing to panic about and definitely, no hurry. There were always happy campers heading up the mountain and Tom was sure that he would catch a lift, even before he reached the Tom Groggin camping area.

Moments later, a truck laden with firewood pulled up and Tom jumped in the passenger side of the cab.

'Gidday mate.' Tom said brightly, grinning like a cat with fresh cream from the dairy.

'You're looking bright mate for this time of day. Heading to Thredbo?'

'You got it. Spot of camping if the weather holds out.'

'Forecast is OK mate. Geoff.' The driver shot Tom an appreciative glance.

'Tom. Nice to meet you. Thanks for the lift!'

'No trouble. You at the Station?'

'Yeah. The rest are back this morning and I'm off for a bit anyway. So this is it.'

'You travel light?'

'Always do. Mind you, you truckies haven't got much extra in the cab.'

'Always have a good sleeping bag and me dog.' Geoff patted his Jack Russell. 'This is Pretzel.' The dog leapt onto its four tiny legs at the sound of its name.

'Cute.'

'Yep. He's a good mate. No trouble. Keeps me awake on the long hauls.'

'Could be handy.'

'You got a dog?'

'Nuh. I've got a nice horse though, Brindy. Had to let another stallion go when the fires came through. Breaking in a few new ones now.'

'Oh?'

'You know. Some of the brumbies are better than you think. Great nick after the fires. Coats look a treat with all that long grass in the bush.'

'There are a few left then?'

'Not as many mobs as before and the mobs are smaller. Except the ones that came out of the fires have produced some pretty good foals. Got my eye on one of the grey stallions. Just haven't gotten around to catching him yet.'

'Reckon you can?'

'Yeah. I reckon. I lost a beauty back there in the fires. Thunder. Magnificent horse. Reckon some of the foals are his. So I'll settle on one of his colts.'

'Let me know if you have any spare. Could do with a couple of mares.'

'You got land?'

'A few acres.'

'Cool.' Tom wished he had a few of his own.

'Well, it's up the mountain slow and steady with this load on board.'

'Alpine Ash?'

'Some of it. Have to be careful these days just to take what's left without depleting the farm.'

'Thought that there would be heaps after the fires.'

'Yeah, but whose gunna let us take it out? What a waste.' Geoff shook his head quietly.

'Still. Could be worse. Looks as though there is a fair bit of regrowth.' Tom said brightly.

'That there is Tom.' Geoff pursed his lips, putting the truck into a very low gear, for the steep climb up the western flank of the mountain.

'Geez mate. Can't thank you enough.' Tom hopped out of the cab and slammed the door shut, his pack swinging onto his back at the same time.

'See you next time then Tom. Nice meeting you.' Geoff bipped the horn as he left Tom standing at the top of the village.

Tom looked for the stairs and made his way quickly towards the village. It was still early and a couple of stabs at breakfast sounded like a good idea, first in the village then later, at Eagle's Nest, to meet his 'contact', Thora.

Thora caught the first chair on the Kosciuszko Express to the top of the mountain then settled in for her first cappuccino for the morning at Eagle's Nest cafe. The mist rose from the valley in a thick veil, swirling lightly about the fractured rocks of the Ramshead Range. She looked idly through the large, single glazed windows of the restaurant, watching as the cloud vapour skidded from east to west. The front moving along the SE Coast sent moisture-bearing winds from the opposite direction, often bringing unprecedented falls of rain or, during the winter, 'wet snow' that would build cornices to breaking point. Now, the weather promised to be a classic summer morning, the cloud evaporating to reveal a perfectly clear, blue sky without the slightest whisper of wind. The fractured rocks emerged from the evaporative morning like tors of eternity; silent and solitary, bearing nothing on their surface other than the deep cracks and scars of their periglacial past. Even the crows were happy, first to laze along the valley floor, content with the morning pick of insects, and then with a sudden decision to form a flock, heading for the tors of the South Ramshead. From a distance, their cries — heralding the unfolding day — rang against the body of rocks, dying into strange echoes deep into the Leatherbarrel Creek Valley. It was a moment of mystical beauty, the mountains suspended in the womb of time, pregnant with promise.

'Hi Thora. What will it be today. The usual?' Paul approached his regular customer with his usual cheery grin.

'Hi Paul. Yes thanks. Might have a look at the menu first.'

'Sure. Nothing new though.'

'Yep.' Thora needed time to collect her thoughts. She had not expected to mount a climbing expedition at this time of year, far less take instructions to meet with a youngster who was more than likely still green about the gills. She grinned. Might as well give him a run for his money, try him out on the sheer tors, abseil him off one of myriad mini cliffs that formed the Ramsheads Range and see what he was made of. The crows would not mind today if their space was disturbed for a short period.

'Climbing today Thora?' Paul returned with the menu.

'Just an abseil. Taking someone out for a friend.'

'Oh?'

'Uh huh.' Thora remained non-committal.

'Half your luck. Beautiful day for it.' Paul smiled and retreated smoothly behind the bar, priming the coffee machine for the inevitable flow of walkers on a day like today.

'Thora flicked the menu over and wondered whether a brunch would be in order rather than her usual big brekky on climbing days. The list was simple, however always to her liking.

'Yeah Paul. That's the one.' Thora called to him as she punched a finger at the cheese melt.

'Coffee too?'

'Mm.' Thora nodded. Her thoughts drifted on the clouds down the valley, the rising warmth tantalising to her senses. The mass of cloud that had settled over Twin Valleys was beginning to disperse and uncover the peaceful vista stretching towards the lake. It was going to be a hot one today she thought. Still, better than climbing in the rain. Her problem was — and she knew all about it — that once she had set her sights on a goal, there would be little to deter her, not even the weather. A flurry of gang gangs passed beside the restaurant then flew down the creek line, cavorting and carolling on the delights of the morning updrafts. Thora knew how they felt, her spirits always higher when the mountains turned on one of their best days.

She pulled the maps out of her climbing pack and placed them on the table. Curiously, the more one studied the maps, the more information seemed to leap out from the neatly drawn contours, the well-marked ridges and occasionally, depending on the scale, shaded valleys and well described streams, lakes and rivers. It was the minute detail that interested her: the flow of rocks, the scatter of boulders, the moraines formed by ancient glaciers that became the hiding and nesting ground for a myriad of tiny alpine creatures. Some, like the pygmy possums, were too delicate to withstand the trampling of human beings on the well-trodden resort tracks, now the domain of the increasing population of mountain bikers. Thora was always glad that the less accessible boulder fields, semi-covered by alpine heaths, were sufficiently remote to deter most walkers. Winter was different. There was nowhere that she could not and would not explore on her solid, metal-edged skies. Equipped for the worst, Thora was always confident in her capacity to navigate in most conditions and return in reasonable safety to her base camp at the set time. This was no real challenge for her, a longish walk followed by a few technical high boulder problems and a relatively straightforward abseil.

The clatter of boots on the metal steps alerted Paul to more custom. He pursed his lips, running steam through the milk for Thora's coffee, then quickly turning off the jet as the milk reached just below boiling point. Paul was an artist at heart and coffee making was part of that. He thumped the metal jug on the bench to settle the froth then expertly poured her coffee, twirling the milk into a neat spiral on top of the cup. A light shake of chocolate powder and he was ready.

'Enjoy Thora. The rest is on the way.' Paul smiled catching Tom in his direct and unabashed gaze, as he climbed the last step into Eagle's Nest. Paul easily judged the mood and nature of his next customer and called him in. 'Hi there. Hungry?'

'Yeah. Thanks.' Tom grinned sheepishly.

'Table with a view?'

'I'm meeting someone actually.' Tom said almost reverently.

'Over here Paul.' Thora caught on fast.

'Right. Paul raised an eyebrow at Tom and walked him to the

table.'

Thora put out her hand. 'Thora.' She greeted Tom with sudden warmth, gauging his awkwardness, as if he had been lost in the wilderness for a month of Sundays. 'Breakfast smells good. You up for it?'

'Yeah. Thanks.' Tom sat down, bumping the table with his hip.

'Steady'. Thora caught her coffee cup in time.

'Sorry.' Tom dropped his head down as he sat down.

Paul tweaked the corner of his lip at Thora and silently gave Tom the menu.

'What you having?' Tom asked Thora shyly.

'Only the best, Tom.' Thora laughed at Paul.

'Same then thanks.' Tom looked up noticing the weathered strength, the easy humor and well-worn creases at the corners of Thora's eyes. 'Those maps of here?'

'Yes they are Tom.' Thora pulled the 1:25000 topographic and orthophoto map closer so that Tom could see as well. 'You got one of these? Angus mentioned you were fully equipped.' Thora was keen to suss Tom without wasting too much time. He was hardly a man, but Angus assured him this one was well on the way.

'Full set in me pack.' Tom offered proudly. 'Picked me gear up from the cache Sean organised at Dead Horse Gap.'

'Good.' Thora nodded quickly.

'Coffee Tom?' Paul called out from behind the counter.

'Yeah. Make it a strong one please.' Tom suddenly buoyed by the sense of a new adventure regained his cheek.

'Coming up. Seconds Thora?' Paul responded keeping his favourite customer well and truly in the loop.

'Thought you'd be offering me a schnapps by now Paul.' Thora shook her head and then buried herself in the detail of the map.

'Later maybe.'

'Yeah. Take you up on that one Paul.' Thora continued to pour over the contours. 'You know this area Tom?'

Tom wasn't sure how to respond. 'Not a lot.' He confessed.

Thora nodded continuing to study the Ramsheads. 'Reckon you can navigate your way through there in a whiteout?'

'Nope. Cass reckons the magnetics are all over the shop.'

'Right. That's the first thing that we will have to sort out then. Nav.' Thora said dryly.

Tom grinned and picked up his head as Paul approached with his coffee. 'Thanks. Nice spot you've got here Paul. You stay up here in winter?'

'No mate. Bit windy.' Paul said quietly. 'Won't even find the crows here then. The tin cladding makes a helluva racket in a gale.'

'Mm.' Tom said wistfully.

Paul smiled and looked at Thora, still tracing contours with her index finger.

'You're not, Thora, going to climb on that side.'

'Nope. Just wondering about the drop. This one will do I think.' Thora stabbed at the South Ramshead. 'Descend to the Leatherbarrel, but not all the way down. Undergrowth is better since the fires. Still it's not my idea of fun, clambering amongst the heath and boulders. Good way to break a leg.'

'Thanks for the warning.' Tom grinned, warming to his 'instructress'.

'You'd better believe it Tom. She'll insist you carry her out if she falls.' Paul turned his back on the map, preferring the infinitely more elegant occupation of window gazing. In his heart, he knew Thora would never fall, and if she did, it would be only to catch someone else, on their way down. This woman was tough, tougher than most of the men he had ever met. There was little that she had not attempted in this part of the world.

'Well Tom. Looks as though you'll be put to the test then.' Thora said with a smile in her voice. 'Hope you're up for it. Making camp tonight?'

'Yep. Drop the gear on the way through I suppose.'

'Got a spot picked out for you. Angus reckons he wants you where you have a good view.'

'Great. You coming too?' Tom said hopefully.

'Nope. You're on your own for this one.' Thora said firmly. 'Keep you posted though. Angus asked me to give you this.' Thora pulled the satellite phone from her pack.

'Cool.' Tom took the phone and turned it over. 'Bit heavy.'

'Better than anything else for now. Get you the rest of the gear later. Heard you like watching movies?'

'Christ. Didn't leave much out did they.'

'Who?' Thora pretended innocence.

'Sean and Angus.'

Thora said nothing and shrugged her shoulders.

'Oh well. Can't complain. Good company, good food and good movies on the way.' Tom grinned.

'Breakfast.' Paul placed 'the same' in front of Tom and Thora.

'That was good.' Tom was back to form after the feed.

'Good. Anything else, Thora?'

'That'll be fine thanks Paul. Might not see you tonight. Could be a bit later than you are here and wouldn't want to leave Tom out there without making sure he's safe from wolves, yetis and foxes!'

'Wolves?'

'Feral dogs mate.' Paul said openly.

'Up here?' Tom was incredulous.

'Yeah. Didn't you know that the dingoes are descended from the wolves? Then they breed with the feral domestic dogs. Nasty!'

'Ohh. Sounds like fun.' Tom looked as floored as he felt.

'That's true Paul but mostly below the tree line. I haven't seen any dogs or wolves or dingoes up here. Have you?'

'Nuh. Just teasing Thora. But brumbies yes and foxes yes.'

'Yetis?' Tom wrinkled his brow.

'Seen the footprints. Yes.' Thora said evenly.

'I thought this would be a picnic.'

'You could be the picnic mate.' Paul joked.

'No way!' Tom said soberly. He knew that the cafe owner was having a lend of him, nevertheless he was happy about the satellite phone that he would carefully stash in his backpack.

Thora stood up, folding and neatly packing the maps into her pack then walked to the counter to pay. 'Thanks Paul.'

'Anytime Thora. See you anon.'

'Yep. See you soon. Come on then Tom. We're off.' Thora strode out of Eagle's Nest and lithely ran down the metal stairway, through the sheltered opening of the building and into the warm sunlight. She turned quickly to the right, heading along the walkway adjusting her pack as she went. Tom followed quickly, sure that this was one lady who would take absolutely no nonsense. If Tom knew Angus and Sean, then Thora would be of the same mould, fast, furious and very competent! The promise of the climb was enticing and in a few paces, he was beside Thora on the walkway.

'How do you keep fit Tom?' Thora said practically.

'Chop wood. Chase brumbies. Work around the farm. The usual.'

'Good. You'll need your arms for this. You'll be roped into a belay but don't count on an easy run. You might need to do it on ice later on.'

'Right.' Tom had nothing further to say.

By mid-morning, Thora had Tom well and truly secured in the climbing harness and was already lowering him over the edge of the western face of the Southern Ramshead. The view to Victoria was as spectacular as usual and there was no sign of a new cold front approaching. They had a few good hours climbing up their sleeves, enough time to show Tom the ropes of the local terrain before setting up his camp. Thora was confident he could handle most of the immediately challenging climbs, however not sure how he would handle the isolation. He could be camped at least for a couple of months at middle earth before they had a fix on the expected insurgents. This abseil and the climb back up were too easy for her and she was sure that Tom was smart enough not to stuff it up with over enthusiasm. She fed the rope out slowly then gave Tom the signal to rappel to the next ledge. He deftly dropped down lightly pushing off the rock face before landing catlike on the grassy ledge.

'That was good Tom!' Thora yelled encouragingly.

'Too easy.' Tom shouted back. 'You coming down?'

'Not yet. I'll just be a minute.' She pulled out her phone and quickly speed dialled Angus.

'Yep it's me Thora.' Angus answered the call evenly.

'All in place Angus. He's a natural.' Thora said.

'Good. Take him through the course. Set him up. Drop in on him over the next few days. It will take us a bit longer on this piece of iced up metal before we're back in Hobart. I've got an appointment in Dubai Thora. Sean will be up the following week. Keep Tom happy. Whatever he wants for now. Over and out.'

Thora pocketed the phone and looked over the cliff. 'On way Tom.'

It was late in the evening by the time Thora had taken Tom 'through the ropes', challenging him to a variety of climbs, abseils, short walks and some navigation tests to determine whether he was fit for the job. He didn't waver for a second in his enthusiasm, keen to please her and keener still to score the DVDs promised by Sean.

By the time the sun began to touch Victoria with a deep pink, Tom was ready to camp. They had more than worked off 'breakfast' and Thora had anyway, made no mention of lunch. She did seem, Tom was happy to note, keen to get him set up and that could mean something like dinner before dark. The late evening stretched over the horizon and for a few moments, Tom was lost in the bliss of being on top of the country, of being able to see in all directions, unobstructed by trees, buildings or clouds.

'This tent is something else Thora. Could fit three of me.'

'Just one for now Tom. Use the space. Keep your pack in the outer vestibule, ready to go. Always.' She added.

'Bit military!' Tom attempted protest.

'This is your new job Tom. That's how we play it. You don't know when you might have to pack down your camp and move fast.'

'OK. I'll miss breaking in the horses though.' Tom decided not to joke with her.

'We know that. Charlie is good for you to be here for the time being. And besides, young Jake is shaping up as one of the best horse handlers in the district.'

'He's pretty rare yeah? Never seen anything like the way he handled Thunder that day.'

'I heard all about it. Angus caught me up with all your news.' Thora grinned.

The climbing had taken a light toll on his energy levels, however it did not seem to phase Thora's strength or presence of mind in the slightest. Within minutes, she had the site pegged and the tent half up before Tom had a chance to assist. Together, they pulled the tent taught and placed the fly over the top, securing the ropes to resist the strongest of the alpine winds.

'This one worked in the Antarctic Tom. It should work here.

Later on, we might find you a pod and perch you somewhere in the rocks. Could be a little more comfortable and it will have a proper floor.'

'Hmm! That could be interesting.' Tom felt as excited about a comfortable camp.

'Dinner?'

'What's on the menu?'

'Stir fry with rice. Semolina pudding to follow. All quick stuff that doesn't use too much fuel. Always soak your pasta and rice. Keep up your carbs.' Thora said efficiently. 'We're setting you up with a portaloo in the rocks. It will be invisible to most. We've organised a carry out so you don't have to think about that. Want to keep you discreet, and clean.' Thora suddenly switched topics. 'Tom. Don't use the phone unless you have to. It's encrypted and your calls are flagged as emergency or important only. Nothing OK? Not unless you have something to report.'

'Right.' Tom went quiet. 'What are we expecting?'

'Keep an eye on the southern and western approaches.' Thora fished into her pack. 'This is your routine surveillance program. Daily basis. Weekly basis.' Thora gave Tom the timetable.

Tom looked down the list of times, days and locations. 'That would keep a man busy.'

'Yep. Night surveillance?'

'Can do.'

'Alarm clock.' Thora handed Tom a wristwatch. 'Also GPS, internal magnetic compass, altitude. Internal light. You should be able to gauge your position when it's pitch black. This is the logbook. Detail on a daily basis please Tom.'

'Cool.' Tom whistled and grinned at Thora.

'Great. That's fixed then. Now dinner. Oh, and something for later.' She pulled out the first of the DVD's and a block of nut chocolate.

Thora picked herself off the rock dinner table and threw her pack across her shoulders. With a quick nod to Tom, she disappeared into the early evening, taking a different route back towards Eagle's Nest. The ground was luminous beneath the ascendant moon and there would be little effort in walking down to the village. The night was clean and the air sweet and cool. Her legs felt supple and despite her age, Thora knew that she had plenty of condition to take her into several more seasons of climbing and ski touring. She broke into a half jog, trotting confidently to the edge of the range, before dropping down towards the ski slopes. She made her way more carefully on the steeper ground, the grass slippery beneath the soles of her all-terrain lightweight boots. They were easy enough to climb in provided she was just scrambling and abseiling. She quickly passed the main slope adjacent to Kareela Hutte then glissaded lightly on her heels, jumping to break her speed from time to time. On skis, this would be no trouble, except that anyone careless enough to go too fast, could turn an ankle on the otherwise steep slopes leading to the village.

Half an hour later, Thora walked softly into the House of Ullr, keeping her eye on the big screen as she drifted towards the bar. There were already a loose collection of locals, drinking, casually watching the rap dance on the screen, chatting and some filtering through to the dining room. Thora blended in easily, arousing no attention, talking to the barman then taking her drink to a stool to join climbing friends who had been out near the western faces for a couple of days.

'Thora! Good day out?' Peter opened.

'Yeah. It was nice. Nice climbs. Nothing unexpected.'

'Good.' He nodded his head appreciatively.

'And your climbs went well?' Thora asked gently.

'Nothing to report Thora. All quiet.'

'That's what we want to hear Peter.'

Two weeks later, Thora would be ensconced at the Kosciuszko Chalet waiting for Sean to arrive and begin their extensive training program in the mountains; navigation, search and rescue, strategic ops.

Tom yawned luxuriously stretching his limbs in the sun as he lay on a broad rock platform casually dropped by an ancient glacier. It was over a week since Thora had delivered the DVD player. He hadn't expected anything so soon and was more than surprised when he received the call to collect the 'back pack' from Eagle's Nest. Curious, Tom arrived to Paul's ready friendship and the good food as he still remembered it. He wasn't anyway, against having a feed from time to time at someone else's expense. Paul had suggested to put what he wanted in his mouth and the expenses would be charged to 'Sean's account'. That suited Tom perfectly. Not that he was going to take advantage of the open house policy. He quickly became accustomed to his own company and preferred poking around quietly, exploring the mountains as he completed his daily and weekly routine surveillance program. When he fronted to the restaurant mid-morning, the smell of fresh scones was enough to sit him down for a bit of a chat with his new friend. Paul obliged, happy also for the company on a slow mid-week morning. Most of the Christmas and New Year holiday makers had bolted and there was an hiatus before the onslaught of the music festival, some of them, happily, booked for his venue.

'Here it is mate. For you. Courtesy of Sean.'

'Thanks. Tell you what is in it?'

'Feels heavy.' Paul said politely. 'Open it and see. Could be a can of worms for all anyone knows.'

'Great fishing up here then.' Tom replied dryly.

'Yep.' Paul sat down at the table while Tom fished into the pack and pulled out the laptop.

'This is what I've been waiting for. Got a solar generator to go with it by the look of it.'

'Nice.'

Tom pulled open the lid and automatically, the system began to tick over. 'Looks pretty neat yeah.' Tom reached further into the pack and pulled out the stash of DVDs.

'Might have to come and join you in the backcountry Tom.' Paul said wistfully.

'You think your girlfriend would mind?'

'She's cool. For a couple of nights that is.'

'Hey, no one sort of knows where I'm camped do they?'

'Thora didn't mention it. Bound to be a few people notice a tent. Nothing unusual this time of year though. So long as you don't set off any firecrackers mate.' Paul suddenly got up from the table and walked into the kitchen, returning with the plate of fresh and steaming scones.

'Tuck in Tom. There's plenty for four of you here.'

'Thanks Paul. Looks like a good DVD player.'

Paul walked to the counter and intercepted his customers with cool efficiency and perfect politeness. Before they had a chance to look around the restaurant, he expertly guided them to a corner table. They would be long engaged with the fabulous view. Paul returned to the counter, deliberately avoiding Tom.

Tom downplayed his new equipment as soon as he found the instructions typed onto a note on the desktop. Thora's cursory language left no room for imagination, yet the instructions were sufficient to set Tom on a different course altogether. The laptop was also a communications device with instructions to link to the International Space Station and the link to the SingSat.

'Jeez. Who needs binoculars when you've this stuff!' Tom thought to himself. Discreetly, he scrolled through the functions and found the weather station dial in using the satellite phone as a modem. Tom closed the laptop and dropped it carefully into his pack then set about sorting out the pile of scones. Having polished off enough for at least three of him, he decided that enough was enough and the rest could go back to camp with him for an afternoon snack. Making a light show of paying the bill to satisfy any curious and wandering eyes, Tom sauntered out of the restaurant and loped around the corner until he could cut across the side of the mountain. He knew a few points of entry into the mountainous and rocky area where he was able to eventually skirt around unnoticed and head back to his camp. There would be no-one out there today anyway, and those who were would simply see him as another walker, a little off the track maybe, more than likely looking for the way back to the main paths. At worst, they would find the tent, however most campers and walkers were respectful of other people's private spaces. Few were likely to look into his tent, far less search his belongings. Climbing gear constantly ready at the vestibule, Tom was to all intents and purposes a happy climber and camper doing his summer holiday thing.

Tom would remain deep undercover until June and no-one would notice. Thora assured him that Paul at Eagle's Nest would remain his point of contact for regular provisions and that he would not ask any unnecessary questions. By the time the weather changed, most of the Easter holiday visitors would have left the national park. Then, the only people wandering around off track would automatically be on Tom's list of possibly suspicious characters up to whatever they had in mind if the surveillance comms Angus reckoned on was true to form. It would be another few weeks before they were back in the country and Tom desperately wanted to see Sean, to catch up with the man with whom he had forged an uncommon and unbreakable bond. The Crucible of Ice

Climbing was always difficult in the first week after the coastal weather fronts assaulted the mountains. The snow was too wet, the overhangs building dangerously and quickly, ready at a moment's notice to fall as the sun quickly softened their structure. This would not be the time to attempt the Blue Lake climb. Thora decided to wait another week until the snow pack consolidated, the crystal formations settling and bonding with the more recent dry snow pack and the now solid base beneath the recent falls. It suited her to give Sean more time to acclimatise. Already they had met at the Chalet, Sean instantly captured by the quiet, light blue eyes of the climber who had taken up residence in the mountains.

'Sean?' She held out her hand warmly greeting her climbing buddy.

'Yes! You must be Thora?' Sean felt himself go numb inside. It was not so much the expectation of a tough training session, it was the impact of Thora's energy, her natural charisma and aura of compassion that caught him off guard. He felt himself choke slightly, the emotion suddenly erupting to the surface.

Thora had felt herself blush. It was a long time since she had responded so suddenly to a man. As soon as Sean walked into the Chalet, she knew that this was the person Angus described to her, the tough, wounded mercenary, who paradoxically, at the core of his being, was sensitive and vulnerable. Thora instantly judged him to have a soul. She walked confidently towards him, attempting to hide from others the impact of what she had seen.

'Come. Lunch is being served.' Thora smiled, her lips open and inviting, eyes creased with natural laughter.

Sean allowed himself to relax. Why not. Out here there was little to worry about. Might as well let her in, let her get to know him. He was curious too as to why Angus had chosen a woman to be his trainer and ultimately his climbing partner.

'So. Angus mentioned that you have plenty of climbing

experience.' Thora, though curious, said matter of factly.

'Oh?' Sean could not resist smiling back at her. He pulled a plate off the stack and walked towards the food warmers.

'Climbing in the Antarctica. That's a pretty hard act to follow!' Thora was half-amused, half-respectful.

'I had Angus with me. The better the company, the better I climb.' Sean said tactfully.

'Then I hope that I'm good company for you Sean.' Thora said.

Lunch was a quiet affair. Thora insisted that they eat inside to avoid the unwanted attention of crows, then continue with coffee outside after that.

Sean sat contentedly, squinting into the brilliant afternoon sunlight reflecting off the slope and glinting on skis as the last of the lunchtime crowd picked their way down the mountain towards the Kosciuszko Chalet. The rough stonework of the perimeter of the Chalet, hewn from the mountains decades before, was already warm, soaking up the long hours of sunlight in the bowl of Charlotte Pass. Today, the tiny resort was well protected from the searing winter winds and blizzards that crossed the mountains. Mostly, as the major storm fronts crossed from west to east, the mountains formed a mechanical barrier to stream-line and tunnel the wind speed and force, before dissipating their energy over the flat broad acres of the Monaro plains. Today was, by comparison, a textbook experience of captured warmth, sufficient to seep into the most scarred and wounded psyches. Sean looked carefully sideways to Thora; her mind was clearly elsewhere, exploring the skies for signs of approaching weather.

'We'll go tonight Sean.' She suddenly announced. 'Head out on sunset.'

'You sure? Night climbing.'

'Full moon.' Thora grinned. 'Nothing like it. Blue Lake is a beautiful crucible of ice during the full moon. The sky will be clear tonight. Nothing like you've ever seen before, not even in the Antarctica.'

At 4.30 p.m. Thora checked their gear and adjusted her climbing helmet to a firm fit. The helmet always accompanied her, even on ski trips, its weight and warmth a critical factor in comfort as well as safety. Sean followed suit, checking his boots, helmet, gloves, the over-gloves in the backpack, food, maps, compass, GPS and satellite phone. There would be no mistakes. With two ice axes apiece as well as unbreakable nylon harnesses, lens-reinforced climbing glasses and head torches, there would be no accidents. Thora had insisted that Sean change his boots for the Celeba plastic mountain boots. This was a different climate where wet snow could make the difference between life and death if they were stranded in the mountains, or if sudden weather forced them to bivvy rather than face an uncertain journey on skis. Thora knew the landscape well, yet it was on more than one occasion that even she found herself travelling in circles rather than traversing the side of a mountain or taking the direct route to the river for the home run to the Chalet. Mountain whiteouts were like that: disorienting, deceptive and dangerous. GPS navigation did not always work in a whiteout. Compass and maps were fine provided there was no local magnetic interference — but there often was.

Thora thumped the back of Sean's pack. Nothing rattled, nothing hung off the sides. She need not have worried; this man was clearly a veteran climber who did not make mistakes. Perhaps Angus had her cast as his 'trainer/partner' simply because she outranked him on service missions in the field. Sean had a good many runs on the board, however Thora had more international experience, especially in war zones and had won the equivalent of a row full of medals for her efforts. She instantly decided that she would not let on about her past successes to Sean. The man, for all his outer roughness and strength was, in her instant estimation, fragile on the inside.

'There won't be much in this department that I can teach you Sean. Except for the plastic boots, you have it sorted already.'

'You never know Thora.' Sean liked her. She did not have any of the rough manners of some of the women climbers that he had met and she had retained a distinct feminine charm that he found attractive. 'Anyone can slip up at any time in this game.'

'Often just the weather will do it Sean. It looks as though it will be a beautiful night tonight, though.' Already, Thora felt lulled by the ascending moon, the clear sky, and the soft sound of distant crows calling as they flew down the valley to the tree line.

'Well, I'm ready if you are?' Sean smiled openly.

'We'll skin up to the Pass then ski down to the river. There are stable snow bridges a little further upstream. Then it's an easy traverse and climb to the lip of the cirque.'

'Half an hour?'

'No, more like an hour and a half if you are feeling reasonably fit. There's no point in burning our energies before we start the climb. I decided not to camp out this time. Want us to develop our endurance and stamina, so the ski home should be good for that.'

'Midnight at the oasis?'

'Oasis of light, snow and ice!' Thora's eyes sparkled at the prospect.

It was less than half an hour before they had reached the top of Charlotte Pass. Thora efficiently removed the skins from her skis, stowing them into the side pocket of her pack. She waited for Sean to follow suit then pushed off through the remaining contorted snow gums, their trunks reflecting a silvery glow from the moon. She took a gentle line, testing Sean's skills with the telemark skis, before descending at speed to her usual snow bridge across the Snowy River. Sean stayed with her most of the way, choosing a longer traverse and kick turn for the final run down to the river. He arrived, slightly out of breath, cheeks shining with the glow of enjoyment and exertion.

'We're making good time Sean. Could only be another hour, at the most, at a steady climb. Stay behind me on the crossing. I know that this bridge is firm. We haven't had the loadings of snow, although it's pretty cold, so don't think about chancing it for now.'

'That's as I thought.'

'I saw you take it slowly on the last couple of turns. You sure that you're up for this?'

'New skis. More turnability than I'm used to.' Sean recovered his breath and composure.

'Bend more at your core to keep the weight on your back foot and ski. Keep your stance a little wider and you'll be fine. You don't need to finesse the turns too much in this terrain. If you need to and it feels safer, just use regular parallel turns.' Thora nodded and pushed off onto the snow-bridge quickly climbing a few metres before signalling for them to put on their climbing skins again.

Sean followed at a distance of a few metres, happy to fall into the rhythm established by Thora on the gradual climb towards the bowl of Blue Lake.

'What do you think Sean?' Thora was visibly elated by the vision of Blue Lake completely ice covered, bordered by impressive cliffs and topped by snow-covered mountains. The light had dropped yet the rising moon shone over the lake and glinted off the ice frozen onto the granite cliffs.

'Beautiful. You are right. No need to compare with the Antarctic. Magnificent in its own way.'

'Wait 'til you start climbing. You feel somehow transported. I can't really explain it Sean.' Thora attempted.

'No matter. I'll be the same. Where do we climb from?'

'We ski to the edge of the lake, or what you can see of the lake. It's pretty well and truly frozen over by the look of it.'

'Deep?'

'Very. Nice place for a swim in summer. But not so at any other time of the year. You want to lead off?' Thora offered.

'Prefer you did this time Thora.' Sean was unsure whether Thora was being charitable, whether she was saving her strength or whether she wanted to gauge his skiing abilities.

'No probs. See you at the bottom.' Thora sped off in a series of deft, swinging parallel turns. Sean followed, clumsily at first until he allowed the skis to run more freely, gently applying pressure on the back ski for each turn.

'That's looking better. Heaps.' Thora was free with compliments. 'Right. Skis on packs. We're climbing with them now so we have a fast exit at the top of the climb.'

Half way up the cliff Thora checked their pace. From this perspective, the moon was a glowing ball in the sky, illuminating the Amphitheatre of the Blue Lake and casting shadows from the prominent rocks. The steep walled granite cliffs plunged with ferocity into the cavern of the cirque, some buttresses exposed, some totally ice covered. There was the occasional slope surrendering to snow, the inclination and underlying grass cover gentler to the eye. Thora felt the magnetic pull on Sean. He could not contain himself, putting secure hand over hand with the ice axes, digging in the crampons sufficiently to hold onto the ice, gently on the thin ice, as if an unseen force were climbing through him. Thora observed in his final few metres the easy grace of the man, the surrender to the wall, the total lack of fear.

Sean paused just below Thora, resting on the tips of her Dartwin icefall crampons, the Quark ice axes providing the additional balance points. His pack nestled easily against his back and Sean felt at peace, suspended like a giant praying mantis against the ice wall. Thora picked up her right arm, swinging it openly above her, connecting with the ice and driving the axe into secure anchorage.

Suddenly the entire slab came away beneath her axe. She swung her weight into the cliff and to the left, throwing the right axe far above her and away from the slab. For a moment, she hung in the balance, then moved her left foot fractionally higher, again, kicking the crampon into the ice, carefully this time. She was off centre from Sean, but the slab extended across the face of the wall to directly above Sean balanced on his crampons and ice axes. Carefully, she selected an ice screw from her harness and began to work it into the ice. She felt the bite and turned the screw until she was sure it would hold a fall. Without hesitating she took a quickdraw from her harness and attached it before clipping the climbing rope. She eased her arms by shifting the position of her feet, front pointing the crampons more securely. In moments she placed the second ice screw and quickdraw and equalised both anchors with her cordelette. She clipped her safety lanyard and relaxed.

'Safe.' Thora attached her belay device to the same anchors. 'On belay, Sean. Climb when ready.'

'Climbing.' Sean's voice reverberated around the Amphitheatre of ice and granite. the sound amplified by the absolute stillness and silence of the night. The steady clink of his ice axes reminded him of the fantastic feeling of topping out in Antarctica. He climbed for three metres to the first anchor and adjusted his feet so both front points of the crampons bit into the ice. With his left hand he secured an ice axe and with the right, quickly unclipped the rope from the carabiner and started to wind out the screw from the ice. He clipped the icescrew to his harness then with a powerful stroke aimed his right ice axe high into the wall above him.

The rhythmic movement of his ice axes, the measured swinging of his legs and the easy progress past the second and third icescrews to the belay with Thora was an absolute joy to Sean. Nothing in the world felt better than this. He remembered for a fraction of a second, Thora's description of the beauty of 'The Crucible of Ice' that was Blue Lake especially now under the full moon.

'Climb on Sean.' Thora nodded as he reached her belay. 'You lead the next pitch.' She smiled and payed out the rope.

'Climbing.' Sean confidently front-pointed into the steep wall and continued two, three metres to the left and above Thora.

The crashing sound of ice hitting the wall below her, the thundering sound of Sean falling, could not have come at a worse time. Thora gritted her teeth, quickly swinging her left leg and driving the crampon in as far as she could into the ice to steel herself for the moment of impact.

It came with an intense jerk on the anchors. Sean fell to the full length of the belay, the fractured ice floating behind him. Suddenly the rope caught him. The anchors were solid. Thora was grateful for her habit of always belaying from the anchors and not her harness. Sean spun his body into the wall to find a point of purchase. He drove in his crampons, first the right foot then the left and then his right axe. He was positioned and balanced, the weight off the rope.

'Are you OK Thora?' This was no time to fall into the abyss that was the Crucible of Ice.

Thora gasped for breath, momentarily stunned by the speed of Sean's intense fall and the sudden weight on the anchors and her reflex actions to hold him on the Grigri. She calmed herself, surprised at how much she was affected, not physically, but emotionally. For a second, she thought that she had lost Sean. In an instant, -ever the professional — she recovered and readied herself for the remainder of the climb.

'Sean. You alright?' Thora yelled, her voice surprisingly reassuring.

'I'm fine Thora. Excellent belay.' Sean's voice echoed around the cliffs.

'Double anchors. Pity you didn't have one in above the belay!' Thora joked to ease the tension.

'Yep. Glad it wasn't you who fell Thora.'

Thora grinned. 'I don't fall. Are you ready?'

'Ready. The ice is more fragile than we thought?'

'Yes. We'll traverse left in a moment. Looks like a stronger line. Climb back to the belay then I'll lead the next pitch.'

'As good as done. Did you catch the view Thora?' Sean's musical voice calmed and soothed her.

'Yes. Beautiful.' Thora whispered more to herself. The moon lifted higher over the Crucible of Ice. The moment had not escaped Thora, the hidden meaning in the moonlight, the sudden tension on the rope connecting them inexorably, binding them close together.

The ski home was initially silent, Thora taking wider turns towards the river, waiting from time to time for Sean to catch her before the final hundred metres or so to the Snowy. This time, she walked rather than skied across the snow-bridge, each step with the skis cautious. Sean, surprised by her sudden care, followed judiciously, seeking out any cracks in the snow-bridge. Safely on the other side, he suddenly caught Thora's shoulder, kissing her softly on the cheek.

'Thanks. I mean it. It could have been my skin out there.'

Thora blushed, glad that the moonlight obscured her face from Sean's intimate gaze.

'You would have done it for me Sean.'

'Yes I would Thora.' Sean said emphatically. 'You're a great climber.'

Thora nodded and allowed the smile to form at the corners of her mouth. 'So are you Sean Keating. So are you. Lead on.' Thora nodded towards the tracks still visible in the moonlight from their earlier approach to the bridge over the Snowy River.

Thora followed Sean, surer of himself this time, on the final run home from the top of the pass as he executed perfect turns, carving the last section of the slope now glittering with hoarfrost under the radiant and star strung sky. She clattered up the steps of the chalet, her skis ensconced in the snow ready for an early departure in the morning. She was keen to test Sean again and build his confidence, strength, and stamina. She knew that there would be little to worry about with this man, it was more a case of closer familiarisation with the terrain.

'Sean? Coffee?'

'Yeah. Thanks Thora. Anythin' hot is good,' he said drawling out the Irish in him. 'Burnt up quite a few kilojoules this evening.'

'It was worth it.' Thora said quietly. 'Well worth it.'

THE KNOCK

'Angus speaking.' Angus put the phone to his ear, careful to mute his voice as he left the hotel.

'We have news for you Angus.' David Morris said quietly. 'We think that the Pakistani men spotted in the Southern Oceans are planning attacks on the power stations. Anything out your way?'

'Tom is out on the main range as we speak, keeping an eye out as it were.'

'Good. Nothing to report?' David sounded more anxious than his usual unruffled self.

'Nothing, David. Everything all right?'

'We know that there is something going on in your patch.'

'I see. Anything I should worry about?'

'Call Tom. See what he's found out from his end. My guess is they will access one of the disused tunnels.'

'Yes. I will call him.'

'Stay in touch Angus.' David suddenly sounded amused. 'We see that Sean had a little fall ice climbing under the full moon.'

Angus chuckled. 'All that experience in Antarctica won't make the ice at Blue Lake any the safer.'

'How is Thora?'

'Just as capable as Sean, if not more so. On Australian thin ice she is better than any of us will ever be.'

'Excellent. Make sure Tom does some more training with her. I heard that he was one of the best alpine skiers at his school. But he will need to get used to back country skis at the first sign of snow.'

'Copy that David.'

'Over and out Angus.'

'Over and out.' Angus signed off from the call with his senior officer.

MORNING GLORY

Tom had settled in for a quiet morning, but the unexpected call from Angus alerted him to activity expected on the main range.

'Yeah. It's me Angus. Tom.'

'Hello son. How are you doing?'

'Pretty quiet so far. Nothing much to report except a fox and a hare that spend most of their lives chasing one another.'

'Good tucker mate!' Angus suggested.

'More like a bit of company. Pretty isolated up here. There are a few day-skiers though.' Tom munched into a muesli bar.

'Right. Good view?'

'Magic!' Tom switched into the visual memories of the sunrises lighting the mountains in a soft pink, the rising of the delicate blue into the sky, the glistening of light on the crystals of ice formed under the clear overnight skies. 'Yeah. Pretty beautiful alright.'

'Good. Should make up for the lack of action then.'

'Well…'

'Got something for you son.' Angus said brightly.

'Cool.'

'A bit of activity on the warning system.'

'Oh?' Tom felt a little nervous in spite of himself. 'You've got the connections.' Tom tried it on.

'You got the laptop and satellite phone. Use them Tom. I need you to think for me now.'

'I already have. Looking good. Four-day forecast clear as.'

'That's better.'

'No sign of the weather coming in at all?' Angus double-checked.

'Nope. Nothing. Should still be a full moon and sky as clear as a bell.'

'That's what we want to hear. OK. Here's the plan.'

Tom left the middle camp early in the afternoon and skied directly towards the Snowy River by the fastest route. The snow was still hard-packed after the sheering winds of the last blizzard had ripped off the loose top layer and left a myriad of tiny wavelets as if part of a giant pavlova. He wanted to check out the best snow bridges on the river, the approach points to Blue Lake before making his way to the western fall. He would spend the rest of the afternoon, slowly climbing to the summit of Mt Twynam from where he would have the best view of most of the mountain range.

Already the sun lazed in the mid-sky sending warming rays onto his limbs and Tom stripped off a layer, stuffing the all-weather shell into his pack. He rolled up his sleeves and pushed off, skiing fast and skating on the slight rise before dropping into the short and steep slope to the river. There was no sound or movement of water. Good. He skated to a point where the river suddenly crashed through a deep and short valley — the falls. Tom watched carefully the line of the river, looking for shadows, or signs of the snow breaking through or being too thin to chance a crossing. He moved carefully past the boulders on a shoulder of the river, and tested the link from bank to bank. The snow held firm. Tom eased himself into the middle of the river. There was no telltale cracking or sudden sinking feeling or collapse into the icy water.

Yet something told him that he was not alone, that he was being, watched. Cautiously, Tom stopped mid-stream and looked upstream. How he had missed her earlier, he did not know.

'Oh!' Tom grinned automatically. He had not expected to find anyone here, let alone Cassandra.'

'Hello too.' Cassandra said softly. 'Long time no see stranger. You look pretty safe there.' She said with a broad grin.

'Thanks. You too!' Tom was not about to be upstaged.

'Yeah I am. Bit tricky sometimes though. Have to dig a bit beneath the snow to reach the river.'

'Why would you want to do that?' Tom admired her for no reason.

'Water sampling. Good to take samples all year around. Not just in the summer.'

'Right. What do you do with that then. Drink it?'

Cassandra laughed. 'Try some?' She held a test tube towards Tom.

'You first!'

'Well, might save this one for the test.' Cassandra capped and pocketed the test tube. 'Mind you, after doing a couple of seasons of this, I have completely changed my mind about supping on the Snowy.'

'Oh?'

'Mostly it happens in summer, however winter is getting worse. Lots of E coli.' Cassandra mused sadly.

'Haven't heard of it myself.' Tom said as if he knew all about it.

'Not surprising. There is, you might say, a virtual dearth of water sampling in the Snowies.'

'Dearth? That rhymes with bath doesn't it?' Tom looked more innocent than he felt. There was something about Cassandra that he desperately wanted to hold close to himself.

'If you are thinking about a bath, then after you!'

'Right. Where are you camped?'

'Where are you camped Tom?'

Tom taken completely by surprise, stammered 'I'm..I'm..Angus didn't tell you?'

'No. Need to know only on this one?' Cassandra said carefully.

'Shit.'

'No mate. That's what's in this river!' Cassandra burst out laughing.

Tom laughed with her, then watched slightly uncomfortably as Cassandra continued to giggle..

'Shit Cassandra!' Tom suddenly interrupted her.

'OK. Tell us.'

'Can't.' Tom was ready to clam up. Completely.

'Sensitive?' Cassandra looked at him, her head cocked to the side as she dipped another test tube into the water where she had created a hole.

'Nope! The information is though.' Tom blustered.

'OK. Well, we're evens then. Which way are you skiing?'

'Jesus. Women. You want to know everything.'

'Mmm. You asked first.' Cassandra reminded him gently.

'Spose.'

'Anyways. I'm heading for Kosi Chalet. You coming?'

'Can't today. Got something on my schedule.'

'Right. You look real busy. Did you bring your diary?'

'Jeezuz! Alright then. I'm heading back to Twynam. Satisfied?'

'Yeah. Bit late to camp if you don't have your gear with you. Where to then?'

'Maybe I should ski over to the Chalet if you reckon that's where the action is happening.' Tom conceded.

'Could be. Where would you stay?'

'Got some friends there.'

'Lucky you Tom. Anyone I know?' Cassandra pulled herself to her full height. She adjusted her backpack and kicked her boots into the skis. 'If you can't find anyone there, you'll find me in the den. Nice joint. Good fire. Looks as though you could use a feed. See ya!' Cassandra pushed off on her skis, setting a fair pace along the line of the river, towards the crossing near Charlotte Pass.

'Damn. Women!' Tom was completely, thrown by Cassandra. He felt disoriented, a bit dizzy. 'Shouldn't let that happen to me.'

Tom pushed over the river, took off his skis, and stuck them upright in the snow. He pulled the skins out of his pack and banged them onto the base of the skis. They looked well and evenly placed where Tom, had already figured, they would give him maximum purchase on the steepest hills. Half an hour later, breathing heavily, he allowed himself to swear, not at Cassandra, but at himself, for falling into the all-time trap all over again. She did seem pretty at home on the snow, capable on skis and clearly in her element. And his feelings towards her definitely had not changed.

The climb past Clark East Ridge, to the Soil Conservation Creek was exhilarating and mildly exhausting, yet Tom reckoned that he needed the exertion to shift the explosive reaction taking place inside of him. The last thing he expected was to be obsessed about Cassandra. Already, he could not stop thinking about her.

From the far side of the Creek, Tom had an easy view to the lip of the Blue Lake Cirque, the cliffs protruding into the skyline. The Lake was as magnetic and enchanting as anywhere on earth could be, however for now he was set on climbing behind the cliffs and up to Twynam. There was nothing better than watching a magnificent sunset, perched on one of the best mountains within reach. From there, he could pick out the campsite of the would-be's, whatever they were up to. It seemed not to matter. Tom whistled happily as he poled rhythmically, climbing where he wanted to be — the high plateau between Watson's Crags and Mt Twynam.

For half an hour, Tom sat on his padded cell mat, designed especially for short trips to insulate him when on obs. This time, he pulled out an extra jacket and quickly donned some overpants, zipping them to the high cuff of his mountaineering boots. This was going to be a long and cold one and there was no way that he was about to get exposure. There was no wind, however as soon as he stopped climbing, his core temperature nevertheless dropped sufficiently to warn him to cover up, to pull out his extra parka and the hood over a warm, knitted skullcap. Over-gloves, the pants and insulation between his butt and the snow completed his sense of comfort. Then food — wraps stuffed with cheese and sun-dried tomatoes, salami — a flask of hot coffee. Tom sipped quietly as he looked towards the west, from time to time picking up the binoculars.

The sun was already dipping well past the zenith towards the horizon, the first signs of pink touching the horizon. The temperature would plummet once the rays angled horizontally and the southern hemisphere time zone was occluded from the sun. Tom mentally plotted his course for a fast and effortless ski back to the Chalet. He waited another 20 minutes. The sun suddenly dropped in an explosion of red, the magnificent play of light briefly illuminating the western fall, its steep aretes, spurs and narrow valleys plunging into the darkness of the Geehi Valley. Tom knew that Cassandra's plan was the only one. He turned quickly, taking the gentle line towards Little Twynam, skirting around the fatal cliffs of Blue Lake then cutting across Hedley Tarn and back to the crossing on the Snowy. He would allow plenty of time to climb to the Pass and arrive, he reckoned in time for a good feed at The Kosciuszko Chalet. Thora would be there, somewhere, and if he knew her, she would sort him out for the night.

Exuberant at the magnificent sunset, the full moon now rising high over the valley, Tom skied down to the Chalet tucked amongst the cluster of lodges nestling at the base of the valley. The ski lifts were quiet, motionless. Nothing moved apart from a single worker on a skidoo returning to base. Tom could not believe the quiet beauty of the valley, the perfect shimmering of moonlight on the snow, the smoke curling from the chimneys, the welcoming ambience of the village. He let out a whoop and shot down the final slope past the twisted snow gums towards the heavy door of Kosciuszko Chalet.

'Gidday. I'm looking for Thora. Have you seen her? Tom announced as he walked up to the bar.

'Thora? She headed out this afternoon with her friend Sean for some ice climbing at Blue Lake. They should be back by now though.'

'Sean? Was he here?'

'Yup. And you are ..?'

'Tom. Me name's Tom.'

'Glad to meet you Tom. You look as if you've been out there yourself.'

'Yeah.' Tom was temporarily lost for words.

'Tom!' Cassandra walked up to the bar.

'Cassandra.' Tom blushed, taking her in for the second time, but now under the muted bar lights.

'You just got back?

'Yeah. Thought someone I know might be here.' Tom said defensively.

'Thora? She's here.' Cassandra grinned.

'You know her?'

'Course. Small world yeah. You must be hungry. Coming in for something to eat?'

'You bet. Hungry as!' Tom said enthusiastically.

'Come on then. Next door. Bistro's still pumping. Thanks Josh.' Cassandra turned to her mate behind the bar.

'You'd better tell me all about it now. Since I'm shouting. By the look of you, you didn't bring any brass with you let alone clobber for tonight.'

'Well…'

'Don't think about it. Chips?'

'Yep.' Tom chirped up. 'The lot thanks Cassie.'

'It's fine.'

Tom smiled. He finally felt a little more at ease with her, no longer completely overwhelmed by the effect she had on him. Still, she was like no other woman he had met before.

'Thora told me a little about the project. She's training Sean of course.'

'I didn't know…'

'Course not. Sean would not give anything away unless he had to. But he must trust you mate if you are on his A list.'

Tom smiled. He felt better already. This girl was good for his spirits, even if she was sharp as rime on granite.

'Sean will be surprised. He probably isn't expecting you to turn up.'

'Nope. Me base is…'

'That way!' Cassandra grinned. 'I know. Thora told me before they headed out for the climb. They think the world of you, you know.'

'Really?'

'Yep. Thora said you were a natural climber and Sean seemed to think that you had the situation under hand.'

'You'll have to come and visit my camp then.' Tom decided that she was a safe bet.

'Thanks. I'd like that Tom. Very much.' Cassandra touched the back of his hand lightly, her eyes warm and cheeks flushed with happiness. 'Budge along. We're nearly at the end of the queue and I'm famished!' Cassandra nudged him forwards, selecting for herself a pile of steamed vegetables and adding them to a fair serve of pasta.

'Tom!' Thora swung on her heel as Tom walked into the dining room. 'Cassandra! I didn't know you two...'

'We didn't. Tom said dryly. 'Cassandra was dipping her test tube into the river this morning and I was on way to Twynam.' Tom smiled and put his hand out to Thora.

'You came back here?' Thora did not attempt to conceal her surprise.

'Cassandra's idea.' Tom deflected her question.

'Hello Sean. Heard you were out moonlighting!' Tom said cheekily.

'Tom. Good to see you Tom. Hi Cass.'

'We all know one another of course.' Thora said simply.

'Mutual interests. Seem to be centring on the Snowy River at the moment.' Sean agreed.

'Yeah, Cassie is into water sampling and stuff.' Tom said proudly.

'Right. Cassandra anything new?' Sean stood up, offering her a seat at their table.

'Thanks Sean.' Cassandra smiled. 'Not a lot. Usual E coli. Dam wall looks as though it should easily manage the spring melt in a month or so.'

'Good. So, Tom, tell us all about it.' Sean grinned. 'I'm all ears.'

'Couldn't see you out there anywhere on the main range!' Tom said deflecting the attention back to Sean.

'Tom, we could have lost Sean last night.' Thora gently touched Sean on his arm.

'Oh? Thought you and Angus were indestructible.' Tom suppressed the surprising tears pricking the backs of his eyes.

'Antarctica is one thing but climbing here is not as much of a snack as I thought.' Sean smiled noticing Tom's sudden emotion. 'Anyway Tom, you can't get rid of us that easily.'

'Here's breakfast. Bacon and eggs Tom?' Thora offered.

THE KAC

The morning light was brighter than Sean expected. This was the day of the race and he wanted to quickly check out the landscape — people, things, spaces, built structures — before the first skiers arrived. He looked sideways at Thora, as he dumped his skis on the snow. He felt the sudden silence in his senses, their tuning to exact and minute differences in sounds, sights, pressure, temperature... Sean was built to survive and his senses were the first point through which information flowed allowing him maximum understanding of the circumstances. Any subtle changes could mean the difference between life and death.

He watched carefully as his quarry moved into the hotel. The man who Angus had described from the Polar Bird surveillance trip was right on cue. The question was, where was his friend?

Sean and Tom caught an early oversnow vehicle to Perisher to join in the race. At the start Sean observed everything and everyone. There was — so far — nothing unexpected, no-one who looked out of place.

Cassie headed out early to ski across the Guthrie Ridge and to the Snowy River. She was determined to capture images of the morning light on the river, where it was frozen, whether the dam remained frozen and how the dam wall was holding up after the earthquake.

Thora sat quietly, unmoving, unsure whether there was anything unusual, anyone out of place. She wanted to appear as she had been, relaxed, engaged in conversation in the sun with no other agendas. But her eyes moved quickly and quietly behind her sunglasses, flicking to either side, watching the slopes for any signs of people who did not seem to belong here. There were none. She relaxed. There was nothing to act on at the moment. She blended into the crowd, chatting to the assembly of race officials and people coming and going with an assortment of prizes into the Chalet.

They waited. The small orange flags marking the course waved in the gentle breeze and the finish line banners fluttered as the wind predictably picked up mid-morning.

'Here they come!' One of the race officials spotted the first classic skiers topping out on the Sugar Loaf before double poling down the long hill towards the Plains of Heaven. Suddenly there were more skiers and a mass of colourful cross-country skiers in the mostly social race "The KAC" surged forwards, the fastest and fittest breaking into long strides over the flats putting distance between themselves and the rest of the pack. The first of the skaters reached the top of the hill powering with longer poles towards the plain.

It was a glorious day, only a few clouds forming in the high atmosphere, the snow still firm from the overnight frost. Sean pushed hard to gain purchase with his lightly stepped skis. He opted against waxes to ensure maximum gain and purchase on the longer uphill sections to the Chalet. He knew that he could outrun most men his age, but made the judicious decision to use his strength rather than waste it fighting icy hills if his level of fitness proved insufficient. He was, happily, surprised that he was now in the first twenty men and women, keeping pace with the third level of good skiers. He arrived at the Chalet in good time, still within the first thirty racers in the pack. Already the skiers were lining up their lightweight skis on the outside wall of the Kosciuszko Chalet, collecting their daypacks dumped on the snow and pulling on warmer jackets before heading up to one of the lodges for hot soup. The parade of skis was a colourful and uplifting sight.

Sean grinned as he crossed the finish line, flicked a quick glance at Thora and shook his head, imperceptible to anyone apart from Thora. Thora waiting discreetly for him not ten metres away smiled, waiting for an appropriate moment of engagement. Then Tom crossed the line, only a minute behind Sean. Sean jammed his skis into the snow, then poles over the tips. He found his daypack and pulled on his jacket then accepted the drink Thora pushed into his hand, immediately moving away.

Sean swung around and saw Tom finish, Thora was already congratulating Tom and fussing over him like a child, finding him an energy bar and drink. He heard them laugh, Tom louder, clearly intoxicated with the race, the result and now, Thora's attentions.

'Come.' Thora pulled him at the elbow.

Thora steered Tom to the race marshall to return his race number, then led him towards the Chalet, careful not to make contact with Sean.

'Tom, we heard that we are expecting a bigger earthquake. The dam may go. US Geoscience called Angus this morning, after you and Sean left on the snowcat. There's been a series of quakes along the fault line.' Thora said quietly.

'No! Cassie's gone to the dam.'

'I thought she was just doing a photo shoot on the Snowy River' Thora felt ice cold in her chest.

'The crack. She said something about following up the crack she reported and that the maintenance people didn't seem to think it was a problem.'

'Can you call her?'

'I don't know.'

'But she's in danger. Now!' Tom tried to keep the panic from his voice.

'We know that Tom. Angus will find her.' Thora said evenly.

'We can't just wait here. I need to find her.'

Thora looked for Sean and made eye contact. She quickly raised a hand as if waving to someone in the distance. He caught the message. They would meet in five.

Sean moved quickly towards the race martial, mixing with the crowd and clapping as skiers crossed the line. 'Good race.' He slapped a skier on the back.

'Thank you. Do I know you?' The skier was surprised, and pleased, by the unexpected congratulations.

'Join me inside.'

'Thank you.'

'I think that one of your friends is here waiting for you.' Sean said carefully, warning the man that there were no secrets kept in the Kosciuszko Chalet.

EVACUATE

'Angus?'

'Yes Cassandra. It is me.'

'That crack looks much the same as last time, but I just don't feel good about it.'

'Well that's good news Cassandra. Heard the boys went for a bit of a run up from Perisher to Charlotte Pass today.'

'Yes. The KAC.'

'You didn't enter Cassandra.'

'Pure intuition Angus. I just don't feel easy about this. Something is clearly not right. My gut tells me so.'

'I think that you and your gut are pretty in tune with the Snowy, Cassandra.'

'I'll keep in touch. Thanks Angus.'

Tom put his skis on and quickly skated along the valley towards Spencers Creek. He fast-tracked down the Spencer's Creek-line almost to the level of the Snowy River. Abruptly he stopped with a spectacular carved telemark turn. He then took a line through the trees towards the Guthega Village and turned onto the skating track leading straight to the bottom ski tow. The small café was still half-filled with late lunchers oblivious to any imminent danger. Tom looked in through the window and recognised no one and nothing. Cassandra was nowhere to be seen. Not here. Tom skied past the café and towards the road, dumping his gear on the snow to ring Sean.

'Nothing mate. Not in the village.'

'OK. Tom listen. I want you to go in very carefully. Use your head and not your heart.'

'Right.'

'Take it steadily. Make it look as if you are just going for a short tour up to Tate. Cross the dam wall. Ring me and tell me exactly what the dam looks like.'

'Shit.'

'Yep. You got it.

'Where's Cassandra?'

'Angus will order her out as soon as he can make contact. She didn't know about the earthquakes when she went in. We hope she has gone from there already.'

'Good. Let's hope her sat phone is on.'

'Now listen. Your job is simply observation. Clear?'

'As crystal Sean.' Tom surprised himself at how sober he felt and sounded.

Sean broke off the connection with a click and Tom snapped into action, running with skis and stocks in hand towards the access road to the Guthega Dam.'

Cassandra walked leisurely across the dam wall, test tube in hand, from time to time, peering over the dam wall. Already, she had spotted a Snowy Hydro worker dressed in company gear. From the far side of the dam, the man saw Cassandra and walked straight towards her.

'What is he doing here?' Cassandra's thoughts whirred into action.

'What are you doing here?' The man asked coldly.

'The usual. Checking the dam for cracks. Checking for water pollution. Nothing new. Same same.'

'For cracks?'

'Yeah. Mind you. A dam of this strength is going nowhere. They tell me piles of geli are not good enough for some of these Snowy works. Amazing engineers.' Cassandra said calmly.

'You seem to know a lot about it.' The voice now hard.

'Well, you know how it can be. Spend long enough in an area and it becomes part of you. The environment does that to you.' Cassandra said brightly.

'You're right of course.' The man reddened suddenly.

'Do you want to help me?' Cassandra asked carefully.

'Actually, I was going to ask you the same.'

'Sure. I don't even know your name.'

'Anton.'

'Nice name. As in Charles Anton?'

The man grinned. 'I guess. But no relation of course.'

Cassandra smiled. 'There you go. Famous despite yourself.'

'I suppose.' Anton began to relax.

'Listen I sure could use a hand here. Need to obtain one final sample. Could you hold this one. I've got to get one from upstream from the dam.' Cassandra pointed towards the Snowy River.

'Oh?'

'Good to take the samples at several positions. Then you get a better picture. The water can become pretty dead if it lies at the bottom of a dam or lake for too long. This one worries me though. Lots of campers so you don't know what is going into the water.'

'As if you would notice it out here.' Anton was not comfortable. 'Look. I can help you. I need to ask a favour though.'

'Go on?' Cassandra attempted to sound interested, surprised.

He turned Cassandra away from the dam, pointing downstream, where the river was barely a trickle, devoid of its natural flow, at this point.

'I'm worried about the seepage through the dam wall.'

'Apparently no one else is concerned about it apart from me.'

'Well I am. I think you should leave. I'm worried that the whole thing will go.'

'Just one last sample.'

'Cassandra…'

'There's a lot at stake here. The Parks are doing nothing about water pollution.'

'I promise I'll help you get the testing done? But not now.'

'For real?' Cassandra stood up and looked the man straight in the eye.

'That's a promise.'

'OK then. I also came here to check on the dam wall. I'm worried' Cassandra moved to cap the test tube and place it back in her pack.

'Well I can tell you, you have a reason to be. Look. The man peered over the edge. The seepage has increased in the last twenty four hours. You have to go.'

Tom schussed down the narrow track to the dam wall. Against his better instincts, he skied straight to the snowed over wall, then stopped, realising that he had almost walked into a perfect trap. 'No way!'

'Tom!' Cassandra sounded the warning. Her voice was powerful and steady.

Tom stopped dead in his tracks.

'Cassandra!'

'We need to go. Looks as though the crack in the wall has opened up.

GAIA

Tom quickly raced through a series of options. Whether or not Cassandra would move quickly enough towards him, whether Angus had called her, whether Sean had organised a backup evacuation, whether she was warm enough. Tom pushed himself forwards. His body felt as though it were in incredibly slow motion, as much as he tried to move faster, he felt rooted to the moment, the horrible realisation that Cassandra was in greater danger than any of them. She could not exit quickly.

'Cassandra!' Tom yelled again. He turned back to Cassandra, the feeling of moving against a wall unable to reach Cassandra fast enough. Time was an agonising reality, the power in his legs, the force of will and effort unfolding excruciatingly slowly. He pushed harder breathing heavily, his shoulders tensed with exertion.

Then he heard the crack, the sound of the wall breaking, the first sign of water surging through the gaping hole. Tom looked back towards Guthega and saw Sean skiing towards him. He followed Tom, legs pumping fast, eyes focussed on the far shore, searching for Cassandra. In three long strides he reached Tom.

'Go high Tom. She'll be alright. Cassandra will climb up further along the creek. Move!' Sean screamed.

Tom burst into extra effort, breaking through the inertia. He suddenly felt powerful, skiing side by side with Sean.

Cassandra saw them, powering over the dam wall. The sound of the crack completely drowned out any thoughts towards her.

They would reach her in moments. Then she looked for Anton. But he had already left the dam minutes before Sean and Tom arrived and was running as fast as he could to Guthega to raise the alarm. The earth trembled and Cassandra felt her feet moving on the unstable ground. This was no explosion, this was the earth cracking beneath them, the tremor deep in the bowels of the fault line shooting down the valley along the line of the Snowy River. This was far worse than she knew was possible. Her sense that the tremor she felt at the campsite was just the first of a series to come, was spot on. Cassandra understood that there was only one option. She had seconds to scramble through the creek for higher ground, steps only ahead of Sean and Tom, both now almost on all fours, ditching their skis as they struggled to gain balance and purchase on the trembling ground.

'Cassandra, keep moving!' Sean yelled at her.

'Tom.'

'Keep moving' Tom ordered.

'Tom.' Sean commanded quietly. 'Son. I've twisted my ankle. Get Cassandra out of here. Keep moving.'

'Sean…'

'Get out of here Tom. Move it!' Sean yelled.

'Cassandra. It's Sean.'

'Come on soldier. You're coming up the hill. With us!' Cassandra flung Sean's arm over her shoulder.

Before Sean had time to shake her off, Tom grabbed the other arm, flinging it over his shoulder and physically forcing Sean to continue moving.

Sean ignored the pain. Despite the sharp stab of pain that took his breath away, he forced himself to partly put weight on the ankle. Cassandra was tiny, and Tom as strong as they came, would be determined no matter what, to drag him out by his hair if humanly possible.

The sudden roar as the dam broke stunned them into temporary immobility.

Tom half-turned to see the pondage surging through the hole now blasting apart under the force and weight of the water.

Stunned, Sean looked at Cassandra, her eyes shocked, at the same time amazed as the Snowy River exploded through the remnants of the dam wall.

ON THE MOUNTAIN

Sean did not waste time watching the dam burst, the water now surging over the steep fall into the riverbed below. The earth felt unstable and his gut feel was that they needed to climb higher, to climb out of the line where the collapsing soil, rock and concrete had sufficient power and pull to drag them under.

'Come on Tom. Cassandra. Up we go.' Sean tried to move himself. The pain in his right leg was indescribable, forcing him to draw in his breath.

Tom was first to move, sensing Sean's cool reasoning, his superb presence of mind in the unfolding disaster that had already loosened tonnes of rock and earth.

Cassandra was mystified, almost entranced by the vision of the Snowy River, liberated at last, the water tumbling, surging in an immense projectile into the narrow channel of the valley. She felt her heart almost leap — the release bringing her for a moment to her knees. Sean felt her fall, grabbing her around the waist and hauling her back to her feet. Then they were moving again, Tom leading, dragging Sean, now hobbling and leaning heavily on Cassandra who had suddenly grown in stature and strength.

'Sean, I'm not sure how far I can go.' Cassandra stopped suddenly out of breath and clearly mesmerised by the major changes taking place around them. Her intuition kicked into overdrive and Cassandra felt the urge to stay where they were, to observe, not to move, or run. 'We'll be safe here Sean.' Cassandra sat herself on the ground, loosening Sean from her supportive hold.

'OK. Just a little rest Cassandra.' Sean slumped on the ground next to her.

Tom remained on his feet, looking down the valley at the surging wave of water filling the gorge to the sides. 'God help anyone camped at Island Bend.' He said softly.

'Tom. Sit with us.' Cassandra asked quietly.

'OK. I just hope that your friends left their camp Cassandra.'

'Gaia has her methods of settling scores whether we like it or not Tom.'

'Sean, what do you think about this tremor?'

'I think that Cassandra's right. We can't be sure what's about to happen, whether or not anyone is safe or not, or where they are at this point in time.'

'Heaven forbid Sean.' Tom did not want to think the unthinkable. 'You don't think…'

'Tom. This is no normal earth movement, no simple earthquake.' Cassandra said emphatically.

'What do you mean by that!' Tom allowed his scepticism to surface.

'Think Tom.' Sean allowed his mind to briefly traverse the landscape.

'You tell me Sean.' Tom shook his head in disbelief.

'Remember the Earthquake. Macquarie Island.'

'Yeah, what of it.'

'Well before that,' Sean stopped to ponder the incredible, 'Before that Angus and I did a climb in the Antarctic we were looking into unusual seismic activity in the Southern Ocean.'

'Can't quite follow your drift there Sean.'

Sean laughed despite the situation. 'You're right there. We think that there were deliberate underwater explosions along the faultline.'

'No way Sean.' Tom's face said it all. He thought the idea was totally nuts. 'As if anyone would think of doing something like that.'

'That's what we thought at first. But now we are not so sure, especially with our friends at Kosciuszko Chalet.'

'Who are they Sean?' Cassie asked curiously.

'The same faces captured on satellite images on the fishing boat that the Polar Bird was following.'

'No way!' Tom said in semi-shock. 'You mean that's the reason you have had me in the high camp, Sean?'

'That's exactly the reason Tom. But these characters are cunning and they slipped through all our nets and turned up for the race day.'

'The KAC?' Cassie asked incredulously.

'We thought that the seismic activity was normal. But it looks as though the charges were planted at a distance along the faultline.'

'So here we are.' Cassandra said.

'Yes and it looks as though for now at least, we three are going to have to hang around here — for tonight anyway.' Sean remarked quietly.

'Well what do we do if the earth continues moves around us, under us?' Cassandra said suddenly.

'Well we won't be skiing anywhere tonight.' Sean said.

Tom pondered. 'Catch a horse and ride it back to the Chalet?'

Cassandra laughed, catching Tom's mood and teasing his irresistible urge to catch hold of her, to kiss her and stroke her hair, still alight in the late afternoon.

The sun dipped suddenly behind the mountain, turning Mt Tate into a broad and shadowy outline resting over the Snowy River Valley.

'Any other bright ideas Tom?' Cassandra said lightly.

'Listen you two.' Sean began. 'No time for idle chatter. We need to make a plan and move.'

'Yeah. You're right Sean.' Tom sprang to his feet. 'Thora? Where is she?'

'My hunch is that she's gone to Blue Lake.' Cassandra burst out.

'Why Blue Lake?'

'Can you make it Sean?' Cassandra let her concern show through.

'I think I can. Pity I didn't have my skis with me. It would be easier.'

'Tighten your boots mate. It will be a support for your ankle.'

'I reckon I can handle it. Project 'heal' into the ankle.' Sean laughed.

'Prefer you project 'fly to Blue Lake'.' Tom said.

'OK guys. We're out of here.'

Two hours later, they sat on the lip of the Blue Lake cirque their eyes now accustomed to the pale glow of the moon, the fleeting images in the mist rising off the lake. Then the darkness descended, drawing them into its surreal shelter, the moon still strong, lighting the main range in an ethereal glow. All the time that they struggled higher, away from the obvious fault lines, they knew that they would be further away from the danger. The fault line of the Snowy River was shearing apart, and they were not about to tumble back into the Sea of Gondwana with it.

Blue Lake glinted softly in the moonlight, the soft crusting of snow covering the hard, translucent ice in the bowl of the cirque. Thora was there, standing amongst the ice falls, tumbling and frozen waterfalls as they cascaded towards the flat plain, the frozen body of water. Already, Thora had carved in her mind a way up and over the cliffs to Mt Twynam. Sean drew in his breath, stunned by the vision of her, standing to her full stature, appearing like a vision of one of the Valkryies. Thora turned to look upward to Sean on top of the cirque, sensing his gaze, the magnetic pull of his feelings. Instinctively, she knew he was hurt. It was late. They needed to shelter now and she would have to move fast to get Sean to the campsite.

Tom walked around the base of the cliff, choosing to explore options that could lead them immediately towards shelter. If Sean were right, then there may be caves within the moraine at the base of the cliffs. He knew one thing and that was that Sean needed help. He was not badly injured, however now that they had stopped moving, he would need food, warmth and rest.

Suddenly Tom stopped as if confronted by a memory of the past. Walking into the centre of the lake, suspended in the ethereal mists was Thunder. The horse looked at Tom, his eyes a soft and dark brown, the black of his coat magnificent in its sheen, his mane and tale silvery in the moonlight.

'Thunder.' Tom whispered, completely awestruck.

'Tom!' Thora swung around to greet him.

'Sean. He needs help Thora. It's his ankle.'

'I know.' Thora said gently. 'Bring him down. Come over the cliff. There's a fixed abseil line and harness. He'll be safe on this one. The tent is on the far side of the lake.' Thora pointed to the western edge of the crucible.

'Will do Thora.' Tom laughed lightly. 'Did you see Thunder?'

'No. I didn't see him. Bring Cassandra down too. She can abseil by herself.'

The light of the moon cast soft shadows onto the cliffs of Blue Lake and penetrated the mist where Thunder stood waiting for Tom. Hours later, the dawn broke through the mist and Thunder was no longer there. Tom looked out of the tent hoping to see him. The horse was gone, descending once more into the deep Valley of the Snowy River, treading over timeless paths worn by his ancestors from ages before.

AFTER THE EARTHQUAKE

Tom reached into his sleeping bag and found his torch. He doubted whether he would need any more light than the moonlight now bathing the Crucible of Ice in a silvery sheen. The night was picture perfect; the clouds scattered and dispersed as the full moon rose high above the lip of the Snowy River Valley. The aftershocks from the earthquake still continued to rumble beneath them, threatening to force their tiny encampment — the scant shelter of the sled, two tents and the make-do snow cave that Thora constructed as extra space for their gear — secured at the base of the ice cliffs of Blue Lake.

Cassandra lay curled into her sleeping bag, knees tucked almost to her chin, her back curved towards him. At first Cassandra was faintly shy, curious at being thrown together with Tom as a matter of survival, wanting his warmth and yet unsure of whether to let him in closer. Then Tom began to stroke her face, his hands exploring her sensuous mouth he so longed to kiss. He pulled her closer so that he could feel her body through the sleeping bags and touched her hair. He caressed the back of her scalp feeling her breath against his mouth, surprised at her sudden passion as he explored her mouth with his fingers, his tongue and then with open lips, drinking in her kiss. He pushed the sleeping bag off his shoulders and legs and tugged at Cassandra's bag, pulling it off her shoulders. He kissed her again, feeling her breasts with his hands and pushing the sleeping bag off her thighs and knees. Cassandra kicked the bag away from her feet and curled her legs around Tom's.

'Cassie.' Tom breathed desire into her ear. 'Cassie, I want ...'

Cassandra felt for him, caressing his torso, his muscles tightening to her touch, her fingers massaged his stomach and she pulled his buttocks towards her. Tom felt his body respond to hers, his desire pushing him into her, the sweat forming in a trickle down his back. Cassandra opened herself to him, no longer letting anything come between them. It was time.

'Tom..' Cassie gasped.

'Cassie. I want you.' Tom murmured through their kisses. 'I want you now Cass.'

Cassandra relaxed, letting her feelings guide her judgement. Their longing for one another was mutual and too strong. They could not go back.

Even in the muted moonlight filtering through the semi-open tent-fly, her hair glittered as if the gods had blessed her with an otherworldly beauty. The sight of her sleeping beside him, her steady breathing, the little pool of moisture building against the inner wall of the tent as she breathed out, was as mesmerizing as the pull of the moon, forcing him awake and into the sitting position.

Then the sound of Thunder crying into the midnight sky broke the utter silence of the deep night. Impossible, yet unmistakable! It was Thunder.

The horse neighed again, this time his call echoing as if inside an amphitheater.

Quickly Tom pushed the sleeping bag off his legs and felt for his boots that were still sitting semi-frozen, in the tent porthole. The slight sound of his movement, the excitement tingling in his every nerve, woke Cassandra.

'Tom?' Cassandra called through her semi-dreaming. 'Tom. It's too early.'

'Shh. You'll wake the others.'

'What's happening Tom?' Cassandra pushed herself up bumping her head against the roof of the tent and dislodging the tiny droplets of moisture.

'Thunder! Can you hear him Cassie?' Tom could not contain his excitement. 'It's my horse that I released back into the wilderness.'

'Out here? It's winter Tom.'

'I know it's him. Listen.' Tom put a finger to her lips.

Thunder called again, this time whickering as if meeting an old friend.

'It can't be.'

'Sound travels on a night like this Cassie. I'd reckon he's well above the Blue Lake cliffs.'

'What are you doing Tom?' Cassandra abruptly pushed herself out of the sleeping bag.

'I'm going to Thunder. Coming?' Tom grinned.

'As if I wouldn't.' Cassandra pushed the curls away from her face, gathering her fleece closer to her slim body before feeling under her sleeping bag for her climbing pants and jacket.

'It's freezing out. You'll need everything Cassie.'

'OK. Balaclava, the lot! Christ it's cold!'

'Let's take the snow shoes, it'll be faster.'

'What about following Thunder?'

'The snow is still pretty hard.' Tom paused reflectively. 'I'd bet Thunder's got more than a second sense when it comes to choosing his track.'

'Why come out here Tom?' Cassandra still wondered whether she was dreaming.

'Must be a reason. I'd reckon he's found a mate.' Tom flashed his trademark grin towards Cassandra. He pulled open the tent flap for the woman of more than his wildest of dreams. 'You ready?'

'Yep. We should head for the saddle first. It's way too steep to climb here and I'm not sure about those cliffs.'

'That's what I reckoned. I think Thunder is high up on Twynam, Cassandra.'

'Hmm. We'll soon see. Hope your theory means that it's safe for us.

'Can't figure him Cassandra. Why would Thunder come out here? Middle of winter almost.' Tom continued as if he had not heard Cassandra's warning.

'Maybe the quake scared him, you know, drove him out of his territory. We don't know how far it stretches and which fault lines opened up.'

Tom paused and laughed softly. 'Romance?' He looked quietly at Cassandra.

'How did you figure that one Tom!' Cassandra blushed despite the cool air now pricking her skin like a million tiny needles.

'Here. Wrap this around …'

Cassandra shot Tom a grateful smile and quickly accepted his spare gortex outer-shell. 'That's better.' She smiled openly, her eyes alight under the southern sky; the moon was still brilliant, its rays touching her cheeks with a haunting glow.

'You look beautiful Cassandra.' Tom said soberly.

'Tom…'

Thunder's more urgent whickering broke the silence.

'Let's go.' Tom set his GPS to backtracking.

The light was magnificent yet Tom knew the mountains well enough to know that in a matter of an hour or less, the weather could dramatically change. Then they would be stranded by poor visibility, or at worst, a searing blizzard that could pin them between the savage western fall of the Kosciuszko massif and the steep descents into the cliffed glacial-cirques. There was no margin and Tom was the last to take a chance now that Cassandra was by his side.

'Yeah. It's looking good for now Tom.' Cassandra quickly slipped in behind Tom, following him step for step up into the moonlight and out of the Blue Lake Cirque.'

Tom checked his speech, conserving his breath and energy. He wanted desperately to see Thunder. The sight of the horse always set his heart pounding, and now was no exception, the image of the stallion clearly etched into his dreams and waking memories. He drew his breath in sharply. The air was chilling to his throat and lungs, cooling the fire burning and tingling in his every nerve. The horse awakened Tom to himself. Recollections of the bushfire and Thunder's flight into the wilderness in search of his mares seared through Tom's mind as powerfully as the fires had raced across the earth scorching everything in their path. Now, Thunder was surrounded by the majesty of the mountains where tiny crystals of ice glittered on the snow reflecting the moonstruck and star-studded night sky.

Tom and Cassandra climbed steadily behind the ice-covered cliffs of the Blue Lake Cirque, working their way carefully along the deep gully between the greater Mt Twynam and Little Twynam. Tom allowed Cassandra to take the lead, understanding and accepting her intuitive feel for the landscape, her almost minute adjustments that kept them away from the steeper sections of Mt Twynam as they headed towards the saddle that would thrust them suddenly into the Geehi Valley. Their regular breathing and the crunch of the snowshoes on the frosted surface consumed them in a soundscape that reverberated and echoed against the myriad of invisible walls created by the frost hanging in the night air.

'Not much further Tom. I think that we should at least reach the saddle then look for Thunder.'

'Good idea Cassie. I think that he would be on the summit though, by the sound of him. Spooky yeah?'

'If you say so Tom. You know him.'

Tom's soul was connected to the horse and Cassandra knew that his horse had returned to him in this land that was long traversed by horses when it was a world only of myths; that was long before they became legends, when the horses were transparent like ghosts from another time, and wild rivers thundered through magnificent mountain gorges on moonlit nights such as this. Tom felt now as immortal as the moonlight, as eternal as Ancient Gondwana and as ethereal as the haunting cry of Thunder resonating into the deepening night.

Thunder stood atop Mount Twynam, his flanks shuddering with expectation and his ears twitching forwards anticipating her arrival. His hooves thundered like the trembling of an aftershock, sending vibrations of hope to his mare Midnight as she carefully completed her ascent from the banks of the Snowy River below Guthega. At first, Midnight had screamed with fear as the shaking of the earth beneath her terrified her every nerve but instinct drove her higher, away from the deep rift that formed in the valley where she had sheltered the previous day. Here, the snow was still firm beneath her dark and neat hooves. The water suddenly thundering along the river had frightened her into a strenuous climb as the earthquake bore its full power along the valley floor.

Midnight felt surer on her feet on the rocky and often icy terrain of the lower slopes. On the mountain tops she was now out of her domain, yet she was glad to be free, glad to be away from the herd and the unwanted interest of the young colts that did not inspire anything in her apart from rage. For months she had enjoyed her privacy and the quietness of the mountains, the gentle lullaby of the alpine streams, the scent of wild heath and herbs in spring, the rejoicing of the earth as the sun rose higher in the sky. And as the days became longer, she was lulled by the rising eddies of air scented by the wildflowers and fresh leaves shooting on the snowy gums.

Autumn came, then winter, forcing Midnight away from her familiar territory, towards the gentle valley of the lower Eucumbene River, before it lost itself in Jindabyne Dam. She sought the shelter of the snow gums, her midnight black flanks stark against their slender white trunks, barriers to eager eyes and ropes searching for her capture. Midnight was alone in her world filled with the symphony of birds and the sound of the river pounding over polished rocks during the spring.

Then, she had heard him. After the earth shook beneath her hooves, after she fled into the darkness of a winter night too young to be lit by the rising full moon, she heard his cry. The wild neighing, the echo of Thunder in the hills and in her heart, sent Midnight into a plunging canter along the line of the Snowy River until she reached the broken waste of the dam wall, bits of concrete sticking out at impossible angles from the bed of the river. She heard his cry high on the mountain tops, even though she could not see, not yet. Midnight sensed in her flanks the presence of Thunder. She felt him draw her upwards, towards the ascending moon that now sat like a Sentinel over the rounded crest of the highest mountains near Kosciuszko. The stallion was to be her mate. He was the one guiding her away from the men with the ropes and metal yards, away from the earth that still shuddered with aftershocks from the earthquake.

Thunder called again, this time sure that Midnight would hear him clearly and come to him. He had not known a mare like her, ever, yet through instinct, he had found her. Thunder saw Midnight clearly in his mind, her beautiful and glossy black coat bright against the snow, her mane flying in the wind and tail held high like a flag of freedom. He wanted her. He wanted Midnight more than any of the mares that he had corralled into his territory near

Tom Groggin. Midnight heard him. She heard his call and Thunder stamped his hooves, dropping his head to the snow, snorting and throwing his mane to the moonlight, then rising on his hind legs and screaming for her to come to him. His front hooves pounded against the frosty air and again plunged onto the snow. Thunder was jubilant and ablaze with freedom as the moon ascended to its full height, lighting Mount Twynam in an eerie glow, and his mare climbed towards him.

Suddenly, he stopped; ears pressed forwards, attuned to a familiar scent. It was Tom. Thunder whickered softly, this time, urging Tom closer before Midnight reached them.

'Tom, that's him!' Cassandra heard the whicker first.

'Thunder!' The joy sprang from Tom's throat into his heart and he almost broke into a run, passing Cassandra, his neck arched and eyes searching the night, mouth open with happiness as he drank in the moonlight. 'Thunder. Is that you boy?' Tom surged forwards. 'Steady boy. Thunder, it's me. Tom.' Tom stopped, his chest heaving as he attempted to catch his breath, his heart pounding against his ribcage. 'Thunder. You came back!' Tom whispered.

'Tom, wait. It's a mare. She's coming up behind us. Move away!' Cassandra spoke urgently, breaking into a run to the left of the horse. 'Come on Tom. Move. Now!' Cassandra put her head down and ran as fast and far away from Thunder as she could. Let's go back to the camp. Come on Tom!' She tore her man away from his horse moments before Midnight reached the col below the summit of Mt Twynam.

Already Thunder had changed from the gentle friend Tom had known him as, into a wild and dangerous stallion pawing the ground as the scent of his mare became more pungent on the winter air

Tom ran quickly and carefully following Cassandra as she fled towards the far north end of the Blue Lake Cirque. He realised that his horse was too wild to ever become his. The mares — especially this mare — called him and Thunder would risk every bone in his body to protect them. He tried to push the horse out of his mind and focus on running, running carefully, placing one snowshoe after the other, making sure the aluminium crampons bit firmly into the firm snow as they made their way down to the Lake.

Months passed and the people of the Snowy River gradually adjusted to the new order. The paddlers delighted in a continual free run on the Snowy River now that the Guthega Dam no longer impounded the river. The bird and animal life returned to the river downstream of the Island Bend Dam Wall as the great river spilled more frequently into the once dry riverbed below.

Cassandra returned to the Island Bend camping ground amazed at how quickly the land regenerated after the great flood. Debris still littered the old landing field and from time to time she would pick up a piece of broken concrete to remind herself how lucky she was — how lucky she and Tom and Sean were — on that fateful afternoon when the river ran through the middle of the Guthega Dam Wall.

As the subalpine spring colours gave way to the olive greens of summer and the alpine wildflowers burst onto the mountain stage, Cassandra prepared herself for a summer of walking and climbing. It was too long until she and Tom could spend the months alone that they craved. So she worked in a range of local jobs including at the Dalgety Pub to keep herself busy.

Tom returned to the farm with Angus and Sean. There was plenty of work in the district crutching and shearing sheep and Sean made sure that he put his hand to as many trades as practically possible. Tom and Brindabella entered a middle distance endurance race and did well. The colt matured into a strong stallion and Malcolm reminded Tom that in good time, he must breed from the horse. Later in the summer, Tom knew he must return to the High Country — to the middle earth campsites — to continue with the surveillance work that Angus, Sean and Thora had entrusted to him. He waited in anticipation for the seasons to turn when he and Cassandra could spend the long evenings alone amongst the rocky peaks and granite tors.

THE RECKONING

'Cassandra?' Angus waited for the phone to answer.

'Angus!' Nice to hear from you 'How's Sean doing?'

'We're both doing fine thanks Cassie. I have a special job for you.'

'Oh?'

'Nothing to do with the Snowy River this time.'

'Then it would have to be very special to get my interest Angus.'

'Special guest you could say.'

'Who?'

'Friend of a friend. Remember Dariyan at the Jillamatong Races?'

'Sure do. He wanted Brindabella.'

'Well one of his distant cousins you might say — a Prince needs a guide to the Summit.'

'A Prince? Wouldn't that be more your line of work, Angus.'

'Not really sunshine. He wants a guide and I reckon someone who is "in tune" with the mountains would work wonders for his soul.'

'You've got be joking Angus. What am I going to say to a Saudi Prince?'

'Talk about the Snowy River if you like.'

'Right. Are they interested in buying the water?'

'Not this mob. But I reckon he might be interested in buying some horses at some time, you know, one's like Brindabella.' Angus joked.

Ricardo Corvini adjusted the thinly woven tan leather belt looped carefully through his moleskin trousers. He looked at his Rolex wristwatch and checked for the fourth time in the last five minutes, how long he had been stationed in the crevasse. He had always revelled in being in the European mountains, mostly during the winter, honing his ice climbing skills on the east face of the Piz Badile as often as time, romance and travel allowed. Now, there was only a single thought in his mind. He wasn't unhappy that this new assignment was in the Snowy Mountains in Australia. Mountains anywhere across the world drew him like a magnet and even though these mountains could hardly be described as anything more than 'hills', they held a certain magic. He waited in the rocky tors above the Kosciuszko walkway for the return of the small group of people walking back from Mt Kosciuszko. He estimated that they would be below him within 12 minutes.

Corvini pulled a silk cloth from the top pocket of his light blue shirt and wiped the telescopic lens clean of tiny flecks of dust. He reached into his trouser pocket for his handkerchief and dusted the imaginary debris from his sturdy leather Scarpa boots. Again, he flicked a glance at his wristwatch then cradled the rifle in his right arm, the left forefinger resting gently against the trigger as he sighted along the metal walkway, now abandoned apart from one or two small groups. A reliable source had informed him that this guide was always on time.

Corvini chose the late afternoon for his operation, to make the most of the gentler light where the sun would not create problems sighting the target by reflecting a tell tale glint of light on metal. He pulled deeper into the shadow of the crevasse. But he knew that he could count on the absence of people in the mountains at this time of year both for cover and to enable his quiet exit from the scene. To be exposed would be fatal. He reached into his pack for the packet of mint gum and placed two pieces into his mouth welcoming the fresh taste,

The walking party was minutes away and he needed to be fully relaxed, sure and steady. His aim was perfect, ninety nine points out of a hundred and on a calm afternoon, where there was hardly a whisper of air in the high peaks, he only needed to adjust the sights for the height and distance of the trajectory. He had one shot and one shot only. Corvini was a dead shot. The fact mildly disturbed him because this was neither sport nor game. This was assassination clear and sure.

The girl came into view at the crest of the last hill as the path descended gradually past the rock tors before crossing the creek and winding to the top of the chairlift. Corvini sighted the purpose-built high powered rifle, shifting his position, tracing the movement of the group down the broad metal stairs. He waited, breathing in and out regularly, softly chewing the gum then spitting it quietly onto the rock. Again he sighted the rifle, this time, keeping the cross-hairs positioned on the target, allowing himself to follow each moment, each second of their progress. He let his left forefinger tighten automatically on the trigger.

The group was in clear range and Corvini knew that he could shoot at any time. He waited another ten seconds, counting down slowly and surely. He breathed in deeply, holding his position without breathing out and sighted to shoot. Corvini's finger tightened reflexly on the trigger as his mind issued the command to kill.

Cassandra paused for a moment to read the interpretive sign and point out to the Saudi Prince and his bodyguard the remnant moraine field, now covered by heath and dotted with the last of the summer wildflowers. The walk had been pleasant and Cassandra was happy to cruise the rest of the trip, pointing out the best features of the ancient landscape, the wealth of natural biodiversity now protected thanks to a legacy of conservation. For a second she paused, looking at a flock of ravens heading towards them. One of the bright eyed birds flew straight towards her. Cassandra dropped onto a knee, unsurprised that the bird nearly touched her head with its wing. The ravens were her friends and she knew them individually almost as well as many of them knew her.

The bodyguard dropped onto the grass as the bullet shattered the right lens of his sunglasses before grazing the side of his nose, the impact throwing him sideways onto the ground. Suddenly, the walkway erupted into a major commotion as the Cassandra knelt beside the man. In an instant, she whipped the first aid kit from her pack then the 'smart' satellite phone from her pocket, simultaneously ripping open a gauze bandage with her teeth and free hand as she speed-dialled Tom.

The Prince's yelled 'What happened?' He stepped astride his prostrate bodyguard.

'Take my glasses.' Cassandra commanded.

The Prince yanked the field glasses from around her neck and searched vainly in a 180 degree arc for the source of the bullet.

Corvini retreated carefully backwards, quickly dismantling his high-powered rifle before concealing it in the purpose made pouch in his backpack. He pulled his buff over his mouth and pulled the hood on his shell jacket over his head. There would be no distinguishing features from any satellite imagery of the scene. Quickly he climbed the short distance through the tor and struck out at a fast trot towards the ridge-line that would take him to the rocky buttress of the Ramshead. He knew exactly where he was and how to move fast to the best vantage point.

'Tom. There's been an accident. Cassandra spoke quickly and

calmly taking off the bodyguard's glasses as she covered the wound with the thick gauze pad.

'Where are you?' Tom barked.

'Just behind the bridge near Eagle's Nest.'

'I'm on my way Cassandra. Don't move.'

Tom flicked his phone to 'search' and dialled Sean.

'Tom.'

'Emergency. Sean, there's been a shooting on the walkway — with Cass.'

'Copy that. You need to go after the problem Tom.

'Will do.'

'Angus will organise a rescue on way Tom. Stay in touch.'

'On my way Sean.' Tom shut the phone off.

Tom reached for his emergency overnight pack already meticulously packed with high energy food and fluids, first aid kit, GPS watch, Iridium Satellite phone, maps, compass and super lightweight bivvy bag. He stuffed in his waterproof shell jacket and overpants, two spare pairs of socks and the high tech military field glasses — a gift from Sean. Last, he reached for the light weight 60 metre 8 mm rope and abseiling glove — a handful of slings and four or five abseiling rings. It was going to be a fast and furious trip if Tom was going to track and capture the killer. In Sean's estimation Tom had less than half an hour and it would be all over. By then the killer would be under the cover of thick vegetation and it would be impossible for any of the heat-sensor equipped helicopters to find him. Even with night vision goggles there would be little chance of detection so it would literally be a race to the site and an educated guess by Tom as to the origin of the bullet and exit plan of the killer.

Within moments, Tom was moving out of the hidden campsite. He dialled Cassandra.

'I'm on the move Cassie.'

'Thank goodness Tom.'

'What happened?'

'Too fast to tell. All I heard was a raven shrieking then the man fell at my feet.'

'I can't come to you now Cassandra. Sean wants me to go after him.'

'Are you crazy? He's armed.'

'I know Cass. I have to do it. We need to get a fix on the problem. Sean will set up the roadblocks. Check out whether he has stashed a vehicle somewhere. We don't know which way he'll come out of the mountains. My reckoning is he won't be travelling down the chairlift.'

'Shit.'

'I'm ready for overnights.'

'Tom. Look after yourself.' Cassandra fought back the tears.

'Be strong Cass. I reckon your crows will look after me.' Tom grinned to himself.

'Ravens Tom.' Cassandra managed a smile in her voice. 'Do you think…'

'I don't know Cass. I don't want to think about that. Rescue chopper is on way. They'll airlift him out. They'll send in a second chopper to search for the shooter. But I reckon this guy has the running shoes on and once he hits the tree line it won't be easy for anyone to find him, not on foot or from the air.'

'OK Tom. I'd better go. The Prince is looking pretty distraught. We need to evac him with his bodyguard.'

'Understandable. Over and out.' Tom flicked off the phone.

Tom took a few deep breaths. He made a mental note to call Cassie, whether or not he was still in pursuit of the assassin or back at base, debriefing with Sean. From the bottom of his heart he wanted to be home, not so much for himself, but for Cassandra. The shock of the assassination had not taken hold yet he knew her and it was only a matter of hours before the she would feel the full impact of the death — and on her watch.

'Well that's pointless Tom.' He admonished himself. Cassandra would not have had any reason to imagine that one of her clients was the target of a deliberate murder. Tom felt mildly disturbed, not because the man was sufficiently high profile to be disliked by someone, somewhere in the world; it was because he had a nagging feeling in the back of his mind that neither the bodyguard or the prince was the target. He pushed the thought away; however it continued to return to him as surely as the shrieking warning of the raven was Cassie's main recollection of events. Tom pushed himself off the chair as quickly as gravity and common sense would allow. He headed past the tin building, pulling the waistband of his pack tight and adjusting the field glasses around his neck so that they would be all but motionless as he jogged. Quickly he assessed the immediate terrain and chose to take the main path for a hundred metres before shortcutting along the Dead Horse Gap track and striking upwards to the high Ramsheads plateaus. He would use a combination of intuition and knowledge of the landscape to predict the escape route of the shooter.

Tom was no slouch when it came to cross country running, yet even so he knew that this was a deadly race against time and the skill of a man who no doubt had a watertight exit strategy. The deal would be to position himself as if he were the man he now pursued. Twenty minutes ago he shot someone. He would need to move quickly and the most likely point of exit would be Dead Horse Gap. That would take at least half an hour from his position in the rocks from where he must have shot the bodyguard. By then, there would be police all over the area with road closures on the Alpine Way. No one in their right mind would move to a known position where they could be easily found. It would be smarter by far to head deeper into the mountains and descend towards the Geehi. That could mean days. How long would the police keep the road blocks in place? How long could he expect to avoid detection in the bush?

There must be another way out.

He could, instead, move fast and make good his escape under the full vision of his pursuers. Disguise! Merge and mingle. The only reasonable route on that front would still be to drop over to the Geehi but then take his chances on the Alpine Way.

Tom struck along the marked route marking time until he made his move into the Ramsheads. It was his judgement call that this would mean capture or escape for the assassin. His own instinct for his survival clearly indicated to him that he would strike a difficult path towards a point where he could continue easily. Immediately Tom turned inwards, almost running along the pathways that he had explored again and again, free from the troubles of needing to be home by a certain time, he knew now that his wild nature and knowledge of the mountain would serve him well. The mountains suited him, in all weathers. This was not going to be any picnic, but the weather was, so far, on his side. Later, he would download the latest satellite radar and cloud images onto his phone. The forecast was still mild with no hint of the strengthening westerly winds that often foretold approaching cold fronts blowing all the way from the Western Australian coast to the Great Dividing Range. Tom decided that he would stop even only for seconds, to drink as often as possible from the fens and streams as there would be no guarantees of water later on if his man were taking the route that he, Tom, would take.

Already he had decided to be extra careful. He could not afford to slip on a rock or run too fast downhill. He adjusted his pace, making fast progress on the uphill sections and moderating on the level or downhill sections. He set a route straight towards the upper bowl of the Leatherbarrel. For a moment, he considered running down the steep side of the bowl and along the course of the Leatherbarrel Creek. The going would be rough and treacherous. Then by instinct he stopped and waited.

Suddenly a single raven wheeled across the rock buttress, turning its eye for a second towards Tom then cawing, before flying straight to the buttress of The Ramshead high above him. Tom followed the flight of the raven then turned and ran towards The Ramshead, taking in the line of rocks on the north-west buttress that would lead him to the summit.

Ricardo Corvini checked his watch again. Half an hour ago, he had removed the silencer and telescopic lens and had dismantled the carefully designed and specially manufactured rifle into his backpack. He still had enough ammunition to survive easily in the bush for a month, killing at least one small beast a day, whether a rabbit or bird, perhaps a possum or small wallaby. But he did not want to leave signs, a trail of carnage that could easily be followed. His plan was to abandon the rifle and ammunition deep in the wilderness where there would only be wombats and foxes — and even then there were many crevasses in the rocks where not even the birds would nest. He planned to leave now with the possible complication of overnighting along the Swampy Plains River or ridge adjacent to the highway, the most easily traversed country that had delivered him to his hiding place. Now, he seriously had to consider staying off the tracks during the day and travelling mostly by night where detection would be possible only with sophisticated night vision lenses. Corvini was sufficiently experienced to realise that the police would not have the capability to track and capture him. If it were only a matter of the girl, then it would be left to the police to find her killer. However in the millisecond that the raven entered the field of view, the bullet that was meant for her had found instead, the Saudi man. The diplomatic fallout would almost certainly bring special forces hunters onto his tail, tracking him to kingdom come. He needed to get out of the country and fast.

Corvini had a sixth sense and he knew he was already being followed. Quietly and quickly he moved towards the Ramshead bluff and withdrew into the shadows, waiting to see if his senses were as true as they almost always were. He trusted them, the sudden pricking sensation on the back of his neck, the tightening of his gut, the reflex pursing of his lips. Corvini knew what it meant to hunt another man. Rarely, it was he who was the hunted. The man following him had his man marked. Corvini knew it instinctively, from the scent of his sweat rising on the warm air, from the feeling coursing through his limbs warning him to hide. This was the scent of a man who was very sure of himself, working physically hard with adrenaline fully pumping as he doggedly came after his prey.

Corvini waited. He pulled his breathing in to short and silent puffs. He looked carefully around him and noted the wall of rock and, behind the wall, a crevasse with deep shadows. There were signs of foxes and that meant he could find reasonable shelter but he knew that he had to be out of these mountains as fast as possible — en-route to civilisation where he could disappear as easily as any one of the thousands of people flocking into the cities every day. He felt as comfortable in civilisation as in wild terrain, not like his pursuer who, he instantly understood, was a man of the mountains.

Tom breathed in and out rhythmically, measuring each step and observing carefully the landscape around him, the fall of the shadows, the movement of the breeze, the slight changes in the scents of the bush that could mean an animal had recently disturbed the heath. So far, the main scent was his of own sweat and Tom cursed that he had not learned to work hard without raising a sweat. Now, every moment and every calorie of energy were as precious to him as the drops of water taken in at careful and regular intervals to keep the body working at maximum efficiency. He could not afford to become overheated. Almost certainly that would mean a sudden drop in the core temperature as the pace and rate of exertion slowed and the fading afternoon light robbed him of critical radiant energy. He needed to stay physically strong. He paused, looking at the sky for signs of the weather changing, observing the scurrying of a brownish bird — a Dr Pippet — towards the rocks. That was a distinct possibility. His quarry would possibly seek shelter at some time and before dark the assassin would need to find somewhere safe without the additional risk of breaking an ankle or leg.

Tom wanted to follow his instinct and rest, however another more compelling motive forced him forwards. Cassandra. Now he was convinced that the flight of the raven was no accident. He had seen it before with his own eyes when Cassandra went bush. The birds came to her as if she had herself summonsed them to her side. Almost always, they signalled their presence to her and Cassandra never had any fear. She knew they would guide her home from the most treacherous and difficult terrain and no matter the weather, even if darkness descended in a winter storm or late summer evening, the birds would lead her back to safety. So it was no accident in his reckoning that the raven flew as close as it could to Cassandra, alerting her to danger. Tom knew that it was also no accident that the raven flew past him near the lip of the Leatherbarrel bowl then flown in a straight line to The Ramshead.

Tom's instinct was that Cassandra was the target, not her client. Her guest on the walk to Mt Kosciuszko, the bodyguard, was the unlucky recipient of the bullet meant for her, the tenacious woman who would not and could not surrender the Snowy Hydro Scheme to the corporates. Since the government had backed down on the Snowy sale, Cassandra had been increasingly on the end of abusive phone calls and emails — always untraceable. It had happened on a number of apparently unrelated occasions and Tom knew in his gut it was a less-than-subtle threat to her to back off.

From time to time, her concerns about being watched and subtly intimidated were raised when there were unexpected problems with government agencies: a 'letter of suspension of registration' from the motor traffic authority, a blow out of the back tyre, the sudden loss of a job, the continual rebuttal of environmental grant applications. All these minor problems were, in fact, an orchestrated plan designed to intimidate her and curtail her public advocacy for the Snowy River. Someone, somewhere in the government did not like Cassandra and even Sean and Angus — her staunch allies being SAS operatives with more clout than the average person — had trouble in finding out who that was.

'So follow the money trail Tom' was all she would say. Who stood to gain from the sale of the Snowy Scheme? Who wanted the energy assets? Who wanted to tie up the water resources? It was about money. That much was clear. Violence was in Tom's opinion, almost always about money and after that, about jealousy. But now his own mood was one of pure, cold rage. There was no jealousy, no motive for money no honour involved in this pursuit of the assassin. He was simply going to bring down the man who had almost killed Cassandra.

Tom paused. This guy was good. He had so far left no signs. Tom could sense the nearness of his prey yet could not gauge exactly where the man was. He listened, straining for the slightest sound of breathing or movement of the now, thickening heath. Then, the most, subtle of aromas reached him. The summer flowers were well past their zenith and only the coarse undergrowth and dew laden gum leaves were capable of emitting strong and distinct fragrances so late in the season. Tom froze then carefully retreated behind a cluster of boulders. He was suddenly too close and unarmed. He remembered that Sean wanted him to locate only, not intercept the killer. Common sense kicked in and Tom fought the rage-primed adrenaline surging through his body. There was no sound. Nothing. His quarry must be onto him, that he was being pursued.

Tom tuned every sense to detecting the slightest movement. His only advantage was intimate knowledge of the terrain; he had no gun. He had the satellite phone with inbuilt GPS and SMS capability. Quietly Tom logged his position taking a reading from the three nearest satellites in the vicinity. He paused, saved the reading as a waypoint then captured the screen image, complete with local map and photographic overlay and messaged the image to Sean. Tom breathed in deeply. His eyes skirted the terrain carefully. There was no movement, no sound.

The western fall, with its relentlessly steep gorges where the snow-fed streams raced in the spring, was quiet. The water moved slowly over the rock falls. spilling a steady flow into the Swampy Plain, Geehi and Murray Rivers. Already Tom had on many occasions explored the treacherously cold and slippery cliff faces, some of them punctuated with giant slabs of granite that would need at least two abseil pitches for safe navigation. Once the assassin had decided on a route, there would be no going back. Tom urgently needed a better vantage point but did not want to become the target. This guy was smart and would have several contingencies. One of them would almost certainly include taking out potential pursuers.

Neither of the Leatherbarrel or Swampy Plains River in the upper reaches was the best route choice. There was little else on offer and Tom reckoned the man would from this position, cut behind the Ramshead into one of the couloirs that fed the Leatherbarrel and would eventually spit him out into the Murray River. From there he could choose a river or bush route to the sea or regional town and make his way to any of the big cities where finding him would be more than just a tracker's job. In the meantime, it would be tough going for both of them, the heath often shoulder or head high, springy and almost impassable underfoot, still making a savage comeback after the fires. From Tom's perspective he should keep the man within a safe and reasonable distance as it would be all too easy to set himself up as the target. It would be a game of cat and mouse. Tom waited, sitting quietly on his haunches, for the first sounds that would indicate that his quarry was on the move again. Nothing happened, there was no sudden rustle of heath or sound of boots on rock. This guy was playing safe and Tom too decided to keep himself well out of sight.

Ricardo Corvini grimaced. This was getting complicated. The journey in to complete the assignment was relatively straight forward if a little arduous. But now, he was faced with exposure in order to quickly escape. He quietly checked the outside flap of his pack. The paraglider was neatly folded. He did not want to descend in darkness; landing would be far too risky. Corvini waited another ten minutes. There were no sounds from within probably a one hundred metre radius. His man had gone to ground. Corvini slid backwards away from the plunging rock crevasse. He only just heard the sound of the river plummeting over the rocks carved by massive earth movements. Swiftly he turned towards the planned launch point that had been examined from every angle from Google Earth. The weather patterns analysed over ten years told him everything he needed to know about late afternoon up-draughts and the lift he could expect for his flight. At almost 2000 metres with an immediate drop off, he would soon have air and like the wedge tail eagles, he would soar far above the trees and cliffs of the Abbotts

Range before descending towards the Geehi flats.

Corvini did not waste time or breath. He moved quietly into position and carefully placed the backpack on the ground. It took him only moments to pull out the paraglider from the backpack and strap on the harness. He checked his watch. There was still at least an hour before the dusk turned into twilight then darkness.

Calm in the knowledge that he had made good his escape, Ricardo Corvini stepped forwards off the rock buttress. The grass cascading down the steep western face of the Ramshead was suddenly far away as the paraglider caught the air rising from deep below the Leatherbarrel Creek and Geehi Valley. Despite his preparations the strength of the up-draught caught him by surprise. Suddenly, he was flying forwards over the tops of the burnt out timber, some of the trunks dressed in grey green as the coppice growth responded to successive seasons of rain and warmer spring temperatures. The vast copses of dead alpine ash, their trunks and branches scalded white by snow, ice and rain washing the remnants of charcoal after the fires, cast a sombre, almost foreboding air over the forest.

Corvini relaxed as the paraglider opened fully. He floated easily, high above the grasping branches of the heath and dead snow gums sweeping down the sides of the bushfire-devastated western range. Below him, the Swampy Plains River was visible, winding steadily towards the open flats. Corvini was momentarily caught up in the scene below him, amazed then appalled at the extent of the burnt forest, the vast swathes of lifelessness contrasting with the bursting of undergrowth as regenerating understory plants fought for space and light. He hoped that his flight would be true and he would not land, amongst the shrubby regrowth, but as planned, on the open grassland that from space and Google Earth, defined the Geehi Flats.

Tom leant quietly against the rock, the high-powered field glasses scanning the visible line of the Leatherbarrel and its many tributaries. The light was fading sufficiently for him to feel more confident that he could avoid detection, evade capture when he moved out. Death would be the only end if that happened. In the shadows of the late afternoon, he stood a far better chance of returning to Cootapatamba Hut, unnoticed and unscathed by bullets from the high powered rifle that had almost certainly been used to target Cassandra. Any moment now, Tom half expected to hear the sound of the helicopter honing in on his GPS fix and clear photographic image of the landscape hiding the quarry. He allowed himself to breathe calmly, thinking of Cassandra, desperately wanting to call her, knowing that he had to wait.

The vibration of the satellite phone thrilled against Tom's right breast. He flipped open the phone.

'Tom. Where is he?'

'You got my position?'

'SMS clear. No sight?'

'Smelt the vegetation Sean. Alpine Mint. It smells pretty strong when someone walks through it.'

'Right.' Sean grinned. 'On way Tom.'

'Good man. How's Cassandra?'

'She's fine Tom. She's fine. Over and out.'

Tom pushed the phone back into his breast pocket. The fine beads of sweat formed on his forehead. His hands felt clammy with the thought of making the first move into the open. Soon his quarry would be on the run again this time with the SAS in pursuit, night vision rifles at the ready to pick out their man. He knew that Sean and Angus would stop at nothing to find the man — the man who had shot a bullet perilously close to Cassandra, the assassin who had killed her guest. The Saudis Prince was, a man of considerable significance to the Australian Government, a man with many friends in high places. Now that his bodyguard had been grazed by a bullet on Australian soil, the fallout would rock the foundations of diplomatic relations across the Middle East. This was now a case of more than just 'find the shooter'. This was an incident with critical diplomatic ramifications, an incident that had the potential to undermine a range of budding commercial contracts between the two nations, the securing of energy and water assets, the bank rolling of no less than several state governments.

Tom heard the slight rustle in the heath. There was movement and it was too close for comfort. He tuned his senses acutely, not sure whether his quarry was on the move or he had discovered his hide out.

Suddenly a faint image descending from the rock buttress caught Tom's attention. The dull hint of camouflage green against the whiteness of the trees was at first a fleeting mirage. Then the mirage took shape with a definite sense of flight and direction as it moved above the bare crowns of the dead trees. As the green paraglider flew across the Leatherbarrel creek then towards the top of the Abbotts Range, Tom snapped his field glasses to just ahead of the flight path. His man was now in the air and disappearing around the western edge of the Abbotts and towards Victoria.

As Corvini flew from the tops of the Australian Alps towards the Upper Murray Valley, the Geehi flats came into view, a safe reprieve in the heavily forested landscape. He looked for the Alpine Way and steered the paraglider as close as he could to the edge of the flats, a safe distance from both the road and Geehi bridge where there were bound to be curious campers or sightseers. Whether his flight went undetected or not was not his immediate concern. Cover on the ground was. As soon as his feet connected with the earth Corvini pulled the paraglider to the ground rapidly rolling the material into a wad and stuffing it back into the pack. The rifle felt hard against his back. Another ten minutes and he would ditch both. He quickly ran through the bush to the road, breathing steadily and listening intently for any sounds of vehicles. Carefully, he crossed the road and skirted along its edge to the head of the Youngal Fire Trail.

The sound of the helicopter engine shattered the late afternoon silence, filling the sweet air with acrid engine fumes. Corvini dived for cover in the copse of trees where his Baltic 370 Frontera rested against the tree, well-hidden, fuelled and ready to go. The chopper was already well past him, circling the Geehi camping grounds then sweeping around to ascend along the Swampy Plains River towards Kosciuszko. Corvini grinned. He swung a leg over the saddle and accelerated full throttle along the fire trail that would take him to Khancoban and Corryong.

Tom hesitated. The chopper clearly had a 'no sighting'. The sound of the rotors slicing the cooling air chilled his heart. The man was still out there — somewhere — and there was very little chance a foot search would bring him to ground before nightfall. He pulled the collar of his fleece jacket higher around his neck. The sun was heading surely onto the western horizon and he wanted to be back at the hut well before nightfall. Suddenly, the chopper ascended towards him. He could see the pilot clearly pointing towards the landing point.

BLOOD ON THE PLATEAU

The man — his nose contused and bleeding — lay on the grass where he fell next to the metal mesh walkway. The wealthy prince, his master, stood mutely next to Cassandra as they waited for the thwup thwup of the helicopter that would whisk them away from this place of beauty. The man who had loved his racing horses with a passion, listened intently and heard his own heart beating. His body guard El Madhouri — dragged from the sands of poverty and anonymity to riches and social prominence beyond his wildest imagination — was now a part of his family. He breathed in and mentally arrested any thoughts of guilt at so unfortunate an accident. He placed his left hand in his breast pocket to pulled out the white handkerchief embroidered with the family emblem and draped it gently over his bodyguard's face. The handkerchief immediately soaked blood into the cotton weave causing the cloth to stick to the gauze bandage that the guide Cassandra had placed over the wound. There was nothing to do except wait and garner his reserves.

Horrified, Cassandra ran the incident through her mind again and again. There was no sense to the shooting. She drew on the simple strategy that always worked for her to relax — breathe in, breathe out, breathe in.... Tom's voice had allowed her to momentarily step back and view the scene with the eye of the professional she was. This was no random shooting. Almost, a clean hit.

Her satellite phone rang and Sean's voice broke into the late afternoon.

'Cass. Are you alright?'

'Sean. Nothing more I can do except wait for you to arrive. You are coming?'

'Of course I am Cass. Listen you'll have to come straight out with the helicopter for debriefing. Please don't speak to anyone who wanders onto the scene, or anyone who phones for that matter. Absolutely no comment until we speak to you.'

'Sean the Prince has already been on the phone two or three times to the family.' Cassandra pursed her lips.

'This will get very sensitive Cassandra.'

'I'm with you Sean.'

'We'll fill you in on the detail later. Angus will, in any case.'

'Glad it wasn't me.'

'Why do you say that?' Sean was suddenly alert.

'Nasty and plenty of blood. Very close to the eye socket.'

'Cassie. Are you safe?'

'No one else is out here Sean. Tom rang to say he's in pursuit.'

'Yes. I know. He'll have his hands full.'

'It's late Sean. I don't think that there would be many people coming out today.'

'OK. Stay close. Don't separate.'

'That's what I was thinking Sean.'

'Good. Chopper on way Cassie. Over and out.'

'Over and out Sean.' Cassandra trembled slightly as she closed her phone.

The chopper's engine noise suddenly blasted into the solemn afternoon air, drowning out Cassandra's thoughts, the air turbulence plucking at her clothes and tossing her hair uncontrollably behind her. She smiled internally. Sean always delivered on time and in style. The SAS operatives on board jumped out ducking below the sweep of the rotors and ran straight towards the tiny party huddled on the Kosciuszko Walkway.

'Come on Cassie. I'm quickly dropping you off under guard then coming back for this mob.'

'But…'

'No buts Cassandra. That's an order. Sean's on the chopper.'

Cassandra watched the small group of men by the side of the walkway, the medic checking vital signs and making notes on his clipboard. A second SAS soldier gently moved the two men away from the scene where a third man — probably, she mused, from Foreign Affairs — sombrely greeted them, bowing slightly to the Prince. Within minutes they were in the air, Cassandra, an armed SAS soldier and Sean casting a concerned eye over her as they flew quickly away from the unexpected scene.

THE TRACKER

Ricardo Corvini rode his Bultaco motorbike easily along the tarmac rode and into the quiet settlement of Corryong. He booked into the local hotel under a different name and chatted excitedly with the receptionist about the festival that drew thousands of people each year from the bush into town.

The following morning, Tom walked across prime farming land in Corryong towards the Man from the Snowy River Festival. The chopper airlifted him to Geehi where they found no sign of the assassin then quickly took off and left him to search the country town of his youth, the place that he knew so well when his grandfather was still alive. Thousands thronged for the annual festival; horses, bush men and women, trucks and animals all crammed into three days of celebrations. Tom grimaced. He drew his bush hat closer down his forehead slightly shading the dark glasses now changing colour under the midday glare. The showground felt hot and the dust ate into the corners of his mouth working into the spittle. He knew that it was more than a long shot, yet instinct told him that his killer would head for the crowds.

Tom wandered aimlessly past the horse floats and small wooden stands seating people keenly watching the festival events. The scent of excitement, dust, sweat, meat and onions hung on the air and Tom felt faintly disgusted. The sight of a yard full of young brumbies ready for roping galled him. Tom wanted to spit on the

Australian spirit that captured wild horses and turned them into domestic pets at best and dogs' dinners at worst. He hoped that Thunder was deep into the bushland, safe with his herd of mares and foals somewhere near The Station. Soon, some of the young stallions would challenge the older horse — those that survived the death-defying descent along the Leatherbarrel Creek.

He kicked the dirt with the toe of his boot — not a riding boot like most of the people at the Challenge — a solid Scarpa walking boot that would protect him in all weathers and all terrain. The clink of metal caught his attention and Tom stooped to pick up a $2 coin. As he stood upright again. Something had set his nerves jangling. Tom whipped around. The slightly built man was already retreating from sight, his leather jacket burnished in the bright midday sun, the sand-coloured moleskin trousers pulled tight over walking boots, the new Akubra hat tilted to the right and gold watch glinting as he slipped past the stands towards the thousands of parked vehicles.

Tom began to run, jogging through the food and produce stalls, pushing past prams and the old people wandering amongst the crowds. He cursed and increased his pace. The sea of cars, trucks and utes appeared endless as he scanned the rows of metal, looking for one Akubra he knew he could recognise amongst the many. He paused briefly to smile at the two young mounted policewomen — steadying their horses as he brushed past them — then turned back to the task of running his eyes systematically over the metal roofs, pacing doggedly between the long lines of vehicles. The sound of a bike engine momentarily broke his concentration. Instinct prompted Tom to chase after the cloud of dust, but the bike was already accelerating away from the showground towards Corryong heading almost certainly towards Melbourne.

'Shit! I'd better ring Sean.' Tom said out aloud. 'Sean.' Tom was breathless with exertion and frustration.

'Tom? You're onto him?'

'Bultaco. Heading towards Melbourne.'

'Well done! We're onto him.'

As soon as he was out of the town limits Ricardo Corvini opened the engine to full throttle. Five minutes later he turned off the highway and in seconds was churning dust through the corners as he bumped along a farm road. Three minutes later he turned into the forest easing the bike off track and behind a cluster of boulders. Corvini wasted no time. He carefully wiped down the Bultaco all-terrain bike leaving it clear of his prints. He walked back to the edge of the forest then jogged determinedly towards the hangar shed. The sun muted the landscape, now silent and devoid of visitors. The plane was already in the open, fuelled and primed to go. Corvini grinned as he stepped into the pilot's seat. The engine purred to life and he taxied onto the dirt runway setting the autopilot for Essendon Airport.

'Very able young man is our Tom.' Sean opened the conversation.

'Tom. He tracked the assassin?' Angus knew he shouldn't be surprised. 'What else did he tell us.'

'Good description. We haven't found the bike, yet. Tom thinks it was a Bultaco. Good design. Fast. We had roadblocks on all the roads out of Corryong within 15 minutes yet he slipped the net I'm afraid. Seems as though he has gone to ground.'

'Or the reverse?'

'You mean…'

'Why not Angus.' Sean said simply. 'Quickest way from A to B and how would we know where he was going to land.'

'Airports?'

'Yes of course. We're onto it. Angus,' Sean said quietly 'Tom thinks that his target was not the Saudi.'

'What?'

'Cassandra. She's a more likely target. There was zero intelligence about any prospective attacks on our guest and there was no motive that we could put our finger on. Cassandra on the other hand…'

'The State does not like her, we know. More precisely, powerful friends who would get their hands on State water and energy assets…' Angus breathed in deeply.

'Cassandra is also one of our best local operatives Angus. There's no question of that. We just can't replace her that easily.'

'Someone clearly thinks the stakes are higher.'

'There's a lot of money tied up in the National Electricity Market.' Sean pursed his lips.

'Cassandra is sure that water is their real objective, the real prize.'

'Big investors lurking in the hills hoping that she will have a short-lived campaign to prevent their — shall we say — investments in the utilities sector.'

'Well there are certainly enough politicians falling over each other for the spoils.' Angus wished it were not so. 'I did mention it to some of our friends.'

'And?' Sean could never be convinced that any politician was worth talking to when it came to matters of national security.

'I said that "the corporatisation of the Scheme was well orchestrated with unprecedented government to government cooperation and across party lines. Should that have not raised any eyebrows Minister?" or words to that effect.'

'And no doubt your observation fell on deaf ears Angus!'

'Well I did also ask him whether he had connected the attempt to seize and sell the Snowy Scheme with water privatisation.'

'Politicians of course getting the wash back in the new water trading market.'

'Billions are involved Sean. Billions.'

'Then it's likely that Cassie is still in danger.'

'From our assassin?' Sean's focus sharpened on the hunt.

'A professional does not like to leave a job unfinished.'

The Government today claimed responsibility for an accident in Kosciuszko National Park. Guests of the Australian Government were walking in the Australian High Country when a stray bullet contacted with one of the walkers. The bullet was identified to be from a licenced gun belonging to a registered shooter commissioned to remove the remaining wild horses in the Ramshead Range adjacent to the Kosciuszko Walkway. The Australian Government has offered to pay considerable compensation and has made an unconditional apology to the family involved. Australian and international intelligence services verified that in no way are visitors from Saudi Arabia at risk in Australia. The family as guests of Australia, had special protection of the Australian security services and its Allies. This was an unfortunate and unexpected accident.

Signed,
Foreign Minister.

The official line came through on Angus's mobile phone.

'"Accidental shooting". That's the official line. Sean.'

'Still, it makes our security services look extraordinarily weak Angus.' Sean shook his head in disbelief.

Angus picked up his satellite phone. 'Tom. Eight hours.'

'Less than. I've just found the motorbike. Better than mine by far.' Tom could not suppress a grin.

'Once we are done and dusted we'll have to find a way for you to keep it Tom.'

'It's parked five minutes hard ride on the bike outside of Corryong. Bush festival kept the cops busy.' Tom remembered the two policewomen on horses.

'So where's our man?'

'The bike is near an airfield Sean.'

'Clever man.'

'This guy has a few toys at his disposal! Reckon it's a light plane so he probably won't attempt crossing the Tasman.'

'Where would you go?'

'Regional airfield. Essendon. Disappear into Melbourne.'

'We're onto it. Good work Tom.'

'Angus?'

'Yep?'

'Sure about the bike?'

'No reason not to.'

'I'll put it in the back of the ute. Think we should let forensics have a look first.' Tom said honestly.

Angus breathed out.

'He's a smart lad Sean. Straight onto our quarry.'

'How so?'

'Found the man's bike. I told him it was his — keepsake if you like. He probably thinks he is Bruce Lee putting his arse on a Bultaco.'

'Bultaco.' Sean whistled softy. 'Forensics?'

'Tom will deal with it.'

'Impressive. Duty before dalliance.'

'Your charge is shaping up.'

'I knew he would cut it.' Sean said emphatically.

'Otherwise a costly mistake for the Australian Government.'

'The State must be cashed up if they can compensate the House of Saud.

'Friends in banking. Close friends.'

'Oh?'

'Shall we say an excellent working relationship between one of our great Australian banks, a State Premier and — ahh — a certain bank in the Middle East.' Angus allowed himself a half-smile.

'Is that so Angus?' Sean cluck clucked in his Irish way.

Angus laughed. 'I thought but nothing would surprise you Sean.'

'No wonder Cassie is concerned.'

'Is she safe?'

'At present. Very.'

'Keep her safe. I want her under guard at all times.'

'Things are hotting up Angus.'

'There's a lot of money going down on this one.'

THE TURNING

Corvini stretched his legs in his Melbourne hotel, relieved that the 'accident' was seen as just that, and that he was still on commission to kill. The girl was still a problem but he did not want her to be his problem any longer. Most targets were easy enough — but — to shoot a woman! He felt despondent and desperately wanted to see his wife, to stroke his child, to feel the northern Italian sun on his shoulders and eat a proper meal, the first for days it seemed. There was little good cuisine in Australia in his opinion apart from the Italian and Greek restaurants in Melbourne and Sydney that housed some of the finest Italian chefs that money could buy. Corvini hungered for the life he loved. He could afford the luxuries that came with the occasional assignment such as this, yet longed for the ordinary, for the subtle and tangible warmth of his home.

He jerked to his feet as the mobile phone rang.

'Corvini.' The voice commanded.

'Speaking.' Corvini replied curtly.

'I hear that you failed to complete the commission.'

'The failure is unexpected, yes.' Corvini kept his tone neutral.

'I hope that you are not planning to leave Australia until you have completed the mission? We have paid you well for your services.'

'Indeed. You have paid me well.'

'Then?'

Corvini hung up on the caller.

THE ITALIAN CONNECTION

'Sean?'

'Tom?' Sean continued to study the map.

'What did the forensics show?'

'So you think he jumped from here?' Sean jabbed a finger at the map.

'Could have been any point along the ridge. All of it is good to fly.' Tom mulled over how close he had come to at least cornering if not capturing the assassin. That was the whole point — it was impossible to corner a fox let alone a man in these mountains.

'He either had good knowledge of the mountains or good map reading skills.'

'Forensics show anything? Tom tried again.

'Maybe his contacts in Australia were good enough to give him the exact exit route, the flight path.'

'You mean you have tracked him?'

'Mmm.' Sean traced an imaginary path to the camping ground. 'Paraglider.'

'You found it?'

'Nope.'

'I found the bike though.'

'You can pick it up tomorrow Tom. I'll ask Thora to drop it around.'

'Thora?' Tom jumped up in indignation.

'Hey. Settle down.' Sean grinned. 'After the forensic testing she

wanted to take it for a test run first to make sure it was safe enough
...'

Tom beat into Sean's shoulder with his fists.

'How's the climbing coming along?'

'Haven't had a chance for the last few weeks.'

'Get yourself a paraglider on my expense account kid. Take it
south to Mt Buffalo. You can climb with the glider on your back
then jump off at the top. Only if Thora is lead climber.'

'Cool!' Tom's eyes glistened with anticipation.

'And since you asked, yes we traced the bike.'

'Whose is it?'

'Not so much a matter of who owned the bike. It is about who
cleaned the bike.'

'What does that mean?'

'Few distinguishing marks. False plates. Signature job.'

'You've seen it before?'

'Not this particular bike, however yes, we've seen similar jobs by
a well known craftsperson of the bike re-birthing business.'

'Craftsperson? What is that supposed to mean Sean?'

'She is a woman Tom. A woman who can take any bike and
make it anonymous so it can find its way to your assassin who does
not have any fear of the machine being linked back to him or her.'

'Are there women rebirthers?'

'There are. Some of them are very clever.'

'So she told you who her customer was?'

'She did indeed and you will be very happy to know that as we
speak Interpol are keeping a close watch on our man.'

'Where?'

'Too much information Tom. Need to know basis only.'

'He nearly killed Cassandra!' Tom exploded.

'All the more reason to keep his identity quiet Tom. We would
hate to see you take off on a wild goose chase to Italy.'

'Italy! I thought so. You could smell it on him. The aftershave.'

Sean suddenly looked alert. 'Aftershave? You know the brand?'

'Of course. Thought Thora would like it.' Tom grinned and pulled a bottle of Mondial 908 Homme from his backpack and thrust it towards Sean.

'Gee thanks. So now I can smell like the man who tried to take out Cassandra! Hope you don't confuse me with our man Tom.'

'In your dreams.'

Sean shook his head 'Simple mistake! You smelt his aftershave.'

'Men can also be vain' Tom said looking politely at Sean.

'You cheeky...' Sean rumbled Tom to the floor locking a leg around Tom's leg and pulling his arm gently behind his back.

Tom rolled quickly protecting his shoulder and reversing the leg lock. Suddenly he was on top of Sean pulling his left arm behind his back.

'OK, OK. I give in.' Sean feigned relaxation then suddenly tensed his stomach muscles flicking Tom off him and sending him flying across the floor.

'Hey!' Tom was lithe as a cat and on his feet fists ready for the first onslaught.

Sean remained totally relaxed and let Tom come towards him. Effortlessly he moved in and threw Tom to the ground.

Tom gasped for air winded by the impact of the fall. 'Didn't know you could do judo.'

'Tom, don't mess with me.'

'That was just a friendly Sean.'

'It's still there.' Sean pursed his lips.

'What's still there?' Tom challenged him.

'The stuff inside me. All of it. And on top of it the training kicks in all by itself.'

'OK, OK! It must have been the aftershave that set you off.' Tom attempted a joke. 'You knew straight away Cassandra was the target. Gut feel?'

Sean breathed heavily for a few moments forcibly calming himself down. 'No intel on the Saudi Prince. He was clean. Friend of the government, ours and the Americans. Here on business. Nothing out of the ordinary.'

'On business? What business?'

'Nothing that can link him immediately to Cassandra. Besides, he was just in the wrong place at the wrong time.'

'They could have taken out Cassandra at any time Sean. Why then?'

'Deflect attention onto the Prince. Spooks would earn some brownie points protecting the Prince and Cassandra's death would be put down to being an accident.'

'Perfect cover.' Tom said angrily.

'There is a link though.' Sean said quietly.

'How?'

'He was here to tie up some investments.'

'Investments?'

'Energy assets, artefacts,' Sean said carefully. 'His fingers are in some very meaty pies.'

'They already have an oil empire though. The stuff that everyone else in the world wants.'

'Look at it this way Tom. What does a desert state need most of all?'

'Water?' Tom shrugged.

'Exactly.'

'So…'

'Tell me Tom, what is Cassandra most passionate about?'

'The Snowy River.'

Sean threw the Sydney Morning Herald in front of him open to a full page advertisement. The water sector is worth billions Tom.'

Tom whistled through his teeth. 'No wonder Cassie is a target.

So you reckon it was the investors who were after her?'

'I'm not sure.' Sean was guarded. 'Could be an organiser, a deal-maker, someone who introduces the investors.'

'To government? It could also be the other way around Sean. Government not wanting any hiccups to their sale.'

'The thought had occurred to me.' Sean said quietly.

'That means who?'

'That's what we need to find out. Who in which government is keen enough to pop off Cassandra to stop her from spoiling their scheme?'

'Our Scheme.'

'So she has converted you also.' Sean laughed relieving the pressure he felt in his chest. The adrenaline rush had sapped him of confidence in his control over some knee jerk training responses.

Tom laughed and slapped his friend on the back. 'First the Pakistanis and now an Italian! Well there are plenty enough in Australia.'

'There are indeed, several well connected and well known influential Italian families living in NSW, some of them with strong bonds to government.'

'Are you talking Mafia?' Tom was incredulous.

'I am.' Sean chewed the inside of his cheek. 'Oh yes. Dare to differ and you won't get pre-selection next time, you suddenly find that funds promised to your electorate are withdrawn, that there is no new hospital or cancer service or the upgrade to the school hall is cancelled!'

'Nasty bunch.' Tom scowled.

'That's just the beginning.' Sean said.

'Enlighten me.' Tom opened his arms.

'The party faithful jump ship once the deed is done. They move to the private sector waiting with open arms to reward them for selling off State assets.'

'You're talking conspiracy theory now.' Tom shook his head.

'Nothing conspiratorial about grabbing assets of the Crown, corporatising them, then selling them to interested international investors! That's precisely what is happening here.'

'Well why haven't the media woken up to the fact?'

'What media. They are nothing more than the propaganda arm of industry. It is PR and spin, not media, there's far less investigative journalism.'

'No wonder Cassie can't get any of her articles published.'

'And nor will she. Look at the bigger picture for now.'

'So who do you think is behind it?'

'Count the days when it is the government of the day that holds power in the country. Count down until the time the financiers, the banks and big corporations own and run entire countries.'

'You mean own and control our water.'

'That's the long and the short of it. Control the water and you control food production and if you control food and water you have control over people. Look at how easily tens of thousands die in Africa and always have. They are dispensable are they not?'

'What does her Majesty think about it?' Tom screwed up his forehead.

Sean chuckled. 'The Crown prefers the State to be the State.'

'So why don't you bring down the government?'

'To do so would cause even more insecurity amongst the people and whenever there is a tremor in national security the lawless minority come out and create fear and havoc in the majority.'

'Well how are you going to get rid of — who did you say it was — the government?'

'Now that is a different matter altogether, a different matter altogether.'

'I thought the Italians built the Snowy Scheme' Tom suddenly blurted out.

'They did; and proudly so.'

'Why don't you ...'

'We are Tom. We are. We are reaching out for the assassin as we speak through some of the first Italian families who came to Australia after the Second World War.'

'Will it work?'

'A man who has pride in his country?'

'All Italians do don't they?' Tom was not sure.

'And proud of the engineering feats of Italian emigrants to Australia.'

'What about the ratbags who are trying to sell the Snowy?'

'That is a matter of internecine warfare. A matter of clan against clan.'

'Are any of them in government, you know, working from the inside?'

'Money smooths the many wheels within and outside of governments.' Sean said simply.

'So Cassandra is fighting a mighty battle against the odds.'

'She is indeed and it is unlikely, Tom, that she will down tools and call it a day. Her safety won't mean as much to her as putting her country first, fighting for the rights of the rivers and rights of the people to own their own water and not have it sold to them at inflated prices by some foreign national, a corporation that has absolutely no allegiance or loyalties to the environment or to Australia.'

'Well she is rare!' Tom grinned broadly.

'Show me a government anywhere who is loyal to their people!'

'Then what about you and Angus? What's your gig if you aren't serving Her Majesty?'

'There are sufficient numbers of good servants of the Crown — in this country also — who understand the fickle nature of politics and politicians. Our intelligence is that we have the odds with us rather than against us when it comes to securing national interests.'

'I hope so. I bloody hope so.' Tom vowed.

'I knew that you would feel that way Tom.' Sean said quietly. 'There's something that you haven't told me though.' Sean smiled.

'Told you? What do you mean.'

'The route you took to track our man.'

'Educated guess.' Tom blushed and shrugged his shoulders.

'And?'

'And what. I smelt his aftershave.'

'It was more than that though, wasn't it.'

'More than what?'

'You took a very direct route.'

'Oh you mean the crow?'

'So you had a little raven magic on your side?'

'Bird was probably just curious and maybe thought that there was a feed in it. You know how Cassandra always feeds the ravens, just in case she needs them to help her out sometime.'

'Hmm.'

'So the bird led you towards our shooter.'

'Could have.' Tom shrugged his shoulders.

THIRST OF THE SNOWY

Far away from the cry of the Little Australian Ravens massing around the Ramshead Range in the antipodes, a handful of Australian diplomats, politicians, ex-politicians and corporate directors, gathered around a beautifully polished ebony table in a boardroom high above the Geneva CBD.

'It's only a hiccough', the tall thin man with an over-prominent nose and chin placated the eminent businessman dressed in a long shirt and loose trousers. The Saudi twiddled the end of his headdress and looked studiously at the paperwork in front of him. He paused looking into the eyes of the main negotiator, an older man with silvery hair, quick to smile, despite the sharp, almost black eyes.

'We want the full suite. The generator, the licence, controls over water for your farmers and of course, land for ourselves and you are now telling me that the generators are no longer for sale?'

'Temporarily Sheik. We have made new arrangements to remove the roadblocks to the sale.'

'Roadblocks?' The Sheik raised an eyebrow above the level of the two massive silver eyebrows in front of him. The man was attempting to assuage his fears. He could easily recognise a dealer in the man in front of him, despite his professional status as an eminent ex-politician.

'A few locals are attached to the memory of the Snowy Scheme days. Nothing more.'

'And these locals…?'

'They are vulnerable and unlikely to present any further impediments to the project.'

'You are sure?'

'We have a friend who is as we speak dealing with the impediments.'

'I hope nothing that will be traced back to here.' The Sheik felt an instant opportunity to seize the bargaining chip.

'He is a professional.'

There was a pause of some moments while the Sheik scanned the roomful of men seated around the burnished table. Most were already known to him or to his friends in the Middle East. The ex-politician with the silvery mane, the tall man with the strange manner of speaking — perhaps too conscientious — and prominent chin, the board directors all of whom had been his personal guests over the last decade, the diplomat who had oiled the wheels of progress ensuring that transactions in Australia would be well facilitated with the law allowing for foreign ownership of any resource; land, water, energy utilities and indeed, ownership of entire political parties if he so desired.

'So gentleman. Perhaps we should begin the final stage of our negotiations. Now, we have secured the land holdings — how kind was the great drought to make vacant farming land, fortune indeed. We have purchased more water licences than we need for the next 50 years and we have access to your decision-makers. It appears that Australia is indeed our friend and with your presence', the Sheik bowed slightly to the representative from the conservation sector, 'connected as you are at the highest levels with the World Wildlife Fund and the British Royal family — a relationship that we value highly — we won't find that a rare species of waterfowl will interrupt our agricultural or mining activities will we?'

'Not at all. You can count on blessings from the international conservation lobbies for the rescue of the wetlands. You will be the talk of activists with your generous donations and science programs. There is nothing the activists like more than more studies and recognition of their endangered frogs, parrots and waterfowl.'

The Sheik chuckled. 'You westerners deceive yourselves. The rest of the world does not care about your nature. It is about oil and now of course, carbon trading that will fund our development projects for decades. Thank you gentlemen. I think that we can reconvene over dinner.'

The Sheik stood up and pushed his chair back from the table. From behind a painted Japanese screen, his aide swiftly emerged taking his hand as if he were a young boy and leading him from the boardroom.

'Well, what do you think about that?' The silver hair spoke first.

'Can't be too hard from here on in. The carbon trading bank is ready to go and the land and water transactions are already underway.'

'Nothing like sovereign debt to facilitate the sale.'

'Well, we didn't need the desalination plants but we did have to buy them to seal the deal.'

'They were a mistake.' One of the board directors cut in. 'If you people had not signed when you were in office, we would not have such a large debt to pay the Saudis in the first place.'

'Debt or no debt, they have us over more than a few barrels of oil after the assassination.'

'Has anyone heard back from our professional?'

The diplomat spoke up 'I have received an encrypted email on my phone. He is already back in Australia. This time he is unlikely to fail.'

'Good. I am thirsty. Anyone else for a beer?' The silver mane swept high off the forehead made the man look like a lion. Although arrogance oozed from every pore, he was oblivious to how the other men saw him. As far as he was concerned, the meeting was a success. It was time to celebrate, and all the better if they had a few drinks before dinner. 'Well?'

The men retreated into the high speed lift and descended to the bar on the 15th floor.

PERFECT STORM

Cassandra gently rolled the quartz bowl in a saline solution, cleansing the remnants of human touch. She lightly tapped the rim then flicked a soft fingernail against its edge. The bowl hummed, for a moment.

'That's weird. Didn't know it was a singing bowl.' Cassandra looked carefully at the rim. The touch of the quartz was surprisingly soft even though nothing less than a diamond would cut it. She had a small collection of Tibetan singing bowls that she bought at the Buddhist ceremony in Jindabyne. From time to time she brought out her singing bowls and played them by an open fire under the starlight at Island Bend. The wooden mallets struck on the rim or run around the surface created a most exquisite calming hum, much like the hum now emanating from the present Tom had given her.

She tried it again, this time giving the bowl a gentle yet firm 'tap' with the metal handle on her hairbrush. The bowl vibrated in her hand singing with a sharper note that sent a thrill through her body. The quartz looked unwashed like the quartz found in the mountains. The mountains were filled with remnants of the last igneous intrusion and hydrostatic lift of granite to the surface of the earth's crust. She turned the bowl over looking for invisible inscriptions, a clue to the maker. Cassandra ran the bowl under the cold water then placed it on the centre of Angus's coffee table. It was good to have the comfort of his home for now and the protection of his "friends" as he called them. She still felt slightly shaken, although not unduly frightened after the shooting on the walkway. Curiously, the raven flew almost to her then shot off into the rocks after the accident. Was it she who was being warned? She was waiting for Angus to update her as to potential suspects. In any case, she had her own ideas and knew that it was only a matter of time before one of the government cronies would try and make her drop the campaign.

She knew that she was onto something when she started the water sampling in the Snowy River. Then, she noticed bit by bit the Snowy infrastructure changing and the increased security. It was only a matter of time until she twigged that this was more than the government had done before to fix up the scheme, so they must have been up to something. Then came the innocuous note in the papers about the sale of the Snowy Scheme and she joined the community campaign to keep the corporate wolves out of the mountains.

She knew that she was onto something big when the initial "light intimidation" became more frequent. But she ignored the threats. No-one was about to steal water from any of the Snowy Mountains rivers. She didn't know exactly who or what was driving her, but she knew she had to keep probing to find out exactly what was going on. It wasn't just the Snowy, it had to be a bigger picture than that, and now it seemed to be more important to someone than she first thought.

Since the earthquake, the veneer of 'business as usual' sickened her. Only for a short time did the Snowy River have the freedom to run through the mountains, through gorges and across the Monaro before the deep descents to the ocean. It was only a matter of time before the wild and free river was once again choked, this time by a new dam.

The Snowy River might be dead in its tracks, but it still held memory and stories. She knew that water was not just water; it was an ancient record, a library of the history and geography of the human and animal history of the continent. The only thing that had changed since the earth movements was the sudden appearance of more quartz in the mountains. That is where she found the bowl. There was no obvious origin except that it was made from the very same materials that she handled every day, the tiny and large pieces of quartz she found, caressed and returned to their places of discovery. Cassandra was the last one to remove rocks or natural artefacts, although some of the quartz pieces 'pulled' her to them and she had to fight the impulse to make them hers. This was different. A gift from Tom. A gift from the 'hall of the mountain king.'

'Hall of the Mountain Queen you mean.' Cassandra heard a voice.

'What?' She turned to see who was speaking.

'Hall of the Mountain Queen,' the voice whispered.

There was no-one there.

'Angus!' Cassie called out.

Angus was already outside kicking around loose gravel, hands thrust deep into his pockets. He tried to flick a large piece of gravel behind him as if it were a soccer ball just as Cassie ran towards him.

'Cass?'

'There's no-one there Angus? There's no-one inside?'

'No of course not. Just a minute.' Angus wheeled around and opened the front door and carefully stepped inside, gun at the ready. He moved quickly into the house swinging open doors keeping himself fully protected. Nothing. Just to make sure he reversed the sweep and stepped outside sheathing his weapon.

'Nothing Cassie. Are you alright?'

'That's the problem Angus I am sure that I heard someone speaking to me.'

'What did they say?' Angus flung an arm around his young friend — more concerned that the stress of her shooting incident was playing tricks on her mind now, than there was any real threat close by.

'You wouldn't believe me Angus if I told you.' Cassandra smiled then laughed.

'Try me Cass.'

That night Cassandra slept as if she were back in her childhood, at her grandmother's place wrapped in a double layer of quilts, the light adjusted to a faint glow, the sound of pigeons cooing in the huge frangipani tree as the dawn entered the sky, the soft call of a pied currawong echoing in her dreams, the sound of a lady singing softly.

"The River of Life The River of Love the River of Life..."

Cassandra woke with a start and thrust the blanket off her. She ran to the window and jerked open the curtain. The dawn light touched the open plains with a golden glow and a flock of white cockatoos flung themselves upwards into the sky. An owl flew past her window and a little raven landed beneath the sill, its bright eye piercing Cassandra's. The memory of the walkway suddenly flooded into her consciousness. She sank to her knees sobbing, oblivious to the starkness of the wooden floor, the flapping of wings, the sound of Angus running into her room.

'Cassie, I'm here. It's OK. I'm here.'

Angus cradled her in his arms stroking her hair, brushing the tears from her cheeks. She looked up at her friend.

Angus smiled. That's my girl, that's my girl. We'll get him Cassandra. Tom's onto him.'

'Thanks Angus. I'm hungry. Can we do breakfast?'

'You bet. And there is someone joining us.' Angus smiled broadly.

'Tom?'

'Cassie!'

Angus walked over to Tom, briefly brushing his shoulder with his hand. He turned back to Cassie and smiled. Breakfast in ten? Sean, can you put the kettle on? Angus called out down the hallway.

Cassie smiled wiping away her tears as Tom grabbed her and pulled her into his arms.

'OK, this is how it works.' Angus pushed away the empty plate and brushed toasted crumbs from the table. 'Heard of the Club of Rome anyone? Sean? Tom? Cassie? Anyone?'

'Club of what?'

'Rome Tom, Rome.'

'Nup. What's that, the head office of our Griffith friends?'

'Not quite Tom.' Sean reached for his third piece of toast. 'The Club of Rome reaches well beyond Griffith my friend, all the way into the heart of our establishments: the police, government, legal firms...'

'What do they have to do with us?'

'Well, there must be a reason, and a someone behind the reason, why the bullet let fly.'

'You mean the bullet that just missed Cassie!' Tom almost exploded into an instant rage.

'Handle it Tom — handle it.' Sean warned

'You can't expect me to sit here and listen to this and remain super calm and laid back like you mob.' Tom retorted.

'You mean like Angus and Sean.' Cassie shot Tom a warning glance.

'It's OK Tom. As you know there is a very fine line in my DNA between calm observation of acts against my people and well...'

Sean started.

'You mean you are planning to take out the establishment Sean.' Suddenly, Tom was laughing making light of the conversation.

'Well we won't go there …'

'We will go there Sean, that's the point, we will go there.' Angus said sombrely. 'Someone has to stop this madness, this mania to grab the country's resources for themselves.'

'You mean the Snowy, Angus' Cassandra's hand shook slightly, hot tea spilling onto the table. 'They're after the Snowy Scheme and they are after the water.'

'Here.' Sean swooped with a tea towel. 'Don't want to make a mess on Angus's clean floor!' Sean's gruff smile brought a sparkle back into Cassandra's eyes.

'Well they won't leave it alone will they Sean. Angus?'

'I'm afraid not Cass and the point is that 'they' are more than a handful of greedy executives — and 'they' don't deserve to be called anything of that sort, they're just executives of their own bank accounts.'

'Club of Rome?' Tom picked up the thread.

'Exactly — well almost exactly — a very well connected band of brothers who cross national boundaries, cross cultures and…'

'Cross international bank accounts!' Tom was totally focussed.

'Right on Tom.' Angus looked mutely into his cup. 'But a bit more sinister. The reality is, boys and girls, that the Club of Rome could be our front for the more entrepreneurial amongst environmentalists.'

'Don't understand a word that you are saying Angus.' Tom sounded unhappy.

'OK let's keep it simple for the dumb and blind amongst us.'

'Oh thanks! Nothing like spending time with mates.'

Angus smirked. 'You're too young and dumb to know much Tom. You always were!'

'Hey you' Tom jumped up pretending to thump Angus on the shoulder.'

'Sit down kiddo. Here's the world as I see it.'

'Humdee dumbdee dumbdee..' Tom tapped his fingers on the table.

'Club of Rome — apparently good ideals, good ideas, good people, noble intentions!'

'And?'

'Concerned about climate change just as you are Cassandra.' Angus allowed himself to smile for the sake of his young charge. 'A New Path for World Development'.'

'You mean rake in the money now and hope somebody can pay later.' Tom cut in.

'Hear him out.' Sean spoke hoarsely surprised by his own emotion.

'I feel the same way as Sean. Here we have at face value a bunch, of apparently enlightened souls planning to put the world back on track through radical changes in the EU — call that global — strategies to combat the current 'perfect storm' of environmental, development and economic crises.'

'Well yeah, that's obvious.'

'Thanks for that Tom,' Angus continued. 'So we have a rapid meltdown or degradation in the earth's ecosystems, and the need for a global strategy to cope with the destruction.'

'You mean a sort of revolution from without.'

'Precisely. Very astute of you Tom. Nationhood means little in the face of global ecological catastrophes.'

'A sort of Global Environmental Crisis to match the GFC?'

'The chicken and the egg with some in the club distinctly aware that environmental collapse precedes economic collapse.'

'So why would they want to take out Cassandra? She loves the environment!' Tom reddened.

'Hear me out Tom. We think that amongst our clever friends are those who simply want to make a fast buck out of nature as you have already alluded to. Look at Copenhagen and the ETS.'

'You mean that is a front as well.'

'No news to anyone here — a whole new banking system with some in the world destined to become very rich indeed.'

'Cassie saw through it and didn't even bother going to Copenhagen.' Tom defended her instantly.

'No she didn't go and very wise not to. Far more important things to do at home are there not Cassie?'

Cassandra nodded and remained silent.

'Behind the rhetoric — the talk -' Angus shot a wisecrack smile at Tom, 'of environmental action is a whole new economic paradigm and a whole new — and old — set of people who want run the world their way!'

'They can't, what about us?'

'What about you, you mean Tom.' Sean shot in the remark. 'What will happen to you if the strings are pulled by someone else?'

'That's exactly the point. It is your future, your country and the decisions are yours to make.' Angus spelt it out clearly.

'So you are saying that this club thing is in the way of me and Cassie?' Tom said.

'Cassie and me, Tom.' Sean corrected.

'OK Cassie and me.'

Cassandra smiled and looked into her cup.

'It's a very long bow to draw, however the very people who plan to narrow the gap between the rich and the poor and put a value on the environment appear to be the very same people who don't like Cassandra.'

'You mean a price on carbon?' Cassandra interjected

'No' Angus said slowly, 'a value on the environment or more specifically, environmental services and biodiversity,' allowing the conversation to move where Cassandra directed it.

'The Snowy?' Cassandra looked more confused than enlightened.

'Yes absolutely, the economic benefits of a healthy river not just for the people here, however, but to the planet as a whole.'

'I see.' Cassandra said cautiously.

'It's possibly a good thing to place an economic value or price on the environment…'

'Then they will attach a price tag and sell off our whole natural environment.' Cassie interjected.

'Yes they will and they have. And they are doing so as we speak!'

'So you think that this club of yours is a front for privatising nature on a grand scale?' Tom demanded.

'Some of the people associated with the club definitely would see it that way.'

'So why would they want to take pot shots at me? Cassandra asked.

'Why, Cassandra? Put it this way — there is a strong fraternity who pretend to have a 'love of the environment' as it were, except they are really interested in grabbing and selling natural resources. Our natural resources' Angus clarified. 'Moreover, they're using the present 'perfect storm' of environmental and economic collapses and the gaping divide between the rich and the poor to put up 'new leaders' or a 'new leadership' for the new millennium.'

'Stuff of conspiracy Angus' Tom bravely challenged. 'Nobody in the club of whatever wants the Snowy and anyway, how would that make them a world whatever leading a club of blind followers down the path to nowhere?'

Sean broke into a gleeful chuckle. 'That's a bit of a mouthful Tom, could you put it more simply for some of the less educated amongst us.'

'They want to sell the Snowy River and Cassandra is in their way!'

Cassandra puzzled her brow into an effort of understanding. In her mind she could hear and see the Snowy River coursing towards the upper falls, bright, clear water tumbling, bubbling in delight over smooth granite boulders, streams of water plunging into carefree pools before gathering into a final surge through narrow rock openings and broadening into the river she knew and loved as the Upper Snowy River. The Snowy was no longer just a sacrificial lamb for the sake of 'irrigation' and 'conservation' — bywords for the constitutional right to capture and store water for farming — the Snowy was the dirty secret of water privatisation with tentacles spreading well beyond the shores of Australia.

'Stinks if you ask me.' Tom offered another simple and obvious truth. 'Nothing short of sacrilege! Smacks of greedy traitors clamouring for the spoils of privatisation' he added in the finest of British accents.

Angus laughed. 'Spot on Tom.'

'The thing is, dear boy', Tom mimicked, 'we can't prove a damn thing! And right know, I can smell fresh bacon ready for the pan.' Tom finished off his 'taking the mickey' out of his best friends.

'Well Tom, you have to. That is, if you don't want me shot at again.' Cassie looked a little scared, a little awed and a little apologetic all at the same time.

As if on cue the three men in her life pushed their chairs away from the table and gave her a collective hug.

'We love you Cassie' Angus said as if announcing a battle plan. 'Don't we Tom.'

'Yes.' Tom mumbled.

'What did you say Tom?' Sean grinned.

'Yes, we love you Cassie' said Tom turning a brilliant shade of tanned crimson red.

The phone jangled loudly breaking the breakfast interlude. In two strides Angus was at the phone cradling it quietly to his ear.

'Thora!'

'Angus, there's some news.'

'Yes? Good news as always Thora?' He winked at Cassandra.

'Not always Angus. This is a little more worrying.'

'Speak.'

'It's about our assassin. He is on the way.'

'Your source?'

'A connection.' Thora was concerned about phone lines. 'I'll be there in 40 minutes.'

'Thora, watch your back. Watch for trucks on the road.' Angus cautioned.

Thora put the phone back on its stand and pulled the roll top of her desk down and locked it. The phone was switched to mute, the wires hidden and message bank silent to potential intruders. She checked the windows before emerging from her newly built mudbrick home, the corners strengthened by granite quarried from deep within the mountains, used for culverts then discarded as new roadworks and engineers planned for more permanent crossings on the otherwise slip-strewn tracks and dirt roads of the Snowy Scheme. The local quarry added materials for the impressive fireplace, big enough to harbour tree trunks felled and quartered to make way for road widening and the relentless 'trimming' by the new authority, the RMS who know no bounds to its jurisdiction, even within the national park.

The mountains were filled with tough survivors and Thora was one of them. Her hand crafted home, built with her own labour and through the occasional help from mates, would withstand bushfires, floods and earth movements. The several underground escape routes led away from the river and the once-permanent springs and streams, towards a deep underground bunker that housed supplies: radios, stretcher-style sleeping quarters, bedding, LED lighting and a plethora of gadgets and tools that Thora knew would be more than just a survival kit into the future. She was no conspiracy theorist, no doomsdayer, just a pragmatist living amongst the blind people who refused to see the inevitable, that the economy was tottering.

Thora had lived through it all: landslides, mudslides, winters as severe as sub-Antarctic storms, scorching summers without so much as a bucketful of water for her horses, and plagues of insects plundering her precious grass. She had survived the wildfires, putting out the spot overs from as far away as Victoria, blown ahead of the fire front on screaming winds sucked into a vortex kilometres and hours in front of the main fire. The slow burning fire that licked the western side of the mountains caught the updrafts of air, suddenly rushed into the crowns of the trees and exploded into canopy fires sending sparks, burning embers and ash into the atmosphere across the backbone of the Great Dividing Range and into valleys and forests on the other side. There people were caught badly off guard. Once alight, the fires were a long time in the ground, more resilient and far deadlier than burning above ground. The underground fires were hidden, burning silently until they popped out of nowhere to once again flare and set the bush ablaze.

Thora had no illusions about nature. Unlike Cassandra, she was far from the mystic engaged with the spiritual dimensions of the ever-changing mountains and its rivers. She was the ultimate 'rock of common sense and reliability' that would produce practical solutions to real physical problems common to farming families across the Monaro — and to threats of other kinds such as now. Thora engaged third gear as she topped Guises' Range, descending carefully on the quickly steepening strip of bitumen that would take her across the Monaro plains towards Dalgety. She approached the corners carefully, watching all the time for kangaroos and cars accelerating as they moved through the last of the blind corners ascending the hill. Angus's warning was no novelty at all. A litany of little accidents were more than mistakes that she might make. They were subtle warnings building to a crescendo culminating in a clear 'back off'.

Angus and Sean were satisfied that Thora could and would take care of herself. There was however a caveat that went with her impressive skills set — the times were becoming strained, the noose was tightening around the neck of the Snowy Scheme in the bid for another attempt at privatisation.

No amount of negotiating with officials and ministers of government would relax the relentless pressure to 'sell' the Snowy to save the NSW Treasury Coffers, that had been serially plundered for ministerial junkets — not the least the overseas jaunts aimed at selling off the electricity sector. Cassandra had innocently stumbled into the pool of sharks savaging the last of the state's assets and natural resources. What was revealed triggered a state of alarm, increasingly a state of emergency, for Thora, Angus and Sean. The assassination attempt signalled that the stakes had risen considerably: the international players were becoming impatient, or worried, or both. The 'fraternity' had its eyes and ears in the Snowy Mountains and Thora was not immune to the seriousness of the subtle threats and now the blatant open shooting. She checked the rear vision mirror for, it seemed, the tenth time and swung the wheel before negotiating the last sharp left turn and the final steep pitch where the road crossed a tiny bridge, then flattened out onto the plains.

He came out of nowhere. There was nothing in her side and rear vision mirrors apart from the trees straggled along the road verge and the sudden flight of a small band of white cockatoos. In moments, the Navara Four Wheel Drive was sitting menacingly on her tail, lights full blaze, the driver hunched over the wheel. Thora pulled slightly to the left slowing her speed to let the big four wheel drive pass. He did not move off her tail, the front bumper a metre at most from her rear bumper. She accelerated slightly fixing her gaze for seconds on the mirror, attempting to catch the eyes of the driver. The sunglasses stared back at her, the designer peaked cap hiding his hair except for a few blonde strands. The sun glanced blows from his windscreen into her eyes. Thora levelled her gaze on the road in front of her and slowly accelerated, picking up speed. The Navara kept pace, this time leaving more distance between the vehicles. Suddenly, she saw the turnoff to the Boloco Church. She desperately wanted shake him off before Angus's farm. She swung the wheel hard right and crossed the road then braked quickly and stopped on the verge in front of the church. The Navara sped past gathering speed towards Dalgety.

Thora got out of the vehicle feeling the weight of the service pistol in the leg holster beneath her jodhpurs. She reached down and released the ankle clasp pulling the pistol free and tucking it into the waistband of her trousers. She leant against the car taking a few deep breaths watching and waiting to see if the vehicle would return. Five minutes, ten. No sign of the man. She got back into the car and drove quickly to Angus's turnoff pausing for seconds to close the gate and hoping that the dew-laden morning air would dampen the dust as she drove to the farmhouse.

THE AMBUSH

Corvini reached the intersection near the Dalgety Bridge, glanced to his right and swung the vehicle into a U-turn. He headed back across the bridge, and swung right at the Y intersection and pressed the accelerator to the floor. The narrow road wound between fields, some with large boulders as if plonked by a giant hand randomly to break the monotonous beauty of the sandy-toned grasses. Soon he sighted the neatly steepled church where the woman had pulled over to let him past. She was clearly fast-thinking and no fool. He adjusted his peak cap noting with pleasure the bronze framed Armani sunglasses. Corvini knew he was vain and to be so was an essential tool of his trade, allowing him easy access to the right circles of people who would pay well for his services. He was neither right or left or moderate in his politics. He was simply a professional who did the job well and expected rewards commensurate with the risks and expenses, but also the guarantees of confidentiality and discretion all the way to the highest levels of many governments. Over the past decade he had moved seamlessly from the intelligence circles serving his country to working for international consortiums, frequented mostly by people with impeccable CVs, but with too much at stake to play by the rules.

Corvini had not objected, seeing the obvious, that national borders and governments were dissolving from within whilst keeping an external facade for the populace. Elections and representatives were nothing more than means and mechanisms to access power and wealth, to steer and direct policies towards a global agenda. Since the war and the forming of the United Nations the world was creeping along to another tune altogether. There were new countries like Israel now on the map, attempting to strongly dominate a different global financial agenda and to draw the United States and Great Britain into its fold. There were a myriad of international organisations and agencies springing up to serve — or keep a close eye on — developing nations and their resources and a host of covert (and even overt) intelligence and diplomatic operations underway aimed at controlling emerging power factions at any point on the planet.

The girl was his problem. She was fairly and squarely in the way of several governments and their friends' plans to sell off an asset for a good profit. It wasn't the profit or the motive that worried Corvini. It was the buyers. He had failed. For the first time in his long and distinguished career, he had failed to achieve his target and he wanted to know why and how this girl had escaped his best planning and equipment, and it was always the best. The crow, or 'Little Australian Raven' as he had come to understand was its correct name, was an unexpected factor. The flight of the crow was something he could never have predicted and had no control over, as it swung into his field of concentration and deflected his aim ever so slightly. The fatal consequences were completely unexpected. Corvini had calibrated the shot to allow for the predicted trajectory. He could not have allowed for the bird.

The fallout after the accident involving the Saudi bodyguard, was already shaking international circles. The repercussions were sending seismic waves into sensitive diplomatic circles in Canberra and the talk of payback was unsettling. The emerging Australian-Gulf consortium, with serious investment opportunities and connections to the highest levels of government on both sides of the world, was unnerved by the shooting.

Corvini shrugged off the implications. He was not concerned about political instability in Australia or the cancellation of key export contracts — live mutton or dairy cattle — or of offending the Australian government with whom he had no quarrel. What concerned him was his professional reputation. What concerned him even more was that since he had missed the target he could not stop thinking about the damned girl. She was constantly inside his head and he hated having an intruder. There was a reason that she was there and he wanted to know what it was.

Corvini allowed himself a moment of annoyance, accelerating towards the church and then pulled in where the woman had parked her car. He killed the engine and alighted from the car, scanning three sixty degrees of the horizon before moving quietly towards the church door. To his surprise, the door was not locked, and swung open against the force of his shoulder.

The short aisle led to an unremarkable altar. On both sides of the Church were hewn stone walls and elegant stained-glass windows. The bright colours warmed the otherwise cold interior of the church, and reminded him surprisingly of country churches in northern Italy, although this one was much smaller, more friendly and unexpectedly pulling on his emotions. The combination of the rural setting and the quiet church triggered in Ricardo Corvini a tinge of defiance against the new establishment that exacted so much from him, the professional, the man who was the means to their end. He cast his eyes upwards at the windows, the soft light caressing the images set gently in glass, gazing compassionately towards him. Corvini felt a new wave of protectiveness rising within him like a spring filling a well. He stopped, caught his breath and coughed, the choking in his throat relieving the sensation for the moment. He stepped outside into the light of the morning. The cockatoos that were settled in the pines flew in a burst of white, a noisy chorus breaking the silence. He walked back to the car and stopped dead in his tracks. There they were, her wheel tracks. The woman had not returned the way she came. She had continued onto the road yet he had not passed her coming the other way. How could he have missed it the first time?

Corvini crossed the road on foot, skirting the grave yard and carefully stepping through the fence. Quickly he found the line down the valley towards the river. The going was fast with high terraces flanking the creek on both sides. Then he heard the sound of thunder on earth; hooves racing along the dry valley as the old mare and young black stallion bolted towards him. There was nowhere to go. Corvini stood his ground and the horses fled past him and along the line of the creek.

The single line of smoke rising from the chimney was all that Ricardo Corvini needed to tell him that this was the only occupied house for several kilometres. It was still early in the morning and too cold to be comfortable. A fire meant people. He stayed stock still watching from the protection of the trees. There was no movement around the house, just the trail of smoke wending upwards as the morning sun warmed the land. The woman's car was parked close near the front door of the cottage, steam still rising from the engine. He pulled out his Zeiss glasses and focussed on the window nearest the smoke. For ten minutes, nothing. Then a slight blur across the window. He focussed the glasses again. A man, two men. He pulled back conscious that the glint of the sun on his field glasses could give him away. He put the glasses back in their case and carefully formed a plan.

Thora hugged Sean perhaps for a moment too long before she withdrew, embarrassed at her unexpected lapse of stoic self-control.

'Hi Thora.' Tom announced cheerfully.

'Tom.' Thora acknowledged him then turned abruptly to privately brush a tear from her cheek and straighten her hair.

'You're looking flushed Thora. You didn't ride your horse over did you?'

Thora swung around and clipped Tom lightly on the ear. 'You know I didn't Tom. The wind and the cold morning brings a blush to the cheeks.' She couldn't help but smile at him.

'Uhh huuh. So how come Sean looks like you do and he hasn't even stepped outside this morning.'

'Knock it off.' Sean joked. 'Come here Thora.' Sean grabbed Thora's arm and pulled her towards him and plunged her into a deep kiss that lasted several moments.'

'Hoooeee!' Tom clapped.

'There. It's official. We're getting married.'

'We're what?' Thora gasped.

'Tomorrow. Boloco Church. Just need the minister and you lot are the rent-a-crowd.'

Angus exploded into laughter. 'That'll do Sean. You'll frighten her away.'

'No chance of that.' Sean suddenly dropped on one knee and took Thora's right hand. 'Thora, do you promise to be my faithful wife until the end of your days?'

'If that's a marriage proposal .....'

'And keep that young upstart Tom in place...'

'I will do that!' Thora said spontaneously.

'So there, it's said and done.' Sean sprang to his feet.

'I meant keeping Tom in line....'

'We'll be married tomorrow! Properly.' Sean announced.

A single shot rang outside the shack.

'Down, everyone down!' Angus yelled.

'What the...'

'Shh. Quiet Cassie.' Tom put a finger to his lips. He crawled on his belly along the kitchen floor towards the door.'

'Tom, don't.' Sean's voice rasped.

'I'm not. I'm havin' a look through that crack under the window sill.'

'Be careful son. Don't show your head and stay away from the door.'

'Copy that Angus.' Suddenly Tom was back to his old form, heart pumping against the wall of his chest, breath flowing in and out and the adrenaline surging. His mind instantly alert and focussed. 'Two of them. One dead, one behind the tree, I can just make out the barrel of his gun. How did we not know about them?'

'No dogs. If we had dogs they would have barked.' Angus said.

'What sort of gun? Anyone else.' Sean asked quickly.

'Hold on. There's another guy, he's running up the hill behind them, he's got a rifle.'

'Cassie, take it nice and easy, crawl over to the linen cupboard in the hall and bring back the rifle. You will need to stay on your knees and elbows. Keep the rifle off the floor. Keep your head down.' Angus warned.

Cassie was already trembling but glad for the sudden task Angus had given her. Her gut tightened reflexly and her eyes focussed on the floor. For a second she felt a surge of anger then a second surge of fierceness. Her life was in danger again and she wasn't going to lose anyone this time. She crawled quickly along the hallway, knees slightly spread and elbows moving quickly until she reached the cupboard. Quietly, she prized open the door and felt on the bottom shelf behind the bagged quilts. A long duffle bag was pressed against the back wall and she could easily feel the shape of Angus's rifle. She worked the duffle sideways and pulled it free of the cupboard and quietly pushed the door closed. She could smell the mix of fear and anger emanating from her sweat and pushed herself on her elbows back to the kitchen, moving the duffle forwards between her elbows.

'Well done Cassie. Load the rifle. I need a moment to check the other side of the house. If anyone comes close to any of the windows or doors, shoot to maim.'

'Angus?'

'Hit them below the waist if you can. But avoid the femoral artery. If you miss, shoot again. We need you to look after the front door Cassie while we work out if there are any more around the back. Can you do it?'

'Yeah. I can do it.' Cassie felt a wave of calm wash over her arms. The rifle was steady. She loaded the magazine and pulled the bolt back. The bullet popped into the breech.

'Thora, main bedroom. Sean backdoor. Take your positions. I'm going to try and draw these two fellas out.'

'Careful Angus. We don't know who they are and what they are.' Sean felt ice-cold inside. He did not want to start shooting at anyone or anything. More to the point, he did not want to set alight the tinderbox of anger that always lurked just below the surface. His gut told him that he was under control, yet with less than a moment's notice the emotions could surface again and turn him into a killing machine with precise and deadly intent that meant he would finish whatever job he'd started. He breathed in carefully, pulling the air deep into his lungs and visualising himself outside, standing in the paddock, searching the horizon in all directions. His eyes closed momentarily. The flicker of movement told him that a fourth man was out there, standing to the side, watching the house, watching the two men beside the tree, looking for the shooter.

'I've got him Angus. Sean whispered hoarsely. He had belly crawled back into the main area of the house where Angus was preparing a diversionary incendiary. '275 degrees. Alone. We need to draw him out.'

'Copy that. Cover the back door. Tell Thora to whistle three times to give the all clear. I'm going out the second bedroom window. With this!' Angus held up a molotov cocktail looking device — a kerosene soaked rag stuffed into a glass bottle. Dropped into the bottom of the bottle was the shot from cartridges.

'Deadly.' Sean grinned despite himself.

'It will do the job. I need to get a bit closer.' Angus patted his leg holster. 'Follow up with this. Plan to wound so we can ask the questions. If I miss, take him Sean. Don't give him a second chance.'

Angus waited, hunched below the window frame, for the 'all clear' from Thora. The whistles came, low yet distinct, one, two, three..... Angus raised the window-sash and carefully stepped through to the creekside of the house. He pressed himself against the wall of the house until he had a view of the cluster of rocks. Two wattle trees abutted the rocks, the branches of one moving ever so slightly. Sean was right, there was another man watching, waiting. Were there more? That was the question gnawing at Angus. Two they could easily handle, but if there were more, he would have to rely on Cassie holding her nerve. Tom was there to back her up and he knew the lad was mature enough to stay inside and not attempt anything stupid. There were shooters out there and strangely, one of them was dead already. They were clearly bent on a siege of his house and he wanted to know who they were and why they were here.

Sean stayed absolutely still keeping his eye pressed lightly against the .333 calibre rifle he had purchased for Tom, for hunting rabbits, wild dogs, feral pigs and now it seemed, snakes in the grass hiding close to Angus's house. He was still trying to piece together how in a moment he had worked out that there was a third man as well, and his exact location. It was as uncanny as it was deadly accurate. He could clearly see the wattle tree through the scope of the rifle and the subtle movement of the branches, the leaves twitching independently of the tree. Sean tensed slightly, his finger feeling the trigger, pausing as he adjusted the cross hair to just left of the movement in the leaves. He breathed in and out, sensing rather than seeing Angus move catlike to the edge of the house where he could fix his best aim. Suddenly, the whirring of the bottle through the air and smell of burning kerosene caught his attention. He breathed out and in once more, waiting for the flash of light and movement. The bottle hit the base of the rock and exploded into fragments, the flames shooting into the wattle tree.

'Aghhh!' The man screamed and stumbled from behind the rock, his hands covering his eyes and face. His trousers were already on fire as Angus ran and dragged him to the ground rolling him quickly into the dust to douse the flames.

Tom pushed Cassie away from the front door of the shack and ran full at full speed towards Angus throwing himself on top of the burning man before he had time to recover and mount a challenge.

'Steady Tom, we've got him covered.'

'Where did the shot come from?' Tom breathed heavily, half from exertion and half from fear grasping his throat and clutching at his lungs and heart.

'Good question. Keep your head down. Let's carry him to the shack — quick and fast. You take his legs.' Angus already had a grasp under the man's armpits and waited for Tom to pick him up by the ankles.

'OK, go, go go.' Angus whispered the order his breath coming in pants as he laboured with the dead weight of the man.

Sean was out the back door standing with the rifle sweeping in 180 degree arcs, his eye locked to the sights. The rifle swept to the right and, before he had time to respond to the man pointing his rifle at Angus, another shot rang out. Another man fell forwards, the bullet penetrating his spine and shattering his sternum. The blood burst from the centre of his chest arcing over his friend before he slumped stone dead on top of the already dead man.

'Back door. Sean has us covered.'

'In here.' Sean commanded pointing towards the bedroom door. 'Put him on the bed. I'm cuffing him.'

'Who is out there shooting Angus?'

'I've got no idea. Let's find out from our prisoner.'

'Cass. We're clear for now. Come into the kitchen.' Tom called her.

Cassandra pushed herself off the floor and walked into the kitchen. She opened her arms to Tom.

'I'm for that.' Tom felt mildly elated as he caught her in his arms.

Suddenly there was a frenzy of sounds and gunfire, screams and swearing, the smell of smoke and flesh burning. Tom! The world whirred past in slow motion, Tom, Angus, Sean ran out the backdoor and to the front of the house where the action was. Cassandra could not help herself. She opened the front door, the crack of light appearing on the wooden floor. She prised the door open just millimetres further with the .22 rifle sighting towards Tom as if she could now protect him from the frenzy of sound and smoke. Feeling almost invincible she stood up and pushed the door open still looking through the rifle sights towards the chaos and confusion. Her world changed in less than an instant. A hand covered her mouth and another wrenched the rifle from her grasp. She could feel her knees buckling. Then her world went dark. She couldn't see or speak. But she could hear, and the voice that whispered in her ear 'don't move, don't make a sound' made it clear that she had no option. He had complete control of her. Cassandra stiffened for a second, then relaxed. She knew that it was no time to fight off her assailant. She felt an arm under her left armpit and across her right shoulder pulling her quickly backwards, almost running backwards then sitting her down sharply. Cassandra felt the small rocks beneath her buttocks, the smell of eucalyptus, the sense of being close to the house, yet far from the reach of Tom.

'Don't make a sound Cassandra.'

'How do you know my name?' The thought raced through her mind.

'I need your help. We are going into the house. Together. You and I.'

Cassandra nodded. She looked into his eyes; bright blue, blonde hair, smooth shave, no smile.

The man put a finger to his lips. He stood her up and showed her the .22 rifle and his revolver.

'Walk'. Corvini pushed her back through the front door of the farmhouse.

Cassandra decided to walk decisively, carefully, without fear and without raising the alarm. The revolver and the calm determination of her captor told her that he still had complete control. She stepped carefully into what had been their sanctuary, their safehouse. Now she had only the clear and present danger of a strange man and his gun.

She felt the revolver shift ever so slightly towards her left kidney. The voice in her ear again.

'Call your boyfriend.'

'How did he know about her, about Tom, about them?' Cassandra felt the panic in her thoughts.

'Tom.'

'Louder.' Corvini whispered.

'Tom.' Cassandra called as loudly as her fear would allow.

'Cassie we're back here.'

'Tom, I need you here.'

Tom surprised by the change in Cassie's voice dropped his guard and shot a quick glance at Angus.

'Go. This fellow is not moving far.' Angus laid the prisoner down on the hallway floor.

Like a cat Tom spun into the hallway and in a few lithe steps was in the kitchen a faint scent setting the hairs on the back of his neck on end. Instinctively Tom stopped dead in his tracks turning towards the sound of Cassie's voice, the scent ...

'Hello Tom.' The voice said quietly.

'Cassie ...'

'It's OK Tom, he hasn't hurt me. I think he wants to talk ...' Cassandra felt her knees weakening again.

'Sit down.' Corvini commanded her. 'Tom, you too.' Corvini commanded.

'How did you find us? You've come back for her.' Tom wanted to know.

It was Corvini's turn to be surprised. 'You guessed?'

'The aftershave. It's the same one.'

'Your girlfriend is safe Tom. Where are your friends?' Corvini's tone was ice cold.

'They're tidying up the people you shot.'

'Tom?' Cassandra was suddenly deeply afraid.

Tom ignored Cassandra keeping his eyes firmly fixed on the ice cold blue eyes, the pupils contracting almost to pinpoints. 'They're in the back of the house.'

'I want you to tell them that I have Cassandra and that she is safe. No tricks. Bring them here.'

Tom stood up carefully and pushed his chair back from the table, soundlessly, both of his hands visible in front of him on the table.'

Corvini understood from Tom's body language that he knew precisely the situation as it was. He relaxed slightly, and nodded towards the back of the house. 'Go. Now.'

Cassandra sat still, stunned, silent, unable to fathom the situation, unable to generate thoughts, movement, even fear. The odour of burnt flesh still stung her nostrils but she was now aware of the soft scent that Tom had clearly recognised. She wanted to vomit and sneeze at the same time, her face reddening with the strain of repressing her involuntary response. A neatly folded, white and gold embossed handkerchief appeared on the table in front of her. She looked up at the blonde man and met his eyes, blue like a summer sky flowing across the mountains. Cassandra could not put the picture together. An almost beautiful man, kind. Yet this man was undoubtedly an efficient and chilling killer and he was her captor. She sat for a moment stunned and unsure.

'Cassandra.' Sean's voice was deep and calm, soothing her before she had time to think or feel. 'Cassandra we are here. Tom told me that the man has returned for you.' Sean felt tears pricking his eyes despite himself.

'Sean,' Cassandra's tears flowed as she turned in her chair once again, the world moving ever so slowly as she watched them walk towards her, Sean, Tom, Angus and Thora, their arms loose and hands empty, stepping into the crucible. She felt a firm hand on her shoulder then Thora's arm around her and Tom catching her hand, Angus placing his hand on her head — the high priest of all things that meant truth, justice and safety — infusing a love she had never felt before into her being. She turned again to the man who still pointed his gun at them as if to say "these are my friends, they have protected me from you and will do so again and again".

'I know.' The words came from Corvini.

'What do you know.' Sean said flatly.

'I know that these people are your protectors Cassandra. They have protected you from me, from the people who paid me to kill you, from the people who want something that you won't relinquish.'

Cassandra's chill was now of anger. The hand on her shoulder squeezed ever so slightly.

'And what would that be then?' The Irish lilt crept into Sean's voice, soft, un-menacing, still no anger.

Corvini looked straight at Sean, his eyes unflinching, his mouth straight and unsmiling. His body language was as silent as the deep water harbour on a still morning where his boat was moored in Sweden.

'Perhaps it is something Cassandra loves almost as much as you Tom.' Thora stepped in.

Corvini swung his eyes to meet hers then back to Cassandra. He pulled the magazine out of the gun and put the gun on the table and the magazine in his pocket.

Sean didn't move. Angus stepped backwards to indicate 'no threat'.

'Sit down' Sean offered, not ready to be friendly, not yet.

Corvini carefully pulled a chair backwards and sat down pulling himself into the table and placing both hands in front of him, turning them inwards to a mini-steeple on the table.

POWER GAMES

'Where shall we start?' Corvini engaged the people sitting before him.

Thora moved quietly back to the table placing the blue ceramic teapot at the centre then returned with mugs, milk, sugar and worn silver teaspoons.

'And you are?' Angus opened.

'Corvini. Ricardo Corvini.'

'Ahh. So we have a name at last.' Sean was pleased that his instincts were on track. 'northern Italy.'

'Precisely.' Corvini continued. 'Truth has many faces. Unfortunately for you, for us, what appears to be the truth is far from it. Those who seem to be the protectors of this land and its assets are not in fact the protectors; indeed they are after the very assets that they pretend to protect.'

'Water.' Cassandra stated simply.

'Water indeed, and water infrastructure. The most valuable of all natural resources — or shall we say products — on the planet. Water that feeds the billions. Water that is worth multi-billions of dollars and increases in value day by day as the planet becomes more polluted, as there are more people born every minute who also need water for life, water to live, water to secure their food for the future, water to keep their bodies healthy and water to sustain the millions upon millions of organisms that make up the environments and ecosystems as we know them.'

'They want the Snowy River.' Cassandra confirmed.

'So they decided to shoot Cassandra.' Tom stated.

'Oh yes and for that matter Tom, they clearly did not trust me to complete the assignment and there you have it, they sent several this time to make sure. You have one on the floor of this house. I have killed three. I was sent to kill Cassandra. Fortunately for her, for us,' Corvini made his move to state his alliance with his once captor and her friends, 'fortunately for us that is no longer the case.'

'Well you had a good shot at her mate!' Tom's face was turning a new shade of red.

'Tom. Calm down.' Sean said sharply.

'So Cassandra is no longer in any danger from me, however, I can't say the same for my employers or indeed, their controllers.' Corvini stated openly.

'What is that supposed to mean!' Tom was back on form.

'Tom for heaven's sake!' Sean stepped in.

'The government, or should I state, the state government has friends in common with some interesting people overseas connected variously with emerging water barons and those who have intimate connections with arms and water suppliers — in Iraq as it happens. Their tentacles stretch far and wide on this planet of ours — all the way to this small part of the world that you so clearly love and dearly want to protect.'

'Iraq! I thought so,' whistled Angus. 'So we are talking about ...'

'Yes we are. The less said the better.' Corvini confirmed.

Sean drew in his breath sharply. 'Chilling.'

'Cassandra?' Thora was sharp to take the hint.

'Definitely time to 'de-camp' is the expression is it not, to somewhere a little safer? You need new cover.' Corvini was quick to set the agenda.

'I know just the place.' Tom couldn't help himself.

'I know.' Cassandra said. 'Whoever they are though Angus, they can also track us. Can't they?'

'Yes, but it is too dangerous to tell you who they are at present. These people — you know how it works — have tentacles in every theatre of war on the planet. Dare I say they probably supply the insurgents to cause a ruckus so that the so-called allied forces have to go in and contain the very terrorists or insurgents using their armaments. They probably supply 'our side' as well.'

'You mean war is not war, it's a money machine?' Tom said.

'Well that is obvious. I think that we need one of Tom's solutions at this stage. Tom?'

RETREAT

Tom, Cassandra and Ricardo Corvini quietly made their way into the heart of the mountains long after the sun had set over the western horizon, well past the time that a flurry of the Little Australian Ravens had competed for the highest roost on the rock tors and settled for the night. Already they had moved a long way behind the glaring light at the top of the Kosciuszko Chairlift signalling, through the most wintry of nights, the location of Thredbo. Tonight, the clouds lifted to reveal a stunning sky, resplendent with white stars that truly blazed against the black velvet of the firmament. The night opened its array of diamonds on jeweller's velvet, the brightest of stars pointing the way to the portal.

'We're here Cassie.'

'Tom it's so dark. Are you sure?'

'Sure as sure.'

'I'm coming in with you.' Corvini had been quiet until now fulfilling his self-made role to protect Tom and Cassandra all the way to the portal.

'What? You won't be able to get out so easily? It's not like that here.'

'What do you mean Tom?' Corvini smiled wryly.

'I mean the magnetics. They are all over the place. There is no sense of up, down, north, east south or west here. It's just a different world.'

'I see. Then I will have to leave a tracer to track backwards.'

'What does that mean Ricardo?' Cassandra was worried. 'If you can trace yourself out of here, couldn't someone trace us into here.'

'It won't be visible. It will be a silent system only detectable by me.'

'OK, if you're sure. We definitely don't want anyone else knowing the way in here. There are only a handful of us on the planet that have any idea…'

'Your secrets are safe with me Tom. Believe me. I want nothing more than to make sure you are both safe. I know what is at stake. I know who these people are and what they are after and what they will do to get what they want. They will stop at nothing. Are we ready?'

Tom carefully uncoiled his rope in the manner that Thora had taught him so long ago. He tied a figure of eight knot into one end of the rope and an overhand knot into the other end and clipped the figure of eight into a carabiner.'

'Cassie, can you pull the rope through the anchor point.'

'OK.' Cassie sprang into action pulling the abseil rope through the hidden ring bolts. 'All done Tom. Ready to go.'

Tom quickly attached his CT Biz Bang descender and a French prussik to the rope.

'Ready to go. Ricardo, come second then Cassie. Keep an eye on him threading the belay device. You will need to haul mine up for him to use, Cassie.'

'Done. Good luck Tom. Don't go too fast.'

Tom whipped his abseiling gloves from his pack. The descent was long and he did not want to burn his hands or find himself letting go of the rope for any reason. Besides, the gloves would be excellent for a little 'interior design work' on the new home. Suddenly, he was gone, disappearing into the void past the immediate grasp of their pursuers.

Cassandra drew breath. She counted the seconds, then minutes it would take Tom to abseil into the hidden cave beneath them. She loved this place. From the first moment that Tom had taken her here secretly in the middle of the night she knew that she had to return.

'The first time is always the best' Tom announced proudly as he guided her into the new world that bore little resemblance to anything they had ever seen before. Cavers had special rights and privileges above mere mortals, access to places that most people could never imagine or even dream about. Here they were, in a cave of the most incredible dimensions, a cave that was not a palace filled with the usual limestone formations — of stalactites and stalagmites — but a cave that had formed during timeless processes when the molten core of the earth rose to the surface and crystallised again and where the ice tore away giant slabs from the hardest of granite formations.

For Tom, it was an eye opener, a revelation of ancient earth mechanics. For Cassie, it was simply a magical world where quartz became a totally new medium for beauty. She had seen and adored the quartz streams above the earth. This was something altogether else.

Suddenly, there was a tug on the rope, a distinct and definite signal from Tom that he was off rope. She took Corvini's descender and attached it to the rope.

'Ricardo, it will be fine. The descender is safe and Tom will bottom brake for you.'

'It's not that Cassie. It's the lights. Look!' Ricardo pointed to a group of flashes on the horizon. 'Looks like we have a tail!"

'Put the gloves on. You have to move quickly. Tom will brake for you near the end. 'Go!' Cassandra virtually pushed him into the void. 'Go!' She counted the seconds, one, two, three... then a minute, a minute thirty. The rope went slack. Corvini had abseiled at twice the speed of Tom. She felt the tug. Quickly, she inserted the rope into her descender and pulled on her gloves. Scanning the exit quickly for any signs of their presence, she pushed over the edge allowing herself to fall into the void confident that Tom would have both hands on the ropes to protect her from free falling. Seconds, a minute, a minute and a quarter and she heard Tom call out to her.

'Bend your knees Cassie. You're here.'

Cassandra instinctively landed in a deep bend.

'Shit, that was fast!' Tom looked approvingly at her in the soft light of his dimmed head torch.

'Quick Tom. Help me pull the rope through.' Cassandra was already hauling on one end of the rope. Suddenly she felt the urgency of Tom and Corvini pulling hard on the rope.

'Heads!' Tom warned as the spare end of the rope whistled into the space above them.

Cassandra breathed a sigh of relief. 'Thank God that's over. Never thought I would get off the top in time.'

'Shhh.' Tom warned. 'Let's move in deeper. We'll sit this out until dawn. This way Cassie. Corvini?'

Corvini simply nodded, acutely aware that any echo could reach their pursuers. It was strange how sound travelled further during the night and on a still night where the sky itself became a vast parabola that amplified the tiny pulses of moon and starlight, the shimmering droplets that formed the fabric of sound, the giant weave of the electromagnetic spectrum with its myriad of particle and wave forms — sound would reach across time and space reducing its invisible terrain to absolute zero.

Tom motioned forwards, pointing also beneath their feet making a mini mountain range with his hands, to indicate that it was neither dead flat nor without obstacles. They proceeded carefully, lifting their feet as if stepping across glass barriers that must neither be broken or stepped upon. Tom came to a narrow section and slid a hand along the wall, feeling for the tell-tale opening into the larger crystal cave. Suddenly they were inside. He flashed his head torch around the vast cavern, its light playing tricks with his memory revealing light of a thousand colours mirroring off the walls. It was a bewitching kaleidoscope now enveloping them in their new beginnings.

Cassandra suddenly stopped dead in her tracks and put her hands to her ears.

'Tom. I can hear her again. The same woman in my dreams.'

'I can't hear a thing Cass.' Tom looked at her dumbly. 'How come I can't hear anything?' Tom was puzzled.

'You're not meant to Tom.'

EPILOGUE

The midnight sky at its zenith was dark blue behind the limitless flourish of stars and planets. From the depths of the Geehi Gorge there was nothing except black walls of vegetation and the night sky to guide the horses to their destination.

Thunder tossed his head and nuzzled his mare, proud of their prize. Midnight's foal Storm was born as the first rays of dawn lit the peaks behind them and the sunlight still glistened on the dew-laden gum leaves. Suddenly, the sound of his herd crashing through the regrowth caught Thunder's attention. He could smell their excitement in the air. The day was young and his herd was growing by the minute as more horses joined them to seek out the stallion.

Tom and Cassandra carved out each day as if it were their first and last. The sunlight streamed into the portal giving them light and life. Eventually they emerged from their hideout and when they did, they heard that Ricardo Corvini had fought off a band of mercenaries on his way to Tom Groggin only to find that his new friends and a small band from the Training Camp had already won several battles to secure the farm and its lands.

Thora rejoiced in finally having Sean to herself. It was time. When the heat was finally off them, Cassie, Tom returned to Angus's farm on the Monaro. Expecting their 'family' to increase, Angus and Sean laboured building a second farmhouse, this time with enough room for a mini-conference and training room and a separate study for Tom. Ever-practical, Angus built escape routes deep into the earth to take them away from danger if ever it came their way again. Sean the master stone-mason, constructed a high courtyard — a wall of local stone — planted fruit trees and built the vegetable gardens that could feed an entire band for years at a time.

Angus finally took Tom with him to Melbourne. It was time for the young man to be fully reconciled with himself. The exposure of well-placed and well-heeled individuals involved in the water profiteering rackets that included his father left Tom feeling sick. He returned to the hotel from where he had escaped with Sean so many years ago. The room was dark with the same carpet and suddenly he felt free, free from the past and any shame that held him in its grasp.

Tom rode Brindabella almost every day. As he had promised Malcolm, he bred high-quality endurance horses from Brindabella that inevitably found their way into the international market. He set up round yards on the farm and with Cassie started a small business breaking in brumbies from the bush and rehoming them as far away as Sydney and the Hunter Valley. Sure-footed ponies were always in demand for families with young children who dreamt about owning their own Silver Brumby. Soon, Cassandra and Tom had a wide band of young people learning the ropes of gentling wild horses. At the same time they found they had freed their own spirits.

Angus, Sean, Thora, Cassie and Tom quietly carried on their surveillance work. From time to time they would run the Mountain Training Camps where they constantly looked for hope amongst the young people otherwise damaged by drugs and despair. Cassie continued to dream about the mountains from eons ago. Jack appeared and disappeared from the farm always carrying a new feather for Tom. In time, Tom fashioned a headdress for himself that belonged more on the wild plains of America than the ancient and subdued Monaro landscapes.

Each season, Cassandra and Tom returned to the Snowy Mountains peaks and valleys they knew and loved. The rending of the earth by vast earthquakes had released underground springs that finally burst above the ground, soaking the mountain watersheds. The Snowy River now took its rightful passage, raging through its upper reaches below Seaman's Hut as if it had collected the waters from ten mountains. Further downstream, the river filled the narrow gorge with breathtaking beauty. As the Snowy spilt onto the floodplain it swelled and pushed through the final dam until it reached the rocky plains. The thundering of the Snowy River could be heard from kilometres away as it finally ran free — its flow unstoppable — untroubled on its endless journey towards the sea.

ACKNOWLEDGEMENTS

All names and events that appear in this book are fictitious, apart from place names and some events, including, reference to Stuart Diver, the Thredbo Road Collapse and "The Guthega Ghost", the Phantom Horse who continues to roam and protect the Snowy Mountains and its peoples. Reference is made also to the Snowy Scheme.

Thank you firstly, to my friendly editor Meredith Goulding whose accurate and gentle eye transformed the first novel series Wind Horse into this edited, consolidated and streamlined version. Also, Anthony Scott whose astute eye picked up the mini-inconsistencies in the story and word errors that needed adjusting and amending and became the the final heroic effort to complete the story.

I would like to thank the individuals who have contributed to the evolution of the story, their personal and artistic experiences and talents adding colour and life to many of the scenes in Wind Horse. Amongst these people are especially, women from Berridale who encouraged the author and brought her into their warm and vibrant circle of friendship during the formative period of writing.

Thanks to the Snowy River Alliance for their dedication since the late 1970s, to fight the good fight and the noble cause of restoring Australia's greatest river to life. Some of the formidable characters include Max and Glenice White, Gil Richardson, Jo Garland, Julie and Ross from the Iona Cafe Dalgety, former Snowy River Shire Council Mayor Richard Wallace (who convinced the Mayors of NSW to vote NO to the proposed sale of Snowy Hydro) and Vickki Wallace who continues to campaign for the river, Louise Crisp and her parents Peter and Lois Crisp. Special thanks to Louise Crisp from the Snowy River Alliance for encouraging me to complete the story.

The Snowy River, although its course may be short by comparison to the Murray, is nevertheless the 'Mighty Snowy River', its volume and course resulting from the once massive glacial and later, snow melts and its fast and furious journey to the sea. Now, with 'global warming' and a determination to extract maximum dollar value from the Snowy River and its tributaries, the river is dying. At the time of writing, the Snowy River needs renewed political will to restore its mountain up-waters and to find a minimum of 28%, average annual natural flow (ANF) below Jindabyne Dam wall. May the Snowy run free and wild again. Long live the Snowy River.

We remember some of the key Snowy River Alliance people who are no longer with us — Paul Leete, Angel John Gallard, Cosmic Carl Drury (a formidable and effective campaigner to restore Snowy River flows). May I note the many scientists who have worked tirelessly to restore the Upper Snowy River, the Snowy River and its Estuary including Professor Sam Lake of Monash University, Teresa Rose, Jane Roberts, Simon Williams, Brett Miners and Tim Fletcher. The ANU Human Ecology Group, Rob Dyball and his group have retained an ongoing interest in the social and environmental drivers and health of the Snowy River. Contemporaneously, Prof Jamie Pittcock from the Fenner School at the ANU has taken a keen interest in restoring Snowy River Flows.

Craig Ingram especially deserves a mention for running on a 'Snowy River' campaign to become successfully elected to the Victorian Parliament from 1999-2010.

Thank you also to the First People from the Monaro and surrounding regions, especially the Members of the Ngarigo upon whose land and waters we now tread and enjoy. No offence is intended as a result of any reference to any Ngarigo ancestors. Reference is made by way of respect.

Thank you especially to my friend and colleague in the outdoor adventure guiding world, Richard Swain from Alpine River Adventures. An Indigenous man with extensive knowledge, Richard has lived on the Monaro and in the Snowy Mountains all his life. He is undeniably the person with the most knowledge of how the Snowy River flows from Dalgety to the sea, paddling and discovering its ancient secrets as a part of his livelihood and clearly as his leading passion. May the Snowy River paddlers enjoy free, running water.

This novel invites Ngarigo People to "Remember" their stories and to share those stories with the contemporary settlers and people visiting the Monaro and the High Country so that we too can learn to respect in new ways, the country we love so much. My understanding is many of the original, Traditional Ngarigo stories need to be relived, revitalised and retold. Our hope is that the Ngarigo People will in time, be able to do this, tell their own stories on their own terms. For the reason that many of these stories appear to be lost for the time being, out of respect, I have limited reference to Ngarigo People, their Stories and Traditions.

Special thanks to Peter Cocker for his insights into mountaineering, his talent for story telling, companionship, and continued support during the evolution and writing of this story. Thank you also to Lincoln Hall for casting a 'friendly eye' over the ice climbing scenes at Blue Lake in the Snowy Mountains. Long live the 'brotherhood of the rope'.

Finally and most importantly, a special tribute to my father Dr Alec Costin for his continued inspiration to restore the Upper Snowy River, to think about the landscape, its geological history, its multitude of macro and micro environments, and about the beautiful Australian Alpine Flora.

Five percent of net profits from the sale of
this book will be dedicated to The Australian
Indigenous Alpine Sport Foundation

aiasf.org.au

www.ingramcontent.com/pod-product-compliance
Lightning Source LLC
Chambersburg PA
CBHW020643110726
47901CB00001B/26